D1108475

THE
COLETTE OMNIBUS

THE COLETTE OMNIBUS

INTRODUCED BY
ERICA JONG

NELSON DOUBLEDAY, Inc.
Garden City, New York

CONTENTS

Viva Colette!   vii

CHÉRI   1

THE LAST OF CHÉRI   117

GIGI   221

THE VAGABOND   265

THE SHACKLE   441

About Colette   583

VIVA COLETTE!

by ERICA JONG

COLETTE has always seemed to me the most authentic feminist heroine of all women writers. Like Aphra Behn and Georges Sand, she made her living by her pen. She was professional in that fundamental sense. Unlike so many others, she did not take her own life, but did the far braver thing of living to a ripe old age (writing all the while). She chronicled every stage of a woman's life—from girlhood to old age. And almost alone of women writers, she presents a pattern for living and working that seems attractive. Not easy, not painless, but rich and varied. Her life contained many lives: writing, performing, running a cosmetics business; three marriages, many lovers of both sexes, the birth of a daughter, a close and enduring relationship with her mother. Colette did not find any secret, magical way to combine love and work; she struggled with the problem all her life. But she never gave up, and her own story is moving precisely because it is the story of a survivor.

Colette achieved the first room of her own almost by accident and certainly at great cost: her first husband, "Willy" (Henri Gauthier-Villars), ran a factory of ghostwriters and urged her to write scandalous (he hoped) memoirs of her youth in Burgundy which he then published under his name—claiming Colette as his "model." It is the classic literary form of woman's oppression: ghostwriting for a man. But instead of being defeated by it, Colette learned from the experience. It was her apprenticeship as a writer, and years later, when she was famous in her own write, she was able to wrest the copyrights from Willy's name.

Colette's fiction is particularly important to the development of contemporary literature because it is self-mythologizing in the way Proust's or Henry Miller's fiction is. It often draws upon the author's life with *seeming* candor, but it is not literal autobiography. The facts of the author's life have been shaped, honed, and elevated to myth.

The Vagabond is perhaps the best example of Colette's self-mythologizing. This great novel about a woman alone obviously reflects details of Colette's life, but was not written when Colette was living alone at all. The themes of autonomy versus fusion, freedom versus sexual bondage, which are so brilliantly depicted in *The Vagabond* were certainly in the head of Colette the writer, but not literally in the life of Colette the woman. Her own temporary solution to the unsatisfactoriness of her first marriage was a long relationship with an older woman, though Renée Néré in *The Vagabond* braves it alone. In this most subtle of feminist novels, the protagonist (who is a writer and a music-hall mime like her creator) chooses loneliness rather than marriage to a good man. The point is not that men are beasts (if anything, they are lapdogs—a bit vague, distracted, and incompetent) but that marriage is an oppressive institution and Renée Néré treasures her freedom. She would rather remain a vagabond, with the perspective given only to solitaries.

The other novels in this collection—*Chéri, The Last of Chéri, Gigi,* and *The Shackle*—show Colette's great range and versatility. In *Chéri* and *The Last of Chéri* Colette projects herself into the consciousness of a character very dissimilar to herself, and shows the rise and fall of a foppish young man with the sort of novelistic accuracy we usually associate with Tolstoy.

What is innovative about Colette's art? One of her earliest commentators, Francis Jammes, put his finger on it: she "dared to be natural." She is also one of the first female writers to write unapologetically out of a female consciousness. It is a sad paradox that when male authors impersonate women (Tolstoy as Anna Karenina, Flaubert as Bovary, Richardson as Clarissa, Lawrence as Constance Chatterly, John Berryman as Mistress Bradstreet) they are said to be dealing with "cosmic, major concerns"—but when we impersonate *ourselves* we are said to be writing "women's fiction" or "women's poetry." Unfortunately, Colette has been the victim of that sort of prejudice in America and to some extent in her native country. The male literary establishment has created the impression that she is slightly precious, supersensitive, effusive, and gushy. She is none of these. In fact there are many reasons why Colette's work has particular relevance to us now: because it tells the story of a soul's quest for liberation—not political liberation, but spiritual liberation (which, of course, is the better part of the same thing); because it is extremely modern in its aims and techniques—it is pseudoautobiography, pseudoconfession, subjective writing which seems artless and utterly natural but is really full of invisible artistry; because it asks all the questions about marriage, love, jealousy, bisexuality, maleness, and femaleness which our generation sometimes flatters itself it has invented; because it is great writing, full of sights, smells, colors, birds, beasts, love, hate, and the beautiful rhythms of words; and, finally, because Colette herself is an inspiration, a survivor, a hardy plant.

If you are tired of reading women's novels that end in madhouses, gas ovens, car crashes, leaps from open windows, then read Colette. She will not present a rosy picture of the world or pretend that life is painless. But she will show you the pure and the impure, the earthly paradise which flourishes in an imperfect world, the pleasures to be snatched from the jaws of mortality. She will show you cats and gardens, cups of chocolate and green grapes, sexual passion and friendship, rivalry and amity, imprisonment and freedom. She might have said with Wallace Stevens, "The imperfect is our paradise." What a pleasure it is to know she's there—volumes and volumes of her!

THE
COLETTE OMNIBUS

CHÉRI

Translated by
ROGER SENHOUSE

"Give it me, Léa, give me your pearl necklace! Do you hear me, Léa? Give me your pearls!"

No answer came from the huge brass-bedecked wrought-iron bedstead that glimmered in the shadows like a coat of mail.

"Why won't you let me have your necklace? It looks every bit as well on me as on you—even better!"

At the snap of the clasp, ripples spread over the lace frilled sheets, and from their midst rose two magnificent thin-wristed arms, lifting on high two lovely lazy hands.

"Leave it alone, Chéri! You've been playing long enough with that necklace."

"It amuses me. . . . Are you frightened I'll steal it?"

He was capering about in front of the sun-drenched rosy pink curtains—a graceful demon, black against a glowing furnace; but when he pranced back towards the bed, he turned white again from top to toe, in his white silk pyjamas and white Moorish slippers.

"I'm not frightened," the soft, deep voice answered from the bed. "But you'll wear out the thread. Those pearls are heavy."

"They certainly are," Chéri said with due respect. "Whoever gave you this lot never meant to make light of you!"

He was standing in front of a pier-glass framed in the space between two windows, gazing at the reflection of a very youthful, very good-looking young man, neither too short nor too tall, hair with the blue sheen of a blackbird's plumage. He unbuttoned his pyjamas, displaying a hard, darkish chest, curved like a shield; and the whites of his dark eyes, his teeth, and the pearls of the necklace gleamed on the over-all rosy glow of the room.

"Take off that necklace!" The female voice was insistent. "Do you hear what I say?"

The young man, motionless in front of his image, laughed softly to himself: "Yes, yes, I heard you. I know so well you're terrified I'll make off with it!"

"No, I'm not. But if I did offer it to you, you're quite capable of taking it."

He ran to the bed and bounded into it. "You bet I am! I rise above the conventions. Personally, I think it's idiotic for a man to allow a woman to give him a single pearl for a tie-pin, or two for a pair of studs, and then to consider himself beyond the pale if she gives him fifty. . . ."

"Forty-nine."

"Forty-nine—as if I hadn't counted! I dare you to say they don't look well on me! Or that I'm ugly!"

Léa sat up in bed. "No, I won't say that. For one thing, because you'd never believe me. But can't you learn to laugh without crinkling up your nose like that? I suppose you won't be happy till you've wrinkles all up the side of your nose!"

He stopped laughing at once, let the skin on his forehead relax, and drew in the fold under his chin like a coquettish old woman. They looked at each other in open hostility—she, leaning on her elbow in a flurry of frills and lace; he, sitting side-saddle on the edge of the bed. He was thinking 'Who's she to talk of any wrinkles I may have one day?' and she 'Why is he so ugly when he laughs?—he who's the very picture of beauty!' She thought for a moment, then finished aloud: "It's because you look so ill-natured when you're joking. You never laugh except unkindly—*at* people, and that makes you ugly. You're often ugly."

"That's not true!" Chéri exclaimed, crossly.

Anger knitted his eyebrows close above his nose, magnified his eyes, glittering with insolence behind a palisade of lashes, and parted the chaste bow of his disdainful mouth. Léa smiled to see him as she loved him best: rebellious only to become submissive, enchained lightly but powerless to free himself. She put a hand on his young head, which impatiently shook off the yoke. Like someone quieting an animal, she murmured, "There, there! What is it? What is it, then?"

He fell upon her big beautiful shoulder, nuzzling and butting his way into his favourite resting-place with eyes already shut, seeking his customary long morning sleep in the protection of her arms. But Léa pushed him away. "None of that now, Chéri! You're having luncheon with our national Harpy, and it's already twenty to twelve!"

"Not really? I'm lunching at the old girl's? You too?"

Lazily Léa settled deeper into the bed.

"Not me, I'm off duty. I'll go for coffee at half-past two, or tea at six, or for a cigarette at a quarter to eight. Don't worry; she'll always see enough of me. And besides, I've not been asked."

Chéri's sulky face lit up with malice.

"I know, I know why! We're going to have high society. We're going to have the fair Marie-Laure, and that poisonous child of hers."

Léa brought her big blue wandering eyes to rest.

"Oh, really! The little girl's charming. Less so than her mother, but charming. Now take off that necklace, once and for all."

"Pity," Chéri sighed, as he undid the clasp. "It would look so well in the trousseau."

Léa raised herself on her elbow: "What trousseau?"

"Mine," Chéri said with ludicrous self-importance. "*My* trousseau, full of *my* jewels, for *my* marriage!"

He bounded in the air, executed a perfect *entrechat-six*, returned to earth, butted his way through the door-curtains, and disappeared, shouting: "My bath, Rose! And quick about it! I'm lunching at the old girl's!"

'That's that,' Léa thought. 'We'll have a lake in the bathroom and eight towels floating in it, and razor scrapings in the basin. If only I had two bathrooms!'

But, as on former occasions, she soon saw that this would mean getting rid of a wardrobe and lopping off a corner of her dressing-room, and so concluded, as on former occasions: 'I shall simply have to put up with it till Chéri gets married.'

She lay down again on her back and noticed that Chéri, undressing the night before, had thrown his socks on the mantelpiece, his pants on the writing-table, his tie round the neck of her portrait bust. She could not help smiling at this hasty masculine disorder, and half closed her large tranquil eyes. Their blue was as beautiful as ever, and so were the thick chestnut lashes.

At the age of forty-nine, Léonie Vallon, called Léa de Lonval, was nearing the end of a successful career as a richly kept courtesan. She was a good creature, and life had spared her the more flattering catastrophes and exalted sufferings. She made a secret of the date of her birth; but willingly admitted—with a look of voluptuous condescension for Chéri's special benefit—that she was approaching the age when she could indulge in a few creature comforts. She liked order, fine linen, wines in their prime, and carefully planned meals at home. From an idolised young blonde she had become a rich middle-aged *demi-mondaine* without ever attracting any outrageous publicity. Not that she went in for any pretences. Her friends remembered a Four-in-Hand Meet at Auteuil, about 1895, when the sub-editor of *Gil Blas* had addressed her as "dear artist" and she had answered: "Artist! Oh come, my good friend, my lovers must have been telling tales. . . ."

Her contemporaries were jealous of her imperturbable good health, and the younger women, whose figures were padded out in front and behind after the fashion of 1912, scoffed at her opulent bust. Young and old alike envied her the possession of Chéri.

"Though, good heavens!" Léa used to say, "there's no reason why they should. They're welcome to him! I don't keep him on a lead. He goes out by himself."

But in this she was not altogether speaking the truth, for she was proud of a liaison—sometimes, in her weakness for the truth, referring to it as "an adoption"—that had lasted six years.

'Trousseau,' Léa said over again. 'Marriage for Chéri! It's not possible, it's not . . . human . . . you can't give an innocent girl to Chéri! Why, it would be throwing a doe to the hounds! People don't know what Chéri is!'

As if telling the beads of a rosary, she ran her fingers over the necklace which Chéri had tossed on the bed. She put it away at night now because, with his passion for fine pearls and his fondness for playing with them in the morning, he would have noticed too often that her throat had thickened and was not nearly so white, with the muscles under its skin growing slack. She fastened the pearls round her neck without getting up, and took a hand-mirror from the bedside-table.

'I look like a gardener's wife,' was her unflattering comment, 'a market-gardener's wife. A market-gardener's wife in Normandy, off to the potato-fields wearing a pearl necklace. I might as well stick an ostrich feather in my nose—and that's being polite!'

She shrugged her shoulders, severely critical of everything she no longer loved in herself: the vivid complexion, healthy, a little too ruddy—an open-air complexion, well suited to emphasise the pure intensity of her eyes, with their varying shades of blue. Her proud nose still won her approval. "Marie-Antoinette's nose!" Chéri's mother was in the habit of saying, without ever forgetting to add: "and in another two years, our Léa will have a chin like Louis Seize'." Her mouth, with its even row of teeth, seldom opened in a peal of laughter; but she smiled often, a smile that set off to perfection the lazy flutter of her large eyes—a smile a hundred times lauded, sung, and photographed—a deep, confiding smile one never tired of watching.

As for her body—"Everyone knows," Léa would say, "that a well-made body lasts a long time." She could still afford to show her body, pink and white, endowed with the long legs and straight back of a naiad on an Italian fountain; the dimpled hips, the high-slung breasts, "would last," Léa used to say, "till well after Chéri's wedding."

She got out of bed, and, slipping into a wrap, went to draw back the long curtains. The noonday sun poured into the gay, rosy, over-decorated room. Its luxury dated: double lace curtains, rose-bud watered silk on the walls, gilded woodwork, and antique furniture upholstered in modern silks. Léa refused to give up either this cosy room or its bed, a massive and indestructible masterpiece of wrought iron and brass, grim to the eye and cruel to the shins.

"Come, come!" Chéri's mother protested, "it's not as bad as all that. Personally, I like this room. It belongs to a period. It has a style of its own. It suggests La Païva."

The remembrance of this dig made Léa smile as she pinned up her hair. She hurriedly powdered her face on hearing two doors slam, and the thud of a male foot colliding with some delicate piece of furniture. Chéri came back into the room in shirt and trousers, his ears white with talcum powder. He was in an aggressive mood.

"Where's my tie-pin? What a wretched hole this is! Have they taken to pinching the jewellery?"

"Marcel must have stuck it in his tie to go to the market," Léa gravely replied.

Chéri, who had little or no sense of humour, was brought up short by the little quip like an ant by a lump of coal. He stopped his angry pacing up and down, and found nothing better to say than: "Charming! and what about my boots?"

"Your what?"

"The calf, of course!"

Léa smiled up at him from her dressing-table, too affectionately. "You said it, not I," she murmured in caressing tones.

"The day when a woman loves me for my brains," he retorted, "I shall be done for. Meanwhile I must have my pin and my boots."

"What for? You don't wear a tie-pin with a lounge suit, and you've got one pair on already."

Chéri stamped his foot. "I've had enough of this! There's nobody here to look after me, and I'm sick of it all."

Léa put down her comb. "Very well, say goodbye to it all for good!"

He shrugged his shoulders, like a young tough. "You wouldn't like it if I did!"

"Be off with you! I hate guests who complain of the cooking and leave bits and pieces all over the place and cream-cheese sticking to the mirrors. Go back to your sainted mother, my child, and stay there."

Unable to meet Léa's gaze, he lowered his eyes, and broke out into schoolboy protests. "Soon I shan't be allowed to open my mouth! Anyhow, you'll let me have your motor to go to Neuilly?"

"No."

"Why not?"

"Because I'm going out in it myself at two, and because the chauffeur is having his dinner."

"Where are you going at two?"

"To say my prayers. But if you need three francs for a taxi . . . Idiot," she added tenderly. "At two I'll probably come to your lady mother's for coffee. Does that satisfy you?"

He tossed his head like a young buck. "You bite my head off, you won't give me anything I ask for; they hide my things away, they . . ."

"Will you never learn to dress yourself?"

She took the tie from Chéri's hands and tied it for him.

"There! And that frightful purple tie. . . . However, it's just the thing for the fair Marie-Laure and family. . . . And you wanted to wear a pearl on top of all that! You little dago. . . . Why not earrings into the bargain?"

His defences were down. Blissful, languid, irresolute, supine, he surrendered again to a lazy happiness and closed his eyes. . . .

"Nounoune darling . . ." he murmured.

She brushed the hair off his ears, combed a straighter parting in the bluish locks of his black hair, dabbed a little scent on his temples, and gave him a quick kiss, unable to resist the tempting mouth so close to her own.

Chéri opened his eyes, and his lips, then stretched out his hands.

She moved away. "No. It's a quarter to one! Be off now, and don't let me see you again!"

"Never?"

"Never," she laughed back at him with uncontrollable tenderness.

Left to herself, she smiled proudly, and a sharp little sigh of defeated desire escaped her as she listened to Chéri's footsteps crossing the courtyard. She saw him open and close the gates, drift away on his winged feet, only to encounter the adoring glances of three shop-girls walking along arm in arm.

"Lawks! He's too good to be true! Let's touch him to see if he's real!"

But Chéri took it all for granted and did not even turn round.

"My bath, Rose! Tell the manicurist she can go, it's far too late now. My blue coat and skirt—the new one—the blue hat with the white under brim, and the little shoes with the straps . . . No, wait . . ."

Léa, with one leg across the other, rubbed her ankle and shook her head.

"No, the blue kid laced boots. My legs are a little swollen to-day. It's the heat."

Her elderly maid, butterfly-capped, raised understanding eyes to Léa. "It's . . . it's the heat," she repeated obediently, shrugging her shoulders as much as to say: "We know . . . Nothing lasts for ever. . . ."

With Chéri out of the house, Léa became herself again, very much alive, cheerful, and on the spot. Within an hour, she had been given her bath, followed by a spirit-rub scented with sandal-wood, and was ready dressed, hatted, and shod. While the curling-tongs were heating, she found time to run through the butler's book and send for Emile, the footman, and call his attention to the blue haze on one of the looking-glasses. She ran an experienced eye—rarely taken in—over everything in the room, and lunched in solitary bliss, with a smile for the dry Vouvray and for the June strawberries, served, with their stalks, on a plate of Rubelles enamel as green as a tree-frog after rain. Someone in the past who appreciated good food must have chosen the huge Louis Seize looking-glasses and the English furniture of the same period, for this rectangular dining-room: light, airy side-boards, high pedestalled dumb-waiters, spindly yet strong Sheraton chairs, in a dark wood with delicate swags. The looking-glasses and the massive silver caught the full light of day, with a touch of green reflected from the trees in the Avenue Bugeaud. Léa, as she ate, examined a fork for any suspicion of pink cleaning-powder left in the chasing, and half-closed one eye the better to judge the

quality of the polish on the dark wood. Standing behind her, the
butler watched this performance nervously.

"Marcel!" Léa said, "for the last week or so, the wax on your floors
has been smeary."

"Does Madame think so?"

"Madame does think so. Add a little turpentine while you're melting it in a double saucepan; it's quite easy to do again. You brought
up the Vouvray a little too soon. Close the shutters as soon as you've
cleared the table; we're in for a heat-wave."

"Very good, Madame. Will Monsieur Ch—Monsieur Peloux be
dining?"

"Probably. . . . No *crème-surprise* to-night. We'll just have a
strawberry water ice. Coffee in the boudoir."

As she rose from the table, straight and tall, the shape of her legs
visible under a dress that moulded her hips, she had ample time to
note the "Madame is beautiful" in the butler's discreet glance, and
this did not displease her.

"Beautiful," Léa whispered on her way up to the boudoir.
"No. . . . No longer. I have now to wear something white near my
face, and very pale pink underclothes and tea-gowns. Beautiful!
Pish. . . . I hardly need to be that any longer."

All the same, she allowed herself no siesta in the painted silk
boudoir, when she had finished with coffee and the newspapers. And
it was with battle written on her face that she gave her chauffeur the
order: "To Madame Peloux's."

The tree-lined road through the Bois, dry beneath the young,
already wind-faded June foliage—the toll-gate—Neuilly—Boulevard
d'Inkermann—'How many times have I come this way?' Léa wondered. She began to count, then tired of counting and softened her
step on the gravel outside Madame Peloux's house to overhear any
sounds coming from it.

'They're in the garden-room,' she concluded.

She had put on more powder before approaching the house and
tightened the fine-meshed, misty blue veil under her chin. Her answer to the manservant's formal request to pass through the house
was: "No; I'd rather go round by the garden."

A real garden—almost a park—completely surrounded the vast
white villa, typical of the outer suburbs of Paris. Madame Peloux's
villa had been called "a country residence" in the days when Neuilly

was still on the outskirts of Paris. This was apparent from the stables, converted into garages, the other offices with their kennels and wash-houses, not to mention the size of the billiard-room, entrance hall and dining-room.

"This is a handsome investment of Madame Peloux's," her female devotees never tired of repeating—the old toadies who, in exchange for a dinner or a glass of brandy, came there to take a hand against her at bezique or poker. And they added: "But then, where has Madame Peloux not got money invested?"

Walking along in the shade of the acacia trees, between trellised roses and huge clumps of rhododendrons in full blaze, Léa could hear the murmur of voices, and, rising above it, Madame Peloux's shrill nasal trumpet notes and Chéri's dry cackle.

'That child's got an ugly laugh,' she thought. She paused a moment to listen more attentively to a new feminine note; weak, pleasing, quickly drowned by the redoubtable trumpeting. 'That must be the girl,' she said to herself, and a few quick steps brought her to the garden-room with its glass front, from which Madame Peloux burst out with a "Here comes our beautiful friend!"

A little round barrel of a woman, Madame Peloux—in reality Mademoiselle Peloux—had been a ballet-dancer from her tenth to her sixteenth year. Occasionally Léa would search for some trace in Madame Peloux that might recall the once chubby little fair-haired Eros, or the later dimpled nymph, and found nothing except the big implacable eyes, the delicate aggressive nose, and a still coquettish way of standing with her feet in 'the fifth position', like the members of the *corps de ballet*.

Chéri, coming to life in the depths of a rocking-chair, kissed Léa's hand with involuntary grace and ruined his gesture by exclaiming: "Hang it all! you've put on a veil again, and I loathe veils."

"Will you leave her alone!" Madame Peloux interposed. "You must never ask a woman why she is wearing a veil. We'll never be able to do anything with him," she said to Léa affectionately.

Two women had risen to their feet in the golden shade of a straw blind. One, in mauve, rather coldly offered her hand to Léa, who looked her over from head to foot.

"Goodness, how lovely you are, Marie-Laure! you're perfection itself!"

Marie-Laure deigned to smile. She was a red-haired young woman with brown eyes, whose physical presence alone was enough to take your breath away. She drew attention, almost coquettishly, to the other young woman, by saying: "But would you have recognised my daughter Edmée?"

Léa held out a hand which the girl was reluctant to shake.

"I should have known you, my child, but a schoolgirl alters so quickly, and Marie-Laure alters only to become always more disconcertingly lovely. Are you quite finished with school now?"

"I should hope so, I should hope so," exclaimed Madame Peloux. "You can't go on for ever, hiding her under a bushel, such a miracle of grace and charm, and she's nineteen already!"

"Eighteen," said Marie-Laure, sweetly.

"Eighteen, eighteen! . . . Yes of course, eighteen! Léa, you remember? This child was just making her first Communion the year that Chéri ran away from school, surely you remember? Yes, yes, you did, you little good-for-nothing, you ran away and Léa and I were driven nearly out of our wits!"

"I remember perfectly," Léa said, and she exchanged an imperceptible little nod with Marie-Laure—something corresponding to the 'touché' of a punctilious fencer.

"You must get her married soon, you must get her married soon!" pursued Madame Peloux, who never failed to repeat a basic truth at least twice. "We'll all come to the wedding."

She brandished her little arms in the air, and the young girl glanced at her with ingenuous alarm.

'She's just the daughter for Marie-Laure,' thought Léa, gazing at her more closely. 'She has all her mother's dazzling qualities, but in a quieter key: fluffy, ash-brown hair, that looks as if it were powdered; frightened, secretive eyes, and a mouth she avoids opening even to speak or smile. . . . Exactly what Marie-Laure needs as a foil—but how she must hate her!'

Madame Peloux insinuated a maternal smile between Léa and the young girl: "You ought to have seen how well these two young people were getting on together in the garden!"

She pointed to where Chéri stood smoking a cigarette on the other side of the glass partition, his cigarette-holder clenched between his teeth, and his head tilted back to avoid the smoke. The three women looked at the young man who—forehead held at an angle, eyes half-shut, feet together, motionless—looked for all the world like a winged figure hovering dreamily in the air. Léa did not fail to observe the expression of fright and subjugation in the girl's eyes, and she took pleasure in making her tremble by touching her on the arm.

Edmée quivered from head to foot, withdrew her arm, and whispered almost savagely, "What?"

"Nothing," Léa replied, "I dropped my glove."

"Come along, Edmée!" Marie-Laure called, negligently.

Silent and docile, the girl walked towards Madame Peloux, who flapped her wings: "Leaving already? Surely not? We must meet again soon, we must meet again soon!"

"It's late," Marie-Laure said, "and you'll be expecting any number of people as it's Sunday afternoon. The child is not accustomed to company."

"Of course not, of course not," Madame Peloux said tenderly. "She's had such a sheltered existence . . . such a lonely life!"

Marie-Laure smiled, and Léa gave her a look as much as to say, "That's one for you!"

"But we'll call again soon."

"Thursday, Thursday! Léa, you'll come to luncheon on Thursday?"

"I'll be here," Léa answered.

Chéri had rejoined Edmée at the entrance to the room and stood beside her, disdaining all conversation. He heard Léa's promise, and turned round: "Splendid, then we can go for a run in the motor."

"Yes, yes, just the thing for you young people," Madame Peloux insisted, touched by his proposal. "Edmée can sit in front next to Chéri, at the wheel, and the rest of us will go at the back. Youth at the helm, youth at the helm! Chéri, my love, will you ask for Marie-Laure's motor?"

Her small stumpy feet kept slipping on the gravel, but she managed to take her two visitors to the corner of the path, where she handed them over to Chéri. On her return, she found that Léa had taken off her hat and was smoking a cigarette.

"Aren't they sweet, those two!" Madame Peloux gasped. "Don't you think so, Léa?"

"Delicious," Léa breathed out in the same puff as her cigarette smoke. "But really, that Marie-Laure!"

"What's Marie-Laure been up to?" asked Chéri, as he rejoined them.

"How lovely she is!"

"Ah! Ah!" Madame Peloux began in formal assent. "That's true, that's true. She has been really lovely."

Chéri and Léa caught each other's eye and laughed.

"Has been?", Léa emphasised the past tense. "But she's the picture of youth. Not a single wrinkle! And she can wear the palest mauve, such a foul colour! I loathe it and it loathes me."

Madame Peloux raised her big pitiless eyes and thin nose from her brandy-glass.

"The picture of youth, the picture of youth!" yapped Madame Peloux. "Pardon me, pardon me! Marie-Laure had Edmée in 1895, no . . . '94. She'd just run away with a singing-teacher, leaving Khalil Bey flat, though he'd given her the famous pink diamond which . . . No, no! Wait! . . . That must have been the year before!"

The trumpet notes were shrill and off key. Léa put a hand over her ear, and Chéri declared, with some feeling: "Everything would be heavenly on an afternoon like this, if only we could be spared my mother's voice!"

She looked at her son with no sign of anger, accustomed to his insolence. Dignified, feet dangling, she settled herself back in a basket chair too high for her short legs. In one hand she warmed her glass of brandy. Léa, rocking herself gently to and fro, glanced occasionally at Chéri, who lay sprawled on a cool cane settee, coat unbuttoned, a cigarette dying between his lips, a lock of hair over one eyebrow. 'He's a handsome young blackguard,' she thought admiringly.

There they remained, peacefully side by side, making no effort to talk or be sociable, happy after their own fashion. Years of close familiarity rendered silence congenial, and Chéri slipped back into his lethargy, Léa into her calm. As the afternoon became hotter, Madame Peloux pulled her narrow skirt up to her knees, displaying her tight little sailor's calves, and Chéri ripped off his tie—reproved by Léa in an audible "Tch, tch."

"Oh! leave the child alone," Madame Peloux protested, as from the depths of a dream. "It's much too hot! Would you care for a kimono, Léa?"

"No, thank you. I'm perfectly comfortable."

Their unbuttoned siestas disgusted her. Never once had her young lover caught her untidily dressed, or with her blouse undone, or in her bedroom slippers during the day. "Naked, if need be," she would say, "but squalid, never!"

She picked up her picture paper again, but did not read it. 'These Pelouxs—mother and son alike!' she thought dreamily. 'They've only to sit themselves down at a good meal or in the heart of the countryside and—snap!—the mother whisks off her stays and the son his waistcoat. They behave like publicans out on a holiday, the pair of them.' She cast a vindictive eye on one of the publicans in question, and saw that he had fallen asleep, his eyelashes spread against his pallid cheeks, his mouth closed. His upper lip, lit from below, reflected two silver pinpoints of light at the twin curves of its delicious Cupid's bow, and Léa was forced to admit that he looked far more like a sleeping god than a licensed victualler.

Without moving from her chair, she gently plucked the lighted cigarette from between Chéri's fingers and put it in the ash-tray. The hand of the sleeper relaxed and the tapering fingers, tipped with cruel nails, drooped like wilting flowers: a hand not strictly feminine, yet a trifle prettier than one could have wished; a hand she had kissed a hundred times—not in slavish devotion—but kissed for the pleasure of it, for its scent.

From behind her paper, she glanced at Madame Peloux. Was she asleep too? Léa always liked to remain awake while mother and son dozed, allowing her a quiet hour's self-communing in the dappled sunlight of a broiling afternoon. But Madame Peloux was not asleep. She was sitting bolt upright in her wickerwork chair, like a Buddha staring into space, and sipping her *fine-champagne* with the absorption of an alcoholic baby.

'Why doesn't she go to sleep?' Léa wondered. 'It's Sunday. She's lunched well. She's expecting her sponging old cronies to drop in for her five o'clock tea. By rights she ought to be having a snooze. If she's not snoozing, it's because she's up to some devilment or other.'

They had known each other for twenty-five years. Theirs was the hostile intimacy of light women, enriched and then cast aside by one man, ruined by another: the tetchy affection of rivals stalking one another's first wrinkle or white hair. Theirs was the friendship of two practical women of the world, both adepts at the money game; but one of them a miser, and the other a sybarite. These bonds count. Rather late in their day, a stronger bond had come to link them more closely: Chéri.

Léa could remember Chéri as a little boy—a marvel of beauty with long curls. When quite small he was known as Fred, and had not yet been nicknamed Chéri.

Sometimes forgotten and sometimes adored, Chéri grew up among wan housemaids and tall sardonic menservants. Although his birth had mysteriously brought wealth to the house, no "Fräulein", no "Miss" was ever to be seen at Chéri's side; and his mother had preserved him, to the accompaniment of piercing shrieks, from "these ghouls".

"Charlotte Peloux, you belong to another age." The speaker was the moribund, mummified, but indestructible Baron de Berthellemy. "Charlotte Peloux, in you I salute the only light woman who ever had the courage to bring up her son as the son of a tart! You belong to another age! You never read, you never travel, you make a point of knowing your neighbour's business, and you abandon your child to the tender mercies of the servants. How perfect! How absolutely About![1] . . . Or, better still, how like a novel by Gustav Droz. . . . And to think that you've never heard of either! . . ."

Chéri had enjoyed the full freedom of a profligate upbringing. When barely able to lisp, he was quick to pick up all the backstairs gossip. He shared in the clandestine suppers of the kitchen. His ablutions varied between milky immersions in his mother's orris-root baths and scanty cat-licks with the corner of a towel. He suffered from indigestion after a surfeit of sweets, or from pangs of hunger when no one remembered to give him his supper. He was wretchedly bored at every Battle of Flowers, where Charlotte Peloux would exhibit him—half-naked and catching cold—sitting on drenched roses; but it so happened, when he was twelve, that he had a glorious adventure in an illicit gambling-den, when an American woman allowed him to play with a fistful of louis d'or, and called him 'a little masterpiece'. At about the same time, Madame Peloux imposed a tutor on her son—an Abbé, whom she packed off at the end of ten months "because," she confessed, "whenever I caught sight of that black robe trailing along the passages, it made me think I was housing a female relation: and God knows there are few things more depressing than having a poor relation to stay!"

At the age of fourteen, Chéri had a taste of school. He didn't believe in it. He broke prison and ran away. Madame Peloux not only found the energy to incarcerate him a second time, but also, when faced with her son's tears and insults, took to her heels with hands over her ears screaming, "I can't bear the sight of it! I can't bear the sight of it!" So sincere were her cries that she actually fled from Paris, in the company of a man who was young but far from scrupu-

[1] Edmond About (*Roman d'un brave homme*, etc.) and Gustav Droz (*Monsieur, Madame et Bébé*, etc.) light popular novelists of the last half of the nineteenth century, some of whose books appeared in English translation. (*Papa, Mamma and Baby*, illustrated by Morin 1887.)

lous. Two years later she came back, alone. It was the last time she succumbed to an amorous impulse.

She found, on her return, that Chéri had shot up too fast; that his cheeks were hollow and his eyes black-ringed; that he dressed like a stable-lad and spoke with a worse accent than ever. She beat her breast, and snatched him back from the boarding school. He utterly refused to work; demanded horses, carriages, jewels; insisted on a substantial monthly allowance; and, when his mother began to beat her breast and shriek like a pea-hen, he put a stop to her cries by saying: "Madame Peloux, ma'am, don't carry on so. My venerable mother, if no one except me drags you down into the gutter, you're likely to die a comfortable death in your downy bed; I don't altogether fancy a trustee for my estate. Your cash is mine. Let me go my own way! Men friends cost next to nothing—a dinner and a bottle of champagne. As for the fair sex, surely Ma'me Peloux, seeing that I take after you, you can trust me not to treat 'em to more than a trinket— if that!"

He pirouetted about while she shed tears and proclaimed herself the happiest of mothers. When Chéri began buying motor-cars, she trembled once more; but he simply advised her: "Keep an eye on the petrol, Ma'me Peloux, if you please!" and sold his horses. He was not above checking the two chauffeurs' books. His calculations were quick and accurate, and the figures he jotted down on slips of paper —dashed off rapidly, round and regular—were in marked contrast to his rather slow and childish handwriting.

At seventeen he was like a little old man, always fussing over his expenses: still good-looking—but skinny and short-winded. More than once Madame Peloux ran into him on the cellar steps, coming up from checking the bottles in the racks and bins.

"Would you believe it?" she said to Léa. "It's too wonderful."

"Much too wonderful," Léa answered, "he'll come to a bad end. Chéri! Show me your tongue!"

He put out his tongue, made a face, and showed other signs of disrespect. Léa took no notice. She was too intimate a friend, a sort of doting godmother, whom he called by her Christian name.

"Is it true," Léa enquired, "that you were seen last night at a bar, sitting on old Lili's knees?"

"Her knees!" scoffed Chéri. "She hasn't had any for ages. They foundered years ago."

"Isn't it true," Léa persisted with greater severity, "that she made you drink gin laced with pepper? You know gin is bad for the breath!"

On one occasion, Chéri, hurt, snapped back at Léa: "I can't think why you bother me with all these questions. You must have seen what I was up to; you were tucked away in that cubby-hole at the back, with Patron your prize-fighter friend."

"That's perfectly correct," Léa answered, unmoved. "There's nothing of the dissipated schoolboy about Patron. He has other attractions, and a good deal more to recommend him than a perky little face and two black rings round his eyes."

That week Chéri had been out on the razzle in Montmartre and les Halles, consorting with ladies of the town who called him "poppet" and "my pet vice", but he had got no kick out of it: he suffered from migraines and a dry cough. Madame Peloux poured out her heart-breaking woes—"Life is nothing but a series of crosses for us mothers"—to her masseuse, to her stay-maker, Madame Ribot, to old Lili, to the Baron de Berthellemy, and thus passed painlessly from the state of being the happiest-of-parents to that of the martyr-mother.

A night in June, when Madame Peloux and Léa and Chéri were together in the garden-room at Neuilly, was to change the destinies of the young man and the middle-aged woman. Chéri's friends had gone off for the evening—little Baxter, a wholesale wine-merchant, and the Vicomte Desmond, a hanger-on of his, barely of age, difficult and arrogant—and so Chéri had returned to the maternal fold, and habit had drawn Léa there also.

For one more evening, in a whole sequence of such occasions, these two women, each suspicious of the other, found themselves together. They had known each other for twenty years; they shared a past made up of similarly dull evenings; they lacked other friends; and, in their later days, they had become mistrustful, self-indulgent, and cut off from the world, as women are who have lived only for love.

Both were staring in silence at Chéri, who never spoke. Madame Peloux lacked the strength to take her son's health in hand, but hated Léa a little more each time she bent her white neck and glowing cheeks over Chéri's pallid cheek and transparent ear. She would willingly have bled that healthy female neck, already wrinkled by the so-called lines of Venus, in order to give a touch of colour to her slim lily-green son: yet it never occurred to her to take her darling away to the country.

"Chéri, why are you drinking brandy?" Léa scolded.

"Out of politeness to Ma'me Peloux—who would otherwise be drinking alone," Chéri answered.

"What are you going to do to-morrow?"

"Dunno, and you?"

"I'm off to Normandy."

"With?"

"That's none of your business."

"With our friend Spéleïeff?"

"Don't be so stupid. That was over two months ago. You're behind the times. Spéleïeff's in Russia."

"Chéri, darling, what can you be thinking of?" sighed Madame Peloux. "Don't you remember going last month to the charming dinner given by Léa to celebrate the end of the affair? Léa, you've never let me have the recipe for those langoustines I enjoyed so much."

Chéri sat up, his eyes sparkling. "Yes, yes, langoustines, swimming in a creamy sauce! How I'd like some now!"

"You see," Madame Peloux said reproachfully, "he's got no appetite to speak of and yet he's asking for langoustines."

"Shut up!" Chéri snapped. "Léa, are you off to the shady woods with Patron?"

"Certainly not, my boy. Patron and I are merely friends. I'm going on my own."

"Nice to be so rich!" Chéri threw out.

"I'll take you with me, if you like: there'll be nothing to do but eat and drink and sleep. . . ."

"Where is this place of yours?" He had risen to his feet and was standing over her.

"You know Honfleur—the Côte de Grâce—don't you? Sit down; you're green in the face. Now as you go down the Côte de Grâce, you know those farm gates where we always say, in passing, your mother and I . . ."

She turned round to where Madame Peloux was sitting. Madame Peloux had disappeared. The discretion with which she had faded away was something so unlike the normal Charlotte Peloux, that they looked at each other and laughed in surprise.

Chéri sat down close to Léa. "I'm tired," he said.

"You're ruining your health."

He drew himself up in his chair, with offended vanity. "Oh! I'm still in good enough fettle, you know."

"Good enough! For others perhaps . . . but not . . . not for me, I'd have you know."

"Too green?"

"The very word I was looking for. So why don't you come down to the country? No nonsense, of course. Ripe strawberries, fresh cream, cakes, grilled spring chicken . . . that's just what you need—and no women."

He let himself snuggle up to Léa's elbow and shut his eyes.

"No women . . . grand . . . Léa, tell me, you're my pal? You are? Then let's be off. Women indeed! I'm fed up with 'em. Women! I've seen all they've got to show."

These vulgarities were muttered in a drowsy voice. Léa listened to his soft tone, and felt his warm breath against her ear. He had taken hold of her long string of pearls and was rolling the larger ones between his fingers. She slipped her arm under his head and so accustomed was she to treating the boy in this way that, almost without thinking, she pulled him towards her and rocked him in her arms.

"How comfy I am!" he sighed. "You're a good pal. I'm so comfy."

Léa smiled, as though hearing praise she valued intensely. Chéri seemed to be ready to drop off to sleep. She looked very closely at his glistening, almost dewy, eyelashes sunk flat against the cheeks, and then at the cheeks themselves, hollowed by his joyless dissipation. His upper lip, shaved that morning, was already bluish, and the pink lampshades lent his mouth an artificial colour.

"No women!" Chéri exclaimed, as though dreaming. "Then . . . kiss me!"

Taken by surprise, Léa made no movement.

"Kiss me, I tell you!"

He rapped out his order, frowning, and Léa felt embarrassed by the rekindled gleam in his eyes. It was as if someone had switched on the light. She shrugged her shoulders and kissed the forehead so close to her lips. He drew his arms tighter around her neck, and pulled her down towards him.

She shook her head only at the very instant that their lips touched, then she remained absolutely motionless, and held her breath like someone listening. When he released his hold, she broke away from him, rose to her feet, took a deep breath, and put a hand up to tidy her unruffled hair. She turned to him, rather pale and with rueful eyes, and said, teasingly: "That was a bright idea!"

He lay far back in the rocking-chair, speechless, and scrutinised her with a suspicious, questioning gaze, so that she asked: "What is it?"

"Nothing," Chéri said. "I know what I wanted to know."

She blushed with humiliation, then skilfully defended herself.

"What do you know? That I like your mouth? My poor child, I've kissed uglier. What does that prove? D'you think I'm going to fling myself at your feet and cry, 'Take me!' You talk as if you've known only nice young girls! D'you imagine I'm going to lose my head because of a kiss?"

She grew calmer while speaking and wished to prove her self-control.

"Listen, child," she persisted, as she leaned over him, "d'you think a handsome mouth means anything to me?"

She smiled down at him, completely sure of herself, but unaware that there remained on her face a sort of very faint quiver, an appealing sadness, and that her smile was like a rainbow after a sudden storm.

"I'm perfectly calm. Even if I were to kiss you again, or even if we . . ." She stopped and pouted with scorn. "No, no, I really can't see you and me doing that."

"Nor could you see us doing what we did just now," Chéri said, taking time over his words. "And yet you don't mind doing it, and not in a hurry, either. So now you're thinking of going further, are you? I never suggested such a thing."

They faced each other like enemies. Léa was afraid to reveal a desire she had not yet had time to develop or to disguise; she resented this child, so suddenly cold and perhaps derisive.

"You're right," she conceded lightly. "Let's say no more about it. Shall we say instead that I'm offering to put you out to grass! And the food will be good . . . my food, in other words."

"We'll see," Chéri answered. "Shall I bring the Renouhard tourer?"

"Of course; you're not going to leave it behind with Charlotte."

"I'll pay for the petrol, but you'll feed the chauffeur."

Léa burst out laughing. "I'll feed the chauffeur! Ha! Ha! There speaks the son of Madame Peloux! Get along with you! You forget nothing. . . . I'm not usually inquisitive, but I should love to eavesdrop when you're making up to a woman."

She sank into a chair and fanned herself. A sphinx-moth and a number of long-legged mosquitoes hovered round the lamps; scents of the countryside drifted in from the garden, now that night had fallen. A sudden waft from an acacia burst in upon them, so distinct, so active, that they both turned round, half expecting to see it advancing towards them.

"It's the rose-acacia," Léa said.

"Yes," Chéri said. "But to-night it has sipped a draught of orange-flower water."

She stared at him, in vague admiration, astonished that he had hit upon such an idea. He was breathing in the scent in helpless rapture, and she turned away, suddenly fearful lest he might call her; but he did call, and she went to him.

She went to kiss him, on an impulse of resentment and selfishness, and half thinking to chastise him. 'Just you wait, my boy. . . . It's all too true that you've a pretty mouth, and, this time, I'm going to take my fill because I want to—and then I'll leave you, I don't care what you may say. Now . . .'

Her kiss was such that they reeled apart, drunk, deaf, breathless, trembling as if they had just been fighting. She stood up again in front of him, but he did not move from the depths of his chair, and she taunted him under her breath, "Well? . . . Well?" and waited for an insult. Instead, he held out his arms, opened his vague beautiful hands, tilted his head back as if he had been struck, and let her see beneath each eyelash the glint of a shining tear. He babbled indeterminate words—a whole animal chant of desire, in which she could distinguish her name—"darling"—"I want you"—"I'll never leave you"—a song to which she listened, solicitous, leaning over him, as if unwittingly she had hurt him to the quick.

WHEN Léa recalled their first summer in Normandy, she would sum it up impartially: "I've had other naughty little boys through my hands, more amusing than Chéri, more likeable, too, and more intelligent. But all the same, never one to touch him."

"It's funny," she confided to the old Baron de Berthellemy, towards the end of the summer of 1906, "but sometimes I think I'm in bed with a Chinee or an African."

"Have you ever had a Chinaman or a Negro?"

"Never."

"Well then?"

"I don't know. I can't explain. It's just an impression."

The impression had grown upon her slowly, also an astonishment she had not always been able to conceal. Her earliest memories of their idyll were abundantly rich, but only in pictures of delicious food, superb fruit, and the pleasure of taking pains over her country larder. She could still see Chéri—paler in the blazing sunlight—dragging along his exhausted body beneath the lime-tree tunnels in Normandy, or asleep on the sun-warmed paving beside a pond.

Léa used to rouse Chéri from sleep to cram him with strawberries and cream, frothy milk, and corn-fed chicken. With wide, vacant eyes, as though dazed, he would sit at dinner watching the mazy motions of the moths round the bowl of roses, and then look at his wristwatch to see whether the time had come to go to bed: while Léa, disappointed but unresentful, pondered over the unfulfilled promises of the kiss at Neuilly and good-naturedly bided her time.

"I'll keep him cooped up in this fattening-pen till the end of August, if need be. Then, back in Paris again—ouf!—I'll pack him off to his precious studies."

She went to bed mercifully early, so that Chéri—after nuzzling against her till he had hollowed out a selfishly comfortable position— might get some sleep. Sometimes, when the lamp was out, she would watch a pool of moonlight shimmering over the polished floor, or listen, through the chorus of rustling aspens and shrilling crickets, unceasing by night or day, to the deep, retriever-like sighs that rose from Chéri's breast.

'Why can't I go to sleep? Is there something wrong with me?' she vaguely wondered. 'It's not this boy's head on my shoulder—I've held heavier. The weather's wonderful. I've ordered him a good plate of porridge for to-morrow. Already his ribs stick out less. Then why can't I go to sleep? Yes, of course, I remember. . . . I'm going to send for Patron, the boxer, to give the boy some training. We've plenty of time between us, Patron and I, to spring a surprise on Madame Peloux.'

She fell asleep, lying stretched out on her back between the cool sheets, the dark head of her naughty little boy resting on her left breast. She fell asleep, to be aroused sometimes—but all too rarely— by a waking desire of Chéri's towards the break of day.

Patron actually arrived after they had been two months in their country retreat, with his suitcase, his small pound-and-a-half dumb-bells, his black tights, his six-ounce gloves, and his leather boxing-boots, laced down to the toe. Patron, with his girlish voice, his long eyelashes, and his splendid tanned skin, as brown as the leather of his luggage—he hardly looked naked when he took off his shirt. And Chéri, by turns peevish, listless, or jealous of Patron's smooth strength, started the slow, oft-repeated movements. They were tiresome, but they did him good.

"One . . . sss . . . two . . . sss . . . I can't hear you breathing . . . three . . . sss. . . . Don't think I can't see you cheating there with your knee . . . sss. . . . ."

An awning of lime foliage filtered the August sunlight. The bare bodies of instructor and pupil were dappled with purple reflections from the thick red carpet spread out upon the gravel. Léa watched the lessons with keen attention. Sometimes during the quarter of an hour's boxing, Chéri, drunk with new-found strength, lost all control and, red-faced with anger, attempted a foul blow. Rock-like, Patron stood up to his swings, and from the height of his Olympian glory let fall oracular words—words of wisdom that packed more weight than his proverbial punch.

"Steady on now! That left eye's wandering a bit! If I hadn't stopped myself in time, it would have had a nasty taste of the stitches on my right glove."

"I slipped," Chéri said, enraged.

"It's not a question of balance," Patron went on, "it's a question of morale. You'll never make a boxer."

"My mother won't let me, isn't that a pity?"

"Whether your mother lets you or not, you'll never make a boxer, because you've got a rotten temper. Rotten tempers and boxing don't go together. Aren't I right, Madame Léa?"

Léa smiled, and revelled in the warm sun, sitting still and watching the bouts between these two men, both young and both stripped. In her mind she kept comparing them. 'How handsome Patron is—as solid as a house! And the boy's shaping well. You don't find knees like his running about the streets every day of the week, or I'm no judge. His back, too, is . . . will be . . . marvellous. Where the devil did Mother Peloux drop her line to fish up a child like that? And the set of his head! quite a statue! But what a little beast he is! When he laughs, you'd swear it's a greyhound snarling!' She felt happy and maternal—bathed in quiet virtue. 'I'd willingly change him for anyone else,' she said to herself, with Chéri naked in the afternoon beside her under the lime-tree-bower, or with Chéri naked in the morning on her ermine rug, or Chéri naked in the evening on the edge of the warm fountain. 'Yes, handsome as he is, I'd willingly make a change, if it weren't a question of conscience!'

She confessed her indifference to Patron.

"And yet," Patron objected, "the lad's very nicely made. There's muscles on him now such as you don't see on our French lads; his are more like a coloured boy's—though he couldn't look any whiter, I must say. Nice little muscles they are, and not too showy. He'll never have biceps like melons."

"I should hope not, Patron! But then, you know, I didn't take him on for his boxing!"

"Of course not," Patron acquiesced, letting his long lashes droop, "there's—your feelings to be considered."

He was always embarrassed by Léa's unveiled allusions to sex, and by her smile—the insistence of the smiling eyes she brought to bear on him whenever she spoke of love.

"Of course," Patron tried another tack, "if he's not altogether satisfactory . . ."

Léa laughed: "Altogether! no . . . but I find being disinterested is its own reward. Just as you do, Patron."

"Oh! me . . ." He waited in fear and hope for the question that did not fail to follow.

"Always the same, Patron? You still won't give way an inch?"

"I won't give way, Madame Léa, and I've just had a letter from Liane by the midday post. She says she's all alone, that I've no good reasons for refusing, and that her two admirers have left her."

"Well?"

"Well, I don't believe it! I won't give way, because she won't give way. She's ashamed, she says, of a man who works for his living—specially when it pulls him out of bed so early every day for his training—a man who gives boxing lessons and teaches Swedish gymnastics. We've only got to meet, and the row starts all over again. 'Anyone'd think,' she shouts at me, 'that I'm not in a position to support the man I love!' That shows very nice feelings, I don't say it doesn't, but it doesn't fit in with my ideas. Everyone's funny about something. It's just like you said, Madame Léa, it's all a question of conscience."

They were talking in low tones under the trees: he prudish and half naked; she dressed in white, the colour flaming in her cheeks. They were enjoying the pleasure of a friendly understanding: they shared the same taste for the simple things of life, good health and a sort of plebeian decency. And yet Léa would not have been shocked had Patron received handsome presents from a beautiful and expensive woman like Liane. "Fair exchange is no robbery." And she did her best to break down Patron's "funny feelings" by arguments based on homespun justice. These leisurely conversations always revealed their worship of the same twin deities—love and money, and would drift away from money and love to come back to Chéri and his deplorable upbringing, to his exceptional good looks ("harmless, after all," as Léa would say) and to his character ("virtually non-existent," as Léa would say). They had a taste for sharing confidences, and a dislike of new words or ideas, which they satisfied in these long talks. They were often disturbed by the preposterous apparition of Chéri, whom they thought either asleep or motoring down some baking hot road—Chéri, looming into sight, half naked, but equipped with an account book, a stylo behind his ear.

"Look at our Mister Adding-machine," Patron said admiringly. "All got up as a clerk in a bank."

"What can this mean?" Chéri shouted from afar. "Three hundred and twenty francs for petrol? Somebody must be swilling the stuff! We've been out four times in the last fortnight—and seventy-seven francs for oil!"

"The motor goes to the market every day," Léa replied. "And while we're on the subject, it appears your chauffeur had three helpings of the joint for his dinner. Don't you think that's stretching our agreement a bit far? . . . Whenever a bill sticks in your throat, you look just like your mother."

At a loss for an answer, he stood uncertain for a moment, shifting from one slender foot to the other, poised with winged grace like a young Mercury. This always made Madame Peloux swoon with delight and yelp, "Me when I was eighteen! Winged feet! winged feet!" He cast about for some insolent retort, his whole face a-quiver, his mouth half-open, his forehead jutting forward, in a tense attitude that showed off to advantage the peculiar and diabolic upward twist of his eyebrows.

"Don't bother to think of an answer," Léa said kindly. "I know you hate me. Come and kiss me. Handsome devil. Fallen angel. Silly goose. . . ."

He came, calmed by the softness of her voice, yet ruffled by her words. Seeing them together, Patron once again let the truth flower on his guileless lips.

"As far as first-rate bodies go, Monsieur Chéri, you have one all right. But whenever I look at it, Monsieur Chéri, I feel that if I was a woman I'd say to myself: 'I'll come back again in ten years' time'."

"You hear, Léa? He says in ten years' time," Chéri said insinuatingly, pushing away the head of his mistress as she leaned towards him. "What do you think of that?"

But she did not deign to listen. The young body owed to her its renewed vigour, and she began patting it all over, touching it anywhere and everywhere, on the cheek, on the leg, on the behind, with the irreverent pleasure of a nanny.

"What d'you get out of being spiteful?" Patron then asked.

Chéri allowed a savage, inscrutable gaze to sweep over every inch of the waiting Hercules before he answered. "I find it comforting. You wouldn't understand."

In fact, Léa herself understood precious little about Chéri after three months' intimacy. If she still talked to Patron, who now came only on Sundays, or to Berthellemy, who arrived without being invited but left again two hours later, about "sending Chéri back to his blessed studies", it was because the phrase had become a kind of habit, and as though to excuse herself for having kept him there so long. She kept on setting a limit to his stay, and then exceeding it. She was waiting.

"The weather is so lovely. And then his trip to Paris last week tired him. And, besides, it's better for me to get thoroughly sick of him."

For the first time in her life, she waited in vain for what had never before failed her: complete trust on the part of her young lover, a self-surrender to confessions, candours, endless secrets—those hours in the depths of the night when, in almost filial gratitude, a young man unrestrainedly pours out his tears, his private likes and dislikes, on the kindly bosom of a mature and trusted friend.

'They've always told me everything in the past,' she thought obstinately. 'I've always known just what they were worth—what they were thinking and what they wanted. But this boy, this brat . . . No, that would really be the limit.'

He was now strong, proud of his nineteen years, gay at meals and impatient in bed; even so he gave away nothing but his body, and remained as mysterious as an odalisque. Tender? Yes, if an involuntary cry or an impulsive hug is an indication of tenderness. But the moment he spoke, he was "spiteful" again, careful to divulge nothing of his true self.

How often at dawn had Léa held him in her arms, a lover soothed, relaxed, with half-closed lids! Each morning his eyes and his mouth returned to life more beautiful, as though every waking, every embrace, had fashioned them anew! How often, at such moments, had she indulged her desire to master him, her sensual longing to hear his confession, and pressed her forehead against his, whispering, "Speak. Say something. Tell me . . ."

But no confession came from those curved lips, scarcely anything indeed but sulky or frenzied phrases woven round "Nounoune"—the name he had given her when a child and the one he now used in the throes of his pleasure, almost like a cry for help.

"Yes, I assure you, he might be a Chinee or an African," she declared to Anthime de Berthellemy, and added, "I can't tell you why." The impression was strong but confused, and she felt lazily incompetent to find words for the feeling that she and Chéri did not speak the same language.

It was the end of September when they returned to Paris. Chéri went straight to Neuilly, the very first evening, to "spring a surprise" on Madame Peloux. He brandished chairs, cracked nuts with his fist, leaped on to the billiard-table and played cowboy in the garden at the heels of the terrified watch-dogs.

"Ouf!" Léa sighed, as she entered her house in the Avenue Bugeaud, alone. "How wonderful!—a bed to myself!"

But at ten o'clock the following night, she was sipping coffee and trying not to find the evening too long or the dining-room too large, when a nervous cry was forced from her lips. Chéri had suddenly appeared, framed in the doorway—Chéri, wafted on silent, winged feet.

He was not speaking or showing any sign of affection, but just running towards her.

"Are you mad?"

Shrugging his shoulders, disdaining all explanations, just running towards her. Never asking "Do you love me?", "Have you already forgotten me?". Running towards her.

A moment later they were lying in the middle of Léa's great brass-encumbered bed. Chéri pretended to be worn out and sleepy. This made it easier to grit his teeth and keep his eyes tight shut, suffering as he was from a furious attack of taciturnity. Yet, through his silence, she was listening as she lay beside him, listening with delight to the distant delicate vibration, to the imprisoned tumult thrumming within a body that sought to conceal its agony, its gratitude and love.

"Why didn't your mother tell me this herself at dinner last night?"

"She thought it better it should come from me."

"No!"

"That's what she said."

"And you?"

"What about me?"

"Do you think it better?"

Chéri raised uncertain eyes to Léa's. "Yes." He appeared to think it over a moment and repeated: "Yes, far better, in fact."

In order not to embarrass him, Léa looked away towards the window.

The August morning was dark with warm rain, which fell vertically on the already rusted foliage of the three plane-trees in the garden court.

"It might be autumn," she said, and sighed.

"What's the matter?" Chéri asked.

She looked at him in astonishment. "Nothing, I don't like the rain, that's all."

"Oh! All right, I thought . . ."

"What?"

"I thought something was wrong."

She could not help giving a frank laugh. "Wrong with me, because you're getting married? No, listen . . . you're . . . you're so funny."

She seldom laughed outright, and her merriment vexed Chéri. He shrugged his shoulders and made the usual grimace while lighting a cigarette, jutting out his chin too far and protruding his lower lip.

"You oughtn't to smoke before luncheon," Léa said.

He made some impertinent retort she did not hear. She was listening to the sound of her own voice and its daily lectures, echoing away down the past five years. 'It's like the endless repetition in opposite looking-glasses,' she thought. Then, with a slight effort, she returned to reality and cheerfulness.

"It's lucky for me that there'll soon be someone else to stop you smoking on an empty stomach."

"Oh! *she* won't be allowed to have a say in anything," Chéri declared. "She's going to be my wife, isn't she? Let her kiss the sacred ground I tread on, and thank her lucky stars for the privilege. And that will be that."

He exaggerated the thrust of his chin, clenched his teeth on his cigarette-holder, parted his lips, and, as he stood there in his white silk pyjamas, succeeded only in looking like an Asiatic prince grown pale in the impenetrable obscurity of palaces.

Léa drew the folds of her pink dressing-gown closer about her—the pink she called "indispensable". She was lazily turning over ideas which she found tiresome, ideas that she decided to hurl, one by one, as missiles against Chéri's assumed composure.

"Well, why are you marrying the child?"

He put both elbows on the table and, unconsciously, assumed the composed features of his mother. "Well, you see, my dear girl . . ."

"Call me Madame or Léa. I'm neither your housemaid nor a pal of your own age."

She sat straight up in her armchair and clipped her words without raising her voice. He wanted to answer back. He looked defiantly at the beautiful face, a little pale under its powder, and at the frank blue light of her searching eyes. But he softened, and conceded, in a tone most unusual for him, "Nounoune, you asked me to explain. . . . It had to come to this in the end. And besides, there are big interests at stake."

"Whose?"

"Mine," he said without a smile. "The girl has a considerable fortune of her own."

"From her father?"

He rocked himself to and fro, his feet in the air. "Oh, how do I know? What a question! I suppose so. You'd hardly expect the fair Marie-Laure to draw fifteen hundred thousand out of her own bank account, would you? Fifteen hundred thousand, and some decent family jewels into the bargain."

"And how much have you?"

"Oh, I've more than that of my own," he said with pride.

"Then you don't need any more money?"

He shook his smooth head and it caught the light like blue watered silk. "Need . . . need . . . ? You know perfectly well we don't look at money in the same way. It's something on which we never see eye to eye."

"I'll do you the justice to say that you've spared me any reference to it during the last five years." She leaned towards him and put her hand on his knee. "Tell me, child, how much have you put by from your income in these five years?"

He cavorted like a clown, laughed, and rolled at Léa's feet, but she pushed him aside with her toe.

"No, tell me the truth . . . fifty thousand a year, or sixty? Tell me, sixty? Seventy?"

He sat down on the carpet facing away from Léa, and laid his head back on her lap. "Aren't I worth it, then?"

He stretched out to his full length, turned his head to look up at her, and opened his eyes wide. They looked black, but their true shade, Léa knew, was a dark almost reddish brown. As though to indicate her choice of what was rarest among so much beauty, she put her forefinger on his eyebrows, his eyelids and the corners of his mouth. At moments this lover, whom she slightly despised, inspired her with a kind of respect by his outward form. 'To be as handsome as that amounts to nobility,' she said to herself.

"Tell me, child, how does this young person feel about you?"

"She loves me. She admires me. She never says a word."

"And you—how do you behave with her?"

"I don't," he answered simply.

"Delightful love duets," Léa said, dreamily.

He sat up, crossing his legs tailor-fashion.

"You seem to me to be thinking a lot about her," he said severely. "Don't you think of yourself at all, in this upheaval?"

She gazed at Chéri with an astonishment that made her look years younger—eyebrows raised and lips half open.

"Yes, you, Léa. You, the victimized heroine. You, the one sympathetic character in all this, since you're being dropped."

He had become rather pale, and his tough handling of Léa seemed to be hurting him.

Léa smiled. "But, my darling, I've not the slightest intention of changing my life. Now and then, during the next week, I'll come across a pair of socks, a tie, a handkerchief on my shelves . . . and when I say a week . . . you know in what excellent order my shelves are kept! Oh, yes, and I'll have the bathroom re-done. I've got an idea of putting in encrusted glass. . . ."

She fell silent and assumed an almost greedy look as she traced a vague outline with her finger. Chéri continued to look vindictive.

"You aren't pleased! What do you want, then? Do you expect me to go to Normandy to hide my grief? To pine away? To stop dyeing my hair? To have Madame Peloux rushing to my bedside?" And she imitated Madame Peloux, flapping her arms and trumpeting: " 'The shadow of her former self, the shadow of her former self! The poor unfortunate creature has aged a hundred years, a hundred years!' Is that what you want?"

He had been listening with a smile that died on his lips, and a trembling of the nostrils that might be due to emotion. "Yes!" he cried.

Léa rested her smooth, bare, heavy arms on Chéri's shoulders.

"My poor boy! But at that rate, I ought to have died four or five times already! To lose a little lover. . . . To exchange one naughty little boy. . . ." She added in lower, lighter tones: "I've grown used to it!"

"We all know that," he said harshly. "I don't give a damn—d'you hear me?—I don't give a single damn that I wasn't your first lover. What I should have liked, or rather what would have been . . . fitting . . . decent . . . is to be your last." With a twist of his shoulders, he shrugged off her superb arms. "After all, what I am saying to you now is for your own good."

"I understand perfectly. You think only of me. I think only of your fiancée. That's all very nice, all very natural. It's clear that we both have hearts of gold."

She rose, waiting for some outrageous rejoinder. But he said nothing, and it hurt her to see for the first time a look of discouragement on his face.

She bent over and put her hands under his armpits.

"Now then, come along, get your clothes on. I've only to put on my dress, I'm ready underneath, and what in the world is there to do on a day like this except to go to Schwabe and choose a pearl for you? You see, I must give you a wedding-present."

He jumped up, his face aglow: "Top-hole! A pearl for my shirt-front! A pale pink pearl. I know the very one!"

"Not on your life! A white one, something masculine for pity's sake! Don't tell me, I know which one just as well as you. It'll ruin me, as usual. However, think of the money I'm going to save when you're out of the way!"

Chéri adopted a more reticent attitude. "Oh, that . . . that depends on my successor."

Léa turned back at the door of her boudoir and gave him her gayest smile, showing her strong teeth and the fresh blue of her eyes skilfully darkened by bistre.

"Your successor? A couple of francs and a packet of cigarettes! And a glass of cassis on Sunday—that's all the job will be worth! And I'll settle money on your children."

THEY both became extremely gay for the next few weeks. Chéri's official duties as a fiancé separated them for a few hours each day, sometimes for a night or two. "We mustn't let them lose confidence," Chéri declared. Léa, kept by Madame Peloux at a safe distance from Neuilly, satisfied her curiosity by plying Chéri with a hundred questions. Whenever he came back to Léa's house, he was full of his own importance and heavy with secrets which he at once divulged. He was like a schoolboy playing truant.

"Oh my sainted aunt!" he shouted one day, cramming his hat down on Léa's portrait-bust. "The goings-on at the Peloux Palace Hôtel ever since yesterday!"

She began by scolding him, laughing already in anticipation.

"Take your hat off that, in the first place. And in the second, don't invoke your wretched aunt in my house. Well, what's been happening now?"

"A riot, Nounoune! A riot's broken out among the ladies. Marie-Laure and Ma'me Peloux are scratching each other's eyes out over the marriage settlement!"

"No!"

"Yes! It was a superb sight. (Look out for the olives. . . . I'm going to impersonate Ma'me Peloux as a windmill. . . .) 'Separate bank accounts! Separate bank accounts! Why not a trustee? It's a personal insult, a personal insult. You forget that my son has his own fortune! . . . May I inform you, Madame . . .'"

"She called her Madame?"

"She most certainly did. 'Let me tell you, Madame, that my son has never had a ha'porth of debts since he came of age and the list of his investments bought since 1910 is worth . . .' is worth this, that and the other, including the skin off my nose, plus the fat off my bottom. In short, Catherine de Medici in person! But even more artful, of course!"

Léa's blue eyes glistened with tears of merriment. "Oh Chéri!

you've never been funnier in your life! What about the other? The fair Marie-Laure?"

"Her? Oh! terrible, Nounoune. That woman must have at least a dozen corpses in her wake. Dolled up in jade green, red hair, painted to look eighteen, and the inevitable smile. The trumpetings of my revered Mamma failed to make her bat an eyelid. She held her fire till the assault was over, then she came out with: 'It might perhaps be wiser, dear Madame, not to talk too loudly about all the money your son put by in 1910 and the years following. . . .'"

"Bang! Straight between the eyes! . . . Between yours. Where were you while all this was going on?"

"Me? In the large armchair."

"You were actually in the room?" She stopped laughing, and eating. "You were there? What did you do?"

"Cracked a joke, of course. Ma'me Peloux had just seized hold of a valuable piece of bric-à-brac, to avenge my honour, when I stopped her without even getting up. 'My adored mother, calm yourself. Follow my example, follow that of my charming mother-in-law, who's being as sweet as honey . . . as sweet as sugar.' And that's how I managed to arrange that the settlement should apply only to property acquired after marriage."

"I simply don't understand."

"The famous sugar plantations that the poor little Prince Ceste left to Marie-Laure by his will. . . ."

"Yes?"

"Forged will! Fury of the Ceste family! Lawsuit pending! Now d'you get it?"

He crowed.

"I get it. But how did you get hold of the story?"

"Ah! I'll tell you! Old Lili has just pounced with her full weight upon the younger of the Ceste boys, who's only seventeen and religious. . . ."

"Old Lili? What a nightmare!"

"And he babbles family secrets in her ear between every kiss. . . ."

"Chéri! I feel sick!"

"And old Lili tipped me off at Mamma's At Home last Sunday. She simply adores me! Besides, she respects me because I've never wanted to go to bed with her. . . ."

"I should hope not!" Léa sighed. "Yet all the same . . ." She broke off to reflect, and it seemed to Chéri her enthusiasm was flagging.

"Well, you must say it was pretty smart of me, eh?"

He leaned across the table; and the sunshine, playing over the silver and the white table-cloth, lit him up like a row of footlights.

"Yes . . ." 'All the same,' she was thinking, 'that poisonous Marie-Laure simply treated him like a ponce . . .'

"Is there any cream cheese, Nounoune?"

"Yes . . ." '. . . and he showed no more surprise than if she had thrown him a flower. . . .'

"Nounoune, will you let me have that address? the address of the place where you get your cream cheese—for the new cook I've engaged for October?"

"Are you mad? It's home-made. I *have* a cook, you know. Think of the *sauce aux moules* and *vol-au-vent!*" '. . . it's true I've practically kept the boy for the last five years. . . . But all the same he has an income of three hundred thousand francs a year. That's the point. Can you be a ponce with three hundred thousand a year? But why ever not? It doesn't depend on the amount, but on the man. . . . There are some men I could have given half a million to, and that wouldn't make them a ponce. But how about Chéri? After all, I have never actually given him any money. All the same . . .'

"All the same," she broke into speech. "She treated you like a gigolo!"

"Who did?"

"Marie-Laure!"

He brightened at once, like a child.

"Didn't she? Didn't she just, Nounoune? That's what she meant, wasn't it?"

"So it seems to me."

Chéri raised his glass of Château-Chalon, almost the colour of brandy. "So here's to Marie-Laure! What a compliment, eh? And if anyone can still say it of me when I'm your age, I shan't ask anything better!"

"If that's enough to make you happy . . ."

She listened to him absent-mindedly till the end of luncheon. Accustomed to her half-silences and her worldly wisdom, he asked for nothing better than the usual maternal homilies—"Take the brownest crusts. Don't eat so much new bread. . . . You've never learnt how to choose a fruit. . . ." All the time, secretly disgruntled, she was reproaching herself, 'I must make up my mind what I want!

What would I really have liked him to do? Get up on his hind legs and hiss "Madame, you have insulted me! Madame, I am not what you take me for!" I'm responsible, when all's said and done. I've spoon-fed him, I've stuffed him with good things. . . . Who in the world would have thought that one day he'd want to play the pater-familias? It never occurred to me! Even supposing it had—as Patron would say, "Nature will out." Even supposing Patron had accepted Liane's proposals, his nature would have come out all right if anyone had hinted at the fact in his hearing. But Chéri . . . has Chéri's nature. He's just Chéri. He's . . .'

"What were you saying, child?" she interrupted her thoughts to ask. "I wasn't listening."

"I was saying that never again—never, do you hear me—will anything make me laugh so much as my scene with Marie-Laure!"

—'There you are,' Léa concluded her thoughts, 'it . . . it merely made him laugh.'

Slowly she rose to her feet, as though tired. Chéri put an arm round her waist, but she pushed it away.

"What day is your wedding to be, now I come to think of it?"

"Monday week."

His candour and detachment terrified her. "That's fantastic!"

"Why fantastic, Nounoune?"

"You don't look as if you were giving it a thought!"

"I'm not," he said, calmly. "Everything's been arranged. Ceremony at two o'clock, saving us all the fuss and rush of a wedding breakfast. Instead, a tea party at Ma'me Peloux's. After that, sleepers, Italy, the Lakes. . . ."

"Are the Lakes back in fashion?"

"They are. There'll be villas, hotels, motor-drives, restaurants, like Monte-Carlo, eh?"

"But the girl! There's always the girl. . . ."

"Of course there's the girl. She's not much, but she's there!"

"And I'm no longer there."

Chéri had not expected her to say this and showed it. His face became disfigured, and he suddenly turned white about the mouth. He controlled his breath to avoid an audible gasp, and became himself again.

"Nounoune, you'll always be there."

"Monsieur overwhelms me."

"There'll always be you, Nounoune . . ." and he laughed awkwardly, "whenever I need you to do something for me."

She did not answer. She bent to pick up a tortoiseshell comb that had fallen to the floor and pushed it back in her hair, humming to herself. She went on humming a little snatch of a song in front of a looking-glass, pleased with herself, proud of having kept her self-control so easily, covered up so successfully the only emotional moment of their separation, proud of having held back words that must never be said: "Speak . . . beg for what you want, demand it, put your arms round my neck. . . . You have suddenly made me happy. . . ."

Madame Peloux must have been talking a great deal and for a long time before Léa appeared. The high colour on her cheeks emphasised the sparkle of her large eyes, which expressed only an indiscreet and inscrutable watchfulness. This Sunday she was wearing a black afternoon dress with a very narrow skirt, and nobody could fail to have observed that her feet were tiny and her stays too tight. She stopped talking, took a little sip from the petal-thin brandy glass warming in her hand, and nodded at Léa in lazy contentment.

"Isn't it a lovely day? Such weather, such weather! Would any one believe we're in the middle of October?"

"Oh, no, never. . . . Most certainly not!" two obsequious voices answered in chorus.

Beside the curving garden path a stream of red salvias wound between the banks of grey-mauve Michaelmas daisies. Golden butterflies flitted as if it were summer and the scent of chrysanthemums, strengthened by the hot sun, was wafted into the garden-room. A yellowing birch tree trembled in the wind above beds of tea roses, where the last of the bees still were busy.

"But what's this weather," yelled Madame Peloux, suddenly waxing lyrical, "but what's this weather, when compared to what *they* must be having in Italy?"

"Yes, indeed! . . . Just what I was thinking!" the attendant voices echoed.

Léa turned with a frown in their direction. 'If only they would hold their tongues,' she thought.

The Baroness de la Berche and Madame Aldonza were sitting at a card-table, playing piquet. Madame Aldonza, an aged ballerina, with legs eternally swathed in bandages, was distorted with rheumatism, and wore her shiny black wig a little askew. Opposite her, a head or more taller, the Baroness squared her rigid shoulders like a country priest's. Her face was large and had grown alarmingly masculine with age. She was a bristling bush of hair—hair in her ears, tufts in her nostrils and on her lip, and rough hairs between her fingers.

"Baroness, don't forget I made ninety," Madame Aldonza bleated like a goat.

"Score it, score it, my good friend! All I want is to see everyone happy."

An endless flow of honied words masked her savage cruelty. Léa looked at her closely as if for the first time, felt disgusted, and turned back to Madame Peloux. 'Charlotte, at least, *looks* human,' she thought.

"What's the matter with you, my Léa? You don't seem your usual self?" Madame Peloux enquired tenderly.

Léa drew up her handsome figure and answered: "Of course I am, Lolotte dear . . . it's so comfortable here in your house, I was merely relaxing," thinking all the while, 'Careful now . . . she's just as cruel as the other,' and she at once assumed an expression of flattering contentment, of dreamy repletion, and accentuated it by sighing, "I lunched too well. . . . I really must get thinner. I shall start a strict diet from to-morrow."

Madame Peloux flapped her hands and simpered.

"Isn't a broken heart enough to do that?"

"Oh, oh, oh! Ha-ha! Ho-ho!" guffawed Madame Aldonza and the Baroness de la Berche. "Ha-ha-ha!"

Léa rose to her full height in her autumn dress of sombre green, handsome under her satin hat trimmed with seal-skin, youthful among these old ruins over whom she cast a gentle eye. "Oh, la-la, my dears! Give me a dozen such heart-breaks, if that would help me to lose a couple of pounds!"

"Léa, you're astounding," the old Baroness shot at her in a puff of smoke.

Madame Léa, think of me, please, when you throw away that hat," old Madame Aldonza begged. "Madame Charlotte, you remember your blue one? It lasted me two years. Baroness, when you've quite finished ogling Madame Léa, perhaps you'll be kind enough to deal the cards to me."

"Very well, my sweet, and may they bring you luck!"

Léa stopped for a moment by the door, then stepped out into the garden. She picked a tea rose, which shed its petals. She listened to the breeze in the birch, to the trams in the Avenue, to the whistle of the local train. The bench she sat on was warm, and she closed her eyes, letting her shoulders enjoy the warmth of the sun. When she opened her eyes again, she hurriedly turned her head in the direction of the house, feeling positive that she was going to see Chéri standing in the garden entrance with his shoulder against the doorway.

'What can be the matter with me?' she wondered. Piercing screams of laughter and a little chorus of greeting from indoors brought her, trembling slightly, to her feet. 'Can I be suffering from nerves?'

"Ah, here they are, here they are!" Madame Peloux trumpeted, and the deep bass of the Baroness chimed in "Here come the happy pair!"

Léa shivered, ran as far as the door and stopped short: there, in front of her, were old Lili and her adolescent lover, Prince Ceste, just arriving.

Perhaps seventy years of age, with the corpulence of a eunuch held in by stays, old Lili was usually referred to as 'passing all bounds', without these 'bounds' being defined. Her round pink painted face was enlivened by a ceaseless girlish gaiety, and her large eyes and small mouth, thin-lipped and shrunken, flirted shamelessly. Old Lili followed the fashion to an outrageous degree. A striking blue-and-white striped skirt held in the lower part of her body, and a little blue jersey gaped over her skinny bosom crinkled like the wattles of a turkey-cock; a silver fox failed to conceal the neck, which was the shape of a flower-pot and the size of a belly. It had engulfed the chin.

'It's terrifying,' Léa thought. She was unable to tear her eyes away from details that were particularly sinister—a white sailor hat, for instance, girlishly perched on the back of a short-cut, strawberry-roan wig; or, again, a pearl necklace visible one moment and the next interred in a deep ravine which once had been termed a "*collier de Vénus*".

"Léa, Léa, my little chickabiddy!" old Lili exclaimed as she did her best to hasten towards Léa. She walked with difficulty on round swollen feet, tightly swaddled in high-heeled laced boots with paste buckles on the ankle-straps, and was the first to congratulate herself on this performance: "I waddle like a duckling! it is a special little way I have. Guido, my passion, you remember Madame de Lonval? Don't remember her too well or I'll tear your eyes out. . . ."

A slim youth with Italian features, enormous empty eyes and a weak receding chin, kissed Léa's hand hastily and retired into the shadows without a word. Lili caught him in flight, pulled his head down to her scaly chest, calling the onlookers to witness: "Do you know what this is, Madame, do you know what this is? This, ladies, is the love of my life!"

"Restrain yourself, Lili!" Madame de la Berche advised in her masculine voice.

"But why? But why?" from Charlotte Peloux.

"For the sake of decency," said the Baroness.

"Baroness, that's not nice of you! I think they're so sweet. Ah!" she sighed, "they remind me of my own children."

"I was thinking of them," Lili said, with a delighted smile. "It's our honeymoon too, Guido's and mine. Indeed, we've just come to ask about the other young couple! We want to hear all about them."

Madame Peloux became stern. "Lili, you don't expect me to go into details, do you?"

"Oh yes, yes, I do," Lili cried, clapping her hands. She tried to skip, but succeeded only in raising her shoulders and hips a little. "That's always been my besetting sin, and always will be! I adore spicy talk! I'll never be cured of it. That little wretch there knows how I adore it."

The silent youth, called to bear witness, did not open his mouth. The black pupils of his eyes moved up and down against the whites, like frantic insects. Léa watched him, rooted to the spot.

"Madame Charlotte told us all about the wedding ceremony," bleated Madame Aldonza. "The young Madame Peloux was a dream in her wreath of orange blossom!"

"A madonna! A madonna!" Madame Peloux corrected at the top of her voice, with a burst of religious fervour. "Never, never, has anyone looked so divine. My son was in heaven! In heaven, I tell you! . . . What a pair they made, what a pair!"

"You hear that, my passion? Orange blossom!" Lili murmured. "And tell me, Charlotte, what about our mother-in-law, Marie-Laure?"

Madame Peloux's pitiless eyes sparkled: "Oh her! Out of place, absolutely out of place. In tight-fitting black, like an eel wriggling out of the water—you could see everything, breasts, stomach—everything!"

"By Jove!" muttered the Baroness de la Berche with military gusto.

"And that look of contempt she has for everybody, that look of having a dose of cyanide up her sleeve and half a pint of chloroform inside her handbag! As I said, out of place—that exactly describes her. She behaved as if she could only spare us five minutes of her precious time—she'd hardly brushed the kiss off her lips, before she said, 'Au revoir, Edmée, au revoir, Fred,' and off she flew."

Old Lili was breathing hard, sitting on the edge of her chair, her little grandmotherly mouth, with its puckered corners, hanging half open. "And who gave the usual advice?" she threw out.

"What advice?"

"The little talk—oh, my passion, hold my hand while I say it!—instruction for the young bride. Who gave her that?"

Charlotte Peloux took offence and stared at her. "Things may well have been done in that way when you were young, but the practice has fallen into disuse."

The sprightly old girl plumped her fists on her thighs: "Disuse? Disuse or not, how would you know anything about it, my poor Charlotte? There's so little marrying in your family!"

"Ha-ha-ha!" the two toadies imprudently guffawed.

But a single glance from Madame Peloux made them tremble. "Peace, peace, my little angels! You're each enjoying your paradise on earth, so what more do you want?" The Baroness stretched out a strong arm, like a policeman keeping order, between the purple faces of Lili and Madame Peloux. But Charlotte scented battle like a war-horse. "If you're looking for trouble, Lili, you don't have to look further than me! Because of your age, I must treat you with respect, and if it weren't for that . . ."

Lili shook with laughter from chin to thigh. "If it weren't for that, you'd get married yourself just to give me the lie? I know—it's not so hard to get married! Why, I'd marry Guido like a shot, if only he were of age!"

"Not possible!" gasped Charlotte, so taken aback that she forgot her anger.

"But, of course . . . Princess Ceste, my dear! *la piccola principessa! Piccola principessa,* that's what my little Prince always calls me!"

She nipped hold of her skirt, and, in turning, displayed a gold curb-chain where her ankle ought to have been. "Only," she continued mysteriously, "his father . . ."

By now out of breath, she made a sign to the silent young man, who took up the tale in a low rapid voice as if he were reciting his piece: "My father, the Duke of Parese, threatens to put me in a convent if I marry Lili."

"In a convent!" Charlotte Peloux squealed. "A man in a convent!"

"A man in a convent!" neighed Madame de la Berche in her deep bass, "Egad! if that isn't exciting!"

"They're barbarians," Aldonza lamented, joining her misshapen hands together.

Léa rose so abruptly that she upset a glass.

"It's uncoloured glass," Madame Peloux observed with satisfaction. "You'll bring good luck to my young couple. Where are you running off to? Is your house on fire?"

Léa managed to squeeze out a sly little laugh: "On fire? In a sense, perhaps. Ssh! no questions! It's a secret."

"What? Already? It's not possible!" Charlotte Peloux cheeped enviously. "I was just saying to myself that you looked as if . . ."

"Yes, yes! You must tell us! Tell us everything," yapped the three old women.

Lili's quilted fists, old Aldonza's deformed stumps, Charlotte Peloux's hard fingers had seized upon her wrist, her sleeve, her gold-mesh bag. She snatched her arm away from all these claws and succeeded in laughing again, teasingly: "No, it's far too early in the day, it would spoil everything! It's my secret." And she rushed away to the hall.

But the door opened in front of her and a desiccated old fellow, a sort of playful mummy, took her into his arms: "Léa, lovely creature, a kiss for your little Berthellemy, or he won't let you pass!"

She gave a cry of fright and impatience, struck off the gloved bones retarding her progress, and fled.

Neither in the avenues of Neuilly, nor on the roads through the Bois, turning to blue in the fast-falling twilight, did she allow herself a moment's reflection. She shivered slightly and pulled up the windows of the motor-car. She felt restored by the sight of her clean house, the comfort of her pink bedroom and boudoir, overcrowded with furniture and flowers.

"Quick, Rose, light the fire in my room!"

"But, Madame, the pipes are already at their winter temperature. Madame should not have gone out with only a fur round her neck. The evenings are treacherous."

"A hot-water bottle in my bed at once, and for dinner a cup of thick chocolate beaten up with the yolk of an egg, some toast, and a bunch of grapes. . . . Hurry, dear, I'm freezing. I caught cold in that junk-shop at Neuilly. . . ."

Once under the sheets, she clenched her teeth to stop them chattering. The warmth of the bed eased her stiffened muscles, but still she did not altogether relax, and she went through the chauffeur's expense book till the chocolate arrived. This she drank at once, frothy and scalding. She chose her *chasselas* grapes one by one, the long greenish-amber bunch dangling by its stem against the light.

Then she turned out the bedside lamp, settled herself in her favourite position, flat on her back, and gave way.

'What can be the matter with me?'

She succumbed again to anxiety and started to shiver. She was obsessed by the vision of an empty doorway, with clumps of red salvia on either side. 'I can't be well,' she thought, 'one doesn't get into a state like this over a door!' Again she saw the three old women, Lili's neck, and the beige rug that Madame Aldonza had trailed about with her for the past twenty years. 'Which of them am I going to look like in ten years' time?'

Though she did not feel alarmed at this prospect, her anxiety increased still further. She let her mind wander from one incident of her past life to another, from this scene to that, trying to rid her thoughts of the empty doorway framed by red salvia. She was growing restless in her bed and trembled slightly. Suddenly she jumped as though shot, racked by a pain so deep that at first she thought it must be physical, a pain that twisted her lips and dragged from them, in a raucous sob, a single name: "Chéri!"

Tears followed, beyond all control at first. As soon as she had regained her self-control, she sat up, wiped her face, and turned on the lamp again. 'Ah! That's what it is! Now I understand!'

She took a thermometer from the drawer of her bedside table and put it under her arm. 'My temperature's normal, so it's nothing physical. I see. I'm just unhappy. Something must be done about it.'

She drank some water, got out of bed, bathed her inflamed eyes, put on a little powder, poked the fire, and went back to bed. She was on her guard, full of mistrust for an enemy she had never known: grief. She had just said goodbye to thirty years of easy living: years spent pleasantly, intent often on love, sometimes on money. This had left her, at almost fifty, still young and defenceless.

She made fun of herself, ceased to feel her grief, and smiled. 'I think I was out of my mind just now. There's nothing wrong with me any longer.'

But a movement of her left arm, which bent automatically to hold and shelter a sleeping head, brought back all her agony, and she sat up with a jump. "Well, this *is* going to be fun!" she said out loud and sternly.

She looked at the clock and saw that it was barely eleven. Overhead passed the slippered tread of the elderly Rose, on her way up the stairs to the attic floor. Then there was silence. Léa resisted the impulse to call out for help to this deferential old body. 'Don't give the servants anything to gossip about. We mustn't have that.'

She left her bed again, wrapped herself up warm in a quilted silk dressing-gown and toasted her feet. Then she half opened her window and listened for she knew not what. A moist and milder wind had brought clouds in its wake, and the lingering leaves in the neighbouring Bois sighed with every gust. Léa shut the window again, picked up a newspaper and looked at the date—'October the twenty-sixth. Exactly a month since Chéri was married?' She never said 'Since Edmée was married.'

Following Chéri's example, she did not yet count his young wraith of a wife as really alive. Chestnut-brown eyes, ashy hair which was very lovely with the vestige of a crimp in it—all the rest melted away in her memory like the contours of a face seen in a dream.

'At this very moment, of course, they'll be in each other's arms in Italy. And . . . and I don't mind that in the least.'

She was not boasting. The picture of the young couple she had called up, the familiar attitudes it evoked—even Chéri's face, as he lay exhausted for a minute, with the white line of light between his tired eyelids—aroused in her neither curiosity nor jealousy. On the other hand, an animal convulsion again racked her body, bending her double, as her eye fell on a nick in the pearl-grey wainscot—the mark of some brutality of Chéri's. "The lovely hand which here has left its trace, has turned away from me for ever," she said. 'How grandly I'm talking! Soon grief will be turning me into a poet!'

She walked about, she sat down, she went to bed again and waited for daylight. At eight o'clock Rose found her writing at her desk, and this upset the old lady's-maid.

"Is Madame not well?"

"So-so, Rose. Age, you know. . . . Doctor Vidal thinks I ought to have a change of air. Will you come with me? It promises to be a cold winter here in Paris. We'll go south to the sun, and eat meals cooked in oil."

"Whereabouts will that be?"

"You want to know too much. Simply have my trunks brought down, and give my fur rugs a good beating."

"Madame will be taking the motor-car?"

"I think so. I'm sure of it, in fact. I'll need all my creature comforts now, Rose. Just think of it, this time I'm going all on my own. It's going to be a pleasure trip."

During the next five days Léa rushed all over Paris; wrote, telegraphed, and received telegrams and answers from the south. And she said goodbye to Paris, leaving behind a short letter addressed to Madame Peloux which she started no less than three times:

My dear Charlotte,

You'll forgive me if I go away without saying goodbye to you, and keep my little secret to myself. I'm making a perfect fool of myself . . . and why not? It's a short life, let's make it a gay one.

I send you an affectionate kiss. Remember me to the child when he comes back.

Your incorrigible
Léa.

PS.—Don't trouble to come and interview my butler or concierge; no member of my household knows anything at all about it.

"Do you know, my adored treasure, I don't think you're looking very well."

"It's the night in the train," Chéri answered shortly.

Madame Peloux did not dare to say just what she thought. She found her son changed. 'He's . . . yes, he's sinister!' she decided; and she ended by exclaiming enthusiastically, "It's Italy!"

"If you like," Chéri conceded.

Mother and son had just finished breakfasting together, and Chéri had condescended to praise with an oath his cup of "housemaid's coffee", made with creamy milk, well sugared, slowly re-heated, with buttered toast crumbled into it and browned till it formed a succulent crust.

He felt cold in his white woollen pyjamas and was clasping his knees to his chest. Charlotte Peloux, anxious to look pretty for her son, had put on a brand new marigold négligée, and a boudoir-cap fitting tight across the forehead. This made her face stand out, bare and macabre.

Finding her son's eye fixed upon her, she simpered: "You see, I've adopted the grandmother style. Very soon, I'll powder my hair. Do you like this cap? Rather eighteenth-century, don't you think? Dubarry or Pompadour? How do I look in it?"

"Like an old convict," Chéri said witheringly. "Next time you must run up a warning signal."

She groaned, then shrieked with laughter: "Ha-ha-ha. You've a sharp tongue in your head and no mistake!"

But he did not laugh. He was staring out at the lawn powdered with snow after last night's fall. His nervous state was visible only in the spasmodic twitching of his jaw muscles. Madame Peloux was intimidated. She, too, was silent. The faint tinkle of a bell sounded.

"That's Edmée, ringing for her breakfast," said Madame Peloux.

Chéri did not answer. "What's wrong with the heating? It's freezing in here!" he said a moment later.

"It's Italy!" Madame Peloux repeated lyrically. "You come back here, your eyes and your heart full of the warm sun of the south, and find you've landed at the Pole—at the North Pole. There hasn't been a flower on the dahlias for the last week. But don't worry, my precious! Your love-nest will soon be finished. If the architect hadn't gone down with paratyphoid, it would be ready for you now. I warned him. If I told him once, I told him twenty times: 'Monsieur Savaron . . .'"

Chéri, who was standing by the window, turned round sharply. "What was the date on that letter?"

Madame Peloux opened her large child-like eyes: "What letter?"

"The letter from Léa you showed me."

"She put no date on it, my love; but I got it the night before my last Sunday At-home in October."

"I see. And you don't know who it is?"

"Who what is, my paragon?"

"Whoever it was she went away with, of course."

Malice clothed Madame Peloux's stark features. "No. Would you believe it, nobody has an idea! Old Lili is in Sicily, and none of my set has a clue! A mystery, an enthralling mystery! However, you know me, I've managed to pick up a few scraps here and there . . ."

Chéri's dark eyes expanded: "What's the tattle?"

"It seems it's a young man . . ." Madame Peloux whispered. "A young man not . . . not particularly desirable, if you know what I mean . . . very well made, of course!" She was lying, careful to insinuate the worst.

Chéri shrugged his shoulders.

"Well made, did you say. Don't make me laugh! My poor Léa! I can see him from here—a hefty little fellow from Patron's training-quarters—black hairs on his wrists and clammy hands. . . . Well, I'm going back to bed now; you make me tired."

Trailing his bedroom slippers, he went back to his room, dawdling in the long corridors and on the spacious landings of the house he seemed to be discovering for the first time. He ran into a pot-bellied wardrobe, and was amazed. 'Damned if I knew that thing was there. . . . Oh, yes, I vaguely remember. . . . And who the devil's this chap?' He was addressing an enlarged photograph, in a deep black frame, hanging funereally near a piece of coloured pottery, equally unfamiliar to Chéri.

Madame Peloux had been installed in this house for the last twenty-five years, and had kept every unfortunate result of her bad taste and acquisitiveness. "Your house looks just like the nest of a magpie gone batty," was old Lili's reproachful comment. She herself had a hearty appetite for modern pictures, and still more for modern painters. To this Madame Peloux had replied: "I believe in letting well alone."

If the muddy green paint—"The green of hospital corridors," Léa called it—flaked off in one of the passages, Madame Peloux would have it repainted a similar muddy green; or if the maroon velvet on a *chaise-longue* needed replacing, she was careful to choose the same maroon velvet.

Chéri paused by the open door of a dressing-room. Embedded in the dark red marble-topped wash-stand were jug and basin of plain white with a monogram, and over the two electric-light fittings were lily-shaped bead shades. Chéri shuddered as though caught in a violent draught—'Good God, how hideous, what an old junk-shop!'

He hurried away. At the end of the passage, he came upon a window edged with small pieces of red and yellow stained glass. 'That's the last straw!' he said grumpily.

He turned to the left and roughly opened a door—the door of his nursery—without knocking. A little cry came from the bed where Edmée was just finishing her breakfast. Chéri closed the door and stared at his wife without going any closer.

"Good morning," she said with a smile. "You do look surprised to see me here!"

She lay bathed in a steady blue light reflected from the snow outside. Her crimped ashy chestnut hair was down, but barely covered her prettily curved shoulders. With her pink-and-white cheeks matching her nightgown, and her rosy lips paler than usual from fatigue, she looked like a light toned picture, not quite finished and rather misty.

"Aren't you going to say good morning to me, Fred?" she insisted.

He sat down close beside his wife and took her in his arms. She fell back gently, dragging him with her. Chéri propped himself on his elbow to look down more closely at her. She was so young that even when tired she still looked fresh. He seemed astonished by the smoothness of her fully rounded lower eyelids, and by the silvery softness of her cheeks.

"How old are you?" he asked suddenly.

Edmée opened her eyes, which she had closed voluptuously. Chéri stared at the brown of their irises and at her small square teeth.

"Oh, come! I shall be nineteen on the fifth of January, and do try and remember it."

He drew his arm away roughly and the young woman slipped into the hollow of the bed like a discarded scarf.

"Nineteen, it's prodigious! Do you know that I'm over twenty-five?"

"But of course I know that, Fred. . . ."

He picked up a pale tortoiseshell mirror from the bed-table and gazed at himself. "Twenty-five years old!"

Twenty-five years of age and a face of white marble that seemed indestructible. Twenty-five, but at the outer corners of the eye and beneath it—delicately plagiarising the classical design of the eyelid —were two lines, visible only in full light, two incisions traced by the lightest, the most relentless, of fingers.

He put back the mirror: "You're younger than I am. That shocks me."

"Not me!"

She had answered in a biting voice, full of hidden meaning. He took no notice.

"Do you know why my eyes are beautiful?" he asked in all seriousness.

"No," Edmée said. "Perhaps because I love them?"

"Stuff!" Chéri said, shrugging his shoulders. "It's because they're shaped like a sole."

"Like what?"

"Like a sole."

He sat down near her to give a demonstration.

"Look—here—the corner next the nose is the head of the sole. And then—the upper curve, that's the back of the sole; whereas the lower line runs perfectly straight and that's its belly. And the other corner that tapers up to my temples, that's the sole's tail."

"Oh?"

"Yes, but if I had an eye shaped like a flounder, that's to say, with the lower part as much curved as the top, then I should look silly. See? You've passed your matric., and you didn't know that?"

"No, I must admit . . ."

She broke off, feeling guilty, because he had spoken sententiously and with exaggerated passion, like someone with a mania. 'There are moments when he looks like a savage,' she thought, 'like a man from the jungle. Yet he knows nothing about plants or animals, and some-times he doesn't seem even to know about human beings.'

Sitting close beside her, Chéri put one arm round her shoulders and with his free hand began to finger the small, evenly matched, very round and very beautiful, pearls of her necklace. Intoxicated by the scent which Chéri used too much of, she began to droop like a rose in an overheated room.

"Fred! Come back to sleep! We're both tired. . . ."

He seemed not to have heard. He was staring at the pearls with obsessed anxiety.

"Fred!"

He shivered, leaped to his feet, furiously tore off his pyjamas and jumped naked into bed, seeking the place to rest his head on a shoul-der where the delicate collar-bone was still youthfully sharp. The whole of Edmée's body obeyed his will as she opened her arms to him. Chéri closed his eyes and never moved. She took care to remain awake, a little smothered under his weight, and thinking him asleep. But almost at once he turned over away from her with a sudden pitch, imitating the groans of someone fast asleep, and rolled himself up in the sheet at the other side of the bed.

'He always does that,' Edmée noted.

All through the winter, she was to awaken in this square room with its four windows. Bad weather delayed the completion of the new house in the Avenue Henri-Martin—bad weather, and Chéri's whims. He wanted a black bathroom, a Chinese drawing-room, a basement fitted up with a swimming pool and gymnasium. To the architect's objections he would answer: "I don't care a damn. I pay, I want the work done. To hell with the cost." But every now and again he would cast a ruthless eye over an estimate and proclaim "You can't bamboozle young Peloux." Indeed, he held forth on stand-ardisation, fibro-cement and coloured stucco with unexpected glibness and a memory for exact figures that compelled the contrac-tor's respect.

Rarely did he consult his young wife, although he paraded his au-thority for her benefit and took pains, when occasion arose, to cover his deficiencies by giving curt commands. She was to find that he possessed an instinctive eye for colour, but had only contempt for beauty of shape and period differences.

"You simply clutter up your head with all that stuff and nonsense, what's your name, yes, you, Edmée. An idea for the smoking-room? All right, here's one: Blue for the walls—a ferocious blue. The carpet purple—a purple that plays second fiddle to the blue of the walls. Against that you needn't be afraid of using as much black as you like and a splash of gold in the furniture and ornaments."

"Yes, you're right, Fred. But it will be rather drastic with all those strong colours. It's going to look rather charmless without a lighter note somewhere . . . a white vase or a statue."

"Nonsense," he interrupted, rather sharply. "The white vase you want will be me—me, stark naked. And we mustn't forget a cushion or some thingumabob in pumpkin-red for when I'm running about stark naked in the smoking-room."

Secretly attracted and at the same time disgusted, she cherished these fanciful ideas for turning their future home into a sort of disreputable palace, a temple to the greater glory of her husband. She offered little resistance, just gently requested "some little corner" for a small and precious set of furniture upholstered with needlework on a white ground—a present from Marie-Laure.

This gentleness masked a determination that was young yet far from inexperienced; it stood her in good stead during the four months of camping out in her mother-in-law's house. It enabled her to evade, throughout these four months, the enemy stalking her, the traps laid daily to destroy her equanimity, her still susceptible gaiety, and her tact. Charlotte Peloux, over-excited at the proximity of so tender a victim, was inclined to lose her head and squander her barbs, using her claws indiscriminately.

"Keep calm, Madame Peloux," Chéri would throw out from time to time. "What bones will there be left for you to pick next winter, if I don't stop you now?"

Edmée raised frightened, grateful eyes to her husband, and did her best not to think too much, not to look too much at Madame Peloux. Then one evening, Charlotte, almost heedlessly, three times tossed across the chrysanthemum table-piece Léa's name instead of Edmée's.

Chéri lowered his satanic eyebrows: "Madame Peloux, I believe your memory is giving way. Perhaps a rest-cure is indicated?"

Charlotte Peloux held her tongue for a whole week, but Edmée never dared to ask her husband: "Did you get angry on my behalf? Was it me you were defending? Or was it that other woman, the one before me?"

Life as a child and then as a girl had taught her patience, hope, silence; and given her a prisoner's proficiency in handling these virtues as weapons. The fair Marie-Laure had never scolded her daughter: she had merely punished her. Never a hard word, never a tender one. Utter loneliness, then a boarding-school, then again loneliness in the holidays and frequent relegations to a bedroom. Finally, the threat of marriage—any marriage—from the moment that the eye of a too beautiful mother had discerned in the daughter the dawn of a rival beauty, shy, timid, looking a victim of tyranny, and all the more touching for that. In comparison with this inhuman gold-and-ivory mother, Charlotte Peloux and her spontaneous malice seemed a bed of roses.

"Are you frightened of my respected parent?" Chéri asked her one evening.

Edmée smiled and pouted to show her indifference: "Frightened? No. You aren't frightened when a door slams, though it may make you jump. It's a snake creeping under it that's frightening."

"A terrific snake, Marie-Laure, isn't she?"

"Terrific."

He waited for confidences that did not come and put a brotherly arm round his wife's slender shoulders: "We're sort of orphans, you and I, aren't we?"

"Yes, we're orphans, and we're so sweet!"

She clung to him. They were alone in the big sitting-room, for Madame Peloux was upstairs concocting, as Chéri put it, her poisons for the following day. The night was cold and the window panes reflected the lamp-light and furnishings like a pond. Edmée felt warm and protected, safe in the arms of this unknown man. She lifted her head and gave a cry of alarm. He was staring up at the chandelier above them with a look of desperation on his magnificent features, and two tears hung glistening between the lids of his half-closed eyes.

"Chéri, Chéri, what's the matter with you?" On the spur of the moment she had called him by the too endearing nickname she had never meant to pronounce. He answered its appeal in bewilderment and turned his eyes down to look at her.

"Chéri, oh God! I'm frightened. What's wrong with you?"

He pushed her away a little, and held her facing him.

"Oh! Oh! You poor child, you poor little thing! What are you frightened of?"

He gazed at her with his eyes of velvet, wide-open, peaceful, inscrutable, all the more handsome for his tears. Edmée was about to beg him not to speak, when he said, "How silly we are! It's the idea that we're orphans. It's idiotic. It's so true."

He resumed his air of comic self-importance, and she drew a breath of relief, knowing that he would say no more. He began switching off all the lights with his usual care, and then turned to Edmée with a vanity that was either very simple or very deceitful: "Well, why shouldn't I have a heart like everybody else?"

"What are you doing there?"

He had called out to her almost in a whisper, yet the sound of Chéri's voice struck Edmée so forcibly that she swayed forward as if he had pushed her. She was standing beside a big open writing-desk and she spread her hands over the papers scattered in front of her.

"I'm tidying up . . ." she said in a dazed voice. She lifted a hand and it remained poised in mid-air as though benumbed. Then she appeared to wake up, and stopped lying.

"It's like this, Fred. You told me that when we came to move house you'd hate to be bothered over what you'd want to take with you, all the things in this room . . . the furniture. I honestly wanted to tidy, to sort things. Then the poison, temptation came . . . evil thoughts . . . one evil thought. . . . I implore your forgiveness. I've touched things that don't belong to me. . . ."

She trembled bravely and waited.

He stood with his forehead jutting forward, his hands clenched in a threatening attitude; but he did not seem to see his wife. His eyes were strangely veiled, and ever after she was to retain the impression of having spoken with a man whose eyes were deathly pale.

"Ah, yes," he said at length. "You were looking . . . you were looking for love-letters." She did not deny it. "You were hunting for my love-letters."

He laughed his awkward, constrained laugh.

Edmée felt hurt, and blushed. "Of course you must think me a fool. As if you were the kind of man not to lock them away in a safe place or burn them! And then, anyhow, they're none of my business. I've only got what I deserved. You won't hold it too much against me, Fred?"

Her pleading had cost her a certain effort, and she tried deliberately to make herself look appealing, pouting her lips a little and keeping the upper half of her face shadowed by her fluffy hair. But

Chéri did not relax his attitude, and she noticed for the first time that the unblemished skin of his cheeks had taken on the transparence of a white rose in winter, and that their oval contour had shrunk.

"Love-letters," he repeated. "That's howlingly funny."

He took a step forward, seized a fistful of papers and scattered them: post-cards, restaurant bills, tradespeople's announcements, telegrams from chorus girls met one night and never seen again, *pneumatiques* of four or five lines from sponging friends; and several close-written pages slashed with the sabre-like script of Madame Peloux.

Chéri turned round again to his wife: "I have no love-letters."

"Oh!" she protested. "Why do you want . . ."

"I have none," he interrupted; "you can never understand. I've never noticed it myself until now. I can't have any love-letters because——" He checked himself. "But wait, wait. . . . Yes, there was one occasion, I remember, when I didn't want to go to La Bourboule, and it . . . Wait, wait."

He began pulling out drawers and feverishly tossing papers to the floor.

"That's too bad! What can I have done with it? I could have sworn it was in the upper left-hand . . . No. . . ."

He slammed back the empty drawers and glowered at Edmée.

"You found nothing? You didn't take a letter which began 'But what do you expect, I'm not in the least bored. There's nothing better than to be separated one week in every month,' and then went on to something else. I don't remember what, something about honeysuckle climbing high enough to look in at the window."

He broke off, simply because his memory refused to come to his aid, and he was left gesticulating in his impatience.

Slim and recalcitrant, Edmée did not quail before him. She took refuge in caustic irritability. "No, no, I *took* nothing. Since when have I been capable of *taking* things? But if this letter is so very precious to you, how is it you've left it lying about? I've no need to enquire whether it was one of Léa's?"

He winced, but not quite in the manner Edmée had expected. The ghost of a smile hovered over his handsome, unresponsive features; and, with his head on one side, an expectant look in his eyes, and the delicious bow of his mouth taut-stretched, he might well have been listening to the echo of a name.

The full force of Edmée's young and ill-disciplined emotions burst forth in a series of sobs and tears, and her fingers writhed and twisted as if ready to scratch. "Go away! I hate you! You've never loved me. I might not so much as exist, for all the notice you take of me! You hurt me, you despise me, you're insulting, you're, you're . . . You think only of that old woman! It's not natural, it's degenerate, it's . . . You don't love me! Why, oh why, did you ever marry me? . . . You're . . . you're . . ."

She was tossing her head like an animal caught by the neck, and as she leaned back to take a deep breath, because she was suffocating, the light fell on her string of small, milky, evenly matched pearls. Chéri stared in stupefaction at the uncontrolled movements of the lovely throat, at the hands clasped together in appeal, and above all at the tears, her tears. . . . He had never seen such a torrent of tears. For who had ever wept in front of him, or wept because of him? No one. Madame Peloux? 'But,' he thought, 'Madame Peloux's tears don't count.' Léa? No. Searching his memory, he appealed to a pair of honest blue eyes; but they had sparkled with pleasure only, or malice, or a rather mocking tenderness. Such floods of tears poured down the cheeks of this writhing young woman. What could be done about all these tears? He did not know. All the same, he stretched out an arm, and as Edmée drew back, fearing some brutality perhaps, he placed his beautiful, gentle, scented hand on her head and patted her ruffled hair. He did his best to copy the tone and speech of a voice whose power he knew so well: "There, there. . . . What's it all about? What's the matter, then? There . . . there. . . ."

Edmée collapsed suddenly, fell back huddled in a heap on a settee, and broke out into frenzied and passionate sobbing that sounded like yells of laughter or howls of joy. As she lay doubled up, her graceful body heaved and rocked with grief, jealousy, fury and an unsuspected servility. And yet, like a wrestler in the heat of a struggle, or a swimmer in the hollow of a wave, she felt bathed in some strange new atmosphere, both natural and harsh.

She had a good long cry, and recovered by slow degrees, with periods of calm shaken by great shudders and gasps for breath. Chéri sat down by her side and continued to stroke her hair. The crisis of his own emotion was over, and he felt bored. He ran his eyes over Edmée as she lay sideways upon the unyielding settee. This straggling body, with its rucked-up frock and trailing scarf, added to the disorder of the room; and this displeased him.

Soft as was his sigh of boredom, she heard it and sat up. "Yes," she said, "I'm more than you can stand. . . . Oh! it would be better to . . ."

He interrupted her, fearing a torrent of words: "It's not that. It's simply that I don't know what you want."

"What I want? How d'you mean, what I . . ."

She lifted her face, still wet with tears.

"Now listen to me." He took her hands.

She tried to free herself. "No, no, I know that tone of voice. You're going to treat me to another of those nonsensical outbursts. When you put on that tone of voice and face, I know you're going to prove that your eye is shaped like a striped super-mullet, or that your mouth looks like the figure three on its side. No, no, I can't stand that!"

Her recriminations were childish, and Chéri relaxed, feeling that after all they were both very young. He pressed her warm hands between his own.

"But you must listen to me! . . . Good God! I'd like to know what you've got to reproach me with! Do I ever go out in the evenings without you? No! Do I often leave you on your own during the day? Do I carry on a secret correspondence?"

"I don't know—I don't think so——"

He turned her this way and that like a doll.

"Do I have a separate room? Don't I make love to you well?"

She hesitated, smiling with exquisite suspicion. "Do you call that love, Fred?"

"There are other words for it, but you wouldn't appreciate them."

"What you call love . . . isn't it possible that it may be, really, a . . . kind . . . of alibi?" She hastened to add, "I'm merely generalising, Fred, of course . . . I said '*may* be', in certain cases. . . ."

He dropped Edmée's hands. "That," he said coldly, "is putting your foot right in it."

"Why?" she asked in a feeble voice.

He whistled, chin in air, as he moved back a step or two. Then he advanced upon his wife, looking her up and down as if she were a stranger. To instil fear a fierce animal has no need to leap. Edmée noticed that his nostrils were dilating and that the tip of his nose was white.

"Ugh!" he breathed, looking at his wife. He shrugged his shoulders, turned, and walked away. At the end of the room he turned round and came back again. "Ugh!" he repeated, "Look what's talking!"

"What are you saying?"

"Look what's talking, and what it says. Upon my word, it actually has the cheek to . . ."

She jumped up in a rage. "Fred," she said, "don't dare to speak to me again in that tone! What do you take me for?"

"For a woman who knows exactly how to put her foot in it, as I've just had the honour of informing you."

He touched her on the shoulder with a rigid forefinger, and this hurt her as much as if he had inflicted a serious bruise. "You've matriculated; isn't there somewhere some kind of a proverb which says, 'Never play with knives or daggers' or whatever it may be?"

"Cold steel," she answered automatically.

"That's right. Well, my child, you must never play with cold steel. That's to say, you must never be wounding about a man's . . . a man's favours, if I may so express it. You were wounding about the gifts, about the favours, I bestow on you."

"You . . . you talk like a cocotte," she gasped.

She blushed, and her strength and self-control deserted her. She hated him for remaining cool and collected, for keeping his superiority: its whole secret lay in the carriage of his head, the sureness of his stance, the poise of his arms and shoulders.

The hard forefinger once more pressed into Edmée's shoulder.

"Excuse me, excuse me . . . It'll probably come as a great surprise when I state that, on the contrary, it's you who have the mentality of a tart. When it comes to judging such matters, there's no greater authority than young Peloux. I'm a connoisseur of 'cocottes', as you call them. I know them inside out. A 'cocotte' is a lady who generally manages to receive more than she gives. Do you hear what I say?"

What she heard above all was that he was now addressing her like a stray acquaintance.

"Nineteen years old, white skin, hair that smells of vanilla; and then, in bed, closed eyes and limp arms. That's all very pretty, but is there anything unusual about it? Do you really think it so very unusual?"

She had started at each word, and each sting had goaded her towards the duel of female *versus* male.

"It may be very unusual," she said in a steady voice, "how could *you* know?"

He did not answer, and she hastened to take advantage of a hit. "Personally, I saw much handsomer men than you when we were in Italy. The streets were full of them. My nineteen years are worth those of any other girl of my age, just as one good-looking man is as good as the next. Don't worry, everything can be arranged. Nowadays, marriage is not an important undertaking. Instead of allowing silly scenes to make us bitter . . ."

He put a stop to what she had to say by an almost pitying shake of the head.

"My poor kid, it's not so simple as that."

"Why not? There's such a thing as quick divorce, if one's ready to pay."

She spoke in the peremptory manner of a runaway schoolgirl, and it was pathetic. She had pushed back the hair off her forehead, and her anxious, intelligent eyes were made to look all the darker by the soft contours of her cheeks now fringed with hair: the eyes of an unhappy woman, eyes mature and definitive in a still undeveloped face.

"That wouldn't help at all," Chéri said.

"Because?"

"Because . . ." He leaned forward with his eyelashes tapered into pointed wings, shut his eyes and opened them again as if he had just swallowed a bitter pill. "Because you love me."

She noticed that he had resumed the more familiar form of addressing her, and above all the fuller, rather choked tones of their happiest hours. In her heart of hearts she acquiesced: 'It's true, I love him. At the moment, there's no remedy.'

The dinner bell sounded in the garden—a bell which was too small, dating from before Madame Peloux's time, a sad clear bell reminiscent of a country orphanage. Edmée shivered. "Oh, I don't like that bell. . . ."

"No?" said Chéri, absent-mindedly.

"In our house, dinner will be announced. There'll be no bell. There'll be no boarding-house habits in our home—you'll see."

She spoke these words without turning round, while walking down the hospital-green corridor, and so did not see, behind her, either the fierce attention Chéri paid to her last words, or his silent laughter.

He was walking along with a light step, stimulated by the rathe spring, perceptible in the moist gusty wind and the exciting earthy smells of squares and private gardens. Every now and again a fleeting glimpse in a glass would remind him that he was wearing a becoming felt hat, pulled down over the right eye, a loose-fitting spring coat, large light-coloured gloves and a terra-cotta tie. The eyes of women followed his progress with silent homage, the more candid among them bestowing that passing stupefaction which can be neither feigned nor hidden. But Chéri never looked at women in the street. He had just come from his house in the Avenue Henri-Martin, having left various orders with the upholsterers: orders contradicting one another, but thrown out in a tone of authority.

On reaching the end of the Avenue, he took a deep breath of the good spring scents carried up from the Bois on the heavy moist wing of the west wind, and then hurried on his way to the Porte Dauphine. Within a few minutes he had reached the lower end of the Avenue Bugeaud, and there he stopped. For the first time in six months his feet were treading the familiar road. He unbuttoned his coat.

'I've been walking too fast,' he said to himself. He started off again, then paused and, this time, trained his eyes on one particular spot: fifty yards or so down the road: bareheaded, shammy-leather in hand, Ernest the concierge—Léa's concierge—was "doing" the brasswork of the railings in front of Léa's house. Chéri began to hum, realised from the sound of his voice that he never did hum, and stopped.

"How are things, Ernest? Hard at work as usual?"

The concierge brightened respectfully.

"Monsieur Peloux! It's a pleasure to see Monsieur again. Monsieur has not changed at all."

"Neither have you, Ernest. Madame is well, I hope?"

He turned his head away to gaze up at the closed shutters on the first floor.

"I expect so, Monsieur, all we've had has been a few post-cards."

"Where from? Was it Biarritz?"

"I don't think so, Monsieur."

"Where is Madame?"

"It wouldn't be easy for me to tell you, Monsieur. We forward all letters addressed to Madame—and there's none to speak of—to Madame's solicitor."

Chéri pulled out his note-case, and cocked an eye at Ernest.

"Oh, Monsieur Peloux, money between you and me? Don't think of it. A thousand francs won't make a man tell what he doesn't know. But if Monsieur would like the address of Madame's solicitor?"

"No thanks, there's no point. And when does she return?"

Ernest threw up his hands: "That's another question that's beyond me. Maybe to-morrow, maybe in a month's time. . . . I keep everything in readiness, just the same. You have to watch out where Madame is concerned. If you said to me now, 'There she comes round the corner of the Avenue,' I shouldn't be surprised."

Chéri turned round and looked towards the corner of the Avenue.

"That's all Monsieur Peloux wants? Monsieur just happened to be walking by? It's a lovely day. . . ."

"Nothing else, thank you, Ernest. Goodbye, Ernest."

"Always at Monsieur's service."

Chéri walked up as far as the Place Victor-Hugo, swinging his cane as he went. Twice he stumbled and almost fell, like people who imagine their progress is being followed by hostile eyes. On reaching the balustraded entrance to the Métro, he leaned over the ramp to peer down into the pink-and-black recesses of the Underground, and felt utterly exhausted. When he straightened his back, he saw that the lamps had been lighted in the square and that the blue of dusk coloured everything around him.

'No, it can't be true. I'm ill.'

He had plumbed the depths of cavernous memories and his return to the living world was painful. The right words came to him at last. 'Pull yourself together, Peloux, for God's sake! Are you losing your head, my boy? Don't you know it's time to go back home?'

This last word recalled a sight that one hour had sufficed to banish from his mind: a large square room—his own nursery; an anxious young woman standing by the window; and Charlotte Peloux, subdued by a Martini.

"Oh, no," he said aloud. "Not that! That's all over."

He signalled to a taxi with his raised stick.

"To the . . . er . . . to the Restaurant du Dragon Bleu."

Chéri crossed the grill-room to the sound of violins in the glare of the atrocious electric light, and this had a tonic effect. He shook the hand of a maître d'hôtel who recognised him. Before him rose the stooping figure of a tall young man. Chéri gave an affectionate gasp.

"Desmond, the very man I wanted to see! Howdydo?"

They were shown to a table decorated with pink carnations. A small hand and a towering aigrette beckoned towards Chéri from a neighbouring table.

"It's La Loupiote," Vicomte Desmond warned him.

Chéri had no recollection of La Loupiote, but he smiled towards the towering aigrette and, without getting up, touched the small hand with a paper fan lying on his table. Then he put on his most solemn "conquering hero" look, and swept his eyes over an unknown couple. The woman had forgotten to eat since he had sat down in her vicinity.

"The man with her looks a regular cuckold, doesn't he?"

He had leaned over to whisper into his friend's ear, and his eyes shone with pleasure as if with rising tears.

"What d'you drink, now you're married?" Desmond asked, "Camomile tea?"

"Pommery," Chéri said.

"And before the Pommery?"

"Pommery, before and after." And, dilating his nostrils, he sniffed as he remembered some sparkling, rose-scented old champagne of 1889 that Léa kept for him alone.

He ordered a meal that a shop-girl out on the spree might choose —cold fish *au porto*, a roast bird, and a piping hot soufflé which concealed in its innards a red ice, sharp on the tongue.

"Hello!" La Loupiote shouted, waving a pink carnation at Chéri.

"Hello," Chéri answered, raising his glass.

The chimes of an English wall-clock struck eight. "Blast!" Chéri grumbled, "Desmond, go and make a telephone call for me."

Desmond's pale eyes were hungry for revelations to come.

"Go and ask for Wagram 17–08, tell them to put you through to my mother, and say we're dining together."

"And supposing young Madame Peloux comes to the telephone?"

"Say the same thing. I'm not tied to her apron-strings. I've got her well trained."

He ate and drank a lot, taking the greatest care to appear serious and blasé; but his pleasure was enhanced by the least sound of laughter, the clink of glasses, or the strains of a syrupy valse. The steely blue of the highly glazed woodwork reminded him of the Riviera, at the hour when the too blue sea grows dark around the blurred reflection of the noonday sun. He forgot that very handsome young men ought to pretend indifference; he began to scrutinise the dark girl opposite, so that she trembled all over under his expert gaze.

"What about Léa?" Desmond asked suddenly.

Chéri did not jump: he was thinking of Léa. "Léa? She's in the South."

"Is all over between you?"

Chéri put his thumb in the armhole of his waistcoat.

"Well, of course, what d'you expect? We parted in proper style, the best of friends. It couldn't last a lifetime. What a charming, intelligent woman, old man! But then, you know her yourself! Broadminded . . . most remarkable. My dear fellow, I confess that if it hadn't been for the question of age . . . But there *was* the question of age, and you agree . . ."

"Of course," Desmond interrupted.

This young man with lack-lustre eyes, though he knew just how to perform the wearing and difficult duties of a parasite, had just yielded to curiosity and blamed himself for such rashness. Chéri, circumspect and at the same time highly elated, never stopped talking about Léa. He made all the right remarks, showed all the sound sense of a married man. He spoke in praise of marriage, while giving Léa's virtues their due. He extolled the submissive sweetness of his young wife, and thus found occasion to criticise Léa's independence of character. "Oh, the old devil, she had her own ideas about everything, I can tell you!"

He went a step further in his confidences, speaking of Léa with severity, and even impertinence. He was sheltering behind idiotic words, prompted by the suspicions of a deceived lover, and at the same time enjoying the subtle pleasure of being able to speak of her without danger. A little more, and he would have sullied her name, while his heart was rejoicing in his own memories of her: sullied the soft sweet name which he had been unable to mention freely during the last six months, and the whole gracious vision he had of Léa, leaning over him with her two or three irreparable wrinkles, and her beauty, now lost to him, but—alas—ever present.

About eleven o'clock they rose to go, chilled by the emptiness of the almost deserted restaurant. However, at the next table, La Loupiote was busy writing letters and had called for telegraph-forms. She raised her white, inoffensive, sheep-like head as the two friends passed by. "Well, aren't you even going to say good evening?"

"Good evening," Chéri condescended to say.

La Loupiote drew her friend's attention to Chéri's good looks. "Would you believe it! And to think that he's got such pots of money. Some people have everything!"

But when Chéri merely offered her an open cigarette-case, she became vituperative. "They have everything, except the knowledge of how to make proper use of it. Go back home to your mother, dearie!"

"Look here," Chéri said to Desmond when they were outside in the narrow street, "Look here, I was about to ask you, Desmond . . . Wait till we get away from this beastly crowd. . . ."

The soft damp evening air had kept people lingering in the streets, but the theatre-goers from the Rue Caumartin onwards had not yet packed the Boulevard. Chéri took his friend by the arm: "Look here, Desmond . . . I wanted you to make another telephone call."

Desmond stopped, "Again?"

"You'll ask for Wagram . . ."

"17–08."

"You're marvellous . . . Say that I've been taken ill in your flat. Where are you living?"

"Hôtel Morris."

"Splendid—and that I won't be back till morning, and that you're making me some mint tea. Go on, old man. Here, you can give this to the telephone-girl, or else keep it yourself. But come back quickly. I'll be sitting waiting for you outside Weber's."

The tall young man, arrogant and serviceable, went off crumpling the franc-notes in his pocket, without permitting himself a comment. When Desmond rejoined him, Chéri was slouched over an untouched orangeade in which he appeared to be reading his fortune.

"Desmond . . . Who answered you?"

"A lady," the laconic messenger replied.

"Which?"

"Dunno."

"What did she say?"

"That it was all right."

"In what tone of voice?"

"Same as I'm speaking to you in."

"Oh, good. Thanks."

'It was Edmée,' thought Chéri.

They were walking towards the Place de la Concorde and Chéri linked arms with Desmond. He did not dare to admit that he was feeling dog-tired.

"Where do you want to go?" Desmond asked.

"Well, old man," Chéri sighed in gratitude, "to the Morris; and as soon as we can. I'm fagged out."

Desmond forgot to be impassive. "What? It can't be true. To the Morris? What d'you want to do? No nonsense! D'you want to . . ."

"To go to bed," Chéri answered. And he closed his eyes as though on the point of dropping off, then opened them again. "Sleep, I want to sleep, got it?"

He gripped his friend's arm too hard.

"Let's go there, then," Desmond said.

Within ten minutes they were at the Morris. The sky-blue and white bedroom and the imitation Empire furniture of the sitting-room smiled at Chéri like old friends. He took a bath, borrowed one of Desmond's silk night-shirts which was too tight for him, got into bed, and, wedged between two huge soft pillows, sank into dreamless bliss, into the dark depths of a sleep that protected him from all attacks.

He began to count the shameful days as they went by. "Sixteen . . . seventeen . . . When three weeks are up, I'll go back to Neuilly." He did not go back. Though he saw the situation quite clearly, he no longer had the strength to cure it. At night, and in the morning sometimes, he flattered himself that he would get over his cowardice within an hour or two. "No strength left? . . . Please, please, I beg of you . . . Not yet strength enough. But it's coming back. What's the betting I'll be in the Boulevard d'Inkermann dining-room at the stroke of twelve? One, two . . ." The stroke of twelve found him in the bath, or else driving his motor, with Desmond at his side.

At every mealtime, he felt optimistic for a moment about his marriage. This feeling was as regular as a recurrent fever. As he sat down facing Desmond at their bachelor table, the ghost of Edmée would appear, and plunge him into silent thoughts of his young wife's inconceivable deference. "Really, that young thing's too sweet! Did you ever see such a dream of a wife? Never a word, never a complaint! I'll treat her to one of those bracelets when I get back. . . . Upbringing, that's what does it! Give me Marie-Laure every time for bringing up a daughter!" But one day in the grill-room at the Morris, abject terror was written on his face when he caught sight of a green dress with a chinchilla collar just like one of Edmée's dresses.

Desmond found life wonderful and was getting a little fat. He reserved his arrogance for moments when Chéri—encouraged by him to pay a visit to some "prodigious English girl, riddled with vice", or to some "Indian potentate in his opium palace"—refused point blank or else consented with unconcealed scorn. Desmond had long since despaired of understanding Chéri's ways; but Chéri was paying —and better than during the best of their bachelor days together. They ran across the blonde La Loupiote a second time, when they visited a friend of hers, a woman who boasted such an ordinary name that nobody ever remembered it; "What's-her-name . . . you know perfectly well . . . that pal of La Loupiote's."

The Pal smoked opium, and gave it to others. The instant you came into her modest, ground-floor flat, you smelt escaping gas and stale drugs. She won the hearts of her guests by a tearful cordiality and by a constant incitement to self-pity—both objectionable traits. She treated Desmond, when he paid her a visit, as "a great big desperately lonesome boy," . . . and Chéri as "a beauty who has got everything and it only makes him more miserable." Chéri never touched the pipe; he looked at the small box of cocaine with the repugnance of a cat about to be dosed, and spent most of the night with his back against the cushioned dado, sitting up on a straw mat between Desmond, who went to sleep, and the Pal, who never stopped smoking. For most of the night he breathed in the fumes that satisfy all hunger and thirst, but his self-control and distrust persisted. He appeared to be perfectly happy, except that he stared now and then, with pained and questioning intensity, at the Pal's withered throat—a skinny, far too red throat, round which shimmered a string of false pearls.

Once, he stretched out a hand and with the tip of his fingers touched the henna-tinted hair on the nape of her neck. He judged the weight of the big light hollow pearls with his hand, then snatched it back with the nervous shiver of someone who catches his finger-nail on a piece of frayed silk. Not long after, he got up and went.

"Aren't you sick to death of all this," Desmond asked Chéri, "sick of these poky holes where we eat and drink and never have any girls? Sick of this hotel with the doors always slamming? Sick of the nightclubs where we go in the evenings, and of dashing in that fast car of yours from Paris to Rouen, Paris to Compiègne, Paris to Ville d'Avray? . . . Why not the Riviera for a change? The season down there isn't December and January, it's March, April, or . . ."

"No," said Chéri.

"Then what?"

"Then nothing."

Chéri affected to become amiable and put on what Léa used to call "his air of worldly superiority".

"Dear old boy . . . you don't seem to appreciate the beauty of Paris at this time of the year. . . . This . . . er . . . indecisive season, this spring that doesn't seem willing to smile, the softness of the light . . . as opposed to the commonplace Riviera. . . . No, don't you see, I like it here."

Desmond all but lost his lackey patience. "Yes, and besides, it may be that the young Peloux's divorce will . . ."

Chéri's sensitive nostrils blenched. "If you've arranged to touch a commission from some lawyer friend, you can drop the idea at once. There'll be no such thing as 'young Peloux's divorce'."

"My dear fellow! . . ." Desmond protested, doing his best to look hurt, "You have a very curious way of behaving to a man who has been a friend since your childhood, and who has always . . ."

Chéri was not listening. Instead, he pushed towards Desmond's face a pointed chin and a mouth pursed like a miser's. For the first time in his life he had heard a stranger disposing of his possessions.

He began to reflect. Young Peloux's divorce? Many nights and days had he spent in thinking over these words till they had come to spell liberty, a sort of second boyhood, perhaps something even better. But Desmond's voice, with its affected nasal twang, had just called up the image he had been looking for: Edmée, resolute in her little hat with its long motoring veil, moving out of the house at Neuilly on her way to an unknown house to join an unknown man. "Of course, that would settle everything," and his Bohemian side was delighted. At the same time a surprisingly timorous Chéri jibbed, "That's not the sort of way one behaves!" The image became focused in sharper colour and movement. Chéri could hear the heavy musical note of the iron gate swinging to, and could see beyond it fingers wearing a grey pearl and a white diamond. "Farewell," the small hand said.

Chéri jumped up, pushing back his seat. "Those are mine, all of them! The woman, the house, the rings . . . they all belong to me!"

He had not spoken out loud, but his features expressed such savage violence that Desmond thought his last hour of prosperity had struck. Chéri spoke to him pityingly but without kindness.

"Poor pussy-cat, did I scare you? What it is to be descended from the Crusaders! Come along, and I'll buy you pants as fine as my shirts, and shirts as fine as your pants. Desmond, is to-day the seventeenth?"

"Yes, why?"

"The seventeenth of March. In other words, spring. Desmond, people who think themselves smart, I mean those in the height of fashion, women or men—can they afford to wait any longer before buying their spring wardrobes?"

"Hardly——"

"The seventeenth, Desmond! Come along at once; everything's all right. We're going to buy a huge bracelet for my wife, an enormous cigarette-holder for Madame Peloux, and a tiny tie-pin for you."

On more than one such occasion he had felt an overwhelming presentiment that Léa was on the point of returning; that she was already back in her house; that the first-floor shutters had been opened, allowing a glimpse of the flowered pink net curtains across the windows, the lace of the full-length curtains at each side and the glint of the looking-glasses. . . . The fifteenth of April went by and still there was no sign of Léa.

The mournful monotony of Chéri's existence was tempered by several provoking incidents. There was a visit from Madame Peloux, who thought she was breathing her last when she found Chéri looking as thin as a greyhound, eyes wandering and mouth tight shut. There was the letter from Edmée: a letter all in the same surprising tone, explaining that she would stay on at Neuilly "until further orders," and had undertaken to pass on to Chéri "Madame de la Berche's best regards." . . . He thought she was laughing at him, did not know what to answer, and ended by throwing away the enigmatic screed; but he did not go to Neuilly.

April advanced, leafy, cold, bright, and scenting all Paris with tulips, bunches of hyacinths, paulownias and laburnums like dropping-wells of gold. Chéri buried himself all the deeper in austere seclusion. The harassed, ill-treated, angry but well-paid Vicomte Desmond was given his orders: now to protect Chéri from familiar young women and indiscreet young men; now to recruit both sections and form a troop, who ate, drank, and rushed screaming at the top of their voices between Montmartre, the restaurants in the Bois, and the cabarets on the left bank.

One night the Pal was alone in her room, smoking opium and bewailing some shocking disloyalty of La Loupiote's, when her door opened to reveal the young man, with satanic eyebrows tapering towards his temples. He begged for "a glass of really cold water" to allay some secret ardour that had parched his beautiful lips. He showed not the slightest interest in the Pal and the woes she poured out. She pushed towards him the lacquer tray with its pipe: he would accept nothing, and took up his usual position on the mat, to share with her the semi-obscurity in silence. There he stayed till dawn, moving as little as possible, like a man who fears that the least gesture may bring back his pain. At dawn, he questioned the Pal: "Why weren't you wearing your pearls to-day; you know, the big ones?" and politely took his leave.

Walking alone at night was becoming an unconscious habit with him. With rapid lengthy strides he would make off towards some positive but inaccessible goal. Soon after midnight he would escape from Desmond, who discovered him again only towards daybreak, asleep on his hotel bed, flat on his stomach, his head pillowed on his folded arms, in the posture of a fretful child.

"Oh, good, he's here all right," Desmond would say with relief. "One.can never be sure with such a crackpot."

One night, when out on a tramp, his eyes wide open in the darkness, Chéri had felt compelled to walk up the Avenue Bugeaud; for during the day he had disregarded the superstition that made him return there once every twenty-four hours. There are maniacs who cannot go to sleep without having first touched the door-knob three times; a similar obsession made him run his hand along the railings, then put his first finger to the bell-push, and call out Hullo! under his breath, as if in fun, before making off in haste.

But one night, that very night, as he stood before the railings, his heart jumped almost into his mouth: there, in the court, the electric globe shone like a mauve moon above the front door steps, the back-door stood wide open shedding a glow on the paved courtyard, while, on the first floor, the bedroom lights filtered through the shutters to make a golden comb. Chéri supported himself against the nearest tree and lowered his head.

"It can't be true. As soon as I look up, it will all be dark again."

He straightened up at the sound of a voice. Ernest, the concierge, was shouting in the passage: "At nine to-morrow, Marcel will help me carry up the big black trunk, Madame."

Chéri turned round in a flash and ran as far as the Avenue du Bois. There he sat down. In front of his eyes danced the image of the electric globe he had been staring at—a dark purple ball fringed with gold, against a black group of trees in bud. He pressed his hand to his heart, and took a deep breath. Early lilac blossom scented the night air. He threw his hat away, undid the buttons of his overcoat and, leaning back on a seat, let himself go, his legs outstretched and his hands hanging feebly by his sides. A crushing yet delicious weight had just fallen upon him. "Ah!" he whispered, "so this is what they call happiness. I never knew."

For a moment he gave way to self-pity and self-contempt. How many good things had he missed by leading such a pointless life—a young man with lots of money and little heart! Then he stopped thinking for a moment, or possibly for an hour. Next, he persuaded himself there was nothing in the world he wanted, not even to go and see Léa.

When he found himself shivering in the cold, and heard the blackbirds carolling the dawn, he got up and, stumbling a little but light-hearted, set off towards the Hôtel Morris without passing through the Avenue Bugeaud. He stretched himself, filled his lungs with the morning air, and overflowed with goodwill to all.

"Now," he sighed, the devil driven out of him, "now . . . Oh now you'll see just how nice to the girl I shall be."

Shaved, shod and impatient—he had been up since eight—Chéri shook Desmond. Sleep gave him a swollen look, livid and quite frightful, like a drowned man. "Desmond! Hey, Desmond! Up you get. . . . You look too hideous when you're asleep!"

The sleeper woke, sat up, and turned towards Chéri eyes the colour of clouded water. He pretended to be fuddled with sleep so that he could make a long and close examination of Chéri—Chéri dressed in blue, pathetic, superb, and pale under the lightest coat of powder.

There were still moments when Desmond felt painfully aware of the contrast between his ugly mask and Chéri's good looks. He pretended to give a long yawn. 'What's he up to now?' he wondered; 'The idiot is in far better looks than yesterday—especially his eyelashes, and what eyelashes he has . . .' He was staring at the lustrous sweep of Chéri's thick lashes and the shadow they shed on the dark pupils and bluish whites of his eyes. Desmond noticed also that, this morning, the contemptuously arched lips were moist and fresh, and that he was breathing through them as if he had just that moment finished making love.

Quickly he relegated his jealousy to the back of his mind—where he kept his personal feelings—and asked Chéri in tones of weary condescension: "May one enquire whether you are going out at this hour of the morning, or just coming in?"

"I'm going out," Chéri said. "Don't worry about me. I'm off shopping. I'm going to the florist's, the jeweller's, to my mother's, to my wife's, to . . ."

"Don't forget the Papal Nuncio!"

"I know what's what," Chéri answered. "He shall have some imitation gold studs and a sheaf of orchids."

It was rare for Chéri to respond to jokes: he usually accepted them in stony silence. His facetious reply proved that he was pleased with himself, and revealed this unaccustomed mood to Desmond. He studied Chéri's reflection in the looking-glass, noted the pallor of his dilated nostrils, observed that his eyes were continually on the rove, and ventured to put the most discreet of questions.

"Will you be coming back for luncheon? . . . Hey, Chéri, I'm speaking to you. Are we lunching together?"

Chéri answered by shaking his head. He whistled softly, arranging himself in front of the pier-glass so that it framed his figure exactly like the one between the two windows in Léa's room—the one which would soon frame in its heavy gold, against a sunny pink background, the reflection of his body—naked or loosely draped in silk—the magnificent picture of a young man, handsome, loved, happy, and pampered, playing with the rings and necklaces of his mistress. 'Perhaps her young man's reflection is already there, in Léa's looking-glass!' This sudden thought cut so fiercely into his exhilaration that it dazed him, and he fancied he had heard it actually spoken.

"What did you say?" he asked Desmond.

"I never said a word," his well-trained friend said stiffly. "It must have been someone talking outside in the courtyard."

Chéri went out, slamming the door behind him, and returned to his own rooms. They were filled with the dim continual hubbub of the fully awakened Rue de Rivoli, and Chéri, through the open window, could see the spring foliage, the leaves stiff and transparent like thin jade knives against the sun. He closed the window and sat down on a useless little chair which stood against the wall in a dingy corner between his bed and the bathroom door.

"How can it be? . . ." he began in a low voice, and then said no more. He did not understand why it was that during the last six and a half months he had hardly given a thought to Léa's lover. "*I'm making a perfect fool of myself,*" were the actual words of the letter so piously preserved by Charlotte Peloux.

'A perfect fool?' Chéri shook his head. 'It's funny, but that's not how I see her at all. What sort of a man can she be in love with? Somebody like Patron—rather than like Desmond, of course. An oily little Argentine? Maybe. Yet all the same . . .' He smiled a simple smile. 'Apart from me, who is there she could possibly care for?'

A cloud passed over the sun and the room darkened. Chéri leaned his head against the wall. "My Nounoune . . . My Nounoune . . . Have you betrayed me? Are you beastly enough to deceive me? . . . Have you really done that?"

He tried to give a sharper edge to his suffering by a misuse of his imagination: the words and sights it presented left him more astonished than enraged. He did his best to evoke the elation of early morning delights when he was living with Léa, the solace of the prolonged and perfect silences of certain afternoons, with Léa—the delicious sleepy hours in winter spent in a warm bed in a freshly aired room, with Léa . . . ; but, all the time, in the suffused cherry-coloured afternoon light aflame behind the curtains of Léa's room, he saw in Léa's arms one lover and one lover only—Chéri. He jumped up, revived by a spontaneous act of faith. 'It's as simple as that! If I'm unable to see anyone but myself beside her, then it's because there is no one else to see.'

He seized the telephone, and was on the point of ringing her up, when he gently replaced the receiver. "No nonsense. . . ."

He walked out into the street, erect, with shoulders squared. He went in his open motor to the jeweller's, where he became sentimental over a slender little bandeau of burning blue sapphires invisibly mounted on blue steel, "so exactly right for Edmée's hair," and took it away with him. He bought some stupid, rather pompous flowers. As it had only just struck eleven, he frittered away a further half-hour, drawing money from the Bank, turning over English illustrated papers at a kiosk, visiting his scent-shop and a tobacconist's that specialised in Oriental cigarettes. Finally, he got back into his motor, and sat down between his sheaf of flowers and a heap of little beribboned parcels.

"Home."

The chauffeur swivelled round on his basket-seat.

"Monsieur? . . . What did Monsieur say? . . ."

"I said Home—Boulevard d'Inkermann. D'you require a map of Paris?"

The motor went full speed towards the Champs-Elysées. The chauffeur drove much faster than usual and his thoughts could almost be read in his back. He seemed to be brooding uneasily over the gulf which divided the flabby young man of the past months— with his "As you like," and his "Have a glass of something, Antonin?"—from young Monsieur Peloux, strict with the staff and mindful of the petrol.

"Young Monsieur Peloux" leaned back against the morocco leather, hat on knees, drinking in the breeze and exerting all his energy in an effort not to think. Like a coward, he closed his eyes between the Avenue Malakoff and the Porte Dauphine to avoid a passing glimpse of the Avenue Bugeaud, and he congratulated himself on his resolution.

The chauffeur sounded his horn in the Boulevard d'Inkermann for the gate to be opened, and it sang on its hinges with a heavy musical note. The capped concierge hurried about his business, the watchdogs barked in recognition of their returning master. Very much at his ease, sniffing the green smell of the newly mown lawns, Chéri entered the house and with a master's step climbed the stairs to the young woman whom he had left behind three months before, much as a sailor from Europe leaves behind, on the other side of the world, a little savage bride.

LÉA sat at her bureau, throwing away photographs from the last trunk to be unpacked. "Heavens, how hideous people are! The women who had the nerve to give me these! And they think I'm going to put them up in a row on the mantelpiece—in plated frames or little folding-cases. Tear them all up quick, and straight into the waste-paper basket!"

She picked up the photographs again and, before throwing them away, subjected each to the closest scrutiny of which her blue eyes were capable. A post-card with a dark background of a powerful lady encased in full-length stays, doing her best to veil her hair and the lower part of her face with a wisp of tulle, in the teeth of a strong sea-breeze. "*To dearest Léa, in memory of exquisite hours spent at Guéthary. Anita.*" Another photograph, stuck on the middle of a piece of cardboard with a surface like dried mud, portrayed a large and lugubrious family. They might have been a penal colony, with a dumpy, heavily-painted grandmother in charge. Holding above her head a tambourine tricked out with favours, she was resting one foot on the bent knee of what looked like a robust and crafty young butcher-boy. "That should never have seen the light of day," Léa said decisively, crumpling the rough-cast cardboard.

She smoothed out an unmounted print, to disclose two old provincial spinsters. An eccentric, loud-voiced and aggressive couple, they were to be found every morning on a bench somewhere along a promenade, and every evening between a glass of Cassis and their needlework-frames, on which they were embroidering black pussy-cats, fat toads, or a spider. "*To our beautiful fairy! From her little friends at Le Trayas, Miquette and Riquette.*"

Léa destroyed these souvenirs of her travels—and brushed a hand across her forehead. "It's horrible. And there'll be dozens and dozens more after these, just as there were dozens before them, all much the same. There's nothing to be done about it. It's life. Maybe wherever a Léa is to be found, there at once spring from the earth a myriad creatures like Charlotte Peloux, de la Berche, and Aldonza, or old horrors who were once handsome young men, people who are . . . well, who are impossible, impossible, impossible. . . ."

She heard, so fresh was her memory, voices that had called out to her from the top of hotel steps or hailed her with a "Hoo-hoo" from afar, across golden sands, and she lowered her head in anger like a bull.

She had returned, after an absence of six months, thinner, more flabby, less serene. Now and again a nervous twitch of the jaw jerked her chin down against her neck, and careless henna-shampooing had left too orange a glint in her hair; but her skin had been tanned to amber by sea and wind. This gave her the glowing complexion of a handsome farmer's wife, and she might have done without rouge. All the same, she would have to arrange something carefully round her neck, not to say cover it up completely; for it had shrunk and was encircled with wrinkles that had been inaccessible to sunburn.

Still seated, she dawdled over tidying away her various odds and ends, and her eyes began to glance round the room, as if some chair were missing. But what she was looking for was her old energy, the old anxiety to see at once that everything was as it should be in her comfortable home.

'Oh! That trip!' she sighed. 'How could I? How exhausting it all is!'

She frowned, once again with that irritable jerk of her chin, when she noticed the broken glass of a little picture by Chaplin which she thought perfectly lovely—the head of a young girl, all silver and rose.

"And I could put both hands through that tear in the lace curtains. . . . And that's only the beginning. . . . What a fool I was to stay away so long! And all in *his* honour! As if I couldn't just as well have nursed my grief here, in peace and comfort!"

She rose, disgruntled, and, gathering up the flounces of her teagown, went over to ring the bell, saying to herself, "Get along with you, you old baggage!"

Her maid entered, under a heap of underclothes and silk stockings.

"Eleven o'clock, Rose. And my face hasn't been done yet. I'm late."

"There's nothing to be late for. There aren't any old maids now to drag Madame off on excursions, or turn up at crack of dawn to pick every rose in the place. There's no Monsieur Roland to drive Madame mad by throwing pebbles through her window. . . ."

"Rose, there's only too much to keep us busy in the house. The proverb may well be true that three moves are as bad as a fire, but I'm quite convinced that being away from home for six months is as bad as a flood. I suppose you've noticed the hole in the curtain?"

"That's nothing. . . . Madame has not yet seen the linen-room: mouse-droppings everywhere and holes nibbled in the floor. And it's a funny thing that I left Émérancie with twenty-eight glass-cloths and I come back to find twenty-two."

"No!"

"It's the truth—every word I say, Madame."

They looked at each other, sharing the same indignation, both of them deeply attached to this comfortable house, muffled in carpets and silks, with its well-stocked cupboards and its shiny white basement. Léa gave her knee a determined slap.

"We'll soon change all that, my friend. If Ernest and Émérancie don't want their week's notice, they'll manage to find those six glass-cloths. And did you write to Marcel, and tell that great donkey which day to come back?"

"He's here, Madame."

Léa dressed quickly, then opened the window and leaned out, gazing complacently at her avenue of trees in bud. No more of those fawning old maids, and no more of Monsieur Roland—the athletic young heavyweight at Cambo. . . . 'The idiot,' she sighed.

She forgave this passing acquaintance his silliness, and blamed him only for having failed to please her. In her memory—that of a healthy woman with a forgetful body—Monsieur Roland was now only a powerful animal, slightly ridiculous and, when it came to the point, so very clumsy. Léa would now have denied that, one rainy evening when the showers were falling in fragrance on the rose-geraniums, a flood of blinding tears had served to blot out Monsieur Roland behind the image of Chéri.

This brief encounter had left Léa unembarrassed and unregretful. In the villa she had taken at Cambo, the "idiot" and his frolicking old mother would have been made just as welcome as before. They could have gone on enjoying the well-arranged meals, the rocking-chairs on the wooden balcony, all the creature comforts that Léa dispensed with such justifiable pride. But the idiot had felt sore and gone away, leaving Léa to the attentions of a stiff, handsome officer, greying at the temples, who aspired to marriage with "Madame de Lonval".

"Our years, our fortunes, the taste we both have for independence and society, doesn't everything show that we were destined for each other?" murmured the colonel, who still kept his slim waist.

She laughed, and enjoyed the company of this dry, dapper man, who ate well and knew how to hold his liquor. He mistook her feelings and he read into the lovely blue eyes, and the trustful, lingering smiles of his hostess, the acceptance he was expecting. The end of their dawning friendship was marked by a decisive gesture on her part: one she regretted in her heart of hearts and for which she was honest enough to accept the blame. 'It's my own fault. One should never treat a Colonel Ypoustègue, descendant of an ancient Basque family, as one would treat a Monsieur Roland. I've never given anyone such a snub. All the same, it would have been gentlemanly, and intelligent too, if he had come back as usual the next day in his dog-cart, to smoke his cigar, meet the two old girls and pull their legs.'

She failed to understand that a middle-aged man could accept his dismissal, but not certain glances—glances appraising his physique, comparing him in that respect so unmistakably with another, unknown and invisible. Léa, caught in his sudden kiss, had subjected him to the searching, formidable gaze of a woman who knows exactly where to find the tell-tale marks of age. From the dry, well cared-for hands, ribbed with veins and tendons, her glance rose to the pouched chin and furrowed brows, returning cruelly to the mouth entrapped between double lines of inverted commas. Whereupon all the aristocratic refinement of the "Baroness de Lonval" collapsed in an "Oh, la la," so insulting, so explicit, so common, that the handsome figure of Colonel Ypoustègue passed through her door for the last time. ·

'The last of my idylls,' Léa was thinking, as she leaned out over her window-ledge. But the weather over Paris was fine, her echoing courtyard was dapper, with its trim bay trees rising ball-shaped in green tubs, and from the room behind her a breath of scented warmth came playing over the nape of her neck: all this gradually helped her to recover her good humour, and her sense of mischief. She watched the silhouettes of women passing on their way down to the Bois. 'So skirts are changing again,' Léa observed, 'and hats are higher.' She planned sessions with her dressmaker, others with her milliner; the sudden desire to look beautiful made her straighten her back. 'Beautiful? For whom? Why, for myself, of course. And then to aggravate old Ma Peloux!'

Léa had heard about Chéri's flight, but knew no more than that. While disapproving of Madame Peloux's private-detective methods, she did not scruple to listen to a young *vendeuse*, who would show her gratitude for all Léa's kindnesses by pouring gossip in her ear at a fitting, or else by sending it to her, with "a thousand thanks for the delicious chocolates" on a huge sheet of paper embossed with the letter-head of her establishment. A postcard from Lili, forwarded to Léa at Cambo—a postcard scribbled by the dotty old harridan in a trembling hand without commas or full stops—had recounted an incomprehensible story of love and flight and a young wife kept under lock and key at Neuilly.

'It was weather like this,' Léa recalled, 'the morning I read Lili's postcard in my bath at Cambo.'

She could see the yellow bathroom, the sunlight dancing on the water and ceiling. She could hear the thin-walled villa re-echoing with a great peal of laughter—her own laughter, rather ferocious and none too spontaneous—then the cries that followed it: "Rose! Rose!"

Breasts and shoulders out of water, dripping, robust, one magnificent arm outstretched, looking more than ever like a naiad on a fountain, she had waved the card with the tips of her wet fingers. "Rose, Rose! Chéri . . . Monsieur Peloux has done a bunk! He's left his wife!"

"That doesn't surprise me, Madame," Rose had said. "The divorce will be gayer than the wedding, when the dead seemed to be burying the dead."

All through that day Léa had given way to unseemly mirth. "Oh! that fiendish boy. Oh! the naughty child! Just think of it!"

And she shook her head, laughing softly to herself, like a mother whose son has stayed out all night for the first time.

A bright varnished park-phaeton flashed past her gates, sparkled behind its prancing high-steppers and vanished almost without a sound on its rubber wheels.

'There goes Spéleïeff,' Léa observed; 'he's a good sort. And there goes Merguillier on his piebald: eleven o'clock. It won't be long be-

fore that dried-up old Berthellemy passes on his way to thaw out his
bones on the Sentier de la Vertu. Curious how people can go on
doing the same thing day after day! I could almost believe I'd never
left Paris, except that Chéri isn't here. My poor Chéri! He's finished
with, for the present. Night-life, women, eating at any hour, drinking
too much. It's a pity. He might have turned into a decent sort, perhaps, if he'd only had pink chaps like a pork-butcher and flat
feet. . . .'

She left the window, rubbing her numbed elbows, and shrugged
her shoulders. 'Chéri could be saved once, but not a second time.'
She polished her nails, breathed on a tarnished ring, peered closely at
the disastrous red of her hair and its greying roots, and jotted down a
few notes on a pad. She did everything at high speed and with less
composure than usual, trying to ward off an attack of her old insidious anxiety. Familiar as this was, she denied its connection with her
grief and called it "her moral indigestion". She began wanting first
one thing, then suddenly another—a well-sprung victoria with a quiet
horse appropriate to a dowager; then a very fast motor-car; then a
suite of Directoire furniture. She even thought of doing her hair
differently; for twenty years she had worn it high, brushed straight
off the neck. 'Rolled curls low on the neck, like Lavallière? Then I
should be able to cope with this year's loose-waisted dresses. With a
strict diet, in fact, and my hair properly hennaed, I can hope for ten
—no, let's say five years more of . . .'

With an effort she recovered her good sense, her pride, her
lucidity. 'A woman like me would never have the courage to call a
halt? Nonsense, my beauty, we've had a good run for our money.'
She surveyed the tall figure, erect, hands on hips, smiling at her from
the looking-glass. She was still Léa.

'Surely a woman like that doesn't end up in the arms of an old
man? A woman like that, who's had the luck never to soil her hands
or her mouth on a withered stick! Yes, there she stands, the "vam-
pire", who needs must feed off youthful flesh.'

She conjured up the chance acquaintances and lovers of her early
days: always she had escaped elderly lechers; so she felt pure, and
proud of thirty years devoted to radiant youths and fragile adolescents.

'And this youthful flesh of theirs certainly owes me a great debt.
How many of them have me to thank for their good health, their
good looks, the harmlessness of their sorrows! And then their egg-
nogs when they suffered from colds, and the habit of making love

unselfishly and always refreshingly! Shall I now, merely to fill my bed, provide myself with an old gentleman of . . . of . . .' She hunted about and finished up with majestic forgetfulness of her own age, 'An old gentleman of forty?'

She rubbed her long shapely hands together and turned away in disgust. 'Pooh! Farewell to all that! It's much prettier. Let's go out and buy playing-cards, good wine, bridge-scorers, knitting-needles— all the paraphernalia to fill a gaping void, all that's required to disguise that monster, an old woman.'

In place of knitting-needles, she bought a number of dresses, and négligées like the gossamer clouds of dawn. A Chinese pedicure came once a week, the manicurist twice, the masseuse every day. Léa was to be seen at plays, and before the theatre at restaurants where she never thought of going in Chéri's time.

She allowed young women and their friends—as well as Kühn, her former tailor, now retired—to ask her to their box or to their table. But the young women treated her with a deference she did not appreciate; and when Kühn, at their first supper together, called her "my dear friend," she retorted: "Kühn, I assure you it doesn't suit you at all to be a customer."

She sought refuge with Patron, now a referee and boxing promoter. But Patron was married to a young person who ran a bar, a little creature as fierce and jealous as a terrier. To join the susceptible athlete, Léa went as far out as the Place d'Italie, at considerable risk to her dark sapphire-blue dress, heavy with gold embroidery, to her birds of paradise, her impressive jewels, and her new rich red-tinted coiffure. She had had enough after one sniff of the sweat, vinegar and turpentine exuded by Patron's "white hopes", and she left, deciding never to venture again inside that long low gas-hissing hall.

An unaccountable weariness followed her every attempt to get back into the bustling life of people with nothing to do.

'What can be the matter with me?'

She rubbed her ankles, a little swollen by evening, looked at her strong teeth, and gums that had hardly begun to recede; and thumped her strong ribs and healthy stomach as if sounding a cask. Yet some undefinable weight, now that the chock had been knocked from under her, was shifting within her, and dragging her down. It was the Baroness de la Berche—met by chance in a "public bar" where she was washing down two dozen snails with cabbies' white wine—who in the end informed her of the prodigal's return to the fold, and of the dawn of a crescent honeymoon in the Boulevard d'Inkermann. Léa listened calmly to this Moral Tale; but she turned pale with emotion the following day when she recognised the blue limousine outside her gates and saw Charlotte Peloux on her way to the house.

"At last, at last! Here you are again, Léa, my beauty! . . . Lovelier than ever! Thinner than last year! Take care, Léa, we mustn't get too thin at our age! So far, and no further! And yet . . . But what a treat it is to see you!"

Never had that bitter tongue sounded so sweet to Léa. She let Madame Peloux prattle on, thankful for the breathing-space afforded by this acid stream. She had settled Charlotte Peloux into a deep armchair, in the soft light of the little pink-panelled salon, as in the old days. Automatically she had herself taken the straight-backed chair, which forced her to lift her shoulders and keep up her chin, as in the old days. Between them stood the table covered by a cloth of heavy embroidery, and on it, as in the old days, the large cut-glass decanter half full of old brandy, the shimmering petal-thin goblets, iced water, and shortbread biscuits.

"My beauty, now we'll be able to see each other again in peace, in peace. You know my motto: 'When in trouble, shun your friends: let them only share your luck!' All the time Chéri was playing truant, I purposely didn't show you any sign of life, you understand. Now that all's well and my children are happy again, I shout it aloud, I throw myself into your arms, and we start our pleasant existence all over again. . . ." She broke off and lit a cigarette, as clever with her pauses as an actress, ". . . without Chéri, of course."

"Of course," Léa acquiesced with a smile.

She was watching and listening to her old enemy in satisfied astonishment. The huge inhuman eyes, the chattering lips, the restless, tight little body—all that was facing her across the table had come simply to test her powers of resistance, to humiliate her, as in the old days, always as in the old days. But, as in the old days, Léa knew when to answer, when to be scornful, when to smile, and when to retaliate. Already that sorry burden, which had weighed so heavily the day before and the days before that, was beginning slowly to lift. The light seemed normal once more, and familiar, as it played over the curtains and suffused the little drawing-room.

'Here we are again,' Léa thought, in lighter vein. 'Two women, both a little older than a year ago, the same habits of backbiting and the same stock phrases; good-natured wariness at meals shared together; the financial papers in the morning, scandalmongering in the afternoon: all this will have to be taken up again, since it's Life, my life. The Aldonzas and the de la Berches, the Lilis and a few homeless old gentlemen: the whole lot squeezed round a card table, with the packs jostling the brandy-glasses, and perhaps, thrown in, a pair of little woollen shoes, begun for a baby who's soon to be born. . . . We'll start all over again, since it is ordained. Let's enter on it cheerfully. After all, it's only too easy to sink back into the grooves of the old life.'

And she settled back, eyes bright and mouth relaxed, to listen to Charlotte Peloux, who was greedily expatiating upon her daughter-in-law.

"My Léa, you should know, if anyone, that what I've always longed for is peace and quiet. Well now, I've got them. Chéri's escapade, you see, was nothing more than sowing a few wild oats. Far be it from me to reproach you, Léa dear, but as you'll be the first to admit, from eighteen to twenty-five he really never had the time to lead the life of a bachelor! And now he's done it with a vengeance!"

"It's a very good thing that he did," Léa said, without the flicker of a smile; "it acts as a sort of guarantee to his wife for the future."

"The very word, the very word I was hunting for!" barked Madame Peloux, beaming. "A guarantee! And ever since that day—one long dream! And, you know, when a Peloux does come home again after being properly out on the spree, he never goes off again!"

"Is that a family tradition?" Léa asked.

But Charlotte took no notice.

"And what's more, he was very well received when he did return home. His little wife—ah, there's a little wife for you, Léa!—and I've seen a fair number of little wives in my time, you know, and I don't mind telling you I've never seen one to hold a candle to Edmée!"

"Her mother is so remarkable," Léa said.

"Think, just think, my beauty—Chéri left her on my hands for very nearly three months! and between you and me she was very lucky to have me there."

"That's exactly what I was thinking," Léa said.

"And then, my dear, never a word of complaint, never a scene, never a tactless word! Nothing, nothing! She was patience itself, and sweetness . . . and the face of a saint, a saint!"

"It's terrifying," Léa said.

"And then, what d'you suppose happened when our young rascal walked in one morning, all smiles, as though he'd just come in from a stroll in the Bois? D'you suppose she allowed herself a single comment? Not one. Far from it. Nothing. As for him, though at heart he must have felt just a little ashamed . . ."

"Oh, why?" Léa asked.

"Well, really! After all . . . He was welcomed with open arms, and the whole thing was put right in their bedroom—in two ticks— just like that—no time lost! Oh, I can assure you, for the next hour or so there wasn't a happier woman in the world than me."

"Except, perhaps, Edmée," Léa suggested.

But Madame Peloux was all exaltation, and executed a superb soaring movement with her little arms: "I don't know what you can be thinking of. Personally, I was only thinking of the happy hearth and home."

She changed her tune, screwed up her eyes and pouted: "Besides, I can't see that little girl frantic with passion, or sobbing with ecstasy. Twenty, and skinny at that. . . . Pah! at that age they stammer and stutter. And then, between ourselves, I think her mother's cold."

"Aren't you being carried away by your sense of family?" Léa said.

Charlotte Peloux expanded her eyes to show their very depths, but absolutely nothing was to be read there.

"Certainly not, certainly not! Heredity, heredity! I'm a firm believer in it. Look at my son, who is fantasy incarnate . . . What? You don't know that he's fantasy incarnate?"

"It must have escaped my memory," Léa apologised.

"Well, I have high hopes for my son's future. He'll love his home as I love mine, he'll look after his fortune, he'll love his children, as I loved him. . . ."

"For goodness' sake, don't paint such a depressing picture," Léa begged. "What's it like, the young people's home?"

"Sinister!" shrieked Madame Peloux. "Positively sinister. Purple carpets. Purple! A black-and-gold bathroom. A salon with no furniture in it, full of Chinese vases larger than me! So, what happens is that they're always at Neuilly. Besides, without being conceited, I must say that girl adores me."

"Her nerves have not been upset at all?" Léa asked, anxiously.

Charlotte Peloux's eyes brightened. "No danger of that! She plays her hand well, and we must face the fact."

"Who d'you mean by 'we'?"

"Forgive me, my beauty, pure habit. We're dealing here with what I call a brain, a real brain. You should see the way she gives orders without raising her voice, and takes Chéri's teasing, and swallows the bitterest pills as if they were lollipops. . . . I begin to wonder, I really begin to wonder, whether there is not positive danger lying ahead for my son. I'm afraid, Léa dear, I'm afraid she may prove a damper on his originality, on his . . ."

"What? Is he being an obedient little boy?" Léa interrupted. "Do have some more of my brandy, Charlotte, it comes from Spéléïeff and it's seventy-four years old—you could give it to a new-born babe."

"'Obedient' is hardly the right word, but he's . . . inter- impertur . . ."

"Imperturbable?"

"That's the word! For instance, when he knew I was coming to see you . . ."

"Did he know, then?"

An impetuous blush leapt to Léa's cheeks, and she cursed her hot blood and the bright daylight of the little drawing-room. Madame Peloux, a benign expression in her eyes, fed on Léa's confusion.

"But of course he knew. That oughtn't to bring a blush to your cheeks, my beauty. What a child you are!"

"In the first place, how did you know I was back?"

"Oh, come, Léa, don't ask such foolish questions. You've been seen about everywhere."

"Yes, but Chéri—did you tell him I was back?"

"No, my beauty, it was he who told me."

"Oh, it was he who . . . That's funny."

She heard her heart beating in her voice and dared not risk more than the shortest answers.

"He even added: 'Madame Peloux, you'll oblige me by going to find out news of Nounoune.' He's still so fond of you, the dear boy."

"How nice!"

Madame Peloux, crimson in the face, seemed to abandon herself to the influence of the old brandy and talked as in a dream, wagging her head from side to side. But her russet eyes remained fixed and steely, and she kept a close watch on Léa, who was sitting bolt upright, armed against herself, waiting for the next thrust.

"It's nice, but it's quite natural. A man doesn't forget a woman like you, Léa dear. And . . . if you want to know what I really think, you've only to lift a finger and . . ."

Léa put a hand on Charlotte Peloux's arm. "I don't want to know what you really think," she said gently.

The corners of Madame Peloux's mouth fell: "Oh, I can understand, I approve," she sighed in a passionless voice. "When one has made other arrangements for one's life, as you have . . . I haven't even had a word with you about yourself!"

"But it seems to me that you have."

"Happy?"

"Happy."

"Divinely happy? A lovely trip? Is *he* nice? Where's his photo?"

Léa, relieved, sharpened her smile and shook her head. "No, no, you'll find out nothing, search where you will. Have your detectives let you down, Charlotte?"

"I rely on no detectives," Charlotte answered. "It's certainly not because anyone has told me . . . that you'd been through another heart-breaking desertion . . . that you'd been terribly worried, even over money. . . . No, no, you know what small attention I pay to gossip!"

"No one knows it better than me. My dear Lolotte, you can go back home without any fears on my behalf. And please reassure our friends, and tell them that I only wish they had made half what I did out of Oil shares between December and February."

The alcoholic cloud-screen, which softened the features of Madame Peloux, lifted in a trice; a clear, sharp, thoroughly alert face emerged. "You were in on Oil? I might have known it! And you never breathed a word to me."

"You never asked me about it. . . . You were thinking only of your family, as was natural. . . ."

"Fortunately, I was thinking of Compressed Fuel at the same time." The muted trumpet resembled a flute.

"Ah! and you never let on to me either!"

"Intrude upon love's young dream? Never! Léa, my dear, I'm off now, but I'll be back."

"You'll come back on Thursday, because at present, my dear Lolotte, your Sundays at Neuilly . . . they're finished for me. Would you like it if I started having a few people here on Thursdays? Nobody except old friends, old Ma Aldonza, our Reverend-Father-the-Baroness—poker for you, knitting for me. . . ."

"Do you knit?"

"Not yet, but it will soon come. Well?"

"I jump for joy at the idea! See if I'm not jumping! And you may be sure I won't say a word about it at home. That bad boy would be quite capable of coming and asking for a glass of port on one of your Thursdays. Just one more little kiss, my beauty. . . . Heavens, how good you smell. Have you noticed that as the skin gets less firm, the scent sinks in better and lasts much longer? It's really very nice."

'Be off, be off . . .' Quivering, Léa stood watching Madame Peloux as she crossed the courtyard. 'Go on your mischievous way! Nothing can stop you. You twist your ankle, yes—but it never brings you down. Your chauffeur is careful not to skid, so you'll never crash into a tree. You'll get back safely to Neuilly, and you'll choose your moment—to-day, or to-morrow, or one day next week—to come out with words that should never pass your lips. You'll try and upset those who, perhaps, are happy and at peace. The least harm you'll do is to make them tremble a little, as you made me, for a moment. . . .'

She was trembling at the knees, like a horse after a steep pull, but she was not in pain. She felt overjoyed at having kept so strict a control over herself and her words. Her looks and her colour were enhanced by her recent encounter, and she went on pulping her handkerchief to release her bottled-up energy.

She could not detach her thoughts from Madame Peloux. 'We've come together again,' she said to herself, 'like two dogs over an old slipper which both have got used to chewing. How queer it is! That woman is my enemy, and yet it's from her I now draw my comfort. How close are the ties that bind us!'

Thus, for a long time, she mused over her future, veering between alarm and resignation. Her nerves were relaxed, and she slept for a little. As she sat with one cheek pressed against a cushion, her dreams projected her into her fast-approaching old age. She saw day follow day with clockwork monotony, and herself beside Charlotte Peloux—their spirited rivalry helping the time to pass. In this way she would be spared, for many years, the degrading listlessness of women past their prime, who abandon first their stays, then their hair-dye, and who finally no longer bother about the quality of their underclothes. She had a foretaste of the sinful pleasures of the old— little else than a concealed aggressiveness, day-dreams of murder, and the keen recurrent hope for catastrophes that will spare only one living creature and one corner of the globe. Then she woke up, amazed to find herself in the glow of a pink twilight as roseate as the dawn.

"Ah, Chéri!" she sighed.

But it was no longer the raucous hungry cry of a year ago. She was not now in tears, nor was her body suffering and rebellious, because threatened by some sickness of the soul. Léa rose from her chair, and rubbed her cheek, embossed by the imprint of the embroidered cushion.

'My poor Chéri! It's a strange thought that the two of us—you by losing your worn old mistress, and I by losing my scandalous young lover—have each been deprived of the most honourable possession we had upon this earth!'

Two days went by after the visit of Charlotte Peloux: two grey days that passed slowly for Léa. She faced this new life with the patience of an apprentice. 'Since this is going to be my new life,' she said to herself, 'I'd better make a start.' But she set about it clumsily, altogether too conscientiously, so that it was a strain on her perseverance. On the second day, about eleven in the morning, she was seized with a desire to go for a walk through the Bois as far as the Lakes.

'I'll buy a dog,' she thought. 'He'll be a companion, and force me to walk.' And Rose had to hunt through the bottom of the summer cupboards for a pair of strong-soled brown boots and a tweed coat and skirt, smelling of alpine meadows and pine forests. Léa set off with the resolute stride proper to the wearer of heavy footwear and rough country clothes.

'Ten years ago, I should not have feared to carry a stick,' she said to herself. When still quite near the house, she heard behind her a brisk light tread, which she thought she recognised. She became unnerved, almost paralysed by a compelling fear; and before she could recover she let herself unwittingly be overtaken, and then passed, by an unknown young man. He was in a hurry, and never even glanced at her.

'I really am a fool,' she breathed in her relief.

She bought a dark carnation to pin on her jacket and started off again. But thirty yards ahead of her, looming out of the diaphanous mist above the grass verges of the Avenue, the silhouette of a man was waiting.

'This time I do recognise the cut of that coat and that way of twirling a cane. . . . Oh, no thank you, the last thing I want is for him to see me shod like a postman and wearing a thick jacket that makes me look stocky. If I must run into him, I'd far rather he saw me in something else . . . and he never could stand me in brown, anyhow. . . . No, no . . . I'm off home. . . . I . . .'

At that moment the waiting man hailed an empty taxi, stepped in, and drove past Léa: he was a young man with fair hair and small close-clipped moustache. But this time Léa did not smile or feel relief. She turned on her heel and walked back home.

"One of my off-days, Rose. . . . Bring me the peach-blossom tea-gown, the new one, and the big embroidered cloak. I'm stifling in these woollen things."

'It's no good being obstinate,' Léa thought. 'Twice in succession it's turned out not to be Chéri: the third time it would have been. I know the little jokes Fate plays on one. There's nothing to be done about it. I've no fight left in me to-day, I'm feeling limp.'

She spent the rest of the day once more trying patiently to learn to be alone. After luncheon she enjoyed a cigarette and a look at the papers, and welcomed with a short-lived joy a telephone call from Baroness de la Berche, then another from Spéleïeff, her former lover, the handsome horse-coper, who had seen her in the street the previous evening and offered to sell her a spanking pair.

There followed an hour of complete and frightening silence. 'Come, come . . .' She began to walk up and down, with her hands on her hips, her arms free of the heavy gold rose-embroidered cloak, its magnificent train sweeping the floor behind her.

'Come, come. . . . Let's try to take stock. This isn't the moment to become demoralised—now that I'm no longer in love with the boy. I've been living on my own now for six months. I managed perfectly well when I was in the south. To start with, I moved about from place to place. And the people I got to know on the Riviera or in the Pyrenees did me good; I felt positively refreshed each time any of them went away. Starch poultices may not cure a burn, but they do bring relief when constantly renewed. My six months of keeping on the move reminds me of the story of that hideous Sarah Cohen, who married a monster of ugliness. "Each time I look at him, I think that I am pretty."

'But I knew what it was like to live alone before these last six months. What sort of life did I lead after I'd left Spéleïeff, for instance? Oh yes, I went chasing round bistros and bars with Patron, and then all of a sudden Chéri came into my life. But before

:leïeff, there was little Lequellec: when his family dragged him
ay from me to lead him to the altar, his beautiful eyes were brimming with tears, poor boy. . . . After him, I was all alone for four
months, I remember. The first month, I cried a great deal. Oh, no, it
was for Bacciocchi I cried so much. But when I was through with my
tears, there was no holding me. It was so delightful to find myself
alone. Yes, but at the Bacciocchi time I was twenty-eight, and thirty
after Lequellec, and in between these two, I had known . . . Well,
no matter. After Spéleïeff, I became disgusted—so much money so ill
spent. Whereas now, after Chéri, I'm . . . I'm fifty, and I was un-
wise enough to keep him for six whole years!'

She wrinkled her forehead, and looked ugly with her mouth in a
sulky droop.

'It serves me right. At my age, one can't afford to keep a lover six
years. Six years! He has ruined all that was left of me. Those six years
might have given me two or three quite pleasant little happinesses,
instead of one profound regret. A liaison of six years is like following
your husband out to the colonies: when you get back again nobody
recognises you and you've forgotten how to dress.'

To relieve the strain, she rang for Rose, and together they went
through the contents of the little cupboard where she kept her lace.
Night fell, set the lamps blossoming into light, and called Rose back
to the cares of the house.

'To-morrow,' Léa said to herself, 'I'll order the motor and drive
out to Spéleïeff's stud-farm in Normandy. I'll take old La Berche, if
she wants to come: it will remind her of the past glories of her own
carriages. And, upon my word, should the younger Spéleïeff cast an
eye in my direction, I'm not saying I . . .'

She carefully smiled a mysterious and provocative smile, to delude
what ghosts there might be hovering round the dressing-table or
round the formidable bed, glimmering in the shadows. But she felt
entirely frigid, and full of contempt for the pleasures other people
found in love.

She dined off grilled sole and pastries, and found the meal a recre-
ation. She chose a dry champagne in place of the Bordeaux, and
hummed as she left the table. Eleven o'clock caught her by surprise,
still taking the measurements of the space between the windows in
her bedroom, where she planned to replace the large looking-glasses
with old painted panels of flowers and balustrades. She yawned,
scratched her head, and rang for her maid to undress her. While
Rose knelt to take off her silk stockings, Léa reviewed her achieve-

ments of the day already slipping into the pages of the past, and was
as pleased with her performance as if she had polished off an imposi-
tion. Protected for the night against the dangers of idleness, she
could look forward to so many hours of sleep, so many when she
would lie awake. Under cover of night, the restless regain the privilege of yawning aloud or sighing, of cursing the milkman's cart, the
street-cleaners, and the early morning sparrows.

During her preparations for the night, she thought over a number
of mild projects that would never come into being.

'Aline Mesmacker has a restaurant bar and is simply coining
money. . . . Obviously, it gives her something to do, as well as being
a good investment. . . . But I can't see myself sitting at a cash-desk;
and if one employs a manageress, it's no longer worth while. Dora
and that fat Fifi run a night-club together, Mother La Berche told
me. Everybody's doing it now. And they wear stiff collars and dinner
jackets, to attract a special clientèle. Fat Fifi has three children to
bring up—they're her excuse. . . . Then there's Kühn, who's simply
kicking his heels, and would gladly take some of my capital to start a
new dressmaker's.' Naked, and brick-pink from the reflection of her
Pompeian bathroom, she sprayed herself with her favourite sandal-
wood, and, without thinking about it, enjoyed unfolding a long silk
nightgown.

'All that's so much poppycock! I know perfectly well that I dislike
working. To bed with you, Madame! You'll never have any other
place of business, and all your customers are gone!'

The coloured lining of the white gandoura she put on was
suffused with a vague pink. She went back to her dressing-table, and
combed and tugged at the hairs stiffened by dye, lifting both her
arms, and thus framing her tired face. Her arms were still so beautiful, from the full deep hollow of the armpit up to the rounded
wrists, that she sat gazing at them in the looking-glass.

"What lovely handles for so old a vase!"

With a careless gesture she thrust a pale tortoiseshell comb into
the back of her hair, and, without much hope, picked a detective
story from the shelf of a dark closet. She had no taste for fine bind-
ings and had never lost the habit of relegating books to the bottom
of a cupboard, along with cardboard boxes and empty medicine bottles.

As she stood smoothing the cool linen sheets on her huge uncovered bed, the big bell in the courtyard rang out. The full, solemn,
unwonted peal jarred on the midnight hour.

"What in the world . . . ?" she said out loud.

She held her breath while listening, her lips parted. A second peal sounded even louder than the first, and Léa, with an instinctive movement of self-preservation and modesty, ran to powder her face. She was about to ring for Rose when she heard the front door slam, followed by footsteps in the hall and on the stairs, and the sound of two voices mingling—her maid's and someone else's. She had no time to make up her mind: the door of her room was flung open by a ruthless hand. Chéri stood before her—his top-coat unbuttoned over evening clothes, his hat on his head—pale and angry-looking.

He leaned back against the door now shut behind him, and did not move. He looked not so much at Léa as all round the room, with the quick shifting glance of a man about to be attacked.

Léa, who that morning had trembled at the half-surmised outline of a figure in the mist, felt at first only the resentment of a woman caught at her toilet. She drew her wrap more closely about her, settled her comb, and with one foot hunted for a missing slipper. She blushed, yet by the time the high colour died down she had already recovered the semblance of calm. She raised her head and appeared taller than the young man who was leaning, all in black, against the white of the door.

"That's a nice way to come into a room," she said in a rather loud voice. "You might at least take your hat off and say good evening."

"Good evening," Chéri said in surly tones.

The sound of his voice seemed to astonish him. He looked all round less like an angry animal, and a sort of smile drifted from his eyes down to his mouth, as he repeated a gentler "Good evening."

He took off his hat and came forward a few steps.

"May I sit down?"

"If you like," Léa said.

He sat down on a pouffe and saw that she remained standing.

"Are you in the middle of dressing? Aren't you going out?"

She shook her head, sat down far away from him, picked up her nail-buffer and never said a word. He lit a cigarette, and asked her permission only after it was alight.

"If you like," Léa repeated indifferently.

He said nothing more and dropped his gaze. Noticing that his hand with the cigarette in it was shaking, he rested it on the edge of a table. Léa continued polishing her nails deliberately and from time to time cast a brief glance at Chéri's face, especially at his lowered eyelids and the dark fringe of his lashes.

"It was Ernest who opened the front door to me as usual," Chéri said at last.

"And why shouldn't it have been Ernest? Ought I to have changed my staff because you got married?"

"No . . . I mean, I simply said that . . ."

Again silence fell, broken by Léa.

"May I know whether you intend to remain for some time, sitting on that pouffe? I don't even ask why you take the liberty of entering my house at midnight. . . ."

"You may ask me why," he said quickly.

She shook her head. "It doesn't interest me."

He jumped up precipitately, sending the pouffe rolling away behind him, and bore down upon Léa. She felt him bending over her as if he were going to strike her, but she did not flinch. The thought came to her: 'What in this world is there for me to be frightened of?'

"So you don't know what brings me here! You don't want to know what brings me here!"

He tore off his coat and sent it flying on to the chaise-longue, then he crossed his arms, and shouted quite close to Léa's face, in a strained but triumphant voice, "I've come back!"

She was using a delicate pair of tweezers, and these she carefully put away before wiping her fingers. Chéri dropped into a chair, as though his strength was completely exhausted.

"Good," Léa said. "You've come back. That's very nice! Whose advice did you take about that?"

"My own," Chéri said.

She got up in her turn, the better to dominate him. Her surging heartbeats had subsided, allowing her to breathe in comfort. She wanted to play her role without a mistake.

"Why didn't you ask me for my advice? I'm an old friend who knows all your clownish ways. Why did it never occur to you that your coming here might well embarrass . . . someone?"

Lowering his head, he searched every corner of the room from under his eyebrows—the closed doors, the bed, metal-girt and heaped with luxurious pillows. He found nothing exceptional, nothing new, and shrugged his shoulders.

Léa expected more than that and drove home her point. "You understand what I mean?"

"Perfectly," he answered. " 'Monsieur' has not come in yet? 'Monsieur' is sleeping out?"

"That's none of your business, child," she said calmly.

He bit his lip and nervously knocked off his cigarette ash into a jewel tray.

"Not in that, I keep on telling you!" Léa cried. "How many times must I . . . ?"

She broke off to reproach herself for having unconsciously adopted the tone of their old familiar quarrels. But he did not appear to have heard and went on examining one of Léa's rings—an emerald she had purchased on her recent trip.

"What's . . . what's this?" he stammered.

"That? It's an emerald."

"I'm not blind. What I mean is, who gave it you?"

"No one you know."

"Charming!" Chéri said bitterly.

The note in his voice was enough to restore Léa's authority, and she pressed her advantage, taking pleasure in leading him still further astray.

"Isn't it charming? I get compliments on it wherever I go. And the setting, you've seen it . . . the filigree of diamonds . . ."

"Enough!" bawled Chéri furiously, smashing his fist down on the fragile table.

A few roses shed their petals at the impact, and a china cup slithered without breaking on to the thick carpet. Léa reached for the telephone, but Chéri caught her hand in a rough grasp. "What are you going to do with that telephone?"

"Call the police," Léa said.

He took hold of both her arms, pretending to be up to some playful nonsense as he pushed her away from the instrument.

"Oh go on with you, that's all right. Don't be silly! Can't I even open my mouth without your getting all melodramatic?"

She sat down and turned her back on him. He remained standing, with nothing in his hands: his parted lips were swollen, giving him the look of a sulky child; one black lock hung down over his eyebrow. Surreptitiously, Léa watched him in a looking-glass, till his reflection vanished when he sat down. In her turn, Léa was embarrassed when she felt him staring at her back, broadened by the loose folds of her gandoura. She returned to her dressing-table, smoothed her hair, rearranged her comb, and, as if for want of something better to do, began unscrewing the top of a scent-bottle. Chéri turned his head as the first whiff reached his nostrils.

"Nounoune!" he called.

She did not answer.

"Nounoune!"

"Beg my pardon," she ordered, without turning round.

"Not likely!" he sneered.

"I can't force you. But you'll leave the house. And at once. . . ."

"I beg your pardon," he said at once, peevishly.

"Better than that."

"I beg your pardon," he repeated, quite low.

"That's better."

She went over to him and ran her hand lightly over his bowed head. "Come, tell me all about it."

He shivered, trembling under her touch. "What do you want me to tell you? It's not very complicated. I've come back, that's all."

"Tell me! Come along, tell me!"

He rocked backwards and forwards on his seat, pressing his hands between his knees, and raised his head towards Léa without meeting her eyes. She watched the quivering of his nostrils, and she heard him trying to control his rapid breathing. She had only to say once more, "Come, tell me all about it," and give him a prod with her finger, as if to push him over. At once he cried out, "Nounoune darling! Nounoune darling!" and threw all his weight upon her, clasping her long legs, so that they gave way under her.

Once seated, she let him slither to the floor and sprawl over her with tears, and inarticulate words, and groping fingers that caught at her lace and her pearls and hunted feverishly under her dress for the shape of her shoulder and under her hair to touch her ears.

"Nounoune darling! We're together again, my Nounoune! Oh, my Nounoune! your shoulder, and your scent, and your pearls, my Nounoune, oh, it's so stunning . . . and that little burnt taste your hair has, oh, it's . . . it's stunning. . . ."

He leaned back to breathe out this silly word with what might have been the last breath of his body: then, still on his knees, he clasped Léa in his arms, offering her a forehead shadowed under tousled hair, a trembling mouth moist with tears, and eyes bright with weeping and happiness. She was so lost in contemplating him, so perfectly oblivious of everything that was not Chéri, that she never thought of kissing him. She twined her arms round his neck and gently hugged him to her, rocking him to the rhythm of murmured words.

"My pet . . . my naughty boy . . . You're here . . . You've come

back again. . . . What have you been up to now? You're so naughty
. . . my pretty. . . ."

He was moaning softly, keeping his lips together and hardly speaking, as he listened to Léa. He rested his cheek on her breast and
begged her to go on, if for a moment she ceased her tender lullaby.
And Léa, fearful that her own tears would flow, went on with her
scolding.

"Wicked monster . . . heartless little devil . . . Get along with
you, you great slut!"

He looked at her in gratitude: "That's right . . . Go on slanging
me! Oh, Nounoune!"

She held him at arm's length to see him properly. "So you love
me, then?"

He lowered his eyes in childish confusion: "Yes, Nounoune."

A little burst of uncontrollable laughter warned Léa that she was
on the verge of giving way to the most terrible joy of her life. An embrace, followed by collapse, the uncovered bed, two bodies joined together like the two living halves of an animal that has been cut
through. 'No, no,' she said to herself, 'not yet, oh, not yet. . . .'

"I'm thirsty," Chéri sighed. "Nounoune, I'm thirsty."

She rose quickly and put a hand on the now tepid jug of water;
hardly had she hurried from the room before she was back again.
Chéri, curled up in a ball, was lying with his head on the pouffe.
"Rose will bring you some lemonade," Léa said. "Don't stay there.
Come and sit on the chaise-longue. Does the lamp hurt your
eyes?"

She was trembling with delight in her imperious solicitude. She sat
down at the other end of the chaise-longue and Chéri half stretched
out to nestle against her.

"Perhaps now you'll tell me a little . . ."

They were interrupted by the entry of Rose. Chéri, without getting up, languidly turned his head in her direction: "Evening,
Rose."

"Good evening, Monsieur," Rose said, discreetly.

"Rose, to-morrow at nine, I'd like . . ."

"Brioches and chocolate," Rose finished for him.

Chéri shut his eyes again with a sigh of contentment. "And that's
that. . . . Rose, where am I going to dress to-morrow morning?"

"In the boudoir," Rose answered accommodatingly. "Only I had
better take the settee out, I suppose, and put back the shaving-mir-
ror, as it used to be?"

She sought confirmation in the eye of Léa, who was proudly displaying her spoilt child, supported by her arm as he drank.

"If you like," Léa said. "We'll see. You can go, Rose."

Rose retired, and during the ensuing moment's silence nothing could be heard except the vague murmuring of the wind and the cry of a bird bewildered by the brightness of the moon.

"Chéri, are you asleep?"

He gave one of his long-drawn sighs like an exhausted retriever. "Oh, no, Nounoune, I'm too happy to sleep."

"Tell me, child . . . You haven't been unkind over there?"

"At home? No Nounoune, far from it. I swear to you."

He looked up at her, without raising his trusting head.

"Of course not, Nounoune. I left because I left. The girl's very nice. There was no fuss at all."

"Ah!".

"I wouldn't swear that she didn't have an inkling all the same. This evening she was wearing what I call her 'orphanage look', you know, pathetic dark eyes under her pretty head of hair. . . . You know how pretty her hair is?"

"Yes."

She threw out these monosyllables in a whisper as if intent on the words of someone talking in his sleep.

"I even think," Chéri continued, "that she must have seen me going through the garden."

"Oh?"

"Yes. She was on the balcony, in her white sequin dress, congealed whiteness. Oh! I don't like that dress. . . . Ever since dinner it had been making me long to cut and run."

"No."

"Yes it had, Nounoune. I can't say whether she saw me. The moon wasn't up. It came up while I was waiting."

"Where were you waiting?"

Chéri waved a vague hand in the direction of the avenue. "There. I was waiting, don't you understand. I wanted to see. I'd waited a long time."

"But what for?"

He hastily jumped away and sat further off. He resumed his expression of primitive distrust. "I wanted to be sure there was nobody here."

"Oh, yes. . . . You thought that . . ."

She could not resist a scornful laugh. A lover in her house! A lover while Chéri was still living! It was grotesque. 'How stupid he is!' she thought in her enthusiasm.

"You're laughing?"

He stood up in front of her and put his hand on her forehead, forcing back her head. "You're laughing! You're making fun of me. You're . . . Then you have a lover! There is someone!"

He leaned over her as he spoke, pushing her head back against the end of the chaise-longue. She felt the breath of an insulting mouth on her eyelids, and made no effort to be free of the hand that was crushing her hair against her forehead.

"I dare you to say you have a lover!"

She fluttered her eyelids, dazzled by the radiance of the face bearing down on her, and finally, in a toneless voice, she said: "No, I have no lover. I . . . love you. . . ."

He relaxed his hold and began pulling off his dinner jacket and waistcoat; his tie whistled through the air and ended up round the neck of Léa's bust—up on the mantelpiece. Meanwhile, he never moved away from her, and kept her, wedged between his knees, where she sat on the chaise-longue.

When she saw him half-naked, she asked, with a note of sadness: "Do you really want to? . . . Do you? . . ."

He did not answer, carried away by the thought of his approaching pleasure and the consuming desire to take her again. She gave way and served her young lover like a good mistress, with devout solicitude. Nevertheless, she anticipated with a sort of terror the moment of her own undoing; she endured Chéri as she might a torture, warding him off with strengthless hands, and holding him fast between strong knees. Finally, she seized him by the arm, uttered a feeble cry and foundered in the deep abyss, whence love emerges pale and in silence, regretful of death.

They remained enfolded in their close embrace and no words troubled the prolonged silence of their return to life. The upper part of his body had slipped down and he lay across Léa's thigh, his pendent head, with eyes closed, resting upon the sheets as if he had been stabbed to death over the body of his mistress. She, meanwhile, partly turned away from him, bore almost the full weight of this unsparing body. She breathed softly but unevenly. Her left arm ached, crushed beneath her. Chéri could feel the back of his neck growing numb. Both were waiting, concentrated and motionless, for the abating tempest of their pleasure to recede.

'He's asleep,' Léa thought. With her free hand, she was still cling-

ing to Chéri's wrist and she squeezed it gently. One of her knees was
being crushed by a knee—how well she knew its lovely shape! About
the level of her own heart she could feel the steady muffled beating
of another. Chéri's favourite scent—insistent, clinging, reminding her
of fat waxy flowers and exotic glades—was all pervasive. 'He is here!'
she whispered, immersed in a feeling of blind security. 'He is here for
ever!' her senses re-echoed. The well-ordered prudence, the happy
common sense that had been her guide through life, the humiliating
vagaries of her riper years and the subsequent renunciations, all beat
a retreat and vanished into thin air before the presumptuous brutality of love. 'He is here!' she thought. 'He has left his own home and
his pretty silly little wife to come back, to come back to me! Who
can take him from me now? Now at last I'll be able to organise our
existence. He doesn't always know what he wants; but I do. No
doubt we shall have to go away. We shan't go into hiding, but we'll
look for somewhere peaceful. For I must find time to look at him.
When I was unaware I loved him, I can't ever have looked at him
properly. I must find a place where there'll be room enough for his
whims and my wishes. I'll do the thinking for both of us—let him do
the sleeping.'

While she was painstakingly withdrawing her left arm, cramped
and pricking with pins and needles, and her numbed shoulder, she
glanced at Chéri's averted face and found that he was not asleep.
She could see the whites of his eyes and the flutter of the little black
wings of his long eyelashes.

"Why, you're not asleep!"

She felt him tremble against her, before he turned over in a single
movement.

"But you're not asleep, either, Nounoune!"

He stretched a hand out to the bedside table and switched on the
lamp: a flood of rosy light covered the big bed, throwing the patterns
of the lace into high relief, hollowing out shadowed valleys between
swelling hills in the quilted folds of the eiderdown. Chéri, stretched
out at full length, surveyed the field of his victory and of his peace.
Léa, leaning on one elbow beside him, stroked his beloved, long eyebrows, and swept back the rebellious locks. Lying with his hair
dishevelled over his forehead, he looked as if he had been blown over
by a raging wind.

The enamel clock struck. Chéri straightened himself at a bound
and sat up. "What time is it?"

"I don't know. What difference can it make to us?"

"Oh, I just asked. . . ."

He gave a short laugh, and did not immediately lie down again. Outside, the first milkcart clinked out its tinkling carillon, and he made a vague movement in the direction of the avenue. The strawberry-coloured curtains were slit through by the cold blade of dawning day. Chéri turned back to look at Léa, and stared at her with the formidable intensity of a suspicious dog or a puzzled child. An undecipherable thought appeared in the depths of his eyes; their shape, their dark wallflower hue, their harsh or languorous glint, were used only to win love, never to reveal his mind. From sheets crumpled as though by a storm, rose his naked body, broad-shouldered, slim-waisted; and his whole being breathed forth the melancholy of perfect works of art.

"Ah, you . . ." sighed the infatuated Léa.

He did not smile, accustomed as he was to accepting personal praise.

"Tell me, Nounoune. . . ."

"What, my pretty?"

He hesitated, fluttered his eyelids, and shivered. "I'm tired . . . and then to-morrow, how will you manage about——"

Léa gave him a gentle push and pulled the naked body and drowsy head down to the pillows again.

"Don't worry. Lie down and go to sleep. Isn't Nounoune here to look after you? Don't think of anything. Sleep. You're cold, I'm sure. . . . Here, take this, it's warm. . . ."

She rolled him up in the silk and wool of a little feminine garment, retrieved from somewhere in the bed, and put out the light. In the dark, she lent him her shoulder, settled him happily against her side, and listened till his breathing was in rhythm with her own. No desires clouded her mind, but she did not wish for sleep. 'Let him do the sleeping; it's for me to do the thinking,' she repeated to herself. 'I'll contrive our flight with perfect tact and discretion; I believe in causing as little suffering and scandal as possible. . . . For the spring we shall like the south best. If there were only myself to be considered, I'd rather stay here, in peace and quiet; but there's Ma Peloux and the young Madame Peloux. . . .' The vision of a young wife in her nightgown, anxiously standing beside a window, checked Léa only long enough for her to shrug her shoulders with cold impartiality. 'I can't help that. What makes one person's happiness . . .'

The black silky head stirred on her breast, and her sleeping lover moaned in his dream. With a zealous arm, Léa shielded him against nightmares, and rocked him gently so that—without sight, without memory, without plans for the future—he might still resemble that "naughty little boy" never born to her.

HE had lain awake for some little while, taking great care not to stir. Cheek on folded arms, he tried to guess the time. Under a clear sky, the avenue must be vibrating with heat too insistent for early morning, since no shadow of a cloud passed across the lambent rose-red curtains. 'Ten o'clock, perhaps?' He was tormented by hunger; he had eaten little the previous evening. A year ago he would have bounded out of bed, roughly aroused Léa from sleep by ferocious shouts for cream-frothed chocolate and butter off the ice.

He did not stir. He was afraid, did he move, of crumbling away what remained to him of his rapture, the visual pleasure he derived from the shining curtains and from the steel and brass spirals of the bed, twinkling in the coloured aura of the room. Last night's great happiness had dwindled, it seemed, had melted, and sought refuge in the dancing iridescence of a cut glass jug.

On the landing, Rose trod the carpet with circumspect step; a discreet besom was sweeping the courtyard; and Chéri heard the tinkle of china coming from the pantry. 'How the morning drags on,' he said to himself. 'I'll get up.' But he remained without moving a muscle, for, behind him, Léa yawned and stretched her legs. He felt the touch of a gentle hand on his back. He shut his eyes again, and, for no good reason, his whole body began to act a lie, feigning the limpness of sleep. He was aware of Léa leaving the bed and of her dark silhouette between him and the curtains, which she drew half apart. She turned round to look at him, and with a toss of the head smiled in his direction—in no sense a smile of triumph, but a resolute smile, ready to accept all dangers. She was in no hurry to leave the room, and Chéri kept watch on her through hardly parted eyelashes. He saw her open a railway time-table and run her finger down the columns; then she seemed absorbed in some calculation, brow puckered and face upturned. Not yet powdered, a meagre twist of hair at the back of her head, double chin and raddled neck, she was exposing herself rashly to the unseen observer.

She moved away from the window, and, taking her cheque-book from a drawer, wrote and tore out several cheques. Then she put a pair of white pyjamas at the foot of the bed, and silently left the room.

Alone, Chéri took several deep breaths, realising that he had hardly dared to breathe since Léa had left the bed. He got up, put on the pyjamas, and opened a window. 'It's stifling in here,' he gasped. He had the vague uncomfortable feeling of having done something reprehensible. 'Because I pretended to be asleep? But I've watched Léa a hundred times just after she's got out of bed. Only, this time, I made the pretence of being asleep.'

The dazzling light restored the rose-pink glow of the room, and the delicate nacreous tints of the picture by Chaplin smiled down at him from the wall. Chéri bowed his head and shut his eyes, in an effort to remember the room as it had looked the night before—the mysterious colour, like the inside of a water-melon, the enchanted dome of lamp-light, and, above all, his exaltation when reeling under the intensity of his pleasures.

"You're up! The chocolate's already on its way."

He was pleased to note that it had taken Léa only these few moments to do her hair, touch up her face, and spray herself with the familiar scent. The room seemed suddenly to be filled with the cheerful sound of her lovely voice, and with the smell of chocolate and hot toast. Chéri sat down beside the two steaming cups and was handed the thickly buttered toast by Léa. She did not suspect that he was trying to find something to say, for she knew that he was seldom talkative, especially when he was eating. She enjoyed a good breakfast, eating with the haste and preoccupied gaiety of a woman who, her trunks packed, is ready to catch her train.

"Your second piece of toast, Chéri?"

"No, thank you, Nounoune."

"Not hungry any more?"

"Not hungry."

With a smile, she shook her finger at him. "You know what you're in for! You're going to swallow down two rhubarb pills!"

He wrinkled his nose, shocked. "Listen, Nounoune. You've got a mania for fussing . . ."

"Ta ti ta ta! That's my look out. Put out your tongue. You won't show it me! Then wipe off your chocolate moustache, and let's have a quick sensible talk. Tiresome subjects can't be dealt with too quickly."

She stretched across the table to take Chéri's hand and hold it between her own.

"You've come back. That was our fate. Do you trust yourself to me? I'll be responsible for you."

She could not help breaking off, and closed her eyes as if hugging her victory. Chéri noticed the flush on his mistress's face.

"Oh!" she continued in a lower voice, "When I think of all that I never gave you, all that I never said to you! When I think that I believed you merely a passing fancy, like all the others—only a little more precious than all the others! What a fool I was not to understand that you were my love, *the* love, the great love that comes only once!"

When she opened her blue eyes, they seemed to have become bluer, gaining depth in the shade of her eyelids, and her breathing was uneven.

'Oh,' Chéri prayed inwardly, 'don't let her ask me a question, don't let her expect an answer from me now! I couldn't speak a single word.'

She gave his hand a little shake. "Come along, let's be serious. As I was saying—we're leaving, we've already left. What will you do about *over there*? Let Charlotte arrange all the settlement details— it's much the wisest—and make her be generous, I beg of you. How will you let them know *over there*? A letter, I imagine. None too easy, but the less ink spilled, the better. We'll see about that between us. Then there's the question of your luggage. I've none of your things here any more. Such little details are far more upsetting than a major decision, but don't worry too much. . . . Will you kindly stop tearing the skin off the side of your toe all the time! That's the way to get an ingrowing toe-nail!"

Automatically, he let his foot drop to the floor. Under the weight of his sullen taciturnity, he found it a strain to focus his jaded attention on what Léa was saying. He stared at his mistress's happy, animated, imperious features, and asked himself vaguely: 'Why does she look so happy?'

His bewilderment became so obvious that Léa stopped in the middle of her monologue on their chances of buying old Berthellemy's yacht from him. "Could anyone believe that you've not got one word of advice to give? Oh, you might still be twelve!"

Chéri, snatched from his stupor, put a hand to his forehead and looked at Léa, his eyes filled with melancholy.

"Being with you, Nounoune, is likely to keep me twelve for half a century."

She blinked her eyes several times as if he had breathed on their lids, and let silence settle again.

"What are you trying to say?" she asked at last.

"Nothing, except what I did say, Nounoune. Nothing but the truth. And can you deny it, you, the most honest person alive?"

She decided to laugh, but her gaiety masked a terrible fear.

"But half your charm lies in your childishness, stupid! Later on it will be the secret of your eternal youth. Why complain of it? And you have the cheek to complain of it to *me!*"

"Yes, Nounoune. Do you expect me to complain to anyone but you?" and he caught hold of the hand she had taken away. "My own Nounoune, dearest, darling Nounoune, I'm not only complaining of myself: I'm accusing you!"

She felt the grip of his firm hand. Instead of looking away, his large dark eyes with lashes gleaming clung pitifully to hers. She was determined not to tremble, yet. 'It's nothing, it's nothing,' she thought. 'It calls only for two or three sharp words and he'll become insulting, then sulky, and then I'll forgive him. . . . It's no more than that.' But she failed to find the quick rebuke which would change the expression on his face. "Come, come, child . . . You know quite well there are certain jokes I will not tolerate." But at the same moment she knew her voice to be sounding false and feeble. 'How badly I said that . . . bad theatre. . . .'

It was half-past ten, and the sun was now shining on the table between them. Léa's polished nails twinkled in its beams; but the light fell also on the soft flabby skin on the back of her well-shaped hands and on her wrists. This emphasised—like criss-crossings on a clay soil when heavy rain is followed by a dry spell—the complicated network of tiny concentric grooves and miniature parallelograms. Léa rubbed her hands absent-mindedly, turning her head to make Chéri look out of the window; but he persisted in his miserable, hang-dog moodiness. The two hands were pretending, as if in disgrace, to toy with a loop of her belt. Brusquely he pounced upon them, kissed and kissed them again, then pressed his cheek against them, murmuring "My Nounoune. . . . Oh, my poor Nounoune . . ."

"Let me alone," she cried with inexplicable anger, snatching her hands away from him.

She took a moment to regain her control, frightened of her weakness, for she had been on the verge of tears. As soon as she was able, she smiled and spoke.

"So now it's me you're sorry for! Why did you accuse me a moment ago?"

"I was wrong," he said, humbly. "For me you have been always . . ." He made a gesture to express his inability to find words worthy of her.

"*You have been?*" she underlined in a biting voice. "That sounds like an obituary notice, my good child!"

"You see . . ." he began reproachfully.

He shook his head, and she saw only too well that she could not rouse any anger in him. She tightened all her muscles, and reined in her thoughts with the help of those few words, ever the same, and inwardly repeated again and again: 'Here he is, in front of my eyes. I've only to look to see he's still there. He's not out of reach. But is he still here, with me, really and truly?'

Her thoughts escaped from the domination of these repeated phrases, only to sink into a great unvoiced lament. 'Oh! if only, if only I could somehow be returned to the moment when I was saying, "Your second piece of toast, Chéri!" for that moment's only just round the corner—it's not yet lost and gone for ever! Let's start again from there. The little that's taken place since won't count—I'll wipe it out, I'll wipe it out. I'm going to talk to him as though we're back where we were a moment ago. I'm going to talk to him about our departure, our luggage.'

She did, in fact, speak, and said, "I see . . . I see I cannot treat as a man a creature who, from sheer feebleness of character, can drive two women to distraction. Do you think that I don't understand? You like your journeys short, don't you? Yesterday at Neuilly, here to-day, but to-morrow! To-morrow, where? Here? No, no, my child, no need to lie, that guilty look would never take in even a woman stupider than I am, if there is one like that over there. . . ."

She threw out an arm to indicate Neuilly with so violent a gesture that she upset a cake-stand, which Chéri picked up again. Her words had sharpened her grief into anguish, an angry jealous anguish pouring forth like a young wife's outburst. The rouge on her cheek turned to the deep purple of wine-lees; a strand of her hair, crimped by the curling-tongs, wriggled down her neck like a small dry snake.

"And even the woman over there, even your wife won't be found waiting there every time you choose to come back home! A wife, my child, may not always be easy to find, but she's much easier to lose! You'll have yours kept under lock and key by Charlotte, eh? That's a marvellous idea! Oh, how I'll laugh, the day when . . ."

Chéri got up, pale and serious. "Nounoune! . . ."

"Why Nounoune? What d'you mean, Nounoune? Do you think you're going to frighten me? You want to lead your own life, do you? Go ahead! You're bound to see some pretty scenes, with a daughter of Marie-Laure's. She may have thin arms and a flat behind, but that won't prevent her from . . ."

"I forbid you, Nounoune!"

He seized her by the arm; but she rose, vigorously shook herself free, and broke into hoarse laughter: "Why, of course, 'I forbid you to say a word against my wife!' Isn't that it?"

He walked round the table, trembling with indignation, and went straight up to her. "No, I forbid you—d'you hear me?—I forbid you to spoil my Nounoune!" She retreated to the end of the room, babbling, "What's that? what's that?" He followed her as though bent on chastising her. "You heard what I said. Is that the way for Nounoune to speak? What do you mean by such behaviour? Cheap little jibes like Madame Peloux's, is that what you go in for? To think they could come from you, Nounoune, from you. . . ."

Arrogantly he threw back his head. "I know how Nounoune should speak. I know how she ought to think. I've had time to learn. I've not forgotten the day when you said to me, just before I married, 'At least don't be cruel. Try not to make her suffer. I have the feeling that a doe is being thrown to a greyhound.' Those were your words. That's really you. And the night before I married, when I ran away to come and see you, I remember you said to me . . ."

He could not go on, but all his features were bright with the memory.

"Darling, pull yourself together." He put his hands on Léa's shoulders. "And even last night," he went on, "it wasn't the first time you asked me whether I might not have hurt somebody *over there!* My Nounoune, I knew you as a fine woman, and I loved you as a fine woman, when we first started. If we have to make an end of it, must you start behaving like all the other women?"

She dimly felt the cunning behind the compliment and sat down, hiding her face in her hands.

"How hard you are, how hard," she stammered. "Why did you come back? . . . I was so calm on my own, getting so used to . . ."

She heard herself lying and stopped.

"Well, *I* wasn't!" Chéri said quickly. "I came back because . . . because . . ."

He raised his arms, let them drop and lifted them again. "Because I couldn't go on without you, there's no point in looking for any other explanation."

For a moment no word was spoken.

Quite overcome, she looked at this impatient young man, who with light feet and open arms, as white as a seagull, seemed poised for flight.

Chéri let his dark eyes rove all over her body.

"Oh, you can be proud of yourself," he said suddenly. "You can be proud of yourself for having made me—and what's more for three months—lead such a life, such a life!"

"I did?"

"Who else, if it wasn't you? If a door opened, it was Nounoune; the telephone rang, Nounoune; a letter in the garden postbox, perhaps Nounoune. . . . In the very wine I drank, I looked for you, and I never found a Pommery to equal yours. And then at nights . . . Oh, heavens above!"

He was walking up and down the carpet with rapid, noiseless steps. "I know now what it is to suffer for a woman, and no mistake! After you, I know what all the other women will be . . . dust and ashes! Oh, how well you've poisoned me!"

She drew herself up slowly in her chair, and, letting her body turn now this way, now that, followed Chéri's movements. Her cheeks were dry, rather shiny, and their fevered flush made the blue of her eyes almost intolerable. He was walking up and down, head lowered, and he never stopped talking.

"Imagine Neuilly with you not there, the first days after my return! For that matter, everything—with you not there! I almost went mad. One night, the child was ill—I no longer remember what it was, headache, pains, something. I felt sorry for her, but I had to leave the room; otherwise nothing in the world could have stopped me saying, 'Wait, don't cry, I'll go and fetch Nounoune and she'll make you well'—and you would have come, wouldn't you, Nounoune? Great heavens, what a life it was. . . . I took on Desmond at the Hôtel Morris, paid him well into the bargain, and sometimes at night I would tell him stories. . . . I used to speak as if you were unknown to him. 'Old boy, there's never been a skin like hers. . . . Take one look at that cabochon sapphire of yours, and then hide it away for ever, because no light can turn the blue of *her* eyes to grey!' I used to tell him how you could be tough when you wanted to be; and that no one had ever got the better of you, least of all me! I used to say, 'That woman, old boy, when she's wearing just the right hat—the dark blue one with the white wing, Nounoune, last summer's—and with the way she has of putting on her clothes—you can match her against any other woman you may choose—and she'll put every one of them in the shade!' And then that wonderful manner you have of walking—of talking—your smile—the erect way you hold yourself, I used to say to him—to Desmond: 'Ah! A woman like Léa *is* something!' "

He snapped his fingers with proprietary pride and stopped, quite out of breath from his talking and walking. 'I never said all that to Desmond,' he thought, 'and yet I'm not telling lies. Desmond understood all right.'

He wanted to go on and glanced at Léa. She was still ready to listen. Sitting bolt upright now, she exposed to him in the full light her noble face in its disarray, the skin shining like wax where the hot tears had dried. Her cheeks and chin were pulled down by an invisible weight, and this added a look of sadness to the trembling corners of her mouth. Chéri found intact amidst this wreckage of beauty the lovely commanding nose and the eyes as blue as a blue flower.

"And so you see, Nounoune, after months of that sort of life, I come back here, and . . ." He pulled himself up, frightened by what he had nearly said.

"You come back here, and find an old woman," Léa said calmly, in a whisper.

"Nounoune! Listen, Nounoune!"

He threw himself on his knees beside her, looking like a guilty, tongue-tied child no longer able to hide his misdemeanour.

"And you find an old woman," Léa repeated. "So what are you afraid of, child?"

She put her arms round his shoulders, and felt his body rigid and resistant, in sympathy with the hurt she was suffering. "Come, cheer up, my Chéri. Don't cry, my pretty. . . . What is it you're afraid of? Of having hurt me? Far from it: I feel so grateful to you."

He gave a sob of protestation, finding no strength to gainsay her.

She put her cheek against his tousled black hair. "Did you say all that, did you really think all that of me? Was I really so lovely in your eyes, tell me? And so kind? At the age when a woman's life is so often over, was I really the loveliest for you, the most kind, and were you really in love with me? How grateful I am to you, my darling! The finest, did you say? . . . My poor child."

He let himself go, while she supported him in her arms.

"Had I really been the finest, I should have made a man of you, and not thought only of the pleasures of your body, and my own happiness. The finest! Oh no, my darling, I certainly wasn't that, since I kept you to myself. And now it's almost too late. . . ."

He seemed to be asleep in Léa's arms; but his obstinately tight-shut eyelids quivered incessantly, and with one lifeless hand he was clutching hold of her négligée and slowly tearing it.

"It's almost too late, it's almost too late. But all the same . . ." She leaned over him. "Listen to me, my darling. Wake up, my pretty, and listen to me with your eyes open. Don't be afraid of looking at me. I am, after all, the woman you were in love with, you know, the finest woman . . ."

He opened his eyes, and his first tearful glance was already filled with a selfish, mendicant hope.

Léa turned away her head. 'His eyes . . . Oh, we must get this over quickly. . . .' She put her cheek against his forehead.

"It was I, child, it was my real self who said to you, 'Don't cause unnecessary pain; spare the doe. . . .' I had quite forgotten, but luckily you remembered. You are breaking away from me very late in the day, my naughty little boy; I've been carrying you next to my heart for too long, and now you have a load of your own to carry: a young wife, perhaps a child. . . . I am to blame for everything you lack. . . . Yes, yes, my pretty, here you are, thanks to me, at twenty-five, so light-hearted, so spoilt, and at the same time so sad. . . . I'm very worried about you. You're going to suffer and make others suffer. You who have loved me. . . ."

His fingers tightened their grip on her négligée, and Léa felt the sharp nails of her "naughty child" bite into her breast.

"You who have loved me," she went on after a pause, "will you be able to? . . . I don't know how to explain what I mean. . . ."

He drew back in order to listen: and she could barely restrain herself from saying, "Put your hand back on my breast and your nails where they have left their mark; my strength abandons me as soon as your flesh is parted from mine." Instead, she leaned over him as he knelt in front of her, and continued: "You have loved me, and you will regret . . ."

She smiled at him, looking down into his eyes.

"What vanity, eh! . . . But you will regret me! I beg of you, when you're tempted to terrify the girl entrusted to your care and keeping, do restrain yourself! At such moments, you must find for yourself the wisdom and kindness you never learned from me. I never spoke to you of the future. Forgive me, Chéri—I've loved you as if we were both destined to die within the same hour. Because I was born twenty-four years before you, I was doomed, and I dragged you down with me. . . ."

He was listening very attentively, which made his face look hard. She put her hand on his forehead to smooth the furrows of anxiety.

"Can you see us, Chéri, going out to lunch together at Armenonville! . . . Can you see us inviting Monsieur and Madame Lili! . . ."

She gave a sad little laugh, and shivered.

"Oh, I'm just about as done for as that old creature. . . . Quick, quick, child, run off after your youth! Only a small piece of it has been snipped off by ageing women: all the rest is there for you and the girl who is waiting for you. You've now had a taste of youth! It never satisfies, but one always goes back for more. Oh, you had started to make comparisons before last night. . . . And what am I up to now, doling out all this advice and displaying the greatness of my soul! What do I know of you two? She loves you: it's her turn to tremble; but her misery will come from passion and not from perverted mother love. And you will talk to her like a master, not capriciously, like a gigolo. Quick, quick, run off. . . ."

She spoke in tones of hasty supplication. He listened, standing planted before her, his chest bare, his hair tempestuous: and so alluring, that she had to clasp her hands to prevent their seizing hold of him. He guessed this, perhaps, and did not move away. For an instant they shared a lunatic hope—do people feel like this in mid-air when falling from a tower?—then the hope vanished.

"Go," she said in a low voice. "I love you. It's too late. Go away. But go away at once. Get dressed!"

She rose and fetched him his shoes, spread out his crumpled shirt and his socks. He stood helpless, moving his fingers awkwardly as if they were numb. She had to find his braces and his tie; but she was careful not to go too close to him and offered him no further help. While he was dressing, she glanced into the courtyard several times, as if she were expecting a carriage at the door.

He looked even paler when he was dressed, and a halo of fatigue round his eyes made them seem larger.

"You don't feel ill?" she asked him. And she added timidly, lowering her eyes, "You could always lie down for a little." But at once she pulled herself together and came over to him, as though he were in great danger. "No, no, you'll be better at home. Hurry, it's not yet midday; a good hot bath will soon put you to rights, and then the fresh air . . . Here are your gloves. . . . Your hat? On the floor, of course. Put your coat on, there's a nip in the air. Au revoir, my Chéri, au revoir. That's right. And tell Charlotte that . . ." She closed the door behind him, and silence put an end to her vain and desperate words. She heard Chéri stumble on the staircase and she ran to the window. He was going down the front steps and then he stopped in the middle of the courtyard.

"He's coming back! He's coming back!" she cried, raising her arms.

An old woman, out of breath, repeated her movements in the long pier-glass, and Léa wondered what she could have in common with that crazy creature.

Chéri continued on his way towards the street. On the pavement he buttoned up his overcoat to hide his crumpled shirt. Léa let the curtain fall back into place; but already she had seen Chéri throw back his head, look up at the spring sky and the chestnut trees in flower, and fill his lungs with the fresh air, like a man escaping from prison.

The LAST of CHÉRI

Translated by
ROGER SENHOUSE

CHÉRI closed the iron gate of the little garden behind him and sniffed the night air: "Ah! it's nice out here!" In the same breath, he changed his mind: "No, it isn't."

The thickly planted chestnut trees weighed heavily upon the heat pent up beneath. A dome of rusted leaves vibrated above the nearest gas-lamp. The Avenue Henri-Martin, close-set with greenery, was stifling; only with the dawn would a breath of fresh air come up from the Bois de Boulogne.

Bare-headed, Chéri turned back to look at the house, empty now but still lit up. He heard the clink of roughly handled glass, followed by the clear ring of Edmée's voice, sharp with reproof. He saw his wife come to the window of the gallery on the first floor and lean out. The frosted beads on her evening dress lost their snowy whiteness, caught for a moment a greenish glint from the lamp, then flamed into yellow as she touched the gold lamé curtains.

"Is that you on the pavement, Fred?"

"Who else could it be?"

"You didn't take Filipesco home, then?"

"No, I didn't; he'd hopped it already."

"All the same, I'd rather have liked . . . Oh well, it doesn't matter. Are you coming in now?"

"Not just yet. Far too hot. I'll just stretch my legs."

"But . . . Oh well, just as you like."

She broke off a moment, and must have been laughing, for he could see the quiver of her frost-spangled dress.

"All I can see of you from here is a white shirt-front and a white face cut out on black. Exactly like a poster for a night club. It looks devastating."

"How you adore my mother's expressions!" he said reflectively. "You can tell everyone to go to bed. I've got my key."

She waved a hand in his direction. He watched the lights go out one by one in all the windows. One particular light—a dull blue gleam—told Chéri that Edmée was going through her boudoir into their bedroom, which looked out on the garden at the back of the house.

'The boudoir will soon come to be known as the study, and no mistake,' he thought.

The clock of Janson-de-Sailly began to strike and Chéri cocked his ear to catch the chiming notes in flight, like drops of rain. 'Midnight! She's in a hurry to get to bed. . . . Yes, of course, she has to be at her Hospital by nine to-morrow morning.' He took a few nervous steps, shrugged his shoulders, and grew calmer.

'It's as if I'd married a ballet-dancer. Nine o'clock sharp, the class: it's sacrosanct. It has to come before everything else.'

He walked on as far as the entrance to the Bois. The day's dust, hanging in the pallid sky, dimmed the brightness of the stars. Step for step, a second tread echoed Chéri's: he stopped and waited for it to catch up with him. He disliked anyone walking behind him.

"Good evening, Monsieur Peloux," said the night-watchman, touching his cap.

Chéri answered by raising a finger to his forehead with the condescension of an officer—a trick he had picked up during the war from his fellow quartermaster-sergeants—and walked on past the night-watchman, who was trying the locks on the iron gates to the little private gardens.

From a couple of lovers on a bench just inside the Bois, came the rustle of crushed clothes and the whisper of smothered endearments. Chéri listened for an instant to the clasped bodies and invisible lips, a sound like the ripple of a ship's prow cleaving calm waters.

'The man's a soldier,' he noticed. 'I've just heard him unbuckle his belt.'

He was not thinking, which left his every sense on the alert. On many a calm night during the war Chéri had derived complex pleasure and subtle terror from his primitive keenness of hearing; his fingers, even when caked with mud and pocket fug, had been quick to distinguish the image on medal or coin, and to tell, by leaf or stalk, plants whose name he did not know. "Hi, there, Peloux lad, just tell us what I've got ahold of here?" Chéri recalled the ginger-headed lad who, under cover of darkness, would push into his hand a dead mole, a small snake, a tree-frog, an over-ripe fruit, or some piece of filth, and then exclaim, "Blimey, he gets it every time!" The memory made him smile, but with no pity for the ginger-headed lad, now

dead. Yet he was haunted sometimes by the picture of his pal
Pierquin, lying there on his back asleep for ever, with a look of distrust still on his face. He often spoke of him.

This very evening, at home, when dinner was over, Edmée had
deftly steered the conversation round to the pathetic little tale, put
together with such studied clumsiness. Chéri had it off by heart and
it ended with the words: "And then Pierquin said to me, 'I had a
dream about cats, old lad; and then I'd another dream about our
river at home and it looked fair mucky. . . . The meaning of that's
pretty clear. . . .' It was at this very moment he was picked off, by
the smallest scrap of shrapnel. I wanted to carry him back. They
found the two of us, him on the top of me, not a hundred yards
from the spot. I tell you about him because he was a rare good sort
. . . and he had quite a lot to do with my being given this."

And, as he ended on this modest note, Chéri had lowered his eyes
to his green-and-red riband and knocked the ash off his cigarette, as
though to keep himself in countenance. He considered it nobody's
business that a chance explosion had thrown one of them across the
other's shoulders, leaving Chéri alive and Pierquin dead. The truth—
more ambiguous than falsehood—was that the terrific weight of a
Pierquin, suddenly struck dead, had kept Chéri alive and half-
suffocated, indignant and resentful. Chéri still bore a grudge against
Pierquin. And, further, he had come to scorn the truth ever since the
day when, years ago, it had suddenly fallen from his mouth like a
belch, to spatter and wound one whom he had loved.

But at home this evening, the Americans—Majors Marsh-Meyer
and Atkins, and Lieutenant Wood—had not appeared to listen to
him. With the vacant faces of athletic first-communicants, with fixed
and expressionless eyes, they had simply been waiting to go to a
night club, waiting with almost painful anxiety. As for Filipesco!
'Needs watching,' Chéri decided laconically.

The lake in the Bois was encircled with a fragrant mist that rose
rather from the scythed slopes of its banks than from the stagnant
water. Chéri was about to lean against a tree, when, from the shadows, a woman boldly brushed against him. "Good evening, kid . . ."
The last word made him start; it was uttered in a low parched voice,
the very voice of thirst, of dusty roads, of this dry hot night. . . .
He made no answer, and the dim figure came a step nearer on soft-
soled shoes. But he caught a whiff of black woollens, soiled linen,
dank hair, and turned back with long springy strides towards his own
home.

The dull blue light was still on: Edmée had not yet left her boudoir-study. In all probability she would still be seated at her desk, signing chits for drugs and dressings, reading through the day's notes and the short reports made by her secretary. Her pretty school-marm head, crimped hair with a reddish tint, would be bent over her papers.

Chéri pulled out the small flat key on the end of its thin gold chain. 'Here we go. In for another carefully measured dose of love. . . .'

As was his habit, he entered his wife's boudoir without knocking. Edmée showed no sign of surprise, but went on with her telephone conversation. Chéri listened.

"No, not to-morrow. . . . You won't want me there for that. The General knows you perfectly well. And at the Ministry of Commerce, there's . . . What do you mean? 'Have I got Lémery?' No, certainly not! He's charming, but . . . Hullo? . . . Hullo? . . ." She laughed, showing her small teeth. "Oh come! that's going too far. . . . Lémery makes up to every woman, provided she's not blind or lame. . . . What? Yes, he's come in, he's here at my elbow. No, no, I'll be very discreet. . . . Goodbye. . . . See you to-morrow. . . ."

A plain white wrap, the white of her pearl necklace, was slipping off one shoulder. She had taken the pins from her chestnut hair, which, slightly frizzed by the dry atmosphere, followed every movement of her head.

"Who was that?" Chéri asked, as she put back the receiver and turned to ask him:

"Fred, you'll let me have the Rolls to-morrow morning, won't you? It will look better for bringing the General back here to lunch."

"What General?"

"General Haar."

"Is he a Boche?"

Edmée frowned. "Really, Fred, you're too old for such jokes! General Haar is coming to inspect my Hospital to-morrow. Then he can go back to America and tell them all that my Hospital can compare with any effort of the sort over there. Colonel Beybert will be showing him round, and they'll both come back here for luncheon afterwards."

Chéri took off his dinner-jacket and sent it flying in the direction of a chair.

"I don't give a damn! I'm lunching out."

"What d'you mean. What's all this?"

A spasm of rage crossed Edmée's face; but she smiled, picked up the dinner-jacket with care, and changed her tone of voice. "Didn't you ask me a moment ago who that was on the telephone? Your mother."

Chéri collapsed into an armchair and said nothing. His features were set in their most beautiful and impassive mould. Over his forehead hovered an air of serene disapproval. This was apparent, too, on his lowered eyelids, faintly shadowed now at the approach of his thirtieth year, and on his mouth, which he was careful never to compress too tightly, keeping his lips gently apart as in sleep.

"You know," Edmée continued, "she wants Lémery, of the Ministry of Commerce, to do something about her three cargo-loads of leather. There are three ships filled with leather, at present held up in harbour at Valparaiso. There is something in the idea, you know! The only thing is that Lémery won't grant the necessary import licence . . . at least, that's what he says. Do you know how much money the Soumabis offered your mother as a minimum commission?"

With a wave of the hand, Chéri brushed aside ships, leather, and commission.

"Not interested," he said simply.

Edmée dropped the subject, and affectionately approached her husband.

"You will have luncheon here to-morrow, won't you? There'll probably be Gibbs—the reporter from *Excelsior*, who's going to photograph the Hospital—and your mother."

Chéri shook his head with no sign of impatience.

"No," he said. "General Hagenbeck . . ."

"Haar."

". . . and a Colonel, and my mother in her uniform. Her tunic—what d'you call it? her jacket?—with its little leather buttons; her elastic uplift-belt; epaulettes; high colonel's collar and her chin cascading over . . . and her cane. No, really, I don't pretend to be braver than I am. I'd rather go out."

He was laughing quietly to himself, and his laugh seemed mirthless. Edmée put a hand, already trembling with irritation, upon his arm; but her touch was light.

"You can't mean that seriously?"

"Certainly I can. I shall go for lunch to *Brekekekex*, or somewhere else."

"With whom?"

"With whom I choose."

He sat down and kicked off his pumps. Edmée leant against a black lacquer cabinet and racked her brain for words to make him behave sensibly. The white satin front of her dress rose and fell in rhythm to the quickened pace of her breathing, and she crossed her hands behind her back like a martyr. Chéri looked at her with an air of pretended indifference. 'She really does look a lady,' he thought. 'Hair all anyhow, in her chemise, on her way to the bath—she always looks a lady.'

She lowered her eyes, caught Chéri's, and smiled.

"You're teasing me," she said plaintively.

"No," Chéri replied. "I shan't lunch here to-morrow, that's all."

"But why?"

He rose, walked as far as the open door into their room—which was in darkness and filled with night scents from the garden—and then came back to her.

"Because I shan't. If you compel me to explain myself, I shall speak out and perhaps be rude. You'll burst into tears, and 'in your distress', as the saying goes, you'll let your wrap slip to the floor and . . . and unfortunately it won't have the slightest effect on me."

Another spasm of rage passed over his wife's features, but her much-tried patience was not yet exhausted. She smiled and shrugged the one bare shoulder peeping from under her hair.

"It's quite easy to *say* that it won't have any effect on you."

He was walking to and fro, clad in nothing but his short white silk pants. All the time he was testing the elasticity of his instep and calf muscles, and kept rubbing his hand over the twin brown scars under his right breast, as if to preserve their fading hue. Lean, with less flesh on his body than he had had at twenty, at the same time in better shape and training, he liked to parade up and down in front of his wife as a rival rather than a lover. He knew himself to be the more perfect specimen and, as a connoisseur, could condescend to admire in her the slim hips, the small breasts, and the graceful, almost imperceptible lines which Edmée knew so well how to clothe in tubular frocks and slinky tunics. "Are you fading away, then?" he would sometimes ask her, just for the fun of annoying her. He would watch her whole body writhe in anger, and note its sudden and un-suspected vigour.

This reply of his wife's was distasteful to him. He wanted her to look well-bred, and to be silent, if not unresponsive, in his arms. He came to a halt, puckered his brow, and looked her up and down. "Pretty manners, I must say. Do you learn them from your Physician-in-charge? The war, Madame!"

She shrugged her bare shoulder.

"What a child you are, my poor Fred! It's lucky we're by our-selves. To go on at me like that just because of a little joke . . . which was really a compliment. And for you to try and teach me manners, you . . . you! And after seven years of marriage!"

"Where do you get the seven years from?"

He sat down, naked as he was, as though for a prolonged discus-sion, his legs wide apart with all the ostentation of an athlete.

"Well . . . really . . . nineteen-thirteen . . . nineteen-nine-teen . . ."

"Excuse me! it's clear that we don't reckon by the same calendar. Now, I count from . . ."

Edmée arched a knee, taking the weight of her body on the other leg, a confession of her weariness; but Chéri interrupted her with: "Where's all this talk leading us? Come on, let's go to bed. You've got your ballet-class at nine to-morrow, haven't you?"

"Oh! Fred!"

Edmée crushed a rose from a black vase and threw away its petals. Chéri fanned the flames of anger still smouldering in her eyes, now moist with tears, by saying: "That's the name I give that job-lot of wounded, when I'm not thinking."

Without looking at him, she murmured through trembling lips: "You brute . . . you brute . . . you loathsome monster!"

He laughed, quite untouched.

"What d'you want me to say? As far as you're concerned, we all know you're carrying out a sacred mission. But what about me? You might just as well *have* to go to the Opera every day and practise in the Rotunda, for all the difference it would make. That would leave me just as much . . . just as much out of it. And those men I called your 'job-lot', well, they're wounded, aren't they? wounded who are a little luckier than others, perhaps. I've got absolutely noth-ing to do with them either. With them, too, I'm . . . out of it."

She turned round to face him so impulsively that it made her hair fly out from her temples: "My darling, don't be so unhappy! You're not out of it at all, you're above all that!"

He got up, drawn towards a jug of iced water, on the sides of which the moisture was slowly condensing into bluish tears. Edmée hurried forward: "With or without lemon, Fred?"

"Without, thanks."

He drank, she took the empty glass from his hands, and he went towards the bathroom.

"By the way," he said. "About that leak in the cement of the bathing-pool. It ought . . ."

"I'm having it seen to. The man who makes those glass mosaics happens to be a cousin of Chuche, one of my wounded, and he won't need to be asked twice, believe me."

"Good." Then, as he was moving away, he turned round. "Tell me, this business of the Ranch shares we were talking about yesterday morning, ought we to sell or not? Supposing I went to see old Deutsch about them to-morrow morning, and had a chin-wag with him?"

Edmée gave a shriek of schoolgirl laughter.

"Do you think I waited for you about that? Your mother had a stroke of genius this morning, while we were giving the Baroness a lift home."

"You mean that old La Berche woman?"

"Yes, the Baroness. Your mother, as you so elegantly put it, had a chin-wag with her. The Baroness is one of the original shareholders, and never leaves the Chairman of the Board alone for a moment. . . ."

"Except to cover her face in flour."

"Must you interrupt me the whole time? . . . and by two o'clock, my dear, the whole lot had been sold—every bit of it! The little flare up on the Bourse this afternoon—it lasted only a very short time—raked us in something like two hundred and sixteen thousand francs, Fred! That'll pay for piles of medicine and bandages. I wanted to keep the news till to-morrow, and then give you one of these topping note-cases. Kiss?"

He stood, naked and white-skinned, holding back the folds of the door-curtain, and looking closely at the expression on his wife's face.

"That's all very well . . ." he said at last, "but where do I come in?"

Edmée gave a mischievous shake of the head: "Your power of at-

torney still stands, my love. 'The right to sell, purchase, draw up or
sign an agreement made out in my name . . . etcetera'—which
reminds me, I must send the Baroness something as a souvenir."

"A briar pipe," said Chéri, after pretending to have given the matter his attention.

"No, don't laugh. The good soul is so valuable to us."

"And who are 'us'?"

"Your mother and me. The Baroness knows how to talk to the
men in a way they understand. She speaks their language. She tells
them rather risky stories, but in such a way . . . They dote on her."

The strangest of laughs trembled on Chéri's lips. He let go his
hold on the dark curtain, and it fell back into place behind him, thus
obliterating him completely, as sleep obliterates the figment of a
dream. He walked along a passage dimly lit by a blue globe, without
making a sound, like a figure floating on air; for he had insisted upon
having thick carpets laid on every floor, from top to bottom of the
house. He loved silence, and furtiveness, and never knocked at the
door of the boudoir, which his wife, since the war, called her study.
She showed no annoyance, and sensing Chéri's presence, never
jumped when he came into the room.

He took a shower bath without lingering under the cool water,
sprayed himself with scent absent-mindedly, and returned to the
boudoir.

He could hear the sound of someone rumpling the sheets in the
bedroom next door, and the tap of a paper-knife against a cup on the
bedside table. He sat down and rested his chin in his hand. On the
little table beside him, he caught sight of the morrow's menu, duly
made out for the butler, according to daily routine. On it he read:
"*Homard Thermidor, Côtelettes Fulbert-Dumonteil, Chaudfroid de
canard, salade Charlotte, Soufflé au curaçao, Allumettes au
Chester.*" . . . 'No alteration required,' he murmured to himself.
"*Six places?*"—'Ah, yes, that I must alter.' He corrected the number,
and once more cupped his chin in his hand.

"Fred, do you know what time it is?"

He did not answer the soft voice, but went into their room and sat
down facing the bed. With one shoulder bare and the other half-hidden by a wisp of white nightgown, Edmée was smiling, despite her
tired state, aware that she looked prettier in bed than out. But Chéri
remained seated, and once again cupped his chin in his hand.

"Rodin's *Penseur*," said Edmée, to encourage him to smile or to
move.

"There's many a true word spoken in jest," he answered sententiously.

He pulled the folds of his Chinese dressing-gown closer over his knees and savagely crossed his arms.

"What the hell am I doing here?"

She did not understand, or had no wish to do so.

"That's what I'd like to know, Fred. It's two o'clock, and I get up at eight. To-morrow's going to be another of those pleasant little days. . . . It's unkind of you to dawdle like this. Do come along; there's a nice breeze rising. We'll go to bed with it on our faces, and imagine we're sleeping out of doors."

He weakened, and hesitated only an instant before hurling his silk wrap to a far corner of the room, while Edmée switched out the remaining light. She nestled up against him in the dark, but he neatly turned her over with her back to him and held her round the waist with strong arms, murmuring, "Like that. That's like being on a bob-sleigh," and fell asleep.

The following day, from the little window of the linen-room where he was hidden, he watched them leave. The duck's-egg green motor and another long American automobile were purring very quietly in the avenue under the thick overhanging chestnut trees. The green shade and the recently watered pavement exuded a pretence of freshness, but Chéri knew very well that in the garden at the back of the house the heat of this June morning—the month that scorches Paris—was already shrivelling the lovely deep blue of a pool of forget-me-nots within their edging of pinks.

His heart began to beat with a sort of nervousness when he saw, approaching the iron gates to his house, two figures in khaki, with gold stars on their breast and crimson velvet bands round their caps. "In uniform, of course, the crackpot!"

This was the nickname Chéri had bestowed on the Physician-in-Charge at Edmée's Hospital, and without really knowing it, he loathed the man and his red-gold hair and the caressing tones he put into technical terms when talking to Edmée. He muttered vague hearty curses, against the Medical Corps in particular, and against all who insisted on wearing uniform in peace-time. The American officer was growing fat, so Chéri sneered: "I thought the Americans went in for sport. What's he doing with a belly like that?" but he said not a word when Edmée, in a white dress and white shoes, vivaciously held out her white-gloved hand to the Doctor. She greeted him in loud, quick, cheerful tones. Chéri had not missed a single word that fell from her red mouth, which parted in a smile over such tiny teeth. She had walked out as far as the motors, come back to tell a footman to fetch a notebook she had forgotten and stood chatting while she waited for it. She had spoken in English to the American Colonel, and lowered her voice, in automatic deference, when replying to Doctor Arnaud.

Chéri was keeping a sharp look-out from behind the muslin curtains. His characteristic mistrust and slyness froze his features into immobility directly he concealed a strong emotion, and he kept a strict watch on himself, even when alone. His eyes travelled from Edmée to the Doctor, and then from the American Colonel back to Edmée, who had more than once looked up to the first floor, as though she knew of his hiding-place.

'What are they waiting for?' he grumbled under his breath. 'Ah, so this is it. . . . God in heaven!'

Charlotte Peloux had arrived, in a sports-car driven by an impersonal and impeccable young chauffeur. Bursting out of her gabardine uniform, she held her head stiffly upright under its little tight-fitting hat with a military peak, and the ends of her bobbed red hair could be seen popping out at the back. She did not set foot to ground, but suffered them to come and pay their respects to her. She received Edmée's kiss and apparently asked after her son, for she too raised her head in the direction of the first floor, thus unveiling her magnificent eyes, over which drifted, as over the huge eyes of an octopus, some dark inhuman dream.

"She's wearing her little military cap," Chéri murmured.

He gave a curious shudder, which made him angry with himself, and smiled when the three motors drove away. He waited patiently until his "bachelor's runabout" drew up against the kerb punctually at eleven o'clock, and he kept it waiting for some considerable time. Twice he stretched out his hand to lift the receiver of the telephone, and twice he let it fall again to his side. His sudden impulse to invite Filipesco soon vanished and he thought he would like to collect young Maudru and his girl. 'Or, better still, Jean de Touzac. . . . But at this hour he'll still be furiously snoring. Gosh! all that lot . . . not one of them, I must be fair, a patch on Desmond. . . . Poor old boy.'

He regarded Desmond as a war casualty; but with greater compassion than he ever vouchsafed the dead. Desmond, who was alive yet lost to him, had the power of inspiring him with an almost tender melancholy, as well as with the jealous respect due to a man with a "job". Desmond ran a night club, and sold antiques to Americans. A gutless wash-out during the whole of the war, when he had carried anything and everything but a rifle—official papers, billy-cans, any dirty hospital receptacle—Desmond had bitten deep into peacetime with a warlike fervour, and rich had been his immediate reward, very much to Chéri's astonishment. *Desmond's* had been started in quite a small way in a private house in the Avenue d'Alma, and now it sheltered frenzied and silent couples behind its heavy ashlar masonry, beneath ceilings decorated with swallows and hawthorn, and hemmed in by the bulrushes and flamingoes of its stained-glass windows. They danced at *Desmond's*, night and day, as people dance after war: the men, young and old, free from the burden of thinking and being frightened—empty-minded, innocent; the women, given over to a pleasure far greater than any more definite sensual delight, to the company of men: that is to say, to physical contact with them, their smell, their tonic sweat, the certain proof of which tingled in every inch of their bodies—the certainty of being the prey of a man wholly alive and vital, and of succumbing in his arms to rhythms as personal, as intimate, as those of sleep.

'Desmond will have got to bed at three, or three-thirty,' Chéri reckoned. 'He'll have had enough sleep.'

But once again he let drop the hand he had stretched out to the telephone. He went down the stairs in double quick time, aided by the springy thick pile that covered every floor board in his house. As he passed by the dining-room he looked without anger at the five white plates set in a diadem round a black crystal bowl, in which floated pink water-lilies, matching the pink of the tablecloth; and he did not pause till face to face with the looking-glass, fixed to the back of the heavy door of the reception-room on the ground floor. He feared, yet was attracted by, this looking-glass, which drew what little light it had from the french windows immediately facing it across the corridor, their opaque blue panes further obscured by the dark foliage of the garden. Every time he bumped into his own image, Chéri was brought up sharp by a slight shock when he recognised it as his own. He never could understand why this glass did not reflect the faithful image of a young man of twenty-four. He could not detect the precise points where time, with invisible finger, marks first the hour of perfection on a handsome face, and then the hour of that more blatant beauty, the herald of a majestic decline.

To Chéri's mind, there could be no question of a decline, and he could never have noticed it on his own features. He had just happened to bump into a thirty-year-old Chéri and failed to recognise him; and he sometimes asked himself "What's wrong with me?" as though he were feeling a little off-colour or had thrown his clothes on anyhow. Now he hurried past the reception-room door, and thought no more about it.

Desmond's, being a properly organised establishment, was up and doing by midday, despite the late hours it kept. The concierge was hosing the paved courtyard, a waiter was sweeping the steps clean, brushing away a heap of high-class rubbish—fine light dust, silver paper, corks with metal caps, stub-ends of gold-tipped cigarettes, and crumpled drinking-straws—rubbish which bore daily witness to the prosperity of *Desmond's*.

Chéri cleared at a bound the residue of last night's brisk business; but the smell inside the house barred further progress like a rope stretched across his path. Forty couples, packed like sardines, had left behind the smell—the memory of their sweat-soaked clothes—stale, and tainted with tobacco fumes. Chéri plucked up courage and leapt up the staircase, narrowed by heavy oak banisters supported on caryatids. Desmond had wasted no money on changing the stuffy sumptuosities of 1880. After removing two dividing walls, installing a refrigerator in the basement, engaging a jazz-band regardless of cost, no further outlay would be necessary for at least another year. "I'll bring it up to date to attract customers," so Desmond said, "when dancing isn't such a rage."

He slept on the second floor, in a room where convolvulus ran riot on the walls and storks on the stained-glass windows; his bath was of enamelled zinc, bordered by a tiled frieze of river-plants, and the ancient heating-apparatus wheezed like a bulldog past its prime. But the telephone shone as brightly as a weapon kept polished by daily use, and Chéri, after bounding up four steps at a time, discovered his friend, lips to the chalice, apparently imbibing the murky breath of its mouthpiece. His wandering glance came down to earth, and hardly settled on Chéri before it was off and up again to the convolvulus-wreathed cornice. His yellow-gold pyjamas cast a blight over a morning-after-the-night-before face, but Desmond was inflated by prosperity and no longer worried about being ugly.

"Good morning," said Chéri. "I came through all right. What a stench there is on your stairs. Worse than a dug-out."

". . . You'll never get *Desmond's* custom at twelve," Desmond was saying to an invisible listener. "I have no difficulty in buying Pommery at that price. And for my private cellar, Pommery ought to be eleven when minus labels . . . hullo . . . yes, the labels that came off in the general rumpus. That's what I want . . . hullo?"

"You're coming out to lunch. I've got the runabout at the door," Chéri said.

"No, and twice times no," said Desmond.

"What?"

"No, and a thousand times no. Hullo? . . . Sherry! What d'you take me for? This isn't a bar. Champagne, or nothing. Don't go on wasting your time and mine. Hullo. . . . That's quite possible. Only I'm all the rage at the moment. Hullo. . . . At two o'clock precisely. A very good day to you, Monsieur."

He stretched himself, before offering a limp hand. He still looked like Alfonso XIII, but thirty summers and the war had rooted this uncertain creature in the soil he needed. To have come through the war without firing a shot, to have eaten regularly, taken every advantage of it, and malingered in general, were so many personal victories from which he had emerged strengthened and self-confident. Assurance and a full pocket had made him less ugly, and you could be sure that, at sixty, he would give the illusion of having once passed for a handsome man with a large nose and long legs. He looked at Chéri condescendingly, but with a friendlier eye. Chéri turned away his head and said: "What! Are you reduced to this? Come on, old boy. It's midday and you're not up yet."

"In the first place, I *am* ready," Desmond replied, unbuttoning his pyjamas to show a white silk shirt and a bronze-coloured bow tie. "And in the second, I'm not going to lunch out."

"So that's it," said Chéri. "Well, of all . . . I'm speechless. . . ."

"But if you like I can give you two fried eggs, and half my ham, my salad, my stout and my strawberries. No extra charge for coffee."

Chéri looked at him in impotent fury. "Why?"

"Business," said Desmond, with a deliberately nasal twang. "Champagne! You heard what I was saying a moment ago. Oh! these wine-merchants! If one didn't put on the screw . . . But I'm a match for them."

He knotted his fingers and the knuckle-joints cracked with commercial pride.

"Yes or no?"

"Yes, you swine."

Chéri chucked his soft felt hat at his head; but Desmond picked it up and brushed it with his forearm, to show that this was not the moment for childish jokes. They had eggs in aspic, ham and tongue, and good black stout with coffee-coloured foam on it. They spoke little, and Chéri, gazing out on to the paved courtyard, was politely bored.

'What am I doing here? Nothing, except that I'm not at home, sitting down to cutlets Fulbert-Dumonteil.' He visualised Edmée in white, the baby-faced American Colonel, and Arnaud, the Physician-in-Charge, in whose presence she acted the docile little girl. He thought of Charlotte Peloux's epaulettes, and a sort of fruitless affection for his host was coming over him, when the latter asked him an abrupt question:

"Do you know how much champagne was drunk here last night, between four o'clock yesterday and four o'clock this morning?"

"No," said Chéri.

"And do you know how many bottles were returned empty from those delivered here between May the first and June the fifteenth?"

"No," said Chéri.

"Say a number."

"No idea," Chéri grunted.

"But say something! Say a number! Have a guess, man! Name some figure!"

Chéri scratched the table cloth as he might during an examination. He was suffering from the heat, and from his own inertia.

"Five hundred," he got out at last.

Desmond threw himself back in his chair and, as it swerved through the air, his monocle shot a piercing flash of sunlight into Chéri's eye.

"Five hundred! You make me laugh!"

He was boasting. He did not know how to laugh: his nearest approach was a sort of sob of the shoulders. He drank some coffee, to excite Chéri's curiosity, and then put down his cup again.

"Three thousand, three hundred, and eighty-two, my boy. And do you know how much that puts in my pocket?"

"No," Chéri interrupted, "and I don't give a damn. That's enough. My mother does all that for me if I want it. Besides . . ."

He rose, and added in a hesitant voice: "Besides, money doesn't interest me."

"Strange," said Desmond, hurt. "Strange. Amusing."

"If you like. No, can't you understand, money doesn't interest me . . . doesn't interest me any more."

These simple words fell from his lips slowly. Chéri spoke them without looking up, and kicked a biscuit crumb along the carpet; his embarrassment at making this confession, his secretive look, restored for a fleeting instant the full marvel of his youth.

For the first time Desmond stared at him with the critical attention of a doctor examining a patient, 'Am I dealing with a malingerer?' Like a doctor, he had recourse to confused and soothing words.

"We all go through that. Everyone's feeling a little out of sorts. No one knows exactly where he stands. Work is a wonderful way of putting you on your feet again, old boy. Take me, for instance. . . ."

"I know," Chéri interrupted. "You're going to tell me I haven't enough to do."

"Yes, it's your own fault." Desmond's mockery was condescending in the extreme. "For in these wonderful times . . ." He was going on to confess his deep satisfaction with business, but he pulled himself up in time. "It's also a question of upbringing. Obviously, you never learned the first thing about life under Léa's wing. You've no idea how to manage people and things."

"So they say." Chéri was put out. "Léa herself wasn't fooled. You mayn't believe me, but though she didn't trust me, she always consulted me before buying or selling."

He thrust out his chest, proud of the days gone by, when distrust was synonymous with respect.

"You've only got to apply yourself to it again—to money matters," Desmond continued, in his advisory capacity. "It's a game that never goes out of fashion."

"Yes," Chéri acquiesced rather vaguely. "Yes, of course. I'm only waiting."

"Waiting for what?"

"I'm waiting. . . . What I mean is . . . I'm waiting for an opportunity . . . a better opportunity. . . ."

"Better than what?"

"What a bore you are. An excuse—if you like—to take up again everything the war deprived me of years ago. My fortune, which is, in fact . . ."

"Quite considerable?" Desmond suggested. Before the war, he would have said "enormous," and in a different tone of voice. A moment's humiliation brought a blush to Chéri's cheek.

"Yes . . . my fortune. Well, the little woman, my wife, now makes that her business."

"Oh, no!" exclaimed Desmond, in shocked disapproval.

"Oh, yes, I promise you. Two hundred and sixteen thousand in a little flare-up on the Bourse the day before yesterday. So, don't you see, the question now arises, 'How am I to interfere?' . . . Where do I stand, in all this? When I suggest taking a hand, they say. . ."

"They? Who are 'they'?"

"What? Oh, my mother and my wife. They start saying: 'Take it easy. You're a warrior. Would you like a glass of orangeade? Run along to your shirt-maker, he's making you look a fool. And while you are going the rounds, you might call in and collect my necklace, if the clasp's been mended . . .' and so on, and so forth."

He was growing excited, hiding his resentment as best he could, though his nostrils were quivering, and his lips as well.

"So must I now tout motor-cars, or breed Angora rabbits, or direct some high-class establishment? Have I got to engage myself as a male nurse or accountant in that bargain-basement, my wife's Hospital?" He walked as far as the window, and came back to Desmond precipitately. "Under the orders of Doctor Arnaud, Physician-in-Charge, and pass the basins round for him? Must I take up this night club business? Can't you *see* the competition!"

He laughed in order to make Desmond laugh; but Desmond, no doubt a little bored, kept a perfectly straight face.

"How long ago did you start thinking of all this? You certainly had no such ideas in the spring, or last winter, or before you were married."

"I had no time for it," Chéri answered quite simply. "We went off on our travels, we began furnishing the house, we bought motors just in time to have them requisitioned. All that led up to the war. Before the war . . . before the war I was . . . a kid from a rich home. I was rich, damn it!"

"You still are."

"I still am," Chéri echoed.

He hesitated once more, searching for words. "But now, it's not at all the same thing. People have got the jitters. And work, and activity, and duty, and women who serve their country—not half they don't—and are crazy about oof . . . they're such thorough-going business-women that they make you disgusted with the word business. They're such hard workers it's enough to make you loathe the sight of work." He looked uncertainly at Desmond, "Is it really wrong to be rich, and take life easy?"

Desmond enjoyed playing his part and making up for past subservience. He put a protective hand on Chéri's shoulder.

"My son, be rich and live your own life! Tell yourself that you're the incarnation of an ancient aristocracy. Model yourself on the feudal barons. You're a warrior."

"*Merde*," said Chéri.

"Now you're talking like a warrior. Only, you must live and let live, and let those work who like it."

"You, for instance."

"Me, for instance."

"Obviously, you're not the sort to let yourself be messed about by women."

"No," said Desmond curtly. He was hiding from the world a perverse taste for his chief cashier—a gentle creature with brown hair scraped well back, rather masculine and hairy. She wore a religious medallion round her neck, and smilingly confessed, "For two pins I'd commit murder: I'm like that."

"No. Emphatically, no! Can't you mention anything without sooner or later dragging in 'my wife, women,' or else 'in Léa's time'? Is there nothing else to talk about in 1919?"

Beyond the sound of Desmond's voice, Chéri seemed to be listening to some other, still unintelligible sound. 'Nothing else to talk about,' he repeated to himself. 'Why should there be?' He was daydreaming, lulled by the light and the warmth, which increased as the sun came round into the room. Desmond went on talking, impervious to the stifling heat, and as white as winter endive. Chéri caught the words "little birds" and began to pay attention.

"Yes, I've a whole heap of amusing connections, with whom, of course, I'll put you in touch. And when I say 'birds', I'm speaking far too frivolously of what amounts to a unique collection, you understand, utterly unique. My regulars are tasty pieces, and all the tastier for the last four years. Just you wait and see, old boy! When my capital is big enough, what a restaurant I'll show the world! Ten tables, at most, which they'll fall over each other to book. I'll cover in the courtyard. . . . You may be sure my lease provides for all additions I

make! Cork-lino in the middle of the dance-floor, spot-lights. . . .
That's the future! It's out there. . . ."

The tango merchant was holding forth like a founder of cities,
pointing towards the window with outstretched arm. Chéri was
struck by the word "future," and turned to face the spot indicated by
Desmond, somewhere high up above the courtyard. He saw nothing,
and felt limp. The reverberations of the two o'clock sun smote
glumly down upon the little slate roof of the old stables, where the
concierge of *Desmond's* had his lodging. "What a ballroom, eh?"
said Desmond with fervour, pointing to the small courtyard. "And it
won't be long now before I get it!"

Chéri stared intently at this man who, each day, expected and received his daily bread. 'And what about me?' he thought, inwardly
frustrated.

"Look, here comes my swipes-merchant," Desmond shouted.
"Make yourself scarce. I must warm him up like a bottle of Corton."

He shook Chéri's hand with a hand that had changed its character: from being narrow and boneless, it had become broad, purposeful, disguised as the rather firm hand of an honest man. 'The war
. . .' thought Chéri, tongue in cheek.

"You're off? Where?" Desmond asked.

He kept Chéri standing on the top of the steps long enough to be
able to show off such a decorative client to his wine merchant.

"Over there," said Chéri, with a vague gesture.

"Mystery," murmured Desmond. "Be off to your seraglio!"

"Oh no," said Chéri, "you're quite wrong."

He conjured up the vision of some female—moist flesh, nakedness,
a mouth. He shuddered with impersonal disgust, and, repeating
'You're quite wrong' under his breath, got into his runabout.

He carried away with him an all too familiar uneasiness, the embarrassment and irritation of never being able to put into words all
that he really wanted to say; of never meeting the person to whom
he would have to confide a half-formed admission, a secret that
could have changed everything, and which, for instance, this afternoon would have dispersed the ominous atmosphere from the
bleached pavements and the asphalt, now beginning to melt under a
vertical sun.

'Only two o'clock,' he sighed, 'and, this month, it stays light till
well after nine.'

The breath of wind raised by the speed of his motor was like a hot
dry towel being flapped in his face, and he yearned for the make-

believe night behind his blue curtains, to the accompaniment of the simple drip-drop-drip of the Italian fountain's sing-song in the garden.

'If I slip quickly through the hall, I'll be able to get in again without being seen. *They'll* be having coffee by now.'

He could almost catch a whiff of the excellent luncheon, of the lingering smell of the melon, of the dessert wine which Edmée always had served with the fruit; and, ahead of time, he saw the verdigrised reflection of Chéri closing the door lined with plate glass.

'In we go!'

Two motors were dozing in the shade of the low-hanging branches just inside the gates, one his wife's and the other American, both in the charge of an American chauffeur who was himself taking a nap. Chéri drove on as far as the deserted Rue de Franqueville, and then walked back to his own front door. He let himself in without making a sound, took a good look at his shadowy form in the green-surfaced mirror, and softly went upstairs to the bedroom. It was just as he had longed for it to be—blue, fragrant, made for rest. In it he found everything that his thirsty drive had made so desirable: and more besides, for there was a young woman dressed in white, powdering her face and tidying her hair in front of a long looking-glass. Her back was turned to Chéri, and she did not hear him enter. Thus he had more than a moment to observe in the glass how flushed luncheon and the hot weather had made her, and to note her strange expression of untidiness and triumph and her general air of having won an emotionally outrageous victory. All at once Edmée caught sight of her husband and turned to face him without saying a word. She examined him critically from top to toe, waiting for him to speak first.

Through the half-open window facing the garden, floated up the baritone notes of Doctor Arnaud's voice, singing, "*Oy Marie, Oy Marie.*"

Edmée's whole body seemed to incline towards this voice, but she restrained herself from turning her head in the direction of the garden.

The slightly drunken courage visible in her eyes might well forebode a serious situation. Out of contempt or cowardice, Chéri, by putting a finger to his lips, enjoined silence upon her. He then pointed to the staircase with the same imperative finger. Edmée obeyed. She went resolutely past him, without being able to repress, at the moment when she came closest to him, a slight twist of the hips and quickening of the step, which kindled in Chéri a sudden impulse to strike her. He leant over the banisters, feeling reassured, like a cat that has reached safety at the top of a tree; and, still thinking of punishing, smashing, and taking flight, he waited there, ready to be wafted away on a flood of jealousy. All that came to him was a mediocre little feeling of shame, all too bearable, as he put his thoughts into words, 'Punish her, smash up the whole place! There's better to do than that. Yes, there's better to do.' But what, he did not know.

Each morning for him, whether he woke early or late, was the start of a long day's vigil. At first he paid but scant attention, believing it to be merely the persistence of an unhealthy habit picked up in the army.

In December, 1918, after putting his knee-cap out of joint, he had eked out in his bed at home a short period of convalescence. He used to stretch himself in the early morning and smile. 'I'm comfortable. I'm waiting for the time when I feel much better. Christmas this year is really going to be worth while.'

Christmas came. When the truffles had been eaten, and the holly twig dipped in brandy set alight on a silver platter, in the presence of an ethereal Edmée, very much the wife, and to the acclamations of Charlotte, of Madame de La Berche, and members of the nursing staff of the Hospital, together with a sprinkling of Rumanian officers and athletic adolescent American colonels, Chéri waited. 'Oh, if only those fellows would go away! I'm waiting to go to sleep, head in the cool air and feet warm, in my own good bed!' Two hours later, he was still waiting for sleep, laid out as flat as a corpse, listening to the mocking call of the little winter owls in the branches—a challenge to the blue light of his unshuttered room. At last he fell asleep; but a prey to his insatiable vigilance from the peep of dawn, he began to wait for his breakfast, and gave utterance to his hearty impatience: "What the hell do they think they're doing with the grub downstairs?" He did not realise that whenever he swore or used "soldiers' slang", it always went with an affected state of mind. His jolliness was a method of escape. Breakfast was brought to him by Edmée; but in his wife's bustling movements he never failed to discern haste and the call of duty, and he would ask for more toast, or for another hot roll which he no longer really wanted, simply from a malicious wish to delay Edmée's departure, to delay the moment when he would once more, inevitably, resume his period of waiting.

A certain Rumanian lieutenant used to be sent off by Edmée to look for concentrated disinfectant and absorbent cotton wool, or again to press a demand upon Ministers—"What the government refuses point-blank to a Frenchman, a foreigner gets every time," she affirmed. He used to bore Chéri stiff by cracking up the duties of a soldier, fit or nearly fit, and the paradisal purity of the Coictier Hospital. Chéri went along there with Edmée, sniffed the smells of antiseptics which relentlessly suggest underlying putrefaction, recognised a comrade among the "Trench Feet" and sat down on the edge of his bed, forcing himself to assume the cordiality prescribed by war novels and patriotic plays. He knew well enough, all the same, that a man in sound health, who had come through unscathed, could find no peer or equal among the crippled. Wherever he looked, he saw the fluttering white wings of the nurses, the red-brick colour of the faces and hands upon the sheets. An odious sense of impotence weighed upon him. He caught himself guiltily stiffening one of his arms as if held in a sling, or dragging one of his legs. But the next moment he could not help taking a deep breath and picking his way between the recumbent mummies with the light step of a dancer. He was forced reluctantly to reverence Edmée, because of her authority as a non-commissioned angel, and her aura of whiteness. She came across the ward, and, in passing, put a hand on Chéri's shoulder; but he knew that the desire behind this gesture of tenderness and delicate possession was to bring a blush of envy and irritation to the cheek of a young dark-haired nurse who was gazing at Chéri with the candour of a cannibal.

He felt bored, and consumed by the feeling of weariness that makes a man jib at the serried ranks of masterpieces before him as he is being dragged round a museum. The plethora of whiteness, thrown off from the ceiling and reflected back from the tiled floor, blotted out all corners, and he felt sorry for the men lying there, to whom shade would have been a charity, though no one offered it. The noonday hour imposes rest and privacy upon the beasts of the field, and the silence of deep woodland undergrowth upon the birds of the air, but civilised men no longer obey the dictates of the sun. Chéri took a few steps towards his wife, with the intention of saying: "Draw the curtains, install a punkah, take away that macaroni from the poor wretch who's blinking his eyes and breathing so heavily, and let him eat his food when the sun goes down. Give them shade, let them have any colour you like, but not always and everywhere this eternal white." With the arrival of Doctor Arnaud, he lost his inclination to give advice and make himself useful.

The Doctor, with his white linen belly and his red gold hair, had taken no more than three steps across the ward, before the hovering non-commissioned angel glided to earth again, to minister as a humble seraph, rosy with faith and zeal. Chéri thereupon turned to Filipesco, who was distributing American cigarettes, shouted "Are you coming?" in contemptuous tones, and bore him away; but not before he had bidden farewell to his wife, to Doctor Arnaud, to nurses male and female, with the haughty affability of an official visitor. He crossed the rough gravel of the little courtyard, got into his car, and allowed himself no more than a dozen words' soliloquy: 'It's the regular thing. The correct move for the Physician-in-Charge.'

Never again did he cross the threshold of the Hospital, and thereafter Edmée invited him on State occasions only, out of official courtesy, much as one might, at a dinner party, politely offer the snipe to a vegetarian guest.

He was now given over to reflection, and a prey to idleness. Before the war his idleness had been so light and varied, with the resonant ring of a flawless empty glass. During the war, too, he had endured periods of inertia under military discipline, inertia modified by cold, mud, risk, patrols, and even, on occasion, a little fighting. Conditioned to indolence by his upbringing and the life of a sensual young man, he had watched, himself untouched, the fresh young vulnerable companions all round him pine away in silence, solitude, and frustration. He had witnessed the ravages inflicted on intelligent people by the lack of newspapers as if they were being deprived of a daily drug. Whereas he had relapsed into contemplative silence—like a cat in a garden at night—content with a short letter, a postcard, or a cunningly packed parcel, other men, so-called superior men, had appeared to him to be showing every symptom of ruinous mental starvation. Thus he had learned to take pride in bolstering up his patience, and had brooded over two or three ideas, over two or three persistent memories, as highly coloured as a child's, and over his inability to imagine his own death.

Time and again, throughout the war, on coming out of a long dreamless sleep or a fitful bout of spasmodically interrupted rest, he would awake to find himself somewhere outside the present time and, his more recent past sloughed off, restored to the days of his boyhood—restored to Léa. Later, Edmée would suddenly rise up from the past, distinct and clear in every detail, and this evocation of her form, no less than its almost immediate disappearance, had always put Chéri in good spirits. "That gives me two of them," he reckoned. Nothing came to him from Léa; he did not write to her. But he received postcards signed by the crabbed fingers of old mother Aldonza, and cigars chosen by the Baroness de La Berche. Sometimes he dreamed of a long soft-wool scarf, as blue as a pair of blue eyes and with a very faint suggestion of the scent associated with it throughout long hours of warmth and slumber. He had loved this scarf and hugged it to him in the dark, until it had lost its fragrance and the freshness of the blue eyes, and he had thought of it no more.

For four years he had not bothered his head about Léa. Her trusty old cronies, had occasion arisen, would have forwarded news of any events in her life. He never imagined anything happening to her. What had Léa in common with sickness, or Léa with change?

In 1918 he could not believe his ears when the Baroness de La Berche casually mentioned "Léa's new flat".

"Has she moved, then?"

"Where have you sprung from?" the Baroness answered. "The whole world knows it. The sale of her house to the Americans was a brilliant deal, you bet! I've seen her new flat. It's small, but it's very cosy. Once you sit down in it, you never want to get up again."

Chéri clung to the words "small, but cosy". Unable to imagine anything different, he supplied an over-all rose-pink background, threw in that huge galleon of gold and steel—the bed with its lace rigging—and hung Chaplin's pearly-breasted nymph from some floating cloud.

When Desmond began looking about for a sleeping partner for his night club, Chéri had spasms of alarm and anxiety. "The blackguard's certain to try and tap Léa, or get her mixed up in some fishy business . . . I'd better tip her off on the telephone." He did nothing of the sort, however. Telephoning to a discarded mistress is riskier far than holding out your hand in the street to a nervous enemy who tries to catch your eye.

He went on biding his time, even after surprising Edmée in front of the looking-glass, after that flagrant exhibition of over-excitement, flushed cheeks, and untidiness. He let the hours slip by, and did not put into words—and so accentuate—his certainty that a still almost chaste understanding existed between his wife and the man who had been singing "*Oy Marie!*" For he felt much lighter in spirit, and for several days stopped uselessly consulting his wrist-watch as soon as daylight began to fade. He developed the habit of sitting out under the trees in a basket-chair, like a newly arrived guest in an hotel garden. There he marvelled to see how the oncoming night blotted out the blue of the monkshood, producing in its stead a hazier blue into which the shapes of the flowers were fused, while the green of their leaves persisted in distinct clumps. The edging of rose-coloured pinks turned to rank mauve, then the colour ebbed rapidly and the July stars shone yellow between the branches of the weeping ash.

He tasted at home the pleasures enjoyed by a casual passer-by who sits down to rest in a square, and he never noticed how long he remained there, lying back with his hands dangling. Sometimes he gave a fleeting thought to what he called "the looking-glass scene" and the atmosphere in the blue room when it had been secretly troubled by a man's sudden appearance, theatrical behaviour, and flight. He whispered over and over, with foolish mechanical regularity, "That's one point established. That's what's called a point-t-established", running the two words together into one.

At the beginning of July he bought a new open motor, and called it his Riviera Runabout. He drove Filipesco and Desmond out along drought-whitened roads, but returned to Paris every evening, cleaving alternate waves of warm and cool air, which began to lose their good smells the nearer the motor drew to Paris.

One day he took out the Baroness de La Berche, a virile companion, who, when they came to the barriers of the Octroi, raised her forefinger to the little felt hat pulled well down on her head. He found her agreeable, sparing of words, interested in wayside inns overgrown with wistaria, and in village wine-shops with their cellar-smell and wine-soaked sand. Rigid and in silence, they covered two hundred miles or more, without ever opening their mouths except to smoke or feed. The following day Chéri again invited Camille de La Berche with a curt "Well, how about it, Baroness?" and whisked her off without further ado.

The trusty motor sped far afield through the green countryside, and came back at nightfall to Paris like a toy at the end of a string. That evening, Chéri, while never taking his eye off the road, could distinguish on his right side the outline of an elderly woman, with a man's profile as noble as that of an old family coachman. It astonished him to find her worthy of respect because she was plain and simple, and when he was alone in her company for the first time and far away from town-life, it began to dawn on him that a woman burdened with some monstrous sexual deformity needs must possess a certain bravura and something of the dignified courage of the condemned.

Since the war this woman had found no further use for her unkindness. The Hospital had put her back in her proper place, that is to say, among males, among men just young enough, just tamed enough by suffering, for her to live serenely in their midst, and forget her frustrated femininity.

On the sly, Chéri studied his companion's large nose, the greying hairy upper lip, and the little peasant eyes which glanced incuriously at ripe cornfields and scythed meadows.

For the first time he felt something very like friendship for old Camille, and was led to make a poignant comparison: "She is alone. When she's no longer with her soldiers or with my mother, she's alone. She too. Despite her pipe and her glass of wine, she's alone."

On their way back to Paris, they stopped at a "hostelry" where there was no ice, and where, trained against the plinths of columns and clinging to ancient baptismal fonts dotted about the lawn, the rambler-roses were dying, frizzled by the sun. A neighbouring copse screened this dried-up spot from any breeze, and a small cloud, scorched to a cherry hue, hung motionless, high in the heavens.

The Baroness knocked out her short briar pipe on the ear of a marble fawn.

"It's going to be grilling over Paris to-night."

Chéri nodded in agreement, and looked up at the cloud. The light reflected from it mottled his white cheeks and dimpled chin, like touches of pink powder on an actor's face.

"Yes," he said.

"Well, you know, if the idea tempts you, let's not go back till to-morrow morning. Just give me time to buy a piece of soap and a tooth-brush. . . . And we'll telephone your wife. Then, to-morrow morning we can be up and on our way by four o'clock, while it's fresh."

Chéri sprang to his feet in unthinking haste. "No, no, I can't."

"You can't? Come, come!"

Down near his feet he saw two small mannish eyes, and a pair of broad shoulders shaking with laughter.

"I didn't believe that you were still held on such a tight rein," she said. "But, of course, if you are . . ."

"Are what?"

She had risen to her feet again, robust and hearty, and clapped him vigorously on the shoulder.

"Yes, yes. You run around all day long, but you go back to your kennel every night. Oh, you're kept well in hand."

He looked at her coldly: already he liked her less. "There's no hiding anything from you, Baroness. I'll fetch the car, and in under two hours we'll be back at your front door."

Chéri never forgot their nocturnal journey home, the sadness of the lingering crimson in the west, the smell of the grasses, the feathery moths held prisoner in the beam of the headlamps. The Baroness kept watch beside him, a dark form made denser by the night. He drove cautiously; the air, cool at faster speeds, grew hot again when he slowed down to take a corner. He trusted to his keen sight and his alert senses, but he could not help his thoughts running on the queer massive old woman motionless at his right side, and she caused him a sort of terror, a twitching of the nerves, which suddenly landed him within a few inches of a waggon carrying no rear lamp. At that moment a large hand came lightly to rest on his forearm.

"Take care, child!"

He certainly had not expected either the gesture or the gentle tone of the voice. But nothing justified the subsequent emotion, the lump like a hard fruit stone in his throat. 'I'm a fool, I'm a fool,' he kept repeating. He continued at a slower speed, and amused himself by watching the refraction of the beams, the golden zigzags and peacock's feathers, that danced for a moment round the headlamps when seen through the tears that brimmed his eyes.

'She told me that it had a hold on me, that I was held well in hand. If she could see us, Edmée and me. . . . How long is it since we took to sleeping like two brothers?' He tried to count: three weeks, perhaps more? 'And the joke about the whole business is that Edmée makes no demands, and wakes up smiling.' To himself, he always used the word "joke" when he wished to avoid the word "sad". 'Like an old married couple, what! like an old married couple . . . Madame and her Physician-in-Charge, Monsieur . . . and . . . his car. All the same, old Camille said that I was held. Held. Held. Catch me ever taking that old girl out again. . . .'

He did take her out again, for July began to scorch Paris. But neither Edmée nor Chéri complained about the dog-days. Chéri used to come home, polite and absent-minded, the backs of his hands and the lower part of his face nut-brown. He walked about naked between the bathroom and Edmée's boudoir.

"You must have been roasted to-day, you poor townees!" Chéri jeered.

Looking rather pale and almost melting away, Edmée straightened her pretty odalisque back and denied that she was tired.

"Oh well, not quite as bad as that, you know. There was rather more air than yesterday. My office down there is cool, you know. And then, we've had no time to think about it. My young man in bed twenty-two, who was getting on so well . . ."

"Oh yes!"

"Yes, Doctor Arnaud isn't too pleased about him."

She didn't hesitate to make play with the name of the Physician-in-Charge, much as a player moves up a decisive piece on the chess-board. But Chéri did not bat an eyelid, and Edmée followed his movements, those of a naked male body dappled a delicate green from the reflected light of the blue curtains. He walked to and fro in front of her, ostentatiously pure, trailing his aura of scent, and living in another world. The very self-confidence of this naked body, superior and contemptuous, reduced Edmée to a mildly vindictive immobility. She could not now have claimed this naked body for her own except in a voice altogether lacking the tones and urgency of desire—that is, in the calm voice of a submissive mate. Now she was held back by an arm covered with fine gold hairs, by an ardent mouth behind a golden moustache, and she gazed at Chéri with the jealous and serene security of a lover who covets a virgin inaccessible to all.

They went on to talk about holidays and travelling arrangements, in light-hearted and conventional phrases.

"The war hasn't changed Deauville enough, and what a crowd . . ." Chéri sighed.

"There's simply no place where one can eat a good meal, and it's a huge undertaking to reorganize the hotel business!" Edmée affirmed.

One day, not long before the Quartorze Juillet, Charlotte Peloux was lunching with them. She happened to speak of the success of some business deal in American blankets, and complained loudly that Léa had netted a half share of the profits. Chéri raised his head, in astonishment. "So you still see her?"

Charlotte Peloux enveloped her son in the loving glances induced by old port, and appealed to her daughter-in-law as witness: "He's got an odd way of putting things—as if he'd been gassed—hasn't he? . . . It's disturbing at times. I've never stopped seeing Léa, darling. Why should I have stopped seeing her?"

"Why?" Edmée repeated.

He looked at the two women, finding a strange flavour in their kindly attention.

"Because you never talk to me about her . . ." he began, ingenuously.

"Me!" barked Charlotte. "For goodness sake . . . Edmée, you hear what he says? Well at least it does credit to his feelings for you. He has so completely forgotten about everything that isn't you."

Edmée smiled without answering, bent her head, and adjusted the lace that edged the low-cut neck of her dress by tweaking it between her fingers. The movement drew Chéri's attention to her bodice, and through the yellow lawn he noticed that the points of her breasts and their mauve aureolas looked like twin bruises. He shuddered, and his shudder made him realise that the conventional beauty and all the most secret details of her charming body, that the whole of this young woman, in fact, so close and so disloyal, no longer aroused in him anything but positive repugnance. Nonsense, nonsense; but he was whipping a dead horse. And he listened to Charlotte's ever flowing stream of nasal burblings.

". . . and then again, the day before yesterday, I was saying in your presence, that motor for motor, well—I'd far rather have a taxi, a taxi, any day, than that prehistoric old Renault of Léa's—and if it wasn't the day before yesterday, it was yesterday, that I said—speaking of Léa—that if you're a woman living on your own and you've got to have a manservant, you might just as well have a good-looking one. And then Camille was saying, only the other day when you were there, how angry she was with herself for having sent a second barrel of Quarts-de-Chaumes round to Léa instead of keeping it for herself. I've complimented you often enough on your fidelity, my darling; I must now scold you for your ingratitude. Léa deserved better of you. Edmée will be the first to admit that!"

"The second," Edmée corrected.

"Never heard a word of it," Chéri said.

He was gorging himself with hard pink July cherries, and flipping them from beneath the lowered blind at the sparrows in the garden, where, after too heavy a watering, the flower beds were steaming like a hot spring. Edmée, motionless, was cogitating on Chéri's comment, "Never heard a word of it." He certainly was not lying, and yet his off-hand assumed schoolboyishness, as he squeezed the cherry stones and took aim at a sparrow by closing his left eye, spoke clearly enough to Edmée. 'What can he have been thinking about, if he never heard a word?'

Before the war, she would have looked for the woman in the case. A month earlier, on the day following the looking-glass scene, she would have feared reprisals, some Red Indian act of cruelty, or a bite on the nose. But no . . . nothing . . . he lived and roamed about innocently, as quiet in his freedom as a prisoner in the depths of a gaol, and as chaste as an animal brought from the Antipodes, which does not bother to look for a kindred female in our hemisphere.

Was he ill? He slept well, ate according to his fancy—that is, delicately, sniffing all the meat suspiciously, and preferring fruit and new-laid eggs. No nervous twitch disfigured the lovely balance of his features, and he drank more water than champagne. 'No, he's not ill. And yet he's . . . something. Something that I should guess, perhaps, if I were still in love with him. But . . .' Once again she fingered the lace round the neck of her bodice, inhaled the warmth and fragrance that rose up from between her breasts, and as she bent down her head she saw the precious twin pink and mauve discs through the material of her dress. She blushed with carnal pleasure, and dedicated the scent and the mauve shadows to the skilful, condescending, red-haired man whom she would be meeting again in an hour's time.

'They've spoken of Léa in front of me every day, and I didn't hear. Have I forgotten her, then? Yes, I have forgotten her. But then what does it mean, "to forget"? If I think of Léa, I see her clearly, I remember the sound of her voice, the scent which she sprayed herself with and rubbed so lavishly into her long hands.' He took such a deep breath that his nostrils were indented and his lips curled up to his nose in an expression of exquisite pleasure.

"Fred, you've just made the most horrible face; you were the spit and image of that fox Angot brought back from the trenches."

It was the least trying hour of the day for the pair of them, awake and in bed with breakfast over. After a refreshing shower-bath, they were gratified to hear the drenching rain—three months ahead of the proper season—falling in sheets that stripped the false Parisian autumn of its leaves and flattened the petunias. They did not bother to find an excuse, that morning, for having wilfully remained behind in town. Had not Charlotte Peloux hit upon the proper excuse the previous evening? She had declared, "We're all good Parigots, born and bred, aren't we! True blue one and all! We and the concierges can claim that we've had a real taste of the first post-war summer in Paris!"

"Fred, are you in love with that suit? You never stop wearing it. It doesn't look fresh, you know."

Chéri raised a finger in the direction of Edmée's voice, a gesture which enjoined silence and begged that nothing should divert his attention while he was in the throes of exceptional mental labours.

'I should like to know if I have forgotten her. But what is the real meaning of "forgotten"! A whole year's gone by without my seeing her.' He felt a sudden little shock of awakening, a tremor, when he found that his memory had failed to account for the war years. Then he totted up the years and, for an instant, everything inside him stopped functioning.

"Fred, shall I never get you to leave your razor in the bathroom, instead of bringing it in here!"

Almost naked and still damp, he took his time in turning round, and his back was silver-flecked with dabs of talcum powder.

"What?"

The voice, which seemed to come from afar, broke into a laugh.

"Fred, you look like a cake that's been badly sugared. An unhealthy looking cake. Next year, we won't be as stupid as we have been this. We'll take a place in the country."

"Do you want a place in the country?"

"Yes. Not this morning, of course."

She was pinning up her hair. She pointed with her chin to the curtain of rain, streaming down in a grey torrent, without any sign of thunder or wind.

"But next year, perhaps . . . Don't you think?"

"It's an idea. Yes, it's an idea."

He was putting her politely at arm's length, in order to return to his surprising discovery. 'I really did think that it was only one year since I'd seen her. I never took the war into reckoning. I haven't seen her for one, two, three, four, five years. One, two, three, four. . . . But, in that case, have I really forgotten her? No! Because these women have spoken of her in front of me, and I've never jumped up and shouted, "Hold on! If that's true—then what about Léa?" Five years . . . How old was she in 1914?'

He counted once more, and ran up against an unbelievable total. 'That would make her just about sixty to-day, wouldn't it? . . . How absurd!'

"And the important thing," Edmée went on, "is to choose it carefully. Let's see, a nice part of the world would be . . ."

"Normandy," Chéri finished for her, absent-mindedly.

"Yes, Normandy. Do you know Normandy?"

"No . . . Not at all well. . . . It's green. There are lime trees, ponds . . ."

He shut his eyes, as though dazed.

"Where do you mean? In what part of Normandy?"

"Ponds, cream, strawberries and peacocks. . . ."

"You seem to know a lot about Normandy! What grand country it must be! What else d'you find there?"

He appeared to be reading out a description as he leaned over the round mirror in which he made sure of the smoothness of chin and cheeks after shaving. He went on, unmoved, but hesitatingly. "There are peacocks. . . . Moonlight on parquet floors, and a great big red carpet spread on the gravel in front of . . ."

He did not finish. He swayed gently, and slithered on to the carpet. His fall was checked halfway by the side of the bed. As his head lay against the rumpled sheets, the overlying tan of his pallid cheeks had the greenish tinge of an old ivory.

Hardly had he reached the floor when Edmée, without uttering a sound, threw herself down beside him. With one hand she supported his drooping head, and with the other held a bottle of smelling-salts to his nostrils, from which the colour was visibly ebbing. But two enfeebled arms pushed her away.

"Leave me alone. . . . Can't you see I'm dying?"

He was not dying, however, and under Edmée's fingers his pulse retained its rhythm. He had spoken in a subdued whisper, with the glib, emphatic sincerity of very young would-be suicides who, at one and the same moment, both court death and fight shy of it.

His lips were parted over gleaming teeth and his breathing was regular; but he was in no haste to come right back to life. Safely ensconced behind his tightly shut eyes, he sought refuge in the heart of that green domain, so vivid in his imagination at the instant of his fainting fit—a flat domain, rich in strawberry-beds and bees, in pools of moonbeams fringed with warm stones. . . . After he regained his strength, he still kept his eyes shut, thinking 'If I open my eyes, Edmée will then see the picture in my mind.'

She remained on one knee, bending over him. She was looking after him efficiently, professionally. She reached out with her free hand, picked up a newspaper and used it to fan his forehead. She whispered insignificant but appropriate words, "It's the storm. . . . Relax. . . . No, don't try to move. . . . Wait till I slip this pillow under you. . . ."

He sat up again, smiling, and pressed her hand in thanks. His parched mouth longed for lemons or vinegar. The ringing of the telephone snatched Edmée away from him.

"Yes, yes. . . . What? Yes, of course I know it's ten. Yes. What?"

From the imperious brevity of her replies, Chéri knew that it was someone telephoning from the Hospital.

"Yes, of course I'm coming. What? In . . ." With a rapid glance she estimated Chéri's term of recovery. "In twenty-five minutes. Thanks. See you presently."

She opened the two glass doors of the french windows to their fullest extent, and a few peaceful drops of rain dripped into the room, bringing with them an insipid river smell.

"Are you better, Fred? What exactly did you feel? Nothing wrong with your heart, is there? You must be short of phosphates. It's the result of this ridiculous summer we're having. But what can you expect?"

She glanced at the telephone furtively, as she might at an onlooker.

Chéri stood up on his feet again without apparent effort. "Run along, child. You'll be late at your shop. I'm quite all right."

"A mild grog? A little hot tea?"

"Don't bother about me. . . . You've been very sweet. Yes, a little cup of tea—ask for it on your way out. And some lemon."

Five minutes later she was gone, after giving him a look, which she believed expressed solicitude only. She had searched in vain for a true sign, for some explanation of so inexplicable a state of affairs. As though the sound of the door shutting had severed his bonds, Chéri stretched himself and found that he felt light, cold, and empty. He hurried to the window and saw his wife crossing the small strip of garden, her head bowed under the rain. 'She's got a guilty back,' he pronounced, 'she's always had a guilty back. From the front, she looks a charming little lady. But her back gives the show away. She's lost a good half-hour by my having fainted. But "back to our muttons", as my mother would say. When I got married, Léa was fifty-one—at the very least—so Madame Peloux assures me. That would make her fifty-eight now, sixty perhaps. . . . The same age as General Courbat? No! That's too rich a joke!'

He tried his hardest to associate the picture of Léa at sixty with the white bristling moustache and crannied cheeks of General Courbat and his ancient cab-horse stance. 'It's the best joke out!'

The arrival of Madame Peloux found Chéri still given over to his latest pastime, pale, staring out at the drenched garden, and chewing a cigarette that had gone out. He showed no surprise at his mother's entrance, "You're certainly up with the lark, my dear mother."

"And you've got out of bed the wrong side, it would seem," was her rejoinder.

"Pure imagination. There are, at least, extenuating circumstances to account for your activity, I presume?"

She raised both eyes and shoulders in the direction of the ceiling. A cheeky little leather sports hat was pulled down like a vizor over her forehead.

"My poor child," she sighed, "if you only knew what I'm engaged on at this moment! If you knew what a gigantic task . . ."

He took careful stock of the wrinkles on his mother's face, the inverted commas round her mouth. He contemplated the small flabby wavelet of a double chin, the ebb and flow of which now covered, now uncovered, the collar of her mackintosh. He started to weigh up the fluctuating pouches under her eyes, repeating to himself: 'Fifty-eight . . . Sixty . . .'

"Do you know the task I've set myself? Do you know?" She waited a moment, opening wider her large eyes outlined by black pencil. "I'm going to revive the hot springs at Passy! *Les Thermes de Passy!* Yes, that means nothing to you, of course. The springs are there under the Rue Raynouard, only a few yards away. They're dormant; all they need is to be revived. Very active waters. If we go the right way about it, it will mean the ruination of Uriage, the collapse of Mont Dore, perhaps—but that would be too wonderful! Already I've made certain of the co-operation of twenty-seven Swiss doctors. Edmée and I have been getting to work on the Paris Municipal Council. . . . And that's exactly why I've come—I missed your wife by five minutes. . . . What's wrong with you? You're not listening to me. . . ."

He persisted in trying to relight his damp cigarette. He gave it up, threw the stub out upon the balcony, where large drops of rain were rebounding like grasshoppers; then he gravely looked his mother up and down.

"I am listening to you," he said. "Even before you speak I know what you're going to say. I know all about this business of yours. It goes by the varying names of company promotion, wheezes, commissions, founders' shares, American blankets, bully-beef, etcetera. . . . You don't suppose I've been deaf or blind for the last year, do you? You are nasty, wicked women, that's all there is to it. I bear you no ill will."

He stopped talking and sat down, by force of habit rubbing his fingers almost viciously over the little twin scars beneath his right breast. He looked out at the green, rain-battered garden, and on his relaxed features weariness battled with youth—weariness, hollowing his cheeks and darkening his eye-sockets, youth perfectly preserved in the ravishing curve and full ripeness of his lips, the downiness of his nostrils, and the raven-black abundance of his hair.

"Very well, then," said Charlotte Peloux at length. "That's a nice thing to hear, I must say. The devil turned preacher! I seem to have given birth to a Censor of Public Morals."

He showed no intention of breaking the silence, or of making any movement whatever.

"And by what high standards do you presume to judge this poor corrupt world? By your own honesty, I don't doubt!"

Buckled into a leather jerkin, like a yeoman of old, she was at the top of her form and ready for the fray. But Chéri appeared to be through with all fighting, now and for ever.

"By my honesty? . . . Perhaps. Had I been hunting for the right word, I should never have hit upon that. You yourself said it. Honesty will pass."

She did not deign to reply, postponing her offensive until a later moment. She held her tongue that she might give her full attention to her son's peculiar new aspect. He was sitting with his legs very wide apart, elbows on knees, his hands firmly locked together. He continued to stare out at the garden laid flat by the lashing rain, and after a moment he sighed without turning his head: "Do you really call this a life?"

As might be expected, she asked: "What life?"

He raised one arm, only to let it fall again. "Mine. Yours. Everything. All that's going on under our eyes."

Madame Peloux hesitated a moment. Then she threw off her leather coat, lit a cigarette, and she too sat down.

"Are you bored?"

Coaxed by the unusual sweetness of a voice that sounded ethereally solicitous, he became natural and almost confidential.

"Bored? No, I'm not bored. What makes you think I'm bored? I'm a trifle . . . what shall I say? . . . a trifle worried, that's all."

"About what?"

"About everything. Myself. . . . Even about you."

"I'm surprised at that."

"So am I. These fellows . . . this year . . . this peace." He stretched his fingers apart as though they were sticky or tangled in overlong hair.

"You say that as we used to say 'This war' . . ." She put a hand on his shoulder and tactfully lowered her voice. "What is the matter with you?"

He could not bear the questioning weight of this hand; he stood up, and began moving about in a haphazard way. "The matter is that everyone's rotten. No!" he begged, seeing an artificial look of indignation on the maternal countenance, "No, don't start all over again. No, present company *not* excluded. No, I do *not* accept the fact that we are living in splendid times, with a dawn of this, a resurrection of that. No, I am *not* angry, don't love you any less than before, and there is nothing wrong with my liver. But I do seriously think that I'm nearly at the end of my tether."

He cracked his fingers as he walked about the room, sniffing the sweet-smelling spray of the heavy rain as it splashed off the balcony. Charlotte Peloux threw down her hat and her red gloves, a gesture intended as a peace-offering.

"Do tell me exactly what you mean, child. We're alone." She smoothed back her sparse hennaed hair, cut boyishly short. Her mushroom-coloured garb held in her body as an iron hoop clamps a cask. 'A woman. . . . She has been a woman. . . . Fifty-eight. . . . Sixty. . . .' Chéri was thinking. She turned on him her lovely velvety eyes, brimming with maternal coquetry, the feminine power of which he had long forgotten. This sudden charm of his mother's warned him of the danger lying ahead, and the difficulty of the confession towards which she was leading him. But he felt empty and listless, tormented by what he lacked. The hope of shocking her drove him on still further.

"Yes," he said, in answer to his own question. "You have your blankets, your macaroni and spaghetti, your légions d'honneur. You joke about the meetings of the Chambre des Députés and the accident to young Lenoir. You are thrilled by Madame Caillaux, and by the hot springs at Passy. Edmée's got her shopful of wounded and her Physician-in-Charge. Desmond dabbles in dance-halls, wines and spirits, and white slavery. Filipesco bags cigars from Americans and hospitals, to hawk them round night clubs. Jean de Touzac . . . is in the surplus store racket. What a set! What . . ."

"You're forgetting Landru," Charlotte put in edgeways.

His eyes twinkled as he gave the slyest of winks, in silent tribute to the malicious humour that rejuvenated his old pugilist of a mother.

"Landru? That doesn't count, there's a pre-war flavour about that. There's nothing odd about Landru. But as for the rest—well . . . well, to cut it short, there's not one who's not a rotter and . . . and I don't like it. That's all."

"That's certainly short, but not very clear," Charlotte said, after a moment. "You've a nice opinion of us. Mind you, I don't say you're wrong. Myself, I've got the qualities of my defects, and nothing frightens me. Only, it doesn't give me an inkling of what you're really after."

Chéri swayed awkwardly on his chair. He frowned so furiously that the skin on his forehead contracted in deep wrinkles between his eyes, as though trying to keep a hat on his head in a gusty wind.

"What I'm really after . . . I simply don't know. I only wish people weren't such rotters. I mean to say, weren't *only* rotten. . . . Or, quite simply, I should like to be able not to notice it."

He showed such hesitancy, such a need of coming to terms with himself, that Charlotte made fun of it. "Why notice it, then?"

"Ah, well. . . . That's just the point, you see."

He gave her a helpless smile, and she noticed how much her son's face aged as he smiled. 'Someone ought constantly to be telling him hard-luck stories,' she said to herself, 'or else making him really angry. Gaiety doesn't improve his looks . . .' She blew out a cloud of smoke and in her turn allowed an ambiguous commonplace to escape her. "You didn't notice anything of that before."

He raised his head sharply. "Before? Before what?"

"Before the war, of course."

"Ah, yes . . ." he murmured, disappointed. "No, before the war, obviously. . . . But before the war I didn't look at things in the same way."

"Why?"

The simple word struck him dumb.

"I'll tell you what it is," Charlotte chid him, "you've turned honest."

"You wouldn't think of admitting, by any chance, that I've simply remained so?"

"No, no, don't let's get that wrong." She was arguing, a flush on her cheeks, with the fervour of a prophetess. "Your way of life before the war, after all—I'm putting myself in the position of people who are not exactly broad-minded and who take a superficial view of things, understand!—such a way of life, after all, has a name!"

"If you like," Chéri agreed. "What of it?"

"Well then, that implies a . . . a way of looking at things. Your point of view was a gigolo's."

"Quite possibly," said Chéri, unmoved. "Do you see any harm in that?"

"Certainly not," Charlotte protested, with the simplicity of a child. "But, you know, there's a right time for everything."

"Yes . . ." He sighed deeply, looking out towards a sky masked by cloud and rain. "There's a time to be young, and there's a time to be less young. There's a time to be happy . . . d'you think it needed you to make me aware of that?"

She seemed suddenly to be upset, and walked up and down the room, her round behind tightly moulded by her dress, as plump and brisk as a little fat bitch. She came back and planted herself in front of her son.

"Well, darling, I'm afraid you're heading for some act of madness."

"What?"

"Oh! there aren't so many. A monastery. Or a desert island. Or love."

Chéri smiled in astonishment. "Love? You want me . . . in love with . . ." He jerked his chin in the direction of Edmée's boudoir, and Charlotte's eyes sparkled.

"Who mentioned her?"

He laughed, and from an instinct of self-preservation became offensive again.

"You did, and in a moment you'll be offering me one of your American pieces."

She gave a theatrical start. "An American piece? Really? And why not a rubber substitute as provided for sailors into the bargain?"

He was pleased with her jingoistic and expert disdain. Since childhood he had had it dinned into him that a French woman demeans herself by living with a foreigner, unless, of course, she exploits him, or he ruins her. And he could reel off a list of outrageous epithets with which a native Parisian courtesan would brand a dissolute foreign woman. But he refused the offer, without irony. Charlotte threw out her short arms and protruded her lower lip, like a doctor confessing his helplessness.

"I don't suggest that you should work . . ." she risked shame-facedly.

Chéri dismissed this importunate suggestion with a shrug of the shoulders.

"Work," he repeated . . . "work, what you mean by that is hob-nobbing with fellows. You can't work alone, short of painting picture post-cards or taking in sewing. My poor mother, you fail to realise that, if fellows get my goat, women can hardly be said to inspire me either. The truth is, that I have no further use for women at all," he finished courageously.

"Good heavens!" Charlotte caterwauled. She wrung her hands as though a horse had slipped and fallen at her feet; but harshly her son enjoined silence with a single gesture, and she was forced to admire the virile authority of this handsome young man, who had just owned up to his own particular brand of impotence.

"Chéri! . . . my little boy! . . ."

He turned to her with a gentle, empty, and vaguely pleading look in his eyes.

She gazed into the large eyes that shone with an exaggerated brilliance, due, perhaps, to their unblemished white, their long lashes and the secret emotion behind them. She longed to enter through these magnificent portals and reach down to the shadowed heart which had first started to beat so close to her own. Chéri appeared to be putting up no defence and to enjoy being balked, as if under hypnosis. Charlotte had, in the past, known her son to be ill, irritable, sly; she had never known him unhappy. She felt, therefore, a strange kind of excitement, the ecstasy that casts a woman at a man's feet at the moment when she dreams of changing a despairing stranger into an inferior stranger—that is to say, of making him rid himself of his despair.

"Listen, Chéri," she murmured very softly. "Listen. . . . You must . . . No, no, wait! At least let me speak. . . ."

He interrupted her with a furious shake of the head, and she saw it was useless to insist. It was she who broke their long exchange of looks, by putting on her coat again and her little leather hat, making towards the door. But as she passed the table, she stopped, and casually put her hand out towards the telephone.

"Do you mind, Chéri?"

He nodded his consent, and she began in a high-pitched nasal shrill like a clarinet. "Hullo . . . Hullo . . . Hullo . . . Passy, two nine, two nine. Hullo . . . Is that you, Léa? But of course it's me. What weather, eh! . . . Don't speak of it. Yes, very well. Everyone's very well. What are you doing to-day? Not budging an inch! Ah, that's so like you, you self-indulgent creature! Oh, you know, I'm no longer my own mistress. . . . Oh no, not on that account. Something altogether different. A vast undertaking. . . . Oh, no, not on the telephone. . . . You'll be in all day then? Good. That's very convenient. Thank you. Goodbye, Léa darling!"

She put back the receiver, showing nothing but the curve of her back. As she moved away, she inhaled and exhaled puffs of blue smoke, and vanished in the midst of her cloud like a magician whose task is accomplished.

WITHOUT hurrying, he climbed the single flight of stairs up to Léa's flat. At six in the evening, after the rain, the Rue Raynouard re-echoed, like the garden of a boarding-school, with the chirrup of birds and the cries of small children. He glanced quickly, coldly, at everything, refusing to be surprised at the heavy looking-glasses in the entrance-hall, the polished steps, the blue carpet, or the lift-cage lavishly splashed with as much lacquer and gold as a sedan-chair. On the landing he experienced, for a moment, the deceptive sense of detachment and freedom from pain felt by a sufferer on the dentist's doorstep. He nearly turned away, but, guessing that he might feel compelled to return later, he pressed the bell with a determined finger. The maid, who had taken her time in coming to the door, was young and dark, with a butterfly cap of fine lawn on her bobbed hair: her unfamiliar face took from Chéri his last chance of feeling moved.

"Is Madame at home?"

The young servant, apparently lost in admiration of him, could not make up her mind.

"I do not know, Monsieur. Is Monsieur expected?"

"Of course," he said, with a return of his old harshness.

She left him standing there, and disappeared. In the half-light, he was quick to take in his surroundings, with eyes blurred by the gloom, and alert sensitive nostrils. There was nowhere a vestige of that light golden scent, and some ordinary pine essence sputtered in an electric scent-burner. Chéri felt put out, like someone who discovers that he is on the wrong floor. But a great peal of girlish laughter rang out, its notes running down a deep descending scale. It was muffled by some curtain or other, but at once the intruder was cast into a whirlpool of memories.

"Will Monsieur please come to the drawing-room."

He followed the white butterfly, saying over to himself as he went:

"Léa's not alone. She's laughing. She can't be alone. So long as it's not my mother." Beyond an open door, he was being welcomed by rosy pink daylight and he waited, standing there, for the rebirth of the world heralded by this dawn.

A woman was writing at a small table, facing away from him. Chéri was able to distinguish a broad back and the padded cushion of a fat neck beneath a head of thick grey vigorous hair, cut short like his mother's. 'So I was right, she's not alone. But who on earth can this good woman be?'

"And, at the same time, write down your masseur's address for me, Léa, and his name. You know what I'm like about names. . . ."

These words came from a woman dressed in black, also seated, and Chéri felt a preliminary tremor of expectation running through him: 'Then . . . where is Léa?'

The grey-haired lady turned round, and Chéri received the full impact of her blue eyes.

"Oh, good heavens, child—it's you!"

He went forward as in a dream, and kissed an outstretched hand.

"Monsieur Frédéric Peloux—Princess Cheniaguine."

Chéri bent over and kissed another hand, then took a seat.

"Is he your . . . ?" queried the lady in black, referring to him with as much freedom as if he had been a deaf-mute.

Once again the great peal of girlish laughter rang out, and Chéri sought for the source of this laugh here, there, and everywhere—anywhere but in the throat of the grey-haired woman.

"No, no, he isn't! Or rather, he isn't any longer, I should say. Valérie, come now, what are you thinking of?"

She was not monstrous, but huge, and loaded with exuberant buttresses of fat in every part of her body. Her arms, like rounded thighs, stood out from her hips on plump cushions of flesh just below her armpits. The plain skirt and the nondescript long jacket, opening on a linen blouse with a jabot, proclaimed that the wearer had abdicated, was no longer concerned to be a woman, and had acquired a kind of sexless dignity.

Léa was now standing between Chéri and the window, and he was not horrified at first by her firm, massive, almost cubic, bulk. When she moved to reach a chair, her features were revealed, and he began to implore her with silent entreaties, as though faced with an armed lunatic. Her cheeks were red and looked over-ripe, for she now disdained the use of powder, and when she laughed her mouth was packed with gold. A healthy old woman, in short, with sagging cheeks and a double chin, well able to carry her burden of flesh and freed from restraining stays.

"Tell me, child, where have you sprung from? I can't say I think you're looking particularly well."

She held out a box of cigarettes to Chéri, smiling at him from blue eyes which had grown smaller, and he was frightened to find her so direct in her approach, and as jovial as an old gentleman. She called him "child", and he turned away his eyes, as though she had let slip an indecent word. But he exhorted himself to be patient, in the vague hope that this first picture would give place to a shining transfiguration.

The two women looked him over calmly, sparing him neither goodwill nor curiosity.

"He's got rather a look of Hernandez . . ." said Valérie Cheniaguine.

"Oh, I don't see that at all," Léa protested. "Ten years ago perhaps . . . and, anyhow, Hernandez had a much more pronounced jaw!"

"Who's that?" Chéri asked, with something of an effort.

"A Peruvian who was killed in a motor accident about six months ago," said Léa. "He was living with Maximilienne. It made her very unhappy."

"Didn't prevent her finding consolation," said Valérie.

"Like anyone else," Léa said. "You wouldn't have wished her to die of it, surely?"

She laughed afresh, and her merry blue eyes disappeared, lost behind wide cheeks bulging with laughter. Chéri turned away his head and looked at the woman in black. She had brown hair and an ample figure, vulgar and feline like thousands and thousands of women from the south. She seemed in disguise, so very carefully was she dressed as a woman in good society. Valérie was wearing what had long been the uniform of foreign princesses and their ladies—a black tailor-made of undistinguished cut, tight in the sleeve, with a blouse of extremely fine white batiste, showing signs of strain at the breast. The pearl buttons, the famous necklace, the high stiff whalebone collar, everything about Valérie was as royal as the name she legitimately bore. Like royalty, too, she wore stockings of medium quality, flat-heeled walking shoes and expensive gloves, embroidered in black and white.

From the cold and calculating way she looked him over, Chéri might have been a piece of furniture. She went on with her criticisms and comparisons at the top of her voice.

"Yes, yes, there is something of Hernandez, I promise you. But, to hear Maximilienne to-day, Hernandez might never have existed . . . now that she has made quite certain of her famous Amerigo. And yet! And yet! I know what I'm talking about. I've seen him, her precious Amerigo. I'm just back from Deauville. I saw the pair of them!"

"No! Do tell us!"

Léa sat down, overflowing the whole armchair. She had acquired a new trick of tossing back her thick grey hair; and at each shake of the head, Chéri saw a quivering of the lower part of her face, which looked like Louis XVI's. Ostensibly, she was giving Valérie her full attention, but several times Chéri noticed a mischievous faltering in one of the little shrunk blue eyes, as they sought to catch those of the unexpected visitor.

"Well, then," Valérie started on her story, "she had hidden him in a villa miles outside Deauville, at the back of beyond. But that did not suit Amerigo at all—as you will readily understand, Monsieur!—and he grumbled at Maximilienne. She was cross, and said: 'Ah! that's what the matter is—you want to be on view to the world and his wife, and so you shall be!' So she telephoned to reserve a table at the Normandy for the following evening. Everyone knew this an hour later, and so I booked a table as well, with Becq d'Ambez and Zahita. And we said to ourselves: 'We're going to be allowed to see this marvel at last!' On the stroke of nine there was Maximilienne, all in white and pearls, and Amerigo. . . . Oh, my dear, what a disappointment! Tall, yes, that goes without saying . . . in point of fact, rather too tall. You know what I always say about men who are too tall. I'm still waiting to be shown one, just one, who is well put together. Eyes, yes, eyes, I've got nothing to say against his eyes. But —from here to there, don't you see (she was pointing to her own face), from here to there, something about the cheeks which is too rounded, too soft, and the ears set too low. . . . Oh, a very great disappointment. And holding himself as stiff as a poker."

"You're exaggerating," said Léa. "The cheeks—well what about cheeks?—they aren't so very important. And, from here to there, well really it's beautiful, it's noble; the eyelashes, the bridge of the nose, the eyes, the whole thing is really too beautiful! I'll grant you the chin: that will quickly run to flesh. And the feet are too small, which is ridiculous in a boy of that height."

"No, there I don't agree with you. But I certainly noticed that the thigh was far too long in proportion to the leg, from here to there."

They went on to thrash out the question, weighing up, with a wealth of detail and point by point, every portion of the fore and hind quarters of this expensive animal.

'Judges of pedigree fat cattle,' Chéri thought. 'The right place for them is the Commisariats.'

"Speaking of proportions," Léa continued, "you'll never come across anything to touch Chéri. . . . You see, Chéri, you've come at just the right moment. You ought to blush. Valérie, if you can remember what Chéri was like only six, or say seven years ago . . ."

"But certainly, of course, I remember clearly. And Monsieur has not changed so very much, after all. . . . And you were so proud of him!"

"No," said Léa.

"You weren't proud of him?"

"No," said Léa with perfect calm, "I was in love with him."

She manœuvred the whole of her considerable body in his direction, and let her gay glance rest upon Chéri, quite innocently. "It's true I was in love with you, very much in love, too."

He lowered his eyes, stupidly abashed before these two women, the stouter of whom had just proclaimed so serenely that she and he had been lovers. Yet at the same time the voluptuous and almost masculine tone of Léa's voice besieged his memory, torturing him unbearably.

"You see, Valérie, how foolish a man can look when reminded of a love which no longer exists? Silly boy, it doesn't upset me in the least to think about it. I love my past. I love my present. I'm not ashamed of what I've had, and I'm not sad because I have it no longer. Am I wrong, child?"

He uttered a cry, almost as if someone had trodden on his big toe. "No, no, of course not! The very reverse!"

"It's charming to think you have remained such good friends," said Valérie.

Chéri waited for Léa to explain that this was his first visit to her for five years, but she just gave a good-humoured laugh and winked with a knowing air. He felt more and more upset. He did not know how to protest, how to shout out loud that he laid no claim to the friendship of this colossal woman, with the cropped hair of an elderly 'cellist—that, had he but known, he would never have come upstairs, never crossed her threshold, set foot on her carpet, never collapsed in the cushioned armchair, in the depths of which he now lay defenceless and dumb.

"Well, I must be going," Valérie said. "I don't mean to wait for crush-hour in the Métro, I can tell you."

She rose to face the strong light, and it was kind to her Roman features. They were so solidly constructed that the approach of her sixtieth year had left them unharmed: the cheeks were touched up in the old-fashioned way, with an even layer of white powder, and the lips with a red that was almost black and looked oily.

"Are you going home?" Léa asked.

"Of course I am. What d'you suppose my little skivvy would get up to if left to herself!"

"Are you still pleased with your new flat?"

"It's a dream! Especially since the iron bars were put across the windows. And I've had a steel grid fixed over the pantry fanlight, which I had forgotten about. With my electric bells and my burglar-alarms . . . Ouf! It's been long enough before I could feel at all safe!"

"And your old house?"

"Bolted and barred. Up for sale. And the pictures in store. My little entresol flat is a gem for the eighteen hundred francs it costs me. And no more servants looking like hired assassins. You remember those two footmen? The thought of them still gives me the creeps!"

"You took much too black a view, my dear."

"You can't realise, my poor friend, without having been through it all. Monsieur, delighted to have met you. . . . No, don't you move, Léa."

She enfolded them both in her velvety barbaric gaze, and was gone. Chéri followed her with his eyes until she reached the door, yet he lacked the courage to follow her example. He remained where he was, all but snuffed out by the conversation of these two women who had been speaking of him in the past tense, as though he were dead. But now Léa was coming back into the room, bursting with laughter. "Princess Cheniaguine! Sixty millions! and a widow!—and she's not in the least bit happy. If that can be called enjoying life, it's not my idea of it, you know!"

She clapped her hand on her thigh as if it were a horse's crupper.

"What's the matter with her?"

"Funk. Blue funk, that's all. She's not the sort of woman who knows how to carry such wealth. Cheniaguine left her everything. But one might say that it would have done her less harm if he'd taken her money instead of leaving her his. You heard what she said?"

She subsided into the depths of a well upholstered armchair, and Chéri hated to hear the gentle sigh of its cushions as they took the weight of her vast bulk. She ran the tip of her finger along the grooved moulding of the chair, blew away the few specks of dust, and her face fell.

"Ah! things are not at all what they were, not even servants. Eh?"

He felt that he had lost colour, and that the skin round his mouth was growing tighter, as during a severe frost. He fought back an overwhelming impulse to burst out in rancour mingled with entreaties. He longed to cry out loud: 'Stop! Show me your real self! Throw off your disguise! You must be somewhere behind it, since it's your voice I hear. Appear in your true colours! Arise as a creature reborn, with your hair newly hennaed this morning, your face freshly powdered: put on your long stays again, the blue dress with its delicate jabot, the scent like a meadow that was so much a part of you. In these new surroundings I search for it in vain! Leave all this behind, and come away to Passy—never mind the showers—Passy with its dogs and its birds, and in the Avenue Bugeaud we'll be sure to find Ernest polishing the brass bars on your front door.' He shut his eyes, utterly worn out.

"And now, my child, I'm going to tell you something for your own good. What you need is to have your urine tested. Your colour's shocking and you've got that pinched look round your lips—sure signs, both of them: you're not taking proper care of your kidneys."

Chéri opened his eyes again, and they took their fill of this placid epitome of disaster seated in front of him. Heroically he said: "D'you really think so? It's quite possible."

"You mean, it's certain. And then, you've not got enough flesh on you. . . . It's no use telling me that the best fighting cocks are scraggy. You could do with a good ten pounds more on you."

"Give them to me," he said with a smile. But he found his cheeks singularly recalcitrant and opposed to smiling, almost as though his skin had stiffened with age.

Léa burst into a peal of happy laughter, and Chéri tasted a pleasure which he could not have borne for long; he listened again to its full and rounded tones, the very laugh which in the old days used to greet some outrageous impertinence on the part of the "naughty little boy".

"That I could well afford! I've certainly been putting on weight, haven't I? Eh? Look . . . here . . . would you believe it? . . . and again here!"

She lit a cigarette, exhaled a double jet of smoke through her nostrils, and shrugged her shoulders. "It's age!"

The word flew out of her mouth so lightly that it gave Chéri a sort of extravagant hope. 'Yes: she's only joking. In a flash she'll reappear as her real self.' For an instant she seemed to take in the meaning of the look he gave her.

"I've changed a lot, haven't I, child? Fortunately, it doesn't much matter. As for you, I don't like the look of you at all. . . . You've been fluttering your wings too much, as we used to say in the old days. Eh?"

He detested this new "Eh?" with which she peppered her sentences so freely. But he stiffened at each interrogation, and each time mastered his rising excitement, preferring to remain in ignorance of both its reason and its aim.

"I don't ask whether you have any troubles at home. In the first place, it's none of my business; and besides, I know your wife as if I were her mother."

He listened to the sound of her voice without paying much attention. He noticed, above all, that when she stopped smiling or laughing, she ceased to belong to any assignable sex. Despite her enormous breasts and crushing backside, she seemed by virtue of age altogether virile and happy in that state.

"And I know your wife to be thoroughly capable of making a man happy."

He was powerless to hide his inward laughter, and Léa quickly went on to say:

"What I said was 'a man', and not 'any man'. Here you are in my house, without a word of warning. You've not come, I take it, just to gaze into my beautiful eyes, eh?"

She turned on Chéri those once "beautiful blue eyes", now so diminished, marbled with tiny red veins, quizzical, neither kind nor unkind, alert and bright certainly, but . . . but where was now the limpid freshness that had laved their whites with palest blue? Where the contour of their orbs, with the roundness of fruit, breast, or hemisphere, and blue as a land watered by many a river?

Jestingly, he said, "Pooh! aren't you sharp! A real detective!" And it amazed him to find that he had fallen into such a carefree posture, with his legs crossed, like a handsome young man with bad manners. For inwardly he was watching his other self, hopelessly distracted and on his knees, waving his arms, baring his breast, and shrieking incoherently.

"I'm not a particularly stupid woman. But you must admit that you don't present me to-day with a very difficult problem!"

She drew in her chin and its lower folds spread over her neck: the kneeling ghost of his other self bowed its head like a man who has received a death-blow.

"You show every known sign of suffering from the disease of your generation. No, no, let me go on. Like all your soldier friends, you're looking everywhere for your paradise, eh! the paradise they owe you as a war hero: your own special Victory Parade, *your* youth, *your* lovely women. . . . They owe you all that and more, for they promised you everything, and, dear God, you deserved it. And what do you find? A decent ordinary life. So you go in for nostalgia, listlessness, disillusion and neurasthenia. Am I wrong?"

"No," said Chéri, for he was thinking that he would give his little finger to stop her talking.

Léa clapped him on the shoulder, letting her hand with its large rings rest there. As he bent his head down towards it, he could feel on his cheek the heat of this heavy hand.

"Oh!" Léa continued, raising her voice. "You're not the only one! I've come across dozens of boys, since the war ended, exactly in your state of . . ."

"Where?" Chéri interrupted.

The suddenness of the interruption and its aggressive character put an end to Léa's parsonic eloquence. She withdrew her hand.

"They're to be met with everywhere, my child. Is it possible to be so vain? You seem to think you're unique because you find the postwar world insipid. Don't flatter yourself to that extent!"

She gave a low chuckle, and a toss to her sportive grey hair, and then a self-important smile like a judge who has a nice taste in wine. "And you do flatter yourself, you know, always imagining that you're the only one of your kind."

She took a step back and narrowed her gaze, adding, perhaps a little vindictively: "You were unique only for . . . for a time."

Behind this veiled but carefully chosen insult, Chéri discovered something of her femininity at last. He sat bolt upright, delighted to find himself suffering less acutely. But by this time Léa had reverted to her milk and honey.

"But you didn't come here to have that said about you. Did you make up your mind on the spur of the moment?"

"Yes," said Chéri.

He could have wished that this monosyllable might have been the last word between the two of them. Shyly, he let his gaze wander to all the things that surrounded Léa. From the nearest plate he took a dry cake shaped like a curved tile, and then put it back, convinced that it would turn to brick-red grit in his mouth were he to take a bite out of it. Léa noticed this action, and the painful way he swallowed his saliva.

"Tut, tut, so we're suffering from nerves, are we? Peeky chin, and dark lines under the eyes. That's a pretty state of affairs!"

He closed his eyes, and like a coward decided to listen and not look.

"Listen to me, child, I know a little restaurant in the Avenue des Gobelins. . . ."

He looked up at her, in the full hope that she was going mad, that in this way he would be able to forgive her for both looking and behaving like an old woman.

"Yes, I know a little restaurant . . . Let me speak! Only, you must be quick, before the smart set and the newspapers take it into their heads to make it fashionable, and the good woman herself is replaced by a chef. She does all the cooking at present, and, my dear . . ." She brought thumb and forefinger together on the tip of her lips, and blew an imitation kiss. Chéri turned away to look out of the window, where the shadow thrown by a branch flicked at the steady shaft of sunlight, impatiently but at regular intervals, much as a bent reed or river-plant appears to strike at the ripples of a regularly flowing current.

"What an odd sort of conversation . . ." he ventured in strained tones.

"No more odd than your presence in my house," Léa snapped back at him.

With a wave of the hand he made it clear that he wanted peace, only peace, with as few words spoken as possible, and preferably none at all. He felt defeated in face of this elderly woman's boundless reserves of energy and appetite. Léa's quick blood was now rising and turning her bulging neck and her ears to purple. 'She's got a crop like an old hen,' he thought, with something of his old enjoyment of cruelty.

"And that's the truth!" she hurled at him excitedly. "You drag yourself round here, for all the world like an apparition, and when I do my best to find some way of putting things to rights, I who, when all's said and done, do happen to know you rather well . . ."

He smiled at her despondently, 'And how in the world should she know me? When far shrewder people than she, and even than I myself . . .'

"A certain kind of sickness of the soul, my child, of disillusion, is just a question of stomach. Yes, yes, you may laugh!" He was not laughing, but she might well think he was. "Romanticism, nerves, distaste for life: stomach. The whole lot, simply stomach. Love itself! If one wished to be perfectly sincere, one would have to admit there are two kinds of love—well-fed and ill-fed. The rest is pure fiction. If only I knew how to write, or to make speeches, my child, what things I could say about that! Oh, of course, it wouldn't be anything new, but I should know what I was talking about, and that would be a change from our present-day writers."

Something worse than this obsession with the kitchen was upsetting Chéri: the affectation, the false tone of voice, the almost studied joviality. He suspected Léa of putting on an act of hearty and sybaritic geniality, just as a fat actor, on the stage, plays "jovial" characters because he has developed a paunch.

As though defiantly, she rubbed her shiny, almost blotchy red nose with the back of her first finger, and fanned the upper part of her body with the aid of the two revers of her long jacket. In so doing, she was altogether too cheerfully inviting Chéri to sit in judgment on her appearance, and she even ran her hand through her thick grey locks as she shook them free of her head.

"Do you like my hair short?"

He deigned to reply only by a silent shake of the head, just like someone brushing aside an idle argument.

"Weren't you saying something just now about a little restaurant in the Avenue des Gobelins . . . ?"

It was now her turn to brush aside an irrelevance. She was beginning to understand, and he could see from the quivering of her nostrils that at last she was piqued. His animal instincts, which had been shocked into dullness, were now on the alert and it was as though a weight had been lifted from his mind. He intended somehow to find a way past this shameless flesh, the greying curls and "merry friar" joviality, and reach the being concealed behind them, to whom he was coming back, as to the scene of a crime. He remained close to this buried treasure, burrowing towards it spontaneously. 'How in the world did old age come upon her? All of a sudden, on waking up one morning? or little by little? And this surplus fat, this extra avoirdupois, under the weight of which armchairs groan? Was it some sudden shock that brought about this change and unsexed her? Could it, perhaps, have been grief on my account?' But he asked these questions of no one but himself, and without voicing them. 'She is piqued. She's on the way to understanding me. She's just going to tell me. . . .'

He watched her rise to her feet, walk over to the bureau, and start to tidy the papers lying on the open hinged flap. He noticed that she was holding herself more upright than when he had first entered the room, and that, under his following eye, she straightened her back still more. He accepted the fact that she was really colossal, her body seeming to run absolutely straight from armpit to hip. Before turning round again to face Chéri, she arranged a white silk scarf tightly round her neck, despite the heat of the room. He heard her take a deep breath, before she came towards him with the slow rolling gait of a ponderous animal.

She smiled at him. "I am not doing my duty as a hostess, it would seem. It's not very polite to welcome someone by giving them advice, especially useless advice."

From under a fold of her white scarf peeped insinuatingly a twisting, coiling, resplendent string of pearls, which Chéri at once recognised.

Held captive beneath the translucent skin, the seven colours of the rainbow flickered with some secret fire of their own all over the surface of each precious sphere. Chéri recognised the pearl with a dimple, the slightly egg-shaped pearl, and the biggest pearl of the string, distinguishable by its unique pink. 'These pearls, these at least, are unchanged! They and I remain unchanged.'

"So you've still got your pearls," he said.

She was astonished by the foolish phrase, and looked as though she wanted to interpret it.

"Yes, in spite of the war. Are you thinking that I could, or should, have sold them? Why should I have sold them?"

"Or 'for whom'?" he answered jokingly, in a tired voice.

She could not restrain a rapid glance towards the bureau and its scattered papers; and Chéri, in his turn, felt he knew the thought behind it, guessing that it was aimed at some yellowish postcard-photograph, probably the frightened features of a beardless boy in uniform. Disdainfully, he considered this imaginary face and said to himself, 'That's none of my concern,' adding a moment later, 'But what is there here that does concern me?'

The agitation which he had brought in his heart was now excited by everything around him; everything added to it—the setting sun, the cries of insect-chasing swallows, and the ember-glowing shafts of light stabbing through the curtains. He remembered that Léa carried with her wherever she went this incandescent rose-pink, as the sea, on its ebb-tide, carries with it far out from shore the earthy smells of pastures and new-mown hay.

No word passed between them for a while, and they were kept in countenance by pretending to listen to the clear fresh notes of a child singing. Léa had not sat down again. Standing massively in front of him, she carried her irretrievable chin higher than before, and betrayed some vague distress by the frequent fluttering of her eyelids.

"Am I making you late? Have you to go out this evening? Do you want to dress?" The questions were abrupt, and forced Léa to look at Chéri.

"Dress? Good Lord, and in what do you wish me to dress? I *am* dressed—irrevocably—once and for all."

She laughed her incomparable laugh, starting on a high note and descending the scale by leaps of equal interval till she got to the deep musical reaches reserved for sobs and amorous moans. Chéri unconsciously raised a hand in supplication.

"Dressed for life, I tell you! And how convenient that is! Blouses, fine linen, and this uniform on top, and here I am in full fig. Equally ready for dinner either at Montagné's or somewhere modest, ready for the cinema, for bridge, or for a stroll in the Bois."

"And what about love—which you're forgetting to mention?"

"Oh, child!"

She blushed: and, though her face was dark with the chronic red of sufferers from arthritis, the blush could not be concealed. Chéri, after the first caddish satisfaction of having said something outrageous, was seized with shame and remorse at the sight of this maidenly reaction.

"I was only joking," he said, in some confusion. "Have I gone too far?"

"Of course not. But you know very well I have never cared for certain kinds of impropriety or for jokes that are not really funny."

She strove to control her voice, but her face revealed that she was hurt, and every coarsened feature gave signs of a distress that could perhaps be outraged modesty.

'Dear God, if she takes it into her head to cry!' and he imagined the catastrophic effect of tears coursing down each cheek into the single deep ravine near the mouth, and of her eyelids reddened by the salt of tears.

He hastened to intercept: "No, no, you mustn't think that! How could you! I never meant. . . . Please, Léa. . . ."

From her quick reaction he realised suddenly that this was the first time he had spoken her name. Proud, as in the old days, of her self-control, she gently stopped him.

"Don't worry, child. I'm not offended. But I've only got you here for a few minutes, so don't spoil them by saying anything I shouldn't care to remember."

Her gentle tone left him cold, and her actual words seemed offensively tactful to him. 'Either she's lying, or she really has become the sort of person she pretends. Peace, purity, and the Lord knows what! She might as well wear a ring in her nose! Peace of heart, guzzling, and the cinema. . . . Lies, lies, all lies! She wants to make me think that women find growing old comfortable, positively enjoyable. How can she expect *me* to swallow that? Let her bore anyone else she likes with her fine talk about how cosy life is, and the little restaurants with the most delicious country dishes. I'm not having any! Before I could toddle, I knew all there is to know about reducing. I was *born* among ageing beauties! All my life I've watched them, my painted pixies, squabbling about their wrinkles, and, well into their fifties, scratching each other's eyes out over some wretched gigolo!'

"You sit there saying nothing, and I'm not used to it any more. I keep on thinking that there's something you want to say to me."

On her feet, separated from Chéri by an occasional table with a decanter and port glasses, she made no effort to defend herself against the severe inspection to which she was being subjected; but from the almost invisible tremors that passed over her body, Chéri noted the muscular effort required to keep in her spreading stomach. 'How many times must she have put on her full-length corset again, left it off, then valiantly put it on again, before abandoning it for ever? . . . How often of a morning must she have varied the shades of her face powder, rubbed a new rouge on her cheeks, massaged her

neck with cold-cream and a small lump of ice tied up in a handkerchief, before becoming resigned to the varnished hide that now
shines on her cheeks!' Impatience alone, perhaps, had made her
tremble, yet this faint tremor led him to expect—so stubbornly blind
was he to reality—some miraculous new blossoming, some complete
metamorphosis.

"Why don't you say something?" Léa persisted.

Little by little she was losing her poise, though she was careful not
to move. She was playing with her rope of large pearls, knotting and
unknotting, round her big well-manicured and wrinkled fingers, their
luminous, indescribably bedewed and everlasting lustre.

'Perhaps it's simply because she's frightened of me,' Chéri mused.
'A man who says nothing must always seem a bit cranky. She's thinking of Valérie Cheniaguine's terrors. If I put my hand out, would
she scream for help? My poor Nounoune!' He lacked the courage to
pronounce this name out loud, and, to protect himself from even a
moment's sincerity, he spoke:

"What are you going to think of me?"

"It all depends," Léa answered guardedly. "At the moment you
remind me of people who bring along a little box of cakes and leave
it in the hall, saying to themselves: 'There'll be plenty of time to
produce these later,' and then pick them up again when they go."

Reassured by the sound of their voices, she had begun to reason
like the Léa of old, quick on the uptake, and as wily as a sharp-wit-
ted peasant. Chéri rose to his feet, walked round the table which separated him from Léa, and the daylight streaming through the pink
curtains struck him full in the face. This made it easy for her to com-
pute the passage of days and years from his features, which were all
of them in danger, though still intact. There was something about so
secret a falling away to tempt her pity and trouble her memory, and
perhaps extract from her the word or gesture that would precipitate
Chéri into a frenzy of humiliation. As he stood there, a sacrifice to
the light, with eyes lowered as if he were asleep, it seemed to him
this was his last chance of extorting from her one last affront, one
last prayer, one final act of homage.

Nothing happened, so he opened his eyes. Once more he had to
accept the true picture—in the shape of his stalwart old friend, who,
prudently keeping her distance, was bestowing on him a certain degree of benevolence from small and slightly suspicious blue eyes.

Disillusioned and bewildered, he looked all over the room for her,
except in the very spot where she stood. 'Where is she? Where is

she? This old woman is hiding her from me. She's bored by me, and she's waiting for me to go, thinking it all an infernal nuisance, these crowding memories and this returning ghost. . . . But if by any chance I did ask for her help, if I beg her to give me back Léa . . .' Deep inside him, his kneeling double was still palpitating, like a body from which the life-blood is being drained. With an effort of which he would never have deemed himself capable, Chéri tore himself away from this tortured image.

"I must be going," he said out loud, and he added on a note of rather cheap wit, "and I'm taking my box of cakes with me."

Léa's exuberant bosom heaved with a sigh of relief. "As you like, my child. But I'm always here, you know, if you're in any little trouble."

Though she seemed so obliging, Chéri could sense an underlying resentment. Within that vast edifice of flesh crowned with silvery thatch, femininity had for a moment reasserted itself in tones resounding with an intelligent harmony. But Chéri could not respond: like a ghost he had come, and with the shyness of a ghost he must vanish, in his own despite.

"Of course," Chéri replied, "and I thank you."

From that moment on, he knew, unerringly and spontaneously, exactly how to manage his exit. All the right words sprang to his lips, fluently, mechanically.

"You do understand, don't you, I came here to-day . . . why not sooner, you may ask? I know I ought to have come a long while ago. . . . But you will forgive me. . . ."

"Of course," Léa said.

"I'm even more hare-brained than before the war, you know, so that . . ."

"I understand, I understand."

And because of this interruption, he thought that she must be impatient to see the last of him. A few words were exchanged during Chéri's retreat, in the intervals of bumping into some piece of furniture, crossing a strip of sunshine from the courtyard window—after the pink light in the drawing-room it seemed by comparison almost blue—kissing a puffy hand bulging with rings when it was raised to his lips. Another of Léa's laughs, which broke off abruptly half way down its usual scale, just like a fountain when the jet is turned off and the crest of the plume, suddenly bereft of its stem, falls back to earth in a myriad separate pearls. . . . The staircase seemed to glide away under Chéri's feet like a bridge connecting two dreams, and

once more he was in the Rue Raynouard. Even the street was unfamiliar.

He noticed that the rosy tints of the sky were wonderfully
reflected in the rain-filled gutters and on the blue backs of the low-
skimming swallows. And now, because the evening was fresh, and because all the impressions he was bringing away with him were slipping back perfidiously into the recesses of his mind—there to assume
their final shape and intensity—he came to believe that he had forgotten all about them, and he felt happy.

ONLY the sound of an old woman's bronchial cough, as she sat over her glass of crème-de-menthe, disturbed the peace of the bar room where the murmur of the Place de l'Opéra died away, as though muffled in an atmosphere too thick to carry any eddies of sound. Chéri ordered a long drink and mopped his brow: this precaution was a carry-over from the days when he had been a little boy and sat listening to the babble of female voices, as, with Biblical gravity, they bandied such golden rules as: "If you want your milk of cucumber with real cucumber in it, you must make it yourself . . .", or "Never rub the perspiration into your face when you're overheated, or the perspiration will get under your skin and ruin it."

The silence, and the emptiness of the bar, created an illusion of coolness, and at first Chéri was not conscious of the couple who, with heads bent close together across a narrow table, were lost in inaudible whisperings. After a few moments his attention was drawn to this unknown man and woman by an occasional hissing sibilant which rose above the main stream of their chatter, and by the exaggerated expressions on their faces. They looked like servants, underpaid, overworked, and patient.

He took a mouthful or two of the fizzy iced drink, leaned his head back against the yellow plush of the banquette, and was delighted to feel a slackening of the mental strain which, for the last fortnight, had been sapping his strength. The dead weight of the present had not accompanied him across the threshold of the bar, which was old-fashioned, with red walls, gilt festoons, plaster roses, and a large open hearth. The cloakroom attendant could be half-seen in her tiled kingdom, counting every stitch as she mended the linen, her white hair bowed beneath a green lamp.

A passer-by dropped in. He did not trespass upon the yellow room, but took his drink standing at the bar as though to be discreet, and left without a word. The Odol odour of the crème-de-menthe was

the only thing distasteful to Chéri, and he frowned in the direction
of the dim old woman. Under a black and battered soft hat, he could
distinguish an old face, accentuated here and there by rouge, wrinkles, kohl, and puffiness—all jumbled together—rather like a pocket
into which have been popped, higgledy-piggledy, handkerchief, keys,
and loose change. A vulgar old face, in short—and commonplace in
its vulgarity, characterised, if at all, only by the indifference natural
to a savage or a prisoner. She coughed, opened her bag, blew her
nose vaguely, and replaced the seedy black reticule on the marble-
topped table. It had an affinity with the hat, for it was made of the
same black cracked taffeta, and equally out of fashion.

Chéri followed her every movement with an exaggerated repugnance; during the last two weeks he had been suffering, more than
he could reasonably be expected to bear, from everything that was at
once feminine and old. That reticule sprawling over the table almost
drove him from the spot. He wanted to avert his eyes, but did nothing of the sort: they were riveted by a small sparkling arabesque, an
unexpected brilliance fastened to the folds of the bag. His curiosity
surprised him, but half a minute later he was still staring at the point
of sparkling light, and his mind became an absolute blank. He was
roused from his trance by a subconscious flash of triumphant certainty, and this gave him back the freedom to think and breathe. 'I
know! It's the two capital L's interlaced!'

He enjoyed a moment of calm satisfaction, not unlike the sense of
security on reaching a journey's end. He actually forgot the cropped
hair on the nape of that neck, the vigorous grey locks, the big nondescript coat buttoned over a bulging stomach; he forgot the contralto
notes of the peal of youthful laughter—everything that had dogged
him so persistently for the past fortnight, that had deprived him of
any appetite for food, any ability to feel that he was alone.

'It's too good to last!' he thought. So, with a brave effort, he returned to reality. He looked more carefully at the offending object,
and was able to reel off: 'The two initials, set in little brilliants,
which Léa had designed first for her suède bag, then for her dressing-
table set of light tortoise-shell, and later for her writing-paper!' Not
for a moment would he admit that the monogram on the bag might
represent some other name.

He smiled ironically. 'Coincidence be blowed! I wasn't born yesterday! I came upon this bag by chance this evening, and to-morrow my
wife will go and engage one of Léa's old footmen—again by chance.
After that I shan't be able to go into a single restaurant, cinema, or

tobacconist's without running up against Léa at every turn. It's my own fault. I can't complain. I ought to have left her alone.'

He put some small change beside his glass, and got up before summoning the barman. He faced away from the old woman as he slipped between the two tables, holding himself in under his waistcoat, like a tomcat squeezing under a gate. This he managed so adroitly that the edge of his coat only just brushed against the glass of green crème-de-menthe. Murmuring an apology, he made a dash for the glass door, to escape into the fresh air beyond. Horrified, but not really in the least surprised, he heard a voice call out after him, "Chéri!"

He had feared—known indeed—that this was coming. He turned to find that there was nothing about the raddled old ruin to help him recall her name; but he made no second attempt to escape, realising that everything would be explained.

"Don't you recognise me? You don't? But how could you? More women were aged by the war than men were killed by it and that's a fact. All the same, it's not for me to complain; I didn't risk losing anyone in the war. . . . Eh! Chéri! . . ."

She laughed; and recognition was complete, for he saw that what he had taken for decrepitude was only poverty and natural indifference. Now that she was holding herself upright and laughing, she did not look more than her age—sixty or thereabouts—and the hand with which she sought Chéri's was certainly not that of a doddering old grandmother.

"The Pal!" Chéri murmured, almost in tones of admiration.

"Are you really pleased to see me?"

"Oh, yes. . . ."

He was not telling a lie. He was gaining assurance step by step and thinking, 'It's only her . . . Poor Old Pal . . . I'd begun to fear . . .'

"Will you have a glass of something, Pal?"

"Just a whisky and soda, my pretty. My! haven't you kept your looks!"

He swallowed the bitter compliment which she tossed to him from the peaceful fringes of old age.

"And decorated, too," she added out of pure politeness. "Oh! I knew all about it, you may be sure! We all knew about it."

The ambiguous plural failed to wrest a smile from Chéri, and the Pal thought she had shocked him.

"When I say 'we', I'm speaking of those of us who were your real friends—Camille de La Berche, Léa, Rita, and me. You may be sure Charlotte would never have told me a word about it. As far as she's concerned, I don't exist. But—and I may as well say so—she doesn't exist for me, either." She stretched out across the table a pale hand that had long forgotten the light of day. "You must understand that Charlotte will never again be anything to me but the woman who contrived to get poor little Rita arrested and detained for twenty-four hours. . . . Poor Rita, who had never known a word of German. Was it Rita's fault, I ask you, if she happened to be Swiss?"

"I know, I know. I know the whole story," Chéri broke in precipitately.

The Pal raised her huge dark watery eyes towards him, full of inveterate complicity and a compassion that was always misplaced. "Poor kid," she sighed. "I understand you. Forgive me. Ah! you've certainly had your cross to bear!"

He questioned her with a look, no longer accustomed to the overstatements that added a rich funereal tone to the Pal's vocabulary, and he feared she might be going to talk to him about the war. But she was not thinking of the war. Perhaps she never had, for it is the concern of two generations only.

She went on to explain. "Yes, I was saying that to have such a mother must have been a heavy cross to bear for a son like you—for a boy, that's to say, with a blameless life, both before marriage and after! A nice, quiet boy and all that; not one to sow his wild oats all over the place, or to squander his inheritance."

She wagged her head, and bit by bit he began to piece together the past. He rediscovered her, though she had the mask of a ravaged tragedy queen. Her old age was without nobility, yet bore no signs of illness, no tell-tale trace that betrayed her addiction to opium. The drug is merciful to those unworthy of it.

"Have you quite given up the pipe?" asked Chéri sharply.

She raised a white untended hand. "What do you suppose? That kind of foolishness is all very well when you're not all on your own. In the days when I used to shock you young men, yes. . . . You remember when you used to come back at nights? Ah! you were very fond of that. . . . 'Dear old Pal,' you used to say to me, 'just let me have another little pipeful, and pack it well!' "

Without turning a hair, he accepted this humble flattery, as he might from an old retainer, who fibs in order to fawn. He smiled knowingly, and scrutinised the folds of black tulle round her neck, looking in the shadows under the faded hat for a necklace of large fake pearls.

Almost mechanically and sip by sip, he drank the whisky which had been put in front of him by mistake. He did not care for spirits as a rule, but this evening he enjoyed the whisky, for it helped him to smile easily and softened to his touch unpolished surfaces and rough materials; it enabled him to listen kindly to an old woman for whom the present did not exist. They met again on the further side of the superfluous war-years and the young, importunate dead: the Pal spanned the gap by throwing across to Chéri a bridge of names—names of old men who bore charmed lives, of old women revitalised for the struggle or turned to stone in their ultimate shape, never to alter again. She recounted in detail a hard-luck story of 1913, some unhappiness that had taken place before August, 1914, and something trembled in her voice when she spoke of La Loupiote —a woman now dead—"The very week of your wedding, dear boy! you see what a coincidence it was? the hand of Fate was upon us, indeed"—dead after four years of a pure and peaceful friendship.

"We slanged each other day in, day out, dear boy, but only in front of other people. Because, don't you see, it gave them the impression that we were 'a couple'. Who would have believed it, if we hadn't gone for each other hammer and tongs? So we called each other the most diabolical names, and the onlookers chuckled: 'Have you ever seen such a devoted pair?' Dear boy, I'll tell you something else that will knock you flat—surely you must have heard about the will Massau was supposed to have made. . . ."

"What Massau?" Chéri asked, languidly.

"Oh, come. You knew him as well as you know yourself! The story of the will—so called—that he handed to Louise MacMillar. It was in 1909, and at the time I am speaking of, I was one of the Gérault pack, his pack of 'faithful hounds'—and there were five of us he fed every evening at *La Belle Meunière* down at Nice; but on the Promenade des Anglais, you must remember, we only had eyes for you— dolled up in white like an English baby, and Léa all in white as well. . . . Ah! what a pair you made! You were the sensation—a miracle, straight from the hands of the Creator! Gérault used to tease Léa: 'You're far too *young*, girlie, and what's worse you're too proud. I shan't take you on for fifteen or twenty years at least. . . .' And to think that such a man had to be taken from us! Not a tear at his funeral that wasn't genuine, the whole nation was in mourning. And now let me get on with the story of the will. . . ."

Chéri was deluged with a perfect flood of incidents, a tide of bygone regrets and harmless resurrections, all declaimed with the ease and rapidity of a professional mourner. The two of them formed a symmetrical pattern as they leaned towards each other. The Pal lowered her voice when she came to the dramatic passages, giving out a sudden laugh or exclamation; and he saw in one of the looking-glasses how closely they seemed to resemble the whispering couple whose place they had taken. He got up, finding it imperative to put an end to this resemblance. The barman imitated his movement, but from afar, like a discreet dog when its master comes to the end of a visit. "Ah! well . . . yes . . ." said the Pal, "well, I'll finish the rest another time."

"After the next war," said Chéri, jokingly. "Tell me, those two capital letters. . . . Yes, the monogram in little brilliants. . . . It's not yours, Pal?"

He pointed at the black bag with the tip of his forefinger, extending it slowly while withdrawing his body, as though the bag were alive.

"Nothing escapes you," the Pal said in admiration. "You're quite right. She gave it to me, of course. She said to me: 'Such bits of finery are far too frivolous for me nowadays!' She said: 'What the devil do you suppose I'd be doing with those mirrors and powder and things, when I've a great face like a country policeman's?' She made me laugh. . . ."

To stem the flood, Chéri pushed the change from his hundred-franc note towards the Pal. "For your taxi, Pal."

They went out on to the pavement by the tradesman's entrance, and Chéri saw from the fainter lamp-light that night was coming on.

"Have you not got your motor?"

"My motor? No. I walked; it does me good."

"Is your wife in the country?"

"No. Her Hospital keeps her in Paris."

The Pal nodded her invertebrate hat. "I know. She's a big-hearted woman. Her name's been put forward for a decoration, I understand from the Baroness."

"What?"

"Here, stop that taxi for me, dear boy, the closed one. . . . And Charlotte's going big guns in her support; she knows people round Clemenceau. It will make up a little for the story about Rita . . . a little, not very much. She's as black as Sin itself, is Charlotte, my boy."

He pushed her into the oven of the taxi, where she sank back and became enveloped in the shadow. She ceased to exist. It was as though he had never met her, now that he heard her voice no longer. He took stock of the night, filling his lungs with the dust-laden air that foretold another scorching day. He pictured, as in a dream, that he would wake up at home, among gardens watered every evening, among the scent of Spanish honeysuckle and the call of birds, resting alongside his wife's straight hips. . . . But the Pal's voice rose up from the depths of the taxi: "Two hundred and fourteen, Avenue de Villiers! Remember my address, Chéri! And you know that I often dine at the *Giraffe*, Avenue de Wagram, don't you, if ever you should want me. . . . You know, if ever you should be looking for me."

'That's really the limit,' thought Chéri, lengthening his step. ' "If I should ever be looking for her." I ask you! Next time I come across her, I'll turn round and walk the other way.'

Cooled off and calmer, he strode without effort along the *quais* as far as the Place de l'Alma, and from there took a taxi back to the Avenue Henri-Martin. The eastern sky was already burnished with dull copper-coloured tints, which seemed rather to betoken the setting of some planet than the dawn of a summer day. No clouds streaked the vault of the heavens, but a haze of particles hung heavy and motionless over Paris, and would presently flare up and smoulder with the sombre glow of red-hot metal. As dawn breaks, the dog-days drain great cities and their suburbs of the moist pinks, floral mauves and dewy blues that suffuse the sky above open country where plant life flourishes in profusion.

Nothing was stirring in the house when Chéri came to turn the tiny key in the lock. The flagged hall still smelt of the previous evening's dinner, and the cut branches of syringa, arranged by the armful in white vases tall enough to hide a man, filled the air with unbreathable poison. A stray grey cat slipped past him, stopped dead in the middle of the passage, and coldly inspected the intruder.

"Come here, little clerk of the Courts," Chéri called in a low voice. The cat glared at him almost insultingly and did not budge. Chéri remembered that no animal—no dog, horse or cat—had ever shown him any signs of affection. He could hear, across a span of fifteen years, Aldonza's raucous voice prophesying: 'A curse lies on those from whom animals turn away.' But when the cat, now wide awake, began to play with a small green chestnut, bowling it along with its front paw, Chéri smiled and went on up to his room.

He found it as dark and blue as a stage night. The dawn penetrated no further than the balcony, bedecked with well trained roses and pelargoniums fastened with raffia. Edmée was asleep, her bare arms and toes peeping out from under a light blanket. She was lying on her side, her head inclined, one finger hooked through her pearls. In the half-light she seemed to be immersed in thought rather than sleep. Her wavy hair strayed over her cheek, and Chéri could hear no sound of her breathing.

'She's enjoying a peaceful sleep,' thought Chéri. 'She's dreaming of Doctor Arnaud, or the Legion of Honour, or Royal Dutch shares. She's pretty. How pretty she is! . . . "Don't you worry, only another two or three hours, and you'll go to find your Doctor Arnaud. That's not so bad, is it? You'll meet again in the Avenue de l'Italie, in your beloved joint with its stink of carbolic. You'll answer 'Yes, Doctor; No, Doctor,' like a good little girl. You'll both of you put on really serious expressions; you'll jiggle with thermometers—ninety-nine point six, a hundred and two point four—and he'll take your small carbolicky paw in his great coal-tarry mitt. You're lucky, my girl, to have a romance in your life! Don't worry. I shan't deprive you of it. . . ." I wouldn't mind, myself. . . .'

All of a sudden Edmée woke up with such a start that Chéri caught his breath, as though rudely interrupted in the middle of a sentence.

"It's you! It's you! Why, it *is* you after all."

"If you were expecting someone else, I offer my apologies," said Chéri, smiling at her.

"That's very clever. . . ." She sat up in bed and tossed back her hair. "What time is it? Are you getting up? Oh no, I see you've not been to bed yet. . . . You've just come in. . . . Oh, Fred! What have you been up to this time?"

"'This time' is a compliment. . . . If you only knew what I've been doing. . . ."

She was no longer at the stage where, hands over her ears, she besought him, "No, no! say nothing! Don't tell me!" But, faster than his wife, Chéri was leaving behind that childishly malicious period when, amidst floods of tears and stormy scenes which ended by her throwing herself into his arms in the early hours of the morning, he would draw her down with him into the deep sleep of reconciled antagonists. No more little games of that sort. . . . No more betrayals. . . . Nothing, now, but this enforced and unavowable chastity.

He chucked his dusty shoes to the other end of the room, and sat down on the soft lace-frilled sheets, offering his wife a pallid face accustomed to dissemble everything except his will to dissemble. "Smell me!" he said. "Come on! I've been drinking whisky."

She brought her charming mouth to his, putting a hand on her husband's shoulder. "Whisky . . ." she repeated wonderingly. "Whisky . . . why?"

A less sophisticated woman would have asked "With whom?" and her cunning did not pass unnoticed. Chéri showed that two could play at that game by answering, "With an old pal. Do you want to hear the whole truth?"

She smiled, now caught in the dawning light which, with growing boldness, touched the edge of the bed, the looking-glass, a picture-frame, and then the golden scales of a fish swimming round and round in a crystal bowl.

"No, Fred, not the whole truth. Only a half-veiled truth, suitable for the small hours." At the same time, her thoughts were busy. She was certain—or nearly so—that Chéri had not been drawn away from her either by love or by lust. She let her acquiescent body fall helplessly into his arms, yet he felt on his shoulder a thin, hard hand, unrelaxed in its guarded prudence.

"The truth is," he went on, "that I don't know her name. But I gave her . . . wait a moment . . . I gave her eighty-three francs."

"Just like that, all at once! The first time you met her? It's princely!"

She pretended to yawn, and slipped softly back into the depths of the bed, as though not expecting an answer. He gave her a moment's pity; then a brilliant horizontal ray brought into sharper relief the almost naked body lying beside him, and his pity vanished.

'She's . . . she has kept her good looks. It's not fair.'

She lay back, her lips parted, looking at him through half-closed eyes. He saw a gleam of the candid, calculating, uncharacteristically feminine expression that a woman bestows on the man who is going to pleasure her, and it shocked his unavowable chastity. From his superior position he returned this look with another—the uncommunicative, enigmatic look of the man who prefers to abstain. Not wishing to move away, he simply looked towards the golden daylight, the freshness of the watered garden, and the blackbirds, weaving liquid sequences of sound round the dry incessant chirps of the sparrows. Edmée could see signs of emaciation and prolonged fatigue on his features. His cheeks were blue with a day's growth of beard. She

noticed that his fine hands were not clean, that his finger-nails had
not been near soap and water since the previous evening, and that
the dark lines which accentuated the hollows under his eyes were
now spreading, in the shape of crow's feet, towards his nose. This
handsome young man—she decided—without collar or shoes, looked
ravaged, as if he had had to spend a night in prison. Without losing
his looks, he had shrunk in accordance with some mysterious scaling
down, and this enabled her to regain the upper hand. She no longer
invited him to join her, sat up in bed, and put a hand on his forehead.

"Ill?"

Slowly he let his attention wander back from the garden to his
wife.

"What? . . . No, no, nothing's wrong with me, except I'm sleepy.
So sleepy that I can hardly bring myself to go to bed—if you know
what I mean. . . ."

He smiled, showing dry gums and lips colourless on the insides.
But, above all, this smile betrayed a sadness that sought no remedy,
modest as a poor man's suffering. Edmée was on the point of questioning him categorically, but then thought better of it.

"Get into bed," she ordered, making room for him.

"Bed? It's water I need. I feel so filthy, I can't tell you."

He just had the strength to lift up a water bottle, take a gulp from
the neck, then throw off his coat, before he fell back like a log on the
bed, and lay there without moving again, drained by sleep.

For some little time Edmée gazed at the half-stripped stranger
lying like a drugged man beside her. Her watchful eye wandered
from bluish lips to hollowed eyes, from outflung hand to forehead
sealed upon a single secret. She summoned her self-control and composed her features, as though afraid the sleeper might take her by
surprise. She got out of bed softly, and, before shutting out the dazzling sunlight, drew a silk counterpane to hide the outstretched untidy body looking like a burglar who had been knocked out. She arranged this so as to give the beautiful rigid features their full
splendour, carefully pulling it down over the drooping hand with a
slight qualm of pious disgust, as though hiding a weapon that perhaps had killed.

He never twitched a muscle—having retired for a few moments
within an impregnable fastness. In any case, Edmée's hospital training had given her fingers a professional touch, which, if not exactly
gentle, was competent to go straight to the required spot without

touching or in any way affecting the surrounding area. She did not get back into bed; but, sitting half-naked, enjoyed the unexpected freshness of the hour when the sun rouses the winds. The long curtains stirred, as if breathing and, dependent on the breeze, stippled Chéri's sleep with fitful flecks of dark blue.

As she gazed at him, Edmée was not thinking of the wounded, or of the dead, whose peasant hands she had joined together upon coarse cotton sheets. No invalid in the grip of a nightmare, not one among the dead, had ever resembled Chéri: sleep, silence, and repose made him magnificently inhuman.

Extreme beauty arouses no sympathy. It is not the prerogative of any one country. Time's finger had touched Chéri only to make him more austere. The mind—whose task it is to curb the splendour of mankind while degrading it piecemeal—respected Chéri as an admirable temple dedicated to instinct. What could avail the Machiavellian deceit, the ardour and the cunning self-sacrifice imposed by love, against this inviolable standard-bearer of light and his untutored majesty?

Patient and, on occasion, subtle as she was, it never occurred to Edmée that the feminine appetite for possession tends to emasculate every living conquest, and can reduce a magnificent but inferior male to the status of a courtesan. Her lower-middle-class wisdom made her determined not to relinquish the gains—money, ease, domestic tyranny, marriage—acquired in so few years and rendered doubly attractive by the war.

She gazed at the limp, worn-out, almost empty-looking body. 'That's Chéri,' she said to herself; 'yes, that's Chéri all right . . . That's how small a thing he is!' She shrugged a shoulder and added: 'That's what he's reduced to, this wonderful Chéri of theirs . . .' doing her best to induce contempt for the man lying thus supine. She called up memories of rapturous nights, of languid early mornings bathed in sunlight and pleasure, and, as a result—since he had progressively grown to disdain her—she saw fit to pay but coldly vindictive homage to this body so sumptuously laid out under the pall of flowered silk and the refreshing wing of the curtains. She put one hand on the small, pointed breast set low on her slender body, and squeezed it like a pulpy fruit, as if calling this most tempting allurement of her young body to witness the injustice of his desertion. 'What Chéri himself needs is doubtless something else. What he needs is . . .'

But vain were her attempts to put her scorn into words. Even a woman loses the desire and the ability to despise a man who suffers in silence and alone.

All of a sudden, Edmée felt satiated with the spectacle: the shadows thrown by the curtains, the pallor of the sleeper, and the white bed helped to invest it with the romantic colouring of death and the nether world. She jumped to her feet, strong and ready to face this world, but determined to avoid any emotional attack upon the traitor lying on the disordered bed, the absentee seeking refuge in sleep, silent, ailing and repulsive. She was neither irritated nor unhappy. Her heart would beat more feverishly in her breast, the blood mount more quickly to her pearl-pale cheeks, only at the thought of the healthy red-haired man whom she called "dear master" or "chief" in tones of serious playfulness. Arnaud's thick gentle hands; his laugh; the points of light that sunshine or the lamp in the operating-theatre caused to twinkle on his red moustache; his very coat—the white surgery-coat he wore and even took off in the hospital, just like an intimate garment that never passes beyond the bedroom door. . . . Edmée sprang up as though for a dance.

'That, oh yes, *that's* my life!' She gave a toss of the head that sent her hair flying out like a horse's mane, and went into the bathroom without turning round.

UNIMAGINATIVE in style, and in its very ordinary proportions, the dining-room made no pretence to luxury except in the panels of yellow stuff starred with purple and green. The grey and white stucco of the surrounding walls deflected too much light on the guests, deprived already of all shade by the merciless glare of the top lighting.

A galaxy of crystal sequins shimmered with every movement of Edmée's dress. For the family dinner, Madame Peloux was still wearing her tailor-made with leather buttons, and Camille de La Berche her nurse's veil, under the cowl of which she bore a striking resemblance to Dante, only far hairier. Because it was so hot, the women spoke little: so did Chéri, because it was his habit. A warm bath followed by a cold shower had triumphed over his fatigue; but the powerful light, ricocheting upon his cheeks, accentuated their cavities, and he kept his eyes lowered, to allow the shadow from his eyebrows to fall directly over the lids.

"To-night, Chéri doesn't look a day over sixteen," boomed the deep bass of the Baroness out of the blue.

No one took up her remark, and Chéri acknowledged it with a slight bow.

"Not for a long time," the Baroness continued, "have I seen the oval of his face so slender."

Edmée frowned imperceptibly. "I have. During the war, of course."

"That's true, that's true," piped Charlotte Peloux in shrill agreement. "Heavens! how worn out he looked in 1916, at Vésoul! Edmée, my dear child," she went on in the same breath, "I've seen you-know-who to-day, and *everything* is going along very nicely. . . ."

Edmée blushed in a docile, unbecoming manner, and Chéri raised his eyes. "You've seen who? And what's going along nicely?"

"Trousellier's pension—my little soldier who's had his right arm off. He left the Hospital on June the twentieth. Your mother's taking up his case at the War Office."

She had not hesitated for words, and she let her calm golden gaze rest on Chéri: yet he knew she was lying.

"It's a question of whether he'll get his red riband. After all, poor boy, it's certainly his turn. . . ."

She was lying to him in front of two friends who knew that she was lying. 'Why don't I pick up the water-bottle and crash it down in the middle of them?' But he made no movement. What strength of feeling would have given him the impetus to brace his body and direct his hand?

"Abzac is leaving us in a week's time," began Madame de La Berche.

"That's not certain," Edmée took her up with an air of knowing better. "Doctor Arnaud isn't at all satisfied that he should be allowed to go off like that on his new leg. You can just see the man, liable to do any sort of silly thing, and always with the possibility of gangrene. Doctor Arnaud knows only too well that it was exactly that sort of thing, all through the war. . . ."

Chéri looked at her, and she stopped abruptly in the middle of her pointless sentence. She was fanning herself with a rose on a leafy stalk. She waved away a dish which she was offered, and put her elbows on the table. In her white dress and bare shoulders, even when sitting still, she was not exempt from a secret contentment, a self-satisfaction, which revealed her true nature. Something outrageous radiated from her soft outlines. Some tell-tale glow betrayed the woman bent on "arriving", who up till the present had met only with success.

'Edmée,' Chéri concluded, 'is a woman who should never grow older than twenty. How like her mother she's getting!'

The next moment the resemblance had vanished. Nothing obvious about Edmée recalled Marie-Laure: only in one respect did her daughter exhibit something of the poisonous, pink and white, impudent beauty exploited by the red-haired Marie-Laure to ensnare her victims during her palmy days—and that was in her shamelessness. Careful as she was not to shock anyone, those who still retained their native shrewdness, by instinct or from lack of education, were shocked by her all the same, as if by a second-rate racehorse, or a jewel that looked too new. The servants, as well as Chéri, were frightened of something in Edmée, whom they guessed to be more vulgar than themselves.

Authorised by Edmée, who was lighting a cigarette, the Baroness de La Berche slowly grilled the tip of her cigar before inhaling the first rapturous puff. Her white Red Cross veil fell over her manly shoulders and she looked like one of those grave-faced men who, at Christmas parties, adorn their heads with tissue paper Phrygian caps, programme-sellers' kerchiefs, or shakos. Charlotte undid the plaited leather buttons of her jacket and drew towards her a box of Abdullas; while the butler, mindful of the customs of the house, pushed within easy reach of Chéri a small conjuror's table on wheels—full of secret drawers, sliding double-bottomed compartments, and liqueurs in silver phials. Then he left the room; and there was no longer against the yellow panels the tall silhouette of an elderly Italian with a face carved out of box-wood, and crowned with white hair.

"Old Giacomo really does look an aristocrat," said the Baroness de La Berche, "and I know what I'm talking about."

Madame Peloux shrugged her shoulders, a movement that had long since ceased to lift her breasts. Her white silk blouse with a jabot sagged under the weight of her bosom, and her short, dyed, but still abundant hair glowed a livid red above large disastrous eyes and high forehead, suggesting a leader of the French Revolution.

"He's got the distinguished looks of all elderly Italians with white hair. They're all Papal Chamberlains, by the look of them, and they can write out the menu for you in Latin; but you've only to open a door and you'll find them raping a little girl of seven."

Chéri welcomed this outburst of virulence as a timely shower. His mother's malice had parted the clouds again, bringing back an atmosphere in which he could breathe. Not so long ago he had begun to enjoy discovering traces of the old Charlotte, who, from the safety of her balcony, would refer to a pretty woman passing below as "a tuppenny-ha'penny tart," and who, to Chéri's "Do you know her, then?" would reply, "No! Whatever next! Do you expect me to know that slut?" Only recently had he begun to take a confused pleasure in Charlotte's superior vitality, and, confusedly, he now preferred her to the other two creatures present; but he was unaware that this preference, this partiality, could perhaps be termed filial affection. He laughed, and applauded Madame Peloux for still being —and quite startlingly so—the woman he had known, detested, feared, and insulted. For an instant, Madame Peloux took on her authentic character in her son's eyes; that is to say, he estimated her at her proper value, a woman high-spirited, all-consuming, calculating and at the same time rash, like a high financier; a woman capable of taking a humorist's delight in spiteful cruelty. "She's a scourge, certainly," he said to himself, "and no more. A scourge, but not a stranger." Looking at the way the points of her hair impinged upon her Jacobin forehead, he recognised a similarity to the blue-black jutting points on his own forehead, which emphasised the whiteness of his skin and the blackbird sheen of his hair.

'She's my mother all right,' he thought. 'No one's ever told me I'm like her, but I am.' The "stranger" was sitting opposite, glimmering with the milky, veiled brilliance of a pearl. Chéri heard the name of the Duchess of Camastra thrown out by the deep voice of the Baroness, and on the stranger's face he saw a fleeting rapacity flicker and die, like the serpent of flame that suddenly flares up along a burnt vine-twig before it is consumed among the embers. But she did not open her mouth, and took no part in the volley of military curses which the Baroness was firing at a hospital-rival.

"They're properly in the soup, it appears, over some new-fangled injection or other. Two men died within two days of being given the needle. That needs some explaining!" said Madame de La Berche with a hearty laugh.

"You've got it wrong," corrected Edmée dryly. "That's an old story of Janson-de-Sailly resuscitated."

"No smoke without fire," sighed Charlotte charitably. "Chéri, are you sleepy?"

He was dropping with fatigue, but he admired the powers of resistance of these three women: neither hard work, the Parisian summer, nor perpetual movement and jabber could put them out of action.

"The heat," he murmured laconically. He caught Edmée's eye, but she made no comment and refrained from contradicting him.

"Pooh, pooh, pooh," chanted Charlotte. "The heat! But, of course. . . . Pooh, pooh, pooh."

Her eyes, which remained fixed on Chéri's, overflowed with blackmailing tenderness and complicity. As usual, she knew everything there was to be known: back-stairs gossip, concierges' chatter. Perhaps Léa herself, for the pleasure of a feminine fib, of winning one last trick, had told Charlotte. The Baroness de La Berche emitted a little neigh, and the shadow of her large clerical nose covered the lower part of her face.

"God in Heaven!" swore Chéri.

His chair fell to the floor behind him, and Edmée, alert and on the watch, promptly jumped to her feet. She showed not the slightest astonishment. Charlotte Peloux and the Baroness de La

Berche at once put themselves on the defensive, but in the old-fashioned way—hands clutching skirts, ready to gather them up and fly. Chéri, leaning forward with his fists on the table, was panting and turning his head to right and left, like a wild animal caught in a net.

"You, to start with, you . . ." he stammered. He pointed at Charlotte; used as she was to such scenes, she was galvanised by this filial threat in the presence of witnesses.

"What? What? What?" she barked in sharp little yelps. "You dare to insult me? a little whippersnapper like you, a wretched little whippersnapper who, were I to open my mouth . . ."

The wine-glasses quivered at the sound of her piercing voice, but her words were cut short by a shriller voice: "Leave him alone!"

After three such abrupt explosions the silence seemed deafening, and Chéri, his physical dignity restored, shook himself, and a smile spread over his green face.

"I beg your pardon, Madame Peloux," he said mischievously.

She was already conferring blessings on him with eye and hand, like a champion in the ring, pacified at the end of a round.

"You're hot-blooded and no mistake!"

"He's a soldier all right," said the Baroness, as she shook hands with Edmée. "I must say goodbye, Chéri; they'll be missing me in my dug-out."

She refused a lift in Charlotte's motor, and insisted on going home on foot. The tall figure, the white nurse's veil, and the glow of her cigar would strike terror at night into the heart of the fiercest footpad. Edmée accompanied the two old women as far as the front door, an exceptional act of courtesy, which allowed Chéri time to draw what conclusions he could from his wife's wary action and her diplomatic peacemaking.

He drank a glass of cold water very slowly, as he stood beneath the cataract of light, thinking the matter over and savouring his terrible loneliness.

'She defended me,' he kept repeating to himself. 'She defended me with no love in her heart. She protected me as she protects the garden against blackbirds, her store of sugar against thieving nurses, or her cellar against the footmen. Little doubt she knows that I went to the Rue Reynouard, and came back here, never to go there again. She's not said a word about it to me, in any case—perhaps because she doesn't care. She protected me, because it wouldn't have done for my mother to talk. She defended me with no love in her heart.'

He heard Edmée's voice in the garden. She was testing his mood from afar. "You don't feel ill, Fred, do you? Would you like to go straight to bed?"

She put her head through the half-open door, and he laughed bitterly to himself: 'How cautious she's being.'

She saw his smile and grew bolder. "Come along, Fred. I believe I'm just as tired as you, or I wouldn't have let myself go just now. I've been apologising to your mother."

She switched off some of the cruel light, and gathered the roses from the table-cloth to put them into water. Her body, her hands, her head bending over the roses and set off by a haze of fair hair from which the heat had taken most of the crimp—everything about her might have charmed a man.

"I said *a man*—I didn't say *any man*," Léa's insidious voice kept ringing in Chéri's ears.

'I can behave as I like to her,' he thought, as he followed Edmée with his eyes. 'She'll never complain, she'll never divorce me; I've nothing to fear from her, not even love. I should be happy enough, if I chose.'

But, at the same time, he recoiled with unspeakable repugnance from the idea of the two of them living together in a home where love no longer held sway. His childhood as a bastard, his long adolescence as a ward, had taught him that his world, though people thought of it as reckless, was governed by a code almost as narrow-minded as middle-class prejudice. In it, Chéri had learned that love is a question of money, infidelity, betrayals, and cowardly resignation. But now he was well on the way to forgetting the rules he had been taught, and to be repelled by acts of silent condescension.

He therefore ignored the gentle hand on his sleeve. And, as he walked with Edmée towards the room whence would issue no sound of endearment or reproach, he was overcome with shame, and blushed at the horror of their unspoken agreement.

He found himself out of doors, dressed for the street and hardly conscious of having put on his soft hat and light raincoat. Behind him
lay the drawing-room, misty with tobacco smoke; the overpowering
scent of women and flowers; the cyanide smell of cherry brandy.
There he had left Edmée, Doctor Arnaud, Filipesco, Atkins, and the
two Kelekian girls, well-connected young women who, having done a
little mild lorry-driving during the war, had no use now for anything
but cigars, motors, and their garage-hand friends. He had left Desmond sitting between a real estate merchant and an Under-Secretary
in the Ministry of Commerce, together with an invalided poet and
Charlotte Peloux. Also a fashionable young married couple, who had
obviously been put wise. Throughout dinner they had looked greedy
but prudish, with a knowing expression and a simple-minded
eagerness to be shocked—as though expecting Chéri to dance stark
naked, or Charlotte and the Under-Secretary to make violent love to
one another in the middle of the carpet.

Chéri had made off, aware that his behaviour had been stoical,
with no other lapse than a sudden loss of interest in the present: an
awkward thing to lose in the middle of a meal. Even so, his trance
could have lasted little more than a moment, had been instan-
taneous, like a dream. But now he was putting a distance between
himself and the strangers who thronged his house, and the sound of
his footfall on the sand was as light as the soft padding of an animal.
His light silver-grey coat shaded into the mist that had fallen over
the Bois; and a few nocturnal loiterers must have envied a young
man who was in such a hurry to go nowhere in particular.

He was haunted by the vision of his crowded house. He could still
hear the sound of voices, and carried with him the memory of faces,
of smiles, and especially of the shape of mouths. An elderly man had
talked about the war; a woman about politics. He remembered, too,
the new understanding between Desmond and Edmée, and the in-

terest his wife had taken in some building scheme. 'Desmond! . . .
Just the husband for my wife!' And then, dancing . . . the strange
effect of the tango on Charlotte Peloux. Chéri quickened his step.

The night was filled with the damp mist of a too early autumn
and the full moon was shrouded. A great milky halo, ringed with a
pallid iridescence, had replaced the planet, and was sometimes itself
hidden by fitful puffs of scudding cloud. The smell of September was
already in the leaves that had fallen during the dog days.

'How mild it is,' Chéri thought.

He rested his weary limbs on a bench, but not for long. He was
rejoined by an invisible companion, to whom he refused his seat on
the bench—a woman with grey hair, wearing a long coat, who
poured forth a relentless gaiety. Chéri turned his head towards the
gardens of La Muette, as though he could hear, even at that distance, the cymbals of the jazz-band.

The time had not yet come for him to go back to the blue room,
where perhaps the two society girls were still smoking good cigars, as
they sat side-saddle on the blue velvet of the bed, keeping the real estate merchant amused with mess-room tales.

'Oh! for a nice hotel bedroom, a jolly pink room, very ordinary
and very pink . . .' But would it not lose its very ordinariness the
moment the light was turned out and total darkness gave the right of
entry—a ponderous, mocking entry—to a figure with vigorous grey
hair, dressed in a long, nondescript coat? He smiled at the intruder,
for he was past the stage of fear. 'There, or in any other place, *she*
will be just as faithful. But I simply can't go on living with those
people.'

Day by day, hour by hour, he was becoming more scornful, more
exacting. Already he was severely critical of the Agony Column he-
roes, and young war widows who clamoured for new husbands, like
the parched for cold water. His uncompromising intolerance extended to the world of finance, without his realising how grave was
the change. 'That Company for transporting raw hides they talked
about at dinner. . . . How disgusting it was! And they don't mind
discussing it at the top of their voices. . . .' But nothing in the
world would have induced him to protest, to reveal that he was fast
becoming a man utterly out of sympathy with his surroundings. Prudently, he kept quiet about that, as about everything else. When he
had taken Charlotte Peloux to task for having disposed of several
tons of sugar in rather a dubious fashion, had she not reminded him
—and in no uncertain terms—of the time when he had shouted,

without a trace of embarrassment, "Hand over five louis, Léa, so that I can go and buy some cigarettes"?

'Ah!' he sighed, 'they'll never understand anything, these women. It wasn't at all the same thing.'

Thus he let his thoughts run on, as he stood, bareheaded, his hair glistening, barely distinguishable in the mist. The shadowy form of a female passed close beside him, running. The rhythm of her steps and the crunch as each foot bit into the gravel betrayed anxiety and haste. Then the shadowy woman fell into the arms of a shadowy man who came to meet her, and down they fell together, breast to breast, as though struck by the same bullet.

'Those two are trying to hide,' Chéri thought. 'They're deceiving someone somewhere. The whole world's busy deceiving and being deceived. But I . . .' He did not finish the sentence, but a repugnance made him jump to his feet, an action that meant, 'But I am chaste.' A faint ray of light, flickering uncertainly over stagnant, hitherto unfeeling regions of his inmost being, was enough to suggest that chastity and loneliness are one and the same misfortune.

As night advanced, he began to feel the cold. From his prolonged, aimless vigils, he had learned that, at night, tastes, smells, and temperatures vary according to the hour, and that midnight is warm in comparison with the hour which immediately precedes the dawn.

'The winter will soon be on us,' he thought, as he lengthened his stride, 'and none too soon, putting an end to this interminable summer. Next winter, I should like . . . let me see . . . next winter . . .' His attempts at anticipation collapsed almost at once; and he came to a halt, head lowered, like a horse at the prospect of a long steep climb ahead.

'Next winter, there'll still be my wife, my mother, old gammer La Berche, Thingummy, What's-his-name, and the rest of them. There'll be the same old gang. . . . And for me there'll never again be . . .'

He paused once more, to watch a procession of low clouds advancing over the Bois, clouds of an indescribable pink, set upon by a gusty wind which buried its fingers in their misty tresses, twisting and dragging them across the lawns of heaven, to carry them off to the moon. Chéri gazed with eyes well used to the translucent magic of the night, which those who sleep regard as pitch-dark.

The apparition of the large, flat, half-veiled moon among the scurrying vaporous clouds, which she seemed to be pursuing and tearing asunder, did not divert him from working out an arithmetical fantasy: he was computing—in years, months, hours and days—the amount of precious time that had been lost to him for ever.

'Had I never let her go when I went to see her again that day before the war—then it would have meant three or four years to the good; hundreds and hundreds of days and nights gained and garnered for love.' He did not fight shy of so big a word.

'Hundreds of days—a lifetime—life itself. Life as it was in the old days, life with my "worst enemy", as she used to call herself. My worst enemy! who forgave me all, and never let me off a single thing.' He seized hold of his past, to squeeze out every remaining drop upon his empty, arid present; bringing back to life, and inventing where necessary, the princely days of his youth, his adolescence shaped and guided by a woman's strong capable hands—loving hands, ever ready to chastise. A prolonged, sheltered, oriental adolescence, in which the pleasures of the flesh had their passing place, like silent pauses in a song. A life of luxury, passing whims, childish cruelty, with fidelity a yet unspoken word.

He threw back his head to look up at the nacreous halo which irradiated the whole sky, and he gave a low cry, 'It's all gone to hell! I'm thirty years old!'

He hurried on his way back home, heaping curses on himself to the rhythm of his quickened steps. 'Fool! The tragedy is not her age, but mine. Everything may be over for her, but, for me . . .'

He let himself in without making a sound, to find the house in silence at last; to be nauseated by the lingering stale smell of those who had dined, wined, and danced there. In the looking-glass fitted to the door in the hall he met face to face the young man who had grown so thin, whose cheeks had hardened, whose sad beautifully moulded upper lip was unshaven and blue, whose large eyes were reticent and tragic. The young man, in effect, who had ceased, inexplicably, to be twenty-four years old.

'For me,' Chéri completed his thought, 'I really do believe that the last word has been said.'

"WHAT I need is somewhere quiet, you understand. . . . Any little place would do. . . . A bachelor flat, a room, a corner. . . ."

"I wasn't born yesterday," said the Pal, reproachfully.

She raised disconsolate eyes towards the festoons on the ceiling: "A little love, of course, of course, a little kiss—something to warm a poor lonely heart. . . . You bet I understand! Any special fancy?"

Chéri frowned. "Fancy? For whom?"

"You don't understand, my pretty. . . . Fancy for any particular district?"

"Ah! . . . No, nothing special. Just a quiet corner."

The Pal nodded her large head in collusion. "I see, I see. Something after my style—like my flat. You know where I rest my bones?"

"Yes."

"No, you don't know at all. I was certain you wouldn't write it down. Two hundred and fourteen Rue de Villiers. It's not big, and it's not beautiful. But you don't want the sort of place where the whole street knows your business."

"No."

"I got mine, of course, through a little deal with my landlady. A jewel of a woman, by the way, married, or as good as. Periwinkle blue eyes, and a head like a bird; but she bears the mark of Fate on her forehead, and I already know from her cards that she can't say no to anything, and that——"

"Yes, yes. You were saying just now that you knew of a flat. . . ."

"Yes, but not good enough for you."

"You don't think so?"

"Not for you . . . not for the two of you!"

The Pal hid a suggestive smile in her whisky, and Chéri turned from its smell—like wet harness. He put up with her quips about his imaginary conquests, for he saw, round her scraggy neck, a string of

large faked pearls which he thought he recognised. Every visual reminder of his past halted him on his downward path, and, during
such respites, he felt at peace.

"Ah!" sighed the Pal, "How I'd love to catch a glimpse of her!
What a pair! . . . I don't know her, of course, but I can just see you
two together! . . . Of course you'll provide everything yourself?"

"For whom?"

"Why, the furniture in your love-nest, of course!"

He looked at the Pal in bewilderment. Furniture . . . What furniture? He had been thinking only of one thing: a refuge of his own,
with a door that opened and closed for him and no one else, safe
from Edmée, Charlotte, all of them. . . .

"Will you furnish it in period or in modern style? La belle Serrano
arranged her entire ground floor with nothing but Spanish shawls,
but that was a bit eccentric. You're old enough, of course, to know
your own mind. . . ."

He hardly heard her, far away in his dreams of a future home that
would be secret, small, warm and dark. At the same time, he was
drinking red currant syrup, like any young "miss", in the red-and-
gold, out-of-date, unchanging bar, just as it used to be when, a small
boy, Chéri had come there to sip his first fizzy drink through a
straw. . . . Even the barman himself had not changed, and if the
woman sitting opposite Chéri was now a withered specimen, at least
he had never known her beautiful, or young.

'They all change, the whole of that set—my mother, my wife, all
the people they see—and they live for change. My mother may
change into a banker, Edmée into a town councillor. But I . . .'

In imagination, he quickly returned to that refuge, existing at
some unknown point in space, but secret, small, warm, and . . .

"Mine's done up in Algerian style," the Pal persisted. "It's no
longer in the fashion, but I don't mind—especially as the furniture is
hired. You'll be sure to recognise many of the photos I've put up:
and then there's the portrait of La Loupiote. . . . Come and have a
look at it. Please do."

"I'd like to. Let's go!"

On the threshold he hailed a taxi.

"But d'you never have your motor? Why haven't you got your
motor? It's really quite extraordinary how people with motors never
have their motor!"

She gathered up her faded black skirts, caught the string of her lor-
gnette in the clasp of her bag, dropped a glove, and submitted to the

stares of the passers-by with the lack of embarrassment of a Negro. Chéri, standing at her side, received several insulting smiles and the admiring condolences of a young woman, who called out: "Lord, what a waste of good material!"

In the taxi, patiently and half asleep, he endured the old thing's tattle. And then some of her stories were soothing: the one about the ridiculous little dog which had held up the return from the races in 1897, and then Mère La Berche eloping with a young bride on the day of her wedding in 1893.

"That's it over there. This door's stuck, Chéri, I can't get out. I warn you, there's not much light in the passage, nor, for that matter, is there much out here. . . . It's only a ground-floor flat, when all's said and done! . . . Wait where you are a second."

He waited, standing in the semi-darkness. He heard the jingle of keys, the wheezy old creature's gasps for breath and then her fussy servant's voice, "I'm lighting up. . . . Then you'll find yourself in a familiar landscape. I've got electricity, of course. . . . There, let me introduce you to my little morning-room, which is also my large drawing-room!"

He went in, and, from kindness—hardly bothering to glance at it—praised the room; it had a low ceiling and reddish walls, kippered by the smoke of innumerable cigars and cigarettes. Instinctively, he looked all round for the window, barricaded by shutters and curtains.

"You can't see in here? You're not an old night-bird like your Pal. Wait, I'll switch on the top light."

"Don't bother. . . . I'll just come in and——" He broke off, staring at the most brightly lit wall, covered with small frames and photographs pinned through the four corners. The Pal began to laugh.

"What did I say about a familiar landscape! I was quite sure you'd enjoy looking at them. You haven't got that one, have you?"

'That one' was a very large photographic portrait-study, touched up with water colours now quite faded. Blue eyes, a laughing mouth, a chignon of fair hair, and a look of calm yet exultant triumph. . . . High-breasted—in a First Empire corselet, legs showing through gauze skirts, legs that never finished, rounded out at the thigh, slender at the knee, legs that. . . . And a fetching hat, a hat that turned up on one side only, trimmed like a single sail to the wind.

"She never gave you that one, not that one, I bet! It makes her a goddess, a fairy walking on clouds! And yet it's absolutely her, of course. This big photo is the loveliest, to my way of thinking, but

I'm still every bit as fond of the others. Here, for instance, look at this little one here—much more recent, of course—isn't it a sight for sore eyes?"

A snapshot, clinging to the wall with the help of a rusty pin, showed a woman standing in the shade against a sunlit garden.

'It's the navy-blue dress and the hat with the seagulls,' Chéri said to himself.

"I'm all for flattering portraits, myself," the Pal went on. "A portrait like this one. Come now—you must confess—isn't it enough to make you join your hands and believe in God?"

A degraded and smarmy art, to lend glamour to the "portrait photograph," had lengthened the neck line and modified those around the sitter's mouth. But the nose, just sufficiently aquiline, the delicious nose with its ravishing nostrils, and the chaste little dimple, the velvety cleft that indented the upper lip under the nose—these were untouched, authentic, respected by even the photographer.

"Would you believe it? She wanted to burn the lot, pretending that nobody to-day is the least interested in what she used to be like. My blood boiled, I shrieked like a soul in torment, and she gave me the whole collection the very same day that she made me a present of the bag with her monogram. . . ."

"Who's this fellow with her . . . here . . . in this one underneath?"

"What were you saying? What's that? Wait till I take off my hat."

"I'm asking you who this is—this fellow—here. Get a move on, can't you?"

"Heavens, don't bustle me about so. . . . That? It's Bacciocchi, come! Naturally, you can hardly be expected to recognise him, he dates from two turns before you."

"Two what?"

"After Bacciocchi, she had Septfons—and yet no—wait . . . Septfons was earlier than that. . . . Septfons, Bacciocchi, Spéleïeff, and you. Oh! do look at those check trousers! . . . How ridiculous men's fashions used to be!"

"And that photo over there; when was that taken?"

He drew back a step, for at his elbow the Pal's head was craning forward, and its magpie's nest of felted hair smelt like a wig.

"That? That's her costume for Auteuil in . . . in 1888, or '89. Yes, the year of the Exhibition. In front of that one, dear boy, you should raise your hat. They don't turn out beauties like that any more."

"Pooh! . . . I don't think it so stunning."

The Pal folded her hands. Hatless, she looked older, and her high forehead was a buttery yellow under hair dyed greenish black.

"Not so stunning! That waist you could encircle with your ten fingers! That lily neck! And be good enough to let your eyes rest on that dress! All in frilled sky-blue chiffon, dear boy, and looped up with little pink moss-roses sewn on to the frills, and the hat to match! And the little bag to match as well—we called them alms-bags at that time. Oh! the beauty she was then! There's been nothing since to compare with her first appearances: she was the dawn, the very sun of love."

"First appearances where?"

She gave Chéri a gentle dig in the ribs. "Get along with you. . . . How you make me laugh! Ah! the trials of life must melt into thin air when you're about the house!"

His rigid features passed unobserved. He was still facing the wall, seemingly riveted by several Léas—one smelling an artificial rose, another bending over a book with medieval hasps, her swan neck rising from a pleatless collar, a white and rounded neck like the bole of a birch-tree.

"Well, I must be going," he said, like Valérie Cheniaguine.

"What d'you mean—you must be going? What about my dining-room? And my bedroom? just glance at them, my pretty! Take a note of them for your little love-nest."

"Ah! yes. . . . Listen; not to-day, because . . ." He glanced distrustfully towards the rampart of portraits, and lowered his voice. "I've an appointment. But I'll come back . . . to-morrow. Probably to-morrow, before dinner."

"Good. Then I can go ahead?"

"Go ahead?"

"With the flat."

"Yes, that's right. See about it. And thanks."

'I really begin to wonder what the world's coming to. . . . Young or old—it's hard to tell which are the most disgusting. . . . Two "turns" before me! . . . and "the first appearances", said the old spider, "the dazzling first appearances". . . . And all quite openly. No, really, what a world!'

He found that he had been keeping up the pace of a professional walker in training, and that he was out of breath. And all the more because the distant storm—which would not burst over Paris—had walled off what breeze there was behind a violet bastion, now towering straight up against the sky. Alongside the fortifications of the Boulevard Berthier, under trees stripped bare by the summer drought, a sparse crowd of Parisians in rope-soled sandals and a few half-naked children in red jerseys seemed to be waiting for a tidal wave to come rolling up from Levallois-Perret. Chéri sat down on a bench, forgetting that his strength was apt to play him tricks. He was unaware that his strength was being sapped in some mysterious manner ever since he had started to fritter it away on night vigils, and had neglected to exercise or nourish his body.

' "Two turns!" Really! Two turns before me! And after me, how many? Add the whole lot together, myself included, and how many turns d'you get?'

Beside a blue-clad, seagull-hatted Léa, he could see a tall, broad Spéléïeff, smiling expansively. He remembered a sad Léa, red-eyed with weeping, stroking his head when he was a small boy and calling him a "horrid little man in the making".

"Léa's lover" . . . "Léa's new pet" . . . Traditional and meaningless words—as common on everyone's lips as talk about the weather, the latest odds at Auteuil, or the dishonesty of servants. "Are you coming, kid?" Spéléïeff would say to Chéri. "We'll go out and have a porto at Armenonville, while we wait for Léa to join us. Nothing would drag her out of bed this morning."

"She's got a ravishing new little Bacciocchi," Madame Peloux had informed her son, aged fourteen or fifteen at the time.

But, a bundle of sophistication and innocence, brought up in the midst of love, yet blinded by its proximity, Chéri, at that tender age, had talked love, as children learn a language by ear, picking up words, pleasant or filthy, merely as sounds without meaning. No vivid or voluptuous vision arose behind the shadow of this huge Spéléïeff so recently risen from Léa's bed. And was there really very much difference between this "ravishing little Bacciocchi" and a "prize Pekingese"?

No photograph or letter, no story from the only lips that might have told him the truth, had blighted the enclosed Paradise in which Léa and Chéri had dwelt for so many years. Next to nothing in Chéri existed which dated back beyond Léa: why, then, should he bother about a man who, before his day, had brought warmth or sadness or riches to his mistress?

A fair-haired little boy with fat knees came and planted his crossed arms on the bench beside Chéri. They glared at each other with identical expressions of offended reserve, for Chéri treated all children as strangers. For some time this boy let his pale blue eyes rest on Chéri, who watched some sort of indescribable smile, full of scorn, mount up from the small anæmic mouth to the flax-blue pupils of the eyes. Then the child turned away, and, picking up his dirty toys from the dust, began to play at the foot of the bench, blotting Chéri out of existence. Then Chéri got up and walked away.

Half an hour later, he was lying in a warm, scented bath, clouded by some milky bath essence. He lay revelling in its luxury and comfort, in the soft lather of the soap, and in the remote faint sounds about the house, as though they were the rewards of an act of great courage, or else blessings he was tasting for the last time.

His wife came into the room humming, broke off at the sight of him, and narrowly failed to disguise her speechless astonishment at finding Chéri at home and in his bath.

"Am I in your way?" he asked, with no irony.

"Not in the least, Fred."

She began to take off her day clothes with youthful abandon, with total disregard for modesty or immodesty, and Chéri was amused by her haste to be undressed and in a bath.

'How completely I'd forgotten her,' he thought, as he looked at the odalisque back, supple but well-covered, of the woman bending down to untie her shoelaces.

She did not speak to him, but went about her business like a woman who believes she is safely by herself, and in front of his eyes rose the figure of the child who, not long since, had been playing in the dust at his feet, resolutely ignoring his presence.

"Tell me . . ."

Edmée raised a surprised forehead, a soft half-naked body.

"What would you say to our having a child?"

"Fred! . . . What are you thinking of?"

It was almost a cry of terror, and already Edmée was clutching a wisp of lawn close to her bosom with one hand, while with the other she groped, fumbling, for the first kimono within reach. Chéri could not hold back his laughter.

"Would you like my revolver? I'm not going to assault you."

"Why are you laughing?" she asked, almost in a whisper. "You should never laugh."

"I seldom laugh. But do tell me . . . now that all is quiet and

peaceful between us . . . do tell me why. Are you really so terrified
at the thought that we could have had, could still have, a child?"

"Yes," she said cruelly, and her unexpected frankness shocked
even herself.

She never took her eyes off her husband, lying full length in a low
armchair, and she murmured distinctly enough for him to hear, "A
child . . . who'd be sure to take after you. You twice over, you twice
over in the single lifetime of one woman? No. . . . Oh, no."

He began a gesture which she misinterpreted.

"No, I beg of you. . . . There's nothing more to be said. I won't
even discuss it. Let's leave things as they are. We've only to be a little cautious, and go on . . . I ask nothing of you . . ."

"That suits you?"

Her only answer was to put on a look, insulting in its misery and
plaintive helplessness, a seraglio look that well suited her nakedness.
Her freshly powdered cheeks, the touch of colour on her youthful
lips, the light brown halo round her hazel eyes, the care bestowed on
every feature of her face, were in striking contrast to the confusion of
her body, bare except for the crumpled silk shift she was clasping to
her breasts.

'I can no longer make her happy,' thought Chéri, 'but I can still
make her suffer. She is not altogether unfaithful to me. Whereas I
am not untrue to her . . . I have deserted her.'

Turning away from him, she began to dress. She had regained her
freedom of movement and her disingenuous tolerance. The palest of
pink frocks now hid from view the woman who, a moment since,
had pressed her last stitch of clothing to her bosom, as though to a
wound.

She had recovered, too, her buoyant determination, her desire to
live and hold sway, her prodigious and feminine aptitude for happiness. Chéri despised her afresh; but a moment came when the rays of
the evening sun, shining through her transparent pink dress, outlined
the shape of a young woman who no longer bore any semblance to
the wounded Circassian: a heaven-aspiring form, as supple and vigorous as a serpent about to strike.

'I can still hurt her, but how quickly she recovers! In this house,
too, I am no longer needed, no longer expected. She has gone far beyond me, and is going further: I am, the old creature would say, her
"first turn". It's now for me to follow her example, if only I could.
But I can't. And then would I, if I could? Unlike some of us, Edmée
has never come up against what one meets only once in a lifetime

and is floored by completely. Spéleïeff was fond of saying that, after a really bad crash—which, however, involved no broken bones—some horses would let themselves be killed rather than take the fence again. I am just the same.'

He cast about for further sporting, and rather brutal, metaphors that would make his own fall and misfortunes seem an accident. But he had started his night too early, and, dog-tired, his dreams were haunted by sweet ghosts in sky-blue flounces, and half-remembered figures from the pages of the imperishable literature which finds its way into tawdry love-nests, from tales and poems dedicated to constancy and to lovers undivided in death: writings irresistible to adolescents and time-worn courtesans, who are akin in their credulity and passion for romance.

"Then she said to me: 'I know who's at the back of all this: it's Charlotte again, making mischief about me. . . .' 'It's no more than you deserve,' I told her, 'you've only to stop going to see Charlotte as much as you do, and trusting her with all your secrets.' She retorted: 'I'm a much closer friend of Charlotte's than of Spéleïeff's and I've known her far longer. I assure you Charlotte, Neuilly, bezique and the child would be a far greater loss to me than Spéleïeff—you can't change the habits of a lifetime.' 'That doesn't prevent your faith in Charlotte costing you a pretty penny,' I said. 'Oh! well,' was her answer, 'what's good is worth paying for.' That's her all over, you'll agree: big-hearted and generous but no fool. And with that she went off to dress for the Races—she told me she was going to the Races with a gigolo. . . ."

"With me!" Chéri exclaimed bitterly. "Am I right? It was me?"

"I don't deny it. I simply tell you things as they took place. A white dress—of white crêpe-de-chine—Oriental-looking, edged with blue Chinese embroidery, the very dress you see her in here, in this snapshot, taken at the Races. And nothing will get it out of my head that this man's shoulder you can see behind her is you."

"Fetch it me!" Chéri ordered.

The old woman got up, pulled out the rusty drawing-pins tacking the photograph to the wall, and brought it back to Chéri. Lolling on the Algerian divan, he raised a tousled head, and, barely running his eyes over it, flung the snapshot across the room.

"When have you seen me wearing a collar that gapes at the back, and a short coat to go to the Races? Come, think again! I don't find that sort of thing at all funny."

She ventured a tut-tut of timid censure, bent her stiff knees to pick up the photograph, and went on to open the door into the passage.

"Where are you going?"

"I can hear the water for my coffee boiling. I'm going to pour it out."

"Good. But come back here again."

She disappeared in a shuffle of rustling taffeta and heelless slippers. Left to himself, Chéri settled his neck against the moquette cushion stamped with Tunisian designs. A new and startlingly bright Japanese kimono, embellished with pink wistaria on a ground of amethyst, had replaced his coat and waistcoat. The fag-end of a too-far-smoked cigarette was almost burning his lips, and his hair, falling fanwise down to the level of his eyebrows, half covered his forehead.

Wearing so feminine and flowered a garment did not make his appearance in any way ambiguous: he merely acquired an ignominious majesty that stamped every feature with its proper value. He seemed bent on death and destruction, and the photograph had flashed like a blade from his hand as he hurled it from him. Hard, delicate bones in his cheeks moved to the rhythm of his working jaws. The whites of his eyes flickered in the darkness round him like the crest of a wave, with the moonbeams interruptedly following its course.

Left alone, however, he let his head sink back against the cushion, and closed his eyes.

"Lord!" exclaimed the Pal coming back into the room, "you'll not look more handsome when laid out on your deathbed! I've brought in the coffee. Would you care for some? Such an aroma! It will waft you to the Isles of the Blest."

"Yes. Two lumps."

His words were curt, and she obeyed with a humility that suggested, perhaps, a deep subservient pleasure.

"You didn't eat anything for dinner?"

"I had enough."

He drank his coffee, without moving, supporting himself on one elbow. An Oriental curtain, draped like a canopy, hung from the ceiling directly above the divan, and in its shade lay an ivory and enamel Chéri, robed in exquisite silks, reclining upon an old worn dust-bedraggled rug.

The Pal set out, piece by piece upon a brass-topped table, the coffee-set, an opium lamp capped with a glass cowl, two pipes, the pot of paste, the silver snuff-box used for cocaine, and a flask, which, tight-stoppered as it was, failed to control the cold and treacherously volatile expansion of the ether. To these she added a pack of tarot cards, a case of poker chips, and a pair of spectacles, before settling herself down with the apologetic air of a trained hospital nurse.

"I've already told you," grunted Chéri, "all that paraphernalia means nothing to me."

Once again she stretched out her sickly white hands in protestation. In her own home she adopted what she called her "Charlotte Corday style": hair flowing loose, and wide white linen fichus crossed over her dusty mourning, looking a mixture of decorum and fallen virtue—like a heroine of the Salpêtrière Prison.

"No matter, Cheri. They're just in case. And it does make me so happy to see the whole of my little armoury set out in its proper order under my eyes. The arsenal of dreams! the munitions of ecstasy! the gateway to illusion!"

She nodded her long head and looked up to the ceiling, with the compassionate eyes of a grandmother who ruins herself on toys. Her guest partook of none of her potions. Some sort of physical sense of honour still survived in him, and his disdain for drugs was akin to his distaste for brothels.

For a number of days—he had kept no count of them—he had found his way to this black hole, presided over by an attendant Norn. Ungraciously, and in terms that brooked no argument, he had paid her for food, coffee and her own liqueurs, and for his personal requirements in the way of cigarettes, fruit, ice and soft drinks. He had commanded his slave to buy the sumptuous Japanese robe, scents and expensive soaps. She was moved less by desire for money than by the pleasure of acting as an accomplice. She devoted herself to Chéri with enthusiasm, a revival of her old zeal as a missionary of vice who, with garrulous and culpable alacrity, would divest and bathe a virgin, cook an opium pellet, and pour out intoxicating spirits or ether. This apostolate was fruitless, for her singular guest brought back no paramour, drank soft drinks only, stretched himself on the dusty divan and delivered only one word of command: "Talk."

She did talk, following, she believed, her own fancies; but, now brutally, now subtly, he would direct the muddied meanderings of her reminiscences. She talked like a sewing-woman who comes in by the day, with the continuous, stupefying monotony of creatures whose days are given over to long and sedentary tasks. But she never did any sewing, for she had the aristocratic unpracticalness of a former prostitute. While talking, she would pin a pleat over a hole or stain, and take up again the business of tarot cards and patience. She would put on gloves to grind coffee bought by the charwoman, and then handle greasy cards without turning a hair.

She talked, and Chéri listened to her soporific voice and the shuffle of her felted slippers. He reclined at ease, magnificently robed, in the ill-kempt lodging. His guardian dared ask no questions. She knew enough: he was a monomaniac, as his abstemiousness proved. The illness for which she was ministering was mysterious; but it was an illness. She took the risk of inviting, as from a sense of duty, a very pretty young woman, childish and professionally gay. Chéri paid her neither more nor less attention than he would a puppy, and said to the Pal, "Are we going to have any more of your fashionable parties?"

She did not require snubbing a second time, and he never had cause to bind her to secrecy. One day she almost hit upon the simple truth, when she proposed asking in two or three of her friends of the good old days; Léa, for instance. He never batted an eyelid.

"Not a soul. Or I'll have to hunt out some better hole."

A fortnight went by, as funereal in its routine as life in a monastery; but it did not pall on either recluse. During the daytime, the Pal set forth on her old woman's junketings; poker parties, nips of whisky, and poisonous gossip, hole-and-corner gambling-dens, lunches of "regional dishes" in the stuffy darkness of a Norman or Limousin restaurant. Chéri would arrive with the first shadow of evening, sometimes drenched to the skin. She would recognise the slam of his taxi-door and no longer asked: "But why do you never come in your motor?"

He would leave after midnight, and usually before daybreak. During his prolonged sessions on the Algerian divan, the Pal sometimes saw him drop off to sleep and remain for an instant or two with his neck twisted against his shoulder, as though caught in a snare. She never slept herself till after his departure, having forgotten the need for repose. Only once, in the small hours of the morning, while he was putting back, meticulously and one by one, the contents of his pockets—key on its chain, note-case, little flat revolver, handkerchief, cigarette-case of green gold—did she dare to ask: "Doesn't your wife begin to wonder, when you come in so late?"

Chéri raised long eyebrows above eyes grown larger from lack of sleep: "No. Why? She knows perfectly well I've been up to no harm."

"No child, of course, is easier to manage than you are. . . . Shall you be coming again this evening?"

"I don't know. I'll see. Carry on as if I were coming for certain."

Once more he gazed long at all the lily necks, all the blue eyes, that flowered on one wall of his sanctuary, before he went his way, only to return again, faithfully, some twelve hours later.

By roundabout ways he considered cunning, he would lead the Pal to talk of Léa, then he would clear the narrative of all bawdy asides that might retard it. "Skip it. Skip it!" Barely bothering to enunciate the words, he relied on the initial sibilants to speed up or curtail the monologue. He would listen only to stories without malice in them, and glorifications of a purely descriptive nature. He insisted upon strict respect for documentary truth and checked his chronicler peevishly. He stocked his mind with dates, colours, materials, and places, and the names of dressmakers.

"What's poplin?" he fired at her pointblank.

"Poplin's a mixture of silk and wool, a dry material . . . if you know what I mean; one that doesn't stick to the skin."

"Yes. And mohair? You said 'of white mohair.' "

"Mohair is a kind of alpaca, but it hangs better, of course. Léa was afraid to wear lawn in the summer: she maintained that it was best for underwear and handkerchiefs. Her own lingerie was fit for a queen, you'll remember, and in the days when that photograph was taken—yes, that beauty over there with the long legs—they didn't wear the plain underclothes of to-day. It was frill upon frill, a foam, a flurry of snow; and the drawers, dear boy! they'd have sent your head whirling. . . . White Chantilly lace at the sides and black Chantilly in between. Can't you just see the effect? But *can* you imagine it?"

'Revolting,' thought Chéri, 'revolting. Black Chantilly in between. A woman doesn't wear black Chantilly in between simply to please herself. In front of whose eyes did she wear them? For whom?'

He could see Léa's gesture as he entered her bathroom or boudoir —the furtive gesture as she drew her wrap across her body. He could see the chaste self-confidence of her rosy body as she lay naked in the bath, with the water turned to milk by some essence or other. . . . 'But, for others, she wore drawers of Chantilly lace. . . .'

He kicked one of the hay-stuffed moquette cushions to the floor.

"Are you too warm, Chéri?"

"No. Let me have another look at that photo . . . the large framed one. Tilt the what's-its-name of your lamp up a bit . . . a bit more . . . that's it!"

Abandoning his usual circumspection, he applied a searching eye to the study of every detail that was new to him, and almost refreshing. 'A high-waisted belt with cameos! . . . Never saw that about the place. And boots like buskins! Was she wearing tights? No, of course not, her toes are bare. Revolting. . . .'

"At whose house did she wear that costume?"

"I don't rightly remember. . . . A reception at the club, I believe . . . or at Molier's."

He handed back the frame at arm's length, to all appearances disdainful and bored. He left shortly afterwards, under an overcast sky, towards the close of a night that smelt of wood smoke and dankness.

He was deteriorating physically and took no account of it. He was losing weight through eating and sleeping too little, walking and smoking too much, thus bartering his obvious vigour for a lightness, an apparent return to youth, which the light of day repudiated. At home, he lived as he pleased, welcoming or running away from guests and callers. All that they knew of him was his name, his almost petrified good looks fined down little by little under an accusing chisel, and the inconceivable ease with which he would ignore them.

So he eked out his peaceful and carefully regimented despair until the last days of October. Then, one afternoon, he was seized by a fit of hilarity, because he caught a glimpse of his wife's unsuspected terror. His whole face lit up with the merriment of a man impervious to all feeling. 'She thinks I'm mad. What luck!'

His merriment was short-lived: for, on thinking it over, he came to the conclusion that, where the brute and the madman are concerned, the brute wins every time. She was frightened of the madman; otherwise would she not have stood her ground, biting her lips and forcing back her tears, in order to worst the brute?

'I am no longer even considered wicked,' he thought bitterly. 'And that's because I am no longer wicked. Oh! the harm the woman I left has done to me! Yet others left her, and she left others. . . . How, I wonder, does Bacciocchi exist at the present time? or Septfons, Spéleïeff, and all the rest of them? But what have we got in common, I and the rest of them? She called me "little bourgeois" because I counted the bottles in the cellar. "Little bourgeois", "faithful heart", "great lover"—those were her names for me—those were my real names: and, though she watched my departure with tears glistening in her eyes, she is still herself, Léa, who prefers old age to me, who sits in the corner by the fire counting over on her fingers: "I've had What's-his-name, and Thingummy-bob, and Chéri, and So-and-so . . ." I thought she belonged to me alone, and never perceived that I was only one among her lovers. Is there anyone left, now, that I am not ashamed of?'

Hardened by now to the exercise of impassivity, he sought to endure the capricious hauntings of such thoughts with resignation, and to be worthy of the devil by which he was possessed. Proud and dry-eyed, with a lighted match held between steady fingers, he looked sideways at his mother, well aware of her watchful eye. Once his cigarette was alight, with a little encouragement he would have strutted like a peacock in front of an invisible public, and taunted his tormentors with a "Good, isn't it?" In a confused way, the strength born of his dissimulation and resistance was gathering in his inmost self. He was beginning now to enjoy his extreme state of detachment, and dimly perceived that an emotional storm could be just as valuable and refreshing as a lull, and that in it he might discover the wisdom which never came to him in calmer moods. As a child, Chéri frequently had taken advantage of a genuine fit of temper, by changing it into a peevishness that would bring him what he wanted. Today he was fast approaching the point at which, having attained to a definite state of unhappiness, he could rely on it to settle everything.

One gusty, wind-swept, September afternoon, with leaves sailing straight across the sky—an afternoon of blue rifts in the clouds and scattered raindrops—Chéri felt an urge to visit his dark retreat and its attendant, garbed in black, with a touch of white on the chest like a scavenging cat. He was feeling buoyant, and avid for confidences, though these would be sickly, like the fruit of the arbutus and as prickly leaved. Words and phrases of special though ill-defined significance kept running in his head: "Her monogram embroidered in hair on all her lingerie, dear boy, in golden hairs from her own head . . . faery handicraft! And, did I tell you, her masseuse used to pluck the hairs from the calves of her leg, one by one. . . ."

He turned round and left the window. He found Charlotte on a chair looking thoughtfully up at him; and in the restless waters of her great eyes he saw the formation of a prodigious, rounded, crystalline, glistening sphere which detached itself from the bronzed iris, and then vanished, evaporating in the heat of her flushed cheek. Chéri felt flattered and cheered. 'How kind of her! She's weeping for me.'

An hour later, he found his ancient accomplice at her post. But she was wearing some sort of parson's hat, bunched up with shiny black ribbon, and she held out to him a sheet of blue paper, which he waved aside.

"What's that? . . . I haven't the time. Tell me what's written on it."

The Pal lifted puzzled eyes to his: "It's my mother."

"Your mother? You're joking."

She did her best to appear offended. "I'm not joking at all. Please respect the departed! She is dead." And she added, by way of an excuse, "She was eighty-three!"

"Congratulations. Are you going out?"

"No; I'm going away."

"Where to?"

"To Tarascon, and from there I take a little branch line train that puts me down at . . ."

"For how long?"

"Four or five days . . . at least. There's the solicitor to be seen about the will, because my younger sister . . ."

He burst out, hands to heaven: "A sister now! Why not four children into the bargain?" He was conscious of the unexpectedly high-pitched tone of his voice and controlled it. "Good, very well. What d'you expect me to do about it? Be off, be off. . . ."

"I was going to leave word for you. I'm catching the 7.30."

"Catch the 7.30."

"The time of the funeral service is not mentioned in the telegram: my sister speaks only of the laying out, the climate down there is very hot, they'll have to get through it very quickly, only the business side can keep me there, and over that one has no control."

"Of course, of course."

He was walking to and fro, from the door to the wall with the photographs and back to the door again, and in doing so he knocked against a squashed old travelling-bag. The coffee-pot and cups were steaming on the table.

"I made you your coffee, come what might. . . ."

"Thanks."

They drank standing up, as at a station, and the chill of departure gripped Chéri by the throat and made his teeth chatter secretly.

"Goodbye, then, dear boy," said the Pal. "You may be sure that I'll hurry things as much as I can."

"Goodbye—pleasant journey."

They shook hands, and she did not dare to kiss him. "Won't you stay here for a little while?"

He looked all round in great agitation. "No. No."

"Take the key, then?"

"Why should I?"

"You're at home here. You've fallen into the habit of it. I've told Maria to come every day at five and light a good fire and get the coffee ready. . . . So take my key, won't you? . . ."

With a limp hand he took the key, and it struck him as enormous. Once outside, he longed to throw it away or take it back to the concierge.

The old woman took courage on her way between her own door and the street, loading him with instructions as she might a child of twelve.

"The electric-light switch is on your left as you go in. The kettle is always on the gas-stove in the kitchen, and all you have to do is to put a match to it. And your Japanese robe—Maria has her instructions to leave it folded at the head of the divan and the cigarettes in their usual place."

Chéri nodded affirmation once or twice, with the look of courageous unconcern of a schoolboy on the last morning of the holidays. And, when he was alone, it did not occur to him to make fun of his old retainer with the dyed hair, who had placed the proper value both on the last prerogatives of the dead and on the little pleasures of one whom all had now deserted.

The following morning, he awoke from an indecipherable dream, in which a crush of people were all running in the same direction. Though he saw only their backs, each was known to him. As they hurried by, he identified his mother, Léa—unaccountably naked, and out of breath—Desmond, the Pal, and young Maudru . . . Edmée was the only one to turn and smile at him, with the grating little smile of a marten. "But it's the marten Ragut caught in the Vosges!" Chéri cried out in his dream, and this discovery pleased him immeasurably. Then he checked and recounted all the one-way runners, saying over to himself: 'There's one missing. . . . There's one missing. . . .' Once out of his dream, on this side of awakening, it came to him that the one missing was none other than himself: 'I must get back into it. . . .' But the efforts of exerting every limb, like an insect caught on flypaper, served only to widen the bar of blue between his eyelids, and he emerged into that real world in which he was frittering away his time and his strength. He stretched out his legs, and bathed them in a fresh, cool part of the sheets. 'Edmée must have got up some time ago.'

He was surprised to see beneath the window a new garden of marguerites and heliotrope, for in his memory there was only a summer garden of blue and pink. He rang, and the sound of the bell brought to life a maid whose face was unfamiliar.

"Where is Henriette?"

"I've taken her place, sir."

"Since when?"

"Why—for the last month, sir."

He ejaculated an "Ah!", as much as to say, "That explains everything."

"Where's your mistress?"

"Madame is just coming, sir. Madame is ready to go out."

Edmée, indeed, did appear, as large as life, but stopped just inside the door in so marked a manner that Chéri was secretly amused. He allowed himself the pleasure of upsetting his wife a little by exclaiming, "But it's Ragut's marten!" and watching her pretty eyes waver under his gaze.

"Fred, I . . ."

"Yes, you're going out. I never heard you get up."

She coloured slightly. "There's nothing extraordinary in that. I've been sleeping so badly these last few nights, that I've had a bed made up on the divan in the boudoir. You're not doing anything special to-day, are you?"

"But I am," he replied darkly.

"Is it important?"

"Very important." He took his time, and finished on a lighter note: "I'm going to have my hair cut."

"But will you be back for luncheon?"

"No; I'll have a cutlet in Paris. I've made an appointment at Gustave's for a quarter past two. The man who usually comes to cut my hair is ill."

He was childishly courteous, the lie flowering effortlessly on his lips. Because he was lying, his mouth took on its boyhood mould—

poutingly provocative and rounded for a kiss. Edmée looked at him with an almost masculine satisfaction.

"You're looking well this morning, Fred. . . . I must fly."

"Are you catching the 7.30?"

She stared at him, struck dumb, and fled so precipitately that he was still laughing when the front door slammed behind her.

'Ah! that does me good,' he sighed. 'How easy it is to laugh when you no longer expect anything from anyone. . . .' Thus, while he was dressing, did he discover for himself the nature of asceticism, and the tuneless little song he hummed through pursed lips kept him company like a silly young nun.

He went down to a Paris he had forgotten. The crowd upset his dubious emotional balance, now so dependent on a crystalline vacuity and the daily routine of suffering.

In the Rue Royale he came face to face with his own full-length reflection at the moment when the brightness of noon broke through the rain-clouds. Chéri wasted no thoughts on this crude new self-portrait, which stood out sharply against a background of newsvendors and shopgirls, flanked by jade necklaces and silver fox furs. The fluid feeling in his stomach, which he compared to a speck of lead bobbing about inside a celluloid ball, must come, he thought, from lack of sustenance, and he took refuge in a restaurant.

With his back to a glass partition, screened from the light of day, he lunched off selected oysters, fish and fruit. Some young women sitting not far away had no eyes for him, and this gave him a pleasant feeling, like that of a chilly bunch of violets laid on closed eyelids. But the smell of his coffee suddenly brought home the need to rise and keep the appointment of which this smell was an urgent reminder. Before obeying the summons, he went to his hairdresser's, held out his hands to be manicured, and slipped off into a few moments' inestimable repose, while expert fingers substituted their will for his.

The enormous key obstructed his pocket. 'I won't go, I won't go! . . .' To the cadence of some such insistent, meaningless refrain, he found his way without mishap to the Avenue de Villiers. His clumsy fumbling round the lock and the rasp of the key made his heart beat momentarily faster, but the cheerful warmth in the passage calmed his nerves.

He went forward cautiously, lord of this empire of a few square feet, which he now owned but did not know. The useless daily arrangement of the armoury had been laid out on the table by the well-trained charwoman, and an earthenware coffee-pot stood in the midst of charcoal embers already dying under the velvet of warm ashes. Methodically, Chéri emptied his pockets and set out one by one his cigarette case, the huge key, his own small key, the flat revolver, his note-case, handkerchief, and watch; but when he had put on his Japanese robe, he did not lie down on the divan. With the silent curiosity of a cat he opened doors and peered into cupboards. His peculiar prudishness shrank back before a primitive but distinctively feminine lavatory. The bedroom, all bed and little else, also was decorated in the mournful shade of red that seems to settle in on those of declining years; it smelt of old bachelors and eau-de-Cologne. Chéri returned to the drawing-room. He switched on the two wall lamps and the beribboned chandelier. He listened to faint far away sounds and, now that he was alone for the first time in this poor lodging, began trying out on himself the influence of its previous inmates—birds of passage or else dead. He thought he heard and recognised a familiar footstep, a slipshod, shambling old animal pad-pad, then shook his head: 'It can't be hers. She won't be back for a week, and when she does come back, what will there be left for me in this world? I'll have . . .'

Inwardly he listened to the Pal's voice, the worn-out voice of a tramp. "But wait till I finish the story of the famous slanging-match between Léa and old Mortier at the Races. Old Mortier thought that with the aid of a little publicity in *Gil Blas* he would get all he wanted out of Léa. Oh! la la, my pretties, what a donkey he made of himself! She drove out to Longchamp—a dream of blue—as statuesque as a goddess, in her victoria drawn by a pair of piebalds. . . ."

He raised his hand towards the wall in front of him, where so many blue eyes were smiling, where so many swan-necks were preening themselves above imperturbable bosoms. '. . . I'll have all this. All this, and nothing more. It's true, perhaps, that this is a good deal. I've found her again, by a happy chance, found her here on this wall. But I've found her, only to lose her again for ever. I am still held up, like her, by these few rusty nails, by these pins stuck in slantwise. How much longer can this go on? Not very long. And then, knowing myself as I do, I'm afraid I shall demand more than this. I may suddenly cry out: "I want her! I must have her! Now! at this very moment!" Then what will become of me?'

He pushed the divan closer to the illustrated wall and there lay down. And as he lay there, all the Léas, with their downward gazing eyes, seemed to be showing concern for him: 'But they only *seem* to be looking down at me, I know perfectly well. When you sent me away, my Nounoune, what did you think there was left for me after you? Your noble action cost you little—you knew the worth of a Chéri—your risk was negligible. But we've been well punished, you and I: you, because you were born so long before me, and I, because I loved you above all other women. You're finished now, you have found your consolation—and what a disgrace that is!—whereas I . . . As long as people say, "There was the War," I can say "There was Léa." Léa, the War . . . I never imagined I'd dream of either of them again, yet the two together have driven me outside the times I live in. Henceforth, there is nowhere in the world where I can occupy more than half a place. . . .'

He pulled the table nearer to consult his watch. 'Half-past five. The old creature won't be back here for another week. And this is the first day. Supposing she were to die on the way?'

He fidgeted on his divan, smoked, poured himself out a cup of luke-warm coffee. 'A week. All the same, I mustn't ask too much of myself. In a week's time . . . which story will she be telling me? I know them off by heart—the one about the Four-in-Hand Meet, the one about the slanging-match at Longchamp, the one about the final rupture—and when I've heard every one, every twist and turn of them, what will there be left? Nothing, absolutely nothing. In a week's time, this old woman—and I'm already so impatient for her, she might be going to give me an injection—this old woman will be here, and . . . and she'll bring me nothing at all.'

He lifted beseeching eyes to his favourite photograph. Already this speaking likeness filled him with less resentment, less ecstasy, less heartbreak. He turned from side to side on the hard mattress, unable to prevent his muscles from contracting, like a man who aches to jump from a height, but lacks the courage.

He worked himself up till he groaned aloud, repeating over and over again "Nounoune", to make himself believe he was frantic. But he fell silent, ashamed, for he knew very well that he did not need to be frantic to pick up the little flat revolver from the table. Without rising, he experimented in finding a convenient position. Finally he lay down with his right arm doubled up under him. Holding the weapon in his right hand, he pressed his ear against the muzzle, which was buried in the cushions. At once his arm began to grow numb, and he realised that if he did not make haste his tingling fingers would refuse to obey him. So he made haste, whimpering muffled complaints as he completed his task, because his forearm was hurting, crushed under the weight of his body. He knew nothing more, beyond the pressure of his forefinger on a little lever of tempered steel.

GIGI

Translated by
ROGER SENHOUSE

"DON'T FORGET you are going to Aunt Alicia's. Do you hear me, Gilberte? Come here and let me do your curls. Gilberte, do you hear me?"

"Couldn't I go there without having my hair curled, Grandmamma?"

"I should think not," said Madame Alvarez, quietly. She took an old pair of curling-irons, with prongs ending in little round metal knobs, and put them to heat over the blue flame of a spirit-lamp while she prepared the tissue-papers.

"Grandmamma, couldn't you crimp my hair in waves down the side of my head for a change?"

"Out of the question. Ringlets at the very ends—that's as far as a girl of your age can possibly go. Now sit down on the footstool."

To do so, Gilberte folded up under her the heron-like legs of a girl of fifteen. Below her tartan skirt, she revealed ribbed cotton stockings to just above the knees, unconscious of the perfect oval shape of her knee-caps. Slender calf and high arched instep—Madame Alvarez never let her eyes run over these fine points without regretting that her granddaughter had not studied dancing professionally. At the moment, she was thinking only of the girl's hair. She had corkscrewed the ends and fixed them in tissue-paper, and was now compressing the ash-blonde ringlets between the heated knobs. With patient soft-fingered skill, she gathered up the full magnificent weight of finely kept hair into sleek ripples which fell to just below Gilberte's shoulders. The girl sat quite still. The smell of the heated tongs, and the whiff of vanilla in the curling-papers, made her feel drowsy. Besides, Gilberte knew that resistance would be useless. She hardly ever tried to elude the authority exercised by her family.

"Is Mamma singing Frasquita today?"

"Yes. And this evening in *Si j'étais Roi*. I have told you before, when you're sitting on a low seat you must keep your knees close to each other, and lean both of them together, either to the right or to the left, for the sake of decorum."

"But, Grandmamma, I've got on my drawers and my petticoat."

"Drawers are one thing, decorum is another," said Madame Alvarez. "Everything depends on the attitude."

"Yes, I know. Aunt Alicia has told me often enough," Gilberte murmured from under her tent of hair.

"I do not require the help of my sister," said Madame Alvarez testily, "to instruct you in the elements of propriety. On that subject, thank goodness, I know rather more than she does."

"Supposing you let me stay here with you today, Grandmamma, couldn't I go and see Aunt Alicia next Sunday?"

"What next!" said Madame Alvarez haughtily. "Have you any other *purposal* to make to me?"

"Yes, I have," said Gilberte. "Have my skirts made a little longer, so I don't have to fold myself up in a Z every time I sit down. You see, Grandmamma, with my skirts too short, I have to keep thinking of my you-know-what."

"Silence! Aren't you ashamed to call it your you-know-what?"

"I don't mind calling it by any other name, only . . ."

Madame Alvarez blew out the spirit-lamp, looked at the reflection of her heavy Spanish face in the looking-glass above the mantelpiece, and then laid down the law.

"There is no other name."

A skeptical look passed across the girl's eyes. Beneath the cockle-shells of fair hair they showed a lovely dark blue, the color of glistening slate. Gilberte unfolded with a bound.

"But, Grandmamma, all the same, do look! If only my skirts were just that much longer! Or if a small frill could be added!"

"That *would* be nice for your mother, to be seen with a great gawk looking at least eighteen! In her profession! Where are your brains!"

"In my head," said Gilberte. "Since I hardly ever go out with Mamma, what would it matter?"

She pulled down her skirt, which had rucked up towards her slim waist, and asked, "Can I go in my everyday coat? It's quite good enough."

"That wouldn't show that it's Sunday! Put on your serge coat and blue sailor-hat. When will you learn what's what?"

When on her feet, Gilberte was as tall as her grandmother. Madame Alvarez had taken the name of a Spanish lover now dead, and

accordingly had acquired a creamy complexion, an ample bust, and
hair lustrous with brilliantine. She used too white a powder, her
heavy cheeks had begun to draw down her lower eye-lids a little, and
so eventually she took to calling herself Inez. Her family pursued
their fixed orbit around her. Her unmarried daughter Andrée,
forsaken by Gilberte's father, now preferred the sober life of a
second-lead singer in a State-controlled theatre to the fitful opulence
of a life of gallantry. Aunt Alicia—none of her admirers, it seemed,
had ever mentioned marriage—lived alone, on an income she pretended was modest. The family had a high opinion of Alicia's judgment, and of her jewels.

Madame Alvarez looked her granddaughter up and down, from
the felt sailor-hat trimmed with a quill to the ready-made cavalier
shoes.

"Can't you ever manage to keep your legs together? When you
stand like that, the Seine could flow between them. You haven't the
shadow of a stomach, and yet you somehow contrive to stick it out.
And don't forget your gloves, I beg of you."

Gilberte's every posture was still governed by the unconcern of
childish innocence. At times she looked like Robin Hood, at others
like a carved angel, or again like a boy in skirts; but she seldom resembled a nearly grown-up girl. "How can you expect to be put into
long skirts, when you haven't the sense of a child of eight?" Madame
Alvarez asked. And Andrée sighed, "I find Gilberte so discouraging."
To which Gilberte answered quietly, "If you didn't find *me* discouraging, then you'd find something else." For she was sweet and
gentle, resigned to a stay-at-home life and seeing few people outside
the family. As for her features, no one could yet predict their final
mould. A large mouth, which showed beautiful strong white teeth
when she laughed, no chin to speak of, and, between high cheekbones, a nose—"Heavens, where did she get that button?" whispered
her mother under her breath. "If you can't answer that question, my
girl, who can?" retorted Madame Alvarez. Whereupon Andrée, who
had become prudish too late in life and disgruntled too soon,
relapsed into silence, automatically stroking her sensitive larynx.
"Gigi is just a bundle of raw material," Aunt Alicia affirmed, "it may
turn out very well—and, just as easily, all wrong."

"Grandmamma, there's the bell! I'll open the door on my way
out. Grandmamma," Gigi shouted from the passage, "It's Uncle
Gaston!"

She came back into the room with a tall, youngish looking man, her arm linked through his, chattering to him with the childish pomposity of a school-girl out of class.

"What a pity it is, Tonton, that I've got to desert you so soon! Grandmamma wishes me to pay a call on Aunt Alicia. Which motor-car are you using today? Did you come in the new four-seater de Dion-Bouton with the collapsible hood? I hear it can be driven simply with one hand! Goodness, Tonton, those are smart gloves, and no mistake! So you've had a row with Liane, Tonton?"

"Gilberte," scolded Madame Alvarez, "what business of yours can that be?"

"But, Grandmamma, everybody knows about it. The whole story was in the *Gil Blas*. It began: *A secret bitterness is seeping into the sweet product of the sugarbeet.* . . . At school all the girls were asking me about it, for of course they know I know you. And I can tell you, Tonton, there's not a soul at school who takes Liane's side! They all agree that she's behaved disgracefully!"

"Gilberte!" repeated Madame Alvarez, "Say goodbye to Monsieur Lachaille, and run along!"

"Leave her alone, poor child," Gaston Lachaille sighed. "She, at any rate, intends no harm. And it's perfectly true that all's over between Liane and me. You're off to Aunt Alicia's, Gigi? Take my motor-car and send it back for me."

Gilberte gave a little cry, a jump of joy, and hugged Lachaille.

"Thank you, Tonton! Just think of Aunt Alicia's face! The concierge's eyes will be popping from her head!"

Off she went, with the chatter of a young filly not yet shod.

"You spoil her, Gaston," said Madame Alvarez.

But in this she was not altogether speaking the truth. Gaston Lachaille did not know how to "spoil" anyone—even himself. His luxuries were cut and dried: motor-cars, a dreary mansion on the Parc Monceau, Liane's monthly allowance and birthday jewels, champagne and baccarat at Deauville in the summer, at Monte Carlo in the winter. From time to time he would drop a fat check into some charity fund, or finance a new daily paper, or buy a yacht only to resell it almost at once to some Central European monarch: yet from none of this did he get any fun. He would say, as he looked at himself in the glass, "That's the face of a man who is branded." Because of his rather long nose and large dark eyes he was regarded on all sides as easy game. His commercial instinct and rich man's caution stood him in good stead, however; no one had succeeded in robbing him of his pearl studs, of his massive gold or silver cigarette-cases encrusted with precious stones, of his dark sable-lined topcoat.

From the window he watched his motor-car start up. That year, fashionable automobiles were being built with a slightly higher body and a rather wider top, to accommodate the exaggerated hats affected by Caroline Otero, Liane de Pougy, and other conspicuous figures of 1899: and, in consequence, they would sway gently at every turn of the wheel.

"Mamita," said Gaston Lachaille, "you wouldn't make me a cup of camomile?"

"Two rather than one," answered Madame Alvarez. "Sit down, my poor Gaston."

From the depths of a dilapidated armchair she removed some crumpled illustrated papers, a stocking waiting to be darned, and a box of liquorice candies known as *agents de change*. The jilted man settled down into the chair luxuriously, while his hostess put out the tray and two cups.

"Why does the camomile they brew at home always smell of faded chrysanthemums?" sighed Gaston.

"It's simply a matter of taking pains. You may not believe it, Gaston, but I often pick my best camomile flowers in Paris, growing on waste ground, insignificant little flowers you would hardly notice. But they have a taste that is *unesteemable*. My goodness, what beautiful cloth your suit is made of! That deep-woven stripe is as smart as can be. Just the sort of material your father liked! But, I must confess, he would never have carried it so elegantly."

Never more than once during the course of a conversation did Madame Alvarez evoke the memory of an elder Lachaille, whom she claimed to have known intimately. From her former relationship, real or invented, she drew no advantage other than the close relationship of Gaston Lachaille, and the pleasure to be derived from watching a rich man enjoying the comforts of the poor when he made himself at home in her old armchair. Under their gas-blackened ceiling, these three feminine creatures never asked him for pearls, chinchillas, or solitaire diamonds, and they knew how to converse with tact and due solemnity on scandalous topics traditional and recondite. From the age of twelve, Gigi had known that Madame Otero's string of large black pearls were "dipped," that is to say, artificially tinted, while the three strings of her matchlessly graded pearl necklace were worth "a king's ransom"; that Madame de Pougy's seven rows lacked "life"; that Eugénie Fougère's famous diamond bolero was quite worthless; and that no self-respecting woman gadded about, like Madame Antokolski, in a coupé upholstered in mauve satin. She had obediently broken her friendship with a school friend, Lydia Poret, after the girl had shown her a solitaire, set as a ring, presented by the Baron Ephraim.

"A solitaire!" Madame Alvarez had exclaimed. "For a girl of fifteen! Her mother must be mad!"

"But, Grandmamma," pleaded Gigi, "it's not Lydia's fault if the Baron gave it to her!"

"Silence! I'm not blaming the Baron. The Baron knows what is expected of him. But plain common sense should have told the mother to put the ring in a safe at the bank, while waiting."

"While waiting for what, Grandmamma?"

"To see how things turn out."

"Why not in her jewel-case?"

"Because one never knows. Especially as the Baron is the sort of man who might change his mind. If, on the other hand, he has declared himself openly, Madame Poret has only to withdraw her daughter from her studies. Until the matter has been properly cleared up, you will oblige me by not walking home with that little Poret. Who ever heard of such a thing!"

"But supposing she marries, Grandmamma?"

"Marries? Marries whom, pray?"

"Why, the Baron!"

Madame Alvarez and her daughter exchanged glances of stupefaction. "I find the child so discouraging," Andrée had murmured. "She comes from another planet."

"My poor Gaston," said Madame Alvarez, "is it really true, then, that you have broken with her? In some way, it may be the best thing for you; but in others, I'm sure you must find it most upsetting. Whom can one trust, I ask you!"

Poor Gaston listened while he drank the scalding camomile. The taste of it gave him as much comfort as the sight of the plaster-rose on the ceiling, still black from the hanging lamp now "converted to electricity," still faithfully retaining its shade—a vast frilly bell of palest green. Half the contents of a work-basket lay strewn over the dining-room table, from which Gilberte had forgotten to remove her copy-book. Above the upright piano hung an enlarged photograph of Gilberte at eight months, as a pendant to a portrait in oils of Andrée, dressed for her part in Si j'étais Roi. The perfectly inoffensive untidiness, the ray of spring sunshine coming through the point-lace curtains, the warmth given out by a little stove kept at a low heat,—all these homely things were like so many soothing potions to the nerves of a jilted and lonely millionaire.

"Are you positively in torment, my poor Gaston?"

"To be exact, I'm not in torment. I'm just very upset, as you say."

"I have no wish to appear inquisitive," said Madame Alvarez, "but how did it all happen? I've read the papers, of course; but can one believe what they say?"

Lachaille tugged at his small waxed moustache, and ran his fingers over his thick, cropped hair.

"Oh, much the same as on previous occasions. She waited for the birthday present, then off she trotted. And, into the bargain, she must needs go and bury herself in such a wretched little hole in Normandy—so stupid of her! Any fool could have discovered that there were only two rooms at the inn, one occupied by Liane, the other by Sandomir, a skating-instructor from the *Palais de Glace*."

"He's Polaire's tea-time waltzing partner, isn't he? Oh, women don't know where to draw the line nowadays! And just after her birthday, too! Oh! it's so tactless! What could be more unladylike!"

Madame Alvarez stirred the teaspoon round and round in her cup, her little finger in the air. When she lowered her gaze, her lids did not quite cover her protuberant eyeballs, and her resemblance to George Sand became marked.

"I'd given her a rope," said Gaston Lachaille. "What you might call a rope—thirty-seven pearls. The middle one as big as the ball of my thumb."

He held out his white, beautifully manicured thumb, to which Madame Alvarez accorded the admiration due to a middle pearl.

"You certainly know how to do things in style," she said. "You came out of it extremely well, Gaston."

"I came out of it with a pair of horns, certainly."

Madame Alvarez did not seem to have heard him.

"If I were you, Gaston, I should try to get your own back on her. I should take up with some society lady."

"That's a nice pill to offer me," said Lachaille, who was absent-mindedly helping himself to the *agents de change*.

"Yes, indeed, I might even say that sometimes the cure may prove worse than the disease," Madame Alvarez continued, tactfully agreeing with him. "Out of the frying-pan into the fire." After which she respected Gaston Lachaille's silence.

The muffled sounds of a piano penetrated through the ceiling.

Without a word, the visitor held out his empty cup, and Madame Alvarez refilled it.

"Is the family all right? What news of Aunt Alicia?"

"Oh, my sister, you know, is always the same. She's smart enough to keep herself to herself. She says she would rather live in a splendid past than an ugly present. Her King of Spain, her Milan of Serbia, her Khedive, her rajahs by the half-dozen—or so she would have you believe! She is very considerate to Gigi. She finds her a trifle backward for her age, as indeed she is, and puts her through her paces. Last week, for instance, she taught her how to eat *homard a l'Américaine* in faultless style."

"Whatever for?"

"Alicia says it will be extremely useful. The three great difficulties in a girl's education, she maintains, are *homard a l'Américaine*, a boiled egg, and asparagus. Bad table manners, she says, have broken up many a happy home."

"That can happen," said Lachaille dreamily.

"Oh, Alicia is no fool! And it's just what Gigi requires—she is so greedy! If only her brain worked as well as her jaws! But she might well be a child of ten! And what breathtaking scheme have you got for the Battle of Flowers? Are you going to dazzle us again this year?"

"O Lord no!" groaned Gaston. "I shall take advantage of my misfortune, and save on the red roses."

Madame Alvarez wrung her hands.

"Oh, Gaston, you mustn't do that! If you're not there, the procession will look like a funeral!"

"I don't care what it looks like," said Gaston gloomily.

"You're never going to leave the prize banner to people like Valérie Cheniaguine? Oh, Gaston, we can't allow that!"

"You will have to. Valérie can very well afford it."

"Especially since she does it on the cheap. Gaston, do you know where she went for the ten thousand bunches thrown last year? She had three women tying them up for two days and two nights, and the flowers were bought in the flower market! In the market! Only the four wheels, and the coachman's whip, and the harness trappings bore the label of Lachaume."

"That's a dodge to remember!" said Lachaille, cheering up. "Good Lord! I've finished the liquorice!"

The tap-tap of Gilberte's marching footsteps could be heard crossing the outer room.

"Back already!" said Madame Alvarez. "What's the meaning of this?"

"The meaning," said the girl, "is that Aunt Alicia wasn't in good form. But I've been out in Tonton's 'tuf-tuf.' "

Her lips parted in a bright smile.

"You know, Tonton, all the time I was in your automobile, I put on a martyred expression—like this—as if I was bored to death with every luxury under the sun. I had the time of my life."

She sent her hat flying across the room, and her hair fell tumbling over her forehead and cheeks. She perched herself on a rather high stool, and tucked her knees up under her chin.

"Well, Tonton? You look as if you were dying of boredom. What about a game of piquet? It's Sunday, and Mamma doesn't come back between the two performances. Who's been eating all my liquorice? Oh, Tonton, you can't get away with that! The least you can do is to send me some more to make up for it."

"Gilberte, your manners!" scolded Madame Alvarez. "Your knees! Gaston hasn't the time to bother about your liquorice. Pull down your skirts. Gaston, would you like me to send her to her room?"

Young Lachaille, with one eye on the dirty pack of cards in Gilberte's hand, was longing simultaneously to give way to tears, to confide his sorrows, to go to sleep in the old armchair, and to play piquet.

"Let the child stay! In this room I can relax. It's restful. Gigi, I'll play you for twenty pounds of sugar."

"Your sugar's not very tempting. I much prefer sweets."

"It's the same thing. And sugar is better for you than sweets."

"You only say that because you make it."

"Gilberte, you forget yourself!"

A smile enlivened the mournful eyes of Gaston Lachaille.

"Let her say what she likes, Mamita. And if I lose, Gigi, what would you like? A pair of silk stockings?"

The corners of Gilberte's big childish mouth fell.

"Silk stockings make my legs itch. I would rather. . . ."

She raised the snub-nosed face of an angel towards the ceiling, put her head on one side; and tossed her curls from one cheek to the other.

"I would rather have an *eau-de-nil* Persephone corset, with rococo roses embroidered on the garters. No, I'd rather have a music-case."

"Are you studying music now?"

"No, but my older friends at school carry their copy-books in music-cases, because it makes them look like students at the Conservatoire."

"Gilberte, you are making too free!" said Madame Alvarez. "You shall have your case, and your liquorice. Cut, Gigi."

The next moment, the heir of Lachaille-Sugar was deep in the game. His prominent nose, large enough to appear false, and his slightly negroid eyes did not in the least intimidate his opponent. With her elbows on the table, her shoulders on a level with her ears, and her blue eyes and red cheeks at their most vivid, she looked like a tipsy page. They both played passionately, almost in silence, exchanging occasional insults under their breath. "*You spindly spider! you sorrel run to seed!*" Lachaille muttered. "*You old crow's beak!*" the girl countered. The March twilight deepened over the narrow street.

"Please don't think I want you to go, Gaston," said Madame Alvarez, "but it's half-past seven. Will you excuse me while I just see about our dinner?"

"Half-past seven!" cried Lachaille, "and I'm supposed to be dining at Larue with de Dion, Feydeau, and one of the Barthous! This must be the last hand, Gigi."

"Why one of the Barthous?" asked Gilberte. "Are there several of them?"

"Two. One handsome and the other less so. The best known is the least handsome."

"That's not fair," said Gilberte. "And Feydeau, who's he?"

Lachaille plopped down his cards in amazement.

"Well, I declare! She doesn't know who Feydeau is! Don't you ever go to a play?"

"Hardly ever, Tonton."

"Don't you like the theatre?"

"I'm not mad about it. And Grandmamma and Aunt Alicia both say that going to plays prevents one from thinking about the serious side of life. Don't tell Grandmamma I told you."

She lifted the weight of her hair away from her ears, and let it fall forward again. "Phew!" she sighed. "This mane does make me hot!"

"And what do they mean by the serious side of life?"

"Oh, I don't know it all off by heart, Uncle Gaston. And, what's more, they don't always agree about it. Grandmamma says: 'Don't read novels, they only depress you. Don't put on powder, it ruins the complexion. Don't wear stays, they spoil the figure. Don't dawdle and gaze at shop windows when you're by yourself. Don't get to know the families of your school friends, especially not the fathers who wait at the gates to fetch their daughters home from school.' "

She spoke very rapidly, panting between words like a child who has been running.

"And on top of that, Aunt Alicia goes off on another tack! I've reached the age when I can wear stays, and I should take lessons in dancing and deportment, and I should be aware of what's going on, and know the meaning of 'caret,' and not be taken in by the clothes that actresses wear. 'It's quite simple,' she tells me, 'of all the dresses you see on the stage, nineteen out of twenty would look ridiculous in the paddock.' In fact, my head is fit to split with it all! What will you be eating at Larue this evening, Tonton?"

"How should I know! *Filets de sole aux moules*, for a change. And of course, saddle of lamb with truffles. Do get on with the game, Gigi! I've got a point of five."

"That won't get you anywhere. I've got all the cards in the pack. Here, at home, we're having the warmed up remains of the *cassoulet*. I'm very fond of *cassoulet*."

"A plain dish of *cassoulet* with bacon rind," said Inez Alvarez modestly, as she came in. "Goose was exorbitant this week."

"I'll have one sent to you from Bon-Abri," said Gaston.

"Thank you very much, Gaston. Gigi, help Monsieur Lachaille on with his overcoat. Fetch him his hat and stick!"

When Lachaille had gone, rather sulky after a regretful sniff at the warmed up *cassoulet*, Madame Alvarez turned to her grand-daughter.

"Will you please inform me, Gilberte, why it was you returned so early from Aunt Alicia's? I didn't ask you in front of Gaston. Family matters must never be discussed in front of a third person, remember that!"

"There's no mystery about it, Grandmamma. Aunt Alicia was wearing her little lace cap to show me she had a headache. She said to me, 'I'm not very well.' I said to her, 'Oh! Then I mustn't tire you out, I'll go home again.' She said to me, 'Sit down and rest for five minutes.' 'Oh!' I said to her, 'I'm not tired. I drove here.' 'You drove here!' she said to me, raising her hands like this. As you may imag-ine, I had kept the motor-car waiting a few minutes, to show Aunt Alicia. 'Yes,' I said to her, 'The four-seater de-Dion-Bouton-with-the-collapsible-hood, which Tonton lent me while he was paying a call on us. He has had a rumpus with Liane.' 'Who do you think you're talking to?' she says to me, 'I've not yet got one foot in the grave! I'm still kept informed about public events when they're important. I know that he has had a rumpus with that great lamp-post of a woman. Well, you'd better run along home, and not bother about a poor ill old creature like me.' She waved to me from the window as I got into the motor-car."

Madame Alvarez pursed her lips.

"A poor ill old creature! She has never suffered so much as a cold in her life! I like that! What . . ."

"Grandmamma, do you think he'll remember my liquorice and the music-case?"

Madame Alvarez slowly lifted her heavy eyes towards the ceiling.

"Perhaps, my child, perhaps."

"But, as he lost, he owes them to me, doesn't he?"

"Yes, yes, he owes them to you. Perhaps you'll get them after all. Slip on your pinafore, and set the table. Put away your cards."

"Yes, Grandmamma. Grandmamma, what did he tell you about Madame Liane? Is it true she ran out on him with Sandomir and the rope of pearls?"

"In the first place, one doesn't say 'ran out on' anyone. In the second, come here and let me tighten your ribbon, so that your curls won't get soaked in the soup. And finally, the sayings and doings of a person who has broken the rules of etiquette are not for your ears. These happen to be Gaston's private affairs."

"But, Grandmamma, they are no longer private, since everyone's talking about them, and the whole thing came out in *Gil Blas.*"

"Silence! All you need to know is that the conduct of Madame Liane d'Exelmans has been the reverse of sensible. The ham for your mother is between two plates: you will put it in the larder."

Gilberte was asleep when her mother—Andrée Alvar, in small type on the Opéra-Comique play-bills—returned home. Madame Alvarez, the elder, seated at a game of patience, inquired from force of habit whether she was not too tired. Following polite family custom, Andrée reproached her mother for having waited up, and Madame Alvarez made her ritual reply.

"I shouldn't sleep in peace unless I knew you were in. There is some ham, and a little bowl of warm *cassoulet.* And some stewed prunes. The beer is on the window-sill."

"The child is in bed?"

"Of course."

Andrée Alvar made a solid meal—pessimists have good appetites. She still looked pretty in theatrical make-up. Without it, the rims of her eyes were pink and her lips colorless. For this reason, Aunt Alicia declared, Andrée never met with the admiration in real life that she gained on the stage.

"Did you sing well, my child?"

"Yes, I sang well. But where does it get me? All the applause goes to Tiphaine, as you may well imagine. Oh dear, oh dear, I really don't think I can bear to go on with this sort of life."

"It was your own choice. But you would bear it much better," said Madame Alvarez sententiously, "if you had someone! It's your loneliness that gets on your nerves, and you take such black views. You're behaving contrary to nature."

"Oh, Mother, don't start that all over again, I'm tired enough as it is. What news is there?"

"None. Everyone's talking of Gaston's break with Liane."

"Yes, they certainly are! Even in the green room at the Opéra-Comique, which can hardly be called up-to-date."

"It's an event of world-wide interest," said Madame Alvarez.

"Is there talk of who's in the running?"

"I should think not! It's far too recent. He is in full mourning, so to speak. Can you believe it, at a quarter to eight he was sitting exactly where you are now, playing a game of piquet with Gigi? He says he has no wish to attend the Battle of Flowers."

"Not really!"

"Yes. If he doesn't go, it will cause a great deal of talk. I advised him to think twice before taking such a decision."

"They were saying at the *Théâtre* that a certain music-hall artiste might stand a chance," said Andrée. "The one billed as the Cobra at the Olympia. It seems she does an acrobatic turn, and is brought on in a basket hardly big enough for a fox-terrier, and from this she uncurls like a snake."

Madame Alvarez protruded her heavy lower lip in contempt.

"What an idea! Gaston Lachaille has not sunk to that level! A music-hall performer! Do him the justice to admit that, as befits a bachelor of his standing, he has always confined himself to the great ladies of the profession."

"A fine pack of bitches!" murmured Andrée.

"Be more careful how you express yourself, my child. Calling people and things by their names has never done anyone any good. Gaston's mistresses have all had an air about them. A liaison with a great professional lady is the only suitable way for him to wait for a great marriage, always supposing that some day he does marry. Whatever may happen, we're in the front row when anything fresh turns up. Gaston has such confidence in me! I wish you had seen him asking me for camomile! A boy, a regular boy! Indeed, he is only thirty-three. And all that wealth weighs so heavily on his shoulders."

Andrée's pink eyelids blinked ironically.

"Pity him, Mother, if you like. I'm not complaining, but all the time we've known Gaston, he has never given you anything except his confidence."

"He owes us nothing. And thanks to him we've always had sugar for our jams, and, from time to time, for my *curaçao*; and birds from his farm, and odds and ends for the child."

"If you're satisfied with that!"

Madame Alvarez held high her majestic head.

"Perfectly satisfied. And even if I was not, what difference would it make?"

"In fact, as far as we're concerned, Gaston Lachaille, rich as he is, behaves as if he wasn't rich at all. Supposing we were in real straits! Would he come to our rescue, do you suppose?"

Madame Alvarez placed her hand on her heart.

"I'm convinced that he would," she said. And after a pause, she added, "But I would rather not have to ask him."

Andrée picked up the *Journal* again, in which there was a photograph of Liane the ex-mistress. "When you take a good look at her, she's not so extraordinary."

"You're wrong," retorted Madame Alvarez, "she is extraordinary. Otherwise she would not be so famous. Successes and celebrity are not a matter of luck. You talk like those scatterbrains who say, 'Seven rows of pearls would look every bit as well on me as on Madame de Pougy. She certainly cuts a dash—but so could I.' Such nonsense makes me laugh. Take what's left of the camomile to bathe your eyes."

"Thank you, Mother. Did the child go to Aunt Alicia's?"

"She did indeed, and in Gaston's motor-car, what's more! He lent it to her. It can go forty miles an hour, I believe! She was in seventh heaven."

"Poor lamb, I wonder what she'll make of her life. She's quite capable of ending up as a mannequin or a saleswoman. She's so backward. At her age, I—"

There was no indulgence in the glance Madame Alvarez gave her daughter.

"Don't boast too much about what you were doing when you were her age. If I remember rightly, at her age you were snapping your fingers at Monsieur Mennesson and all his flour-mills, though he was perfectly ready to make you your fortune. Instead, you must needs bolt with a wretched music master."

Andrée Alvar kissed her mother's lustrous plaits.

"My darling mother, don't curse me at this hour, I'm so sleepy. Goodnight, Mother. I've a rehearsal tomorrow at a quarter to one. I'll eat at the dairy during the entr'acte; don't bother about me."

She yawned and walked in the dark through the little room where her daughter was asleep. All she could see of Gilberte in the obscurity was a bush of hair and the Russian braid of her nightdress. She locked herself into the exiguous bathroom and, late though it was, lit the gas under a kettle. Madame Alvarez had instilled into her progeny, among other virtues, a respect for certain rites. One of her maxims was, "You can, at a pinch, leave the face till the morning, when travelling or pressed for time. For a woman, attention to the lower parts is the first law of self-respect."

The last to go to bed, Madame Alvarez was the first to rise, and allowed the daily cleaning woman no hand in preparing the breakfast coffee. She slept in the dining-sitting room, on a divan-bed, and, at the stroke of half-past seven, she opened the door to the papers, the quart of milk, and the daily maid—who was carrying the others. By eight o'clock she had taken out her curling-pins, and her beautiful coils of hair were dressed and smooth. At ten minutes to nine, Gilberte left for school, clean and tidy, her hair well-brushed. At ten o'clock Madame Alvarez was "thinking about" the midday meal, that is, she got into her mackintosh, slipped her arm through the handle of her shopping net, and set off to market.

Today, as on all other days, she made sure that her granddaughter would not be late; she placed the coffee-pot and the jug of milk piping hot on the table, and unfolded the newspaper while waiting for her. Gilberte came in fresh as a flower, smelling of lavender-water, with some vestiges of sleep still clinging to her. A cry from Madame Alvarez made her fully wide awake.

"Call your mother, Gigi! Liane d'Exelmans has committed suicide."

The child replied with a long drawn-out "Oooh!" and asked, "Is she dead?"

"Of course not. She knows what she's about."

"How did she do it, Grandmamma? A revolver?"

Madame Alvarez looked pityingly at her granddaughter.

"The idea! Laudanum, as usual. *'Doctors Morèze and Pelledoux, who have never left the heart-broken beauty's bedside, cannot yet answer for her life, but their diagnosis is reassuring . . .'* My own diagnosis is that if Madame d'Exelmans goes on playing that game, she'll end by ruining her stomach."

"The last time she killed herself, Grandmamma, was for the sake of Prince Georgevitch, wasn't it?"

"Where are your brains, my darling? It was for Count Berthou de Sauveterre."

"Oh, so it was. And what will Tonton do now, do you think?"

A dreamy look passed across the huge eyes of Madame Alvarez.

"It's a toss-up, my child. We shall know everything in good time, even if he starts by refusing to give an interview to anybody. You must always start by refusing to give an interview to anybody. Then later you can fill the front page. Tell the concierge, by the way, to get us the evening papers. Have you had enough to eat? Did you have your second cup of milk, and your two pieces of bread and butter? Put on your gloves before you go out. Don't dawdle on the way. I'm going to call your mother. What a story! Andrée, are you asleep? Oh, so you're out of bed! Andrée, Liane has committed suicide!"

"That's a nice change," muttered Andrée. "She has only the one idea in her head, that woman, but she sticks to it."

"You've not taken out your curlers yet, Andrée?"

"And have my hair go limp in the middle of rehearsal? No thank you!"

Madame Alvarez ran her eyes over her daughter, from the spiky tips of her curlers to the felt slippers. "It's plain that there's no man here for you to bother about, my child! A man in the house soon cures a woman of traipsing about in dressing-gown and slippers. What an excitement, this suicide! Unsuccessful, of course."

Andrée's pallid lips parted in a contemptuous smile: "It's getting too boring—the way she takes laudanum as if it was castor oil!"

"Anyhow, who cares about her? It's the Lachaille heir who matters. This is the first time such a thing has happened to him. He's already had—let me see. He's had Gentiane, who stole his private papers; then that foreigner, who tried to force him into marriage, but Liane is his first suicide. In such circumstances, a man so much in the public eye has to be extremely careful about what line he takes."

"Hm! He'll be bursting with pride, you may be sure."

"And with good reason, too," said Madame Alvarez. "We shall be seeing great things before very long. I wonder what Alicia will have to say about the situation."

"She'll do her best to make a mountain of a molehill."

"Alicia is no angel. But I must confess that she is long-sighted. And that without ever leaving her room!"

"She's no need to, since she has the telephone. Mother, won't you have one put in here?"

"It's expensive," said Madame Alvarez, thoughtfully. "We only just manage to make both ends meet, as it is. The telephone is of real use only to important businessmen, or to women who have something to hide. Now, if you were to change your mode of life—and I'm only putting it forward as a supposition—and if Gigi were to start on a life of her own, I should be the first to say, 'We'll have the telephone put in.' But we haven't reached that point yet, unfortunately."

She allowed herself a single sigh, pulled on her rubber gloves, and coolly set about her household chores. Thanks to her care, the modest flat was growing old without too many signs of deterioration. She retained, from her past life, the honorable habits of women who have lost their honor, and these she taught to her daughter and her daughter's daughter. Sheets never stayed on the beds longer than ten days, and the combination char- and washerwoman told everyone that the chemises and drawers of the ladies of Madame Alvarez' household were changed more often than she could count, and so were the table napkins. At any moment, at the cry of "Gigi, take off your shoes!" Gilberte had to remove shoes and stockings, exhibit white feet to the closest inspection, and announce the least suspicion of a corn.

During the week following Madame d'Exelmans' suicide, Lachaille's reactions were somewhat incoherent. He engaged the stars of the National Musical Academy to dance at a midnight fête held at his own house, and, wishing to give a supper party at the Pré-Catalan, he arranged for that restaurant to open a fortnight earlier than was their custom. The clowns, Footit *et* Chocolat, did a turn: Rita del Erido caracoled on horseback between the supper tables, wearing a divided skirt of white lace flounces, a white hat on her black hair with white ostrich feathers frothing round the relentless beauty of her face. Indeed, Paris mistakenly proclaimed, such was her beauty, that Gaston Lachaille was hoisting her astride a throne of sugar. Twenty-four hours later, Paris was undeceived. For in the false prophecies it had published, *Gil Blas* nearly lost the subsidy it received from Gaston Lachaille. A specialized weekly, *Paris en amour*, provided another red herring, under the headline: "Young Yankee millionairess makes no secret of weakness for French sugar."

Madame Alvarez' ample bust shook with incredulous laughter when she read the daily papers: she had received her information from none other than Gaston Lachaille in person. Twice in ten days, he had found time to drop in for a cup of camomile, to sink into the depths of the now sagging conch-shaped armchair, and there forget his business worries and his dislike of being unattached. He even brought Gigi an absurd Russian leather music-case with a silver-gilt clasp, and twenty boxes of liquorice. Madame Alvarez was given a *pâté de foie gras* and six bottles of champagne, and of these bounties Tonton Lachaille partook by inviting himself to dinner. Throughout the meal, Gilberte regaled them rather tipsily with tittle-tattle about her school, and later won Gaston's gold pencil at piquet. He lost with good grace, recovered his spirits, laughed, and, pointing to the child, said to Madame Alvarez, "There's my best pal!" Madame Alvarez' Spanish eyes moved with slow watchfulness from Gigi's reddened cheeks and white teeth to Lachaille, who was pulling her hair by the fistful. "You little devil, you had the fourth king up your sleeve all the time!"

It was at this moment that Andrée, coming back from the Opéra-Comique, looked at Gigi's disheveled head rolling against Lachaille's sleeve, and saw the tears of excited laughter in her lovely slate-blue eyes. She said nothing, and accepted a glass of champagne, then another, and yet another. After her third glass, Gaston Lachaille was threatened with the Bell Song from *Lakmé*, at which point Andrée's mother led her away to bed.

The following day, no one spoke of this family party except Gilberte, who exclaimed, "Never, never in all my life, have I laughed so much! And the pencil is real gold!" Her unreserved chatter met with a strange silence, or rather with "Now then, Gigi, try to be a little more serious!" thrown out almost absent-mindedly.

After that, Gaston Lachaille let a fortnight go by without giving a sign of life, and the Alvarez family gathered its information from the papers only.

"Did you see, Andrée? In the Gossip Column it says that Monsieur Gaston Lachaille has left for Monte Carlo. *The reason for this seems to be of a sentimental nature—a secret that we respect.* What next!"

"Would you believe it, Grandmamma, Lydia Poret was saying at the dancing class that Liane travelled on the same train as Tonton, but in another compartment! Grandmamma, do you think it can be true?"

Madame Alvarez shrugged her shoulders.

"If it was true, how on earth would those Porets know? Have they become friends with Monsieur Lachaille all of a sudden?"

"No, but Lydia Poret heard the story in her aunt's dressing room at the Comédie Française."

Madame Alvarez exchanged looks with her daughter.

"In her dressing room! That explains everything!" she exclaimed, for she held the theatrical profession in contempt, although Andrée worked so hard. When Madame Emilienne d'Alençon had decided to present performing rabbits, and Madame de Pougy—shyer on the stage than any young girl—had amused herself by miming the part of Columbine in spangled black tulle, Madame Alvarez had stigmatised them both in a single phrase, "What! have they sunk to that?"

"Grandmamma, tell me, Grandmamma, do you know him, this Prince Radziwill?" Gilberte went on again.

"What's come over the child today? Has she been bitten by a flea? Which Prince Radziwill, to begin with? There's more than one."

"I don't know," said Gigi. "The one who's getting married. Among the list of presents, it says here, '*are three writing-sets in malachite.*' What is malachite?"

"Oh, you're being tiresome, child. If he's getting married, he's no longer interesting."

"But if Tonton got married, wouldn't he be interesting either?"

"It all depends. It would be interesting if he were to marry his mistress. When Prince Cheniaguine married Valérie d'Aigreville, it was obvious that the life she had led him for the past fifteen years was all he wanted; scenes, plates flung across the room, and reconciliations in the middle of the restaurant Durand, Place de la

Madeleine. Clearly, she was a woman who knew how to make herself valued. But all that is too complicated for you, my poor Gigi."

"And do you think it's to marry Liane that they've gone away together?"

Madame Alvarez pressed her forehead against the window pane, and seemed to be consulting the spring sunshine, which bestowed upon the street a sunny side and one with shade.

"No," she said, "not if I know anything about anything. I must have a word with Alicia. Gigi, come with me as far as her house; you can leave me there and find your way back along the quais. It will give you some fresh air, since, it would seem, one must have fresh air nowadays. I have never been in the habit of taking the air more than twice a year, myself, at Cabourg and at Monte Carlo. And I am none the worse for that."

That evening Madame Alvarez came in so late that the family dined off tepid soup, cold meat, and some cakes sent round by Aunt Alicia. To Gilberte's "Well, what did she have to say?" she presented an icy front, and answered in clarion tones.

"She says that she is going to teach you how to eat ortolans."

"Lovely!" cried Gilberte. "And what did she say about the summer frock she promised me?"

"She said she would see. And that there's no reason why you should be displeased with the result."

"Oh!" said Gilberte, gloomily.

"She also wants you to go to luncheon with her on Thursday, sharp at twelve."

"With you, too, Grandmamma?"

Madame Alvarez looked at the willowy slip of a girl facing her across the table, at her high, rosy cheekbones beneath eyes as blue as an evening sky, at her strong even teeth biting a fresh-colored but slightly chapped lip, and at the primitive splendor of her ash-gold hair.

"No," she said at last. "Without me."

Gilberte got up and wound an arm about her grandmother's neck.

"The way you said that, Grandmamma, surely doesn't mean that you're going to send me to live with Aunt Alicia? I don't want to leave here, Grandmamma!"

Madame Alvarez cleared her throat, gave a little cough, and smiled.

"Goodness gracious! what a foolish creature you are! Leave here!

Why, my poor Gigi, I'm not scolding you, but you've not reached the first stage towards leaving."

For a bell-pull, Aunt Alicia had hung from her front door a length of bead-embroidered braid on a background of twining green vine-leaves and purple grapes. The door itself, varnished and revarnished till it glistened, shone with the glow of a dark brown caramel. From the very threshold, where she was admitted by a "man-servant," Gilberte enjoyed in her undiscriminating way an atmosphere of discreet luxury. The carpet, spread with Persian rugs, seemed to lend her wings. After hearing Madame Alvarez pronounce her sister's Louis XV little drawing room to be "boredom itself," Gilberte echoed her words by saying: "Aunt Alicia's drawing room is very pretty, but it's boredom itself!" reserving her admiration for the dining room, furnished in pale almost golden lemon wood dating from the Directoire, quite plain but for the grain of a wood as transparent as wax. "I shall buy myself a set like that one day," Gigi had once said in all innocence.

"In the Faubourg Antoine, I dare say," Aunt Alicia had answered teasingly, with a smile of her cupid's bow mouth and a flash of small teeth.

She was seventy years old. Her fastidious taste was everywhere apparent: in her silver-grey bedroom with its red Chinese vases, in her narrow white bathroom as warm as a hot-house, and in her robust health, concealed by a pretence of delicacy. The men of her generation, when trying to describe Alicia de Saint-Efflam, fumbled for words and could only exclaim, "Ah, my deah fellow!" or "Nothing could give you the faintest idea . . ." Those who had known her intimately produced photographs which younger men found ordinary enough. "Was she really so lovely? You wouldn't think so from her photographs!" Looking at portraits of her, old admirers would pause for an instant, recollecting the turn of a wrist like a swan's neck, the tiny ear, the profile revealing a delicious kinship between the heart-shaped mouth and the wide-cut eyelids with their long lashes.

Gilberte kissed the pretty old lady, who was wearing a peak of black Chantilly lace on her white hair, and, on her slightly dumpy figure, a tea-gown of shot taffeta.

"You have one of your headaches, Aunt Alicia?"

"I'm not sure yet," replied Aunt Alicia, "it depends on the luncheon. Come quickly, the eggs are ready! Take off your coat! What on earth is that dress?"

"One of Mamma's, altered to fit me. Are they difficult eggs today?"

"Not at all. *Oeufs brouillés aux croutons.* The ortolans are not difficult, either. And you shall have chocolate cream. So shall I."

With her young voice, a touch of pink on her amiable wrinkles, and lace on her white hair, Aunt Alicia was the perfect stage marquise. Gilberte had the greatest reverence for her aunt. In sitting down to table in her presence, she would pull her skirt up behind, join her knees, hold her elbows close to her sides, straighten her shoulder blades, and to all appearances become the perfect young lady. She would remember what she had been taught, break her bread quickly, eat with her mouth shut, and take care, when cutting her meat, not to let her fore-finger reach the blade of her knife.

Today her hair, severely tied back in a heavy knot at the nape of her neck, disclosed the fresh line of her forehead and ears, and a very powerful throat, rising from the rather ill-cut opening of her altered dress. This was a dingy blue, the bodice pleated about a let-in piece, and to cheer up this patchwork, three rows of mohair braid had been sewn round the hem of the skirt, and three times three rows of mohair braid round the sleeves, between the wrist and the elbow.

Aunt Alicia, sitting opposite her niece and examining her through fine dark eyes, could find no fault.

"How old are you?" she asked suddenly.

"The same as I was the other day, Aunt. Fifteen and a half. Aunt, what do you really think of this business of Tonton Gaston?"

"Why? Does it interest you?"

"Of course, Aunt. It worries me. If Tonton takes up with another lady, he won't come and play piquet with us any more or drink camomile tea—at least not for some time. That would be a shame."

"That's one way of looking at it, certainly."

Aunt Alicia examined her niece critically, through narrowed eyelids.

"Do you work hard, in class? Who are your friends? Ortolans should be cut in two, with one quick stroke of the knife, and no grating of the blade on the plate. Bite up each half. The bones don't matter. Go on eating while you answer my question, but don't talk with your mouth full. You must manage it. If I can, you can. What friends have you made?"

"None, Aunt. Grandmamma won't even let me have tea with the families of my school friends."

"She is quite right. Apart from that, there is no one who follows you, no little clerk hanging round your skirts? No schoolboy? No older man? I warn you, I shall know at once if you lie to me."

Gilberte gazed at the bright face of the imperious old lady who was questioning her so sharply.

"Why, no, Aunt, no one. Has somebody been telling you tales about me? I am always on my own. And why does Grandmamma stop me from accepting invitations?"

"She is right, for once. You would only be invited by ordinary people, that is to say, useless people."

"And what about us? Aren't we ordinary people ourselves?"

"No."

"What makes these ordinary people inferior to us?"

"They have weak heads and dissolute bodies. Besides, they are married. But I don't think you understand."

"Yes, Aunt, I understand that we don't marry."

"Marriage is not forbidden to us. Instead of marrying 'at once,' it sometimes happens that we marry 'at last.' "

"But does that prevent me from seeing girls of my own age?"

"Yes. Are you bored at home? Well, be a little bored. It's not a bad thing. Boredom helps one to make decisions. What is the matter? Tears? The tears of a silly child who is backward for her age. Have another ortolan."

Aunt Alicia, with three glittering fingers, grasped the stem of her glass and raised it in a toast.

"To you and me, Gigi! You shall have an Egyptian cigarette with your coffee. On condition that you do not wet the end of your cigarette, and that you don't spit out specks of tobacco—going *ptu, ptu*. I shall also give you a note to the *première vendeuse* at Béchoff-David, an old friend of mine who was not a success. Your wardrobe is going to be changed. Nothing venture, nothing gain."

The dark blue eyes gleamed. Gilberte stammered with joy.

"Aunt! Aunt! I'm going to . . . to Bé—"

"—choff-David. But I thought you weren't interested in clothes?"

Gilberte blushed.

"Aunt, I'm not interested in home-made clothes."

"I sympathize with you. Can it be that you have taste? When you think of looking your best, how do you see yourself dressed?"

"Oh, but I know just what would suit me, Aunt! I've seen—"

"Explain yourself without gestures. The moment you gesticulate you look common."

"I've seen a dress . . . oh, a dress created for Madame Lucy Gérard! Hundreds of tiny ruffles of pearl-grey silk muslin from top to bottom. And then a dress of lavender-blue cloth cut out on a black velvet foundation, the cut-out design making a sort of peacock's tail on the train."

The small hand with its precious stones flashed through the air.

"Enough! Enough! I see your fancy is to be dressed like a leading _comédienne_ at the Théâtre Français,—and don't take that as a compliment! Come and pour out the coffee. And without jerking up the lip of the coffee-pot to prevent the drop from falling. I'd rather have a foot-bath in my saucer than see you juggling like a waiter in a café."

The next hour passed very quickly for Gilberte: Aunt Alicia had unlocked a casket of jewels to use for a lesson that dazzled her.

"What is that, Gigi?"

"A marquise diamond."

"We say, a marquise-shaped brilliant. And that?"

"A topaz."

Aunt Alicia threw up her hands and the sunlight, glancing off her rings, set off a myriad scintillations.

"A topaz! I have suffered many humiliations, but this surpasses them all. A topaz among my jewels! Why not an aquamarine or a chrysolite? It's a yellow diamond, little goose, and you won't often see its like. And this?"

Gilberte half opened her mouth, as if in a dream.

"Oh! That's an emerald. Oh, how beautiful it is!"

Aunt Alicia slipped the large square-cut emerald on one of her thin fingers and was lost in silence.

"Do you see," she said in a hushed voice, "that almost blue flame darting about in the depths of the green light? Only the most beautiful emeralds contain that miracle of elusive blue."

"Who gave it to you, Aunt?" Gilberte dared to ask.

"A king," said Aunt Alicia simply.

"A great king?"

"No. A little one. Great kings do not give very fine stones."

"Why not?"

For a fleeting moment, Aunt Alicia proffered a glimpse of her tiny white teeth.

"If you want my opinion, it's because they don't want to. Between ourselves, the little ones don't either."

"Then who does give great big stones?"

"Who? The shy. The proud, too. And the bounders, because they think that to give a monster jewel is a sign of good breeding. Sometimes a woman does, to humiliate a man. Never wear second-rate jewels, wait till the really good ones come to you."

"And if they don't?"

"Well, then it can't be helped. Rather than a wretched little diamond full of flaws, wear a simple, plainly inexpensive ring. In that case you can say, 'It's a memento. I never part with it, day or night.' Don't ever wear artistic jewelry, it wrecks a woman's reputation."

"What is an artistic jewel?"

"It all depends. A mermaid in gold with eyes of chrysoprase. An Egyptian scarab. A large engraved amethyst. A not very heavy bracelet said to have been chased by a master-hand. A lyre or star, mounted as a brooch. A studded tortoise. In a word, all of them, frightful. Never wear baroque pearls, not even as hat-pins. Beware, above all things, of family jewels!"

"But Grandmamma has a beautiful cameo, set as a medallion."

"There are no beautiful cameos," said Alicia, with a toss of the head. "There are precious stones and pearls. There are white, yellow, blue, blue-white or pink diamonds. We won't speak of black diamonds, they're not worth mentioning. Then there are rubies—when you can be sure of them; sapphires, when they come from Kashmir; emeralds, provided they have no fatal flaw, or are not too light in color, or have a yellowish tint."

"Aunt, I'm very fond of opals, too."

"I am very sorry, but you are not to wear them. I won't allow it."

Dumbfounded, Gilberte remained for a moment open-mouthed.

"Oh! Do you too, Aunt, really believe that they bring bad luck?"

"Why in the world not? You silly little creature," Alicia went bubbling on, "you must pretend to believe in such things. Believe in opals, believe—let's see, what can I suggest—in turquoises that die, in the evil eye . . ."

"But," said Gigi, haltingly, "those are . . . are superstitions!"

"Of course they are, child. They also go by the name of weaknesses. A pretty little collection of weaknesses, and a terror of spiders, are indispensable stock-in-trade with men."

"Why, Aunt?"

The old lady closed the casket, and kept Gilberte kneeling before her.

"Because nine men out of ten are superstitious, nineteen out of twenty believe in the evil eye, and ninety-eight out of a hundred are afraid of spiders. They forgive us—oh! for many things, but not for the absence in us of their own failings," she said. "What makes you sigh?"

"I shall never remember all that!"

"The important thing is not for *you* to remember, but for me to know it."

"Aunt, what is a writing-set in . . . in malachite?"

"Always a calamity. But where on earth did you pick up such terms?"

"From the list of presents at grand weddings, Aunt, printed in the papers."

"Nice reading! But, at least you can gather from it what kind of presents you should never give, or accept."

While speaking, she began to touch here and there the young face on a level with her own, with the sharp pointed nail of her index finger. She lifted one slightly chapped lip, inspected the spotless enamel of the teeth.

"A fine jaw, my girl! With such teeth, I should have gobbled up Paris, and the rest of the world into the bargain. As it was, I had a good bite out of it. What's this you've got here? A small pimple? You shouldn't have a small pimple near your nose. And this? You've pinched a blackhead. You've no business to have such things, or to pinch them. I'll give you some of my astringent lotion. You mustn't eat anything from the pork-butchers' except cooked ham. You don't put on powder?"

"Grandmamma won't let me."

"I should hope not. You go you-know-where regularly? Let me smell your breath. Not that it means anything at this hour, you've just had luncheon."

She laid her hands on Gigi's shoulders.

"Pay attention to what I'm going to say. You have it in your power to please. You have an impossible little nose, a nondescript mouth, cheeks rather like the wife of a moujik—"

"Oh, Aunt!" sighed Gilberte.

"But, with your eyes and eyelashes, your teeth, and your hair, you can get away with it, if you're not a perfect fool. As for the rest—"

She cupped her hands like conch-shells over Gigi's bosom and smiled.

"A promise, but a pretty promise, neatly moulded. Don't eat too many almonds, they add weight to the breasts. Ah! remind me to teach you how to choose cigars."

Gilberte opened her eyes so wide that the tips of her lashes touched her eyebrows.

"Why?"

She received a little tap on the cheek.

"Because—because I do nothing without good reason. If I take you in hand at all, I must do it thoroughly. Once a woman understands the tastes of a man, cigars included, and once a man knows what pleases a woman, they may be said to be well matched."

"And then they fight," concluded Gigi with a knowing air.

"What do you mean, they fight?"

The old lady looked at Gigi in consternation.

"Ah!" she added, "You certainly never invented the triple mirror! Come, you little psychologist! Let me give you a note for Madame Henriette at Béchoff."

While her aunt was writing at a miniature rose-pink escritoire, Gilberte breathed in the scent of the fastidiously furnished room. Without wanting them for herself, she examined the objects she knew so well but hardly appreciated: Cupid, the Archer, pointing to the hours on the mantel-piece; two rather daring pictures; a bed like the basin of a fountain and its chinchilla coverlet; a rosary of small seed pearls and the New Testament on the bedside table; two red Chinese vases fitted as lamps—a happy note against the grey of the walls.

"Run along, my little one. I shall send for you again quite soon. Don't forget to ask Victor for the cake you're to take home. Gently, don't disarrange my hair! And remember, I shall have my eye on you as you leave the house. Woe betide you if you march like a guardsman, or drag your feet behind you!"

The month of May fetched Gaston Lachaille back to Paris, and brought to Gilberte two well-cut dresses and a light-weight coat—"a sack-coat like Cléo de Mérode's" she called it—as well as hats and boots and shoes. To these she added, on her own account, a few curls over the forehead, which cheapened her appearance. She paraded in front of Gaston in a blue and white dress reaching almost to the ground. "A full seven and a half yards round, Tonton, my skirt measures!" She was more than proud of her slender waist, held in by a grosgrain sash with a silver buckle; but she tried every dodge to free her lovely strong neck from its whale-bone collar of "imitation Venetian point" which matched the tucks of the bodice. The full sleeves and wide flounced skirt of blue and white striped silk rustled deliciously, and Gilberte delighted in picking at the sleeves, to puff them out just below the shoulder.

"You remind me of a performing monkey," Lachaille said to her. "I liked you much better in your old tartan dress. In that uncomfortable collar you look just like a hen with a full crop. Take a peep at yourself!"

Feeling a little ruffled, Gilberte turned round to face the looking-glass. She had a lump in one of her cheeks caused by a large caramel, out of a box sent all the way from Nice at Gaston's order.

"I've heard a good deal about you, Tonton," she retorted, "but I've never heard it said that you had any taste in clothes."

He stared, almost choking, at this newly fledged young woman, then turned to Madame Alvarez.

"Charming manners you've taught her! I congratulate you!"

Whereupon he left the house without drinking his camomile tea, and Madame Alvarez wrung her hands.

"Look what you've done to us now, my poor Gigi!"

"I know," said Gigi, "but then why does he fly at me? He must know by now, I should think, that I can give as good as I get!"

Her grandmother shook her by the arm.

"But think what you've done, you wretched child! Good heavens! when will you learn to think? You've mortally offended the man, as likely as not. Just when we are doing our utmost to—"

"To do what, Grandmamma?"

"Why! to do everything, to make an elegant young lady of you, to show you off to advantage."

"For whose benefit, Grandmamma? You must admit that one doesn't have to turn oneself inside out for an old friend like Tonton!"

But Madame Alvarez admitted nothing; not even to her astonishment, when, the following day, Gaston Lachaille arrived in the best of spirits, wearing a light colored suit.

"Put on your hat, Gigi! I'm taking you out to tea."

"Where?" cried Gigi.

"To the *Réservoirs*, at Versailles!"

"Hurrah! Hurrah! Hurrah!" chanted Gilberte.

She turned towards the kitchen.

"Grandmamma, I'm having tea at the *Réservoirs*, with Tonton!"

Madame Alvarez appeared, and without stopping to untie the flowered satinette apron across her stomach, interposed her soft hand between Gilberte's arm and that of Gaston Lachaille.

"No, Gaston," she said simply.

"What do you mean, No?"

"Oh! Grandmamma!" wailed Gigi.

Madame Alvarez seemed not to hear her.

"Go to your room a minute, Gigi. I should like to talk to Monsieur Lachaille in private."

She watched Gilberte leave the room and close the door behind her; then, returning to Gaston, she met his dark, rather brutal stare without flinching.

"What is the meaning of all this, Mamita? Ever since yesterday, I find quite a change here. What's going on?"

"I shall be glad if you will sit down, Gaston, I'm tired," said Madame Alvarez. "Oh, my poor legs!"

She sighed, waited for a response that did not come, and then untied her apron, under which she was wearing a black dress with a large cameo pinned upon it. She motioned her guest to a high-backed chair, keeping the armchair for herself. Then she sat down heavily, smoothed her greying black coils, and folded her hands on her lap. The unhurried movement of her large dark lambent eyes, and the ease with which she remained motionless, were sure signs of her self-control.

"Gaston, you cannot doubt my friendship for you!" Lachaille emitted a short, businesslike laugh, and tugged at his moustache. "My friendship and my gratitude. Nevertheless, I must never forget that I have a soul entrusted to my care. Andrée, as you know, has neither the time nor the inclination to look after the girl. Our Gilberte has not got the gumption to make her own way in the world, like so many. She is just a child."

"Of sixteen," said Lachaille.

"Of nearly sixteen," consented Madame Alvarez. "For years you have been giving her sweets and playthings. She swears by Tonton, and by him alone. And now you want to take her out to tea, in your automobile, to the *Réservoirs!*"

Madame Alvarez placed a hand on her heart.

"Upon my soul and conscience, Gaston, if there were only you and me, I should say to you, 'Take Gilberte anywhere you like, I entrust her to you blindly.' But there are always the others. The eyes of the world are on you. To be seen tête-à-tête with you, is, for a woman—"

Gaston Lachaille lost patience.

"All right, all right, I understand. You want me to believe that once she is seen having tea with me, Gilberte is compromised! A slip of a girl, a flapper, a chit whom no one knows, whom no one notices!"

"Let us say, rather," interrupted Madame Alvarez gently, "that she will be labeled. No matter where you put in an appearance, Gaston, your presence is remarked upon. A young girl who goes out alone with you is no longer an ordinary girl, or even—to put it bluntly—a respectable girl. Now our little Gilberte must not, above all things, cease to be an ordinary young girl, at least not by that method. So far as it concerns you, it will simply end in one more story to be added to the long list already in existence but, personally, when I read of it in *Gil Blas*, I shall not be amused."

Gaston Lachaille rose, paced from the table to the door, then from the door to the window, before replying.

"Very good, Mamita, I have no wish to vex you. I shan't argue," he said coldly. "Keep your precious child."

He turned round again to face Madame Alvarez, his chin held high.

"I can't help wondering, as a matter of interest, whom you are keeping her for! A clerk earning a hundred a year, who'll marry her and give her four children in three years?"

"I know the duty of a mother better than that," said Madame Alvarez composedly. "I shall do my best to entrust Gigi only to the care of a man capable of saying, 'I take charge of her and answer for her future.' May I have the pleasure of brewing you some camomile tea, Gaston?"

"No, thank you. I'm late already."

"Would you like Gigi to come and say goodbye?"

"Don't bother, I'll see her another time. I can't say when, I'm sure. I'm very much taken up these days."

"Never mind, Gaston, don't worry about her. Have a good time, Gaston."

Once alone, Madame Alvarez mopped her forehead, and went to open the door of Gilberte's room.

"You were listening at the door, Gigi!"

"No, Grandmamma."

"Yes, you had your ear to the key-hole. You must never listen at key-holes. You don't hear properly and so you get things all wrong. Monsieur Lachaille has gone."

"So I can see," said Gilberte.

"Now you must rub the new potatoes in a cloth. I'll sauté them when I come in."

"Are you going out, Grandmamma?"

"I'm going round to see Alicia."

"Again?"

"Is it your place to object?" said Madame Alvarez severely. "You had better bathe your eyes in cold water, since you have been silly enough to cry."

"Grandmamma!"

"What?"

"What difference could it make to you, if you'd let me go out with Tonton Gaston in my new dress?"

"Silence! If you can't understand anything about anything, at least let those who are capable of using their reason do so for you. And put on my rubber gloves before you touch the potatoes!"

Throughout the whole of the following week, silence reigned over the Alvarez household, except for a surprise visit, one day, from Aunt Alicia. She arrived in a hired brougham, all black lace and dull silk with a rose at her shoulder, and carried on an anxious conversation, strictly between themselves, with her younger sister. As she was leaving, she bestowed only a moment's attention on Gilberte, pecked at her cheek with a fleeting kiss, and was gone.

"What did she want?" Gilberte asked Madame Alvarez.

"Oh, nothing . . . the address of the heart specialist who treated Madame Buffetery."

Gilberte reflected for a moment.

"It was a long one," she said.

"What was long?"

"The address of the heart specialist. Grandmamma, I should like a cachet. I have a headache."

"But you had one yesterday. A headache doesn't last forty-eight hours!"

"Presumably my headaches are different from other people's," said Gilberte, offended.

She was losing some of her sweetness, and, on her return from school, would make some such remark as "My teacher has it in for me!" or complain of not being able to sleep. She was gradually slipping into a state of idleness, which her grandmother noticed, but did nothing to overcome.

One day Gigi was busy applying liquid chalk to her white canvas button boots, when Gaston Lachaille put in an appearance without ringing the bell. His hair was too long, his complexion sun-tanned, and he was wearing a broad check summer suit. He stopped short in front of Gilberte, who was perched high on a kitchen stool, her left hand shod with a boot.

"Oh! Grandmamma left the key in the door, that's just like her!"

As Gaston Lachaille looked at her without saying a word, she began to blush, put down the boot on the table and pulled her skirt down over her knees.

"So, Tonton, you slip in like a burglar! I believe you're thinner. Aren't you fed properly by that famous chef of yours who used to be with the Prince of Wales? Being thinner makes your eyes look larger, and at the same time makes your nose longer, and—"

"I have something to say to your grandmother," interrupted Gaston Lachaille. "Run into your room, Gigi."

For a moment she remained open-mouthed, then she jumped off her stool. The strong column of her neck, like an archangel's, swelled with anger as she advanced on Lachaille.

"Run into your room! Run into your room! And suppose I said the same to you? Who do you think you are here, ordering me to run into my room? All right, I'm going to my room! And I can tell you one thing; so long as you're in the house, I shan't come out of it!"

She slammed the door behind her, and there was a dramatic click of the bolt.

"Gaston," breathed Madame Alvarez, "I shall insist on the child apologising, yes, I shall insist; if necessary, I'll . . ."

Gaston was not listening to her, and stood staring at the closed door.

"Now, Mamita," said he, "let us talk briefly and to the point."

"Let us go over it all once again," said Aunt Alicia. "To begin with, you are quite sure he said, 'She shall be spoiled, more than—'"

"Than any woman before her!"

"Yes, but that's the sort of vague phrase that every man comes out with. I like things cut and dried."

"Just what they were, Alicia, for he said that he would guarantee Gigi against every imaginable mishap, even against himself, by an insurance policy; and that he regarded himself more or less as her godfather."

"Yes, hmm . . . Not bad, not bad. But vague, vague as ever."

. She was still in bed, her white hair arranged in curls against the pink pillow. She was absent-mindedly tying and untying the ribbon of her night-dress. Madame Alvarez, pale and wan under her morning hat as the moon behind passing clouds, was leaning cross-armed against the bedside.

"And he added, 'I don't wish to rush anything. Above all, I am Gigi's best pal. I shall give her all the time she wants to get used to me.' There were tears in his eyes. And he also said, 'After all, she won't have to deal with a savage.' A gentleman, in fact. A perfect gentleman."

"Yes, yes. Rather a vague gentleman. And the child, have you spoken frankly to her?"

"As was my duty, Alicia. This is no time for us to be treating her like a child from whom the cakes have to be hidden. Yes, I spoke frankly. I referred to Gaston as a miracle, as a god, as—"

"Tut, tut, tut," criticised Alicia, "I should have stressed the difficulties rather: the cards to be played, the fury of all those ladies, the conquest represented by so conspicuous a man."

Madame Alvarez wrung her hands.

"The difficulties! The cards to be played! Do you imagine she's like you? Don't you know her at all? She's very far from calculating, she's—"

"Thank you."

"I mean she has no ambition. I was even struck by the fact that she did not react either one way or the other. No cries of joy, no tears of emotion! All I got from her was, 'Oh, yes! Oh, it's very considerate of him.' Then, only at the very end, did she lay down, as her conditions—"

"Conditions, indeed!" murmured Alicia.

"—that she would answer Monsieur Lachaille's proposals herself, and discuss the matter alone with him. In other words, it was her business, and hers only."

"Let us be prepared for the worst! You've brought a nitwit into the world. She will ask for the moon and, if I know him, she won't get it. He is coming at four o'clock?"

"Yes."

"Hasn't he sent anything? No flowers? No little present?"

"Nothing. Do you think that's a bad sign?"

"No. It's what one would expect. See that the child is nicely dressed. How is she looking?"

"Not too well, today. Poor little lamb—"

"Come, come!" said Alicia heartlessly. "You'll have time for tears another day—when she's succeeded in ruining the whole affair."

"You've eaten scarcely anything, Gigi."

"I wasn't too hungry, Grandmamma. May I have a little more coffee?"

"Of course."

"And a drop of Combier?"

"Why, yes. There's nothing in the world better than Combier for settling the stomach."

Through the open window rose the noise and heat from the street below. Gigi let the tip of her tongue lick round the bottom of her liqueur glass.

"If Aunt Alicia could see you, Gigi!" said Madame Alvarez lightheartedly.

Gigi's only reply was a disillusioned little smile. Her old plaid dress was too tight across the breast, and under the table she stretched out her long legs well beyond the limits of her skirt.

"What can Mamma be rehearsing today that's kept her from coming back to eat with us, Grandmamma? Do you think there really is a rehearsal going on at her Opéra-Comique?"

"She said so, didn't she?"

"Personally, I don't think she wanted to eat here."

"What makes you think that?"

Without taking her eyes off the sunny window, Gigi simply shrugged her shoulders.

"Oh, nothing, Grandmamma."

When she had drained the last drop of her Combier, she rose and began to clear the table.

"Leave all that, Gigi, I'll do it."

"Why, Grandmamma? I do it as a rule."

She looked Madame Alvarez straight in the face, with an expression the old lady could not meet.

"We began our meal late, it's almost three o'clock and you're not dressed yet; do pull yourself together, Gigi."

"It's never before taken me a whole hour to change my clothes."

"Won't you need my help? Are you satisfied your hair's all right?"

"It will do, Grandmamma. When the door bell rings, don't bother, I'll go and open it."

On the stroke of four, Gaston Lachaille rang three times. A childish, wistful face looked out from the bedroom door, listening. After three more impatient rings, Gilberte advanced as far as the middle of the hall. She still had on her old plaid dress and cotton stockings. She rubbed her cheeks with both fists, then ran to open the door.

"Good afternoon, Uncle Gaston."

"Didn't you want to let me in, you bad girl?"

They bumped shoulders in passing through the door, said "Oh, sorry!" a little too self-consciously, then laughed awkwardly.

"Please sit down, Tonton. D' you know, I didn't have time to change. Not like you! That navy blue serge couldn't look better!"

"You don't know what you're talking about! It's tweed."

"Of course. How silly of me!"

She sat down facing him, pulled her skirt over her knees, and they stared at each other. Gilberte's tomboy assurance deserted her; a strange woebegone look made her blue eyes seem twice their natural size.

"What's the matter with you, Gigi?" asked Lachaille softly. "Tell me something! Do you know why I'm here?"

She assented with an exaggerated nod.

"Do you want to, or don't you?" he asked, lowering his voice.

She pushed a curl behind her ear, and swallowed bravely.

"I don't want to."

Lachaille twirled the tips of his moustache between two fingers, and for a moment looked away from a pair of darkened blue eyes, a pink cheek with a single freckle, curved lashes, a mouth unaware of its power, a heavy mass of ash-gold hair, and a neck as straight as a column, strong, hardly feminine, all of a piece, innocent of jewelry.

"I don't want what you want," Gilberte began again. "You said to Grandmamma . . ."

He put out his hand to stop her. His mouth was slightly twisted to one side, as if he had the toothache.

"I know what I said to your grandmother. It's not worth repeating. Just tell me what it is you don't want. You can then tell me what you do want. I shall give it to you."

"You mean that?" cried Gilberte.

He nodded, letting his shoulders droop, as if tired out. She watched, with surprise, these signs of exhaustion and torment.

"Tonton, you told Grandmamma you wanted to make me my fortune."

"A very fine one," said Lachaille firmly.

"It will be fine if I like it," said Gilberte, no less firmly. "They've drummed into my ears that I am backward for my age, but all the same I know the meaning of words. 'Make me my fortune,' that means I should go away from here with you, and that I should sleep in your bed."

"Gigi, I beg of you!"

She stopped, because of the strong note of appeal in his voice.

"But, Tonton, why should I mind speaking of it to you? You didn't mind speaking of it to Grandmamma. Neither did Grandmamma mind speaking of it to me. Grandmamma wanted me to see nothing but the bright side. But I know more than she told me. I know very well that if you make me my fortune, then I must have my photograph in the papers, go to the Battle of Flowers and to the races at Deauville. When we quarrel, *Gil Blas* and *Paris en amour* will tell the whole story. When you throw me over once and for all, as you did Gentiane des Cevennes when you'd had enough of her—"

"What! You've heard about that? They've bothered you with all those old stories?"

She gave a solemn little nod.

"Grandmamma and Aunt Alicia. They've taught me that you're world-famous. I know too that Maryse Chuquet stole your letters, and you brought an action against her. I know that Countess Pariewsky was angry with you, because you didn't want to marry a *divorcée*, and she tried to shoot you. I know what all the world knows."

Lachaille put his hand on Gilberte's knee.

"Those are not the things we have to talk about together, Gigi. All that's in the past. All that's over and done with."

"Of course, Tonton, until it begins again. It's not your fault if you're world-famous. But I haven't got a world-famous sort of nature. So it won't do for me."

In pulling at the hem of her skirt, she caused Lachaille's hand to slip off her knee.

"Aunt Alicia and Grandmamma are on your side. But as it concerns me a little, after all, I think you must allow me to say a word on the subject. And my word is, that it won't do for me."

She got up and walked about the room. Gaston Lachaille's silence seemed to embarrass her. She punctuated her wanderings with, "After all, it's true, I suppose! No, it really won't do!"

"I should like to know," said Gaston at last, "whether you're not just trying to hide from me the fact that you dislike me. If you dislike me, you had better say so at once."

"Oh no, Tonton, I don't dislike you at all! I'm always delighted to see you! I'll prove it by making a suggestion in my turn. You could go on coming here as usual, even more often. No one would see any harm in it, since you're a friend of the family. You could go on bringing me liquorice, champagne on my birthdays, and on Sunday we should have an extra special game of piquet. Wouldn't that be a pleasant little life? A life without all this business of sleeping in your bed and everybody knowing about it, losing strings of pearls, being photographed all the time and having to be so careful."

She was absent-mindedly twisting a strand of hair round her nose, and pulled it so tight that she snuffled and the tip of her nose turned purple.

"A very pretty little life, as you say," interrupted Gaston Lachaille. "You're forgetting one thing only, Gigi, and that is, I'm in love with you."

"Oh!" she cried, "you never told me that."

"Well," he owned uneasily, "I'm telling you now."

She remained standing before him, silent and breathing fast. There was no concealing her embarrassment; the rise and fall of her bosom under the tight bodice, the hectic flush high on her cheeks, and the quivering of her close pressed lips—albeit ready to open again and taste of life.

"That's quite another thing!" she cried at last. "But then you are a terrible man! You're in love with me, and you want to drag me into a life where I'll have nothing but worries, where everyone gossips about everyone else, where the papers print nasty stories. You're in love with me, and you don't care a fig if you let me in for all sorts of

horrible adventures, ending in separations, quarrels, Sandomirs, revolvers, and lau . . . and laudanum."

She burst into violent sobs, which made as much noise as a fit of
coughing. Gaston put his arms round her to bend her towards him
like a branch, but she escaped and took refuge between the wall and
the piano.

"But listen, Gigi! Listen to me!"

"Never! I never want to see you again! I should never have
believed it of you. You're not in love with me, you're a wicked man!
Go away from here!"

She shut him out from sight by rubbing her eyes with closed fists.
Gaston had moved over to her and was trying to discover some place
on her well guarded face where he could kiss her. But his lips found
only the point of a small chin wet with tears. At the sound of sobbing, Madame Alvarez had hurried in. Pale and circumspect, she had
stopped in hesitation at the door to the kitchen.

"Good gracious, Gaston!" she said. "What on earth's the matter
with her?"

"The matter!" said Lachaille. "The matter is that she doesn't
want to."

"She doesn't want to!" repeated Madame Alvarez. "What do you
mean, she doesn't want to?"

"No, she doesn't want to. I speak plainly enough, don't I?"

"No. I don't want to," whimpered Gigi.

Madame Alvarez looked at her granddaughter in a sort of terror.

"Gigi! It's enough to drive one raving mad! But I told you, Gigi.
Gaston, as God is my witness, I told her—"

"You have told her too much!" cried Lachaille.

He turned his face towards the child, looking just a poor, sad,
lovesick creature, but all he saw of her was a slim back shaken by
sobs and a disheveled head of hair.

"Oh!" he exclaimed hoarsely, "I've had enough of this!" and he
went out, banging the door.

The next day, at three o'clock, Aunt Alicia, summoned by
pneumatique, stepped out from her hired brougham. She climbed
the stairs up to the Alvarez' floor—pretending to the shortness of
breath proper to someone with a weak heart—and noiselessly pushed
open the door which her sister had left on the latch.

"Where's the child?"

"In her room. Do you want to see her?"

"There's plenty of time. How is she?"

"Very calm."

Alicia shook two angry little fists.

"Very calm! She has pulled the roof down about our heads, and she is very calm! These young people of today!"

Once again she raised her spotted veil and withered her sister with a single glance.

"And you, standing there, what do you propose doing?"

With a face like a crumpled rose, she sternly confronted the large pallid face of her sister, whose retort was mild in the extreme.

"What do I propose doing? How do you mean? I can't, after all, tie the child up!" Her burdened shoulders rose on a long sigh. "I surely have not deserved such children as these!"

"While you stand there wringing your hands, Lachaille has rushed away from here and in such a state that he may do something idiotic!"

"And even without his straw hat," said Madame Alvarez. "He got into his motor bare-headed! The whole street might have seen him!"

"If I were to be told that by this time he's already become engaged, or is busy making it up with Liane, it would not surprise me in the least!"

"It is a moment fraught with destiny," said Madame Alvarez lugubriously.

"And afterwards, how did you speak to that little brat?"

Madame Alvarez pursed her lips.

"Gigi may be a bit scatter-brained in certain things and backward for her age, but she's not what you say. A young girl who has held the attention of Monsieur Lachaille is not a little brat."

A furious shrug of the shoulders set Alicia's black lace quivering.

"All right, all right! With all due respect, then, how did you handle your precious princess?"

"I talked sense to her. I spoke to her of the family. I tried to make her understand that we sink or swim together. I enumerated all the things she could do for herself and for us."

"And what about nonsense? Did you talk nonsense to her? Didn't you talk to her of love, travel, moonlight, Italy? You must know how to harp on every string. Didn't you tell her that on the other side of the world the sea is phosphorescent, that there are humming-birds in all the flowers, and that you make love under gardenias in full bloom beside a moonlit fountain?"

Madame Alvarez looked at her spirited elder sister with sadness in her eyes.

"I couldn't tell her all that, Alicia, because I know nothing about it. I've never been further afield than Cabourg and Monte Carlo."

"Aren't you capable of inventing it?"

"No, Alicia."

Both fell silent. Alicia, with a gesture, made up her mind.

"Call the chit in to me. We shall see."

When Gilberte came in, Aunt Alicia had resumed all the airs and graces of a frivolous old lady and was smelling the tea-rose pinned near her chin.

"Good afternoon, my little Gigi."

"Good afternoon, Aunt Alicia."

"What is this Inez has been telling me? You have an admirer? And *what* an admirer! For your first attempt, it's a master-stroke!"

Gilberte acquiesced with a guarded, resigned little smile. She offered to Alicia's darting curiosity a fresh young face, to which the violet-blue shadow on her eyelids and the high color of her mouth gave an almost artificial effect. For coolness' sake, she had dragged back the hair off her temples with the help of two combs, and this drew up the corners of her eyes.

"And it seems you have been playing the naughty girl, and tried your claws on Monsieur Lachaille! Bravo, my brave little girl!"

Gilberte raised incredulous eyes to her aunt.

"Yes, indeed! Bravo! It will only make him all the happier when you are nice to him again."

"But I am nice to him, Aunt. Only, I don't want to, that's all."

"Yes, yes, we know. You've sent him packing to his sugar refinery, that's perfect. But don't send him to the Devil, he's quite capable of going. The fact is, you don't love him."

Gilberte gave a little childish shrug.

"Yes, Aunt, I'm very fond of him."

"Just what I said, you don't love him. Mind you, there's no harm in that, it leaves you free to act as you please. Ah, if you'd been head over heels in love with him, then I should have been a little anxious. Lachaille is a fine figure of a man. Well built—you've only to look at the photographs of him taken at Deauville in bathing costume. He's famous for that. Yes, I should feel sorry for you, my poor Gigi. To start by having a passionate love-affair—to go away all by your two selves to the other side of the world, forgetting everything in the arms of the man who adores you, listening to the song of love in an eternal spring—surely things of that sort must touch your heart! What does all that say to you?"

"It says to me that when the eternal spring is over Monsieur Lachaille will go off with another lady. Or else that the lady—me if you like—will leave Monsieur Lachaille, and Monsieur Lachaille will hurry off to blab the whole story. And then the lady, still me if you like, will have nothing else to do but get into another gentleman's bed. I don't want that. I'm not changeable by nature, indeed I'm not."

She crossed her arms over her breasts and shivered slightly.

"Grandmamma, may I have a *cachet faivre*? I want to go to bed, I feel cold."

"You great goose!" burst out Aunt Alicia, "a silly little milliner's shop is all you deserve! Be off, go and marry a bank clerk!"

"If you wish it, Aunt. But I want to go to bed."

Madame Alvarez put her hand on Gigi's forehead.

"Don't you feel well?"

"I'm all right, Grandmamma. Only I'm sad."

She leaned her head on Madame Alvarez' shoulder, and, for the first time in her life, closed her eyes pathetically like a grown woman. The two sisters exchanged glances.

"You must know, my Gigi," said Madame Alvarez, "that we won't torment you to that extent. If you say you really don't want to—"

"A failure is a failure," said Alicia caustically. "We can't go on discussing it for ever."

"You'll never be able to say you didn't have good advice and the very best at that," said Madame Alvarez.

"I know, Grandmamma, but I'm sad, all the same."

"Why?"

A tear trickled over Gilberte's downy cheek without wetting it, but she did not answer. A brisk peal of the door bell made her jump where she stood.

"Oh, it must be him," she said. "It is him! Grandmamma, I don't want to see him! Hide me, Grandmamma!"

At the low, passionate tone of her voice, Aunt Alicia raised an attentive head, and pricked an expert ear. Then she ran to open the door and came back a moment later. Gaston Lachaille, haggard, his eyes bloodshot, followed close behind her.

"Good afternoon, Mamita. Good afternoon, Gigi!" he said airily. "Please don't move, I've come to retrieve my straw hat."

None of the three women replied, and his assurance left him.

"Well, you might at least say a word to me, even if it's only How-d'you-do?"

Gilberte took a step towards him.

"No," she said, "you've not come to retrieve your straw hat. You have another one in your hand. And you would never bother about a hat. You've come to make me more miserable than ever."

"Really!" burst out Madame Alvarez. "This is more than I can stomach. How can you, Gigi! Here is a man who, out of the goodness of his generous heart—"

"If you please, Grandmamma, just a moment, and I shall have finished."

Instinctively she straightened her dress, adjusted the buckle of her sash, and marched up to Gaston.

"I've been thinking, Gaston. In fact, I've been thinking a great deal—"

He interrupted her, to stop her saying what he was afraid to hear.

"I swear to you, my darling—"

"No, don't swear to me. I've been thinking I would rather be miserable with you than without you. So . . ."

She tried twice to go on.

"So . . . There you are. How d'you do, Gaston, how d'you do?"

She offered him her cheek, in her usual way. He held her, a little longer than usual, until he felt her relax, and become calm and gentle in his arms. Madame Alvarez seemed about to hurry forward, but Alicia's impatient little hand restrained her.

"Leave well alone. Don't meddle any more. Can't you see she is far beyond us?"

She pointed to Gigi, who was resting a trusting head and the rich abundance of her hair on Lachaille's shoulder.

The happy man turned to Madame Alvarez.

"Mamita," he said, "will you do me the honor, the favor, give me the infinite joy of bestowing on me the hand. . . ."

The VAGABOND

Translated by
ENID McLEOD

PART ONE

ONE

TEN THIRTY. . . . Once again I'm ready too soon. My friend Brague, who helped me when I first began acting in pantomimes, often takes me to task for this in that salty language of his:

"You poor boob of an amateur! You've always got ants in your pants. If we listened to you we'd be putting on our make-up base at half-past seven in the middle of bolting the *hors-d'œuvre!*"

After three years of music-hall and theatre I'm still the same: always ready too soon.

Ten thirty-five. . . . I'd better open that book lying on the make-up shelf, even though I've read it over and over again, or the copy of *Paris-Sport* the dresser was marking just now with my eyebrow pencil; otherwise I'll find myself all alone, face to face with that painted mentor who gazes at me from the other side of the looking-glass, with deep-set eyes under lids smeared with purplish grease-paint. Her cheek-bones are as brightly coloured as garden phlox and her blackish-red lips gleam as though they were varnished. She gazes at me for a long time and I know she is going to speak to me. She is going to say:

"Is that you there? All alone, there in that cage where idle, impatient, imprisoned hands have scored the white walls with interlaced initials and embellished them with crude, indecent shapes? On those plaster walls reddened nails, like yours, have unconsciously inscribed the appeal of the forsaken. Behind you a feminine hand has carved *Marie*, and the name ends in a passionate mounting flourish, like a cry to heaven. Is it you there, all alone under that ceiling booming and vibrating beneath the feet of the dancers, like the floor of a mill in action? Why are you there, all alone? And why not somewhere else?"

Yes, this is the dangerous, lucid hour. Who will knock at the door of my dressing-room, what face will come between me and the painted mentor peering at me from the other side of the looking-glass? Chance, my master and my friend, will, I feel sure, deign once again to send me the spirits of his unruly kingdom. All my trust is now in him—and in myself. But above all in him, for when I go under he always fishes me out, seizing and shaking me like a life-saving dog whose teeth tear my skin a little every time. So now, whenever I despair, I no longer expect my end, but some bit of luck, some commonplace little miracle which, like a glittering link, will mend again the necklace of my days.

Faith, that is what it is, genuine faith, as blind as it sometimes pretends to be, with all the dissembling renunciations of faith, and that obstinacy which makes it continue to hope even at the moment of crying. "I am utterly forsaken!" There is no doubt that, if ever my heart were to call my master Chance by another name, I should make an excellent Catholic.

How the floor vibrates this evening! It's obvious that it's a cold night: the Russian dancers are warming themselves up! When they all shout "Yoo!" in chorus, in voices as shrill and hoarse as those of young pigs, it will be ten past eleven. My clock is infallible, it does not vary by so much as five minutes in a month. Ten o'clock: I arrive; Mme Cavalier is singing her three songs, The Little Guttersnipes, The Farewell Kiss, and The Little You-know-what. Ten ten: Antonieff and his dogs. Ten twenty-two: shots, barks, end of dog-act. The iron staircase creaks and someone coughs: Jadin is coming down. She swears in the middle of her coughing because she's treading on the hem of her frock; it happens every time. Ten thirty-five: Whimsical Bouty. Ten forty-seven: the Russian dancers, and, finally, eleven ten: me!

Me. As that word came into my head, I involuntarily looked in the mirror. There's no getting away from it, it really is me there behind that mask of purplish rouge, my eyes ringed with a halo of blue grease-paint beginning to melt. Can the rest of my face be going to melt also? What if nothing were to remain from my whole reflection but a streak of dyed colour stuck to the glass like a long, muddy tear?

It's absolutely freezing in here! I rub my hands together, grey with cold under the wet white which is beginning to crack. Good Lord! the radiator pipes are icy; it is Saturday and on Saturdays here they rely on the high-spirited popular audience, rowdy and slightly drunk, to warm the auditorium. No one has given a thought to the artistes' dressing-rooms.

The door shudders under a blow from a fist, which makes my very

ears quiver. I open it to my pal Brague, dressed as a swarthy
Roumanian bandit, and conscientious as ever.

"You know it's our turn next?"

"Yes I know. And about time too! I'm frozen to death!"

At the top of the iron staircase leading to the stage, the good, dry,
dusty warmth wraps me round like a comfortable dirty cloak. While
the ever-meticulous Brague keeps an eye on the setting of the scene
and sees to the raising of the stage lights—for a sunset effect—I mechanically glue my eye to the luminous peephole in the drop curtain.

There's a grand Saturday house in this favourite local *café-concert*.
The auditorium is dark, as the projectors are not strong enough to il-
luminate it, and you might bet a shilling you would not find a collar
from the tenth row of the stalls to the second gallery! A pall of
reddish smoke floats over it all, full of the horrible smell of stale tobacco and twopenny cigars smoked too far down. The stage-boxes,
on the other hand, look like four flowerstands. It is indeed a fine Saturday house but, as little Jadin vigorously puts it: "To hell with the
house, I don't get a rake-off on the takings!"

As soon as the first bars of our overture strike up, I feel soothed
and ready for anything, grown all of a sudden gay and irresponsible.
With my elbows propped on the canvas balcony, I calmly consider
the layer of powdered dirt—composed of mud from shoes, dust, hairs
of dogs and crushed gum—covering the boards where soon my bare
knees will be crawling, and sniff an artificial red geranium. From that
moment I no longer belong to myself, and all is well. I know that I
shall not fall when I dance, that my heel will not catch in the hem
of my skirt, and that when Brague handles me roughly I shall collapse without grazing my elbows or flattening my nose. I shall keep a
straight face when I vaguely hear the little scene-shifter making
noises like farts behind the wings at the most dramatic moments to
make us laugh. The harsh light sustains me, the music governs my
gestures, a mysterious discipline controls and protects me . . . all is
well.

All is indeed well! Our dun-coloured Saturday public has rewarded
us with an uproar compounded of bravos, catcalls, shrieks and well-
meant ribaldries, and I received, plumb on a corner of my mouth, a
little bunch of cheap carnations, those anaemic white carnations
which the street flower-sellers dip in carmine-tinted water to dye
them. I take it home, pinned to the lapel of my jacket; it smells of
pepper and wet dog.

I take home also a letter which has just been handed to me:

"Madame, I was in the first row of the stalls. Your gifts as a mime incline me to think that you must possess others, more special and still more captivating. Give me the pleasure of supping this evening with me."

It is signed "Marquis de Fontanges"—yes, it really is—and written from the Café du Delta. What a number of descendants of noble families which one had thought extinct long ago have taken up residence at the Café du Delta! Unlikely as it seems, I can't help suspecting a close relationship between this Marquis de Fontanges and a Comte de Lavallière who, last week, offered me a "five o'clock" in his bachelors' chambers. Commonplace impostures though these are, one can divine in them that romantic admiration for high life, that respect for a title, which lurks in this tough neighbourhood under more than one battered cap.

TWO

As always, I give a great sigh when I close the door of my ground-floor flat behind me. Is it a sigh of weariness, or relaxation, or relief? Or does it spring from the bitterness of solitude? Better not think of it, far better not!

But what on earth is the matter with me tonight? It must be this icy December fog, like particles of frost hanging in the air, quivering in an iridescent halo round the gas lamps and melting on one's lips with a taste of creosote. And besides, this new quarter where I live, looming up all white behind Les Ternes, is enough to discourage both one's eyes and one's spirit.

My street, under the greenish gas at this hour, is a morass of toffee-like, creamy mud—coffee-coloured, maroon and caramel yellow—a sort of crumbling, slushy trifle in which the floating bits of meringue are lumps of concrete. Even my house, the only one in the street, has a sort of "it can't be true" look. But its new walls and thin partitions offer, at a modest rent, a shelter sufficiently comfortable for "ladies on their own" like me.

When you are a "lady on your own", in other words the landlords' abomination, outcast and terror all rolled into one, you take what you find, lodge where you may and put up with newly plastered walls.

The house where I live compassionately shelters quite a colony of "ladies on their own". On the mezzanine floor we have the acknowledged mistress of Young, of Young-Automobiles; above, the girl-friend, very much "kept", of the Comte de Bravailles; higher up are two fair-haired sisters, both of whom are visited every day by the same man, a very-correct-gentleman-in-industry; higher still a terrible little tart makes as much of a racket night and day as an unleashed fox-terrier, screaming, playing the piano, singing and throwing empty bottles out of the window.

"She's a disgrace to the house," Madame Young-Automobiles said one day.

Finally, on the ground floor, there is myself who neither screams, nor plays the piano, nor ever receives gentlemen and still less ladies. The little tart on the fourth floor makes too much noise and I not enough, as the concierge does not fail to remark to me. "It's funny, one never knows whether Madame is there because one doesn't hear her. One would never think she was an artiste!"

What an ugly December night it is! The radiator smells of iodoform, Blandine has forgotten to put my hot-water bottle in my bed, and even my dog is in a bad mood. Grumpy and shivering, she merely casts one black and white glance at me, without leaving her basket. I must say! I don't expect triumphal arches and illuminations, but all the same . . .

No need to search the place, to peer in the corners or look under the bed, there is no one here, no one but myself. What I see in the big looking-glass in my bedroom is no longer the painted image of an itinerant music-hall artiste. It reflects only—myself.

Behold me then, just as I am! This evening I shall not be able to escape the meeting in the long mirror, the soliloquy which I have a hundred times avoided, accepted, fled from, taken up again and broken off. I feel in advance, alas, the uselessness of trying to change the subject. This evening I shall not feel sleepy, and the spell of a book—even a brand-new book with that smell of printers' ink and paper fresh from the press that makes you think of coal and trains and departures—even that spell will not be able to distract me from myself.

Behold me then, just as I am. Alone alone, and for the rest of my life, no doubt. Already alone; it's early for that. When I turned thirty I did not feel cast down because mine is a face that depends on the expression which animates it, the colour of my eyes, and the defiant smile that plays over it—what Marinetti calls my *gaiezza volpina*. But if I look like a fox, it's a fox without guile, which a hen could catch! And a fox without rapacity, one that remembers only the trap and the cage. A gay-looking fox, if you like, but only because the corners of its mouth and eyes look as if they were smiling. A captive fox, tired of dancing to the sound of music.

It is true enough that I do look like a fox. But a slender, pretty fox is not an ugly thing, is it? Brague says too that I look like a rat when

I purse my lips and blink my eyelids so as to see better. I see nothing to mind in that.

But how I dislike seeing myself with that drooping mouth and those slack shoulders, the weight of my whole sad body slumped on one leg! My hair hangs dank and lank and in a little while I shall have to brush it for a long time to give it back its shining beaver brown. My eyes are still faintly ringed with blue eye-shadow and there's a wavering trace of red on my nails. It will take me at least fifty good minutes of bathing and grooming to get rid of all that.

It is one o'clock already. What am I waiting for? A smart little lash with the whip to make the obstinate creature go on again. But no one will give it me because . . . because I am alone. How clearly one sees, in that long frame which holds my reflection, that I'm used already to living alone!

No matter what visitor, for a mere tradesman, or even for my char-woman Blandine, I should raise this drooping neck, straighten that slouching hip and clasp those empty hands. But tonight I am so alone.

Alone! Indeed one might think I was pitying myself for it!

"If you live all alone," said Brague, "it's because you really want to, isn't it?"

Certainly I "really" want to, and in fact I *want* to, quite simply. Only, well . . . there are days when solitude, for someone of my age, is a heady wine which intoxicates you with freedom, others when it is a bitter tonic, and still others when it is a poison which makes you beat your head against the wall.

This evening I would much prefer not to say which it is; all I want is to remain undecided, and not to be able to say whether the shiver which will seize me when I slip between the cold sheets comes from fear or contentment.

Alone . . . and for a long time past. The proof is that I am giving way to the habit of talking to myself and of holding conversations with my dog, and the fire, and my own reflection. It is an idiosyn-cracy which recluses and old prisoners fall into; but I'm not like them, I'm free. And if I talk to myself it is because I have a writer's need to express my thoughts in rhythmical language.

Facing me from the other side of the looking-glass, in that mysteri-ous reflected room, is the image of "a woman of letters who has turned out badly". They also say of me that I'm "on the stage", but they never call me an actress. Why? The nuance is subtle, but there is certainly a polite refusal, on the part both of the public and my friends themselves, to accord me any standing in this career which I have nevertheless adopted. A woman of letters who has turned out badly: that is what I must remain for everyone, I who no longer write, who deny myself the pleasure, the luxury of writing.

To write, to be able to write, what does it mean? It means spending long hours dreaming before a white page, scribbling unconsciously, letting your pen play round a blot of ink and nibble at a half-formed word, scratching it, making it bristle with darts and adorning it with antennae and paws until it loses all resemblance to a legible word and turns into a fantastic insect or a fluttering creature half butterfly, half fairy.

To write is to sit and stare, hypnotised, at the reflection of the window in the silver ink-stand, to feel the divine fever mounting to one's cheeks and forehead while the hand that writes grows blissfully numb upon the paper. It also means idle hours curled up in the hollow of the divan, and then the orgy of inspiration from which one emerges stupefied and aching all over, but already recompensed and laden with treasures that one unloads slowly on to the virgin page in the little round pool of light under the lamp.

To write is to pour one's innermost self passionately upon the tempting paper, at such frantic speed that sometimes one's hand struggles and rebels, overdriven by the impatient god who guides it— and to find, next day, in place of the golden bough that bloomed miraculously in that dazzling hour, a withered bramble and a stunted flower.

To write is the joy and torment of the idle. Oh to write! From time to time I feel a need, sharp as thirst in summer, to note and to describe. And then I take up my pen again and attempt the perilous and elusive task of seizing and pinning down, under its flexible double-pointed nib, the many-hued, fugitive, thrilling adjective. . . . The attack does not last long; it is but the itching of an old scar.

It takes up too much time to write. And the trouble is, I am no Balzac! The fragile story I am constructing crumbles away when the tradesman rings, or the shoemaker sends in his bill, when the solicitor, or one's counsel, telephones, or when the theatrical agent summons me to his office for "a social engagement at the house of some people of very good position but not in the habit of paying large fees".

The problem is, since I have been living alone, that I have had first to live, then to divorce, and then to go on living. To do all that demands incredible activity and persistence. And to get where? Is there, for me, no other haven than this commonplace room done up in gimcrack Louis XVI? Must I stay for ever before this impenetrable mirror where I come up against myself, face to face?

Tomorrow is Sunday: that means afternoon and evening performances at the *Empyrée-Clichy*. Two o'clock already! High time for a woman of letters who has turned out badly to go to sleep.

THREE

"Look alive, for Heaven's sake, look alive! Jadin's not here!"

"How d'you mean, not here? Is she ill?"

"Ill? I'll say! On the spree, more like. The result's the same for us: we go on twenty minutes sooner!"

The mime Brague has just emerged from his dressing-room as I pass, a frightening sight under his khaki-coloured make-up base, and I rush to my dressing-room, full of dismay at the thought that, for the first time in my life, I may be late.

Jadin's not here! I hurry, trembling with nerves, for you can't trifle with our local public, especially at a Sunday matinée. If, as our wild-beast tamer of a stage-manager says, we let it "get hungry" for five minutes between two acts, hootings and cigarette ends and orange peel automatically begin to fly.

Jadin not here! We might have known it would happen one of these days.

Jadin is a little singer, so new to the *café-concert* that she has not yet had time to peroxide her light brown hair; she came straight to the stage from the outer boulevards, flabbergasted at being able to earn two hundred and ten francs a month by singing. She is eighteen. Luck—should one call it?—immediately got her in its grip, and everything about her, the elbows with which she defends herself and her whole obstinate person bent forward like a gargoyle, looks as if it were warding off the blows of a brutal and fraudulent fate.

She sings like a little seamstress or a street singer, and it never occurs to her that there is any other way of singing. In her artless way she forces her harsh, seductive contralto which goes so well with her face, the face of a pink and sulky young apache. The public adores her just as she is, with her dress that is too long and bought goodness knows where, her light brown hair not even waved, her hunched shoulder which looks as if it were still lugging along the laundry basket, and the down on her upper lip all white with cheap powder.

The manageress promises her, for next season, her name in lights twice over, and as for a raise—well we'll see, after that. When she is on the stage Jadin is radiant and exultant. Every evening she recognises, among the public of the upper galleries, some pal of a childish escapade, and she can never resist interrupting her sentimental ditty to greet him with a joyful shout, a shrill schoolgirl laugh or even a resounding slap on her thigh.

And this is the girl who is missing from today's programme. In half an hour they will be rampaging in the house, calling "Jadin! Jadin!", stamping their boots and rattling their mazagran spoons against their glasses.

It was bound to happen. Jadin, they say, is not ill, and our stage-manager grumbles:

"'Flu, my foot! She's come a cropper into a bed, that's what she's done! And someone's using his wallet as a compress to keep her there! Otherwise she'd have let us know."

Jadin has found a fancier who does not belong to this district. A girl must live. But she was living already, with Tom, Dick and Harry. Shall I ever again see her little gargoyle silhouette, with one of those "modish" forage caps she used to fabricate herself, coming right down to her eyebrows? Only last night she thrust her badly-powdered little mug into my dressing-room to show me her latest creation: an "imitation white fox" toque of rabbit fur, so tight fitting that it pressed her little pink ears down on each side.

"You look the dead spit of Attila," Brague told her, with never a smile.

And now she's gone. The long corridor, perforated with little square dressing-rooms, buzzes with derisive laughter: it seems that everyone except me suspected this flight. Bouty, the little funny-man who sings the songs that Dranem made famous, walks up and down outside my dressing-room, made up like an ape, with a glass of milk in his hand, and I hear him prophesying: "It was a cert! But I couldn't help thinking Jadin would hold out another five or six days, or even a month! The boss must be livid! But it'll take more than that to make her decide to raise the screw of us artistes who make the reputation of her house for her. Just you mark my words: we'll be seeing Jadin back again; it's only a jaunt, that's all. She's a girl who knows where she belongs, she'll never be able to keep a fancy chap."

I open my door to speak to Bouty while I am putting the wet

white on my hands: "Didn't she tell you she was going away, Bouty?"

He shrugs his shoulders, turning towards me his red gorilla mask, with its white-rimmed eyes: "Not likely! I'm not her mother." Whereupon he starts gulping his glass of milk, as blue as starch, in little sips.

Poor little Bouty, trailing about with him everywhere his chronic enteritis and his bottle of tested milk! When he removes that white and vermilion mask he reveals a gentle, sickly face, delicate and intelligent, with beautiful tender eyes, and the heart of an ownerless dog ready to devote itself to anyone who will adopt it. His illness and his exacting profession are killing him, he lives on milk and boiled macaroni, and has just enough strength to sing and dance Negro dances for twenty minutes. When he leaves the set he falls exhausted in the wings, unable immediately to go down to his dressing-room. Sometimes his slender body, stretched out there as if dead, bars my way, and I have to harden myself not to stoop and pick him up and call for help. His fellow actors and the old stage-setter content themselves with shaking their heads with an important air as they pass him, and saying: "Bouty's an artist who 'tires' quickly."

"Come on now, we must get a move on, full speed ahead! The house didn't yell for Jadin as much as they might. That's a bit of luck for us!"

Brague hustles me up the iron staircase: the combination of dusty heat and stage-lighting makes me dizzy; this matinée has been like one of those dreams full of incident, half the day has melted away I don't know how, leaving me with nothing but the kind of nervous chill and contraction of the stomach which follow awakenings and rapid risings in the middle of the night. In an hour it will be time for dinner, then a taxi, and it starts all over again.

And that's how it will be for a month! The present show is quite a success and anyhow we must keep it going until the *Revue* begins.

"We're in clover here," says Brague. "Forty days with nothing to think about!"

With nothing to think about. . . . If only I could do as he does! I've got forty days, the whole year, a lifetime for thinking in. How long am I going to spend trailing round, from music-hall to theatre, and from theatre to casino, "gifts" that everyone politely agrees to consider interesting? They admit in addition that my mimicry is "exact", my diction "clear", and my figure "impeccable". It's very kind of them. It goes even beyond what is necessary. But . . . where does it lead?

It's no good, I can see I'm in for a bad fit of the blues. I await it calmly, with a heart that is used to it, knowing I shall recognise its normal phases and get the better of it once again. No one will know anything about it. This evening Brague gives me a quizzical look with his penetrating little eyes, but merely says: "Wool-gathering, aren't you?"

Back in my dressing-room I wash my hands, stained red-currant colour to simulate blood, in front of the looking-glass where my painted mentor and I gravely take stock of each other like well-matched adversaries.

I know there's no escaping what's coming: suffering, regrets, and the insomnia and solitary musings that make the deepest hours of the night longer still. So I go to meet it with a kind of grim gaiety, and with all the serenity of a creature still young and resistant, who has been through it before. Two habits have taught me how to keep back my tears: the habit of concealing my thoughts, and that of darkening my lashes with mascara. . . .

"Come in!"

Someone has just knocked and I answered mechanically, my thoughts elsewhere.

It is neither Brague nor the old dresser, but an unknown person, tall, gaunt and dark, who bows his bare head, announces, without pausing for breath: "Every night this week, Madame, I have come here to applaud you in *The Pursuit*. If my visit appears to you somewhat . . . out of place I hope you will forgive it, but I feel that my admiration for your talent and . . . your figure . . . is sufficient excuse for my presenting myself so . . . unconventionally and that . . ."

I do not answer this imbecile. Damp with sweat and still out of breath, with my dress half undone, I look at him, while I wipe my hands, with such evident ferocity that his fine phrases falter and die suddenly on his lips.

Ought I to slap his face and leave on both cheeks the marks of my fingers still wet with carmine-tinted water? Ought I to raise my voice and hurl at that angular, bony face, barred with a black moustache, the words I have learnt behind the scenes and in the street?

He has the eyes of a sad coal-miner, this intruder. I have no idea how he interprets my look and my silence, but all of a sudden his expression changes.

"Oh my goodness, Madame, what a clumsy creature I am, nothing but a noodle and I've only just realised it. Turn me out, do, I've richly deserved it, but not before I've laid my respectful compliments at your feet."

He bows once more, like a man who is just about to go—and does not go. With that somewhat harlot-like artfulness that men have, he waits for half a second to see if his changed approach may have brought him any reward and—after all I'm not so terrible—it has.

"Well then, Monsieur, I will say to you politely what a moment ago I would have said harshly: please go!"

As I show him the door I laugh in a jolly way. But he does not laugh. He remains where he is, craning forward, his free hand hanging down with the fist clenched. In this attitude he looks awkward and almost menacing, with the slightly clumsy air of a wood-cutter on his best behaviour. The ceiling light is reflected in his sleek, almost lacquered-looking black hair brushed back at the sides; but his eyes are so deep set I cannot see their expression.

The reason why he does not laugh is because he desires me. He does not want my well-being, this man, he merely wants me. He is not in a mood for jests, even smutty ones. In the end this makes me uncomfortable and I would prefer him to be unashamedly lustful, like a man who has dined well and thoroughly enjoyed an eyeful in the front row of the stalls.

He is as hampered by his ardent desire for me as if it were a weapon getting in his way.

"Well, Monsieur, aren't you going?"

His answer bursts out as if I had awakened him: "Of course, of course, Madame! Certainly I'm going. I beg you to accept my excuses and . . ."

". . . and believe me to be your humble servant!" I could not help ending.

It is not very funny, but he laughs, at last he laughs, and changes that obstinate expression which I had found so disconcerting.

"It's kind of you to help me out, Madame! There's another thing too I wanted to ask you . . ."

"Oh no, you don't, you're going right away this minute. I've been amazingly long-suffering with you already, and if I don't soon take off this dress, after sweating in it like three furniture-removers, I shall get bronchitis!"

I push him out with the tip of my first finger, for as soon as I spoke of taking off my dress his face went dark and set again. Even after the door is shut and bolted, I can hear his muffled voice begging: "Madame! Madame! I wanted to know if you like flowers, and if so which ones?"

"Monsieur! Monsieur! leave me in peace! I don't ask you which are your favourite poets or if you prefer the sea to the mountains. Go away!"

"I'm going, Madame! Good evening, Madame!"

Ouf! This great noodle of a man has driven away my black mood; that is something at any rate.

For the last three years my amorous conquests have all been like this. The gentleman in the eleventh stall, the gentleman in the fourth box, the gigolo in the upper circle. A letter, two letters, a bouquet, another letter . . . and that's the end of it. Silence soon discourages them and I have to admit to myself that they are not over-persistent.

Fate, by way of sparing my energies for the future, seems to keep away from me those obstinate lovers, those hunters who pursue a woman until she physically does not know which way to turn. Those whom I attract do not write me love letters. Their letters are urgent, brutal and awkward, betraying their desires, not their thoughts. The one exception was a wretched youth who covered twelves pages with his abashed and garrulous love. He must have been very young. He used to dream of himself as a Prince Charming, poor lad, rich and powerful too: "I am writing you all this at the table in a pub where I'm having my lunch, and every time I raise my head I see my ugly mug in the looking-glass opposite."

At least that little admirer with the "ugly mug", lost in his azure palaces and enchanted forests, could dream of someone. But there is no one waiting for me on the road I follow, a road leading neither to glory nor riches nor love. Not that anything, as I well know, leads to love. It is love who throws himself across your path. And then he either blocks it for ever or, if he abandons it, leaves it in rack and ruin.

What remains of my life reminds me of the pieces of a jigsaw puzzle. Have I got to try and reconstruct, piece by piece, the original scene of it: a quiet house in the middle of a wood? No, no, I can't, someone has jumbled together all the outlines of that sweet landscape; I should never even be able to find again the bits of the blue

roof patterned with yellow lichen, nor the virginia creeper, nor the
deep forest without birds. . . .

Eight years of marriage and three of separation: that accounts for
a third of my whole existence.

My ex-husband? You all knew him, Adolphe Taillandy, the pas-
tellist. He has been doing the same portrait of a woman for the last
twenty years. She is always in evening dress, posed against a misty
gold background borrowed from Lévy-Dhurmer, and her hair, like
floss silk, forms a halo round the velvety bloom of her face. The flesh
on her temples, in the shadow of her neck, and between the swelling
curves of her breasts, glows with the same impalpable bloom, the
dusky blue of luscious grapes which tempt one's lips.

"Even Potel and Chabot can't improve on it!" said Forain one day
before a pastel of my husband's.

Apart from his famous "bloom" I do not think that Adolphe
Taillandy has any talent. But I freely admit that his portraits are irresistible, especially to women. To begin with, he resolutely sees everything in a rosy light. He has even found—goodness knows where—
some red and golden glints to beautify the hair of that withered and
superannuated brunette, Madame de Guimont-Fautru. These flecks
of light, scattered over her lustreless face and Greek nose turn her
into a voluptuous Venetian courtesan.

Once upon a time Taillandy did my portrait too. No one now remembers that I was the model for his picture of the little bacchante
with the shiny nose, where a splash of sunlight, falling full on her
face, makes it look like a mask of mother-of-pearl. I still remember
my surprise at finding myself so blonde. I remember, too, the success
of this pastel and of those which followed it. There were the portraits of Mme de Guimont-Fautru, of Baroness Avelot, of Mme de
Chalis, of Mme Robert-Durand, and of the singer Jane Doré. Then
we come to those which were less illustrious because of the
anonymity of the sitters: the portraits of Mlle J.R., of Mlle S.S., of
Mme U., of Mme Van O., and of Mrs F.W.

That was the period when Adolphe Taillandy used to declare,
with that typical effrontery of the handsome man which became him
so well: "I want no models but my mistresses, and no mistresses but
my models!"

As far as I am concerned, the only genius he had was for lying. No
woman, none of his women, could possibly have appraised and ad-

mired, feared and cursed his passion for lying as much as I did. Adolphe Taillandy used to lie feverishly, voluptuously, untiringly, almost involuntarily. For him, adultery was merely a type of falsehood, and by no means the most delectable.

He luxuriated in lies, with a strength and prodigality that was undiminished by the passing years. And while he was busy elaborating some ingenious piece of perfidy, designed with infinite care and embellished with all the studied refinements at the command of this arch-deceiver, I would see him squandering his passion for cunning in crude and vulgar deceptions that were quite unnecessary, and stories that were childish to the point of imbecility.

I met him, married him, lived with him for eight years . . . and what do I know of him? That he paints pastels and has mistresses. I know, too, that he achieves daily the disconcerting feat of being, for one person, a "plodder" who thinks of nothing but his art; for one woman a seductive and unscrupulous ruffian; for another a fatherly lover who seasons a passing infatuation with a piquant flavour of incest; for still another the tired, disillusioned and aging artist seeking to adorn his autumn with a delicate idyll. There is even the woman for whom he is, quite simply, an unchartered libertine, still vigorous and as lecherous as could be desired; and finally there is the silly little goose, well brought up and deeply enamoured, whom Adolphe Taillandy taunts, torments, spurns and takes back again with all the literary cruelty of an "artist" in a society novel.

This same Taillandy slips without transition into the no less conventional but more old-fashioned "artist" who, in order to overcome the last resistance of the little woman who is married and the mother of two children, throws down his chalks, tears up his sketch, weeps real tears which wet his Kaiser-like moustache and, seizing his broad-brimmed felt, rushes off to the waters of the Seine.

There are still many more Taillandys whom I shall never know, not to mention one of the most shocking: Taillandy in his business dealings, the shady juggler in money matters who is brazen and brutal, or smooth and shifty as occasion demands.

Among all those men which is the real one? I humbly declare that I have no idea. I believe there is no *real* Taillandy. There came a day when this prolific genius of a liar suddenly lost the power to make me despair and even ceased to interest me. Time was when he had been for me a sort of terrifying Machiavelli; perhaps after all he was only Fregoli.

In any case he still continues as before. There are times when I think of his second wife with a faint compassion. Is she still in love and blissfully savouring what she calls her victory over me? No, by this time, terrified and helpless, she must be beginning to find out what manner of man she has married.

Sometimes I sigh: "Heavens, how young I was and how I loved that man! And how I suffered!" But when I do, it is not at all a cry of pain or vengeful lamentation. It is rather as though I were saying: "If you knew how ill I was four years ago!" And when I admit: "I've been jealous to the point of wanting to kill, and die", I do it in the same way as those people who tell you: "I ate rats in '70!" They remember they did, but the memory of it is all they have. They know they ate rats, but they can no longer conjure up in themselves the shiver of horror, nor the anguish of famine.

After the first betrayals, the revolts and submissions of a youthful love determined to hope and to endure, I settled down to suffering with an unyielding pride and obstinacy, and to producing literature.

Just for the pleasure of taking refuge in a still recent past, I wrote *The Ivy on the Wall*, a cheerful little provincial novel, as clear and unruffled as the pools in my part of the world, a chaste little novel of love and marriage, slightly insipid and very agreeable, which had an unexpected and extravagant success. I found my photo in all the illustrated papers, *Life Today* awarded me its annual prize, and Adolphe and I became "the most interesting couple in Paris", the couple one invites to dinner and points out to distinguished foreigners. "You don't know the Taillandys? Renée Taillandy is extremely gifted." "Really? And what about him?" "He? Oh, he's irresistible!"

My second book, *Next Door to Love*, did not sell nearly as well. Yet in giving birth to it I had savoured the voluptuous pleasure of writing, the patient struggling with a phrase until it becomes supple and finally settles down, curled up like a tamed animal, the motionless lying in wait for a word by which in the end one *ensnares* it. Yes, my second volume sold very little. But it managed to win me the—what is the expression one uses? oh yes, of course—"the esteem of the literary world". As for the third, *The Forest Without Birds*, it fell flat and never picked up again. Yet this one is my favourite, my private "unrecognised masterpiece". It was considered diffuse and muddled, incomprehensible and long. Even now, whenever I open it, I love it and wholeheartedly admire myself in it. Incomprehensible? Perhaps it is for you. But for me its warm obscurity is clear as day;

for me a single word is enough to create again the smell and colour of hours I have lived through. It is as sonorous and full of mystery as a shell in which the sea sings, and I should love it less, I think, if you loved it too. But rest assured, I shall not write another like that, I never could.

At present other tasks and cares fill my time, especially that of earning my living, bartering my gestures, my dances and the sound of my voice for hard cash. I have got very quickly into the way of that and enjoy it, having a characteristically feminine fondness for money. And earn my living I certainly do. On my good days I joyfully say over and over again to myself that I earn my living. The music-hall where I became mime, dancer and even on occasion, actress, turned me also, despite my astonishment at finding myself reckoning, haggling and bargaining, into a tough but honest little business woman. The least gifted of women soon learns how to be that when her life and liberty depend upon it.

No one could understand our separation at all. But would anyone in the least have understood my patience and my utter complacency, so cowardly and long-lasting, before it came to that? It is, alas, only the first forgiveness which is difficult. Adolphe soon learnt that I belonged to the true, the best breed of females: in other words, that I was the kind of woman who, having forgiven on the first occasion, can gradually and cleverly be let to become one who submits and then finally accepts. What an expert master I had in him! How skilfully he alternated between indulgence and exigence! When I showed myself too intractable he even went so far as to beat me, though I believe he never really wanted to do that. A man who has lost his temper does not beat as well as he did, and he only struck me from time to time to keep up his prestige. At the time of our divorce the world was almost ready to lay all the blame on me, in order to exculpate "that good-looking Taillandy", whose only fault was that he was attractive and faithless. I was within an inch of giving in and letting myself be intimidated and reduced to my habitual submissiveness by the turmoil which the whole thing created around us.

"D'you mean to say that he's been deceiving her for eight years and it's only now that she's thought of complaining?"

I received visits from domineering friends, superior persons who know "what life is"; and others from aged relations whose most serious argument was: "What do you expect, my dear child!"

What did I expect? At bottom I knew very well. I had had enough of it. What did I want? To die, rather than prolong that humiliating life of a woman "who has everything to make her happy"; to die, yes, and risk misery before suicide, but never again to see Adolphe Taillandy, the Adolphe Taillandy who only showed himself in domestic privacy, the one who, without raising his voice, thrusting that formidable adjutant's chin of his towards me, knew so well how to warn me: "Tomorrow I'm beginning the portrait of Mme Mothier. You'll be good enough, I am sure, to take that expression off your face in future when you're looking at her."

To die, risking utter ruin first, but never again to surprise the sudden gesture which conceals a crumpled letter, nor the falsely commonplace conversation on the telephone, nor the glance of the servant who is in the know, and never again to hear myself told in a casual tone: "Oughtn't you to go and stay with your mother for a couple of days this week?"

To go away, but never again to lower myself to taking one of my husband's mistresses out for a walk all day, while he, reassured and protected by me, was embracing another. To go away, and die, but no longer to pretend ignorance, no longer to endure the nightly waiting, the vigil when one's feet grow cold in the too-big bed, no longer to think out those plans for vengeance which, born in the dark and inflated by the beatings of a lacerated heart, poisoned by jealousy, collapse at the rattle of a key in the lock and feebly let themselves be mollified when a familiar voice cries: "What? Not asleep yet?"

I had had enough.

You can get used to not eating, to having toothache or a pain in your stomach, you can even get used to the absence of a beloved person; but you cannot get used to jealousy. And so there happened what Adolphe Taillandy, who thinks of everything, had not foreseen: one day when without courtesy he had shown me *my own* door, so that he might better entertain Mme Mothier on the big divan in the studio, I did not return.

I returned neither that night, nor the next, nor on any night thereafter. And that is where my story ends—or begins.

I will not dwell on a short and gloomy period of transition during which I received, with the same peevish humour, blame, advice, sympathy and even congratulations.

I discouraged the few persistent friends who came and rang at the door of a tiny flat I had chanced to rent. I felt so outraged to think that, in order to see me, anyone should appear to be defying that sacrosanct, all-powerful and vile thing, public opinion, that I severed, with a furious gesture, the last remaining links that still bound me to my past.

And what followed? Isolation? Yes, isolation, except for three or four friends, obstinate, burr-like creatures who had resolved to put up with all my rebuffs. How ill I received them, but how I loved them, and how frightened I was, when I watched them go, that they might not come again.

Isolation indeed. I was scared of it, as of a remedy which may kill. And then I discovered that all I was doing was to go on living alone. My training in that had begun long ago, in my childhood, and the first years of my marriage had barely interrupted it. Then it had started anew, severe this time and harsh enough to draw tears; and that is the most ordinary part of my story. What numbers of women have experienced that retreat into themselves, that patient withdrawal which follows their rebellious tears! I will do them this justice, which flatters me too: it is only in pain that a woman is capable of rising above mediocrity. Her resistance to pain is infinite; one can use and abuse it without any fear that she will die, as long as some childish physical cowardice or some religious hope keeps her from the suicide that offers a way out.

"She is dying of grief. . . . She has died of grief. . . ." When you hear those clichés you can shake your head, more in disbelief than compassion: a woman can never die of grief. She is such a solid creature, so hard to kill! You think that grief eats into her? Not at all. Very often, though born weak and sickly, she gains from grief indestructible nerves, an inflexible pride, a capacity for waiting and dissimulating which increases her stature, and a contempt for those who are happy. She grows supple in the practice of suffering and dissimulation, as if they were daily exercises full of risks. For she is always on the verge of that keenest and sweetest and most seductive of all temptations, the temptation of revenge.

Sometimes, if she is too weak or too loving, she kills. And when that happens she will be able to astonish the whole world with an example of that disconcerting feminine resistance. Like a cunning animal leading on inexperienced dogs, she will wear out her judges in the course of interminable sessions and finally leave them exhausted. You can be certain that long patience, and griefs jealously hidden have tempered and sharpened and toughened this woman till every-

one cries "She's made of steel!" No, she is merely made "of woman"
—and that is enough.

Solitude, freedom, my pleasant and painful work as mime and
dancer, tired and happy muscles, and, by way of a change from all
that, the new anxiety about earning my meals, my clothes, and my
rent—such, all of a sudden, was my lot. But with it too went a savage
defiance, a disgust for the milieu where I had lived and suffered, a
stupid fear of man, of men, and of women too. I felt a morbid need
to ignore what was happening round me, to have near me none but
rudimentary creatures who would hardly think at all. Very quickly,
too, there came to me that odd sensation that only on the stage was
I really alone and safe from my fellow-creatures, protected from the
whole world by the barrier of light.

FOUR

SUNDAY again! But now the murky cold has given place to a bright cold, so we have taken our exercise, my dog and I, in the Bois between eleven and twelve. There is a matinée after lunch. The creature is ruining me. If it were not for her I could get to the Bois in the Metro, but she gives me pleasure in return for my three francs on the taxi. Black as a truffle, polished with a brush and a flannel rag, she gleams in the sun; the whole wood is hers and she takes possession of it, grunting like a pig and barking as she scatters the dry leaves.

How lovely it is, the Bois de Boulogne on a fine Sunday! For Fossette and me, city tramps who hardly know the country now, it is our forest and our park. Fossette runs faster than I do, but I walk faster than she does, and when she is not playing at "inner circle" with mad bulging eyes and her tongue hanging out, she bounds along after me in short rushes of little trotting gallops which make everyone laugh.

One can gaze full at the tarnished sun because its light is filtered by a fine rosy mist. A quivering, silvery incense, smelling faintly of mushrooms, rises from the open stretches of grass. My veil clings to my nose as I rush along, my whole body glowing with running and tingling with the cold. Am I in truth any different from what I was at twenty? On such a winter morning as this, surely even in the full flower of adolescence I was neither more firm nor more supple nor more sensually happy?

I can believe it as long as I am running through the Bois, but when I return home my fatigue undeceives me. It is no longer the *same* fatigue. When I was twenty I should have enjoyed my temporary lassitude, sunk in a half-dream without any mental reserves. But nowadays I begin to find fatigue irksome, like a sort of bodily distress.

Fossette is a born luxury-dog and play-actress: the *boards* thrill her and she has a craze for jumping into every elegant car she sees. Yet it was Stephen-the-Dancer who sold her to me, and at no time did Fossette ever belong to a successful actress. Stephen-the-Dancer is one of my comrades working at the moment in the same "dump", the *Empyrée-Clichy*. A prey to tuberculosis which year by year is eating him up, this fair Gaul witnesses the gradual dissolution of his biceps, his rosy thighs gleaming with golden down, and the beautiful chest muscles of which he is so justly proud. Already he has had to give up boxing for dancing and roller-skating. He *rinks* here on the sloping stage; in addition he has set up as a dancing teacher, and on the side he also breeds domestic bulldogs. This winter he is coughing a great deal. Often in the evenings he comes to my dressing-room, coughs, sits down and suggests that I should buy "a brindled, grey, bulldog bitch, a perfect beauty, who missed the first prize this year because of some jealousy".

It so happens that I arrive today in the underground corridor, honey-combed with square cells, which leads to my dressing-room, just at the moment when Stephen-the-Dancer is leaving the stage. With his slender waist, broad shoulders, tight-fitting Polish dolman of myrtle-green edged with imitation chinchilla, and fur cap over one ear, the young man still draws the eyes of the women, with his blue eyes and slightly rouged cheeks. But he is getting slowly thinner and thinner and his successes with women hasten his disease.

"Hullo!"

"Hullo, Stephen! Good house?"

"I'll say! But I can't think why the buzzards muck around here when it's so lovely in the country. By the way you don't happen to need a schipperke bitch who weighs just over a pound—a bargain I could get hold of through an acquaintance . . ."

"Just over a pound! Thanks, my flat's too small!"

He immediately laughs and does not insist. I know them well, those schipperke bitches, weighing just over a pound, that Stephen sells. They weigh round about six pounds. It is not dishonesty, it is business.

What will Stephen-the-Dancer do when he's down to his last lung, when he can't dance any more or sleep any longer with kind-hearted little women who buy him cigars, ties and drinks? What hospital, what institution will take in his beautiful hollow carcass? How far from funny all that is! And indeed what a lot of people there are whose misery doesn't bear thinking of!

"Hullo, Bouty! Hullo, Brague! Any news of Jadin?"

Brague shrugs his shoulders without answering, so intent is he on
the tricky job of making up his eyebrows; he paints them dark violet
because "that gives a fiercer look". He has a particular blue for wrinkles, a particular orangy-red for the inside of lips, a particular ochre
for make-up base, a particular syrupy carmine for dripping blood,
and above all a particular white for Pierrot masks, "the recipe for
which", he avers, "I wouldn't give to my own brother!" There's no
denying that he makes a very skilful use of this multi-coloured mania
of his, and it is the only absurdity I know of in this intelligent, almost over-conscientious pantomimist.

Bouty, looking skinnier than ever in his loose checked garment,
makes a mysterious sign to me. "I say, I've seen that kid Jadin. I saw
her on the boulevard, with a bloke. She had feathers like that! And a
muff like that! And a look as though she was bored to death at the
rate of a pound a minute!"

"Well, if she's getting a pound a minute she's got nothing to complain of," interrupts Brague, always logical.

"I didn't say she was, old chap. But she won't stay on the boulevard; she's a girl who has no idea of money. I've kept my eye on
Jadin for a long time, I have; she and her mother used to live in my
court. . . ."

From my open dressing-room, opposite that of Brague, I can see
little Bouty, who has suddenly fallen silent in the middle of his sentence. He has put his half-litre of tested milk to warm on the hot-
water pipe which runs through the dressing-rooms just above floor
level. You can't make out much of his real face behind the brick-red
and chalk-white mask of his make-up; but I can't help thinking that,
since Jadin's departure, poor little Bouty is more wretched than
ever.

When I get to the stage of whitening and powdering my shoulders, and my knees which are a mass of bruises—for Brague is not exactly gentle when he throws me to the ground—I close the door, feeling sure in any case that Bouty will say no more. Like the rest of
them, and myself too, he hardly ever speaks of his private life. It was
this silence, this obstinate modesty, which gave me the wrong impression of his comrades during my early days at the music-hall. The
most expansive and the vainest of them talk of their successes and
their artistic ambitions with the emphasis and gravity that their code
demands; the most malicious go as far as running down the "dump"
and their pals; the most talkative are always repeating old stage and

green-room jokes; but only one in ten feels the need to say: "I've got a wife—I've got two kids—my mother's ill—I'm awfully worried about my girl friend. . . ."

This silence about their private lives seems like a polite way of saying: "The rest is no concern of yours!" As soon as they have removed their grease-paint and put on their hats and scarves, they separate and disappear with a promptitude which I like to think comes as much from pride as discretion. Proud they nearly all are, and poor: the pal who is always bumming a loan is an exception in the music-hall. My silent sympathy, which has been making discoveries and learning during these last three years, goes out to all of them without any preferences.

How unrecognised they are, these *café-concert artistes*, how disparaged and how little understood! Fanciful, proud, and full of an absurd and outmoded faith in Art, they are the only people left who still dare to assert with passionate belief "An *artiste* must not . . . an *artiste* cannot accept . . . an *artiste* will not consent . . ." Proud they certainly are, for though they often exclaim: "Lousy job, ours!" or "What a dog's life!", I have never heard one of them sigh "How unhappy I am!"

Proud, and resigned to existing for only one hour in the twenty-four since, even when it applauds them, the unjust public forgets them afterwards. A newspaper may enquire with discreet solicitude into the way Mlle X. of the *Comédie Française* spends her time, and beguile the leisure hours of the whole world with her opinions on fashion, politics, cooking and love; but who will condescend to wonder what you do, poor intelligent, sensitive little Bouty, and what you think and do not say when darkness has swallowed you up and you are hurrying, towards midnight, along the Boulevard Rochechouart, so thin you are almost transparent in your long "English style" overcoat, which comes from the Samaritaine?

For the twentieth time I ponder, all alone to myself, on these things that are so far from cheerful. And while I do so my fingers briskly and unconsciously perform their accustomed task: white grease, pink grease, powder, dry rose, blue, brown, red, black. . . . I have barely finished when a hard claw scratches the bottom of my door. I open at once because it is the begging paw of a little Brabançon terrier who "has a part" in the first half of the show.

"Hullo, Nelle!"

In she comes, confident and as grave as a trusted employee, and lets me pat her little flanks, hot with exercise, while her teeth, slightly yellowed with age, crumble a biscuit. Nelle has a gleaming sandy coat, with a face like a black marmoset's, in which shine beautiful squirrel's eyes.

"Want another biscuit, Nelle?"

Well brought up, she accepts without a smile. Behind her, in the corridor, her family is waiting for her. Her family consists of a tall, lean man, silent and impenetrable, who speaks to no one, and two courteous white collies who look very much like their master. Where does he come from? What paths have led him and his collies here, like three disinherited princes? His gestures, his way of raising his hat, his long hatchet face—everything about him suggests a man of the world. It was perhaps some gift of divination which made my comrades christen him "the Archduke".

He waits in the corridor till Nelle has finished her biscuit. Nothing could be sadder, more dignified or more disdainful than this man and his three creatures, proudly resigned to their wandering lot.

"Goodbye, Nelle."

I close the door and the tinklings of the little dog's bell grow faint. Shall I see her again? A fortnight's programme comes to an end this evening and perhaps it is the end of an engagement for "Antonieff and his dogs". Where will they go next? Where will Nelle's beautiful brown eyes be shining, those eyes which say to me so clearly: "Yes, I know, you fondle me, you love me, you keep a box of biscuits for me. But tomorrow, or the day after, we shall leave. So don't expect any more of me than the civility of a nice little dog who knows how to walk on her front paws and perform a risky jump. Tenderness, like rest and security, is for us an inaccessible luxury."

FIVE

In bright weather my ground floor, between its two cliffs of new houses, enjoys a shaft of sunshine from eight in the morning until two in the afternoon. First a glittering pencil touches my bed, then it spreads out there like a square cloth of light and the coverlet throws a pink reflection up to the ceiling.

I wait, lazily, until the sunlight reaches my face, dazzling me through my closed eyelids, and the shadow of each pedestrian passes swiftly over me like a dark blue wing. Or perhaps, roused to action, I jump out of bed and begin some feverish scouring: Fossette's ears undergo a delicate probing and her coat gleams under the hard brush. Or perhaps I take advantage of the brilliant, pitiless light to inspect what is already showing signs of age in me: the delicate silk of my eyelids, the corner of my mouth where my smile has already begun to engrave a sad line, and round my throat that triple necklace of Venus which an invisible hand presses a little more deeply into my flesh every day.

Today this severe examination is interrupted by the visit of my comrade Brague, brisk, sober and on the spot as usual. I receive him as I do in my dressing-room, with nothing on but a crêpe kimono on which Fossette's paws, one rainy day, printed some little grey, four-petalled flowers.

No need to powder my nose for Brague, nor to lengthen my eyelids with blue pencil. Brague never looks at me except at rehearsals, to say "Don't do that: it's ugly. Don't open your mouth vertically: you look like a fish. Don't blink your eyes: you look like a white rat. Don't wobble your behind when you walk: you look like a mare."

It was Brague who guided, if not my first steps, at least my first gestures on the stage; and if I still show him the trust of a pupil, he for his part often continues to treat me as an "intelligent amateur", by which I mean that he is slightly impatient of discussion and considers that his opinion ought to prevail.

As he comes in this morning he plasters his hair against his neck as though he were pulling down a wig; and since that alert but sober expression, so characteristic of his clean-shaven, Catalan face, remains unchanged, I begin to wonder whether it is good news he is bringing, or bad. He eyes my ray of sunshine as though it were some precious object and looks at the two windows.

"What d'you pay for this ground floor of yours?"

"I've told you already: seventeen hundred."

"And you've got the lift too! Topping sunshine, might think you were in Nice! But that's not what I've come about: we've got an evening engagement."

"When?"

"When? Why, tonight."

"Oh!"

"Why 'Oh'? Is it awkward for you?"

"No. Do we take our act?"

"No, not the act, it's too important for that. Your dances. And I shall do my *Neurotic Pierrot* for them."

I jump up, really scared.

"My dances! But I can't! And besides, I lost my music at Aix! And then the girl who accompanies me has changed her address. If we'd at least had two days' notice. . . ."

"Out of the question," says Brague, unmoved. "They had Badet on the programme and she's ill."

"So that's it, a fill-in! If that isn't the limit! Do your *Pierrot* if you like, I'm not going to dance!"

Brague lights a cigarette and lets fall these two words: "Five hundred."

"For the two of us?"

"For you. And the same for me."

Five hundred! A quarter of my rent. Brague goes on smoking without looking at me: he knows I shall accept.

"Well of course, five hundred. What time do they want us?"

"Midnight, of course. You'll get busy about your music and everything, won't you? So long then, till this evening. Oh, by the way, Jadin's come back!"

He was closing the door, but I pull it open again: "She hasn't! When?"

"Yesterday, at midnight, you'd just gone. She looked awful! You'll see her; she's singing at our dump again. . . . Seventeen hundred, did you say? It's amazing. And women on every floor!" And off he goes, grave and ribald.

An evening reception. . . . A social engagement. Those three words are quite enough to demoralise me. I don't dare say so to Brague, but I admit it to myself as I look at my funereal face in the glass, while a little shiver of cowardice grips the skin of my back.

To see *them* again . . . them whom I left so abruptly, those who once upon a time called me "Madame Renée", because it was their affectation never to give me my husband's name. Those men—and the women! The women who betrayed me with my husband, and the men who knew I was betrayed.

The time is past now when I used to see in every woman one of Adolphe's mistresses, actual or probable, and to such an adoring wife as I was, men were never much of a menace. But I have retained an idiotic and superstitious terror of those drawing-rooms where I might meet witnesses or accomplices of my past unhappiness.

This social engagement begins by spoiling my tête-à-tête lunch with my faithful old friend Hamond, a painter already old-fashioned and in poor health, who comes from time to time to eat his boiled macaroni with me. We don't talk much. He leans his head, like that of a sick Don Quixote, against the back of an armchair, and after lunch we play at making each other miserable. He talks to me about Adolphe Taillandy, not to hurt me, but to recall a time when he himself was happy. And I discuss with him his cruel young wife whom he foolishly married, and who went off four months later with I don't know whom.

These afternoons of melancholy in which we indulge leave us worn out, with faces so aged and bitter, and mouths so dry from having said all over again so many distressing things, that we swear never to do it again. But the next Saturday finds us reunited at my table, glad to see each other again and quite impenitent: Hamond has discovered an unknown anecdote about Adolphe Taillandy and, in order to enjoy the sight of my best friend sniffing back his tears, I have dug out of a drawer an amateur snapshot in which I am holding the arm of a little, fair-haired aggressive Madame Hamond, as upright as a serpent on its tail.

But this morning our lunch isn't going well. Although Hamond, numb with cold but gay, has brought me some beautiful December grapes, blue as plums, every grape a little skinful of sweet, tasteless water—this accursed evening engagement casts its shadow over my whole day.

At a quarter to twelve Brague and I arrive in the Avenue du Bois. It's a splendid house, they must be most sumptuously bored in it. The imposing footman who leads us to the "sitting-room reserved for the artistes" offers to help me off with my fur coat. I refuse tartly: does he suppose I am going to await the good pleasure of these ladies and gentlemen, dressed in four blue necklaces, a winged scarab and a few yards of gauze?

Much better brought up than I, the imposing footman does not insist and leaves us alone. Brague, looking so thin as to be almost insubstantial in his loose Pierrot's smock, under his white mask, stands stretching in front of a looking-glass. He likes this social engagement no better than I do. Not that he misses the "barrier of light" between himself and *them* as much as I do, but he has a poor opinion of what he calls drawing-room "clients", and treats the fashionable audience with something of the malicious indifference which he shows us.

"D'you suppose it's ever entered these people's heads to try to write my name properly?" says he, holding out a little card to me. "They call me Bragne on their programmes!"

Very much hurt, at heart, he disappears, pursing up his thin, blood-red mouth, behind a door-curtain of greenery, for another imposing footman has that moment courteously called him by his mangled name.

In a quarter of an hour it will be my turn. I look at myself in the mirror and find myself ugly, deprived of the harsh electric-light which, in my dressing-room, floods the white walls, bathes the mirrors, penetrates one's make-up and gives it a velvety look. Will there be a carpet on the platform? If they could have risen, as Brague puts it, to a small row of footlights. This Salome wig grips my temples and makes my headache worse. I feel cold.

"Your turn, old girl! Go and do your stuff for them!"

Back again, Brague has already sponged his white face streaked with lines of sweat, and put on his coat while he is speaking.

"They're obviously people of standing. They don't make too much row. They talk, of course, but they don't laugh too loud. By the way, here's the two francs fifteen for my share of the taxi. I'm off."

"Aren't you going to wait for me?"

"What's the point? You go to Les Ternes and I to Montmartre, it's not the same way. Besides, I've got to give a lesson at nine tomorrow. So long, till tomorrow."

Now is the moment for my turn. My misshapen little pianist is already seated. With a hand trembling with stage-fright, I wrap round myself the veil which constitutes almost my whole costume, a circular veil of blue and violet measuring fifteen yards round.

At first I cannot distinguish anything through the fine mesh of my gauze cage. My bare feet are aware that they are treading on the short, firm pile of a fine Persian carpet. There are, alas, no footlights.

The bluish chrysalis which I represent awakens at the sound of a short prelude, and begins to writhe as my limbs slowly loosen. Little by little, the veil unwinds, fills, billows out and falls, revealing me to the eyes of the beholders, who have stopped their frantic chatter to gaze at me.

I see them. In spite of myself I see them. As I dance and crawl and turn, I see them, and I recognise them!

In the first row is a woman, still young, who was for quite a long time the mistress of my ex-husband. She was not expecting to see me this evening, and I was not thinking of her. Her sorrowful blue eyes, her one beauty, express as much fear as amazement. It is not me she fears; but my sudden presence has confronted her, brutally, with her own memories, she who suffered for Adolphe, she who was ready to leave everything for him, and wanted, with loud cries and noisy, imprudent tears, to kill her husband, and me too, and flee with Adolphe. By then he had already ceased to love her, and found her heavy on his hands. He used to confide her to my care for whole days together, charging me—what am I saying, ordering me—not to bring her back till seven o'clock; and never were there more harrowing tête-à-têtes than those of those two betrayed women who hated each other. Sometimes the poor creature, at the end of her tether, would burst into humiliated tears, and I would watch her weep, without pity for her tears, proud of controlling my own.

There she is, in the front row. They have used every inch of space and her chair is so close to the platform that I could bestow an ironical caress on her hair, which she dyes blonde because it is growing grey. She has aged in the past four years, and she looks at me with terror. She is looking through me at her sin, her despair, and her love which has perhaps ended by dying.

Behind her I recognise another woman too . . . and then one more. They used to come and have tea every week at my house in the days when I was married. Perhaps they slept with my husband; it does not matter if they did. None of them gives any sign of knowing me, but something reveals that they have recognised me, since one of them pretends to let her attention wander and talks very animatedly in a low voice to her neighbour, another exaggerates her short-sightedness, and a third, busy fanning herself and shaking her head, keeps whispering: "How hot it is, how terribly hot!"

They have changed their hair styles since the year when I abandoned all these false friends. Every one of them now conforms to the mode of swathing the hair round over the ears like a cap, binding it with a wide bandeau of ribbon or metal, which makes them look as though they were convalescent and not very clean. One no longer sees tempting napes of necks, or temples haloed in curls; one sees nothing but little muzzles—jaws, chins, mouths and noses—to which this year's fashion undeniably gives a markedly bestial appearance.

Round the sides and at the back there is a dark row of men, standing. Packed closely together they crane forward with that curiosity, that cynical courtesy which men of the world display towards a woman who is considered "déclassée", the woman whose finger-tips one used to kiss in her drawing-room and who now dances, half-naked, on a platform.

Come now, this won't do, I'm too clear-sighted this evening, and if I don't pull myself together my dancing will suffer for it. I dance and dance. A beautiful serpent coils itself along the Persian carpet, an Egyptian amphora tilts forward, pouring forth a cascade of perfumed hair, a blue and stormy cloud rises and floats away, a feline beast springs forwards, then recoils, a sphinx, the colour of pale sand, reclines at full length, propped on its elbows with hollowed back and straining breasts. I have recovered myself and forget nothing. Do these people really exist, I ask myself? No, they don't. The only real things are dancing, light, freedom and music. Nothing is real except making rhythm of one's thought and translating it into beautiful gestures. Is not the mere swaying of my back, free from any constraint, an insult to those bodies cramped by their long corsets, and enfeebled by a fashion which insists that they should be thin?

But there is something more worth while than humiliating them; I want, for one moment only, to charm them! It needs only a little more effort: already their heads, under the weight of their jewels and their hair, sway vaguely as they obediently follow my movements. At any moment now the vindictive light in all those eyes will go out, and the charmed creatures will all give in and smile at the same time.

The end of the dance, and the noise of the very controlled applause, break the spell. I disappear, to return and bow with a smile all round the room. At the back of the room a man's silhouette gesticulates and calls out "Bravo!" I know that voice and that tall black figure.

Why, it's my imbecile of the other evening! It's the Big-Noodle! Any doubts I may have about it are soon dispelled when I see him enter, with bent head, the little room where my pianist rejoins me. He is not alone, he is accompanied by another tall black noodle, who has the air of being the master of the house.

"Madame . . ." says he, bowing.

"Monsieur . . ."

"Will you permit me to thank you for having been so kind as to take part, on the spur of the moment, in . . . and to express to you all the admiration . . ."

"Really, Monsieur . . ."

"I am Henri Dufferein-Chautel."

"Ah, of course."

"And this is my brother, Maxime Dufferein-Chautel, who is extremely anxious to be presented to you."

My Big-Noodle of yesterday bows once more and manages to seize and kiss a hand which was busy gathering up the blue veil. Then he remains standing and saying nothing, much less at his ease than in my dressing-room.

Meanwhile Dufferein-Chautel No. 1 is awkwardly crumpling a closed envelope:

"I . . . I'm not sure whether it is to Monsieur Salomon, your impresario, or to you yourself that I should hand . . ."

Dufferein-Chautel No. 2, suddenly crimson under his brown skin, casts a furious, hurt glance at him, and there they both stand, each as foolish-looking as the other!

What is there embarrassing about all that? I cheerfully put them out of their misery: "Why, to me myself, Monsieur, it's quite simple! Give me that envelope, or rather slip it in with my music—for I will confess to you in confidence that my dancer's costume has no pockets!"

They both burst into relieved and slightly naughty laughter whereupon, declining the sly offer of Dufferein-Chautel No. 2, who fears on my behalf the toughs of Les Ternes, I am at last free to go home alone, joyfully clasping the five hundred francs that are my share, and to go to bed and sleep.

SIX

THIS Friday evening, in order to slip my hand into the box where they put the letters—a little case nailed to the side of the box-office—I have to disturb a fine "pimp" in a cap, one of those classic types that abound in this district.

Even though his costume has been popularised in pictures and caricatures, in the theatre and the *café-concert*, the "bully" remains faithful to his sweater or his coloured, collarless shirt, to his cap and the jacket which he strains flatteringly tight round his hips by plunging his hands in the pockets, to his fag-end and his noiseless slippers.

On Saturdays and Sundays these gentlemen fill half our *Empyrée-Clichy*, outlining the gallery and stumping up two francs twenty-five to reserve in advance the cane-bottomed seats that practically touch the stage. They are the faithful, the devotees, who exchange remarks with the artistes, hiss or applaud them, and have a gift for interjecting the ribald criticism, the lewd exclamation that set the whole house in a roar.

Sometimes their success goes to their heads and then the whole thing becomes a riot. From one gallery to another they exchange prearranged remarks in spicy slang, followed by cat-calls and missiles which in turn lead to the prompt arrival of the police. It is as well for the artist on the stage to await the end of the storm with an expressionless face and a modest bearing, if he does not want to see the oranges, the programmes rolled into a ball, and the small coins change their direction. Simple prudence also cautions him not to go on with his interrupted song.

But these, I repeat, are brief storms, skirmishes reserved for Saturdays and Sundays. Order is very well maintained at the *Empyrée-Clichy*, where one feels the hand of Mme la Directrice—the Boss!

Dark and lively, covered with jewels, the Boss presides this evening, as every evening, in the box-office. Her brilliant, darting eyes miss nothing, and the theatre cleaners, in the mornings, do not dare to forget the dust in the dark corners. At the moment of my arrival those terrible eyes are withering a genuine apache, a hefty fellow not to be spurned, who has come to reserve one of the best cane-bottomed seats, close to the stage, those in the front row whose occupants squat like toads, with their arms on the railing in front and their chins on their crossed hands.

The Boss is turning him away, without any fuss, but with the demeanour of a lion-tamer!

"Pick up your money and hop it!"

The stalwart swings his arms and rocks like a bear: "What for, Madame Barnet? What've I done?"

"You and your, 'What've I done?' D'you think I didn't see you last Saturday? It was you in seat No. 1 in the gallery, wasn't it?"

"As if I could remember!"

"It was you who stood up during the pantomime, wasn't it, shouting out: 'She's only showing one tit, I want to see the two of 'em! I've paid two francs, one for each tit!' "

The stalwart turns crimson and protests, with his hand on his heart: "Me? Me? Now look here, Madame Barnet, I know how to behave, I know what's not done! Cross my heart, Madame Barnet, it wasn't me who . . ."

The queen of the *Empyrée* raises an inexorable right hand: "No fibs! I saw you, didn't I? So that's enough. There'll be no place for you for a week from today. Pick up your money and don't let me see you before Saturday or Sunday next. And now get out!"

The exit of the stalwart, barred for eight days, is well worth my losing a few minutes more. He goes off on his noiseless felt shoes, his back humped, and does not resume his insolent expression until he is on the pavement again. But his heart is not in it, his bearing is forced and, for a short while, there is no difference between this dangerous brute and a small boy deprived of his favourite pudding.

On the iron staircase, mingling with the air rising from the hot pipes, which smells of plaster, coal and ammonia, the voice of Jadin reaches me in snatches. The little wretch has found her familiar public again and got back her hold on them! You only have to hear, in the distance, the stormy laughter and the contented muttering with which they accompany and support her.

That warm harsh contralto, husky already from dissipation and perhaps the beginnings of consumption, finds its way to one's heart by the lowest and surest paths. If a "discriminating and artistic" producer were to stray in here and listen to Jadin singing, he would cry: "I'll take her and launch her, and in three months you'll see what I'll make of her!"

An arrogant and embittered failure, that is what he would make of her. Experiences of that kind are never encouraging; where could the ill-kempt Jadin shine better than here?

There she is on the staircase, just as she went away, would you believe it, with her over-long frock frayed out by her heels, and her Marie-Antoinette fichu, yellowed by the smoke of the auditorium, gaping open to show her gaunt, youthful thinness, her hunched shoulder, and her sulky mouth with its curled upper lip on whose down a moustache of powder lingers.

It gives me a keen and genuine pleasure to see that foul-mouthed child again, and she on her side rushes down the last steps to fall on me and squeeze my hands in her warm paws: for some unknown reason her "spree" has brought us closer together.

She follows me into my dressing-room where I risk a discreet reproach. "You know, Jadin, it was a rotten thing to do! You don't let people down like that!"

"I went to see my mother," says Jadin with great gravity.

But on catching sight of herself in the mirror in the act of lying, her whole childish face breaks into laughter and becomes one wide slit, like the faces of very young Persian cats.

"That's a good 'un, ain't it? . . . How bored you must all have been here without me!"

She radiates confident pride, surprised at heart that the *Empyrée-Clichy* had not put up its shutters during her absence.

"Haven't changed, have I? . . . Oh what lovely flowers! 'Scuse me."

With the swift gesture of a pickpocket, skilled from childhood at stealing oranges from the stalls, she seizes a huge purple rose before I have even opened the little envelope fastened to the side of a great sheaf of flowers which is standing waiting for me on the little make-up shelf.

MAXIME DUFFEREIN-CHAUTEL

With his respectful compliments

Dufferein-Chautel! At last I have found again the name of the Big-Noodle! Ever since the other evening, too lazy to open a *Tout-*

Paris, I have called him successively Thureau-Dangin, Dujardin-Beaumetz, or Duguay-Trouin!

"Those are flowers all right, I'll say!" says Jadin while I undress. "They from your friend?"

I protest, with useless sincerity: "Dear me, no! Just someone thanking me . . . for an evening performance. . . ."

"That's a pity!" declares Jadin, as one who knows all about these things. "Only a gentleman gives flowers like that. The chap I ran off with the other day gave me just that kind."

I burst out laughing: Jadin airing her views on the quality of flowers and "chaps" is irresistible. She turns quite red under her flour-powder and takes offence:

"What is it? P'raps you don't believe he was a gentleman? All right then, ask Canut, the stage-setter, to let you see what I brought back in the way of brass, last night when you'd just gone!"

"How much?"

"Sixteen hundred francs, dearie! Canut saw them, it isn't a yarn!"

Do I look sufficiently impressed? I fear not.

"And what are you going to do with it, Jadin?"

She plucks unconcernedly at the threads hanging from her old blue and white dress: "Don't suppose there'll be any for savings. I stood the stage hands a round of drinks. And then I lent—as she calls it—fifty francs to Myriame to pay for her coat. And the girls keep asking one after the other and saying they haven't got a bean. I really don't know! I say, there's Bouty! Hullo, Bouty!"

"Hullo, reveller!"

Bouty, having politely assured himself that my deshabille is covered by a kimono, pushes open the door of my dressing-room and shakes the hand that Jadin holds out, repeating "Hullo!" in a tender voice but with a rough gesture. But Jadin immediately forgets him and continues her conversation, standing behind me, and addressing herself to my image in the glass: "You know it makes me feel quite sick to have *as much money as that!*"

"But . . . won't you buy yourself some frocks . . . at least one . . . to replace this one?"

With the back of her hand she thrusts aside the straggling locks of her thin, straight hair: "What an idea! This dress'll do very well till the *Revue* comes on. Whatever would *they* say, if they saw I'd gone off up town to pick up enough brass to bring back a swell new outfit!"

She is right. *They* means her famous local public, exigent and jealous, whom she has slightly betrayed but who forgive her on condition that she reappears before them badly turned out, badly shod, got up like an old rag-bag, but just the same as before her escapade, before her lapse.

After a pause Jadin goes on, quite at ease before the embarrassed silence of Bouty: "You see I bought myself what I needed most: a hat and a muff, as well as a scarf. And what a hat! You'll see it soon. . . . So long. You staying, Bouty? You know, Bouty, I'm rich, I'll stand you anything you like!"

"Not my line, thanks."

I've never seen Bouty so cold and disapproving. If I were to say aloud that he loves Jadin I should cover myself with ridicule; so I must be content to think it.

The little comedian departs soon after and I am left alone with my sheaf of roses, a large commonplace sheaf tied with pale green ribbon, just the sheaf one would expect from a "big noodle" such as my new admirer.

"With his respectful compliments. . . ." During the past three years I have received a good many compliments, if I may say so, but there was nothing respectful about them. And my old middle-class respectability, always vigilant, is secretly gratified, just as if those compliments—however veiled with respect they hope they are—were not asking for the same thing, always the same thing.

My short-sightedness does not prevent me from seeing, in the front row of the stalls, M. Dufferein-Chautel, junior, stiff and grave, with his black hair shining like the silk of a top-hat. Happy because he has seen from my look that I have recognised him, he follows my movements, my comings and goings on the stage, with his head, just as my dog Fossette does when I am dressing to go out.

SEVEN

THE days pass. There is nothing new in my life, except a patient man lying in wait for me.

We have just got over Christmas and the first of January. The Christmas evening performance was a hectic affair which shook the whole "dump" to its foundations. The public, more than half drunk, yelled like one man; the bespangled stage-boxes hurled mandarines and twopenny cigars at the upper galleries; Jadin, tipsy from lunch time on, lost the thread of her song and danced a frightful cancan on the stage, pulling up her skirts over her laddered stockings, a great lock of hair flapping down her back. A gala evening with our Boss presiding in her box, totting up the princely takings, with one eye on the sticky glasses cluttering the little shelves nailed to the backs of the stalls.

Brague also had been tipsy since dinner and was bubbling over with lewd fantasies like a little black goat. Alone in his dressing-room he improvised an extraordinary monologue of a moonstruck person defending himself against spectres, with cries of "Oh no, stop, let me alone!" or "Not that! Not that! Well, just once then . . ." and sighs and protests as of a man tortured by diabolical voluptuousness.

As for Bouty, writhing with the cramp his enteritis gave him, he sat sipping his bluish milk.

By way of a New Year's Eve celebration, I ate the beautiful hot-house grapes which my old friend Hamond had brought me, all alone with Fossette, who was crunching sweets sent by the Big-Noo-dle. But it needed a great deal of self-mockery not to fall a prey to the hurt jealousy of a child whom they have forgotten to ask to the party.

What in fact would I have liked? To have supper with Brague, or with Hamond, or with Dufferein-Chautel? Heavens, no! Well then, what? I am neither better nor worse than the rest of the world, and there are times when I should like to forbid others to enjoy themselves when I am bored.

It is a fact worth remarking that all my friends, the real, true ones like Hamond, are people who never have any luck and are incurably sad. Is it the "solidarity of ill-fortune" which binds us together? I don't think so. It seems to me rather that I attract and keep the friendship of those melancholy, solitary persons who are pledged to loneliness or the wandering life, as I am. Birds of a feather . . .

I brood on these cheerful ideas on my way back from visiting Margot. Margot is the younger sister of my ex-husband. Ever since childhood she has lugubriously borne this playful pet name which suits her about as well as a ring in the nose. She lives alone and, with her bobbed hair turning grey, her shirt blouse adorned with Russian embroidery, and her long black jacket, she looks rather like a Rosa Bonheur, turned Nihilist.

Fleeced by her husband, sponged on by her brother, robbed by her lawyer and cheated by her servants, Margot has taken refuge in a grim serenity made up of incurable kindness of heart and silent contempt. Everyone around her is so used to exploiting her that they continue to eat into her income and she lets it happen, merely giving way sometimes to sudden rages and dismissing her cook for a too-flagrant overcharge of a penny.

"I don't mind being robbed," she says, "but I do think they should take care how they do it." After which she relapses for days on end into her all-embracing contempt.

During my married life I knew Margot very little. Kind though she was, she was always cold and far from talkative, and this reserve of hers did not encourage me to confide in her. But on the day when my break with Adolphe seemed final, she politely and briefly closed the door to my astonished husband and never saw him again. It was then I learnt that I had in Margot an ally, a friend and a support, since it is from her that I get the fifteen louis a month which keep me from destitution. "Go on, take it!" said Margot. "You won't be doing me any harm. It's only the ten francs a day that Adolphe has always touched me for!"

It is true that I should never turn to Margot for consolation or for that tonic cheerfulness that they tell me will be good for me. But at least Margot loves me in her own way, her discouraged and discouraging way, though prophesying that I shall come to a wretched end.

"As for you, my girl," she said to me once again today, "you'll be lucky if you don't get caught up all over again with a man just like Adolphe. Like me, you're made to be imposed on. But it's a waste of my time talking to you. Burnt child though you are, you'll go back to the fire, you mark my words! You're so obviously one of those who need more than one Adolphe to teach them."

"Really, Margot, you're extraordinary! Every time I see you, you take me to task like this," I reproached her, laughingly. " 'You're this, you're that, you're one of those who, one of those that . . .' Do at least wait until I've sinned, it'll be time enough to blame me for it afterwards."

Margot put on one of those expressions that make her look very tall, so lofty do they seem.

"I'm not blaming you, my girl. And I shan't blame you any more when you have sinned, as you put it. Only, it will be very difficult for you to refrain from committing *the* folly, for there is only one: the folly of beginning all over again. I know what I'm talking about. Even though," she added with a strange smile, "I never had any senses!"

"Well then, Margot, what ought I to do? What do you feel is wrong with my present life? Do you think I ought to shut myself up, as you do, for fear of a worse ill, and like you love nothing but little short-haired Brabançon terriers?"

"Take jolly good care you don't!" burst out Margot, with a sudden childlike gaiety. "Little Brabançon terriers indeed! They're the nastiest brutes possible. Look at that creature," she went on, pointing to a little tawny bitch who looked like a shorn squirrel. "I sat up with her for fifteen nights when she had bronchitis. Yet if I happen to leave her alone for an hour in the house, the little horror pretends not to recognise me and growls at my heels as if I were a tramp. . . . But apart from all those things, are you well, my child?"

"Very well, thank you, Margot."

"Tongue? Whites of the eyes? Pulse?"

She turns back my eyelids and presses my wrist with an assured, professional hand, exactly as if I were a little Brabançon. For Margot and I both know the value of health, and the misery of losing it. One manages to live alone and one gets used to it; but to languish alone in fever, to cough through an interminable night, to stagger on tottering legs to a window whose panes are lashed with rain, and then to return to a rumpled, sagging bed—alone, alone, alone!

For a few days last year I knew the horror of lying, vaguely delirious, and dreading, in my half-lucidity, that I might die slowly, far from everyone and forgotten. Ever since then, following Margot's example, I take good care of myself and look after my insides, my throat, my stomach and my skin, with the slightly fanatical strictness of a proprietor who is devoted to his possessions.

I have been thinking today of that odd remark of Margot's, that she for her part "never had any senses". And what about me and my senses? Now I come to think of it, it's a very long time since I thought of them.

Margot appears to think that the whole "question of the senses" is important. If I am to believe literature—the best and the worst too—no voice can compete with the voice of the senses. What is one to believe?

Brague once said to me, in the tone of one giving medical advice: "You know, it's not healthy to live as you do." And, like Margot, he added: "Anyway, you'll come to it, like all the others. Remember what I'm telling you."

I don't like thinking of that. Brague is always ready to lay down the law and play at being infallible. It doesn't mean a thing. All the same I don't like thinking of it.

At the music-hall I join, without the slightest affectation of prudery, in conversations where they discuss "the question of the senses" with statistical and surgical precision, and I take the same detached and respectful interest in them as I do in reading in a newspaper of the ravages of the plague in Asia. I am quite ready to be moved but I prefer to remain half incredulous. All the same I don't much like thinking of it.

And besides, there is that man—the Big-Noodle—who contrives to live in my shadow and tread in my footsteps with the obstinacy of a dog. I find flowers in my dressing-room and Fossette gets a little nickel trough for her meals; three minute animal mascots sit chatting nose to nose on my writing-table: an amethyst cat, a chalcedony elephant and a turquoise toad. A circlet of jade, green as a tree-frog, bound the stalks of a bunch of greenish lilies which was handed to me on New Year's Day. And in the street I too often run into that same Dufferein-Chautel, who bows with a look of surprise that would deceive no one.

He forces me to remember, too often, the existence of desire, that imperious demi-god, that unleashed faun who gambols round love and does not obey love; and to remember that I am alone, healthy, still young, and rejuvenated by my long, moral convalescence.

Senses? Yes, I have them . . . or I had them in the days when Adolphe Taillandy condescended to concern himself with them. Shy senses they were, normal senses, glad of the conventional caress which was enough for them, afraid of any refinements or erotic complications, slow to rouse but slow to quench, in short, healthy senses.

Betrayal and long-drawn-out grief have anaesthetised them . . . for how much longer, I wonder? On days when I am gay and light-hearted, the pleasure of feeling myself pure, and cut off from what made me a woman like any other, is enough to make me say to myself "For ever!" But there are also lucid days when I reason harshly with myself. "Take care! Be always on guard! Everyone who approaches you is suspect, but you are your own worst enemy. Don't proclaim that you are dead, empty, light: the beast whom you forget is hibernating, and fortifying himself with a long sleep."

And then I forget once again the memory of what I was, in the fear of becoming once more *alive*; I want nothing, I regret nothing . . . until the next time my confidence lands me in disaster, until that inevitable moment of crisis when, with terror in my eyes, I see advancing towards me, with gentle, powerful hands, the sadness that guides and accompanies one in all the pleasures of the flesh.

EIGHT

For several days past Brague and I have been rehearsing a new act. There will be a forest, a grotto, an old troglodyte, a young hamadryad, and a faun in the prime of life.

The faun is Brague, I am to be the woodland nymph, and as for the old troglodyte, we haven't yet thought about him. He only appears at intervals, and to play this part, Brague says: "There's a young ruffian of eighteen among my pupils who'll make a perfect prehistoric!"

They have kindly lent us the stage at the *Folies* from ten to eleven in the mornings for our rehearsals. Stripped of its backcloths, the whole of the deep, bare stage is visible. How sad and grey it all looks when I arrive, with no corset on, a sweater instead of a blouse, and black satin knickers under my short skirt.

I envy Brague for being, at no matter what hour, always himself, alert, swarthy and authoritative. I struggle feebly against the cold, and the sluggish, sickening atmosphere not yet rid of the stale smells of the night before and still smelling of humanity and sour punch. The tinny old rehearsal piano grinds out the new music, my hands grip each other and part with difficulty, my gestures are constricted, close to my body, I hunch my shoulders with the cold and feel myself mediocre, awkward, lost.

Brague, used to my morning inertia, has also learnt the secret of how to cure it. He badgers me without respite, running round me like a terrier, showering brief encouragements and sharp exclamations which make me tingle as though I had been lashed.

A cloud of dust rises from the auditorium: it is the hour when the cleaners are brushing away the mud that has dried on the carpets, together with all the rubbish dropped the evening before: papers, cherry-stones, cigarette-ends, and dried dung from the soles of shoes.

Towards the back of the stage—for we are only lent a section of it, a strip about two yards wide—a troupe of acrobats are at work on their thick carpet: they are handsome, fair-haired, rosy Germans, silent and intent on the job. Their working tights are dirty, and by way of relaxation and pastime during the intervals of their act, they keep on exercising; two of them, laughing sleepily, attempt a miracle of unattainable equilibrium . . . which they will perhaps achieve next month. When the rehearsal is over, they concentrate very seriously on the perilous education of the youngest of the troupe, an urchin with the face of a little girl, beneath long fair curls, whom they throw in the air and catch on a foot or a hand, an airy little creature who seems to fly, with his locks streaming out horizontally behind him or standing on end like a flame above his head while he falls back to earth, feet together and pointing downwards and arms glued to his body.

"As you were!" cries Brague. "You've bungled that movement again! Of all the lackadaisical rehearsals! Can't you possibly attend to what you're doing?"

It's difficult, I must admit. Overhead now there are some gymnasts swinging on three trapezes, and exchanging shrill cries like the cries of swallows. The glittering nickel of the metal trapezes, the squeak of rosined hands on the polished bars, all that expenditure of elegant and supple strength going on around me, that methodical contempt of danger, finally exalt and fire me with the desire to emulate them. And that is the moment when they turn us out, just when I was beginning to be conscious of the beauty of a perfected gesture, the rightness of an expression of horror or desire, suddenly adorning my body like a rich ornament.

Roused thus too late, I use up the rest of my energy in returning on foot with Fossette, whom rehearsals fill with a silent rage which she works off outside on dogs bigger than herself. Like a brilliant mime, she terrorises them with a single twitch of her Japanese dragon-mask, a hideous grimace which makes her black eyes start out of her head, and curls back her lips to reveal, beneath their pink undersides, a few white teeth set askew like palings of a fence blown in all directions by the wind.

As a result of having grown up in the profession, Fossette knows the music-hall better than I do; she trots about in dark basements, bowls along corridors, and finds her way by the familiar smell of soapy water, rice powder and ammonia. Her brindled body is used to

being clasped in arms coated with pearl white; she condescends to
eat the sugar that the supers scrounge from the saucers in the café
downstairs. A creature of whims, sometimes she insists that I should
take her with me in the evenings, and on other days, coiled round
like a turban in her basket, she watches me go with the contempt of
a dowager who, for her part, likes to digest her meal slowly.

"It's Saturday, Fossette, we must hurry! Hamond will have arrived
before us!"

Instead of taking a cab, we have run like two mad creatures, because the air, this morning, is full of that soft and surprising
sweetness that comes before the spring. We catch up with Hamond
just as he reaches my white box of a house, the colour of sculptured
butter.

But Hamond is not alone: he is talking on the pavement with . . .
with Dufferein-Chautel, junior, christened Maxime, and *known* as
the Big-Noodle.

"What! You again!"

Without giving him time to protest, I questioned Hamond severely. "You know M. Dufferein-Chautel?"

"Certainly I do," says Hamond calmly. "So do you, I see. But I
knew him when he was quite small. I still have in a drawer a photograph of a boy with a white armband: 'In memory of the First Communion of Maxime Dufferein-Chautel, May 15th 18 . . .'"

"So you have!" cries the Big-Noodle. "Mother sent it you because
she thought I looked so beautiful."

I don't join in their laughter. I am not pleased that they know
each other. And I feel uncomfortable under the strong, noonday
light, with my hair out of curl under my fur cap, my nose shiny for
lack of powder, and my mouth dry with hunger and thirst.

I hide my shapeless, laced rehearsal boots under my skirt. The kid
is so rubbed now that it shows the blue, but they grip my ankles well
and their worn soles are as supple as those of dancing slippers. Especially as the Big-Noodle is looking me over as if he had never seen
me before.

I stifle a sudden childish longing to cry and instead I ask him, as if
I were about to bite him: "What is it? Have I got a smut on my
nose?"

He takes his time to reply: "No . . . but . . . it's odd . . . when one has only seen you in the evening one would never believe you have grey eyes. They look brown on the stage."

"Yes, I know. I've been told so before. You know, Hamond, the omelette will be cold. Goodbye, Monsieur."

Come to that, I too had never seen him so well, in full daylight. His deep-set eyes are not black, as I thought, but a rather tawny brown, like the eyes of sheep-dogs.

I thought they would never stop shaking hands! And that little tart, Fossette, saying "goodbye to the gentleman", and grinning like an ogress from ear to ear! And the Big-Noodle putting on the look of a beggar at the pastry-cook's window, just because I spoke of an omelette! If he thinks I'm going to invite him!

Quite unfairly, I lay the blame for all of it on Hamond. So I remain silent as I hurriedly give my face and hands a brief wash before rejoining my old friend in the little study where Blandine is laying the table. For I have suppressed once and for all that sad and useless room known as a dining-room and used for only one hour in the twenty-four. But I must admit that Blandine sleeps in, and that an extra room would have cost me too much.

"Well, well, so you know Maxime!" cries Hamond as he unfolds his napkin.

I was expecting that!

"I? I don't know him at all! I had an evening engagement at his brother's house, where I met him. That's all."

I forbear—why, I wonder?—to mention the first interview, when the Big-Noodle, in a state of excitement, burst into my dressing-room.

"Well, he knows you. And he admires you a great deal. In fact I rather think he is in love with you."

Subtle Hamond! I look at him with that sly, feline mirth that masculine naïvety inspires in us.

"He knows you like roses, and sweets flavoured with pistachio. He's ordered a collar for Fossette . . ."

I spring to my feet: "He's ordered a collar for Fossette! . . . Oh well, after all that's nothing to do with me!" I say, laughing. "Fossette's a creature with no morals: she'll accept, she's quite capable of it!"

"We spoke of you, naturally. I thought you were very good friends."

"Oh Hamond, I would have told you!"

His friendly jealousy flattered, my old friend lowers his eyes.

"He's a very nice chap, I assure you."

"Who is?"

"Maxime. I met his mother, who is a widow, in . . . let's see now, it must be thirty . . . no, thirty-five. . . ."

Off he goes, and I have to endure the history of the Dufferein-Chautels, mother and son. A managing woman, she runs the whole estate, saw mills in the Ardennes, acres of forest land. Maxime, rather lazy, is the youngest and most spoilt of her sons, much more intelligent than he seems, thirty-three and a half years old. . . .

"Fancy! Just like me!"

Hamond leans towards me, over the little table, with the attention of a miniaturist: "Are you thirty-three, Renée?"

"Alas!"

"Don't say it. No one would know."

"Oh, I know very well that on the stage . . ."

"Nor in everyday life either."

That is as far as his compliment gets and Hamond goes on with the history of the Dufferein-Chautels. Displeased, I suck some grapes. The Big-Noodle is insinuating himself into my life more than I have allowed him. At this hour Hamond and I ought, as our custom is, to be stirring up those bad old memories that blossom weekly in the bitter aroma of our steaming cups.

Poor Hamond! It is for my sake that he is departing from his beloved, gloomy habit. I well know that my solitude makes him anxious; if he dared he would say to me, like a paternal go-between:

"There is the lover you need, my dear! Good health, doesn't gamble, doesn't drink, well-enough off. . . . You'll thank me!"

NINE

Four days more and I leave the *Empyrée-Clichy!* Every time I come to the end of a rather long engagement at a *café-concert*, I have the odd impression, during the last days, of being given a freedom I have not desired. Happy though I am to be free and able to spend my evenings at home, I am not in a hurry to enjoy it, and when I stretch and say "At last!" there is a lack of spontaneity about it.

All the same this time I really believe I am glad, and as I sit in Brague's dressing-room I give him a list, at which he mocks, of the urgent tasks which are going to fill my holidays.

"I'm having all the divan cushions re-covered, you know. And then I'm pushing the divan itself right into the corner, and I'm going to have an electric lamp fixed above it."

"Splendid! It'll look just like a brothel," says Brague gravely.

"Silly ass! And besides that, oh well, I've heaps of things to do. It's such ages since I paid any attention to my home."

"It certainly is!" agrees Brague, drily. "And who are you doing all this for?"

"What d'you mean, who for? For myself, of course!"

Brague turns from the mirror a moment, showing a face in which the right eye, the only one he has rubbed with blue, looks as if it were ringed with terrific bruises.

"For yourself? Just for yourself? You'll forgive me but I find that a bit . . . fatuous. Besides, d'you suppose I'm going to let *The Pursuit* lie dormant? You'd better be ready to be off at a moment's notice for one of those first-rate establishments in the provinces and abroad. And by the way, Salomon, the agent, asked me to tell you to drop round and see him."

"Oh! already?"

Brague shrugs his shoulders and says, sharply: "There you go as usual, with your 'Oh! already?' Yet if I were to tell you there was nothing doing, you'd keep on like a mosquito: 'When do we start? When do we start?' You're all exactly alike, you womenfolk."

"My view too," agrees the melancholy voice of Bouty, behind us.

He has grown thinner than ever this past month, has Bouty, and he "tires" more and more. I steal a glance at him when he is not looking, so as not to hurt him; but what can one make out under that red mask with the white-rimmed eyes? Silently we listen to the voice of Jadin above us:

> "My sweet little Mignonet-te
> I pray you may never regret
> The wonderful day
> When I gave you a spray,
> A spray—of mignonette!"

The composer of the *Waltz of the Mignonette*, an experienced man who knows his job, has cunningly contrived a suggestive pause in the middle of the last line of the chorus.

"So in four days more you'll be making tracks?" asks the little funny-man abruptly, raising his head.

"Yes, in four days. I've enjoyed being here. It's so peaceful."

"So peaceful!" protests Bouty, sceptically. "I can think of places more peaceful than this. You'll easily find better. I'm not running down our public, but all the same they're a pretty low lot. Oh, I know one can keep up one's standard anywhere," he goes on, seeing me shrug as if I thought that unimportant. "But all the same . . . just listen to them bawling now! How d'you suppose a woman, a young woman I mean, with no proper notions, always up to larks and ready to go on the spree, can learn good behaviour in the middle of all that? When she's a scatterbrained, rackety girl, I mean . . . like Jadin, for instance?"

Poor little Bouty, it is your unhappy love that has suddenly given you these aristocratic ideas, this contempt for a public which applauds you; and in seeking and finding an excuse for Jadin, you spontaneously invent the theory of the influence of environment, in which I don't believe!

The Russian dancers have gone, and Antonieff—the "grand-duke" —and his dogs have gone too. Where? No one knows. None of us has had the curiosity to find out. Other turns have come to take their place, some engaged for seven days and others for four, since the

Revue is now so imminent; on the stage and in the corridors I run into new faces with which, by way of a friendly and discreet greeting, I exchange a half-smile or a questioning look.

The only ones who remain from the former programme are ourselves, Jadin, who is to create—Heavens above!—various roles in the *Revue*, and Bouty. We chat in a melancholy way in the evenings, like veterans of the *Empyrée-Clichy* forgotten when the young regiment marched away.

Where shall I find again those whom I have known here? In Paris, Lyons, Vienna or Berlin? Perhaps never, perhaps nowhere. We shall meet for five minutes in the office of Salomon, the agent, with noisy greetings and stagey handclasps, just long enough to know that we still exist and to utter the indispensable "What are you doing?" and to learn in reply that "things are going nicely" or that "things aren't shaping too well".

Things aren't shaping too well. . . . This is the vague circumlocution my wandering companions use to cover hard times, "restings", money troubles, and destitution. Puffed up and sustained by that heroic vanity which endears them to me, they never admit. A few of them, at the end of their tether, find a little part to fill in a *real* theatre, and oddly enough they never boast of this. Patient and obscure, they wait there for the renewal of luck which will bring them an engagement at a music-hall, the blessed hour which will see them in a spangled skirt again, or evening clothes smelling of benzine, once more facing the spotlight *in their repertoire!*

"No, things aren't shaping well," some will tell me, adding: "I'm trying the films again."

The motion picture, which threatened the humble *café-concert* artistes with ruin, is now their salvation. In it they adapt themselves to an anonymous labour which brings them no fame, which they do not like, which upsets their habits and changes the times of their meals, their leisure and their work. Hundreds live by it in times of unemployment, and many settle down in it. But if the films become glutted with supers and stars, what will they do?

"Things aren't shaping well . . . no, things aren't shaping well."

They utter the phrase in a casual but at the same time serious way, without overdoing it and without whining, swinging their hat or a pair of old gloves in their hands. They swagger, tightly buttoned in a full-skirted overcoat of the fashion of two seasons ago; for the essential, the indispensable thing, is not the possession of a clean suit but of a "really classy" overcoat which covers everything: threadbare waistcoat, shapeless jacket, trousers yellowed at the knees; a dashing, flashy overcoat, which makes an impression on the director or the agent, and which in the last resort enables one to throw off a "things aren't shaping well" in the jaunty tone of a man of means.

Where shall we be next month? In the evenings Bouty prowls aimlessly up and down the corridor of the dressing-rooms, and keeps up a gentle coughing until I half open my door to invite him to sit down for a moment in my room. He squeezes his flanks, like a lean dog's, into a rickety chair with its white paint flaking off, and tucks his feet under him so as not to interfere with my movements. Brague comes to join us and crouches like a gipsy, with his behind against the hot pipes. Standing between them, I finish dressing, and my red skirt, embroidered with yellow, fans them as I pass. Though we have no wish to talk, we chatter to overcome a brooding longing to be silent, to huddle against each other and grow sentimental.

Brague manages better than the rest of us to remain clear-sighted, interested and active; he is still commercially eager for the future. For me the future, whether it is here or there, is . . . My lately acquired and rather artificial liking for uprootings and travel fits in happily with the peaceful fatalism natural to the bourgeoise that I am. A gipsy henceforth I certainly am, and one whom tours have led from town to town, but an orderly gipsy, careful to mend her well-brushed garments herself; a gipsy who nearly always carries her slender fortune on her person; but in the little suède bag, the coppers are in one compartment, the silver in another, while the gold is preciously hidden in a secret pocket.

A vagabond, maybe, but one who is resigned to revolving on the same spot like my companions and brethren. It is true that departures sadden and exhilarate me, and whatever I pass through—new countries, skies pure or cloudy, seas under rain the colour of a grey pearl—something of myself catches on it and clings so passionately that I feel as though I were leaving behind me a thousand little phantoms in my image, rocked on the waves, cradled in the leaves, scattered among the clouds. But does not a last little phantom, more like me than any of the others, remain sitting in my chimney corner, lost in a dream and as good as gold as it bends over a book which it forgets to open?

PART TWO

ONE

"What a charming, cosy nest! I must say it's hard to imagine your existence in the music-hall when one sees you here between this rosy lamp and that vase of carnations."

Such was the parting remark of my admirer the first time he came to dinner at my flat, with Hamond the go-between. For I have an admirer. Only this old-fashioned name seems to suit him: he is neither my lover, nor my flame, nor my gigolo; he is my admirer.

"What a charming, cosy nest!" That evening I laughed bitterly behind his back. To think that a shaded lamp, a crystal vase filled with sparkling water, an easy chair drawn up close to the table, and a divan whose shabbiness is masked by a cunning disorder of cushions —to think that all that can so dazzle the casual visitor as to make him imagine, between these faded green walls, the secluded, contemplative and studious life of a gifted woman. Ah, but he hasn't noticed the dusty inkpot, the dry pen and the uncut book on the empty box of stationery!

An old spray of holly, contorted as though it had been through fire, curls over the edge of an earthenware pot. The cracked glass of a little pastel (one of Adolphe Taillandy's sketches) waits in vain to be replaced. Round the electric bulb which lights the fireplace I have carelessly pinned, and then forgotten, a torn sheet of paper. A pile of five hundred postcards—scenes from *The Pursuit*—, banded with grey paper, lies on a fifteenth-century carved ivory and threatens to crush it.

The whole place gives an impression of indifference, neglect, hopelessness, almost of imminent departure. Cosy? Could one so describe anything that happens in the evening here, under the lamp with its faded shade?

After my two guests had left I laughed, and sighed with weariness, and the night that followed was so troubled by an obscure sense of shame, born of the very admiration of the Big-Noodle, that it seemed endless. His belief in me, the innocent belief of a man very much in love, enlightened me about myself that evening just as an unexpected mirror, at a street corner or on a staircase, suddenly reveals blemishes and saggings in one's face and figure.

But since then there have been other evenings when Hamond came with my admirer, or my admirer without Hamond. My old friend conscientiously performs what he calls his sordid task. Sometimes he presides with the brilliant ease of a former wit over the visits of his pupil who, without him, I admit in all sincerity, would be too much for me. Sometimes he effaces himself, though not for long, or keeps us waiting, just long enough, exercising on my behalf that social diplomacy of his which was getting rusty.

I do not dress up for them, and change neither my pleated white blouse nor my plain dark skirt. I "let my face go" when they are there, mouth tired and shut and eyes deliberately dull, and to my admirer's persistence I oppose the passive bearing of a girl whom her parents want to marry against her will. The only thing I take trouble over, for my own sake more than theirs, is the sketchy, deceptive interior where I live so little; Blandine has condescended to explore the dusty corners of the study, and the cushions of the armchair in front of the table are still flattened from the last time I rested there.

I have an admirer. Why should it be this one and not another? I have no idea. I look in astonishment at this man who has managed to worm his way into my flat. My word, how desperately he wanted to! Luck was on his side every time, and Hamond helped him. One day, when I was all alone, I opened the door to a timid ring; and how could I possibly have thrust out this creature standing there awkwardly waiting, his arms full of roses, with Hamond beside him gazing imploringly at me? He has managed to worm his way in here, and no doubt it was bound to happen.

Every time he comes now, I have to get to know his face as though I had never seen it before. On each side of his nose there is a crease, already quite deep, which disappears under his moustache, and he has the rather swarthy red lips which you find in people who are almost too dark. His hair and his eyebrows and lashes are as black as the devil, and it needed a very bright ray of sunshine one day to show me that, beneath all that black, my admirer's eyes are a tawny brown, and very deep set.

Standing up, he really is a Big-Noodle, stiff, awkward and nothing but bones. Sitting, or half-reclining on the divan, he seems to grow supple all of a sudden, and to enjoy the pleasure of being quite a different man, lazy and relaxed, moving his hands gracefully as he settles his head indolently back against the cushions.

When I know that he cannot see me, I observe him, feeling vaguely shocked at the thought that I do not know him at all and that the presence of this young man in my flat is as unexpected as a piano in a kitchen.

How is it that he, who is in love with me, is not in the least disturbed that he knows me so little? He clearly never gives that a thought, and his one idea is first to reassure me and afterwards to conquer me. For if he has very quickly learnt—on Hamond's advice, I'll bet—to hide his desire and subdue his look and his voice when he speaks to me, if he pretends, cunning as an animal, to have forgotten that he wants to possess me, neither does he show any eagerness to find out what I am like, to question me or read my character, and I notice that he pays more attention to the play of light on my hair than to what I am saying.

How strange all that is! There he sits close to me, the same ray of sun gliding over his cheek and mine, and if it makes his nostrils glow ruby-red, it must be tinting mine bright coral. He is not there, he is a thousand leagues away! I keep wanting to get up and say to him: "Why are you here? Go away!" And I do nothing of the kind.

Does he think? Does he read? Does he work? I believe he belongs to that large rather commonplace class of persons who are interested in everything and do absolutely nothing. Not a trace of wit, a certain quickness of comprehension, a very adequate vocabulary enhanced by a beautiful rich voice, that readiness to laugh with a childish gaiety that one sees in many men—such is my admirer.

To be entirely honest, let me mention what I like best in him: a look that is sometimes absent and seeking, and that kind of private smile in the eyes which one sees in sensitive people who are both violent and shy.

He has travelled, but just like everyone else: not very far and not often. He has read what everyone reads, he knows "quite a few people" and cannot name three intimate friends, in addition to his elder brother. I forgive him all this ordinariness for the sake of a simplicity which has nothing humble about it, and because he finds nothing to say about himself.

His glance rarely meets mine, which I turn aside. I cannot forget the reason for his presence and for his patience. And yet what a difference between the man sitting there on this divan and the cruel animal, full of fierce desire, who forced the door of my dressing-room! Nothing about me shows that I remember our first meeting, except the fact that I hardly talk to the Big-Noodle. Whatever subject he tries, I answer him briefly, or else I address to Hamond the reply destined for my admirer. This type of indirect conversation gives our meetings a slowness and a false gaiety that are quite indescribable.

TWO

I AM still rehearsing the new act with Brague. Sometimes in the mornings the *Folies-Bergère* takes us in, or else the *Empyrée-Clichy* lends us its stage for an hour; or else we wander from the *Brasserie Gambrinus*, which is used to the noise of Baret's tours, to the Cernuschi dancing-hall.

"It's beginning to look like something," says Brague, as eager for compliments for others as for himself.

The Old Troglodyte rehearses with us: he is a famished-looking youth of eighteen, whom Brague assists, dumbfounds and shatters with insults till I am moved to pity: "You're really going too far, Brague, he's going to cry!"

"Just let him cry and I'll boot him in the backside! He's got to work, not weep!"

Perhaps he is right. The Old Troglodyte gulps back his tears, humps his back in what he hopes is a "prehistoric" way, and sets himself to guarding a Hamadryad attitudinising in a white knitted sweater.

One morning last week Brague took the trouble to come in person to warn me that there would be no rehearsal the following day. He found Hamond, Dufferein-Chautel and myself finishing lunch. I had to keep Brague a few minutes, offer him coffee and introduce him to my guests. And I saw his bright little black eyes linger furtively on my admirer with a curious satisfaction, a sort of security, which made me feel stupidly uncomfortable.

When I accompanied him to the door again my comrade did not question me or permit himself any familiar allusions, and my embarrassment was redoubled. It would have been too absurd to explain:

"That's a friend of Hamond's who came to lunch. He's just a pal, you know."

Fossette is now wearing a collar of red morocco with gilded studs, in deplorable sporting taste. I have not dared to say that I found it ugly. Wretched little servile female that she is, she fawns on the well-dressed gentleman who smells of man and tobacco, and knows just the right way to pat her back.

Blandine outdoes herself, cleaning the windows and, without being asked, bringing in the tea-tray when my admirer is there.

All of them, following the example of my old friend Hamond, look as if they are plotting against me in favour of Maxime Dufferein-Chautel. Alas, it costs me so little effort to remain invulnerable! Invulnerable, and worse than insensitive: shrinking. For when I give my hand to my admirer, the touch of his long hand, warm and dry, surprises and displeases me. I cannot brush against the stuff of his jacket without a little nervous shudder, and when he speaks I involuntarily avoid his breath, healthy though it is. I could never bring myself to tie his tie, and I would rather drink from Hamond's glass than from his. Why?

It is because . . . this fellow is *a man*. In spite of myself I cannot forget that he is *a man*. Hamond is not a man, he is a friend. And Brague is a comrade; so is Bouty. The slender, muscular acrobats who reveal, beneath their shimmering tights, the most flattering details of their anatomy, well, they are just acrobats!

Has it ever occurred to me that Brague, who in *The Pursuit* clasps me hard enough to bruise my ribs, and looks as if he were crushing my mouth under a passionate kiss, had a sex? No. And yet the most fleeting glance from my admirer, the most correct handshake, remind me why he is there and what he hopes. What a delightful pastime he would be for a coquette! What an agreeable flame, provocative and determined!

The trouble is that I do not know how to flirt. I have neither the disposition, nor the experience, nor the light touch necessary, and above all—oh above all—I have the memory of my husband.

If for a single instant I call to mind Adolphe Taillandy when he was on the job, by which I mean working, with that ruthless unswerving pursuit characteristic of him, to seduce a woman or a young girl, I immediately grow frigid, shrinking, and utterly hostile to "the business of love". I see again, too well, his look of conquest, with lowered lids, sly, childish mouth, and that trick of dilating his nostrils when a particular perfume drifted by. Ugh! All that manœuvring, those elaborate preparations for love, for a goal that one cannot even call love, am I to encourage and even to imitate that sort of thing? Poor Dufferein-Chautel! Sometimes it seems to me that it is you who are being deceived here, and that I ought to tell you . . . to tell you what? That I have become an old maid again with no temptations, and that the four walls of my dressing-room at the music-hall are for me a cloister?

No, I shall not tell you that because, like those who have got to the tenth lesson at the Berlitz School, we only know how to exchange elementary phrases where the words *bread, salt, window, temperature, theatre* and *family* play a great part.

You are a *man*, so much the worse for you! Everyone in my house seems to remember it, not in the way I do, but in order to congratulate you because of it, from Blandine who gazes at you with a never-wearying satisfaction, to Fossette whose wide doggy smile says just as clearly: "At last *a man* in the house—behold THE MAN!"

I don't know how to talk to you, poor Dufferein-Chautel. I hesitate between my own *personal* language, which is rather brusque, does not always condescend to finish its sentences, but sets great store on getting its technical terms exact—the language of a one-time blue-stocking—and the slovenly, lively idiom, coarse and picturesque, which one learns in the music-hall, sprinkled with expressions like: "You bet!" "Shut up!" "I'm clearing out!" "Not my line!"

Unable to decide, I choose silence.

THREE

"DEAR Hamond, how happy I am to be lunching with you! No rehearsal today, but sunshine, and you, it's all perfect!"

My old friend, who is suffering from stabs of rheumatism, smiles at me, flattered. He is at present very thin and looks older and somehow light. Being very tall, too, all that, and his bony, aquiline nose gives him a great resemblance to the Knight of the Dolorous Countenance.

"Yet I rather think we have already had the pleasure of lunching together this week? What overflowing affection for my old carcass, Renée!"

"That's just it, I *am* overflowing! It's a fine day, I feel gay, and . . . we're all alone!"

"Which means?"

"That the Big-Noodle isn't here, you've guessed it!"

Hamond shakes his long, melancholy head: "It's an aversion, there's no doubt of it!"

"Not at all, Hamond, not at all! It's . . . it's nothing. All right then, I'll tell you, I've been thinking of being frank with you for some days past: the trouble is I can't discover that I have the slightest feeling for Dufferein-Chautel, unless perhaps it is distrust."

"That's something."

"I haven't even any opinion about him."

"Well then it'll be a pleasure for me to offer you mine. The honest creature has no history."

"Not enough!"

"Not enough? You're really too difficult! You don't encourage him to tell you what he has."

"That would be the last straw! Can't you see him, with his large hand on his large heart: 'I am not a man like other men. . . .'

That's what he'd say, isn't it? Men always say the same thing as women do, at such times."

Hamond's eyes dwell on me with an ironic look.

"I always like you, Renée, when you assume an experience which —happily—you lack. 'Men do this . . . men say that. . . .' Where did you glean such assurance? Men! Men! Have you known so many?"

"Only one. But what a one!"

"That's just it. But you aren't accusing Maxime of reminding you of Taillandy, are you?"

"Heavens, no! He reminds me of nothing at all. Nothing, I tell you! He isn't witty . . ."

"People in love are always a bit idiotic. Take me, for instance, when I was in love with Jeanne . . ."

"Not to mention me, when I was in love with Adolphe! But that was a conscious idiocy, almost voluptuous. Do you remember the evenings when we dined out, Adolphe and I, and I would put on my poor look, my 'look of a dowerless daughter', as Margot used to say? My husband held forth, smiled, laid down the law and shone. No one had eyes for anyone but him. If anyone cast a glance at me I am sure it was to pity him. I was made to understand so well that, without him, I didn't exist."

"Oh, come now, that's a bit exaggerated."

"Not very much, Hamond! Don't protest! I wholeheartedly tried to efface myself as much as possible. I was so fatuously in love with him!"

"I was just the same, just the same!" says Hamond, warming up. "D'you remember when my small chit of a Jeanne used to give her opinion on my pictures? 'Henri was born conscientious and old-fashioned', she would declare. And I never said a word."

We laugh and feel happy, rejuvenated by this stirring up of humiliating and bitter memories. Why must my old friend spoil this Saturday, so much in harmony with all our traditions, by bringing in the name of Dufferein-Chautel?

I make a cross face. "There you go again! Do give me a bit of a rest from that gentleman, Hamond! What do I know about him? That he's clean, well brought up, is fond of bulldogs and smokes cigarettes. That he happens, into the bargain, to be in love with me is not—to be modest—a very special characteristic."

"But you do everything in your power never to get to know him!"

"Well, I have every right."

That irritates Hamond, who clucks his tongue disapprovingly: "Your right, your right! My dear friend, you argue like a child, I do assure you!"

I take away my hand, which he had covered with his own, and speak fast, in spite of myself: "You do assure me of what? That he's a gilt-edged security? What is it you really want? That I should go to bed with this gentleman?"

"Renée!"

"Well, one might as well say it! You want me to act like everyone else? To make up my mind? Him or someone else, what's it matter! You want to upset my newly-recovered peace, to make me exchange the keen, invigorating, natural care of earning my own living for a care of a different kind? Or perhaps you're advising me to take a lover for health reasons, as a blood-purifier? But what for? I'm in good health and, thank God, I love no one, no one, and never again will I love anyone, anyone, anyone!"

I shouted that so loud that all of a sudden I fall silent, quite abashed. Hamond, who is not so carried away as I, gives me time to get a grip on myself while my blood, which had risen to my cheeks, runs slowly back to my heart.

"You'll never again love anyone? Alas, that may be true! And that would be saddest of all. To think of you, young and strong, and affectionate. . . . Yes, that would be saddest of all."

Indignant, and on the verge of tears, I gaze at the friend who dares to speak thus to me: "Oh Hamond, can it be you who say that to me! After what has happened to you . . . to us, could you still hope for love?"

Hamond turns away his gaze, stares at the window with those eyes that are so young in his old face, and replies vaguely: "Yes. It's true I'm very happy as I am. But just because of that, to answer for myself and definitely say: 'I shall never love again,' good lord no, I wouldn't dare!"

That strange answer from Hamond put an end to our discussion, for I don't like talking of love. The broadest of broad jokes doesn't scare me, but I don't like talking of love. If I had lost a beloved child, it seems to me that I should never again be able to pronounce its name.

FOUR

"COME and have a bite at Olympe's this evening," said Brague to me at the rehearsal. "And afterwards we'll go and say hullo to the boys in the *Revue* at the *Emp'-Clich'*."

There's no danger of my misunderstanding: this is not an *invitation* to dinner; we are two *comrades*, and the protocol—for there is one—governing comradeship between artistes banishes all ambiguity.

So I rejoin Brague this evening at Olympe's bar, whose doubtful reputation does not in the least disturb me. Now that I need give no thought to my own reputation, I feel neither apprehension nor pleasure when I enter this little Montmartre restaurant, which is silent from seven to ten and resounds all the rest of the night with what seems rather a deliberate din made up of shouts, the clatter of crockery and the twanging of guitars. I sometimes used to go and dine there in haste, alone or with Brague, last month, before we went on to the *Empyrée-Clichy*.

This evening a waitress from the country, tranquil and slow in the midst of the calls for her, serves us with pickled pork and cabbage, a filling, nourishing dish, rather heavy for the stomachs of the poor little local prostitutes who sit eating near us, by themselves, with that aggressive look which animals and under-nourished women adopt when a heaped plate is put before them. No, indeed, the place is not always gay!

Brague, mocking but compassionate at heart, speaks slightingly of two thin young women who have just entered, with idiotic hats balanced precariously on their curly heads. One of them is striking, and carries her head with a kind of angry insolence; every line of her exaggerated slenderness shows, in all its grace, beneath a tight sheath of pink Liberty silk, bought from the second-hand clothes woman. On this freezing February evening all she has to cover her is a cloak, a sort of light cape, also of Liberty silk, blue and embroidered with tarnished silver. She is frozen, almost beside herself with cold, and her furious grey eyes repulse all compassion; she is ready to insult, or even to claw, the first person who says to her, sympathetically, "Poor child!"

Young women of this kind, slowly dying of misery and pride, beautiful in their stark poverty, are by no means uncommon in this district of Montmartre. I meet them here and there, trailing their flimsy garments from table to table at supper-time on the Butte, gay, drunk, and fierce, always ready to bite, never gentle, never affectionate, resenting their profession and "working" all the same. The men call them "wretched little sluts", with a contemptuous but admiring laugh, because they belong to a breed which never gives in, never admits to cold or hunger or love; little sluts who die saying: "I'm not ill," who may bleed under blows, but hit back all the same.

Yes, I know something of those girls, and it is of them that I am reminded as I watch the proud, frozen young girl who has just come into Olympe's.

A hungry half-silence reigns in the bar. Two painted young men exchange barbed repartee from opposite ends of the room, without any conviction. A street-girl with short legs, who is dining on a crème-de-menthe with water while awaiting a problematical supper, throws out a few half-hearted retorts. A bulldog bitch, in pup to bursting point, pants painfully on the threadbare carpet, her balloon of a stomach studded with knob-like teats.

Brague and I chat, relaxed by the warmth of the gas. I think of all the mediocre restaurants in all the towns which have seen us thus seated at table, tired, indifferent and curious, before strange meats. The hog-wash of station buffets and hotel restaurants is never too much for Brague's iron stomach; but as for me, if the plain veal or the leg of mutton *bonne femme* are so leathery that they defeat me, I make up on the cheese and the omelette.

"I say, Brague, that man over there with his back to us, isn't it Stephen-the-Dancer?"

"Where? Yes, that's him all right . . . with a tart."

Such a "tart", in fact, that I remain flabbergasted at the sight of that fifty-year-old brunette with her dark moustache. And as if he felt our eyes on him, Stephen-the-Dancer half turns to throw us one of those knowing looks which are used in the theatre to convey: "Not a word! It's a mystery!" discreetly enough to be noticed by the whole house.

"Poor wretch, he certainly earns any money *he* gets," whispers Brague. "Coffee, Mademoiselle," he calls, "we've got to skedaddle."

The coffee is an olive-black ink which leaves a clinging stain on the sides of the cups. But as a result of never drinking good coffee any more, I have come to like these hot, bitter brews which smell of liquorice and quinine. In our profession we can do without meat but not without coffee.

Quickly as they serve us ours, Stephen-the-Dancer "skedaddles" before us—he is *rinking* in the *Revue* at the *Emp'-Clich'*—in the wake of his companion. Behind her back he shamelessly imitates for us the gesture of the athlete who "heaves" the four hundred pound weight, and we are cowardly enough to laugh. Then we leave this sad, so-called "pleasure" haunt, where by this time everyone is getting drowsy under the pink lights: the pregnant bitch, the exhausted street-girls, the waitress from the country and the manager with his waxed moustache.

Once outside, the outer boulevard and the Place Blanche, round which an icy wind circles, revive us, and I feel myself joyfully seized once more with an active passion, a real need to *work*, a mysterious and undefined need which I could satisfy equally well by dancing, writing, running, acting, or pulling a hand-cart.

As if the same desire had seized him, Brague suddenly says to me: "By the way, I've had a word from the agent, Salomon. The tour I spoke about's taking shape. He's fixing up one day here and two there, a week in Marseilles and another in Bordeaux. You can still go?"

"Me? Right away! Why not?"

He darts a sharp sideways glance at me.

"Oh, I don't know. Sometimes a mere trifle . . . I know what life is . . ."

So that's it! My comrade remembers Dufferein-Chautel and thinks that . . . My sudden laugh, instead of undeceiving him, bewilders him still further, but this evening I feel in a gay and teasing mood, and as light-hearted as if we had set off already. Oh, how lovely to go away, to move from one place to another, to forget who I am and the name of the town which sheltered me the day before, scarcely to think, to receive and retain no impressions but that of the beautiful landscape which unfolds and changes as the train runs past, of the lead-coloured pool in which the blue sky is reflected green, and the open-work spire of a belfry encircled with swallows.

I remember a day, a May morning, when I was leaving Rennes. The train very slowly followed a track under repair between coppices of white hawthorn, pink apple-trees which cast a blue shadow, and very young willows with leaves of jade. A child, standing at the edge of the wood, watched us pass, a little girl of twelve whose resemblance to myself struck me. A serious child with frowning brows, and tanned round cheeks—as mine were—, and hair a little bleached by the sun, she was holding a leafy shoot in her sunburnt hands covered with scratches—as mine were. Her unsociable look, too, and those ageless, almost sexless, eyes which seemed to take everything seriously, were mine also, really mine. It was indeed my own shy childhood which stood there, dazzled by the sun, at the edge of that coppice and watched me pass.

"Whenever you like, then!"

My comrade's curt invitation brings me back to earth in front of the *Emp'-Clich'*, glittering with mauve lights, whose glare, as Brague says, hurts "the back of your eyes". We descend to the basement, where the familiar smell of plaster, ammonia, *Crème Simon* and rice-powder, rouses in me a disgust that is almost pleasant. We've come to see our pals in the *Revue*, we have, and not the *Revue* itself!

I find my old dressing-room, at present inhabited by Bouty, and Brague's, which is now filled with the dazzling presence of Jadin who is playing three parts in the *Emp'-Clich'-Revue*.

"Stir your stumps!" she calls to us. "You're just in time for my song, *Night-time in Paris*."

Alas, they have dressed Jadin as a street-walker! A black skirt, a low-cut black bodice, cobweb-fine stockings, a red ribbon round her neck and, on her head, the traditional helmet-shaped wig with a blood-red camellia in it. There is not a trace left of the endearing, guttersnipe charm of that young girl with the hunched shoulder.

It was, I suppose, inevitable that they should quickly turn my sulky young apache into the ordinary little *café-concert* singer. While we exchange the "How goes it?" "What's the news?" "Things shaping?" I watch her moving about her dressing-room, and realise with a shock that Jadin walks like a tart, as all of them do, with her stomach drawn in and her chest out, that she is careful to *pitch* her voice when she speaks, and that she has not once said "Bitch!" since we arrived.

Bouty, who is to dance the inevitable cancan with her, beams at us under his silk cap and says nothing. One feels he might at any moment say "Now what about it?", and point at the little creature with a proprietary gesture. Has he at last vanquished his comrade? At any rate I guess that it is he who is making Jadin commonplace and now there they both are, talking of doing a "sensational turn", very well paid, at the Crystal Palace in London!

How quickly everything changes, especially women! In a few months this one will lose nearly all her piquancy, her natural and unconscious pathos. Will that hare-brained, eighteen-year-old Jadin, so prodigal of herself and her scanty cash, suddenly reveal an upsurge of craftiness, the craftiness of concierges and grasping small tradesmen? Why in her presence am I reminded of the Bells, German acrobats with an English name, whom Brague and I knew in Brussels? Of unequalled strength and grace in their cerise tights which made their fair skin look paler still, the five of them lived in two rooms without furniture, where they cooked for themselves on a little iron stove. And all day long, the impresario told us, it was nothing but mysterious discussions, consultings of financial newspapers, and fierce disputes concerning gold-mines, railway shares and the Egyptian Land Loan. Money, money, money.

Jadin's empty chatter enlivens our visit, which needs enlivening. After Bouty, who is slightly less thin, has given us news of his health and announced that "things are shaping" for the following winter, we fall silent and embarrassed, chance friends whom chance has separated. I fiddle with the grease-paint and pencils on the little shelf, with that greedy exasperation, that itch for make-up, familiar to anyone who has ever trodden the boards. Fortunately, the little bell tinkles and Jadin jumps to her feet: "Look sharp, up we go! The fireman'll give you his stage-box and you'll see what a hit I make in my *Night-time in Paris* song."

The sleepy fireman does in fact lend me his straw-bottomed stool and his little box. Sitting there, with my nose to the grating which frames a square of warm, reddish light, I can see, without myself being seen, half of two rows of the stalls and three uncurtained boxes, as well as a stage-box. In this stage-box I can make out a lady in an enormous hat, with pearls, rings and sequins, and two men who are Dufferein-Chautel senior and Dufferein-Chautel junior, both of them looking very black and white, and very sleek and smart. They are relentlessly illuminated and, framed by my grating, they take on an extraordinary importance.

The woman is not a woman, she is a *lady*: Madame Dufferein-Chautel senior, no doubt. My admirer, for his part, seems to be greatly amused by the march past of the girl rag-pickers, and of the girl cabbies who follow them and, after singing a couplet, dance casually off.

Finally comes Jadin, who announces herself: "And I—I am the Queen of Night-time Paris: I am the Street Walker!"

I see my admirer bend rather eagerly over the programme and then raise his head and study my little comrade closely, from her helmet of hair to her open-work stockings.

By a curious transposition, he it is who becomes the spectacle for me, for I can only see little Jadin in profile; the blinding footlights make her face look like a skull, with black nostrils and a lip foreshortened above a gleaming row of teeth, as if her face had been eaten by the light. With her neck stretched out gargoyle-fashion, a red rag knotted round it, this young girl suddenly resembles some lewd spectre by Félicien Rops.

When, at the end of her number, she twice returns to take her call, her heels together and her fingers to her lips, my admirer claps her with his big brown hands so loudly that, before she disappears, she throws him a little kiss all for himself, with a forward thrust of her chin.

"What's the matter, are you asleep? This is the second time I've told you that you can't stay there; they're setting the scene for Heliopolis!"

"All right, all right, I'm coming."

I think in fact that I must have fallen asleep, or else I am just emerging from one of those moments when one's mind goes blank before some painful idea is set in motion, moments which are the prelude to a slight loss of morale.

FIVE

"COME on now, either make up your mind or don't. Does it seem to you all right, or doesn't it?"

There they both are, Brague and Salomon, harrying me with their looks and their voices. Salomon laughs to reassure me, while Brague keeps muttering. Then Salomon lays his heavy hand on my shoulder and says: "As contracts go, it's pretty good, I think!"

I have the typed contract in my hand, and I re-read it for the tenth time for fear there may be some hidden snare, some suspicious clause, lurking among its fifteen short lines. Above all I re-read it to gain time. And then I look at the window, the curtains of starched net, and behind them the sad, clean courtyard.

I look as if I am reflecting, but I am not reflecting. Hesitating is not reflecting. Absentmindedly, I examine the contents of the English-type desk I have seen so many times before, covered with foreign photographs: half-length portraits of ladies in low-necked frocks, with Viennese smiles; men in evening dress who might equally well be singers or acrobats, clowns or ring-masters—impossible to say which.

A six weeks' tour at a hundred and fifty francs a day, that makes six thousand francs. Pretty good. But . . .

"But," I finally say to Salomon, "I don't want to put six hundred francs in your fat purse. Ten per cent, all said and done, is sheer murder."

I have found my voice again and the art of using it, and the right vocabulary for the occasion. Salomon turns the colour of his hair, brick-red; even his shifty eyes go bloodshot, but from his full, pleasant mouth pours a flood of almost amorous supplications.

"My darling, my pet, don't start saying silly things. I've been working at your itinerary for a month now, a whole month. Ask Brague! For a month I've been wearing myself out to find first-class houses for you, absolutely first-class. And posters like . . . like Madame

Otéro, think of it! And that's the way you thank me! Haven't you got a heart? Ten per cent? Why it's twelve, not ten, you ought to give me, d'you hear?"

"Yes, I hear. But I don't want to put six hundred francs in your fat purse. You aren't worth such a sum."

Salomon's little red eyes grow smaller still. The heavy hand caressing my shoulder would like to crush me.

"Oh, you ungrateful wretch! Look at her, Brague! A child who owed her first engagement to me!"

"A child who's now jolly well of age, my friend, and in need of some new clothes. D'you realise my costume for *The Pursuit* is worn out? Thirty pounds for a character costume, plus the slippers, plus the veil for my dance—all the accessories, in short. You're not going to pay me for all those separately, are you, old skinflint?"

"Look at her, Brague!" repeats Salomon. "I feel ashamed for her in front of you. Whatever will you think of her?"

"I think," says Brague tranquilly, "that she would be right to accept the tour and wrong to give you six hundred francs."

"All right then. Give me back the papers."

The fat hand lets go of me. Frowning and pale, Salomon goes back to his English-style desk without a glance at us.

"Come now, Salomon, let's stop pretending. I'm an absolute bitch when I want to be, and if anyone irritates me I don't care a fig if the whole thing goes down the drain!"

"Madame," answers Salomon, very dignified and stiff, "you've spoken to me as though you despised me, and I've taken it to heart."

"Silly ass!" interrupts Brague, without raising his voice. "Stop playing the fool! Six hundred for her share, four hundred and forty for mine . . . d'you take us for German acrobats? Give me the forms; we aren't going to sign today. I want twenty-four hours to consult my family."

"In that case, it's up the spout," splutters Salomon excitably. "All those people are directors of very smart houses, people who don't like being trifled with, people . . ."

"Yes, yes, I know, who go up in smoke if you cross them," interrupts my comrade. "All right, then, tell them I'll be back tomorrow. Coming, Renée? Salomon, it's seven and a half per cent for the two of us. And I call that big and generous."

Salomon wipes his dry eyes and his damp forehead.

"There you go again, I still think you're a pretty pair of sharpers."

"Well, Salomon, I can't say you're so very handsome yourself."

"Leave him alone, Renée, he's a dear creature really. He'll do as we want. In the first place, he loves you. Don't you, Salomon?"

But Salomon is sulking. He turns his back like a big child and says in a tearful voice: "No. Take yourselves off. I don't want to see you any more. I'm really hurt. It's the very first time, since I started to book engagements, that anyone has inflicted such a humiliation on me. Off with you! I want to be alone. I don't want to see you any more."

"Right you are. Till tomorrow!"

"No, no! It's all over between us three."

"Five o'clock?"

Seated at his desk, Salomon lifts his tearful pink face towards us. "Five o'clock? Well I'm blowed, I suppose I must now miss my rendezvous at the Alhambra for you? Not before six, d'you hear?"

Disarmed, I squeeze his stubby fist, and we leave.

The street is so crowded that conversation is impossible, so we are silent. I dread the comparative solitude of the Boulevard Malesherbes, where Brague will begin to argue and convince me. I am convinced in advance and have made up my mind to go. Hamond will not be pleased. Margot will say to me: "You're quite right, my girl!" though she will be quite sure I am not, but she will give me excellent advice, and three or four boxes of "specialities" against headaches, fever and constipation.

And to come down to Dufferein-Chautel, what will he say? It amuses me to think of his face. He will console himself with Jadin, that's all. And I shall depart . . . already I begin to ask how soon.

"What was the date, Brague? I paid no attention to that, just fancy!"

Brague shrugs his shoulders and stands close to me among the cluster of pedestrians waiting submissively until the white baton cleaves the line of carriages, and opens a passage for us from the pavement of the Boulevard Haussmann to the island on the Place Saint-Augustin.

"If we had to depend on you to button up the engagements, my poor friend! Madame rants, and mounts her high horse, Madame wants this, won't have that, and then, at the end of it all, 'Fancy, I paid no attention to the date!'"

Deferentially, I let him enjoy his superiority. It is one of Brague's keenest pleasures to treat me as a novice, a blundering pupil. Protected by the policeman's baton, we hurry as far as the Boulevard Malesherbes.

"From April 5th to May 15th," finishes Brague. "You've nothing against that? Nothing to keep you?"

"Nothing."

We walk up the boulevard, panting a little because of the steam which rises from the damp pavement as from a warm bath. The thaw has set in with a slight, almost stormy, shower; the lights are reflected, elongated and iridescent, in the blackish pavement. The top of the avenue is lost to view in a blurred mist, faintly rosy in the lingering dusk. Involuntarily I look back and all about me, searching for . . . what? Nothing. No, nothing keeps me here, or elsewhere. No dear face will rise from the mist, like a flower emerging from dark water, to beg tenderly: "Don't go away!"

So I shall leave, once again. The fifth of April is a long way off—it is now February 15th—but it is as if I had already left, and I pay no heed as Brague lists in my ear the names of towns and hotels and figures, figures, figures. . . .

"Are you at least listening to me?"

"Yes."

"So you're not doing anything between now and April 5th?"

"Not that I know of!"

"You wouldn't consider a little act, just any kind of little silly thing, something rather elegant, to occupy you between now and then?"

"My goodness, no."

"If you like, I'll look for a little weekly engagement for you?"

I thank my comrade, on parting from him, because I feel touched that he should want to save me from hard times and the idleness which demoralises out-of-work actors, diminishing their powers and making them go to pieces.

Three heads are raised when I enter my study: Hamond's, Fossette's, and Dufferein-Chautel's. All three huddled round a little table under the pink lampshade, they were playing *écarté* while they waited for me. Fossette knows how to play cards in the bulldog manner: perched on a chair, she follows the come and go of hands, ready to seize as it flies past any card thrown too far.

Hamond cries "At last!", Fossette "Wuff!", and Dufferein-Chautel says nothing, but he very nearly barked too.

To leave the fetid fog outside, for this joyful welcome under the softly-shaded light, so raises my spirits that in a burst of affectionate joy I cry: "Greetings! What d'you think, I'm going away!"

"You're going away? How d'you mean? When?"

In spite of himself a slightly curt and inquisitorial note has crept into my admirer's voice; but I pay no attention to that as I roll up my gloves and take off my hat.

"I'll tell you all about it over dinner. You'll both stay: it's almost a farewell dinner already. Stay where you are and go on with your little game; I'll send Blandine to get some cutlets and go and slip into a dressing-gown; I'm worn out!"

When I return, enveloped in the folds of a rose-coloured flannel kimono, I notice that both Hamond and Dufferein-Chautel have the too-casual look of people who have been plotting something. What does it matter? My adorer this evening is reaping the benefit of an optimism which embraces every living thing: I invite him to offer us some of the Saint-Marceaux from the grocer next door, to "drink to the tour", and he runs off at once without his hat, returning with two bottles under his arm.

Feeling feverish and a little tipsy, I bend on my admirer a trustful look which he has never seen on my face before. I laugh aloud with a laugh he has never heard, I roll the wide sleeves of my kimono back to my shoulder, revealing arms which he says are "the colour of a peeled banana". I feel kind and gentle, and for two pins I would offer him my cheek: what does it matter? I'm going away, I shall never see this young man again! It's only for forty days? Oh, but we shall certainly all be dead by the time they're over!

Poor admirer, how badly I've treated him, all the same! Now he seems to me pleasant, clean, well-groomed, and considerate . . . like someone one will never see again! For when I come back I shall have forgotten him, and he too will have forgotten me . . . with little Jadin, or with someone else. But more likely with little Jadin.

"I say, what about that little Jadin!"

I have uttered this remark, which seems to me extremely funny, at the top of my voice. My admirer, who finds it difficult to laugh this evening, wrinkles his coal-miner's eyebrows as he looks at me: "What d'you mean, that little Jadin?"

"She rather took your fancy the other day, didn't she? At the *Emp'-Clich'*?"

Dufferein-Chautel bends towards me, intrigued. As his face

emerges from the zone of shadow cast by the lampshade, I can see the exact shade of his brown eyes, tawny and gold-flecked like certain agates from the Dauphiné.

"Were you in the audience? I didn't see you."

I empty my glass before replying, mysteriously: "Ah, you see!"

"Well, well, so you were there! Yes, she's charming, is little. Jadin. You know her? I find her very charming."

"More than me?"

This imprudent, idiotic remark, so unworthy of me, might well have deserved a different reply from the astonished silence with which he greeted it. I could have kicked myself. Oh well, what does it matter? I'm going away! I describe my itinerary: a complete tour of France, but only the big towns! Posters like . . . like Madame Otéro! And the lovely places I shall see, and the sun I shall find in the South, and . . . and . . .

The champagne—three glasses, but that is quite enough—finally lulls my happy chatter. What an expenditure of energy talking is for someone who remains silent for days together! My two friends are smoking now, and slowly, slowly, they recede behind their veil of smoke. How far away I feel, as if I had already left, cut adrift, and taken refuge in my journey! Their voices grow muffled and fade into the distance, mingling with the rumbling of trains, with whistlings and the lulling swell of an imaginary orchestra. Ah, what a delicious departure, what a sweet sleep, which wafts me towards an invisible shore!

"Hullo? is it six o'clock? Good, thank you. . . . Ah, it's you?"

I was asleep and dreaming of the journey: a hotel servant was knocking with his fist against the door of my dream, and calling out that it was six o'clock. And I come to, sitting up with a start in the hollow of my old divan where weariness and my slight tipsiness have made me doze off. Standing beside me, the Big-Noodle looms as high as the room. My eyes, opened too soon, blink at the lamp; the edges of the lampshade and the corners of the lighted table are like gleaming blades which wound my sight.

"It's you? Where's Hamond?"

"Hamond's just gone."

"What time is it then?"

"It's midnight."

"Midnight!"

I've slept for more than an hour! Mechanically I push up my flattened hair, combing it with my fingers, and then pull down my dressing-gown to the very tips of my bedroom slippers.

"Midnight? Why didn't you leave with Hamond?"

"We were afraid you might feel alarmed at finding yourself alone here. So I stayed."

Is he making fun of me? His face is so far above me in the shadow that I can't make it out.

"I was tired, you understand."

"I understand very well."

What is the meaning of this curt and scolding tone? I am quite staggered. Really, if I were easily frightened, this might seem just the moment to call for help, finding myself alone with this black-visaged creature addressing me from such a height! Perhaps he has been drinking, too.

"I say, Dufferein-Chautel, are you ill?"

"I'm not ill."

Thank goodness, he begins to move about; I had had enough of seeing him towering so close to me!

"I'm not ill, I'm angry."

"Oh, that's it!"

I consider for a moment, and then add, stupidly enough: "Is it because I'm going away?"

Dufferein-Chautel stops short.

"Because you're going away? I never gave it a thought. Since you're still here, there's no need for me to think that you're going away. No. I'm cross with you. I'm cross with you because you were sleeping."

"Really?"

"It's crazy to fall asleep like that! Before Hamond, and even before me! It's obvious you've no idea how you look when you're asleep. Unless you do it on purpose, and that's unworthy of you."

He sits down abruptly, as though he were breaking himself in three, and this brings him close to me, with his face on a level with mine.

"When you sleep you don't look as though you were asleep. You look . . . well, to be frank, you look as though you had closed your eyes to hide a joy that is too much for you. You really do. You haven't the face of a woman asleep, you . . . well, damn it, you know very well what I'm trying to say! It's revolting. When I think that you must have slept in that way before a heap of people, I don't know what I couldn't do to you!"

He is seated sideways on a flimsy chair, and he half turns away his distracted face, divided by two great wrinkles, one on his forehead and the other running down his cheek, as though the explosion of his wrath had just cracked him. I am not afraid; on the contrary, it is a relief to me to find him sincere, like the man who entered my dressing-room two months earlier.

Once again, then, there reappears before me, with his childish rage, his bestial persistence, his calculated sincerity, my enemy and my tormentor: love. There is no mistaking it. I have already seen that forehead, those eyes, and those hands convulsively gripping each other, yes, I have seen all that . . . in the days when Adolphe Taillandy desired me.

But what am I going to do with this one? I am not offended, I am not even moved—or only a very little! But what am I going to do? How shall I answer him? This continuing silence becomes more embarrassing than his avowal. If only he would go away . . . but he does not budge. I dare not risk the slightest movement, for fear a sigh, or a ripple of my gown, might be enough to rouse my adversary; I no longer dare say my admirer, no, he loves me too much.

"That's all you have to say to me?"

The sound of his voice, softened, causes me such keen pleasure that I smile with relief at being released from the suffocating silence.

"Well, I really don't see . . ."

He turned towards me with the clumsy gentleness of a big dog.

"That's quite true, you don't see. You have an absolute talent for not seeing. Whenever I'm concerned, you don't see, you see nothing. You look through me, you smile above my head, you speak to one side of me. And I act as though I didn't see that you don't see. How clever that is! And how worthy of you and of me!"

"Listen, Dufferein-Chautel . . ."

"And you call me Dufferein-Chautel! I know very well I've got a ridiculous name, the sort of name for a member of Parliament or an industrialist, or a director of a discount bank. It isn't my fault. All right, go on, laugh! It's a bit of luck, anyway," he adds in a lower tone, "that I can make you laugh."

"Well, then, what d'you want me to call you? Dufferein or Chautel? Or Duduffe? Or . . . just Maxime, or Max? I say, do pass me the hand-mirror, there, on the little table, and the powder puff: I must look a sight, what with the champagne, and sleeping, and no powder on my nose."

"That doesn't matter," he says impatiently. "Whoever d'you want to put powder on for, at this hour?"

"For myself, in the first place. And then for you."

"There's no need to bother on my account. You treat me like a man who is paying court to you. What if I were, quite simply, a man who loves you?"

I look at him, more distrustful than ever before, disconcerted to find in this man, as soon as it is a question of love between us, a remarkable intelligence and ease which his Big-Noodle-like appearance entirely belies. What I divine in him is, in fact, an aptitude for love, by virtue of which he both surpasses and embarrasses me.

"Tell me frankly, Renée, is it hateful, or a matter of indifference, or vaguely agreeable to you to know that I love you?"

He is neither insulting, nor humble, nor plaintive, nor is there anything timid or cunning about him. Copying his simplicity, I pluck up courage to reply: "I simply don't know."

"That's just what I thought," he said gravely. "Well then . . ."

"Well then?"

"There's nothing for me to do but to go away."

"It's half an hour after midnight."

"No, you haven't understood me. What I mean is: not to see you any more, to leave Paris."

"Leave Paris? Why?" I say, simply. "There's no need for that. And I haven't forbidden you to see me again."

He shrugs his shoulders.

"Oh, I know myself! When things aren't going well, when I have . . . well, worries, I go off home."

There was something provincial and tender in the way he said "home".

"Is it pretty, where you live?"

"Yes. It's forest land. Lots of firs and quite a few oaks. I love the new fellings, you know, when they've thinned out the woods, and all that remains is the saplings and the great circles left by the charcoal fires, where wood strawberries will grow the next summer."

"And lilies of the valley . . ."

"And lilies of the valley. And foxgloves too. You know? They're as tall as that, and when you're a kid you poke your fingers in the bells."

"I know."

He describes it badly, my wood-cutter from the Ardennes, but I see so well what he describes!

"I motor down there during the summer. I shoot a little too, in the autumn. It's mother's house, of course. Mother Ever-Cut!" says he, laughing. "She cuts and cuts and saws and sells."

"Oh!"

"But she doesn't damage anything, you know. She knows what wood is, she's as knowledgeable about it as a man, better than a man."

I listen to him with a new attraction, glad that he should forget me for a moment, and that he should talk, like a worthy wood-cutter, of his mother's forest. I had not remembered that he was from the Ardennes, and he had not bothered to inform me that he loved his countryside. Now I know why he has the look of a noodle! It is because he wears his clothes rather as if they were "party clothes", with an ineradicable and endearing awkwardness, like a handsome peasant in his Sunday best.

". . . Only, if you send me away, Renée, my mother will understand at once that I have come for her to 'look after' me, and she'll want once again to get me married. Look what you're exposing me to!"

"Let yourself get married."

"You don't say that seriously?"

"Why not? Because I've had an unfortunate experience myself? What does that prove? You ought to get married, it would suit you very well. You look married already. Though you're a bachelor, you have all the appearance of a young father of a family, you adore a fireside, you're affectionate and jealous and obstinate, as lazy as a spoilt husband, a despot at heart, and monogamous from birth!"

Stupefied, my admirer stares at me without saying a word, then leaps to his feet.

"I'm all that!" he cries. "I'm all that! She's said it! I'm all that!"

I coldly check his cries and gestures.

"Do be quiet! What's possessed you? Why should being . . . well, egoistical, and lazy, and a fireside-lover make you want to dance?"

He sits down again opposite me, very meekly, but his sheep-dog's eyes rest on me with a look of victorious sagacity.

"No. It doesn't matter a bit to me that I am all you say: what makes me want to dance is the fact that you know it!"

Ah, fool that I am! There he is, triumphant, encouraged by my confession, the confession of my curiosity, if not of a sharper interest. There he is, arrogant, trembling with the longing to reveal himself further. If he dared, he would cry: "Yes, I am all that! So you have deigned to see me, while I was losing hope that I should ever exist in your eyes? Look at me again! Reveal me completely, invent weaknesses and absurdities in me, overwhelm me with imaginary vices! My worry is not that you should know me as I am: create your admirer according to your liking, and afterwards, artfully and little by little, I will make myself resemble him, as a master touches up and re-does the mediocre work of a beloved pupil."

Shall I speak my thought aloud to him to embarrass him? Careful! I nearly did another clumsy thing. He will not be embarrassed, he will listen, ravished, to his soothsayer, and praise to the skies the second sight that love confers. And what is he waiting for now? For me to fall into his arms? Nothing astonishes a man in love. I could wish him far off. I'm struggling with the need to rest, to relax, to raise my hand and beg: "Pax! Stop! I don't know the game. If I find I want to, we'll begin again another time; but I haven't the strength to follow you, and I shall get caught every time, as you well see."

His watchful eyes dart rapidly from my eyelids to my mouth, from my mouth to my eyelids, and seem to read my face. Suddenly he rises and turns aside, with brusque discretion.

"Goodbye, Renée," he says in a lower voice. "I ask your pardon for staying so late, but Hamond suggested to me . . ."

With a sense of social embarrassment, I protest: "Oh, it doesn't matter at all . . . on the contrary . . ."

"Does your concierge sleep very soundly?"

"I hope not."

This is so pitifully silly that I recover some of my gaiety.

"Listen!" I say suddenly. "I would rather you didn't waken the concierge: you shall leave by the window."

"By the window? Oh, Renée!"

"It's the ground floor."

"I know. But aren't you afraid that . . . that I shall be seen? One of the other tenants might return just at that moment."

"Whatever d'you suppose that would matter to me?"

In spite of myself, there is so much contemptuous indifference in the way I answered him and shrugged my shoulders, that my admirer no longer dares to rejoice. In his heart, this exit at one in the morning by the window—from my bedroom, if you please—must make him feel as gleeful as a student. Ah, what youthfulness!

"Jump! That's right. Goodbye!"

"Till tomorrow, Renée?"

"If you like, my friend."

What youthfulness! Yet he is thirty-three, this man. I too. Thirty-four in six months.

I heard him running along the pavement, under a fine, clinging rain which makes the paving stones sticky and moistens the window-sill where I remain propped on my elbows, like a lover. But, behind me, no one has rumpled the big, commonplace bed, with its fresh, uncreased sheets on which my uncomplaining insomnia will leave no trace.

He has gone. He will return tomorrow, and the following days, since I have given him permission. He will return almost happy, awkward but full of hope, with that look as though he were saying: "I'm not asking for anything", which, in the end, has the same exasperating effect on me as the mechanical prayer of a beggar. And to think it would have been so simple to wound him with a refusal before he had got to the dangerous stage, and to let him go while the cut was fresh and curable!

The thin rain, falling past the square of my lighted window, looks like damp, finely-sifted flour, white against the black background of the road.

I must confess that, in allowing this man to return tomorrow, I was giving way to my desire to keep, not an admirer, not a friend, but an eager spectator of my life and my person. "One has to get terribly old," said Margot to me one day, "before one can give up the vanity of living in the presence of someone else."

Could I sincerely declare that, for a few weeks past, I have not taken pleasure in the attention of this passionate spectator? I denied him my brightest look, my freest smile; I was careful of the tone of my voice when I spoke to him, and my whole face remained closed against him. But was it not so that, distressed and humbled, he should realise that all my reticences were addressed to him, and that for his sake I was taking the trouble to exist less? There is no disguise without coquetry, and it needs as much care and vigilance to make oneself ugly all the time as to adorn oneself.

If my admirer, in the shadow, is watching my open window, he has reason to be proud. I am neither regretting him nor wanting him, but I am thinking of him. I am thinking of him as though I were taking stock of my first defeat.

The first? No, the second. There was an evening—oh, what a bitter memory, and how I curse it for rising up at this moment—an evening when, propped on my elbows like this, I was leaning out over an invisible garden. My long, long hair hung down from the balcony like a silk rope. The certainty of love had just swooped down on me, and, far from weakening under it, my young strength bore it proudly. Neither doubt, nor even the sweetest melancholy sobered that triumphal and solitary night, crowned with wisteria and roses. What did the man who aroused it do with that blind, that innocent exaltation?

Shut the window, shut the window! I tremble too much lest I should see rising, through the veil of the rain, a country garden, green and black, silvered by the rising moon across which passes the shadow of a young girl dreamily winding her long plait round her wrist, like a caressing snake.

SIX

"Marseilles, Nice, Cannes, Toulon . . ."

"No, Mentone before Toulon . . ."

"And Grenoble! We've got Grenoble too!"

We reckon up the towns of our tour like children counting their marbles. Brague has decided that we should take two "numbers": *The Pursuit* and *The Dryad*.

"For the big burgs where we do four or six days," he declares, "it's just as well to have a second string."

I readily agree to that. I readily agree to anything. No one could be kindlier and more appreciative than I am this morning. There is hardly a sound to be heard at Cernuschi's studio, where we are working, except Brague's outbursts and the laughter of the "Old Troglodyte" who is thrilled with the idea of going on tour and earning fifteen francs a day: his famished young face, with its sunken blue eyes, beams with uninterrupted happiness, and goodness knows he is paying for it!

"You fat-headed louse!" yells Brague. "Take that ballet-dancer's smirk off, can't you? Anyone'd think you'd never seen a troglodyte. Twist your mug sideways, I tell you! More still! And make your eyes start out! And your jaw quiver! Sort of like Chaliapine, that's the kind of thing."

He wipes his forehead and turns towards me, discouraged: "I can't think why I wear myself out over that clod; when I talk to him of Chaliapine, he thinks I am using rude words to him. And you too, what are you up to, gaping at the ceiling?"

"Oh, so it's my turn now? I was just saying to myself, it's a long time since Brague murmured some love-words to me."

My comrade-professor eyes me with a look of theatrical contempt: "Love-words! I leave those to others: I don't suppose you're short of them, are you? And now, off with you! The meeting's adjourned. To-morrow, dress rehearsal with scenery and accessories, which is to say that you'll have a veil for your dance, while this gentleman here will carry a packing-case full of candles to represent the rock he brandishes over our heads. I'm tired of seeing you both, you with a handkerchief the size of one of my buttocks, and him with his *Paris-Journal* rolled into a ball instead of his lump of granite. Ten o'clock tomorrow, here. Them's my orders."

Just when Brague stops speaking, a ray of sunshine gilds the glass ceiling, and I raise my head as if I had suddenly heard someone calling me from above.

"D'you hear me, you chit of a Renée?"

"Yes."

"Yes? Well then off with you. It's time for grub. Go and wallow in the sun outside. You're dreaming of the country, isn't that it?"

"Nothing escapes you. Till tomorrow."

I'm dreaming of the country, yes, but not in the way that my infallible companion supposes. And the joyful hubbub of the Place Clichy at midday in no wise dispels a nagging memory that is still fresh and keen.

Yesterday Hamond and Dufferein-Chautel took me to the woods at Meudon, like two art-students taking out a little milliner. My admirer was showing off a new car that smelt of morocco leather and turpentine: a magnificent toy for grown-ups. His dark youthful face was alight with longing to offer me this beautiful, gleaming, vibrating object for which I had not the slightest wish. But I laughed because, for this outing to Meudon, Hamond and Dufferein-Chautel were wearing identical wide-brimmed brown hats with a dint in the crown, and I looked so small between those two tall creatures.

Sitting opposite me on one of the tip-up seats, my admirer tucked his legs discreetly under him so that my knees should not touch his. The clear, grey day, very mild and spring-like, showed me all the details of his face, darker than ever under the bronze felt, with the smoky tone of his eyelids and the double row of stiff, thick eyelashes. His mouth, half-hidden under his rusty-black moustache, intrigued me, as did the faint network of little wrinkles below his eyes, and the thick, rather untidy eyebrows that extended beyond their orbit, bristling rather like those of hunting griffons. I suddenly began to grope, with an anxious hand, for the looking-glass in my little bag.

"Have you lost something, Renée?"

But I had already changed my mind: "No, nothing; thank you."

What would be the sense of examining, in front of him, the blemishes of a face which is losing the habit of being looked at in daylight? And what could my mirror have taught me, since yesterday, as on all other days, a skilful make-up of brown pencil, bluish kohl, and red lipstick managed to draw attention to my eyes and my mouth, the three lights, the three loadstars of my face. No rouge on my rather hollow cheeks, nor beneath the eyelids which weariness and frequent blinking have already delicately chequered.

The happiness of Fossette, who sat on my knees craning towards the door, provided us with occasional conversation, as did also the charm of that still wintry wood, with its grey twigs against a chinchilla sky. But whenever I leant forward to drink in a little of the gentle breeze, laden with the bitter musk of old, decayed leaves, I felt the gaze of my admirer dwelling confidently on my whole person.

Between Paris and the woods of Meudon we had not exchanged a hundred phrases. The country never makes me talkative, and my old Hamond feels bored as soon as he passes beyond the fortifications. Our silence might have cast a gloom over anyone but an admirer, sufficiently recompensed by the private satisfaction of having me there under his eyes, a passive prisoner in his car, vaguely enjoying the outing and smiling at the bumps in the damp and rutted road.

With a short bark, Fossette imperiously decided that we should go no further, and that some urgent business was calling her from the depths of those bare woods, on that forest road where the pools left by a recent downpour shone like round mirrors. We all three followed her without protest, with the long strides of people used to walking.

"It smells good," says the Big-Noodle suddenly, sniffing the air. "It smells like it does at home."

I shook my head: "No, not like *your* home, like mine! Hamond, what does it smell like?"

"It smells like autumn," says Hamond in a weary voice.

Whereupon we said no more and stood still, gazing up at a rivulet of sky imprisoned between very tall trees, and listening to the liquid call, clear and quavering, of a blackbird defying the winter, that came to us through the living, whispered murmur that rises from a forest.

A little red-brown creature started up from under our feet, a stoat or a weasel Fossette pretended she had put to flight, and we followed the stupid, excited bitch who kept showing off and barking: "I see it! I've got it!" as she followed an imaginary track.

In the end, catching the excitement, I set off after her down the path, giving myself up to the animal pleasure of the chase, my skunk cap pulled well down to my ears, and grasping my skirt in both hands to leave my legs free. When I stopped, out of breath, I found Maxime behind me.

"Oh, you followed me? Why didn't I hear you running?"

He was breathing fast, his eyes shining under his uneven eyebrows, his hair ruffled by the chase, very much the amorous wood-cutter and rather alarming.

"I followed you . . . I was careful to run at the same pace as you so that you shouldn't hear my steps. It's quite simple."

Yes, it's quite simple. But it had to be thought of. For my part I shouldn't have thought of it. Provoked and imprudent, a nymph-like brutality took possession of me and I laughed full in his face, defying him. I was tempted, and wanted to light again the wicked yellow light in the depths of those beautiful eyes flecked with grey and red-brown. The menace duly appeared in them, but I refused to yield, obstinate as a cheeky child who expects and asks for a slap. And the chastisement came, in the form of a badly-planted, irascible kiss, a bungled kiss in short, which left my mouth punished and disappointed.

As I follow the Boulevard des Batignolles, I carefully weigh all the moments of the day out yesterday, not in order to re-live them complacently, nor to find an excuse. There is no excuse, except for the man whom I provoked. "How unlike me that was!" I mentally exclaimed to myself, yesterday, while we were returning towards Hamond, dissatisfied with each other and in a defiant mood. But was it? How do I know? "You have no more redoubtable enemy than yourself!" A pretended thoughtlessness, a pretended imprudence—these are to be found at the bottom of the most mischievously impulsive women, and I am not one of them. One should be severe with those of them who cry: "Oh, I no longer know what I am doing!" and realise that there is in their confusion a large admixture of premeditated cunning.

I do not at all say that I am not responsible, even partly. What shall I say to this man, this evening, if he wants to clasp me in his arms? That I do not want, that I never did want to tempt him, and that it is a game? That I offer him my friendship for the period of one month and ten days which separates us from the tour? No, the time has come to make up my mind, the time has come to make up my mind.

I walk on and on, quickening my steps every time I see my reflection in a shop window, because the expression of anxious determination which I see on my face looks to me rather too theatrical, with eyes not sufficiently in earnest under frowning brows. I know that face. It puts on a mask of austerity, of renunciation, the better to wait for the little miracle, the sign of my master, Chance, the phosphorescent word that he will write on the black wall when I turn out my light tonight.

How good the air smells round these little barrows full of wet violets and white jonquils! An old man all mossy with beard is selling up-rooted snowdrops with their bulbs clotted with earth and their pendant flowers shaped like a bee. Their scent resembles that of the orange-flower, but so faint as to be almost imperceptible.

Come now, come, the time has come to make up my mind! I walk and walk as if I did not know that, in spite of my bursts of energy, my scruples and all that inner penitence which I try to inflict on myself, as if I did not know, already, that I shall not take *that* course, but the *other!*

SEVEN

HEAVENS, how tired I am, absolutely worn out! I fell asleep after lunch, as I sometimes do on rehearsal days, and I've wakened up utterly weary, feeling as though I had come from the ends of the earth, astonished and sad and barely able to think, eyeing my familiar furniture with a hostile gaze. Just such an awakening, in fact, as the most horrible of those I used to experience in the days of my suffering. But since I am not suffering now, what can the reason be?

I feel unable to move. I look at my hand hanging down as though it did not belong to me. I don't recognise the stuff of my frock. Who was it, while I slept, who loosened the coronet of plaits coiled about my brows like the tresses of a grave young Ceres? I was . . . I was . . . there was a garden . . . a peach-coloured sunset sky . . . a shrill childish voice answering the cries of the swallows . . . yes, and that sound like distant water, sometimes powerful and sometimes muffled: the breath of a forest. I had gone back to the beginning of my life. What a journey to catch up with myself again, where I am now! I cry for the sleep that has fled, the dark curtain which sheltered me and now has withdrawn itself, leaving me shivering and naked. Sick people who think they are cured experience these fresh attacks of their malady which find them childishly astonished and plaintive: "But I thought it was over!" For two pins I could groan aloud, as they do.

O dangerous and too-kindly sleep which in less than an hour obliterates the memory of myself! Whence come I, and on what wings, that it should take me so long, humiliated and exiled, to accept that I am myself? Renée Néré, dancer and mime. . . . Was my proud childhood, my withdrawn and passionate adolescence, which welcomed love so fearlessly, to lead to no end but that?

O Margot, my discouraging friend, if only I had strength to get up, and run to you, and tell you. . . . But my courage is the only thing you admire and I should not dare to falter before you. I feel pretty sure that your direct gaze and the clasp of your dry little hand, chapped by cold water and household soap, would know better how to reward a victory over myself than to help me in my daily efforts.

And what of my approaching departure? And freedom? Ah, no! The only moment when freedom is truly dazzling is at the dawn of love, of first love, when you can say, as you offer it to the person you love: "Take! I wish I could give you more."

As for the new cities and new countrysides, so briefly glimpsed, so quickly passed that they grow blurred in the memory, are there such things as new countries for one who spins round and round in circles like a bird held on a string? Will not my pathetic flight, begun anew each morning, inevitably end up each evening at the fatal "first-class establishment" which Salomon and Brague praise so highly to me?

I have seen so many *first-class establishments* already! On the side of the public there is an auditorium cruelly flooded with light, where the heavy smoke hardly tones down the gilt of the mouldings. On the artistes' side there are sordid, airless cells, and a staircase leading to filthy lavatories.

Must I really, for forty days, endure this struggle against fatigue, the bantering ill-will of the stage-hands, the raging pride of provincial conductors, the inadequate fare of hotels and stations? Must I discover and perpetually renew in myself that rich fund of energy which is essential to the life of wanderers and solitaries? Must I, in short, struggle—ah, how could I forget it?—against solitude itself? And to achieve what? What? What?

When I was small they said to me: "Effort brings its own reward", and so, whenever I had tried specially hard, I used to expect a mysterious, overwhelming recompense, a sort of grace to which I should have surrendered myself. I am still expecting it.

The muffled trill of a bell, followed by the barking of my dog, delivers me at last from this bitter reverie. And suddenly I am on my feet, surprised to find I have jumped lightly up and begun quite simply to live again.

"Madame," says Blandine in a low voice, "may M. Dufferein-Chautel come in?"

"No . . . just a minute."

To powder my cheeks, redden my lips, and comb out the tangled locks which hide my forehead is a rapid mechanical task which does not even need the help of a mirror. One does it as one brushes one's nails, more for manners than vanity.

"Are you there, Dufferein-Chautel? You can come in. Wait a moment. I'll turn on the light."

I feel no embarrassment at seeing him again. The fact that our mouths met yesterday, abortively, does not make me feel the least awkward at this moment. A bungled kiss is much less important than an understanding exchange of looks. And I almost feel surprise that he for his part should look unhappy and frustrated. I called him Dufferein-Chautel as usual, as though he had no Christian name. I always call him "You" or "Dufferein-Chautel". Is it for me to put him at his ease? I suppose it is.

"So there you are! Are you well?"

"Thank you, I'm well."

"You don't look it."

"That's because I'm unhappy," he does not fail to reply.

Really, what a Big-Noodle! I smile at his unhappiness, the trifling unhappiness of a man who has embraced clumsily the woman he loves. I smile at him from rather far away, from the other side of the chaste black stream where I was bathing a while back. I hand him a little vase filled with his favourite cigarettes, made of a sweet, golden tobacco which smells like spice-bread.

"You're not smoking today?"

"Yes, of course. But I'm unhappy all the same."

Sitting on the divan, with his back against the low cushions, he exhales at regular intervals long jets of smoke from his nostrils. I smoke too, for something to do and to keep him company. He looks better bare-headed. A top-hat makes him uglier and a soft felt handsomer to the point of flashiness. He smokes with his eyes on the ceiling, as though the seriousness of the words he is preparing prevented him from paying any attention to me. His long, shining eyelashes—the one sensuous, feminine ornament of that face whose fault is excess of virility—blink frequently, betraying agitation and hesitancy. I can hear him breathing. I can also hear the tick-tock of my little travelling-clock, and the screen in the fireplace which the wind suddenly rattles.

"Is it raining outside?"

"No," he says with a start. "Why do you ask me that?"

"So's to know. I haven't been out since lunch, I don't know what the weather's like."

"Just ordinary . . . Renée!"

All of a sudden he sits up and throws away his cigarette. He takes my hands and looks very closely at me, so closely that his face appears to me almost too big, with the details strongly emphasised, the texture of the skin, and the moist and quivering corner of his large eyes. What love there is, yes, love, in those eyes! How speaking they are, and gentle, and wholly enamoured! And those big hands which clasp mine with such steady, communicative strength, how much in earnest I feel them!

It is the first time that I leave my hands in his. At first I feel I have to overcome my repugnance, then their warmth reassures and persuades me, and in a moment I shall yield to the surprising, brotherly pleasure, for so long unfamiliar, of confiding without words in a friend, of leaning for a moment against him, of finding comfort in the nearness of a warm, motionless being, affectionate and silent. Oh, to throw my arms round the neck of a creature, dog or man, a creature who loves me!

"Renée! What is it, Renée, you're not crying?"

"Am I crying?"

He's quite right, I am! The light dances in my brimming tears in a thousand broken, criss-cross rays. I wipe them quickly with a corner of my handkerchief, but I don't dream of denying them. And I smile at the idea that I was about to cry. How long is it since last I cried? It must be years and years.

My friend is overcome. He draws me towards him and forces me—not that I protest much—to sit beside him on the divan. His eyes, too, are moist. After all he is only a man, capable of feigning an emotion, no doubt, but not of hiding it.

"My darling child, what is the matter?"

Will he forget the stifled cry, the shudder which answers him? I hope so. "My darling child!" His first word of tenderness is "My darling child!" The same word and almost the same accent as *the other* . . .

A childish fear wrenches me from his arms, as if *the other* had just appeared at the door with his Kaiser William moustache, his false, veiled gaze, his terrible shoulders and his short, peasant's thighs.

"Renée, my darling, if only you would talk to me a little!"

My friend is quite pale and does not try to take me in his arms again. May he at least never know the pain he has just, so innocently, given me! I no longer want to cry. My delicious, cowardly tears slowly return to their source, leaving a burning sensation in my

eyes and throat. While I wait for my voice to steady itself, I reassure
my friend with a nod.

"I've made you angry, Renée?"

"No, my friend."

I sit down beside him again, of my own accord, but timidly, for
fear my gesture and my words should provoke another tender exclamation as familiar and hateful as the last.

His instinct warns him not to rejoice at my sudden docility. I feel
no desire to embrace me in the arm which supports me, and the dangerous, grateful communicative warmth is no longer there. No doubt
he loves me enough to guess that, if I lay an obedient head on his
strong shoulder, it is a question of a trial more than a gift.

Can this be my forehead on a man's shoulder? Am I dreaming? I
am neither dreaming nor wandering. Both my head and my senses
are calm, ominously calm. Yet there is something better and more
than indifference in the ease which keeps me there, and the fact that
I can let my hand play innocently and unthinkingly with the plaited
gold chain on his waistcoat shows that I feel myself sheltered and
protected, like the lost cat one rescues, who only knows how to play
and sleep when it has a house.

Poor admirer . . . I wonder what he is thinking of as he sits there
motionless, respecting my silence? I lean my head back to look at
him, but immediately lower my lids, dazzled and abashed by the expression on this man's face. Ah, how I envy him for loving so deeply,
for the passion that confers such beauty on him!

His eyes meet mine and he smiles bravely.

"Renée . . . do you think a time will ever come when you will
love me?"

"Love you? How I wish I could, my friend! *You*, at least, don't
look cruel. Don't you feel that I am beginning to get fond of
you?"

"To get fond of me . . . that's just what I'm afraid of, Renée; that
hardly ever leads to love."

He is so profoundly right that I do not protest.

"But . . . be patient . . . you never know. It may be that, when I
come back from my tour . . . And then, after all, a great, great
friendship . . ."

He shakes his head. Obviously he has no use for my friendship.
For my part I should be very glad to have a friend who was less old,
less *worn out*, than Hamond, a real friend. . . .

"When you come back. . . . In the first place, if you really hoped to love me one day, Renée, you wouldn't think of going away from me. In two months' time, just as now, it will be the same Renée who will stretch out her cold little hands, with eyes that shut me out, and that mouth which, even when it offers its lips, does not surrender itself."

"It's not my fault. Yet here it is, this mouth. See . . ."

With my head on his shoulder once more, I close my eyes, more resigned than curious, only to open them again at the end of a moment, surprised that he does not swoop down with the greedy haste of yesterday. All he has done is to turn a little towards me and encircle me comfortably with his right arm. Then he gathers my two hands into his free hand and bends forward, and I see slowly approaching the serious unfamiliar face of this man whom I know so little.

Now there is hardly any space or air between our two faces, and I try and jerk myself free, breathing fast as if I were drowning. But he holds my hands and tightens his arm round my waist. In vain I bend my neck back, just at the moment when Maxime's mouth reaches mine.

I have not closed my eyes. I frown in an attempt to threaten those eyes above me, which try to subjugate and extinguish mine. For the lips which kiss me are just the same as yesterday, gentle, cool and impersonal, and their ineffectiveness irritates me. But all of a sudden they change, and now I no longer recognise the kiss, which quickens, insists, falters, then begins again with a rhythmical movement, and finally stops as if waiting for a response which does not come.

I move my head imperceptibly, because of his moustache which brushes against my nostrils with a scent of vanilla and honeyed tobacco. Oh! . . . suddenly my mouth, in spite of itself, lets itself be opened, opens of itself as irresistibly as a ripe plum splits in the sun. And once again there is born that exacting pain that spreads from my lips, all down my flanks as far as my knees, that swelling as of a wound that wants to open once more and overflow—the voluptuous pleasure that I had forgotten.

I let the man who has awakened me drink the fruit he is pressing. My hands, stiff a moment ago, lie warm and soft in his, and my body, as I lie back, strives to mould itself to his. Drawn close by the arm which holds me, I burrow deeper into his shoulder and press myself against him, taking care not to separate our lips and to prolong our kiss comfortably.

He understands and assents, with a happy little grunt. Sure at last

that I shall not flee, it is he who breaks away from me, to draw
breath and contemplate me as he bites his moist lips. I let my lids
fall, since I no longer need to see him. Is he going to undress me and
take possession of me completely? It doesn't matter. I am lapped in
a lazy, irresponsible joy. The only urgent thing is that that kiss
should begin again. We have all our time. Full of pride, my friend
gathers me up in his arms as though I were a bunch of flowers, and
half lays me on the divan where he rejoins me. His mouth tastes of
mine now, and has the faint scent of my powder. Experienced as it
is, I can feel that it is trying to invent something new, to vary the caress still further. But already I am bold enough to indicate my preference for a long, drowsy kiss that is almost motionless—the slow
crushing, one against the other, of two flowers in which nothing
vibrates but the palpitation of two coupled pistils.

And now comes a great truce when we rest and get our breath
back. This time it was I who left him, and got up because I felt the
need to open my arms, to draw myself up and stretch. Anxious to arrange my hair and see what my new face looked like, I took up the
hand-mirror, and it makes me laugh to see we both have the same
sleepy features, the same trembling, shiny, slightly swollen lips. Maxime has remained on the divan and his mute appeal receives the
most flattering of responses: my look of a submissive bitch, rather
shame-faced, rather cowed, very much petted, and ready to accept
the leash, the collar, the place at her master's feet, and everything.

EIGHT

He has gone. We dined together, rather a scratch meal; Blandine did us some cutlets in gravy, with gherkins. I was consumed with hunger. "*Et l'amour comblant tout, hormis . . .*", said he, to show he had read Verlaine.

We did not fall into each other's arms when dinner was over, and we have not become lovers, since he is shy and I dislike doing things on the spur of the moment. But I have pledged and promised myself, joyfully and without coquetry.

"We've got plenty of time, haven't we, Max?"

"Not too much, darling. I've grown so old while I've been waiting for you!"

So old! He does not know how old I am.

He has gone, and he will return tomorrow. He could hardly tear himself away from me, and I was so afraid I might weaken that I held him at arms' length. I felt warm and he sniffed me ecstatically, as though he were about to bite me. But at last he has gone. I say "at last", because now I shall be able to think about him, and about us.

"Love" was what he said. Is it love? I should like to be sure of it. Do I love him? My sensuality frightened me; but perhaps it will prove to be only a moment of crisis, an overflowing of forces pent up for such a long time, and afterwards no doubt I shall find I love him. What if he were to come back and knock on my shutter? Yes, certainly I love him. I brood tenderly over the memory of certain inflexions in his voice today—the echo of his little amorous grunt is enough to make me catch my breath—and then how good and strong he was, and what a comfort in my solitude when I laid my head on his shoulder! Oh yes, I do love him. What is it that has made me so timorous? I did not make so much fuss when . . .

Imprudently my train of thought has stumbled on a grave. Too late to flee, I find myself once again face to face with that pitiless mentor who speaks to me from the other side of the looking-glass:

"You didn't make so much fuss when love swept down on you and found you so mad and brave. You didn't ask yourself, that day, *if it was love*. You couldn't mistake it; it was love indeed, *first love*. That was what it was and never again will be. Your maiden simplicity recognised love without hesitation, and begrudged him neither your body nor your childish heart. It was then love made his appearance unannounced, unchosen, unquestioned. And never again will it be he. He took from you what you can only give once: trust, the religious wonder of the first caress, the novelty of your tears, the flower of your first suffering. Love, if you can; no doubt this will be granted you, so that at the summit of your poor happiness you may again remember that nothing counts, in love, except the first love, and endure at every moment the punishment of remembering, and the horror of comparing. Even when you say: 'Ah, this is better!' you will feel the pang of knowing that nothing which is not unique is good. There is a God who says to the sinner: 'You would not seek me if you had not already found me!' But Love is not so merciful. 'You, who have found me once,' he says, 'you shall lose me for ever!' Did you think, when you lost him, that you had reached the limit of suffering? It is not over yet. In striving now to be again what once you were, you will realise the height from which you fell; and the first, the only love will instil its poison into each feast of your new life, if you do not stem its flow."

NINE

I SHALL have to speak to Margot and tell her of this event, this touch of the sun which sets my life aflame. For it has come to that, we love each other. It has come to that and, besides, I have made up my mind to it. I have sent to the devil all my memories-and-regrets, and my obsession about what I call sentimental high-water marks, and my *ifs* and *fors* and *buts* and *howevers*.

We spend every moment together, he sweeps me off my feet, dazes me with his presence and prevents me from thinking. He decides, he almost commands, and I surrender to him not only my liberty but my pride too, since I let him fill my flat with a wasteful abundance of flowers and of next summer's fruits, and I wear a little glittering arrow, pinned against my neck as though it were driven into my throat, all bleeding with rubies.

And yet we are not lovers. Max has grown patient now, and imposes on himself and me a curiously exhausting period of betrothal which in less than a week has already made us languid and slightly thinner. It is not vice in him which makes him act thus, but the coquetry of a man who wants to make himself desired and, at the same time, leave me an illusory "free will" for as long as I want.

In any case there is not much left for me to desire. And the only thing which makes me tremble at present is that unsuspected ardour which leapt into life at the first contact and is always fiercely ready to obey him. I agree he is right to postpone the hour which will unite us completely. I know my value now, and the splendour of the gift which he will receive. I shall surpass his wildest hopes, I am sure of it. In the meantime let him cull a little of the fruit in his orchard if he wants.

And he does often want. For my pleasure and to my disturbance chance has willed that in this tall young man, with his straightforward, symmetrical good looks, there is a subtle lover, born for women, and so skilled at divining that his caresses seem to know the thoughts behind my desire. He makes me think—and I blush for it—of the saying of a lascivious little music-hall comrade who boasted of the cleverness of a new lover: "My dear, one couldn't do better oneself!"

But . . . I shall have to let Margot know! Poor Margot, whom I was forgetting. As for Hamond, he has disappeared. He knows everything, thanks to Max, and keeps away from my house like a discreet relation.

And Brague! I can't forget how he looked at our last rehearsal. He greeted me on my arrival in Max's car with his best Pierrot's grimace, but he still says nothing. He even displayed an unusual and undeserved courtesy, for that morning I was blundering and absentminded, and kept blushing and excusing myself. Finally he burst out: "Be off with you! Go back to it! Take your fill and don't come back here till you've had all you can take!"

The more I laughed, the more he fulminated, looking like a little oriental fiend: "Laugh away, go on, laugh! If you could see the look on your face!"

"My look?"

"Yes, a look that's absolutely asking for it, craving for it. Don't raise your eyes to me, Messalina! Look at her," he cried, calling invisible gods to witness, "she shows those orbs there in broad daylight. And when I ask her to put that much and a bit more too into the Dryad's love scene, and to hot the whole thing up a bit, she trots out the chilly charm of a young girl at her first communion."

"Does *that* really show?" I asked Max, who was taking me home. The same mirror which the other evening reflected a countenance glorying in its defeat, now frames a pointed face with the defiant smile of a friendly fox. Yet an indefinable flame keeps flickering over it, painting it, as it were, with a kind of tormented youthfulness.

I have decided to confess everything to Margot: my relapse, my happiness, and the name of the man I love. It won't be easy. Margot is not a woman to say: "I told you so!" but I feel pretty sure that I shall sadden and disappoint her, although she will not show it. "Burnt child though you are, you'll go back to the fire!" I am indeed going back to it, and with what joy!

I find Margot unchangeably true to herself in the big studio where she sleeps, eats and breeds her Brabançon dogs. Tall and upright, in her Russian blouse and long black jacket, she bends her pale face, with its lean cheeks framed in her rough grey bobbed hair, over a basket in which a minute dog in a flannel shirt, a little yellow monster, is groping about and gazing up at her with the beautiful, imploring eyes of a squirrel, under the bumpy forehead of a bonze. Round me yap and wriggle six cheeky little creatures whom a crack of a whip sends scampering to their straw kennels.

"What, Margot, another Brabançon? It's a passion!"

"Lord, no!" says Margot, sitting down opposite me and cradling the sick animal on her knees. "I don't love this poor little wretch."

"Someone gave her to you?"

"No, I bought her, of course. That will teach me not to walk in future past that old blackguard of a Hartmann, the dog-dealer. If you'd seen this Brabançon in the window, with her little face like a sick rat's and this spine protruding like a rosary, and above all those eyes. . . . Hardly anything touches me now, you know, except the expression of a dog for sale. So I bought her. She's half dead with enteritis; that never shows at the dealer's; they dope them with cacodylate. . . . Well now, my child, it's a long time since I saw you; are you working?"

"Yes Margot, I'm rehearsing."

"I can see that, you're tired."

With that familiar gesture of hers, she takes hold of my chin to tilt my face up and draw it towards her. Embarrassed, I close my eyes.

"Yes, you're tired. You've got older," she says in a very grave tone.

"Older! Oh, Margot!"

In that cry of pain and the flood of tears that follows it, my whole secret leaks out. I bury myself against my stern friend, and she strokes my shoulder and comforts me with the same "Poor little one!" that she used a moment ago to the sick Brabançon.

"There, there now, poor little one, there, there. It'll soon be all right. Look, here's some boracic lotion to bathe your eyes, I'd just prepared it for Mirette's. Not with your handkerchief! Take some cotton-wool . . . there! Poor little one, so your beauty's very necessary to you at present, is it?"

"Oh yes! . . . Oh Margot!"

" 'Oh, Margot!' Anyone might think I'd beaten you. Look at me. Are you very sore with me, poor little one?"

"No, Margot."

"You know very well," she goes on in her gentle, level voice, "that you can always count on finding here every kind of help, even the kind that hurts most: the truth. What was it I said to you? I said, you've got older."

"Yes . . . Oh, Margot . . ."

"Now don't begin again! But you've got older *this week*. You've got older *today*. Tomorrow, or in an hour's time, you'll be five years younger, ten years younger. If you'd come yesterday, or tomorrow, no doubt I should have said: 'My word, you've got younger!' "

"Just think, Margot, I shall soon be thirty-four."

"Don't expect me to pity you, I'm fifty-two!"

"It isn't the same thing, Margot, it's so important for me to be pretty, and young, and happy. I've . . . I . . ."

"You've got a lover?"

Her voice is still gentle, but the expression of her face has changed slightly.

"I haven't got a lover, Margot. Only, it's certain that I . . . I shall have one. But . . . I love him, you see!"

This kind of silly excuse amuses Margot.

"Ah, you love him? And he, too, loves you?"

"Oh!"

With a proud gesture, I protect my friend from the least suspicion.

"That's good. And . . . how old is he?"

"Just my age, Margot: very nearly thirty-four."

"That's . . . that's good."

I can't find anything else to add. I am horribly ill at ease. I had hoped, once the first embarrassment was over, to chatter about my happiness, and to tell everything about my friend, the colour of his eyes, the shape of his hands, his goodness, his honesty.

"He's . . . he's very nice, you know, Margot," I risked, shyly.

"So much the better, my child. You've made some plans, the two of you?"

"Plans? No . . . we haven't yet thought of anything. There's time."

"Yes of course, there's plenty of time. And what's happening about your tour, with all this?"

"My tour? Oh, this makes no difference to that."

"You're taking your . . . your fellow with you?"

Bathed in tears though I am, I can't help laughing when Margot refers to my friend with such squeamish discretion, as if she were speaking of something dirty.

"Taking him along, taking him . . . well . . . as a matter of fact, Margot, I don't at all know. I'll see."

My sister-in-law raises her eyebrows.

"You don't at all know, you have no plans, you'll see! My word, what an astonishing pair you are! What can you be thinking about? After all, it's the only thing you've got to do, to plan and prepare your future."

"The future. . . . Oh, Margot, I don't like preparing the future. It prepares itself without any help, and it comes so soon!"

"Is it a question of marriage or living in sin?"

I do not answer all at once, embarrassed for the first time by the chaste Margot's rather crude vocabulary.

"It isn't a question of anything. We're getting to know each other, finding out what we're like. . . ."

"You're finding out what you're like!"

With her mouth pursed and a cruel gaiety in her bright little eyes, Margot observes me.

"You're finding out what you're like! I see, you're at the stage when you're showing off to each other, is that it?"

"I assure you, Margot, we hardly show off at all," I say, forcing myself to smile. "That game's well enough for very young lovers, but he and I are no longer very young lovers."

"All the more reason," answers Margot, pitilessly. "You have more things to hide from each other. My little one," she added gently, "you know well enough you must laugh at my mania. Marriage seems to me such a monstrous thing. Haven't I often enough made you laugh by telling you how, from the very first days of my married life, I refused to share a bedroom with my husband because I thought it immoral to live at such close quarters with a young man who was a stranger to my family? I was born that way, that's the trouble, and I shall never change. . . . You haven't brought Fossette to see me today?"

Like Margot, I make an effort to cheer up.

"No, Margot. Your pack gave her such a poor welcome last time!"

"That's true. My pack isn't in very good shape at present. Come along, cripples!"

They do not have to be asked twice. From a row of kennels there emerge half a dozen dogs, a shivering, miserable little bunch, the biggest of which could be held in the crown of a hat. Saved by Margot from the "dog-dealer", wrested from that stupid, noxious trade which pens together in a window creatures that are sick, fattened up, starving or doped, I know nearly all of these. A few of them have become again, in her house, healthy, gay, robust animals; but others never get rid of their upset stomachs, their scabby skins, and their ineradicable hysteria. Margot looks after them as well as she can, discouraged by the thought that her charity is all to no purpose and that there will everlastingly be "luxury dogs" for sale.

The sick bitch has gone to sleep. I can find nothing to say. I look at the big room which, with its uncurtained windows, always has somewhat the appearance of an infirmary. On a table there are rows of chemists' bottles, rolled bandages, a diminutive thermometer, a tiny little rubber pear for dogs' enemas. The room smells of iodine and Jeyes fluid. I suddenly feel I must go away, I must find again without an instant's delay my warm narrow room, with the hollowed divan, and the flowers, and the friend I love.

"Goodbye, Margot, I'm going."

"Off you go then, my child."

"You're not too cross with me?"

"What about?"

"For being so foolish, and ridiculous, for being in love, I mean. I had so sworn to myself . . ."

"Cross with you? My poor little one, that would be too unkind. A new love . . . you mustn't feel uncomfortable. Poor little one!"

I am in a hurry to get home. I feel frozen, shrunken, and so sad. Never mind, it's done, what a relief! I've told Margot everything. I have received the cold douche I expected and I run to shake it off, to dry myself and expand in the warmth again. I lower my veil to hide the traces of my upset, and I run—run to him!

TEN

"Monsieur Maxime is here, waiting for Madame." My charwoman Blandine now says "Monsieur Maxime" in a tender tone, as if she were speaking of her foster-child.

He is here!

I rush to my room and shut myself in: he mustn't see my face! Quick! Rice-powder, kohl, lip-stick. . . . Oh dear, look at that shiny groove under my eye, still moist from my tears! "You've got older." Silly thing, to go and cry like a little girl! Haven't you learnt to suffer "dry-eyed"? Where are the days when my glistening tears rolled down the velvet of my cheeks without wetting it? There was a time when, to conquer my husband all over again, I knew how to adorn myself with my tears, weeping with my face lifted towards him and my eyes wide open, and shaking but not drying the slow pearls which made me more beautiful. How poor I have become!

"There you are at last, my darling, my scented one, my appetising one, my . . ."

"Goodness, how silly you are!"

"Thank Heaven, yes!" sighs my friend in a tone of blissful conviction.

He begins to indulge in his favourite game of lifting me up in his arms till I touch the ceiling, and then kissing my cheeks, chin, ears and mouth. I resist enough to force him to show his strength, but he gets the upper hand in the struggle and then he tips me right over on his arm, head down and feet in air until I cry "Help!", when he sets me upright again. The dog rushes to my defence and mingles her hoarse barks with our laughter and cries, in this rough game which I much enjoy.

What a good thing this healthy silliness is! And what a gay companion I have in him, as little concerned to appear clever as to avoid rumpling his tie. How warm it is here, and how quickly our laughter changes from the laughter of two opponents, confronting each other, to a voluptuous challenge. He devours his "appetising one", tasting her slowly, like a gourmet.

"How good you would be to eat, my darling. Your mouth is honeyed, but your arms, when I bite them, are salty, just a tiny bit, and so are your shoulders and knees. I feel sure you're salty from head to foot, like a cool shell, aren't you?"

"You'll know that only too soon, Big-Noodle!"

For I still call him "Big-Noodle", but . . . in a different tone.

"When? This evening? It's Thursday today, isn't it?"

"I think so . . . yes . . . why?"

"Thursday . . . that's a very good day."

Lying back among the cushions, and very happy, he says foolish things. A lock of his hair has fallen over his eyes, which have the vague look that a great wave of desire gives them, and he half opens his mouth to breathe. Whenever he adopts an abandoned attitude, he turns again into a handsome country lad, a wood-cutter "taking a nap" on the grass—not that I dislike that!

"Get up, Max; we must talk seriously."

"I don't want to be hurt!" he sighs plaintively.

"Really, Max!"

"No! I know what talking seriously means. Mother always calls it that when she wants to speak of business, or money-matters, or marriage."

He snuggles into the cushions and closes his eyes. It is not the first time that he has shown that determination to be frivolous.

"Max, you've not forgotten that I'm going away on the fifth of April?"

He half opens his eyelids with their feminine lashes, and favours me with a long look.

"You're going away, darling? Whoever decided that?"

"Salomon, the impresario, and I."

"Good. But I haven't yet given my consent. Well, so be it then, you're going away. But if so, you're going away with me."

"With you!" I say, alarmed. "Don't you know what a tour is, then?"

"Of course I do. It's a journey . . . with me."

"With you?" I repeat. "For forty-five days! But haven't you anything to do, then?"

"Certainly I have. Since I've known you, I haven't a minute to myself, Renée."

That is prettily answered, but . . .

I gaze, disconcerted, at this man who has nothing to do, who always finds money in his pocket. He has nothing to do, that is a fact, I had never thought about it. He has no profession and no sinecure behind which to conceal his lazy freedom. How strange that is! Till I met him I never knew an idle man. He can give himself up entirely, day and night, to love, like. . . like a prostitute.

This quaint idea that, of the two of us, it is he who is the courtesan, causes me a sudden gaiety, and he quickly draws his touchy eyebrows together in a frown.

"What's the matter? Are you laughing? You shan't go!"

"I like that! And what about my forfeit?"

"I'll pay it."

"And Brague's forfeit? And the Old Troglodyte's?"

"I'll pay them."

Even if it is a joke, I do not altogether like it. Can I any longer doubt that we love each other? Here we are on the verge of our first quarrel.

I was mistaken, for here is my friend close to me, almost at my feet.

"My Renée, you shall do whatever you want, you know that."

But he has laid his hand on my forehead, and his eyes are fixed on mine, to read obedience there. Whatever I want? Alas! for the moment all I want is him.

"Is it still *The Pursuit* that you're taking on tour?"

"We're taking *The Dryad* too. Oh, what a lovely violet tie you have! It makes you look quite yellow."

"Leave my tie alone! *The Pursuit*, and *The Dryad*, and everything else, is an excuse to show your beautiful legs, and the rest."

"It's not for you to complain. Wasn't it on the boards that the 'rest' had the honour of being introduced to you?"

He presses me to him until it hurts.

"Be quiet! I remember. Every evening for five days I said hurting things to myself, final things every time. I thought I was a fool to go to the *Emp'-Clich'* as you call it, and when your act was over I would leave, calling myself every kind of name. And then next day I would weakly compromise: 'This truly is the last evening I shall be seen at that dump! But I just want to make sure what colour Renée Néré's eyes are. And besides, yesterday I didn't manage to arrive for the beginning.' In short, I was idiotic already."

"Idiotic already! You have a gift for putting things attractively,

Max. It seems so queer to me that anyone can fall in love with a woman merely by looking at her."

"That depends on the woman one looks at. You know nothing about these things, Renée Néré. Just imagine, after I'd seen you mime *The Pursuit* for the first time, I spent at least an hour trying to sketch a diagram of your face. I succeeded, and I repeated I don't know how many times, in the margins of a book, a little geometric design that conveyed something to me alone. There was also, in your mime, a moment that filled me with unbearable joy: the moment when you sat on the table and read the threatening letter from the man you were deceiving. D'you know? You slapped your thigh, throwing back your head to laugh, and one could hear that your thigh was bare under your thin dress. The gesture was so robust you might have been a young fishwife, but your face glowed with a wonderfully sharp, refined wickedness, worlds apart from your accessible body. D'you remember?"

"Yes, yes . . . like this. Brague was pleased with me in that scene. But that, Max, is . . . is admiration, desire! Has it changed into love since then?"

"Changed?" He looked at me, very surprised. "I've never thought about it. I expect I loved you from that very moment. There are lots of women more beautiful than you, but . . ."

With a gesture of his hand he expresses all that is incomprehensible and irremediable in love. . . .

"But Max, what if, instead of a nice little bourgeoise like me, you'd chanced on a cold and calculating shrew, as tormenting as the itch! What then? Didn't the fear of that hold you back?"

"It never occurred to me," he said, laughing. "What a comic idea! When you love you don't think of so many things, you know."

He sometimes makes remarks like that which I, who think of so many things, feel as a rebuke.

"Little one," he murmurs, "why do you go in for this *café-concert* business?"

"Big-Noodle, why don't you go in for cabinet-making? Don't answer that you have the means to live otherwise, I know you have. But as for me, what would you have me do? Sewing, or typing, or street-walking? The music-hall is the job of those who never learnt one."

"But . . ."

I can hear from his voice that he is going to say something serious and embarrassing. I raise my head, which was resting on his shoulder, and gaze attentively at that face with its straight, firm nose, its fierce eyebrows sheltering the tender eyes, and the thick moustache under which hides a mouth with experienced lips.

"But, darling, you no longer need the music-hall now that I am there, and that . . ."

"Shh!"

Agitated and almost terrified, I urge him to stop. Yes, he is there, and ready for every kind of generosity. But that doesn't concern me, I don't want it to concern me. I cannot see that the fact that my friend is rich has anything to do with me. I cannot manage to fit him in to my future in the way he would like. No doubt that will come. I shall get used to the idea. I ask nothing better than to mingle my mouth with his and feel in advance that I belong to him, yet I can't associate his life with mine. If he were to announce to me: "I'm getting married," I feel I should answer politely: "All my congratulations!", thinking in my heart: "That doesn't concern me." And yet I wasn't exactly pleased, a fortnight ago, that he should eye little Jadin with such attention.

All these sentimental complications, fusses, hair-splittings, and psychological soliloquies, goodness how absurd I am! Would it not at bottom be more honest, and more worthy of a woman in love, to answer him: "Yes indeed you're there, and since we love each other, I'll ask you for everything. It's so simple. If I truly love you, you owe me everything, and any bread which does not come to me from you is impure."

What I have just thought is the right way to look at it. I ought to say it out loud, instead of remaining wheedlingly silent, rubbing my cheek against his shaven cheek, which has the smoothness of a very smooth piece of pumice-stone.

ELEVEN

My old Hamond had persisted for so many days in remaining at home, pleading rheumatism, influenza, or urgent work, that I ordered him to come at once. He delayed no longer and, when he came, his discreet and casual air, like that of a relation visiting some newly-weds, doubled my joy at seeing him again.

So here we are again, in affectionate tête-à-tête, like the old days.

"Like the old days, Hamond. Yet what a change!"

"Thank goodness, my child. Are you at last going to be happy?"

"Happy?"

I look at him with genuine astonishment.

"No, I shan't be happy. I don't even think of it. Why should I be happy?"

Hamond clacks his tongue; that is his way of scolding me. He thinks I have an attack of neurasthenia.

"Oh, come now, Renée. Isn't it going as well as I thought, then?"

I burst out laughing, very gay.

"Yes, of course it's going well, Hamond, only too well. I'm afraid we're beginning to adore each other."

"Well then?"

"Well then! D'you think that's a reason why I should be happy?"

Hamond cannot help smiling, and now it is my turn to look on the gloomy side.

"What torments you've thrust me into all over again, Hamond! For you'll admit it was your doing. Torments," I added in a lower tone, "that I wouldn't exchange for the greatest joys."

"Well," bursts out Hamond, relieved, "at least you're saved from that past which was fermenting inside you. I'd really had enough of seeing you gloomy and defiant, entangled in your memory and fear of Taillandy. Forgive me, Renée, but I would have stooped to pretty low things to endow you with a new love."

"You would, would you! D'you think that a new love, as you call it, destroys the memory of the first or . . . resuscitates it?"

Disconcerted by the asperity of my question, Hamond does not know what to say. But he has touched my sore spot so clumsily! And besides, he is only a man: he does not understand. He must have loved so many times: he no longer understands. His consternation makes me relent.

"No, my friend, I'm not happy. I'm . . . better or worse than that. Only . . . I don't at all know where I'm going. I want to say that to you before I become Maxime's mistress completely."

"Or his wife!"

"His wife?"

"Why not?"

"Because I don't want to."

My quick answer flies ahead of my reasoning, like an animal jumping wide of the snare before it sees it.

"Anyway that's of no importance," says Hamond carelessly. "It's the same thing."

"You think it's the same thing? For you, perhaps, and for many men. But for me! D'you remember, Hamond, what marriage was for me? No, I'm not thinking of the betrayals, you mistake me. I'm thinking of conjugal domesticity, which turns so many wives into a sort of nurse for a grown-up. Being married means . . . how shall I put it? It means trembling lest Monsieur's cutlet should be overdone, his Vittel water not cold enough, his shirt badly starched, his stiff collar soft, or the bath too hot! It means playing the exhausting part of an intermediary buffer between Monsieur's ill humour, his avarice, his greed, his laziness . . ."

"You're forgetting lust, Renée," interrupts Hamond gently.

"No, I jolly well am not! The part of mediator, I tell you, between Monsieur and the rest of humanity. You can't know, Hamond, you've been so little married! Marriage means . . . means: 'Tie my tie for me! . . . Get rid of the maid! . . . Cut my toe-nails! . . . Get up and make me some camomile! . . . Prepare me an emetic. . . .' It means: 'Give me my new suit, and pack my suit-case so that I can hurry to join her!' Steward, sick-nurse, children's nurse—enough, enough, enough!"

I end by laughing at myself and at the long scandalised face of my old friend.

"Oh, for goodness' sake, Renée, if you knew how this mania of yours for generalising gets on my nerves! 'In this country all the servant-girls are red-haired.' One doesn't always marry Taillandy! And I give you my word that, for my humble part, I should have blushed to ask a woman one of those petty services which . . . very much the contrary!"

I clap my hands. "Oh fine, I'm going to learn everything! Very much the contrary: I'm sure there was no one to touch you at buttoning up boots or flattening the press-studs on a tailored skirt? Alas, everyone can't marry Hamond!"

After a silence, I go on in a tone of weariness: "Let me generalise, as you say, even though I've had only one experience, as a result of which I'm still feeling shattered. I'm no longer young enough, or enthusiastic enough, or generous enough to go in for marriage again, or married life, if you prefer. Let me stay alone in my closed bedroom, bedecked and idle, waiting for the man who has chosen me to be his harem. I want to know nothing of him but his tenderness and his ardour, I want nothing from love, in short, but love."

"I know a good many people," says Hamond after a silence, "who would call that kind of love libertinism."

I shrug my shoulders, vexed at having made myself so little understood.

"Yes," insists Hamond, "libertinism. But since I know you . . . a little, I'd rather suppose that there is in you a fanciful, childish longing for the unrealisable: the loving couple, imprisoned in a warm room, isolated by four walls from the rest of the world—the normal dream of any young girl very ignorant of life."

"Or of a woman already mature, Hammond."

He protests, with a polite, evasive gesture, and avoids a direct answer.

"In any case, my dear child, it is not love."

"Why?"

My old friend throws away his cigarette almost angrily.

"Because! You said to me just now: 'Marriage for a woman means accepting a painful and humiliating domesticity; it means *tie my tie, prepare me an emetic, keep an eye on my cutlet, put up with my bad temper and my betrayals.*' You ought to have said *love* and not *marriage.* For only love makes the bond-service you speak of easy and joyful and glorious. You hate it at present, you repudiate it and spew it from you, because you no longer love Taillandy. But remember the time when, in the name of love, the tie, the footbath and the camomile tea became sacred symbols, revered and terrible. Remember the miserable part you played! I used to shake with indignation at seeing you being used almost like a go-between, aiding and abetting Taillandy and his women friends, but when one day I lost all discretion and all patience, you answered me: 'To love is to obey.' Be frank, Renée, be clear-sighted, and tell me whether all your sacrifices haven't only lost their value in your eyes since you recovered your free will? You assess them at their true worth *now that you no longer love*. Before—I've seen you at it, I know you, Renée—did you not unconsciously enjoy the merciful numbness which love dispenses?"

What is the good of answering? Nevertheless I am ready to argue, with all the unfairness in the world: the only thing that could rouse my pity today is this poor man who lists my conjugal misfortunes while thinking of his own. How young and "hurtable" he is, and quite saturated with the poison he longed to get rid of! We've moved a long way from my adventure and from Maxime Dufferein-Chautel.

I wanted to confide in Hamond and ask his advice. What is it that always leads us, scratched all over with dead thorns, invincibly back to the past? I have the feeling that, if Maxime came in, Hamond and I would not have time enough to change those faces of ours that no one ought to see: Hamond is all yellow with bile, with a little nervous tic in his left cheek, and as for me, my brows are knitted as if in the throes of a migraine, and my neck is thrust tensely forward, that strong neck that is beginning to lose the smooth suppleness of its youthful flesh.

"Hamond," I say very gently, "to change the subject, you aren't forgetting that I have to go off on tour?"

"To go off. . . . Yes, of course," he says, like a man being wakened from sleep. "What of it?"

"What of it! What about Maxime?"

"You're taking him, naturally?"

" 'Naturally!' It's not as simple as you seem to think. Life on tour is terrible . . . for a couple. There are the awakenings and departures in the early hours or the middle of the night, and interminable evenings for the one who waits, and then the hotel! What a beginning for a honeymoon! Even a woman of twenty wouldn't dare to risk being surprised at dawn, or sleeping in the train, that sleep that comes at the end of exhausting days, when one looks like a slightly swollen corpse. No, no, that's too great a danger for me. And besides, he and I deserve better than that. I'd vaguely thought of postponing our . . ."

"Heart-to-heart . . ."

"Thank you . . . until the end of the tour, and then to begin a life, oh! such a life! Not to think any more, Hamond, to go to ground somewhere, with him, in a country where, within reach of my mouth and my hands, I should find everything that offers itself and then escapes from me on the other side of the train window: moist leaves, flowers nodding in the wind, fruits with the bloom on their skins, and above all, streams of free, wayward, living water. You know, Hamond, when you've been living in a train for thirty days, you can't think how the sight of running water, between banks of new grass, parches your whole skin with a kind of indefinable thirst. During my last tour, I remember, we used to travel all morning and often all afternoon too. At noon, the farm girls would be milking the cows in the fields: I could see, in the deep grass, pails of burnished copper where the foaming milk squirted in thin straight jets. What a thirst, what an agonised longing I used to feel for that warm milk, topped with foam. It was a real little daily torture, I assure you. That is why I want to enjoy, all at the same time, everything I lack: pure air, a generous country where everything is to be found, and my love."

Involuntarily, I stretch out my arms, with my hands clasped, in the effort to invoke all I desire. Hamond goes on listening as though I had not stopped speaking.

"And then, my child, afterwards?"

"What d'you mean, 'afterwards'?" I say vehemently. "Afterwards? But that's all. I don't ask for anything more."

"That's fortunate," he murmurs to himself. "I mean, how will you live after, with Maxime? You'll give up your tours? You won't . . . work any longer in the music-hall?"

This question of his, so natural, is enough to bring me up short, and I look at my old friend defiantly, anxiously, almost intimidated:

"Why shouldn't I?" I say, feebly.

He shrugs his shoulders.

"Come now, Renée, think for a moment. Thanks to Maxime you can live comfortably, even luxuriously, and take up again, as we all hope, that witty pen which is growing rusty. And then perhaps a child; what a fine little chap he would be!"

Rash Hamond! Is he yielding to his impulse as an ex-genre painter? This little picture of my future life, between a faithful lover and a beautiful child, produces in me the most inexplicable and disastrous effect. And he elaborates it, the poor wretch. He labours the point, without noticing the horrid gaiety dancing in my eyes which avoid his, and that the only replies he is getting from me are an occasional bored "yes", and the "I don't know, I suppose so", of a schoolgirl who is finding the lesson too long.

TWELVE

A BEAUTIFUL child; a faithful husband; after all there was nothing to laugh at in that. I am still wondering what was the reason for my cruel hilarity. A beautiful child; I confess that I have never thought of it. When I was married I had not the time, being occupied first with love and then with jealousy, monopolised, in a word, by Taillandy, who in any case was not at all anxious to encumber himself with an expensive progeny.

So here am I, having spent thirty-three years without ever considering the possibility of being a mother. Am I a monster? A beautiful child: grey eyes, a sharp little nose, and the look of a little fox, like his mother, big hands and broad shoulders, like Maxime. It's no good; no matter how much I try I can't *see* him and I don't love him, the child I might have had, that I perhaps shall have.

"Tell me, what d'you feel about it, darling Big-Noodle?"

He has just come in, very quietly, already so much a part of my mind that I go on with my soul-searching in his presence.

"What d'you feel about the child we might have? It's Hamond who wants one, would you believe it!"

My friend opens enormous eyes and a round, astonished Pierrot mouth, and cries: "Long live Hamond! He shall have his kid, right away if you like, Renée."

I defend myself, for he goes for me with a mixture of roughness and passion, biting a little and kissing a lot, with that famished air which makes me feel just pleasantly frightened.

"A child!" he cries, "a little one of our own! I'd never thought of it, Renée. How intelligent Hamond is! It's a brilliant idea."

"D'you think so, my darling? Selfish brute that you are! It doesn't matter a scrap to you that I should be deformed and ugly, and that I should suffer, does it?"

He laughs again and pins me down on the divan at arms' length.

"Deformed? Ugly? What a goose you are, Madame! You'll be

magnificent, and so will the little one too, and it will all be the greatest fun."

Then all at once he stops laughing and draws his fierce eyebrows together above his gentle eyes.

"And then, at least, you'd never be able to leave me and go gadding about the world all alone, would you? You'd be caught."

Caught. I give in, and play lazily with the fingers which hold me. But giving in is also a ruse of the weak. Caught. He did indeed say that, in a transport of egoism. I summed him up correctly, the time when I laughingly called him a monogamous bourgeois, and a home-loving paterfamilias.

So I might end my days, peacefully, dwarfed by his large shadow? Would his faithful eyes still love me when my graces had faded one by one? Ah, what a difference, what a difference from *the other!* Except that *the other* also spoke as a master and knew how to say under his breath, as he gripped me with a rough grasp: "Keep your head up and walk on, I'm holding you!" How I suffer! Their differences hurt me and so do their resemblances. And I stroke the forehead of this one, so unaware and innocent, and call him "my little one".

"Don't call me your 'little one', darling, it makes me ridiculous."

"I'll make you ridiculous if I want to. You are my little one because you're younger than . . . than your age, because you've suffered very little, and loved very little, because you aren't cruel. . . . Listen to me, my little one: I'm going away."

"Not without me, Renée!"

How he cried out! It makes me shiver with pain and pleasure.

"Without you, my darling, without you. I must. Listen to me. No . . . Max . . . I shall speak all the same, after . . . Listen Max. D'you mean you don't want to, you can't, wait for me? Don't you love me enough then?"

He tears himself from my hands and draws violently away from me.

"Not enough, not enough! Oh, these womanish reasonings! I don't love you enough if I follow you, and not enough if I stay. Admit it: if I'd answered you: 'Very well, darling, I'll wait for you', what would you have thought of me? And you, who go away when you could quite well not go away, how d'you expect me to believe that you love me? After all . . ."

He plants himself in front of me, head thrust forward and suddenly suspicious: "After all, you've never said it to me."

"Said what?"

"That you love me."

I feel myself blushing as if he had caught me out in something.

"You've never said it to me," he repeats obstinately.

"Oh Max!"

"You've said to me . . . you've said to me: 'Darling . . . my beloved Big-Noodle . . . Max . . . my darling love', and you groaned aloud, as though you were singing, the day when . . ."

"Max!"

"Yes, that day when you couldn't prevent yourself from calling me 'My love', but you've never said to me: 'I love you.'"

It is true. I had desperately hoped that he would not notice it. One day, another lovely day, I sighed so loudly in his arms that the words "love you" breathed from me like a slightly louder sigh, and all at once I became silent and cold.

"Love you." I don't want to say it again, never again. I never want to hear again that voice, my voice of other days, broken and low, irresistibly murmuring that word of long ago. Only, I know no other that will do. There is no other.

"Tell me, tell me that you love me. Tell me, I implore you."

My lover has knelt down before me and his imperious prayer will give me no peace. I smile in his face, as if I were resisting him for fun, and all of a sudden I want to hurt him so that he may suffer a little too. But he is so gentle, so far away from my suffering. Why should I hold him responsible for it? He doesn't deserve that.

"Poor darling, don't be naughty, don't be sad. Yes, I love you, I love you, oh, I do love you. But I don't want to say it to you. I'm so proud at heart, if you only knew."

Leaning against my breast, he closes his eyes, accepts my lie with a fond assurance, and goes on hearing me say "I love you" when I have ceased to speak.

What a strange burden he seems to these arms that have been empty for so long! I don't know how to rock so big a child, and how heavy his head is! But let him rest there, sure of me. Sure of me because he is a prey to a time-honoured delusion which makes him jealous of my present and my roving future, but lets him rest trustfully against this heart that another inhabited for so long. Rash and honest lover that he is, it does not occur to him that he shares me with a memory, and that he will never taste that best of all glories, the glory of being able to say to me: "I bring you a joy and a sorrow that you have never known."

There he is, on my breast. Why he, and not another? I don't know. I gaze down at his brow, I feel I want to protect him against myself, to excuse myself for giving him only a heart that has been deconsecrated, if not cleansed. I would like to safeguard him against the harm I can do him. Well, there it is as Margot foretold: I'm going back to the fire. But a reliable fire this time, with nothing infernal about it; in fact much more like a family kettle.

"Wake up, darling."

"I'm not asleep," he murmurs, without lifting his beautiful lashes. "I'm breathing you in."

"You'll wait for me in Paris, while I'm on tour? Or will you go to your mother's in the Ardennes?"

He gets up without answering and smooths his hair with the flat of his hand.

"Well?"

He takes his hat from the table and turns to go with lowered eyes, still silent. With a bound I am on him, clinging to his shoulders: "Don't go away, don't go away! I'll do whatever you want, come back, don't leave me alone, oh, don't leave me alone!"

Whatever has happened to me? I've suddenly become nothing but a poor wisp of a thing, drenched with tears. It seemed to me that if he went away, with him would go warmth and light and that second love all mingled with the burning ashes of the first, but so dear, so unhoped for. I cling to my lover with the hands of a drowning person, and stammer over and over again without hearing it: "Everyone leaves me, I'm all alone."

Loving me as he does, he well knows that there is no need of words or reasonings to calm me, but only cradling arms, a warm murmur of vague caressing words, and kisses, endless kisses.

"Don't look at me, my darling, I'm ugly, my eye-black has got rubbed off and my nose is red. I'm ashamed to have been so foolish."

"My Renée, my little, little one, what a brute I've been. Yes, yes, I'm just a big brute. You want me to wait for you in Paris? I will. You want me to go to mother's? I'll go to mother's."

Undecided, and embarrassed by my victory, I no longer know what I want.

"Listen, Max darling, this is what we must do. I shall go away, alone, about as eagerly as a whipped dog. We'll write to each other

every day. And we'll put up with it heroically, won't we, so as to get
to the date, the beautiful fifteenth of May, which will reunite us?"

The hero agrees sadly, with a resigned nod.

"The fifteenth of May, Max! I feel," say I in a lower voice, "that
that day I shall throw myself into your arms as I would throw myself
into the sea, as freely and as irremediably."

He replies to this with a look and an embrace which make me lose
my head a little.

"And then, listen. If we can't wait, well never mind, you'll come
and join me, I'll send for you. Now are you happy? After all, it's silly
to be heroic and life's so short. That's fixed then. Whoever is the
unhappier will join the other, or write to the other to come. But
we'll still try, because a honeymoon in the train . . . Is it all right
now? What are you looking for?"

"I'm thirsty, can you believe it, absolutely dying of thirst. Would
you mind ringing for Blandine?"

"No need for her. You stay there and I'll go and get the things."

Happy and passive, he lets himself be waited on, and I watch him
drinking as though he were granting me a great favour. If he wants
me to, I'll tie his tie and decide what we'll have for dinner. And I'll
bring him his slippers. And he shall ask me: "Where are you going?"
as though he were my master. A female I was and, for better or
worse, a female I find myself to be.

Relying on the dusk to hide my face whose ravages I have hastily
restored, I sit on his knee and let him drink from my lips the breath
that is still uneven from my sobs of a moment ago. One of his hands
slides down from my forehead to my breast and I kiss it as it passes.
Held in his arms, I fall back again into the state of a cherished victim who protests feebly against something she would not prevent if
she could.

But all of a sudden I spring to my feet, struggle with him for a few
seconds without saying a word, and finally manage to free myself crying "No!"

I had very nearly let myself be taken by surprise, there on that
corner of the divan, his attempt was so swift and so clever. Out of
reach, I look at him without anger and merely reproach him with:
"Why did you do that? That was very naughty, Max."

Obedient and repentant, he sidles towards me, knocking over a little table and some chairs on his way, and murmuring "Forgive me

. . . won't do it again . . . darling, it's so hard to wait . . ." in a somewhat exaggerated tone of childish supplication.

It is nearly dark now and I can no longer make out his features clearly. But I suspected that the suddenness of that attempt a moment ago was due as much to calculation as loss of control. "You would have been caught, and then you would no longer have gone off wandering about the world all on your own."

"Poor Max," I say to him, gently.

"Are you laughing at me? Have I been silly?" He humbles himself nicely, and cleverly. He wants to bring my thoughts back to the gesture itself, and so to prevent me from thinking of his true motives. And I lie a tiny bit, to reassure him.

"I'm not laughing at you, Max. There are precious few men, you know, who would risk losing all their prestige by throwing themselves on a woman as you did, you great idiot. It's your clumsy peasant air which saves you, and those eyes, like an amorous wolf's. You looked like a day labourer tumbling a girl by the roadside on his way home from work at nightfall."

I leave him, to go and encircle my eyes again with the blue outline which makes them velvety and shining, to put on a coat and to pin on my head one of those bell-shaped hats whose form and whose colours remind Max of Champfleury's "Animated Flowers", those little flower-fairies who wear on their heads a poppy inside-out, the cup of a lily-of-the-valley, or a big iris with drooping petals.

We go off together for a gentle drive in the motor in the darkness of the Bois. These evening promenades are dear to me, when I hold my love's hand in the dim light, to know that he is there and for him to know that I am there. Then I can close my eyes and dream that I am going away with him to an unknown country where I shall have no past and no name, and where I shall be born again with a new face and an untried heart.

THIRTEEN

ONE week more and I leave.

Shall I really leave? There are hours and days when I doubt it. Especially days of premature spring, when my love takes me to those parks outside Paris, flattened and rutted with motors and bicycles, yet made mysterious all the same by the sharp, fresh season. Towards the end of the afternoon, a mauve mist veils the avenues so that you do not know where they end, and the unexpected discovery of a wild hyacinth, with its three slender bells of artless blue swaying in the wind, has all the charm of a stolen joy.

On a sunny morning last week we went for a long walk in the Bois, where the grooms gallop their horses. Walking side by side, we felt energetic and happy but not very talkative, and I was humming a little song which makes you walk fast. At a bend in a deserted riding-track we stopped, nose to muzzle before a very young hind with a golden coat, who lost countenance at sight of us and stopped short instead of fleeing.

She was panting with emotion and her delicate knees trembled, but her long eyes, made longer still by a brown line—like mine— expressed more embarrassment than fear. I would have liked to touch her ears, which were pointed towards us and plushy like the leaves of mullein, and that soft velveteen muzzle. But when I stretched out my hand, she turned her forehead away timidly and disappeared.

"You wouldn't have killed her, out hunting, Max?"

"Kill a hind? Why not a woman?" he answered, simply.

That day we lunched at Ville-d'Avray, like everyone else, in that restaurant with the curious terraces, terraces for eating and sleeping, that overhang the edge of the water, and we were as sensible as lovers already surfeited with pleasure. I was glad to find that the open air and the pure wind and the trees inspired in Max the same exhilarating serenity with which they always fill me. I gazed at the

smooth water of the pool, turbid water with patches of iridescence
on its surface, and at the hazel bushes with their hanging catkins.
Then my eyes returned to this good comrade who had come into my
life, full of the firm hope that I might build for him a happiness that
would endure as long as that life itself.

Shall I really leave? There are times when I busy myself, as if in a
dream, with my departure. My sponge-bag, my rolled-up rug and my
waterproof, unearthed from cupboards, have reappeared in the light
of day, streaked and shapeless and looking as though they were worn
out with travelling. Full of disgust, I turned out containers filled
with rancid cold cream and yellowed Vaseline stinking of paraffin.

For the time being I take no pleasure in handling these tools of
my trade. And when Brague came round to see how I was getting on,
I received him so absent-mindedly and offhandedly that he departed
in a huff and, much more serious, with a very polite "au revoir, dear
friend". Never mind, there will be plenty of time to see him and
smooth him out during those forty days. I am expecting him very
soon now, to give me my final instructions. Max will come a little
later.

"Good-morning, dear friend."

I thought as much; my comrade is still ruffled.

"No really, Brague, that's enough. That high-falutin' style doesn't
suit you at all. We're here to talk business. You remind me of
Dranem as the Sun-King when you call me 'dear friend'."

Quickly amused, Brague protests: "High-falutin' style indeed, and
why not? I can outdo Castellane when I want to. Have you never
seen me in a dress suit?"

"No."

"Neither have I. I say, it's dark in this little . . . boudoir of yours.
Why don't we go into your bedroom? We could see better to talk."

"All right, let's go into my bedroom."

Brague immediately spots, on the mantelpiece, a photograph of
Max: Max looking stiff in a new suit, the black of his hair too black,
the white of his eyes too white, formal and slightly absurd but very
handsome all the same.

Brague examines the portrait, as he rolls his cigarette.

"Definitely your 'friend', this chap, isn't he?"

"It's . . . my friend, yes." And I simper, idiotically.

"He's smart, there's no denying it. You'd take him for someone in the government. What are you laughing at?"

"Nothing. Just the thought that he might be in the government. That's hardly his line."

Brague holds a match to his cigarette and watches me out of the corners of his eyes.

"Taking him with you?"

I shrug my shoulders: "No, of course not. I couldn't. How could you expect . . ."

"But I don't *expect*, that's just it," cried Brague, his equanimity restored. "I think that's very right of you, my girl. You wouldn't believe how many tours I've seen bitched up because Madame wouldn't leave Monsieur, or because Monsieur wanted to keep an eye on Madame. It's nothing but arguments, billings and cooings, quarrels, reconciliations when they simply can't get out of bed, or else they totter feebly about the stage with black-ringed eyes: in short, it ruins the whole thing. Give me a cheerful trip where we're all pals. You know how I've always said that love and work don't go together, and I've never changed my mind about that. Besides, after all, forty days isn't eternity; you write to each other and when it's over you meet and team up again. Has he got an office, your friend?"

"An office? No, he hasn't got an office."

"Well, does he . . . make motor-cars? I mean, he's got some sort of business?"

"No."

"He does nothing?"

"Nothing."

Brague lets out a whistle that might be interpreted in at least two ways.

"Absolutely nothing at all?"

"Nothing. That's to say, he owns some forests."

"It's staggering."

"What staggers you?"

"That anyone can live like that. No office. No factory. No rehearsals. No racing stables. Doesn't it seem comic to you?"

I look up at him with an embarrassed and slightly conspiratorial air. "Yes."

I cannot make any other answer. My friend's idleness, that mooning about like a schoolboy on perpetual holiday, often fills me with dismay and almost scandalises me.

"It would kill me," declares Brague, after a silence. "A matter of habit."

"No doubt."

"Now," says Brague, sitting down, "let's be brief and to the point. You've got everything you need?"

"Of course I have! My Dryad's costume, the new one, is a dream. Green as a little grasshopper and weighs less than a pound. The other's been done up and re-embroidered and cleaned, and you'd swear it was new: it can do another sixty shows without showing any signs of wear."

Brague purses his mouth.

"H'm . . . you sure? You ought to have managed to stump up a new rig for *The Pursuit*."

"That's right, and you'd have paid me for it, wouldn't you? And talking about *The Pursuit*, what about your embroidered buckskin breeches that have taken on the colour of all the boards that have covered them with polish, am I reproaching you with them?"

My comrade lifts a dogmatic hand: "Don't let's confuse things, if you don't mind. My breeches are magnificent. They've taken on a patina, a richness; they have the colour of fine earthenware. It would be a crime to replace them."

"You're just a skinflint," I tell him, shrugging my shoulders.

"And you're a harpy."

It does us a world of good to go for each other a bit, it refreshes us. We're both just sufficiently roused for the dispute to seem like a lively rehearsal.

"Break it up!" cried Brague. "The costume question is settled. Now for the baggage question."

"As if I needed you for that! This isn't exactly the first time we've been away together, you know. Are you going to teach me how to fold my chemises?"

From between eyelids wrinkled by his grimaces on the stage, Brague casts on me a crushing look.

"You poor thing. Lop-sided and ill-shaped brain, go on. Talk, natter away, rouse your bee and let it buzz. Am I going to teach you? As if I could teach you! Listen, and try to take it in: we have to pay for our excess baggage ourselves, don't we?"

"Shh!"

I sign to him to stop, agitated because I have heard two discreet rings on the bell in the antechamber. It is *he*, and Brague is still there. After all, they know each other.

"Come in, Max, come in. It's Brague. We're talking of the tour; it won't bore you?"

No, it does not bore him; but it embarrasses me a little. These music-hall matters are poor, precise, commercial things, which I want to keep separate from my love, my darling lazy love.

Brague, very nice when he wants to be, smiles at Max.

"You don't mind, sir? It's our professional mixture we're stirring, and I pride myself on being an economical cook who wastes nothing and doesn't make a bit on the side."

"Oh, please go on," cries Max. "On the contrary, it will amuse me, since it's all new to me. I shall learn."

Liar. For a man who is being amused, he looks very bad-tempered and very sad.

"As I was saying," Brague begins, "on the last tour, the September one, if you remember we got through ten or eleven francs for excess baggage every day, as if we'd been Carnegie."

"Not all the time, Brague."

"No, not all the time. There were days when we paid three francs or four francs excess. Even that's too much. As far as I'm concerned, I've had enough of it. What have you got in the way of luggage, besides your suitcase?"

"My black trunk."

"The big one? It's madness. I won't have it."

Max coughs.

"This is what you'll do: you'll use mine. In the top-layer: stage costumes. Second compartment; our underthings, your chemises, your knickers and your stockings, my shirts, my pants, etcetera."

Max fidgets.

". . . and at the bottom, shoes, change of suit for you and me, oddments, etcetera. Understand?"

"Yes, not a bad idea."

"All the same . . ." says Max.

"Like that," goes on Brague, "we've got just one piece of big luggage (the Troglodyte'll manage somehow. His mother, who's a poultry plucker, will lend him a basket) one, in all and for all. That means no excess, and reduction of tips to station porters, stage hands, etcetera. If we don't each make five francs a day on that, I'm a Dutchman. You change your underwear every how often, on tour?"

I blush, because of Max.

"Every two days."

"That's your affair. We can get our washing done in the big burgs, Lyons, etcetera. So I reckon twelve chemises and twelve little pantikins, and the rest in proportion; isn't that big and generous? In short, I rely on you to be reasonable."

"Don't worry."

Brague gets up and grasps Max's hand.

"You see it doesn't take long to button up, sir. As for you, rendezvous at the station, at quarter past seven on Tuesday morning."

I accompany him as far as the antechamber and, when I come back, a tempest of protestations, lamentations and reproaches greets me.

"Renée, it's monstrous, it isn't possible, you've lost your head. Your chemises, your own chemises, and your far-too-short little pantaloons, my darling love, hugger-mugger with the underdrawers of that individual. And your stockings with his socks, I dare say. How contemptible and how sordid!"

"How d'you mean, how sordid? It mounts up to two hundred francs."

"That's just what I mean, it's all so paltry."

I restrain a reply which would wound him: where could he, the spoilt child, have learnt that money, the money one earns, is a respectable, serious thing which one handles with care and speaks about solemnly?

He wipes his forehead with a beautiful handkerchief of violet silk. For some time past my friend has shown a great concern for elegance: he has magnificent shirts, handkerchiefs to match his ties, and shoes with doe-skin spats. I have not failed to notice this for, on this dear Big-Noodle with his somewhat heavy build, the slightest detail of dress takes on an almost shocking importance.

"Why do you agree to it?" he asks me reproachfully. "It's odious, this promiscuity."

Promiscuity. I was expecting that word. It is widely used. The "promiscuity of the stage".

"Tell me, darling," I say, tapering the points of his silky, rusty-black moustache between two fingers, "if it were a question of *your* shirts and *your* underdrawers, that wouldn't be *promiscuity*? You must remember that I'm only a very sensible little 'caf' conc' ' who lives by her job."

He suddenly embraces me, crushing me a little on purpose.

"The devil take your job. Ah, when I have you all to myself, you'll see. I'll absolutely load you with first-class carriages, and racks full of flowers, and frocks and frocks, and every beautiful thing I can find and everything I can invent."

His beautiful sombre voice ennobles this commonplace promise. Beneath the words I can hear, vibrating in it, his desire to lay the whole universe at my feet.

Frocks? I realise he must find my tailored suits of grey, brown and dark blue very monotonous and severe, a kind of neutral chrysalis which I exchange, once the footlights are lit, for painted gauzes, shining spangles, and iridescent swirling skirts. First-class carriages? What for? They don't go any further than the others.

Fossette has squeezed between us her monk-like skull, which gleams like rosewood. My little companion scents a departure. She has recognised the suitcase, with its rubbed corners, and the waterproof, she has seen the black-enamelled English tin box and the make-up case. She knows that I shall not take her, and resigns herself in advance to a life, petted it must be added, of rambles on the fortifications, evenings with the concierge, dinners in town and teas in the Bois. "I know you'll come back," say her slit eyes, "but when?"

"Max, she's very fond of you; you'll look after her?"

There now, the mere fact of bending together over this anxious little creature makes our tears overflow. I hold mine back with an effort which makes my throat and nose sting. How beautiful my love's eyes look, enlarged by the two lustrous tears which wet his eyelashes. Ah, why leave him?

"In a little while," he murmurs in a stifled voice, "I'll go and fetch a . . . beautiful little handbag . . . that I've ordered for you . . . very strong . . . for the journey. . . ."

"Oh, Max, have you?"

"In . . . pigskin. . . ."

"Max, come now, be a bit braver than I am."

He blows his nose, rebelliously.

"Why should I? I don't want to be brave, I don't. On the contrary."

"We're absurd. Neither would have dared to give way to our feelings on our own account, but Fossette has set us off. It's the trick of the 'little table' in *Manon*, and of the one-armed man in *Poliche*, d'you remember?"

Max dries his eyes, very slowly and carefully, with the simplicity with which he does everything, and which saves him from ridicule.

"I daresay you're right, my Renée. Anyway, if ever you want to turn me into a fountain, you need only talk to me of everything

which surrounds you here in this little flat, everything that I shan't
see again until you return. This old divan, the armchair where you sit
to read, and your portraits, and the ray of sunshine gliding over the
carpet from midday until two o'clock." He smiles, very moved.
"Don't talk to me of the coal-shovel, of the hearth or the tongs or I
shall break down!"

He has gone to get the beautiful little pigskin handbag.

"When we live together," he said to me wheedlingly, before he
went out, "will you give me the furniture of this little sitting-room?
I'll have some more made for you."

I smiled, to avoid refusing. These bits and pieces at Max's? For
lack of money I have never replaced these relics of my conjugal
home, which Taillandy let me take by way of contemptible compen-
sation for the author's rights of which he formerly cheated me.
What a "little table" aria I could sing about that would-be Dutch
fumed oak, about that old divan worn into hollows by wanton games
to which I was not bidden! Haunted furniture it is, amidst which I
have often awakened with the mad fear that my liberty was only a
dream. A strange wedding-present for a new lover. A shelter, and not
a home, that is all I leave behind me: first- and second-class travelling boxes, hotels of every type, and sordid music-hall dressing-rooms
in Paris and the provinces and abroad, have been more familiar and
more benevolent to me than this place which my love calls "a
charming, cosy nest".

How many times, in fleeing from myself, have I not fled from this
ground floor? Today when, beloved and in love, I am leaving, I
would like to be still more loved, still more loving, and so changed as
to be unrecognisable in my own eyes. No doubt it is too soon, and
the time has not yet come. But at least I am leaving with a troubled
mind, overflowing with regret and hope, urged to return and
reaching out towards my new lot with the glorious impulse of a serpent sloughing off its dead skin.

PART THREE

ONE

"Goodbye, my dear love. My trunk is shut. My lovely pigskin bag, my travelling costume, and the long veil to go over my hat are laid out on our big divan, looking sad and sensible and awaiting my awakening tomorrow. Out of reach of you and my own weakness, I feel I have left already, so I give myself the joy of writing you my first love-letter.

"You'll receive this express-letter tomorrow morning, just at the time when I'm leaving Paris. It's merely an au revoir, written before I sleep, to let you know that I love you so much, that you mean so much to me! I am desolate at leaving you.

"Don't forget that you've promised to write to me 'all the time', and to console Fossette. And on my side I promise to bring you back a Renée tired of touring, grown thinner with solitude, and freed from everything, except you.

Your
Renée."

The swift shadow of a bridge passes rapidly over my eyelids which I was keeping closed, and I open them again to see, receding rapidly on the left of the train, that little field of potatoes that I know so well, huddled against the high wall of the fortifications.

I am alone in the compartment. Brague, severely economical, is travelling second with the Old Troglodyte. A wet day, languid as a grey dawn, lies heavy over the countryside with its trails of smoke from factories. It is eight o'clock and the first morning of my trip. After a short period of dejection, following the agitation of departure, I had fallen into a glum immobility which made me hope for sleep.

I pull myself together and proceed to make my preparations, mechanically, like an old campaigner: I unfold the camel-hair travelling-rug, blow up the two silk-covered rubber cushions—one for my back and one for the nape of my neck—and hide my hair under a

veil of the same bronze colour. I do all that methodically and carefully, though a sudden indescribable anger makes my hands tremble
the while. A real fury, yes, and against myself. I am leaving, each
turn of the wheel carries me further from Paris, I am leaving, while
an icy spring adorns the tips of the oak branches with frozen pearls;
all is cold and damp, with a mist which smells of winter still, and I
am leaving when I might at this hour be lying, relaxed with pleasure,
against the warm side of a lover. I feel as though my anger were
whetting in me a devouring appetite for all that is pleasant, luxurious, easy and selfish, a need to let myself slide down the softest
slope, and embrace with arms and lips a belated happiness that is
tangible and ordinary and delicious.

How tedious to me is everything that I see in this familiar suburb,
with its pallid villas where the yawning housewives in their chemises
rise late to shorten the empty days. I would have done better not to
have left Brague, to have remained with him in the dirty, blue-
cushioned seats of the second-class carriages, among the good-natured chatter, the human odour of the crowded compartment, and
the smoke of cigarettes at sixpence the packet.

The ta-ta-tam of the train, which I hear in spite of myself, acts as
an accompaniment to the dance motif of *The Dryad*, which I hum
with the persistence of one possessed. How long will this impression
of having dwindled last? For I feel myself diminished, and weakened, as though I had been bled. During my saddest days the sight
of a quite ordinary landscape, as long as it was receding rapidly to
right and left, and as long as it was veiled from time to time with a
ribbon of smoke that got torn on the thorn hedges, acted all the
same on me like a health-giving tonic. I am cold. A wretched morning sleep numbs me, and I feel as though I were fainting rather than
sleeping, agitated by childish arithmetical dreams in which this weari-
some question keeps recurring: "if you have left half of yourself
behind, does that mean you have lost fifty per cent of your original
value?"

TWO

Dijon, April 3rd.

"Yes, yes, I'm well. Yes, I found your letter; yes, I'm having a success. Ah, my darling, know the whole truth. When I left you I sank into the most absurd, the most impatient despair. Why did I go away? Why did I leave you? Forty days! I shall never be able to bear that, now. And I'm only at the third town.

>At the third town
>Her lover puts on her
>A gown of gold and a silver gown.

"Alas, my lover, I need neither silver nor gold, but only you. It rained at my first two stopping-places, to make me realise better my hateful desertion, there between hotel walls papered with chocolate and beige, and in those imitation oak dining-rooms which the gas makes darker still.

"You don't know what discomfort is, you spoilt son of Madame Ever-Cut. When we're together again, just to rouse your indignation and make you cherish me still more, I'll tell you of the returns at midnight to the hotel, with the make-up box weighing heavily on my tired arm, the waiting at the door under the fine mist while the night-porter slowly wakes, the horrible room with its badly-dried sheets, the minute jug of hot water which has had time to get cold. And should I make you share these daily joys? No, my darling, let me exhaust my own powers of resistance before I cry to you 'Come, I can't bear it another minute!'

"Anyway, it's fine here at Dijon, and I welcome this sun timidly, like a present that's going to be quickly taken away from me.

"You promised me to console Fossette. She's yours as much as mine. Take care not to overwhelm her with attentions while I'm away, or she won't forgive you. Her bulldog sensibility is such as to impose on her an exquisite repression of her feelings, and when I de-

sert her, she greatly resents it if some affectionate third person notices her grief, even by an attempt to distract her from it.

"Goodbye, goodbye, I kiss you and I love you. Such a cold twilight
today, you can't imagine. The sky's as green and pure as it is in January when it's freezing hard. Write to me, love me, warm your

Renée."

April 10th.

"My last letter must have made you unhappy. I'm not pleased
with myself, nor with you either. You have a beautiful writing, bold
and round, and at the same time slender, elegant and curly, like the
plant that in my part of the world we call 'flowering osier'; it fills
four or even eight pages with loving maledictions and the most burning regrets and a few 'I adore you's'. It can be read in twenty seconds
and I'm sure you genuinely think you've written me a long letter.
Moreover, you talk of nothing but me in it.

"My darling, I've just passed through, without stopping, a region
which belongs to me because I spent my childhood there. I felt as
though a long caress were stroking my heart. One day, promise me,
we'll go there together? No, no—what am I writing—we won't go
there. In your memory your Ardennes forests would put to shame my
coppices of oaks and brambles and whitebeam, and you would not
see, as I do, trembling above them and the shadowy waters of the
springs, and above the blue hill adorned with the tall flowers of the
thistle, the slender rainbow which magically enshrines all things in
the place where I was born.

"Nothing has changed there. A few new roofs, bright red, that's
all. Nothing has changed in my part of the world—except me. Ah,
my darling love, how old I am! Can you really love such an old
young woman? I blush for myself, here. Why did you not know the
tall child who used to trail her regal braids here, silent by nature as a
wood nymph? All that, which once I was, I gave to another, to another than you! Forgive me for this cry, Max, it is the cry of my torment, which I've kept in ever since I loved you. And now that it's
too late, are not the things you love in me the things which change
me and deceive you, my curls clustering thick as leaves, my eyes
which the blue kohl lengthens and suffuses, the artificial smoothness
of my powdered skin? What would you say if I were to reappear, if I
appeared before you with my heavy, straight hair, with my fair lashes
cleansed of their mascara, in short with the eyes which my mother
gave me, crowned with brief eyebrows quick to frown, grey, narrow,

level eyes in the depths of which there shines a stern, swift glance
which I recognise as that of my father?

"Don't be afraid, my darling love, I shall return to you more or
less as I left you, a little more weary, a little more tender. Every time
I touch the fringes of it, my own country casts a spell on me, filling
me with sad, transitory rapture; but I would not dare to stop there.
Perhaps it is only beautiful because I have lost it.

"Goodbye, dear, dear Max. We have to leave very early tomorrow,
for Lyons, otherwise we shouldn't have our rehearsal with the orchestra, which I look after while Brague, never tired, sees to the
programmes, the putting of our posters in the frames, and the sale of
our postcards.

"Oh, how cold I was, last night again, in the flimsy dress I wear
for The Pursuit. Cold is my enemy, it paralyses my life and my
thoughts. You know that, you in whose hands my own seek refuge,
curled up like two leaves under the frost. I miss you, my dear
warmth, as much as I miss the sun.

Your
Renée."

THREE

On we go. I eat, sleep, walk, mime and dance. No zest, but no effort.
There is just one moment of excitement in the whole day, the moment when I ask the porter at the music-hall if there is "any post"
for me. I read my letters like one starved, leaning against the greasy
doorpost of the artistes' entry, in the foetid draught that smells of
cellars and ammonia. But they make time hang more heavily afterwards, when there is no more left to read, when I have deciphered
the date of the postmark and turned the envelope inside out as if I
hoped to see a flower or a photo fall out of it.

I pay no attention to the towns where we play. I know them and
have no wish to explore them again. So I just tack on to Brague, who
goes about like a good-humoured conqueror taking possession once
more of those familiar "little old burgs"—Rheims, Nancy, Belfort
and Besançon.

"That little coffee shop's still at the corner of the quay, did you
notice? I bet they recognise me when we go and dig in to their sau-
sage with white wine this evening."

He takes deep breaths, darts down the streets with the joy of a
vagabond, loiters round the shops, and climbs up to the cathedrals.
Last year it was I who led him, but now I accompany him. He trails
me along in his shadow, and sometimes we take the Old Troglodyte
in tow too, though normally he goes off alone, gaunt and seedy-look-
ing in his thin jacket and over-short trousers. Where does he sleep?
Where does he eat? I don't know. When I asked Brague he answered briefly: "Where he likes. I'm not his nurse."

The other evening, at Nancy, I caught sight of the Troglodyte in
his dressing-room. He was standing there biting into a pound loaf
and holding a slice of brawn delicately between two fingers. The
sight of that poor man's meal, and the voracious movement of his
jaws, made my heart contract and I went to find Brague.

"Brague, has the Troglodyte enough to live on on tour? He really does earn fifteen francs, doesn't he? Why doesn't he feed better?"

"He's saving," answers Brague. "*Everyone* saves on tour. *Everyone* isn't Vanderbilt or Renée Néré, to treat themselves to rooms at five francs and *café-au-laits* served in their rooms. The Troglodyte owes me for his costume, which I advanced him; he pays me for it at the rate of five francs a day. In twenty days he'll be able to guzzle oysters and wash his feet in cocktails if he likes. That's his affair."

Thus rebuked, I say no more. And I too "save", first out of habit and then to imitate my companions, so as to excite neither their jealousy nor their contempt. Can she be Max's love, that woman with the calm, indifferent, unsociable look of those who belong neither here nor elsewhere, reflected in the smoke-blackened mirror of a "Brasserie Lorraine" where she is dining, that traveller with the dark-ringed eyes, a travelling veil knotted under her chin, and everything about her, from her hat to her boots, the colour of the road? Can she be Max's lover, the pale lover whom he used to embrace half-naked in a rose-coloured kimono, that tired comedienne who comes along, in corset and petticoat, to hunt in Brague's trunk for her chemise, her linen for the next day, and to put away her spangled draperies?

Every day I wait for my love's letter. Every day it consoles me and disappoints me at the same time. He writes simply but obviously not with ease. His beautiful flowery writing slows up the natural impetus of his hand. And then his tenderness and his sadness both constrain him, as he ingenuously laments: "When I've told you a hundred times that I love you and that I'm horribly cross with you for having left me, what more can I say? My darling wife, my little blue-stocking of a wife, you'll laugh at me but I don't care. My brother is leaving for the Ardennes and I'm going with him. Write to me at Salles-Neuves, care of my mother. I'm going to collect some money, some money for us, for our home, little sweetheart."

This is the way he tells me of his doings and what is happening to him, with no commentary and without frills. He associates me with his life and calls me his wife. He has no idea that by the time his warm solicitude reaches me it has become no more than a beautifully even writing, all cold on the paper; so far apart, what help to us are words? One needs—oh, I don't know—perhaps some passionate drawing, all glowing with colour.

FOUR

"So now you're getting Blandine to tell your fortune from the cards! This really is the limit. My darling, you're lost. Whenever I leave the house, that girl always prophesies the most picturesque catastrophes. If I go on tour she dreams of cats and serpents, turbid waters and folded sheets, and reads in the cards the tragic adventures of Renée Néré (the Queen of Clubs) with the False Young Man, the Soldier and the Rustic. Don't listen to her, Max. Count the days as I do, and smile—oh, that smile that makes hardly perceptible wrinkles in your nostrils—to think that the first week is almost over.

"I myself prophesy to you that, in one month and four days, I shall 'steer my course' to rejoin the 'Big-hearted Man' and that 'you will have great joy of it' and that the False Young Man will be 'thwarted', as will also the mysterious 'Woman of Ill-Fame', by whom I mean the Queen of Diamonds.

"Here we are for five days at Lyons. That'll be a rest, did you say? Yes, if by that you mean that for four mornings running I shall be able to wake up with a start at daybreak, scared to death of missing my train, and then fall back on my bed in a state of exhausted laziness that drives sleep away, and listen for a long time to the servants getting up round me, to the bells, and the traffic in the street. It is much worse, my darling, than the daily departure at dawn. I have the impression that I'm looking on, from the depths of my bed, at a fresh start from which I'm excluded, that the world is beginning to 'turn' without me. And then it is in the depths of my bed, too, when I'm a prey to my memories and overcome with boredom, that I most long for you.

"O dear enemy, we might have spent five days together here. Don't mistake this for a challenge; I don't want you to come. Don't worry, I shan't die of it, lord no! You always seem to think that *being away from you has killed me already. My handsome peasant, all it does is to benumb me, I'm hibernating.*

"It's stopped raining and it's mild and damp and grey, the best kind of Lyons weather. It's rather absurd, the way these meteorological reports crop up in all my letters, but if you only knew how, on tour, both our fate and our moods hang on the colour of the sky. 'Wet weather, dry pocket,' says Brague.

"In the last four years I've spent seven or eight weeks in Lyons. My first visit was to see the deer in the park of Saint-Jean, those little blonde fawns with their unseeing, tender gaze. There are so many of them, and all so alike, that I can't single one out; they follow me down the length of the wire-netting with a trot which pits the soil like hail, and beg black bread with clear, persistent, timid bleats. The smell of the turf, of the churned-up earth, is so strong in this garden, under the still air at the end of the day, that it would be able to carry me back to you if I attempted to escape.

"Goodbye, darling. Here in Lyons I've run again into some wanderers of my own sort whom I met here or elsewhere. If I were to tell you that one is called Cavaillon, a comic singer, and the other Amalia Barally, who plays the duennas in comedies, you wouldn't be much the wiser. Yet Barally is almost a friend, for we played together in a three-act play all round France, two years ago. She is a one-time beauty, a dark woman with a Roman face, an accomplished trouper, who knows by name every inn in the world. She has sung in operetta in Saigon, acted in comedies in Cairo, and enlivened the evenings of I don't know what khedive.

"What I appreciate in her, in addition to her gaiety which is proof against poverty, is her protective nature, that skill in looking after people, a delicate motherliness in her gestures which you find in women who have sincerely and passionately loved women; it confers on them an indefinable attraction which you men will never perceive.

"Heavens, how I write to you! I could spend my whole time writing to you, I believe I find it easier to write than to talk to you. Take me in your arms; it's nearly dark now, the worst moment of the day; hold me very close, very close.

Your
Renée."

April 15th.

"My darling, how kind of you! What a good idea! Thank you,

thank you with all my heart for that badly-developed snapshot, yellow with hyposulphite; you're both there, my dear ones, ravishing, the pair of you. And now of course I can't any longer scold you for having taken Fossette to Salles-Neuves without my permission. She looks so happy in your arms. She's put on her photograph face, that makes her look like a beefy wrestler, holder of the Gold Belt.

"It's clear—as I observe with a slightly jealous gratitude—that at that moment she had no thoughts at all for me. But what about your eyes, that I can't see because they're gazing paternally down at Fossette, what were they dreaming about? The tender awkwardness of your arms holding that little dog both moves and amuses me. I slip this portrait of you, with the two others, into the old leather pocketbook—you remember?—which you thought had a mysterious and sinister air.

"Send me still more photos, will you? I've brought four with me and I compare them, examining you in them with a magnifying glass, to find again in each one, notwithstanding the smears of the retouching and the exaggerated lighting, a little of your secret self. Secret? Heavens no, there's nothing deceptive in you. It seems to me that any little goose would know you at a glance, as I do.

"I say that, you know, but I don't believe a word of it. Behind my teasing there's a nasty little desire to simplify you, to humiliate in you the old adversary: that's what I've always called the man who is destined to possess me.

"Is it true there are so many anemones in your woods, and violets? I saw some violets near Nancy when I was crossing that undulating eastern countryside, blue with firs and slashed with bright, sparkling rivers where the water is green-black. Was that you, that tall boy standing bare-legged in the icy water, fishing for trout?

"Goodbye. Tomorrow we leave for Saint-Etienne. I must grumble to you about Hamond, who hardly ever writes to me, so you must try and write to me a lot, my dear, in case I should complain to Hamond. I kiss you.

                                                              Renée."

FIVE

We have just dined at Berthoux's—an artistes' restaurant—Barally,
Cavaillon, Brague, I and the Troglodyte, whom I had invited. He
does not talk, his one idea is to eat. It was a typical "barnstormers'"
dinner, noisy but with rather a false gaiety. Cavaillon stood us a bottle of Moulin-à-Vent.

"You must be horribly bored here," chaffed Brague, "to fork up
the price of such a classy wine."

"I'll say," replied Cavaillon briefly.

Cavaillon, young but already famous in the music-hall world, is
envied by everyone there. They say of him that "Dranem is afraid of
him", and that "he earns whatever he chooses". We have run into
this tall young man of twenty-two once or twice already; he walks
like a human serpent, as though he had no bones, his heavy fists
swinging at the end of his frail wrists. His face, under his fair hair
cut in a fringe, is almost pretty, but his mauve glance, anxious and
restless, reveals acute neurasthenia, near to madness. His favourite
expression is: "I'm killing myself." He spends his whole day waiting
till it is time for his act, and while it lasts he forgets, enjoys himself,
and carries the public away. He neither drinks nor goes on the loose.
He invests his money and is bored.

Barally, who is "spinning out" a season at the *Celestins*, has
laughed so much, showing her beautiful teeth, and talked so much,
relating terrific binges when she was young, that it has gone to her
head. She tells us of the colonial theatres of twenty years ago, when
she used to sing in operetta in Saigon, in a hall lit by eight hundred
oil lamps. Penniless and already old, she is the old-fashioned Bohemian incarnate, likeable and incorrigible.

A pleasant dinner all the same: we work each other up and come
close together for an instant round the over-small table, and then
goodbye. A goodbye without regrets, for the next day, or the next

moment, we forget each other. . . . At last we are off again. Five days in Lyons can be interminable.

Cavaillon accompanies us to the Kursaal; it is too early for him since he only takes ten minutes to make up; but, a prey to solitude and grown silent and gloomy again, he clings to us. The Troglodyte, transported and slightly tipsy, sings to the stars, and I dream, and listen to the black wind rising and sweeping up the banks of the Rhone with a roar like the sea. Why do I feel as though I were rocked on an invisible swell like a ship set afloat by the sea? It is the kind of evening that makes one want to sail to the other side of the world. My cheeks are cold, my ears frozen and my nose moist: my whole animal self feels fit and vigorous and adventurous . . . until we get to the threshold of the Kursaal, where the musty warmth of the basement chokes my cleansed lungs.

As glum as government clerks, we arrive at those peculiar artists' dressing-rooms which resemble at the same time lofts in provincial houses, and servants' attics, papered in cheap grey and white. Cavaillon, who shed us on the staircase, is already in his dressing-room where I see him, sitting before his make-up shelf, his elbows propped on it and his head in his hands. Brague tells me that that is how this comic actor passes his lugubrious evenings, utterly worn out and silent. I shiver. I should like to shake off the memory of that man sitting there and hiding his face. I am afraid of becoming like him, that wretched, stranded creature, lost in our midst and conscious of his solitude.

SIX

"You're afraid I'm forgetting you? That's a new idea! Max darling, don't start 'playing the tart', as I call it. I think of you and gaze at you from far off with such keen attention that you ought, every now and again, to feel some mysterious intimation of it. Don't you? Across the distance that separates us I watch you intently, unwearyingly. I see you so clearly. The hours of our rapid intimacy have now yielded up all their secrets to me, and I slowly unfold all our words, all our silences, our looks and our gestures, faithfully recorded with all their pictorial and musical values. And this is the time you choose to complain coquettishly, a finger in the corner of your mouth: 'You're forgetting me, I feel you've gone further away from me!' Really, the second sight of lovers!

"It is true I'm going further away, my dear. We have just left Avignon behind, and when I woke in the train yesterday after a nap of two hours, I might have thought I had slept for two months; spring had come to meet me, a spring such as one imagines in fairy-tales, the exuberant, ephemeral, irresistible spring of the South, rich and fresh, springing up in sudden bursts of greenery, in plants already tall which sway and ripple in the wind, in mauve Judas trees and paulownias the colour of grey periwinkles, in laburnums, wistarias and roses.

"The first roses, my dear one! I bought them in the station at Avignon, little more than buds, of sulphur yellow touched with carmine, transparent in the sun as an ear aglow with bright blood, adorned with tender leaves and curved thorns of polished coral. They are on my table now. They smell like apricot and vanilla, like a very fine cigar, and like some dark, curled and scented beauty—the exact scent, Max, of your dry, dark-skinned hands.

"Dear one, I'm letting myself be dazzled and revived by this new season, this hard, strong sky, and that rare, gold colour of rocks that *have been caressed by the sun all the year round. No, no, don't pity me for leaving at dawn, since dawn in this country breaks, naked and rosy, from a milky sky, filled with the sound of bells and flights of white pigeons. . . . Oh I beseech you, do understand that you mustn't write me 'thought out' letters, that you mustn't think of what you are writing to me. Write no matter what, the kind of weather you're having, what time you woke up, how cross you feel with your 'salaried gipsy'; fill your pages with the same tender word, repeated like the cry of a mating bird. My dear lover, I want you to feel the same disturbance as this spring which has thrust its way out of the earth and is burning itself up with its own haste."*

I rarely re-read my letters, but I've re-read this one and let it go with the strange impression that I was doing a clumsy thing, making a mistake, and that it was on its way to a man who ought not to have read it. I have felt a bit light-headed since we left Avignon. The regions of mist have melted away behind the curtains of cypress that bend under the mistral. That day the silky rustle of the long reeds came in through the lowered window of the compartment, together with a scent of honey and pine, of varnished buds and unopened lilac, that bitter scent of the lilac before it flowers, like turpentine and almond mingled. The cherry trees cast a violet shadow on the reddish earth already cracking with thirst. The train cuts across or runs along beside white roads where a chalky dust rolls in low clouds and powders the bushes. A pleasantly exciting murmur, like that of a distant swarm of bees, buzzes incessantly in my ears.

Alive to that excess of scent and colour and warmth, and unable to resist although I had foreseen it, I let myself be taken by surprise, carried away and conquered. Can it be that there is no danger in such sweetness?

Below the balcony, the deafening Canebière teems at my feet, that Canebière which rests neither day nor night, and where idling takes on the importance and assurance of a job. If I bend forward I can see the water of the port glittering at the end of the street behind the geometrical lace of the riggings, a fragment of dark blue sea dancing in little short waves.

My hand, on the edge of the balcony, crumples the last note from my love, in answer to my letter from Lyons. Unluckily he recalls from it that my comrade Amalia Barally was not a lover of men and, like the "normal" and "well-balanced" being that he is, he has not failed to cast a bit of a slur on my old friend, by poking fun at her, and to vilify something that he does not understand. What would be the good of explaining to him? Two women enlaced will never be for him anything but a depraved couple, he will never see in them the melancholy and touching image of two weak creatures who have perhaps sought shelter in each other's arms, there to sleep and weep, safe from man who is so often cruel, and there to taste, better than any pleasure, the bitter happiness of feeling themselves akin, frail and forgotten. What would be the good of writing, and pleading, and discussing? My voluptuous friend can only understand love.

SEVEN

April 24th.

"Don't do that, I implore you, don't do that! Landing here without a word of warning, you haven't seriously thought of it, have you?

"What should I do if I saw you suddenly entering my dressing-room, as you did five months ago at the Empyrée-Clichy? Goodness me, I should keep you here, you can be sure of that. But that is why you mustn't come. I should keep you, my darling, against my heart, against my breast that you have so often caressed, against my mouth which is wilting from not being kissed any more. Ah, how I should keep you! That is why you must not come.

"Stop invoking our common need of taking fresh courage, of drawing from each other the strength for a new separation. Let me devote myself wholly to my job, which you do not like. After all, it's only twenty days more before I return. Let me finish my tour, putting into it an almost soldierly sense of duty and that sort of honest worker's application with which one mustn't mix our happiness. Your letter frightened me, my darling. I thought I was going to see you walk in. Take care not to overwhelm your love and do not lavish on her unexpected sorrows, or joys either.

Renée."

The canvas awning flaps above our heads, chequering with light and shade the terrace of the restaurant on the port where we have just been lunching. Brague reads the newspapers, uttering exclamations from time to time and talking to himself. I don't hear him, I scarcely see him. A habit already of long standing has suppressed all politeness, coquetry and modesty between us—all the insincere things. We have just been eating sea-urchins, tomatoes, and a *brandade* of cod. In front of us, between the oily sea lapping the sides of the boats and the perforated wooden balustrade which encloses this terrace, there is a stretch of pavement where busy people with the happy faces of idlers pass up and down; there are fresh flowers, carnations tied up in stiff bunches, like leeks, soaking in green pails; there is a street-stall loaded with black bananas smelling of ether, and shell-fish dripping with sea-water: sea-urchins, "*violets*", clams, blue mussels and cockles, dotted about with lemons and little flasks of pink vinegar.

I cool my hand on the belly of the white water-cooler, ribbed like a melon, which stands exuding moisture on the table. Everything there belongs to me and possesses me. I shall not think tomorrow that I am taking this picture away with me, but it seems to me that a shadow of myself, detached from me like a leaf, will remain here, a little bowed with fatigue, its transparent hand stretched out and laid on the side of an invisible water-cooler.

I contemplate my changing kingdom as though I had almost lost it. Yet nothing threatens this easy, wandering life, nothing, except a letter. It is there, in my little bag. My word, how my love writes when he wants to! How clearly he makes himself understood! Here, in eight pages, is something that I can at last call a real love-letter. It has the incoherence of a love-letter, the spelling groggy in places, the tenderness and . . . the authority. A superb authority which disposes of me, my future, and the whole of my little life. Absence has done its work; he has suffered without me and so he has thought things out and carefully planned a lasting happiness: he offers me marriage as if he were offering me a sunny enclosure, bounded by solid walls.

"*My mother certainly cried a little, but I let her cry. She has always done what I wanted. You will win her heart, and besides, we shan't be spending much time with her. You love travelling, don't you, my darling wife? You shall have so much that you'll get tired of it; the whole world shall be yours, until you come to love nothing but a little corner of our own where you will no longer be Renée Néré but My Lady Wife. You'll have to be content to be billed as that in future! I'm already arranging to . . .*"

What is he already arranging? I unfold the thin sheets of foreign writing-paper which rustle like bank notes: he is arranging to move, since the second floor of his brother's house was never suitable for anything but a bachelor flat. He has his eye on something in the neighbourhood of the *Rue Pergolèse*.

Impelled by a cruel hilarity, I crumple the letter, exclaiming to myself: "That's all very well, but what about me, am I not to be consulted? What do I become in all that?"

Brague raises his head, then takes up his paper again, without a word. It takes more than that to startle him out of his discretion, which is part reserve and part indifference.

I was not lying when I wrote to Max two days ago: "I see you so clearly, now that I'm far away." I only hope I do not see him too clearly. Young, too young for me, idle, free, affectionate, but spoilt: "My mother has always done what I wanted." I hear his voice pronouncing those words, his beautiful sombre voice with its seductive modulations, as though he had learnt in the theatre how to use it, that voice which gives beauty to the words, and I hear, like a diabolical echo, another voice which rises, muffled, from the depths of my memories: "The woman who will order me about is not yet born." Coincidence, if you will, but all the same it seems to me as though I had just swallowed a small piece of sharp glass.

Yes, what do I become in all that? A happy woman? This sunlight, imperiously penetrating the "dark room" of my inmost being, makes it difficult to think.

"I'm going in, Brague, I'm tired."

Brague looks at me over the top of his paper, his head on one side to avoid the thread of smoke rising from the half-extinguished cigarette in the corner of his mouth.

"Tired? Not ill? It's Saturday you know. The public at the *Eldo* will be pretty lively, so keep up to the mark."

I don't deign to answer. Does he take me for a beginner? We know all about this Marseilles public, decent but excitable, despising timidity and punishing conceit, not to be won over unless one throws one's whole self into it.

The migraine which was beginning vanishes as I get undressed and feel on my skin the coolness of a bluish shantung kimono, that has been washed twenty times. I do not lie down on my bed, for fear of going to sleep; I have not come here to rest. Kneeling on an armchair against the open window, I prop my elbows on the back of it and rub my bare feet against each other behind me. A few days ago I fell again into the habit of planking myself down on the edge of a table, perching on the arm of an easy chair, and remaining for a long time in awkward attitudes on uncomfortable seats, as though for these brief pauses on my way it was not worth while installing myself, or taking trouble to rest properly. Anyone might think that, with my coat thrown here and my hat there, I was only spending a quarter of an hour in the bedrooms where I sleep. It is in railway carriages that I show myself to be methodical to the point of mania, surrounded by my handbag, my rolled rug, my books and papers, the rubber cushions which support me when, with the promptitude of a hardened traveller, I fall into a rigid sleep which disturbs neither my veil, tied like a nun's head-band, nor my skirt drawn down to my ankles.

I am not resting. I want to force myself to think, and my mind jibs, escapes, darts down a path of light that a sunbeam, falling on the balcony, opens before it, and goes on its way across a mosaic roof of green tiles down below, where it childishly stops to play with a reflection, the shadow of a cloud. I struggle, lashing myself on. Then I give up for a minute, only to begin again. It is duels such as this which give to exiles like me those wide-open eyes, so slow to detach their gaze from some invisible lure. These are the gloomy gymnastics of the solitary.

Solitary! How can I think such a thing when my lover is calling to me, ready to take care of me all my life long? But I don't know what "all my life long" means. Three months ago I pronounced those terrible words "ten years", "twenty years", without understanding. Now the time has come when I must understand. My lover offers me his life, the improvident and generous life of a young man of about thirty-four, like me. He thinks I am young too, and he does not see the *end*—my end. In his blindness he will not admit that I must change and grow old, although every second, added to the second that is fleeting, is already snatching me away from him.

I still have what it takes to please him, and more still, to dazzle him. I can put off this face of mine as one takes off a mask; I have another, more beautiful face, which he has glimpsed. And where others adorn themselves, I disrobe, trained as I have been, first as Taillandy's model and then as a dancer, to avoid the dangers that lie in nudity and to move naked under the light as though it were a complicated drapery. But for how many years more am I still thus armed?

My friend offers me his name and his fortune, with his love. Decidedly my master Chance is doing things handsomely, and is anxious to reward by one large gesture my desultory worship of him. It is both unexpected and crazy; it is also a bit too much!

Dear good man, he will be awaiting my reply impatiently and watching for the postman on the road, in company with Fossette, my Fossette who is thrilled at acting the Lady of the Manor, riding in a motor and playing inner circle round the saddled horses. I am sure his joy must be intensified by the naïve legitimate pride of a gentleman who has been decent enough to raise from below stage at the *Emp'-Clich'* to his own level on the white terrace of Salles-Neuves, a nice little *"caf'-conc'"* actress.

Dear, dear, heroic *bourgeois!* Ah, why doesn't he love one of his own kind? How happy she would make him! It seems to me that I shall never be able to.

If it were only a question of giving myself! But voluptuous pleasure is not the only thing. In the limitless desert of love it holds a very small place, so flaming that at first one sees nothing else; but I am not a green young girl, to be blinded by the brilliance of it. All about this flickering hearth there lies the unknown, there lies danger. What do I know of the man whom I love and who wants me? After we have risen from a short embrace, or even from a long night, we shall have to begin to live at close quarters to each other, and in dependence on each other. He will bravely hide the first disappointments that I shall cause him, and I shall keep silent about mine, out of pride and shame and pity, and above all because I shall have expected them, *because I shall recognise them.* I who shrink right up when I hear myself called "my darling child", I who tremble before certain gestures of his, certain intonations that rise up from the past, what an army of ghosts is lying in wait for me behind the curtains of a bed that is still unopened?

No reflection dances now on the green-tiled roof down below. The sun has started to sink; a lake of sky, azure a moment ago between two spindles of motionless cloud, now pales serenely, passing from turquoise to lemon-green. My arms, propped on their elbows, and my bent knees, have gone to sleep. The unprofitable day is drawing to its end and I have decided nothing and written nothing, nor have I torn from my heart one of those irresistible impulses whose wild guidance I once upon a time accepted, without further thought, ready to call it "divine".

What shall I do? For today I'll write—briefly, for time is short—and lie to him.

"My darling, it is nearly six o'clock and I've spent the whole day struggling against a terrible migraine. The heat is so great and so sudden that it makes me groan but, like Fossette before too bright a fire, without resentment. And then your letter on top of all that! You

and the sky overwhelm me with your gifts, it's just too much sun, too much light at the same time; that's all I have strength for today, to sigh 'It's too much!' A friend like you, Max, and lots of love and lots of happiness and lots of money . . . how strong you must think me! I am, usually, it is true, but not today. Give me time.

"Here is a photograph for you. I've just received it from Lyons where Barally took this snapshot. Don't you think I look terribly dark and small, and sort of lost dog, with those folded hands and that beaten look? Frankly, my dear love, that humble stray feels ill-equipped to bear the excess of honour and wealth that you promise her. She is looking in your direction and her defiant fox's muzzle seems to say to you 'Is it really for me, all that? Are you sure?'

"Goodbye, my darling love. You are the best of men, and you deserved the best of wives. Will you not regret having chosen only

Renée Néré?"

I have forty-eight hours before me.

And now I must hurry and get ready to dine on the terrace at Basso's, in the cool breeze and the scent of lemons and wet mussels, and then rush to the *Eldorado* along avenues bathed in pink electric light, snapping, at last, for a few hours, the thread which unceasingly draws me away back there.

EIGHT

Nice, Cannes, Mentone. . . . On I spin, followed by my ever-growing torment: a torment so lively, so ever-present, that I sometimes fear I may see the shape of its shadow beside mine on the pale freestone of the jetties that enclose the sea, or on the hot pavement where banana skins lie fermenting. My torment tyrannises over me; it comes between me and the joy of living, contemplating, and breathing deeply. One night I dreamt that I did not love, and that night, released from all bonds, I lay as though in a kind of soothing death.

To my ambiguous letter from Marseilles Max replied with a calm and happy one, full of thanks from beginning to end without a word crossed out, and friendly, confident love proud of giving everything and receiving more; in short a letter which might have made me suppose I had written: "On such a day, at such an hour, I will be yours and we will go away together."

Is it really settled then? Am I as much committed as that? And this bad mood which makes me find the time drag so between one day and another, one town and another, one night and another, is it due to impatience or to haste? At Mentone yesterday I was listening, in a boarding-house drowsing among gardens, to the birds and the flies waking up, and the parakeet on the balcony. The dawn wind made the palm trees rustle like dead reeds and I recognised all the sounds, the whole music, of a similar morning the year before. But this year the whistling of the parakeet, the buzzing of the wasps as the sun rose, and the stiff breeze in the palms all receded far away from me and seemed like a murmured accompaniment to my anxiety, acting as a pedal to my obsession, love.

In the garden, under my window, an oblong bed of violets which the sun had not yet touched made a blue patch in the dew, beneath mimosas yellow as a chick. And against the wall there were climbing roses, too, which I guessed were scentless from their colour, greenish and sulphury yellow, the same indeterminate shade as the sky, which was not yet blue. The same roses and the same violets as the year before; but why was I not able to greet them yesterday with that involuntary smile, reflecting a harmless, half-physical felicity, in which the silent happiness of solitary people expresses itself?

I suffer. I cannot attach myself to what I see. For just a minute longer, just one more, I cling to what would be the greatest folly, the irremediable unhappiness of the rest of my existence. Clinging and leaning, like a tree which has grown over an abyss, and the weight of whose blossoming bends it towards its destruction, I still resist, and who can say if I shall succeed?

As soon as I grow calmer and accept the thought of my brief future, in which I shall belong utterly to the man who awaits me back there, a little picture, a little photographic picture casts me back into my torment, and into prudence. It is a snapshot of Max playing tennis with a young girl. It has no significance: the young girl is a casual acquaintance, a neighbour come for tea at Salles-Neuves, and he was not thinking of her when he sent me his photograph. But I think of her and I was already thinking of her before I saw her. I do not know her name, I can hardly see her face, turned up to the sun, and dark, with a cheerful grin revealing a shining line of white teeth. Ah, if I had my lover there at my feet, between my hands, I should say to him. . . .

No, I should say nothing to him. But to write is so easy. To write, to write, to cover white pages with the rapid, uneven writing which he says is like my mobile face, exhausted from expressing too much. To write sincerely, almost sincerely! I hope it may bring me relief, that sort of interior silence which follows a sudden utterance, a confession.

"*Max, my dear love, I asked you yesterday the name of that young girl playing tennis with you. I need not have bothered. As far as I am concerned she is called a girl, all the girls, all the young women who will be my rivals a little later on, soon, tomorrow. She is called the unknown, my junior, the one with whom I shall be cruelly and lucidly compared, yet with less cruelty and clearsightedness than I shall use myself.*

"*Triumph over her? How often? And what is triumph when the struggle is exhausting and never-ending? Understand me, please understand me! It is not suspicion, not your future betrayal, my love, which is devastating me, it is my own inadequacy. We are the same age; I am no longer a young woman. Oh my love, imagine yourself in a few years' time, as a handsome man in the fullness of your age, beside me in mine! Imagine me, still beautiful but desperate, frantic in my armour of corset and frock, under my make-up and powder, in my young, tender colours. Imagine me, beautiful as a full-blown rose which one must not touch. A glance of yours, resting on a young woman, will be enough to lengthen the sad crease that smiling has engraved on my cheek, but a happy night in your arms will cost my fading beauty dearer still. I am reaching—you know it—the age of ardour. It is the age of fatal imprudences. Understand me! Will not your fervour, if I let it convince and reassure me, lead me into the fatuous security of women who are loved? I have seen satisfied, amorous women in whom, for a few brief and dangerous minutes, the affected ingénue reappears and allows herself girlish tricks which make her rich and heavy flesh quiver. I have shuddered at the lack of awareness of a friend in her forties who, unclothed and all breathless with love, clapped on her head the cap of her lover, a lieutenant of Hussars.*

"Yes, I know, I'm rambling, and frightening you. You don't understand. What this letter lacks is a long preamble containing all the thoughts I am hiding from you, the thoughts that have been poisoning me for so long. Love is so simple, isn't it? You never supposed it had this ambiguous, tormented face? We love and give ourselves to each other, and there we are, happy for life, isn't that it? Ah, how young you are, and worse than young, you whose only suffering is waiting for me! Your hell is limited to not possessing what you desire, a thing which some people have to put up with all their lives. But to possess what one loves and every minute to feel one's sole treasure disintegrating, melting, and slipping away like gold dust between one's fingers! And not to have the dreadful courage to open one's hand and let the whole treasure go, but to clench one's fingers ever tighter, and to cry and beg to keep . . . what? a precious little trace of gold in the hollow of one's palm.

"Don't you understand? My little one, I would give anything in the world to resemble you, I wish I might never have suffered except because of you, and that I could fling away my old, well-tried distress. Help your Renée, as you can if you will, but, my love, if I no longer hope except in you, am I not already half-way to despair?"

My hand still grips the wretched, over-thin penholder. On the table, four large sheets of paper bear witness to the haste with which

I have written, no less than does the untidiness of the manuscript where the writing slopes upwards and downwards, sometimes bigger and sometimes smaller, responsive to my mood. Will he be able to make me out in all this untidiness? No. I am still concealed in it. To speak the truth is one thing, but the whole truth, that cannot, must not, be said.

Before me, on the square, swept by a wind which was keen a short while back but now weakens and drops like a tired wing, the arched wall of the arena at Nîmes rears its red-brown, rugose substance against a stretch of opaque, slate-coloured sky which foretells a storm. The burning air drifts about my room. I want to see again, under this heavy sky, my Elysian refuge, the Gardens of the Fountain.

A ramshackle cab and a worn-out horse take me as far as the black railings which protect this park where nothing changes. Can last year's spring have lasted magically until this hour, to wait for me? It is so fairy-like in this place, where the spring hangs motionless over all things, that I tremble lest I should see it swallowed up and melt into a cloud.

Amorously, my hand caresses the warm stone of the ruined temple and the varnished leaves of the spindle-trees, which seem damp. The baths of Diana, over which I lean, still, as always, reflect the Judas trees, the terebinths, the pines, the paulownias with their mauve flowers, and the double purple thorns. A whole garden of reflections is spread out there below me, turning, as it decomposes in the aquamarine water, dark blue, the violet of a bruised peach, and the maroon of dried blood. Oh beautiful garden and beautiful silence, where the only sound is the muted plashing of the green, imperious water, transparent and dark, blue and brilliant as a bright dragon.

A harmonious double alley, between walls of clipped yew, leads up to the Tour Magne, and I stop to rest for a moment on the edge of a stone trough full of stagnant water, green with fine watercress and chattering tree-frogs with tiny delicate hands. At the top, the very top, a dry bed of scented pine-needles receives us, me and my torment.

The beautiful garden lies spread out below, with open spaces in a geometrical design. The approach of the storm has driven away all intruders, and the hurricane, with its hail, rises slowly from the horizon, borne along in the billowing flanks of a thick cloud rimmed with white fire.

All this is still my kingdom, a small portion of the splendid riches which God distributes to passers-by, to wanderers and to solitaries. The earth belongs to anyone who stops for a moment, gazes and goes on his way; the whole sun belongs to the naked lizard who basks in it.

Underlying all my anxiety there is a great bargaining going on, a kind of bartering which weighs up undisclosed values and half-hidden treasures; and this dispute is slowly rising up and forcing its way into the daylight. Time presses. The whole truth, which I could not tell to Max, I owe to myself. It is not a beautiful truth, and it is still a bit feeble and scared, and slightly perfidious. So far all it can do is to whisper to me in short sighs: "I don't want . . . I mustn't . . . I'm afraid."

Afraid of getting old, of being betrayed, of suffering. A subtle choice guided my partial sincerity while I was writing that to Max. That particular fear is the hair-shirt which clings to the skin of nascent Love and contracts there as he grows. I have worn that hair-shirt; one does not die of it. I would wear it again if . . . *if I could not do otherwise.*

"If I could not do otherwise. . . ." This time the formula is clear. I saw it written in my mind and I see it there still, printed like a judgment in small, bold capitals. Now at last I have taken the true measure of my paltry love and brought my real hope into the open: the hope of escape.

But how to achieve it? Everything is against me. The first obstacle I run into is the female body lying there, which bars my way, a voluptuous body with closed eyes, deliberately blind, stretched out and ready to perish rather than leave the place where its joy lies. That woman there, that brute bent on pleasure, is I myself. "You are your own worst enemy." Don't I know it, my word, don't I know it! Shall I also be able to overcome the lost child, a hundred times more dangerous than that greedy beast, who trembles inside me, weak and nervous and ready to stretch out her arms and implore: "Don't leave me alone!" She is afraid, that child, of night, solitude, illness and death, in the evenings she draws the curtains over the dark window pane which frightens her, and pines merely because she is not cherished enough. And you, Max, my well-beloved adversary, how will lacerating myself help me to get the better of you? You would only have to appear and . . . But I am not calling to you to come!

No, I am not calling to you to come. It is my first victory.

Now the stormy cloud is passing over my head, letting fall, one by one, sluggish, scented drops of water. A star of rain plops on the corner of my mouth and I drink it, warm and sweetened with a dust that tastes of jonquils.

NINE

NÎMES, Montpellier, Carcassonne, Toulouse . . . four days without respite, and four nights. We arrive, wash, eat, dance to the accompaniment of an orchestra reading at sight and not sure of itself, go to bed—is it worth while?—and leave again. We grow thin with weariness and no one complains, pride before everything. We change music-halls, dressing-rooms, hotels and rooms with the indifference of soldiers on manœuvres. The make-up box is peeling and showing its tin. The costumes are beginning to wear and, hastily cleaned with petrol before the show, give out a sour smell of rice-powder and cleaning-spirit. I re-paint with carmine my cracked sandals for *The Pursuit*; my tunic for *The Dryad* is losing its acid, grass-green, grasshopper shade. Brague is superb in dirt of all colours: his Bulgarian breeches of embroidered leather, stiff with the artificial blood which spatters them each night, look like the hide of a newly-skinned ox. The Old Troglodyte spreads terror on the stage in a tow-wig which is moulting and some discoloured and evil-smelling hare-skins.

Hard days indeed, where we gasp between a blue sky swept with occasional long clouds, wispy as though they had been frayed by the mistral, and an earth cracking and splitting with thirst. And besides, I have a double burden to bear. My two companions, when they land in a new town, free their shoulders from the strap that bows them, and then, light of heart, think of nothing but a foaming half-pint and an aimless stroll. But for me there is the hour when the post arrives. The post: that means Max's letters.

In the glass-fronted rack and on the greasy tables where the porter scatters the papers with the back of his hand, I see, immediately and electrically, the round, flowery script and the bluish envelope: farewell to rest!

"Give it me, that one! Yes, yes, I tell you it's for me." Oh my goodness, what will there be in it? Reproaches, prayers, or perhaps merely: "I'm coming . . ."

I have waited four days for Max's reply to my letter from Nîmes; and for four days I have written tenderly to him, hiding my profound agitation under a wordy gentleness, as though I had forgotten that letter from Nîmes. At such a distance any epistolary dialogue is bound to be disjointed, and a sad note creeps in by fits and starts when things happen not to go well. Four days have I waited for Max's answer, and felt impatient and ungrateful when all I found was the tall, old-fashioned, graceful Italian hand of my friend Margot, the microscopic scribble of my old Hamond, and Blandine's postcards.

Ah, that letter from Max, I've got it at last, and I read it with a too-familiar palpitation, made more painful by a certain memory: was there not a period in my life when Taillandy "the man whom no woman ever dropped", as he always said, got suddenly furious at my absence and my silence and wrote me lover's letters? The mere sight of his spiky writing used to make me turn pale, and I would feel my heart bounding about like something very small and hard and round —just like today, just like today.

What if I were to crumple up this letter from Max without reading it, fill my lungs with air like a hanged man taken down in time, and flee? But I can't. It was only a passing temptation. I must read.

Thank my stars, my friend has not understood. He thought the whole trouble was a fit of jealousy, the coquettish alarm of a woman who wants to receive, from the man she loves, an explicit assurance in the most flattering terms. And so he gives me this assurance and I cannot help smiling because he praises his "beloved soul", sometimes as though she were a very respected sister, and sometimes as though she were a beautiful mare. "You will always be the most beautiful!" he writes, and no doubt he thinks it too. But could he answer anything else? Perhaps, at the moment of writing those words, he raised his head and looked at the deep forest before him, with a hardly perceptible hesitation, a suspension of thought. And then he will have shaken his shoulders, as one does when one is cold, and written bravely and slowly: "You will always be the most beautiful!"

Poor Max! The best of myself seems to conspire against him now. The day before yesterday we left before dawn and, as soon as we were in the train, I was just resuming my shattered sleep, broken and begun again twenty times, when a breath of salt air smelling of fresh seaweed made me open my eyes again: the sea! Sète and the sea! There it was again, running along beside the train, when I had quite forgotten it. The seven o'clock sun, still low on the horizon, had not yet penetrated it; the sea was refusing to let itself be possessed and, hardly awake, still kept its nocturnal colour of ink-blue crested with white.

Salt-pans filed past, edged with grass glittering with salt, and sleeping villas, white as the salt, between their dark laurels, their lilacs and their Judas trees. Half asleep, like the sea, and yielding to the swaying of the train, I thought I was skimming the waves, so close at hand, with a swallow's cutting flight. And then I experienced one of those perfect moments, the kind of happiness that comes to a sick person, unable to think, when a sudden *memory*, an image, a name, turned me once again into an ordinary creature, the creature of yesterday and the days before. How long had it lasted, that moment when for the first time I had forgotten Max? Yes, forgotten him, as though I had never known his gaze, nor the caress of his mouth, forgotten him as if the one dominating anxiety in my life were to seek for words, words to express how yellow the sun is, how blue the sea, and how brilliant the salt like a fringe of white jet. Yes, forgotten him, as if the only urgent thing in the world were my desire to possess through my eyes the marvels of the earth.

In that same hour an insidious spirit whispered to me: "And if indeed that were the only urgent thing? If everything, save that, were merely ashes?"

TEN

I LIVE in a turmoil of thoughts which go round and round unceasingly, and only with difficulty and patience do I find again my vocation of silence and dissimulation. Once more it is easy for me to follow Brague across a town, from top to bottom, through squares, cathedrals and museums, and into the smoke of little taverns where "one eats amazingly well". Our form of cordiality speaks little and rarely smiles, but sometimes shouts with laughter as if gaiety came more naturally to us than gentleness. I laugh easily at Brague's stories and make my laughter as shrill as I can, just as he, when he speaks to me, exaggerates a coarseness that is quite unnatural.

We are both sincere but not always very simple. We have time-honoured jests which provoke time-honoured amusement: Brague's favourite—which exasperates me—is the Game of the Satyr, which is played in trams, where my comrade chooses as a victim sometimes a timid young woman and sometimes an aggressive old maid. Sitting opposite her and lolling back, he fixes a lustful gaze on her to make her blush and cough, fidget with her veil and turn her head aside. The "satyr's" look persists, lasciviously, and then all the features of his face—mouth, nostrils, eyebrows—combine to express the particular joy of an erotomaniac.

"It's a wonderful facial exercise," Brague declares. "When the Conservatoire founds a miming class for me, I shall make all my feminine pupils rehearse it together and separately."

I laughed because the poor scared lady never fails to leave the tram very quickly, but the grimacing perfection of the wicked game gets on my nerves. My body, rather exhausted, has fits of unreasonable chastity, out of which I fall into a brazier lit in a second by the remembrance of a scent, a gesture or a tender cry, a brazier which kindles delights which I have not had and in whose flames I let myself be consumed, motionless and with my knees together, as though at the slightest movement I were in danger of enlarging my burns.

Max. . . . He writes to me and waits for me. How hard to bear his trustfulness is! Harder to bear than to deceive, for I too write, with a fullness and a freedom difficult to explain. I write on wobbly pedestal tables, sitting sideways on chairs that are too high, I write with one foot shod and one bare, the paper lodged between the breakfast tray and my open handbag, all among the brushes, the bottle of scent and the button-hook; I write sitting at a window that frames part of a courtyard, or the most delicious gardens, or misty mountains. I feel myself at home amid this disorder of a camp, this no matter where and no matter how, and freer than among my haunted furniture.

ELEVEN

"SOUTH AMERICA, what d'you say to that?"

This odd question from Brague fell like a stone yesterday into my after-dinner reverie, during that brief hour when I struggle against sleep and my reluctance to undress and put on my make-up just when I'm in the middle of digesting.

"South America? That's a long way away."

"Slacker!"

"You don't understand, Brague. I say 'it's a long way away' as I would say 'it's beautiful'."

"Oh well, all right if that's it. Salomon's been sounding me about going there. Well?"

"Well?"

"Can we consider it?"

"We can consider it."

Neither of us is taken in by our feigned indifference. I have learnt, to my cost, not to "put ideas" into the impresario's head about a tour, by showing my eagerness to go. Brague, on the other hand, unfailingly takes care not to present the matter to me in an advantageous light, for fear I will ask for a greater share of "the gross fee".

South America! At the sound of those two words I felt the dazzlement of an illiterate person who sees the New World through an enchanted web of falling stars, giant flowers, precious stones and humming birds. Brazil, the Argentine . . . what glittering names! Margot told me that she was taken there when she was quite small, and the longing and amazement she evoked remain fixed to the picture she gave me of a spider with a silver stomach and a tree covered with fireflies.

Brazil, the Argentine, but . . . what about Max?

What about Max? Ever since yesterday I've been prowling round this question mark. What about Max? What about Max? It is no longer a thought, it is a refrain, a noise, a little rhythmic croaking which inevitably brings on one of my "fits of coarseness". Who is the foul-mouthed ancestor who goes on barking inside me with a violence not only verbal but sentimental? I have just crumpled up the letter I had begun to my love, swearing under my breath.

"What about Max! What about Max! What, again? However long am I going to go on finding this creature getting under my feet? What about Max! What about Max! What about me, then, do I merely exist to bother my head about this cumbersome capitalist? A truce, Lord, I beseech you, I've had enough fusses and idylls and lost time, and enough of men! Look at yourself, my poor girl, look at yourself, you're not an old woman, by a long chalk, but you're already a kind of confirmed bachelor. You've got the fads of such, and the difficult character, and the finicking sensibility—enough of them to cause you suffering and make you unbearable. What will you do in that galley, or rather in that tub of a houseboat, firmly moored, in solemn attendance on the master's needs? If you could just manage to indulge in a nice little infatuation for the chap, say fifteen days, three weeks or two months and then goodbye! No strings on either side, just a mutual enjoyment. You ought to have learnt, when you were with Taillandy, how to drop people!"

On and on I rant. I display a crude and wicked ingenuity in finding ways to insult my friend and myself; it is a kind of game in which I provoke myself to say true things that I do not think, that I have not so far thought. And it goes on until the moment when I notice that it is raining in torrents: the roofs on the other side of the road are streaming, and the gutter overflowing. A long, cold waterdrop rolls down the window and falls on my hand. Behind me the room has grown dark. How good it would be to lean now against the shoulder of the man I was humiliating a moment ago by calling him a cumbersome capitalist.

I switch on the ceiling-light and, for something to do, try a temporary arrangement of the writing-table, opening the blotter between the cheval-glass and the bunch of narcissus; I'm trying to make the place look like home and what I long for is hot tea, golden bread, my familiar lamp with its pink shade, the barking of my dog and the voice of my old Hamond. A large sheet of white paper lying there tempts me, and I sit down:

"Max, my darling, yes, I'm coming back; I return a little every day. Is it possible that only twelve nights separate me from you? Nothing is less sure; it seems to me that I shall never see you again. How terrible that would be! And how wise!"

I stop short: is it not too clear? No. Besides, I wrote "it would be", and no lover would ever take a conditional tragically. I can continue in the same reassuring vein, risking a few melancholy generalities and a few timorous taboos. And since, all the same, I dread a brusque decision which would bring Max here in less than twelve hours, I do not forget to drown the whole letter in a flood of tendernesses which, alas, draw me on.

Rather disgusting, all that.

TWELVE

How time flies! Where are the Pyrenees with their blossoming cherries, the great austere mountain which seemed to follow us, glittering with a snow which makes you thirsty, slashed with vertiginous shadows, rent with blue chasms and blotched with bronze forests? Where are the narrow valleys, turf-carpeted, and the wild orchids white as gardenias, and where the little Basque village square where we drank steaming dark chocolate? How far away already is the icy Gave, that graceful dangerous river with its waters clouded by the melting of the snows to the milky transparency of moonstones!

We are leaving Bordeaux now, after giving five shows in three days. "A nice town," sighed Brague at the station. "I treated myself to a little Bordelaise . . . a dainty dish! One of those small helpings you can get for the asking in all the main streets, can't you just see? High as your heart, plenty of breast, short in the leg, a plump little foot, and so plastered with eye-black and powder and frizzed hair that I defy you to tell whether they're pretty or not. They sparkle and chatter and wriggle—they're just my dish!"

He exuded tranquil happiness and I looked at him with a rather disgusted hostility, as I look at people eating when I am no longer hungry.

The timid spring flees before us, growing younger hour by hour and closing again leaf by leaf and flower by flower as we get further north. In the sparser shade of the hedges, the April daisies have reappeared, and the last faded violets. The paler blue of the sky, the shorter grass and an acid humidity in the air give one the illusion of growing younger and going back in time.

If only I could wind back again the months that have expired up to that winter day when Max walked into my dressing-room. . . . When I was small and learning to knit, they made me undo rows and rows of stitches until I had found the little unnoticed fault, the dropped stitch, which at school was called "a lapse". A "lapse"! That's all that he would have been in my life, then, this poor second love of mine whom I used to call my dear warmth, my light. He is there, quite close at hand, I can take hold of him—and I flee.

For I shall flee. A premeditated escape is being organised far away, down in the depths of my being, without my taking so far any direct part in it. At the decisive moment, when all that remains will be to cry, as though in panic: "Quick, Blandine, my suitcase and a taxicab!" I shall perhaps be taken in by my own confusion, but O dear Max, whom I wanted to love, I confess here, with the most genuine sorrow, that from this moment all is resolved.

Except for this sorrow, have I not become again *what I was*, that is to say free, horribly alone and free? The momentary grace which touched me now withdraws itself from me, since I refused to lose myself in it. Instead of saying to it: "Take me!" I ask it: "What are you giving me? Another myself? There is no other myself. You're giving me a friend who is young, ardent, jealous and sincerely in love? I know: that is what is called a master, and I no longer want one. He is good and simple, he admires me and he is straightforward? In that case he is my inferior and I should be making a misalliance. A look of his can rouse me and I cease to belong to myself if he puts his mouth on mine? In that case he is my enemy, he is the thief who steals me from myself. I shall have everything, everything that money can buy, and I shall lean over the edge of a white terrace smothered with the roses of my gardens? But it is from there that I shall see the lords of the earth, the wanderers, pass by! Come back to me, beseeches my love, leave your job and the shabby sadness of the surroundings where you live, come back among your equals. I have no equals, I have only my fellow wayfarers."

Windmills revolve on the horizon. In the little stations through which the train passes, Breton head-dresses, the first white head-dresses, blossom like daisies. Dazzled, I enter into the yellow kingdom of the brooms and the gorses. Gold, copper, and vermilion too —for the pale rape is there as well—set these poor heathlands ablaze with an unendurable light. I press my cheek and my outspread hands against the carriage windows, surprised not to feel it warm. We are crossing the conflagration, leagues and leagues of gorse in flower, wasted riches which rebuff even the goats, and where butterflies, made languorous by the warm scent like half-ripe peaches and pepper, flutter about with torn wings.

THIRTEEN

At Caen, two days before our return, I find a letter from Max consisting of only one line, with no signature: "My Renée, do you no longer love me?"

That is all. I had not foreseen that gentleness and the simplicity of that question, which confound all my literature. What was it I wrote then, the last time?

That doesn't matter. If he loves me, it is not in my letters that he read the warning. If he loves me, he knows those mysterious shocks, that light, hurtful finger which strikes the heart, those small thunderbolts which suddenly arrest a gesture or cut short a burst of laughter. He knows that treason, desertion and lies can strike from a great way off, and he knows the brutality and infallibility of a *presentiment*.

Poor, poor friend that I wanted to love! You might have died, or deceived me, and I should have known nothing of it, I whom the best-hidden treachery wounded by telepathy once upon a time.

"My Renée, do you no longer love me?" I did not melt into passionate tears, but I jotted down on a sheet of paper the abbreviated message of a vaguely reassuring telegram: "*Shall be home five o'clock day after tomorrow. All love.*"

I am subtly jealous of this man who is suffering. I re-read his complaint and talk to this letter as if I were speaking to him, with his firm mouth and angry eyebrows.

"*You love and suffer and complain. That makes you just as I was when I was twenty. I am leaving you and, thanks to me, you may perhaps acquire what now you lack. Already you can see through protecting walls; does that not astonish you, you great, dense male? Nerves grown sensitive, an innocent, burning, suffering, hope for ever renewing itself, green and strong, like a mown field, all that was my portion and now it will be yours. I cannot take it away from you, but I begrudge it you.*"

There was a packet of letters with that of Max. Even Blandine writes: "*Madame, Monsieur Maxime has brought Fossette back, she has another new collar. Monsieur Maxime asks for news of Madame, he doesn't look very happy and one can see he's been missing Madame.*"

There's a letter from Hamond, who talks simply but writes with an almost ceremonious courtesy; and a letter from Margot who has nothing to tell me and fills two sheets with a nun-like tittle-tattle. They are all in a hurry to write to me now I am about to return, as if their conscience were pricking them slightly for having neglected me for such a long time.

Whom shall I confide in when I get back? In Hamond? In Margot? In neither. I tear up all this trifling stuff before leaving the stifling tomb known as the "star's dressing-room" at the *Folies-Caennaises,* to go up on to the stage. We are in an old-style *café-chantant:* to reach the stage door one has to cross a part of the auditorium, and this is the worst moment of the evening. The public elbows us and bars our way on purpose so as to stare at us longer; my bare arm leaves its powder on a jacket, a hand slyly pulls at my embroidered shawl, and furtive fingers feel my hips. With heads high, we bear like proud prisoners the contempt and desire of this suffocating crowd.

FOURTEEN

A HALF-HOUR strikes, very far away. The train from Calais, which is to take me back to Paris, is not due for fifty minutes.

I am returning alone, by night, without warning anyone. Brague and the Old Troglodyte, their thirst slaked thanks to me, are now asleep somewhere in Boulogne-sur-Mer. We killed three-quarters of an hour in doing our accounts, and chattering, and discussing plans for our South American tour, and then I found myself in this station at Tintelleries, so deserted at this hour that one might think it was no longer in use. They have not switched on the electric globes of the platform, just for me. A cracked bell tinkles timidly in the shadows, as though it were hanging from the neck of a paralysed dog.

The night is cold and moonless. Near by, in an invisible garden, there are scented lilacs which rustle in the wind. Far away I can hear the call of foghorns at sea.

Who would guess that I am here, right at the end of the platform, huddled in my coat? How well hidden I am! Neither darker nor lighter than the shadows.

With the first light I shall let myself noiselessly into my flat, like a thief, for I am not expected so soon. I shall wake Fossette and Blandine and then will come the hardest moment.

I deliberately imagine the details of my arrival; I conjure up, with necessary cruelty, the memory of the twofold scent which clings to the hangings: English tobacco and rather too-sweet jasmine; in imagination I press the satin cushion with its two pale stains, the traces of two tears which fell from my eyes in a moment of very great happiness. I can hardly hold back the little stifled "ah!" of one who has been wounded and jolts her wound. I am doing it on purpose. It will hurt me less by and by.

From far away I am saying my goodbyes to all which would keep me there, and to him who will have nothing left of me, except a letter. A cowardly, rational wisdom persuades me not to see him again:

no "frank explanations" between us! A heroine who is only human, like myself, is not strong enough to triumph over all the demons. Let him despise me and even curse me a little, it will be all the better if he does; poor dear, he'll recover more quickly. No, no, there mustn't be too much honesty. And not too many phrases either, since by keeping silent I shall spare him.

A man crosses the rails with sleepy steps, pushing a trunk on a hand-cart, and suddenly the electric globes of the station come on. I get up, feeling numb, I had not noticed I was very cold. At the end of the platform a lantern jerks in the darkness, swinging from an invisible arm. A distant whistle answers the harsh foghorns: it is the train. Already!

FIFTEEN

"Goodbye, my darling. I am going away, to a village not very far from here; after that I shall no doubt leave for America, with Brague. I shall not see you again, my darling. When you read this you will not think it is a cruel game, since the day before yesterday you wrote to me; 'My Renée, do you no longer love me?'

"I am going away, it is the least hurt I can do you. I am not cruel, Max, but I feel myself quite worn out, as though unable to resume the habit of loving and afraid lest I should have to suffer again because of it.

"You did not think I was so cowardly, my darling? What a small heart mine is! Yet once upon a time it could have been worthy of yours, which offers itself so simply. But now . . . what could I give you, oh my darling? In a few years' time the best of myself would be that frustrated maternity that a childless woman transfers to her husband. You do not accept that and neither do I. It is a pity. There are days when I, who watch myself growing older with a resigned terror, think of old age as a recompense.

"My darling, one day you will understand all this. You will understand that I must not belong to you or to anyone, and that in spite of a first marriage and a second love, I have remained a kind of old maid, like some among them who are so in love with Love that no love appears to them beautiful enough, and so they refuse themselves without condescending to explain; who repel every sentimental misalliance and return to sit for life before a window, bent over their needle, in solitary communion with their incomparable vision. Like them, I wanted everything; a lamentable mistake punished me.

"I no longer dare, my darling, that is the whole trouble, I no longer dare. Don't be cross if I have hidden so long from you my efforts to resuscitate in myself the enthusiasm, the adventurous fatalism, the blind hope, the whole cheerful escort of love. The only delirium I feel is that of my senses. And alas, there is none whose in-

tervals are more lucid. You would have consumed me to no purpose, you whose gaze, whose lips, whose long caresses, whose moving silence cured, for a little while, a distress which is not your fault.

"*Goodbye, my darling. Seek far from me that youth, that fresh, unspoilt beauty, that faith in the future and in yourself, in a word, the love that you deserve, the love that once upon a time I could have given you. Don't seek me out. I have just enough strength to flee from you. If you were to walk in here, before me, while I am writing to you . . . but you will not walk in.*

"*Goodbye, my darling. You are the one being in the world whom I call my darling, and after you I have no one to whom to give that name. For the last time, embrace me as if I were cold, hold me very close, very close, very close. . . .*

Renée."

I have written very slowly; before signing my letter I re-read it, rounded the loops, added the dots and the accents, and dated it: *May 15th, 7 a.m.*

But though signed and dated and finally stuck down, it still remains an unfinished letter. Shall I open it again? I suddenly shiver as if, in closing the envelope, I had blocked out a luminous opening through which a warm breath of air was still blowing.

It is a sunless morning and the winter cold seems to have taken refuge in this little sitting-room behind the shutters that have been padlocked for forty days. Crouching at my feet, my dog is silent, her eyes on the door: she is waiting. She is waiting for someone who will not come again. I can hear Blandine shifting the casseroles, I smell the smell of ground coffee; hunger gnaws sullenly at my stomach. A worn sheet covers the divan, a damp, blue mist tarnishes the mirror. I was not expected so soon. Everything is shrouded in old linen and dampness and dust, everything here still wears the slightly funereal air of departure and absence, and I pass furtively through this refuge of mine without taking off the white dust-sheets, without writing a name on the bloom of dust, without leaving any other trace of my passage than that letter, unfinished.

Unfinished. Dear intruder, whom I wanted to love, I spare you. By going away, I leave you your one chance of growing bigger in my eyes. Reading my letter will only give you pain. You will not know the humiliating comparison you are escaping, nor the dispute of which you were the prize, the prize which I disdain.

For I reject you and I choose . . . all that is not you. I have met you before, and I recognise you. Are you not he who, thinking he is giving, takes for himself? You came to share my life. To share, yes: *to take your share!* To be a partner in everything I do, to insinuate yourself at every moment in the secret temple of my thoughts, isn't that it? Why you, more than another? I have barred it to every-one.

You are good and, with the best faith in the world, you meant to bring me happiness, since you saw me deprived and solitary. But you counted without my beggar-woman's pride: I refuse to see the most beautiful countries of the world microscopically reflected in the amorous mirror of your eyes.

Happiness? Are you sure that happiness is enough for me hence-forward? It is not only happiness that gives value to life. You wanted to brighten me with that commonplace dawn, for you pitied me in my obscurity. Call it obscurity, if you will: the obscurity of a room seen from without. I would rather call it dark, not obscure. Dark, but made beautiful by an unwearying sadness: silvery and twilit like the white owl, the silky mouse, the wings of the clothes-moth. Dark, with the red gleams of an agonising memory. But you are he in whose presence I should no longer have the right to be sad.

I escape from myself, but I am still not free of you, I know it. A vagabond, and free, I shall sometimes long for the shade of your walls. How many times shall I return to you, dear prop on which I rest and wound myself? How many times shall I cry for what you were able to give me: a long-drawn-out voluptuousness, suspended, fanned, renewed, the winged fall, the swooning in which one's strength is renewed by its own death . . . the musical drumming of the maddened blood . . . the scent of burning sandal-wood and trod-den grass. . . . Ah, how long shall I not thirst for you upon my road!

I shall desire you as I desire in turn the fruit that hangs out of reach, the far-off water, and the blissful little house that I pass by. In each place where my desires have strayed, I leave thousands and thousands of shadows in my own shape, shed from me: one lies on the warm blue rocks of the ledges in my own country, another in the damp hollow of a sunless valley, and a third follows a bird, a sail, the wind and the wave. You keep the most enduring of them: a naked, undulating shadow, trembling with pleasure like a plant in the stream. But time will dissolve it like the others, and you will no longer know anything of me until the day when my steps finally halt and there will fly away from me a last small shadow.

The SHACKLE

Translated by
ANTONIA WHITE

ONE

It is not the calm circle of light thrown by a lamp lit every night on the same table that shows a woman what little she can perceive of herself: yet by changing the table, the lamp and the room, what have I acquired? Only the suspicion, soon to become a certainty, that all countries are going to be exactly alike unless I find the secret of making them new again by renewing my own self. I can no longer rely on my sturdy reason—the sturdy reason of a woman! At the moment she is feeling neither sturdy nor reasonable, but very tremulous and emotional—all because of a trivial encounter on the Promenade des Anglais.

Yet it was so obvious that it was bound to happen sooner or later; it was amazing it had not happened before. Here he was, right beside me, the man who had wanted to give me his name, his love, the support of his steady heart. And he passed by without even seeing me. On one side of him he had a young woman; on the other a very small, plump child who could barely walk. He did not see me because he was giving his entire attention—his touching, slightly owlish attention—to the stumbling child. "Big Booby!" He passed so close that I could see his long, stiff eyelashes and his tie knotted as if he had knotted it for life. He was so like himself that I could have put out my hand, just as in the old days, to loosen that tie a little and thrust the too visible corner of a handkerchief further down into his jacket pocket. It frightens me now to think of the gesture I might have made. He was so utterly unaware of me that I had the impression of being no longer a living person but an insubstantial ghost he was going to walk right through. It is odd that I did not think of looking at his wife and child. All three of them continued their stroll along the sea front.

What has shaken me so much? Not love, not grief. How much does regret account for my disturbance? I have no idea. The shock, the flash of revelation have just made me far more aware of my frailty than the insane daily reverie in which I delude myself I am wise. Call it meditation, if you like. There is no such thing as wise meditation. All habitual meditation contains a germ of delirium. It borders on hysteria, on artificially-induced ecstasy, painful or otherwise.

And there I go, generalising in a typically feminine way. So much the better! There are moments like this when I am quite glad to find myself reacting like a female. It is as if I were establishing the fact that I may still be good for something—from the sexual point of view.

Would I have liked him to see me? No, not really. I repeat his name, his cumbersome name, uneasily: Maxime Dufferein-Chautel . . . I am sure I do not love him. But all the same, that man represents love in my life. Not only love, but adventure, even sensual pleasure. No doubt that is what is keeping me in a tremor and feeling vaguely shocked. That mouth, those hands, that great warm body—all those things taken together very nearly constituted a lover for me three years ago. If he had been alone, just now, and had spoken to me, should I have called him Max, or "darling" or just "you"? He had on his most married look, but that, if I may presume to say so, is a look he was born with. He was displaying that wife and child of his as if they were new purchases he had just made in the Place Masséna.

Let me try to be sincere. I did not fly from him, but I hid myself in the only way that could conceal me from his eyes, in complete immobility; the startled hare squats close to the ground and knows perfectly well that it is the colour of a ploughed furrow. The slightest flutter of my white glove against my dark dress would have attracted his eye; I even dreaded that my scent, still the same scent, might suddenly make him turn round. I did not want him to, no, I did not want him to. I blushed like a woman caught with her hair in curl-papers. And, besides, *he* had such an air of wealth, of having acquired so many new things: a brand-new child, a befurred and befeathered wife, a walking-stick I did not recognise; whereas *I!* He humiliated me with his air of having made a fortune. I had nothing to show him but a tailored suit, and, naturally, a pretty hat, and a slightly different way of doing my hair. Perhaps he would have looked for something new on me and about me, with an expression of disappointment: "Is that all?"

I felt, yes, I did feel as self-conscious as a poor person. This year, in Nice, he would not have seen the big orange and black posters announcing the appearance of Renée Néré, because Renée Néré is not "touring" any more. If he had asked what I was doing, I should have had to tell him that I had become a lady of leisure. A lady of leisure, living on a small private income; neither rich nor poor—not young, but not old either; not happy, but not depressed. Tonight, something comes back to me—something Brague said in one of his sallies.

"One never looks anything but what one is. Therefore, even when I am well-dressed, I look like . . . precisely, I look like a great actor. Whereas you don't look like a great actress, nor like a little one. Neither do you look like a 'lady'. Or a tart. You have an air—so—of folding your paws under you because the world disgusts you, but that's no indication. The fact is you go through life like those customers who don't know what they want to buy in a shop, those women the people behind the counter are longing to kick in the arse all the time they're saying politely: 'Take your time, Madam: have a good look round before you make up your mind.' Real swine of customers, you know!"

He laughed, and, to please him, I pretended to be very indignant.

At the end of a cloudless day, it is raining. The Promenade des Anglais glistens and the noise of the shower on the palm-trees and on the pavement drowns the rhythmic murmur of the sea. Where is the couple that went by at three o'clock, in front of the hotel, bending over the small child all in white? They cannot live here. I can picture them better on the outskirts of Cannes, in a villa surrounded by a garden, like the rich, respectable bourgeois they are. They must have come into Nice to have tea, in a comfortable closed limousine, with Baby on their knees. He must have married in haste, that man who was my friend, very nearly my lover, since his child is already walking. He cannot have lamented for long over the letter I left him one cold, grey spring morning: "My darling Max, I am going away . . ." Well! I'm obviously fated to think of nothing else tonight and there's no great harm in that.

True, I didn't look at his wife but now I can see their group again in all its details. A young woman, of the type people probably think pretty when they get to know her. She struck me as someone who went about absent-mindedly, with an irresponsible, slightly cowlike placidity. "Ask my husband. . . ." And I'm prepared to bet "my husband" deals with everything, from Baby's nurse, to the chauffeur waiting for orders. He opens the laundry book every Monday morning and flattens down the page with the palm of his big brown hand; he confers with the cook. Perhaps there are days when he remembers me and those days he orders "pork cutlets in sauce, with gherkins". Perhaps, sometimes, his young wife calls him "Max"—in a voice he thinks he recognises, and, if he makes her laugh, she may happen to shrug her shoulders and say "Big booby!" When she does that, he must lean his head against her and close his eyes so as to hide two things, a flicker of emotion and the perverse pleasure of lying without saying a word, the pleasure all men savour when they subtly deceive us at the moment they are most passionately embracing us.

There I am, off again. Guessing, or inventing. Penetrating, thanks to my memories, my former lover's new marital life. I am probing it with all the spiteful curiosity of an abandoned mistress, whereas, on the contrary, it was I who . . . Worse still, I am using the erotic and varied imagination of the chaste, reinforced by an all too precise memory. I am raising—and by what right?—a ghost between Max and his wife; the ghost of an unforgotten, unforgettable Renée Néré. Unforgettable, no! But I ask you, in what way am I any better than that cold, lovely blockhead of a Villepreux, the singer who used to sigh every time she heard a man's name mentioned: "Poor fellow! He's mad about me . . . he tried to kill himself . . . he's gone into exile . . ."? At least Villepreux, faithful to her illusions, enjoyed the rich satisfaction of lunatics in padded cells who believe they are reincarnations of Jesus Christ or Napoleon Bonaparte.

It is raining harder than ever. I shall not leave my room again. Yet tonight the posters of the Eldorado display the name of one of my ex-colleagues in the music-hall world: I would have liked to have gone round behind and had a word with her in her dressing-room, given her a surprise. I shan't go. The nearest lighthouse is drawing a neat little silver paintbrush over the rainy sea. I have taken my hair down while I was watching the beam and, instead of leaving it loose for the night, here I am mechanically putting it up again in the way I did it three years ago, pulled down in tufts over my ears and rolled on my nape to give the effect of a medieval page's curled locks. Have I aged? Yes, no, yes and no. Something in the colour and texture of my face reminds me of the distinguished, parched look that is the penalty of women who have to restrict liquid to a minimum in their diet. I no longer like this heavy, pulled-down curtain of hair. Nowadays I show the "fresh areas" that have not often been exposed to the light: ears, temples, a triangle of forehead, the nape of the neck. As to the hollow of my back, the upper part of my arms and chest, I cannot yet bring myself to uncover them, as Brague used to say "in mufti". The skin of one's arms and legs, the roundness of one's breasts, is a kind of fabric one exhibits on the stage, and only on the stage, covered with a sticky foundation that holds the powder; a cold fabric offered from a distance, out of reach of hands or lips; merely a rather striking part of one's costume. And I have noticed it over and over again in actresses I have played with in the theatre or on the music-halls—this curious, professional distortion of the sense of modesty which allows them to face the glare of the footlights naked, with perfect confidence, but forbids them to appear off the stage except behind ramparts of stiff, severe silk and opaque lace.

Although it is a year since I left the theatre my decorum remains strictly professional, and I hide this, that and the other which people might well envy me. The beautiful dancer Bastienne, a superb, placid, nymph-like creature, also used to insist on her dressmaker putting a triple layer of ninon in the neck of a dinner dress. She used to say, slapping her rigidly corseted breasts, "all *that* only concerns my job and my lover!"

I no longer have a job . . . and I have no lover. Nevertheless this afternoon's encounter made me put on that dress again for dinner just now, as if out of defiance—that black dress I did not dare wear, almost a real "low-cut" dress that reveals such a wide, deep triangle of white neck. Stiff with nervousness, my teeth clenched, I walked heroically to my little table at the far end, well away from the gypsy band—and no one paid any attention either to my dress or to me. Was I expecting Max—"Monsieur Dufferein-Chautel and family"— to dine at the Hôtel Impérial? Honestly no one, except the inevitable gentleman-on-his-own who is interested in the lady-on-her-own, follows her about for a few days, tries to make her acquaintance, succeeds or does not succeed—and goes off.

As a Lady-on-her-own, in fact a positively classic type of Lady-on-her-own, with dresses a little too respectable for my kind of face, it was impossible for me to avoid the Gentleman-on-his-own. I have had one for the past week. I could not describe him, for I have not seen him. When I look at the spot where he is, it is not him that I see; I see through him as if through an empty water-jug. I only know the shape of his back, because he promptly turns away from me with an affectation of politeness. Seen from the front, he is a stranger; I can only distinguish him from the others when he turns his back to me. It is at mealtimes he embarrasses me most because I can *hear* him thinking about me while he is eating. Tonight, yielding to that vaguely amorous will, I smiled at him, with my thoughts on Max. I ought not to have done it. But it's so utterly unimportant!

The rain has stopped lashing the windows and the silence wakes me up again. Silence, here, is the sputter of the short waves as they dissolve on the pebbles, the trot of the lively little hoofs of a countryman's horse, the hooting of car-horns. I open the window and lean out to see two lighted windows on the floor below: my friend May's room. Shadows pass over the curtains. There are two tempestuous lovers down there for whom a quarrel, followed by fisticuffs, constitutes a kind of Swedish gymnastics. If I went down to them, they would not stop for such a trifling interruption. I could sit down and score the hits until the disturbing, ferocious moment, when, both covered with bruises, these peculiar lovers can think of no better punishment for each other than a passionate embrace.

Or else I might climb up two floors where, behind another white door, I should find the stifling, scented room of two other nomad friends. Wherever these two go, they take their opium lamp, their flat cushions which smell of precious wood and their white Indian mat, smooth and cold as a lizard's skin. There, too, I could sit down, as a spectator, or lie down and share, not the poison I keep away from, but the warm silence, the air heavy with the dark aroma, the slightly hallucinated repose.

Above and below, I should be welcome—someone who takes nothing from and gives nothing to anyone. Ah! I have no illusions, either, about what I receive from my *friends*. Not a cadger, but not a giver, that's what they must say of me. And what could I give? It is true that a woman who obstinately refuses to sleep with anyone always seems miserly, whatever she does. My "friends", idlers of the Riviera, flotsam and jetsam of the theatre world, easily-shocked illicit couples who value my good behaviour, deny me what they readily grant to May: that vaguely contemptuous trust, that affectionate covetousness which she maintains and satisfies with a coarse love-word and a crude gesture that her childish laugh robs of offence.

On the floor above, on the floor below, the same gay welcome awaits me. But when I get up to go back to my room—157—my departure will distress nobody, either upstairs or down. I can come and go as I like, do whatever I fancy. Only, as a little girl said: "I haven't got a fancy." So I shall go to bed, but not at once, because the air is so good to breathe, still all damp. It smells of gardens and sea-shells. There is a young moon over the sea, a slender moon that sheds no light.

After all, it is a pleasant enough thing, just because of an emotional encounter, or the clear, scented interval between two showers or for nothing, for no reason at all, to feel a little foolish and agitated and weak, to feel oneself melting all over like a young girl who has just received her first love-letter.

TWO

"So then?"

"So it went on like that till three in the morning. At three o'clock, grand beating-up. Six hundred francs' worth of tortoise-shell hairpins left on the carpet!"

"Ah! And after that?"

"After that, naturally . . . I'm sleepy."

May laughed and stretched. She had just come up to my room, wearing only a Roumanian shirt under her Japanese kimono, her bare feet thrust into large man's slippers. She radiated a perishable, impersonal freshness. May has no features and immensely thick hair of unequal degrees of fairness; light on the nape of her neck, silvery on the temples, elsewhere almost brown. Twenty-five! What a waste of precious youth! Anyone would think this vehement creature had sworn to ruin her looks before she was thirty: the tips of her long eyelashes are discoloured by mascara and her beautiful hair is daily scorched with hot tongs. May never goes to bed, forgets to eat lunch, smokes, drinks and takes cocaine. But what does it matter? In spite of it all the absurd little thing has the clear skin of a twenty-five year old blonde, horse-chestnut coloured eyes whose irises leave hardly any space for the whites and a charming, imbecile way of exaggerating fashions which are crazy enough already.

She goes off in the morning—the "morning" being between twelve-thirty p.m. and four o'clock—in broadly-striped skirts that reveal her stubby, tortured little feet, her ankles and even her calves; the waistline is somewhere under her armpits, defined by the edge of a tight, skimpy little jacket which never did look as if it had been cut for May and which, in front, shows the little pot-belly she has recently acquired. A cascade of soft linen opens on to the parting between her breasts and a straw helmet conceals her right eye. Such is the outfit which May calls "ever such a simple little run-about suit".

I have known May for over a year—from eternity according to her

—through having met her at a nightclub where Brague and I were performing as honest wage-earners. She was having supper at the next table and behaved outrageously to make an impression on me. She laughed, dipped her hair in the champagne, displayed the rudeness of a child and the cynicism of a young Negress, wept deliciously for no reason, threw coins into the bodice of a Spanish dancer and ruined everything by those simple words: "I'm a real character, aren't I?"

The "real character" walked to and fro in front of my dressing-table, cutting off the sunlight every other instant with the fluttering shadow of her huge sleeves. Dazzled, I powdered my face as best I could. If May trails about in her lover's slippers which make her feet look like Little Tich's, it is neither by mistake nor out of carelessness; it is "to shock the old fogeys in the corridors".

"Look at that," she said abruptly, thrusting her downy arm under my nose. "That'll be black tomorrow."

I examined, with the proper interest, two yellowish-brown bruises circling each of May's arms like bracelets.

"The filthy brute!" she muttered, not without deference. "And, you know, he ruined my dress, a dress that cost fifty louis—all because I felt in a lucky mood and I wanted to go and play at Monte Carlo. He's going to find out what it costs him, that dress! I've already played one good trick on him before I came up!"

"Now, now May, no details!"

"Don't worry, it's not what you think. I took advantage of him being asleep to pull a hair out of his nose. You ought to have heard the yell the brute gave—I thought the porter was going to come up! Do you think that made him get out of bed? He went straight back to sleep! There he is, flat on his back in that purple nightshirt like a tart's, and he said he wouldn't get up unless you came and pulled him out by his feet."

It is almost impossible for me to avoid knowing the most intimate details of May's domestic life. She has such a crude, vivid way of describing her lover to me that I know how that man washes, goes to sleep and wakes up, and May does not restrict herself to information of that kind. However, today, I was not interested in smutty talk.

"And what about lunch?"

"What lunch?" yawned May. The little tongue that showed between the shining teeth was not moist enough and was white in the middle.

"Why, ours of course! You wanted us to lunch together. Well, it's a quarter to one and you've got no further than putting on *his* bedroom slippers! So whatever time are we going to have lunch?"

May planted herself in front of the window with her legs and arms outspread in the shape of an X; her cloudy hair looked as if it was smoking in the sunlight.

"What time? How on earth do I know? This woman never talks about anything else; the time it is, the time it's going to be, the time it ought to be! One lunches when one feels like it, one goes to bed when one feels like it—— Time's only for flunkeys and stationmasters! That's what I say. Oh my, what a face! Listen—because it's you—I'll just dash upstairs to the others. If they're chockful of the drug, I'll leave them and come haring down again and wake my man up with a good glass of Vittel water—nice and cold—delicately poured over all his most sensitive spots. After that, thirty-five minutes and I'm ready! Oh, you make me sick, the whole lot of you! By the way, would you like me to get the hors d'oeuvre sent up to you?"

She departed in calculated disorder, slithering about in her man's slippers, catching her Japanese sleeves on the door-key.

What a beautiful Riveria day lies in front of me and below me! As yesterday, this noonday hour in Nice gives us all it can; sunshine that prevents one from thinking or taking action and a summer breeze. There are two sails slanting over the sea and, above the sea, a distant aeroplane. The road, freshly sprinkled, makes a dark track, restful to the eyes. There is no traffic on it but the long motor-cars that dart past like fishes and the slow horse-drawn cabs with their drivers chewing a sprig of mimosa. Beyond, the blinding white Promenade is thronged with strollers and dogs on leads. There are hardly any children in the crowd. You could easily count the little bare legs running about or the uncertainly toddling bundles of snowy lace and batiste like that one yesterday. Nice is a town for grown-up people.

My eye is caught by vivid hats, by the fresh, acid green of a passing dress. I can see immaculate costumes of light, far too light silk. They make me think of those butterflies which the first treacherous rays of spring lure to their death. Alongside them, I can see women heavily swathed in furs and, sitting on the benches, prudent strollers armed with green umbrellas and woollen shawls. I am reminded of those restaurants where the head-waiter offers you a fan while the page-boy slips a hot-water bottle under your feet.

In front of the hotel, mandolines and Italian singers make a musical buzzing that the wind carries away in gusts, and I think I can smell something slightly sickening to my famished stomach, the scent of flat straw baskets loaded with violets and red carnations.

When are we going to have lunch? Down below, on the jetty, a fox-terrier whose barking is so continuous that one does not notice it keeps obstinately trying to bring back a pebble too big for him as a souvenir of the beach. That is the fiftieth time a red hat, encircled by a green cord fastened with a purple rosette has gone by. And how many times have I counted the return of those two short-skirted young women—less chic versions of May—one in green, the other in yellow, teetering along with tiny, painful steps on their absurd heels? They do not go far; in any case, you would think that, some five hundred yards away, there is an invisible barrier which nearly all the strollers come up against and which forces them to turn back. Yet, further on, there is a fine, tempting stretch where one can step out and hear the sound of the sea.

I am also gazing at a bright little restaurant, moored to the edge of the Promenade like a house-boat. Brague and I used to lunch there in the old days; silent, contented, stupefied with sunshine . . . I'm hungry. My friends will quite likely be another hour. As to the two above, I don't expect them.

The two down below will arrive quarrelling; she with that perfume which is so strong as to be slightly pharmaceutical; he well-scrubbed, with his hair damp and his hand warm from his bath. And they will exchange insults or kisses that smell of mouth-wash. Their quarrels and their caresses which demand neither darkness nor privacy will continue until lunch, for we *shall* have lunch. Oh yes, we shall end up lunching in the almost empty room that will smell of cold fried food, the onions of the hors d'oeuvre, and tangerines. We shall lunch in spite of the indefatigable gypsy band, in spite of May's contradictory orders to the head-waiter.

By the time they pour out our coffee, the four o'clock sun will be reddening over the sea. Then we shall set off in the car for "a little outing for the good of our health" through a glacial, mauve twilight. Round about seven, May, shivering and bad-tempered, will demand her tea at Cap Martin, and I shall have seen yet another beautiful day crumble away goodness knows how, useless, shrunk to nothing and ruined.

Bonsoir, Madame la Lune,
Bonsoir!
C'est votre ami Pierrot qui vient vous voir.

May sings in tune, but, in my opinion, the planet's rising could well have done without the Montmartre serenade. The moon rising over the sea, the red misty moon, not yet full, was the same slender one that had sailed between two clouds the other night when I had given up trying to go to sleep. The brief, anguished awareness of time flying by so fast, empty, made me all the more sensitive to the chilly hour. It was still daylight, but the light was withdrawing from the clumps of trees and even from the dusty verges of the road. The last vestiges clung obstinately to the white façades of buildings, to the winding road, to our own pale cheeks. It was that fugitive moment when one becomes aware, underneath the clustered villas and the artificial gardens, of the rather depressing and austere aridity of this rocky coast. Why did May have to sing *Bonsoir, Madame la Lune?*

There were four of us in the hired car that was bringing us back to Nice; May and myself in the back; Jean, her lover, and Masseau on the pull-down seats. As a keen wind was blowing our own dust, as well as that of the cars we passed, back in our faces, we were all of us half-masked with goggles. Now that May had woken me up, I amused myself by studying these three half-faces. The twilight hid the eyes behind a glitter of glass, but mouth, chin and nostrils became all the more eloquent. Had I not been masked myself, I would have been embarrassed by watching only the lips of the people to whom I was talking.

May suffered most under the mask with its big oval lenses: you realised that she had hardly any nose. Yet how young and mobile her rather flat mouth is! Looking at her full cheeks whose rich down holds the powder so well, I worried about my own slightly dried-up mask. But a yawn from Jean, May's Jean, suddenly interested me in this masculine face. I had never noticed before how the clean-shaven, sulky mouth, full-lipped but finely chiselled at the corners, revealed both the weaknesses and charms of his character, nor that the chin was at once obstinate and feminine, nor that the neck showing above the low collar was strong but so smoothly rounded that no muscles were visible. I decided that, when he removed his mask, I must take a better look at his eyes.

Masseau, of course, had been smoking opium the night before.

You had only to look at the bad colour of his wry, sad, intelligent
lips and the swelling on the lower part of his green cheeks between
the big nose and the old-fashioned pointed beard. He was silent,
waiting. Waiting to get back to Nice and smoke. He had made a
slight, nervous grimace when May had started singing *Bonsoir, Madame la Lune*, and I thought—though I was not quite sure—that an
extremely malicious smile had hovered on Jean's lips at the same moment.

Instinctively, I kept my mouth tight shut. I had all too good
reason to fear that, with my eyes no longer there to give it the lie,
people might read my real feelings on it; weariness, disgust at a day
badly begun, spent in meaningless activity and ending up in our sullen silence.

The car in which we were travelling was not a particularly good
one and the road itself anything but comfortable. Its rough, twisting
course flung us now to the left, now to the right; I had to keep myself rigid to avoid collapsing on May and May kept flopping on to
my shoulder. Our intellectual conversation was restricted to exclamations that were meant to be gay or that deplored the state of the
roads. The lights of Monte Carlo wrenched a sigh from me; more
than fifty minutes' drive ahead!

The lights woke May up. She removed her goggles, revealing her
beautiful, blinking eyes and her scrap of a nose barred with a red
groove.

"Jean! Jean! Suppose we stop and have dinner at Monte Carlo?
Just as we are, all disgustingly filthy and messy? No? Why not? Oh,
of course, as soon as I want to do something a bit amusing, I can't
find a soul to back me up. Jean, look at the place where you hit me
last year. Yes, dear, that's what he did to me, the brute! Jean, did
you see that little villa on the corner, the Gonzalez's villa? Must be
ruinous to rent a place like that in Monte Carlo!"

I too was reviving old memories as we drove through, but in silence. There was the Villa des Bananiers, a mediocre hotel for modest purses, where Brague and I used to put up along with other stage
people, old women gamblers in black lace mantles and dowdy foreigners. Just by the Théâtre des Beaux-Arts, I know a shady and
agreeable little English pub where I used to drink scalding lemonade
or velvety hot grog after the daily matinées. Round about five
o'clock, I only met one Englishman there, patiently getting drunk.
He had a dark red face, burnished by heavy drinking, and he used to
hum a quavering little song. I can conjure it up so vividly—it's still

all so close to me—the smell of hot canvas and damp earth that triumphed over the smell of grease-paint in the striped tents where we used to dress, at the Beaux-Arts, on those hot afternoons.

In front of the Hôtel de Paris, the car slowed down and hesitated, as if inviting us to get out.

"Jean, I tell you we ought to dine here."

The masked man shook his head, then changed his mind and turned his expressive half-face to me.

"Do you want to?"

"Oh! don't ask *me!*"

I wanted to return to Nice but, if I admitted it, I should start May off and, like a coward, I recoiled at the thought of three-quarters-of-an-hour of insults and tears.

"You know *I* . . ."

"I know," said Jean peremptorily. "Drive on, chauffeur, we're returning to Nice."

"Idiot," squeaked May into the wind. "It wouldn't have hurt you to be nice to me for once, would it? May I ask why you didn't want to stay and have dinner here?"

"Because I didn't feel like it," said Jean placidly.

A rusty laugh greeted this reply. It came from Masseau, who had not uttered a word for hours.

"Oh, so *you've* come to life!" May snapped at him aggressively. "Seems you're feeling better, then?"

Masseau removed his goggles and the passing lights played on his small, red-rimmed eyes. They were blinking and satanic, the eyes of a demon bureaucrat.

"I feel better, certainly, than if I were feeling worse. For if you say: 'I am feeling better', you appear to imply that at some previous, though unspecified period, you were feeling worse. However, since in general I am dissatisfied with my state of health, I can only reply: Yes, I am feeling better, better than if I were feeling worse."

He has an old man's voice and an ageless face. He is frail, but only rarely tired; capriciously doped or prostrated by the "drug". May addresses him as "tu"—but she does that to so many men—yet she does not seem to know him any better than I do who have met him fourteen or fifteen times in a fortnight. When I questioned her once about Masseau, she replied: "Don't ask *me!* He's just an old chap, a colonial."

Now, revived by the darkness and the anticipation of the poison, he was waking up from his long and lugubrious muteness. He put up a fine-boned yellow hand, stroked the little goatee that looked like dried hay and said, glancing sidelong at me, "The gesture of the ladies' man."

He spread out his beard fanwise and said, "Henri IV."

He removed his soft hat, twisted a lock of hair into a horn above his forehead and said, "*Louis Dix*, the Headstrong."

Then he relapsed into his silence and his shivering, huddled immobility until the night, blacker after the lights of Monte Carlo, enveloped us again. The head-lamps that had just been switched on opened a tunnel of brightness in front of us, ringed with a pale, quivering rainbow. The dry, less chilly air expanded my nostrils and I leant the nape of my neck against the fold of the lowered hood with the relaxed, secure feeling that came from knowing that, till we reached Nice, I was invisible; the darkness veiled me better than my glass-eyed mask.

"Sorry," said the voice of Jean, whose knees had just brushed against mine.

"That's right, go on!" May reproached him. "Play footie-footie with her, that would be just the end!"

"Why 'the end'? You're not very polite to Madame Renée Néré, May!"

"What," murmured the voice of Masseau on the breeze, "is the end of the non-dining in Monte Carlo? Answer: the end of the non-dining in Monte Carlo is to play footie-footie with Madame Renée Néré."

I could feel May fidgeting with exasperation beside me.

"You're both too disgusting for words! To think I'm supposed to have an intelligent lover and that there are people cracked enough to say Masseau's got a distinguished mind! Honest, I'm still wondering what's so special about you and him! When did you last see yourself, you intelligent lover you, trying to do something to please me and putting yourself out for me?"

"Never," replied the intelligent lover very emphatically. "You're not an old lady and you're not one of my relatives. Consequently . . ."

Once again I was amused and dumbfounded by this couple in which the woman was treated *as* a woman only in bed.

Upright, May finds all the prerogatives of her sex withdrawn from her and the harmony of lovers transformed into school children's rivalries. People like that are new to me. I endured my husband's tyranny when I was a young and silly bride and Maxime Dufferein-Chautel would have liked to impose a tender, traditional middle-class authority upon me. I have seen my old friend Hamond submit to the lunatic caprices of an imperious child and, backstage, I have seen the primitive fervour which prostrates the female before a tribal chieftain. But never have I anywhere seen anything resembling May and Jean.

Apart from money, apart from love-making—if even in that!—she receives nothing from him in the way of masculine homage.

"What's more," May said suddenly, as if she had read my thoughts, "as from tomorrow morning, I'm taking a room and a bathroom for myself at the Impérial. I've had enough of you always bagging the first bath and finding a shaving-brush full of soap stuck beside my tooth-brush. My dear"—May turned her small face, which I could only make out as a pale blur, towards me—"I don't know if you're like me . . ."

"No," said Jean.

"What d'you mean, no?"

"I say: no, she's not like you. She doesn't find a shaving-brush stuck beside her tooth-brush. Moreover, she isn't my mistress."

"Say you wish she were. Go on, say it at once!"

"Oh, why at once? May, when are you going to stop being in such a violent hurry? Always this haste that ruins all the best things in life! Why, only yesterday morning, to quote only one example . . ."

"Yesterday morning? What did I do, yesterday morning?"

"Do you want me to tell?"

Masseau, who had appeared to be asleep, became interested. As we passed through the lights of Beaulieu, he assumed, in order to listen, the dreamy pose of a sentimental "portrait-study" by Disderi. With one finger at the corner of his mouth, and his eyes and ears agog, he announced, "I am the Empress Eugénie."

But he was not destined to hear any scandalous revelations, for May provided a few peaceful passers-by in Beaulieu with the unwonted spectacle of a young woman standing up in an open red car, scientifically boxing with a gentleman sitting opposite her and screaming at him: "I forbid you! I absolutely forbid you to tell about yesterday morning. Otherwise I'll tell you about your boil above your thigh and the story of the cotton-wool!"

These words produced a smart blow that sent her sprawling on to the back seat where I was keeping out of the way as best I could. I was thoroughly exasperated. This return by night, along the sea swept by horizontal luminous trails, could have been charming. The night had come on so quickly that one could hardly divine the black water rippling under the flotilla of lights and almost imperceptibly rocking it. The two lovers, originally locked together in combat, were still carrying on some kind of tussle. It was Masseau's obvious interest in it, rather than prudishness, that made me avert my head.

At last we were getting near Nice. That garland of living flame ahead of us was the Promenade des Anglais, and there on the Promenade was my temporary refuge, admittedly only an hotel bedroom, but at least somewhere where I could lock the door behind me, where I could smell my own perfume.

"What time is it?"

The question had burst out in spite of myself, as we were passing the minute theatre whose name in red electric bulbs lights up the last trees of the Jardin Public. Such a tiny theatre! How cosy it was in there, last year, while the December showers lashed the pavement and the leaves of the mimosas drooped like bedraggled feathers!

"Pay a forfeit!" cried May. "She's asked the time, she can't get away with less than a louis!"

"Paid to whom?" demanded Masseau.

The motor drew up in front of the entrance to the Impérial, but May was too astonished to get out at once.

"To whom? Why, me of course. When I'm about, who else do you expect people to pay money to?"

Jean shrugged his shoulders and leapt out without a word. No remark, however stinging, no cane, however supple, is capable of curing May of her inborn defect: she scrounges and sponges, and, when she returns from a banquet, she does not exclaim: "There were avalanches of flowers and fruit on the table!" but estimates their cost precisely. "Peaches at five francs apiece, my dears, and fifty louis' worth of orchids on the table." May makes use of other people's purses, not like a sponger but like a distinguished guest who must be served first with every dish.

Ah, there we were at last! We had got back. Once again, we had got back. Here we were again, caparisoned in furs and goggled like Arctic explorers, after having driven sixty miles along the Corniche. We stood blinking in the white vestibule under the stares of the English bachelors with their short pipes and of the roulette players—twenty sous on the 5, twenty on the 10, and . . . hard luck! twenty sous on the 40 that never turns up—all of whom had had their dinner punctually and left the dining-room. Nevertheless, it was for this unappreciative audience that May snatched off her chinchilla cap and shook out her hair, releasing a snow-storm of hairpins and Jean rewarded her with a sharp surreptitious kick on the shin. Masseau, indifferent to fashion and even to good manners, yawned so violently that tears came into his eyes, his goatee thrust up by the extraordinary Medici collar of his antique caped Ulster that looked like a German professor's.

He caught sight of himself in a glass, pinched the corners of his lips in an affected smile and, leaning towards me, said confidentially, "Henri Trois."

The lift seemed a long while coming. I felt slightly shamed at being subjected to the curiosity of these strangers who were dividing up our group according to their fancy and speculating: "Which of the two men is the younger woman going up with?"

Finally the cage carried off all four of us, thus putting an end to a moment of general uneasiness, of false intimacy, almost antipathy. We said: "See you later" firmly and coldly as if we had no intention of meeting again.

"Oh! those people, those people!" I can find nothing to add, so I repeat once more: "Oh! those people! I've had enough of them!"

The waiter who brought me a tray of tea and a macedoine of fruit has gone off with a brief note of excuse to May.

"May dear, I must have caught a chill. I don't feel at all well so shan't have dinner, but go straight to bed. So sorry. See you tomorrow."

Now, with my door locked and bolted, I can go on pacing to and fro and working up my bad temper. "I'm sick of those people!" A scalding, aromatic bath which awaits me exhales its pungent steam. I am trailing about in old bedroom slippers and my dressing-gown gapes open over a crumpled chemise, whose slotted insertion is empty of ribbon; it is only too obvious that I put up meekly with the disastrous laundering one gets in hotels. In the days when I earned my own living, humbler lingerie never lacked ribbons or buttons. "Oh, *how* sick of those people I am!" But I name no names, for fear of accusing myself.

How can I blame Masseau, that cultured bibliomaniac, foundering in opium? Why accuse May, any more than Jean, of hooking on to me, when they only seek me out because I am as idle as they are?

She is not spiteful and he is quite pleasant, a cautious man who laughs a great deal and never talks. Among the number of "those people" of whom I am so heartily sick ought I to include my poor Gentleman-on-his-own, and the staff of the hotel, and the strollers on the jetty? Yes, I prefer to. It's wiser—and less unjust. Poor May, who's done me no harm. . . . At this moment, she is dining with Jean at the Bonne Hôtesse or the Casino, or else Room 82 is resounding with the shrieks and blows of another "grand beating-up".

As I stretched my limbs and relaxed in my scalding-hot bath, I laughed unkindly imagining the May of tomorrow morning, battered and mercenary: "My dear, just look if he hasn't given me fifty louis' worth of bruises!"

Yes, I've had enough of those people, it's true. But, besides beginning to know myself, I am also beginning to know the advantages and disadvantages of this extraordinary part of the world where the mornings are enchanting and the nights, however starry, make one shiver in the discomfort of a double climate. Here cold nights are not invigorating and warm nights throb with fever rather than with passion. Have I, in so few days, become acclimatised to all the caprices of a Mediterranean winter or—far more likely—was my own temperament not already like its weather? The sun here would ripen the grapes in January, if a breath of wind or a patch of icy shade were not enough to wither everything. Max, lying in your arms was like lying in a tomb made to my measurements and yet I rose up from that tomb and fled!

All that does not mean that I need stay on any longer with "those people". The only bond between us is idleness. Last year, May had another lover, less attractive and more considerate than this one. This one I accepted rather coldly and with a touch of embarrassment, whereas May flung herself into this new liaison with all the ardour and organising zeal that usually go into furnishing a new house.

May? I could do without her as well as without Jean. In a year, our intimacy has made no progress. We have discussed love, hygiene, dresses, hats, beauty creams and cooking without acquiring any more affection and esteem for each other. A dozen times I have left May, with no regrets: a dozen times she has gone off with no more affectionate goodbye than a handshake. And a dozen times chance has brought her back to me, turning up unexpectedly to wreck all my plans for an orderly life, my resolutions to settle down into wise, sober middle-age; turning up with the invariable exclamation: "I *am* a character, aren't I?" The moment she appears, the open book shuts of its own accord, the flow of thought and imagination dries up, the mind that was trying to soar is brought rudely back to earth. Even words themselves take flight; all that remain are two or three hundred everyday terms, some of them slangy, with which one can ask one's way, demand food and drink and make love, terms such as you find in a phrase-book for foreigners. And I don't assert my independence. I close the book, and I put on a dress to go off with May and Jean to some commonplace *boîte*.

I am perfectly well aware that May has not a will that overcomes mine, but an inner mechanism superior to my own, a whirling driving-power that is never slowed down by thoughts. She has taught me that one can dine without being hungry, talk without saying anything, laugh from sheer force of habit, drink out of human respect and live with a man in a state of complete servility while maintaining all the appearances of frantic independence. She is no stranger to bouts of neurasthenia and black depression but she knows two great physicians of the soul; the manicurist and the hairdresser. Should they fail, there is only the higher resort of opium and cocaine. If May, looking pale and heavy-eyed, drags herself from chair to chair, yawns, shivers, bursts into tears at a word and tries vainly not to think about her empty past and her empty future, she exclaims fervently: "Tell the manicurist to come up!" or "I'm going to have my hair washed". Then, reassured and relaxed, she abandons her stubby little paws or her golden hair to clever hands that know how to knead, how to scratch delicately, how to brush and polish and wave. Under their soothing, healing magic passes, May smiles, lends her ears to gossip and vague, flattering words and drifts off into the light doze of convalescence.

Is she gay? Men assure me that she is, but personally I do not find her so. Nature has drawn all the features of laughter itself in her round childish face; a Cupid's bow mouth that tilts up at the corners like her mischievous eyes, a short little nose with quivering nostrils. But gaiety is not a perpetual fidgeting that betrays a lack of security, it is not chatter full of recriminations, nor is it a craving for everything that intoxicates. Gaiety, it seems to me, is something calmer, something healthier, something more serious.

Fundamentally, perhaps, Jean is gayer than May. One does not often hear him speak and he scowls as readily as he smiles, but I recognise in him the serenity of those who have a good digestion. And, whereas May, who goes crazy the moment they start quarrelling, looks about and reaches for a pair of scissors or a hat-pin, Jean simply strikes her with the flat of his heavy hand, not viciously but with a kind of athletic heartiness.

Decidedly, most decidedly, the time has come to leave these people! Whether I like it or not, they take up too much space, too much time in my life. True, my life is an empty waste, but every time May passes through it, she leaves a trodden-down goat-track where nothing will grow. Why linger on any longer? I go on and on repeating: "The fact is, I don't know these people", while every minute, this evening, is showing me them in a worse light—I know them too well.

Besides, I can guess what people must already be saying about our trio; a woman on her own, too intimate with a pair of dissipated lovers. Ah, how typical of me that is! The mere idea that I—nowadays an obscure nonentity—might have been misjudged makes me feel that Paris, the provinces, and various foreign courts are all staring at me with an accusing eye. I feel so hot with virtuous indignation that I am making my bed warm. It was so cool just now with its sheets, glossy from being ironed by cylindrical rollers; sheets whose chaste smell of chlorine is not wholly disguised by my perfume.

I had almost got to sleep, when someone in the room next door returned and banged the door with callous brutality. Then two shoes fell with a thud, probably hurled from one end of the room to the other and so heavy that the man might have been wearing hobnailed clogs. Now he is walking about in his socks but the warped floorboards creak under the carpet and I can tell when the traveller goes from the dressing-table to the bedside table, from the bedside table into the bathroom. In the bathroom that backs on to mine, I can hear the clinking of the tooth-glass, the clattering fall of some silver or nickel object, the gush of water splashing into the bath. Alas, I cannot avoid being aware of the belated traveller's every movement and action. Steeling myself to weary resignation, I wait for sleep to plunge him, at least for a few hours, into oblivion. How I execrate that unknown guest, how I wish Mr. X would be stricken by sudden paralysis, even by death! I wait till he has finished prowling about, emitting bellowing yawns, coughing, spitting, testing his baritone voice with "Hmms" that make glassware on my bedside table vibrate.

Above my head, the ceiling shudders under muffled footsteps. The room on the other side of mine comes to life with the sound of pit-a-patting and a shrill, aggressive woman's voice. She is talking to someone whose whispered replies I cannot hear; it sounds as if she were having a quarrel over the telephone . . . I wait. I set up an opposition to all these various noises by remaining as rigidly still as a thief and hardly breathing, as if to set an example of silence.

The bell in the corridor shrills twice, three times, ten times under the pressure of a nervous finger; the lift stops with a reverberating "poum" that shakes the landing and the iron gate is violently slammed. A night typical of any hotel and in this life of mine, going from hotel to hotel, I have lost count of these ruined nights whose slow hours are registered by the dropping of boots, the banging of doors, coughing, and all the other clatter of the human stable. Now and then, above the sustained pedal bass of snores, my ear has caught violent overtones: the madman's revolver, the abominable scream of a hysterical woman and the choking nightmare of a gambler in Monte Carlo! The papier-mâché partitions have often let me overhear softer moanings; the sighs and rustlings of tempestuous love making which I have rudely disturbed by a deliberate cough or a bang on the wall, for I have become severe towards other people's sexual pleasures.

Nothing obliges me to go on enduring the trivial round of petty tortures that hotel life imposes on me. Tomorrow, if I liked, I could take refuge from them in a peaceful villa or a comfortable flat in Paris, for the death of my sister-in-law Margot has left me with a private income. Twenty-five thousand francs a year, for a woman like me, is riches. But there it is; for some reason or other, I don't want to. When a dog has been kept a long time on a lead, it does not go prancing off the moment you undo the catch of its chain; it goes on walking at a measured pace, instinctively calculating the length of an imaginary shackle. I go on with my hotel life, and why not? Broken, fitful sleep, meals at odd hours, chicory coffee and blueish milk, all that is part and parcel of my lot.

Besides, since I have given up my profession, I have acquired the rather selfish, perverse taste of lying in bed in the mornings while others all about me are up and doing. I admit it is a pleasure to me, at that hour when the growing daylight is drawing blue streaks between the slats of the shutters, to hear a valet rapping harshly on neighbouring doors, to imagine the weary awakenings and disgusted yawns, the hurry, the rainy morning, the missed train. A perverse, revengeful joy makes me stretch myself between my warm sheets and I have just time to murmur drowsily: "It's *their* turn now . . ." before drifting off into the shallow, almost conscious sleep of broad daylight, lit up from within by the strange planets of a succession of dreams and from without by the light that forces its way through my half-closed eyelids.

I know it is probably late, but the electric clock only marks the time by an imperceptible click every sixty seconds. May and Jean must have finished their quarrel, perhaps even their reconciliation? Someone is snoring next door, a majestic ample snore as he breathes in, interrupted, as he breathes out, by a comic, macabre little *cloc*. It is a variety of snoring not unknown to me; I prefer it to the progressive snore which begins low, grows louder and reaches its climax in a violent fit of coughing. No doubt, at this moment, Masseau's big nose is reverberating with a hollow din, unless the opium lamp is still alight, its short flame flickering at moments as a drop of sizzling syrup falls into it.

I shall not sleep, but I shall not get impatient. This particular night will be no longer and no shorter than any other similar night. A night always comes to an end, something which most insomniacs do not sufficiently realise. I excuse them, because nearly all of them are ill. I am not ill, I am simply accustomed to not sleeping. I do not turn on the light and I do not open a book; excellent methods both of banishing shy sleep and withering the eyelids. I merely wait. They are odious, all those people behind the walls and above the ceiling, wallowing in repose like glutted barbarians; they are odious, but . . . they are there. Who can say whether, instead of wanting to fly from their presence, it is precisely their presence I seek? I may well have deceived myself the day when, by leaving my home and renouncing every domestic comfort, I supposed I was taking one more step towards solitude. Flanked by as many odious guardians as there are walls to a room, I keep repeating, as if to convince myself more firmly that they are there: "They're odious". And, thus surrounded, thus reassured, I wait the cool rise of dawn over the sea, the higher surge of the waves under the morning wind and that indistinct paleness that creeps slowly into the room till it reaches my bed, my forehead, and finally my eyes, which from then on will be closed and insensible.

THREE

THEY say it is difficult for a woman to remain indifferent to the spectacle of a man in tears. I do not remember that Max's tears, the day he wept so ingenuously over my approaching departure, seemed to me particularly moving.

But I do think, for a woman, that the sight of another woman's suffering is often poignant. It tends to arouse the sharp, egotistical fear we call presentiment, for it is nearly always herself a woman sees reflected in another woman's misery. She can almost formulate her presentiment, like a temporarily sober man looking at a sprawling drunk: "That's how I may well be on Sunday".

May is unhappy. I would have gladly dispensed with knowing this but a "real character", a "child of nature" prides herself on her frankness and regards the pouring out of the most embarrassing confidences as simple honesty.

Poor "real character"! There she was, in the room she had insisted on having to herself. There she was, miserable, among a gay, colourful disorder of silk chemises, open-work stockings, dresses with pointed trains or abbreviated skirts. Trunk-trays were strewn on the bed, a hat-box gaped open and May's chambermaid, a mulish Basque girl, was bustling about, looking sullen and disapproving. I also perceived, beside the tea-tray, two boxes of pills and a stubby little bottle full of white powder. May was yawning and sniffing; her nose was stopped up by the cold morning gloom with flying clouds, by tears and, above all, by having taken cocaine.

"Blow your nose, May."

"What, and make my nose red! I'd much rather sniff!"

She laughed hoarsely, like a child who has screamed too much, for her grief—and I commend her for it—had not gushed out in lamentations. She had merely said: "There. That's that. It had to happen," then swore like a trooper and called Jean the vilest names. She had brought away with her, rolled up in her fist, a photograph of Jean on a postcard and a handful of banknotes, pilfered from her lover's waistcoat under cover of the general confusion. I would much have preferred to go up to my room again. My legs were bare under my dressing-gown and I was shivering from not having dried myself properly after my bath. I felt I was lacking in pity, in warmth—in other words, in affection—and I forced myself to be hearty.

"Now, now, May . . . it isn't serious, all this. Anyway, it's not the first time, is it?"

"The first time what? That I have taken a separate room? Goodness me, if I had as many thousand francs a year as Jean and me have had quarrels! I know perfectly well it isn't serious."

Nevertheless, she was settling herself in as if it were serious. She dragged the new dressing-table over to the window, tilted the mirror and began to do her face, a performance she will go through shamelessly in front of Jean, of myself, of the waiter or the little page-boy. She made a thorough job of it. There was a supplementary scouring of the ears and the corners of the mouth; even the eyelids were raised and turned up with the tip of a finger, as one does to the gills of a dubiously fresh fish.

Then May thrust her forefinger, wrapped in the corner of a handkerchief, into either nostril and cleaned them both out as vigorously as a rinser washing out tall champagne glasses. She scraped her tongue with an ivory spatula, cruelly squeezed out a minute blackhead between two nails, then set to work with the tweezers, plucking out hairs here and there.

"I've learnt by experience it isn't serious. But, after all, I know men, and, above all, I know Jean and I live with him. What did you say?"

I had said nothing. I had only turned away to hide the smile that was neither malicious nor kindly at hearing May say: "I know men". Why do women always utter this classic phrase not after a triumph but after a mortifying failure which would seem to prove just the contrary? I had said nothing, I do *not* know men.

"I've been living with him for a year," May went on, "and I can say without blowing my own trumpet he's not the sort that usually sticks to one woman for long."

With her hair scraped back like a Chinese woman's under a scarf twisted round her head, May was smoothing a liberal amount of cold cream into her cheeks and her forehead. However, she was so desperately anxious to convince me that she interrupted her massage and continued her speech, gesticulating with all her fingers outspread. I thought of the old days of putting on and removing make-up; I thought of the time when Brague used to call me, when my face was all shiny with Vaseline, "the rat that tumbled into the oil".

"A year with a man: that begins to look like a permanent set-up, even though we've only actually lived together at the sea-side or in water places. Sharing a flat together . . . no, that wouldn't suit us. He's got his affairs to see to and I've got my own ideas. There are things I just won't accept. What did you say?"

I had said nothing. But May's fine instinct warned her each time she came up against my incredulity. Things she just won't accept? What things? She takes money, accepts blows, swallows insults—all, it is true, with the imperious air of a little tyrant.

"The fact is, if Jean stops with me . . . oh, don't worry, I'm not getting myself into a state! Perhaps it's more out of vanity than because he's fond of me, because he knows I'm a character too, in my own way, and not an easy-going one either. I can be led, but I can't and won't be driven. There's the proof of it!" May wound up proudly, pointing to her open trunks. "I said to him: 'Au revoir, my boy, in this world or the next'. There!"

She was lying. Her bluff was touching, poor little May. At least it *ought* to have been touching. A man would have been sorry for her, or even a woman—any other than myself.

For she was talking about this lover whom she boasted of having said goodbye to and whom she reckoned to see again tonight, tomorrow, almost at once, as if she had just lost him for ever. She was running him down and remembering him and regretting him as if he was already part of her past.

I did what I could for May, that is to say I listened to her and nodded from time to time. By now her face was powdered mauve and touched with bright pink under the eyes that she had accentuated with grey eye-shadow to make them look voluptuously heavy. Eyelashes . . . mouth . . . a big velvet beauty-spot at the corner of her mouth. It was finished.

She smiled at me absent-mindedly in the glass and said, "How you're staring at me, Renée! You make me think of Jean when he says: 'What an ugly sight a pretty woman's toilet is!' He can be very difficult sometimes, the filthy brute!"

"Then why do you do all this redecorating in front of him?"

Her charming eyes opened wide with surprise between the stiff hedges of eyelashes.

"My dear! I don't say that when I'm thirty-five or forty, I won't hide when I do up my face, but now! I haven't got pimples, have I? Or wrinkles, or red-rimmed eyes? Nothing to hide, anyone can have a good look at it! Either one's natural, or one isn't. Shh!"

"What is it?"

"I thought I could hear his footsteps."

She listened. But he did not come.

"Tell me, May, has there been something more serious than usual between you?"

She looked at me; perplexed and, this time, sincere.

"Why . . . no . . . that's just it. On the contrary. That staggers me a little. You could almost say that practically nothing's happened. We didn't have a fight. I haven't got any marks. It's funny. For some days he's been nasty underneath. He's been putting on his dreamy, far away look—you know, what I call his gigolo's face."

She chewed the bright red lipstick on her lips and stared out over the sea, that was shadowed with grey and a bilious green, with a gaze in which I thought I could read the astonishment and incomprehension of a creature unjustly threatened. And suddenly I saw again, very clearly, Jean's half-masked face; the mouth with the deeply-incised corners, the faun-like cheekbones, the chin cleft with a dimple and the robust neck, padded with soft flesh. Suddenly I saw again that mysterious eyeless visage, and I was sorry for little May, for that man's face revealed all the characteristics of guile, of slightly brutal power and of a weakness attractive enough to obtain all he wanted. In other words, there was no doubt that he was the *stronger*.

"May we come in?"

"Who is 'we'?"

"Us!"

It was a reedy voice which I did not recognise as May's pretty mezzo-soprano; she has a tone of voice that lends charm to her speech. I opened the door and found myself face to face with two men. The one who was speaking in falsetto was Masseau. Either he had got up early or he had not gone to bed at all, for Jean had met him taking a walk on the beach, looking, as usual, like a bilious judge. He was wearing grey kid gloves, a soft felt hat, a perfectly ordinary tie, yet, for some reason, worn by him they took on an air of extravagant oddity. Moreover he had just walked along the Promenade and through the vestibule of the hotel decked in a wrinkled strand of seaweed, as broad as two fists, which he had found down by the sea and pinned round his neck. Going over to the looking-glass on my dressing-table, he arranged this piece of marine frippery in the form of a ruff and murmured, as if to himself, "Columbine!"

"Masseau, are you mad? Take that thing off, you smell of raw mussels."

"One of two things," said Masseau. "Either you are the slave of a prejudice known as 'Fashion' and I spurn you. Or else, in the depths of your heart, you are offering me what every woman radiates at the sight of me: love. In which case, you adore my caprice, the whim of a gladsome morn. Or else again . . . But I should have said: 'One of *three* things.' I shall begin all over again. One of three things . . ."

"Jean, can't you take that object off him?"

"Good heavens, no. I don't know what he's done to me but I'm powerless against Masseau. If we lived on the other side of the world, I'd be a king and I'd set Masseau up as a holy man, stark naked under a baobab."

"I've been one," said Masseau coldly. "One soon gets tired of it, and the health of a holy man on the other side of the world is bound to be deplorable. Innumerable offerings of the faithful, fruit, rice with saffron, mutton with rice, rice with sugar: it's the dilatation of the stomach that ruins the profession."

Normally I am terrified of mad people, but, like Jean, I feel the attraction of this monomaniac. It is impossible to know, with Masseau, where pretence begins. He confided to me once that he is far enough gone to *see*, written in front of him, the sentence he is uttering and he cannot restrain himself from making little dabs in the air to mark its punctuation. When at moments he recovers, as he did just then, a rapid, clipped speech, with no grammatical redundancies, it is always for brief anecdotes, shorn of all verisimilitude, yet which I feel prepared to accept as authentic. May detests Masseau, for she can manage neither to allure him nor to pierce his shell. In his presence, she is like a dog confronted with an impregnable hedgehog.

"Is May coming on after you, Jean, or are we picking her up on the way?"

"No to both questions," replied Jean, who was automatically correcting the alignment of my silver-backed brushes. "May's not feeling well, she isn't having lunch."

"Is she ill? I'll go and . . ."

He turned round sharply.

"It's very nice of you, but don't budge. She wants to sleep. All she's asked for is an egg and some consommé."

He took not the slightest pains to make me believe him; he merely said what was necessary, without pressing the point. He looked as healthy as a dark man with a slightly greenish tinge to his skin can look, and, with his typical impertinence, he was taking the stoppers, one by one, out of my scent bottles. I did not press the point either.

"Right! We'll enquire after the child after lunch. Shall we go down? Masseau! Goodness, now he's busy with his correspondence! Masseau!"

"I'm all yours," said Masseau. "All yours and . . ." (he pointed to the letter he was writing) . . . "and Its."

I waited, irritated. I didn't like his using my writing table nor Jean's opening and sniffing my perfumes and my boxes of powder. I didn't very much like someone coming into my untidy, scented bedroom, nor someone indicating a loose strand of hair on my nape by brushing it with his finger, nor someone removing a thread clinging to my skirt, just a little above the knee. I have developed a physical intransigence which is justifiable, if not amiable, and I had considerable difficulty in hiding it under a forced good fellowship.

Luckily, it was fine. In this part of the world, fine weather makes up for everything and can take the place of a happy love life as well as a topic of conversation.

"Isn't it a lovely day? What a pity that May . . . They say it's snowing in Paris. . . . Where's Masseau?"

"Leaving his seaweed in the cloakroom. Hors d'oeuvre?"

"No, not this morning. Isn't this heat incredible?"

Instinctively, I held up my face to a shaft of sunlight, as if to let it kiss me; then, instinctively too, I quickly withdrew it. "When I'm thirty-five or forty . . ." May had said. And, as she was saying it, I was staring at her uncovered forehead and temples and her clear-cut jawline. I lowered my head so that my hat should cast a little more shadow over my cheeks and I pulled my hands a little further forward on the table-cloth, my well-groomed hands that are no longer ruined by wet-white or by wresting with trunk-straps.

"Nice diamond," observed Jean.

"You might at least have said: 'Nice hands,' you uncivil man!"

"I might indeed have said so, but anyone can pay you a compliment on your hands, whereas there are very few men who really appreciate good stones."

I laughed, and, as I did so, I released something: though I had often found myself alone with May, without Jean, this was the first time that May's absence had left Jean and myself alone together.

"Jean, before Masseau comes back, what's the matter with May? Are you still furious with each other? They're so absurd, all these dramas over a shaving-brush or a button-hook! Honestly, you ought . . ."

On hearing me use the word "ought" to him, May's lover assumed a peculiarly insolent attitude. He put his hands in his pockets, flung back his head and whistled, looking at me under his lashes. I blushed, having been unaccustomed for years to a certain type of masculine rudeness. May, however bitterly she might have regretted it later, would have slapped that "gigolo's face" whose expression is nearly always more youthful than its features.

"I beg your pardon. I'm meddling in something that doesn't concern me."

"For one thing. And for another," he added, sitting upright again, "what does it matter to you?"

"What do you mean, what does it matter to me? You tell me that May's ill, I saw her yesterday morning—ah, here comes Masseau!—I saw her all to pieces in the middle of moving her things, so . . ."

"Ah, of course, so it's out of friendliness? Masseau, we haven't ordered anything for you. *Entrecôte béarnaise* do you?"

"It appeals to me passionately."

"Good! So it's out of friendliness, my dear Renée Néré, that you're making this attempt at reconciliation?"

I liked nothing about that particular moment, neither our table which seemed too big in the absence of May, nor this argument in which I did not want to be involved, nor Jean's manner. Having dealt so abruptly with Masseau, he was now talking with the precision and the affected restraint of a man in a rage.

"So it was out of friendship? Friendship for May rather than myself, I presume. But you haven't any genuine friendship for May, have you?"

"That's an idiotic question!"

It was easier to lose my temper than to lie. I could not make out what he was driving at; was he hoping to induce me to speak ill of his mistress? My appetite deserted me. All at once I had a distressing sensation of being divorced from reality. Everything receded far away and became very small, distinct and dissociated from me; the place where I was, the people eating at other tables, the treacherous sunlight and the man sitting opposite me, his bright eyes, of a mutable grey, fixed on mine.

"It's idiotic, and insulting. Yes, insulting—both to her and to me. There's no need to laugh. Masseau, I appeal to you."

But all I could see of Masseau, who had taken refuge behind a newspaper, was a bony hand raised to disclaim all responsibility. I weakened, and, like a coward, asked Jean, "Why did you say such a thing to me?"

"To amuse myself, and also because it's what I think. Come now, May's a nice little thing, but a woman like you . . ."

His unfinished sentence contained exactly what was most calculated to arouse my distrust; a compliment to myself and the worst possible insult to his mistress. He had already called her, in front of me, "an unattractive little tart" and even "a poseuse", but to go as far as accusing her, with false commiseration, of being "a nice little thing"! Masseau reappeared from behind his paper, blinking satanically, as if he hoped for some more unforgivable words.

"What do you mean—a woman like me? To begin with, I'm not in the least a woman-like-me. I'm a creature who adores the good things of this world and who likes soufflé potatoes when they're hot."

Masseau had taken a fountain-pen out of his pocket and was inscribing on his soufflé potatoes—they were as big and round as beach-pebbles—*Souvenir of Tréport; Biarritz, Queen of Resorts; Dieppe, Summer 1912*. Then he arranged them round the rim of his plate, but ate nothing. When he was handed the dish of steak, he gasped "What is this dead animal?" in such a horrified tone that I refused my almost raw meat, to the immense delight of Jean, who burst out laughing. He laughs, not like a light-hearted man but like a rather malicious child.

"It must ruin anyone's temper to live with you, Jean! You never laugh except at catastrophes. No! I definitely *don't* want this meat. Order me all sorts of cheese, a pot of cream and some fruit. As for you, Masseau, I hope your worthy companion burns all the pipes she cooks for you tonight. Anyway, are we going to go on sitting here for ever? We seem to be taking an interminable time over lunch today!"

Jean began to think of the afternoon that lay ahead, of May waiting for him, and became gloomy. The excellent coffee, with cream on it, along with our cigarettes, brought all three of us back to a state of euphoria, all the more precious and perfect for being fleeting. My nostrils were filled only with the pleasant aromas of peeled oranges, scalding coffee and fine tobacco. Jean was smoking with epicurean pleasure, and looking thoroughly cheerful again. He has a sensitive, impenetrable face, in which everything registers, but only in black and white, without tell-tale transitions.

The cropped head of one of the Impérial's little page-boys, knee-high to a gnat, suddenly appeared level with the top of the table and announced to Jean: "A letter for you, Sir. The lady said I was to give it you as soon as she'd gone."

"Gone?"

Jean gave us both a brusque, interrogating look before he opened the letter. He merely glanced at it, then thrust it under our noses. It was a pencilled note.

"*Enjoy your lunch. I'm off. Goodbye.*
                    May."

"What does this mean, Jean?"

The little page, who had not been running, pretended to be out of breath in his zeal to deliver the message and blinked his white rabbit's eyes. Jean shot a "Right, you needn't wait" forceful enough to knock him down and the white rabbit scuttled away.

"But, Jean, this is impossible! Suppose I go and ask at the desk?"

"Ask what? My dear woman, I implore you sit down and take off that expression of a lady who has lost her Belgian griffon. Your coffee will get cold."

He shifted back a little from the table, crossed his legs, and resumed his cigarette. But his nostrils were quivering and I could count his quickened heartbeats by the little jerks of his raised foot. We were almost alone in the dining-room and I would gladly have obeyed the secret wish of the waiters who were clearing the neighbouring tables and laying them for afternoon tea. Stealthily, I studied Jean's face, searching for the painful, heroic grimace that must have distorted Max's when, nearly three years ago now, he read my farewell letter: "*My darling Max, I'm going away . . .*" But all I could catch on Jean's features was an ambiguous expression of fluttering expectation, of indecision, an air of listening rather than brooding. And this gave him a new, tender face, averted from us and gazing out at the sea; a beautiful, lover's face brimming over not with tears but with hope.

"Masseau?"

Although I had spoken very low, nodding in the direction of the exit, Jean noticed it.

"You're not going? Why? Out of discretion? You . . . respect my grief? I don't demand so much from either of you, especially from you, Renée."

"Is that a dismissal, Sir?" said Masseau, theatrically flinging an imaginary *capa* over his shoulder.

"Of course not, old man, of course not. We're not going to make a tragic scene, just because poor little May . . ."

"Ah! Jean, don't start speaking ill of her again!"

I laughed, perfectly aware that I was not saying what I ought to say and that my slightest word was justifying what Jean had affirmed just now: "You are not May's friend."

"Heavens, no!" he sighed through the smoke. "At heart, there wasn't a better little creature living than that child."

Relieved, I pounced on the opening he offered me.

"Wasn't she? Wasn't she? . . . a thoroughly good little creature . . . with tremendous simplicity under her sophisticated air of 'knowing life' as she used to say. Isn't that true, Masseau? When you teased her, she used to go scarlet with rage, she took you dead seriously, like a child."

"Oh, certainly, certainly!" agreed Masseau with dangerous effusiveness. "Even if we were not always of the same opinion, she confided some delightful ideas of her own to me notably on foreign politics. On so many other things too, in particular on the rôle of religious feeling in modern music."

He rubbed his dry hands together, malicious as an old woman.

"That sort of joke's completely out of date, Masseau! At this moment, you look exactly like an aged fox contemplating a beautiful white grape. And that other one there, laughing! Oh! these men! Twenty-five, golden hair, flawless teeth, lovely eyes! All that's flung into their arms, and still they're not satisfied! Good heavens, what *do* you want?"

"I'm asking *you*," said Jean, in an artificial voice.

"After all, she loved you, that child! And you yourself, Jean. . . ."

I had to take immense pains to keep up my factitious anger which was meeting with no response.

"I can still hear her complaining about you the other day and I am sure she had plenty of grievances!"

"Three or four thousand francs a month's worth, to talk like her. No, no, I'm not being a cad, I'm only joking. Poor little May. And poor little abandoned me."

What was the deep thought that lay behind those grey eyes? Ever since the arrival of the letter, Jean had not let himself go in one single spontaneous gesture. There had been no tear welling up on his lashes, no bang of his fist that threatened to smash the crockery, no furious exclamation that reveals wounded love in the act of denying it.

"Jean, what are you going to do? She can't be impossible to find, this child. Why, she's only just left. In two hours, in twelve at the most, you can catch her up."

"Me!"

There it was, at last, the spontaneous exclamation. But it was not the one I was expecting; it was an indignant bark, followed by a burst of outraged, angry laughter that made the glittering water dance in the carafes.

"Me, go after her? You think I'd do that when the thing . . . the thing . . . I can't find the right word . . . has happened to me . . . whatever it is that makes one want to say: 'It was decreed!' Go back, when I've barely begun to savour an amazing sense of . . . no, not liberty, it isn't that . . . yes, promise! I feel as if the mere fact of being on my own gives me the right to the whole world, and all the women in it. It's as if they were being promised to me, as if fate were on my side, and when I say *all women*, that means the one, the only one I want. Go after May when . . . when I'm here!"

A warm, strong hand pounced on mine, imprisoning it and enclosing it like a living shell. The gesture had been so sudden and the pressure so despotic that I was silent, as if he had struck me a violent blow. All I did was raise my eyes and stare stupidly at Jean, as he repeated in a lower voice: "Go after May!"

"You wouldn't have very far to go," said Masseau's old voice. "She's upstairs in her room. And it is at this point, my friends, I must ask you to excuse me. Senile student that I am . . . anaemic scion of a race which provided the world with Mister E. Man and all his ilk. I caused a line of poorly imitated handwriting to be transmitted to Jean. Now you know all."

He blinked, rubbed his dry fingers together till the joints cracked, and waited. He showed some courage, or else considerable insensibility, in waiting, for a rush of blood had darkened Jean's cheeks. My hand was still a prisoner and I felt as if I could not move as long as that hand was smothering mine. At last I felt free, and I heard Jean's slightly forced laugh.

"Incredibly funny! But why the hell did you do it, Masseau?"

"To see . . ." replied Masseau enigmatically.

Then his mania for buffoonery overcame him again. He put his table-napkin, that had been folded into a mitre, on his head, lowered his eyebrows, tightened his lips to make a thin, cruel mouth and announced himself, "Torquemada!"

FOUR

THE room is over-heated, but the open window lets in a dampness that mists one's hair and moistens one's nostrils. After the stuffy train, after Nice, dry and blazing with premature sunshine, it is a delight, in this more northerly air, to breathe in the smell of rain no longer mixed with salt or iodine or with the enervating scent of mimosa. The wind wafts it to me across the grey Lake Leman, over which hang low clouds which part now and then to show a patch of clear sky against which Mont Blanc glitters, quite close.

I know this room, I recognise these pink walls set off by a lilac frieze, and the sky-blue doors. This is a decorous Swiss hotel, similar to innumerable other Swiss hotels along the lake and elsewhere. Paris did not appeal to me at all, and I remembered that Geneva, fanned by the wings of tame seagulls, is often mild at the end of February; I remembered too that Brague was giving his annual series of his repertoire there this week.

Twenty spots in the Midi might have tempted me, rather than Geneva; warm beaches between two red rocks, an Italian village, a little Provençal town fragrant with violets and jonquils. But I could not forget that these paradises, once the moment comes that deprives them of their only attraction, the sunshine, turn into sinister prisons. The tourist's evenings in them drag out interminably between the terrace and the out-of-tune piano, the reading-room haunted by ancient, bespectacled Anglo-Saxon ghosts, and the drawing-room, the refuge of young and old spinsters, reduced to a state of boredom that makes them want to scream and bite.

I am glad I came here. The chill sweetness of the air; the grey water, so smooth after the rain that the wake of a steamer stretches out behind it in a thin, narrow streak like a trailing rope: everything takes me far away from Nice, from May and from Jean. There is not a single thing here, down to the stiff, bare grace of a wintry bunch of barely budding chimonanthus branches, that does not rejuvenate me, that does not relieve me of the oppressive memory of my stay on the Riviera and of the scene that put an end to it.

I endured the company of the two lovers for another forty-eight hours. May, once again gay and amorous, had worn that overweening air of triumph she assumes in public every time she knuckles under and humiliates herself in private. Jean, instead of adopting a moral attitude which would have set him up in my eyes, had taken the wise course of reverting to what he had been the day before and all the previous days.

It was on the eve of my departure that, having secretly packed my trunks, I consented to spend half the night in Masseau's bedroom-opium den, on the white mat and the chilly, smooth silk cushions. I myself do not smoke opium, but I allowed myself this night with those who do as a slightly shameful indulgence and also, as Masseau would say, "to see".

May flung herself ravenously on the opium, less anxious to savour the pleasure than to demonstrate her endurance. She talked of "the drug" and "the bamboo" and praised the syrupy opium with the competence of an old Chinese addict.

Jean set about smoking without conviction and without getting much out of it; he smoked hurriedly, as if anxious to arrive at the blessed moment when one lays one's drowsy, swimming head on the cushions. When he dropped his last pipe, he stretched out and gave a look aimed only at me, a look in which there was neither covetousness nor anxiety but a security as peaceful as death.

I was not lying so prone as the rest of them, and I was separated from Jean by May, who was recumbent but fidgety, tortured by migraine and cramps in the stomach. I liked the muffled light of the red silk lantern and the silent busyness of the woman Masseau called his "congaï", a humble, ugly creature with beautiful, slave-like eyes. I could not really understand why those people, apart from Masseau, were smoking opium, but I forgave Jean when, overcome by it, he fell asleep like a man who has got drunk on purpose for the good of his health.

The short, almond-shaped flame in the glass bowl kept bringing my wandering gaze back to it and playing with the barely perceptible shadow of a rock-crystal Buddha that stood beside the lamp. Beyond Jean's body, Masseau's parched small hands, pale in the dusk, moved slowly to and fro, endowed with the precision, the intelligent carefulness that guides the hands of the blind.

Only one other painful hour, after that night; the one that

preceded my leaving for the station. In front of an impassive Jean, I had to endure a hundred questions from a stupefied May.

"But why? But what's come over you? Jean, don't you think she's crazy? I bet ten louis that we'll see you back in these parts within a fortnight! There you see, it's the old urge to go 'on tour' coming over her again. At heart, she's every bit as much of a character as me!"

She addressed her remarks and exclamations, now to me, now to Jean and I was afraid she might compare our two faces, both of which looked equally determined to remain silent or to lie. Yet I had not exchanged a single word of connivance with her lover and he made no attempt to prevent my going.

My mind is at rest. I am delighted to have left those people in a civilised way, lightly, without being involved either in a dramatic scene or a base flirtation. Chaste Switzerland is already imbuing me with a desire for a kind of retreat, a literary cure. Piled up in front of me, like slabs of solid nourishment, are the *Grande Revue*, the *Revue des Revues*, the *Revue de Paris*, the *Mercure de France*, and any number of less famous ones! I have enough to read, night and day, for the entire week! Already, before cutting their pages, I have extracted enough from them to despise the companions I have left, with the exception of the irresponsible, well-read, mysterious Masseau. I withdraw myself from them, thinking, with conceited amazement: However could I have lived three whole weeks with those people and made do with the five hundred unvarying words of their vocabulary?

Two hundred words to order food and drink; a hundred, plus a few numbers, to evaluate a passing dress and the woman inside it; a hundred to suffice for all the smutty stories; the final hundred for the subjects that "elevate the mind", art, literature and morality: they suffice for all that and more. Why, it was enough to make one forget one's mother tongue, living in that verbal desert! Brague's slang, the backstage pidgin-English of the music-halls, anything was preferable to the conversation of May and Jean which I had put up with, goodness knows why!

A shower, hurrying across the sky towards the two, has extinguished Mont Blanc which, up till then, was glittering with a harsh incandescence under a distant shaft of sunlight. Against the low, dark sky all the whirling seagulls have turned into snowflakes and, though I have just picked up a thick orange *Revue* from the pile, my thoughts take on a different hue.

Yes, I put up with those people. I put up with them out of cool arrogance, the inveterate arrogance of a former blue-stocking who could smile with ironic compassion at May's linguistic "bricks", at Jean's slipshodness, often too lazy to finish a sentence. Two days out of three, I went about with them only to indulge in the silent disdain of a poor schoolmistress for the idle rich. The third day, I probably justified their idea that I was exactly like them, a gay eating and drinking animal, conditioned to expensive meals, flower-decked tables and motor-cars, to the whole slightly meretricious surface of this life made for light women and wealthy men.

It is not enough to say I put up with those people, because I tried to charm them. For whom, if not for them, did I use such means as I have, a stock-in-trade which every passing year restricts or changes? The attractions I stressed were gaiety—the ready gaiety of women who are no longer very young and who laugh on the least provocation—and the conscious radiance of a serene temperament and a healthy appetite; those were the qualities that might humiliate May's agitated, unsure-of-itself, twenty-five. Twenty-five is not the age of serenity; adolescence is still too close—excitable adolescence, prone to suicide one moment, prone to extravagant hopes the next. A May of twenty-five wastes time in tears and dramatics, in little illnesses, in black depression. A Renée Néré of thirty-six demands nothing, and, merely by being herself, seems to offer everything.

I was not always unaware that, in the public eye, even my defects could stand me in good stead, for a woman is only beautiful by comparison. When I was seen in May's company, I cunningly affected a serene silence, a harmonious stillness, so that she should evoke the image of a half-ripe fruit hanging on a wind-tossed branch.

By so doing, I made use of an adroit defence, which did not pass unnoticed, for Jean's words are still ringing in my ears: "The fact is, you're not fond of May, are you?" Had I not merely deserved but invited them as a slightly stinging retribution for my malicious showing-off?

Thank heaven, I have left those people in time and with nothing to blame myself for except thoughtlessness in not considering Jean's feelings enough. I do not attribute much importance to his behaviour the other day. It is typical of many susceptible lovers, when their mistress leaves them, to exclaim to another woman: "*You're* the one I really wanted, how lucky this is!" What was imprudent was letting myself drift into practically living in common with Jean and May. It was inevitable that the normal, basic instinct of polygamy would be aroused in Jean by the habit and the demands of living between two women and that desire would eventually follow. . . . You are a man, you are the friend of a woman without a lover, you invite her out and seek her company because she is neither stupid nor heavy on the hand. When your mistress is bored, you rely on the friend to amuse her, and then, some night or other, when you stretch out two listless arms, the two arms close about the necks of both women and everything is spoilt—or everything settles into a new pattern.

I have settled everything in the best possible way. There are no broken bones anywhere and now I am perfectly free to . . . Perfectly free to do what? The wildest dissipations of Geneva are within my reach. Shall I go and throw bread to the tame seagulls? Shall I take a boat and have lunch at Nyon at that little inn where Brague and I indulged in tepid tea and raspberry wine?

There are also the cinemas. A positive orgy! as May would say. After that, it would be time to have dinner and then to cross a few bridges to go and see Brague at the *Eden* and enjoy his surprise.

Perhaps I would have taken the boat, but the seagulls detained me. At the first piece of bread, there are one, two, five, then a hundred, before one has time to see where they appear from. They snatch it swarming, now swerving, now rising, now soaring; clever as trained pigeons, but with the fierce little heads of wild birds and wary, malicious eyes. They scream, fight, plummet head first on to the water at the same moment as the pieces of bread. One was always cheekier than the others and would hover at the level of my face, standing in the air and beating its wings, displaying the tempting whiteness of its belly and its feet with their outspread claws. I could have touched it, if it had been willing, merely by stretching out my arm, but it did not want to be touched. It stared at me with stern greed and never once let a piece of bread fall past its infallible beak.

Down below, on the transparent water, pierced by shafts of light now the sun had come out again, the heavy swans, white ones and black ones, rocked gently to and fro and gobbled up what the seagulls missed. Little black water-fowl, whose name I do not know, dived after fish with brilliant accuracy. The water was so clear that you could follow their plunging bodies right to the bottom, heads arrow-straight, wings glued to their indrawn sides, the delicate webbed feet closed and inert.

Time slid by and I almost drifted off to sleep on the bench of the landing-stage, dazed by the whirling of the seagulls, the ripples on the water, the swaying of the swans. I wanted nothing so much in the world as to touch and clutch one of those living creatures, warm under its feathers off which the water rolled in round beads, to lay my finger on its impetuous little heart and my lips on its smooth head. Or else I would have liked to satisfy myself by painting them— if I could paint—by modelling them—if I were a sculptor. Lacking hands that could mould and create, I sought vainly for words to describe the reflection of blue water in the hollow of a white wing; brand-new words to render the richness and silkiness of plumage that defies waves and showers.

Those sudden cravings to touch, those tender, nervous thrills aroused by contact with a smooth, soft animal, I know very well what they are: the overflow of the unused force of pent-up desire. I think no one feels them so deeply as an old maid or a childless woman.

"The Rat! The golden Rat!"

"The Celebrated Mime!"

"Give us a kiss, Rat!"

"Not on your life! Dry your paws first, and then your snout. There! Now, I insist on being left in peace till after the show."

I shrieked, I exaggerated my defensive gestures and my disgusted grimaces to hide the fact that I was moved. How could seeing him again, the man who had been my stage-partner for six years, leave me cold? Seeing him too in these familiar surroundings, in this seedy cabin of a dressing-room with walls of bare boards! The *Eden* is a former Circus which has long lost the friendly reek of dung and warm litter. Given over now to sporadic cinema shows, music-hall turns and light comedies, none of its ephemeral managements has taken the trouble to embellish it or to make it comfortable. Tonight, between two films, Brague is giving *Black Magic* which is none other than our old *Capture* remodelled, gingered up with "lascivious" dances, a chaste imitation of a Black Mass, and a new set. Mademoiselle la Carmencita, my successor, displays her curves in black on an orange poster, Renée Néré's own posters, but the public does not examine them as closely as all that. All the same, I could not help looking for my name in lights, over the porch of the *Eden*, and I arrived in Brague's dressing-room feeling something of the jealousy of a betrayed mistress.

For nowadays he tours without me, this man who was my gruff, honest friend; he tours with another woman. Does he regret me? Was it the moisture of a tear or the streak of violet grease-paint that made his black eyes so brilliant? He would never tell me and our first words were ironical, almost spiteful: he called me Golden Rat because of Margot's legacy and I called him Celebrated Mime in memory of a hand-out he had written himself. But our genuine delight manifested itself in laughter, in expressive noises that were once ritual—the giggle of an English clown to which the reply was the purr of an amorous tom-cat—in sparring that revived my thrill of jealousy.

The dynamos rumbled under our feet and sent up fumes of coal and oily iron as well as intolerable heat: the place felt and smelt like a furnace. I undid my coat.

"Oho! The Rat's all dolled up like a lady," observed Brague.

"I could hardly stroll about Nice, where I've just come from, in the costume I wore in *The Capture*, old boy."

"Why not? Splendid publicity!"

At heart, he disapproved of my get-up as "fancy dress". He would have liked to see me in my regulation uniform of the old days; a prim, severe tailormade of the type only worn nowadays by governesses in austere households and Royal Princesses.

I studied his appearance, too.

"Brague! Honestly, it isn't possible! You've still got those same buckskin breeches in which you created *The Capture!*"

"I shall die in them," announced Brague simply.

He was finishing his make-up with little touches of mysterious ingredients. I laughed with pleasure to see the same old litter on the shelf, the well-known litter of little brownish bottles, ochre-stained rags, paint-brushes. It bears not the slightest resemblance to a make-up box; you could swear Brague was preparing to varnish furniture or to do the brasses or even to polish his shoes.

"And . . . are things going well, Brague?"

"Not too bad, not too bad. I battle on, like the rest. It gets less and less easy."

"Oh!"

Facing me, ferocious from head to foot, from his black crêpe-hair moustache to his red leather moccasins, was the most fearsome Moldo-Walachian, wearing a Roumanian shirt, a Montenegrin belt in which glittered a long Greek pistol. In truth it was not difficult to believe this "Balkan Peril" when he asserted that he "battled on".

"Yes. You know, touring's coming to the end of its days. So I do odd jobs in cinemas, for a change. However, the main thing is I've started up a marvellous racket."

"Ah?"

"Yes. I'm teaching society women and girls deportment. Three or four Persian feasts and other *tableaux vivants* I've produced on the stage, and two or three mimes I've put on in the drawing-rooms of boot kings or tinned-vegetable princes were enough to launch me. These women want me."

"Ah?"

"You realise, every woman with b—— all to do in life has a mania to learn something totally useless and that costs a lot of money. Well, I teach them deportment! I've got a marvellous technique. To begin with, I get them together at eight in the morning till nine in the Cernuschi studio. The mere fact of getting out of bed so early makes them straight away imagine they're working. Once in the studio, I put myself at one end and them at the other and I shout at them: 'Come towards me, *walking naturally*'. You know the result. They start advancing as if they were on a tight-rope and quite likely fall flat on their faces in the process. It's an infallible way to start off."

"Really?"

"And even the ones who soon get discouraged or prefer to go off to another place to learn the tango—the frivolous ones, naturally— even those don't leave me without having learnt three indispensable things; to drape themselves in a scarf seven yards long—I don't provide the scarf; how to walk down a staircase without looking at their feet and how to hang garlands on the pedestal of a statue of Eros. If with all that, they're not armed for life!"

Brague was jubilant, overjoyed at being able to despise the "customer" who paid and had no understanding and to astonish the Rat, the Rat listening deferentially, sitting sideways on a wicker stool, like a lady paying a call.

"And . . . apart from that, are you pleased with the towns you're playing?"

"The towns are fine, it's the managements that aren't worth a button. Didn't I tell you about the business in Bordeaux?"

He came closer, his hand on the grip of his Greek pistol.

"Why, of course! You don't know about the Bordeaux affair! The third day we were there, the manager—and when I call him that, I'm being polite—decamps with the cash-box! You can see the picture:

twenty-two poor devils out on the street, and the *diseuse* having hysterics and the woman-shot-from-a-cannon snivelling and all and sundry talking about going to the police and the Public Prosecutor, as if *they'd* ever been the slightest use! So what did I do? I called everyone together and I said to them . . ."

I listened, less attentively than I appeared to, but I listened all the same. I raised my eyebrows to signify astonishment, I nodded my head, and, though I slapped my thigh to show incredulity, I was convinced that the Bordeaux affair would be straightened out to the glory of the wise, astute Brague. And all during that time, I was thinking: "He hasn't asked *me* if things were going well. He hasn't asked me what I've been doing these last six months. That doesn't interest him because I've gone off on a path that isn't his, above all because I'm not working any more, because I'm finished. I don't exist any more, I'm no longer good for anything but pushing five francs through the box-office window if I want to see the show. Well, I'd better go off and do it!"

"Where are you dashing off to, Rat? That's only the bell for the interval you hear. We've still got a good ten minutes."

To force me to sit down again, Brague stretched out a hand covered with ochre grease-paint on which he had drawn, in blue pencil, gnarled veins and salient tendons that no one would see from the front of the house. This detail of useless conscientiousness softened my heart and I stayed, all the more because there was something I really wanted to know.

"Tell me, Brague, are you satisfied . . . I mean . . . are you satisfied with . . . my successor?"

He suddenly gave a beaming smile, or as beaming a one as his glued-on crêpe moustache permitted.

"Ah, that one!"

"What d'you mean, that one!"

"My dear Rat, you know I'm not easily staggered? Well, that girl does stagger me! She'd put it across to God the Father, she'd put it across to Senator Bérenger, if those two venerable personages frequented the halls. She's got something—I can't describe it—in her skin, in her eyes, in her hips. At the moment—you know the one— when I tear off her dress and raise the knife—at that moment, she bends her head back, thrusts the tip of her tongue between her teeth and makes eyes at the blade! It produces such an effect on the audience. I daren't say too much about it. I try to tell myself, among other clap-trap, that she has a special interpretation of the part . . .

at bottom, I'm slightly ashamed of myself. Wait, I'll let you see the Object for yourself. Hi, you kid!"

He banged his fist against the board partition. A shrill voice from behind it replied "Yes", and the Object promptly made her entrance.

A very dark little person, whose Bordeaux origin sufficiently justified the Spanish name. She had thick, frizzy hair, eyes so brilliant that one would not venture to doubt they were expressive, flawless little teeth and a tongue reddened with liquid carmine. A plump behind and rather short in the leg; in fact, a sturdy little pony, with more mettle than breeding.

"Madame."

"Pleased to meet you, Madame. . . ."

"Brague tells me you're having a great success."

"Yes. I'm quite pleased. Obviously *The Capture* doesn't give me the same opportunities as creating a brand-new part. Still, I've tried to vary it, to adapt it to my style."

She fingered her hair in which she had stuck a pomegranate-flower and studied herself in the glass to avoid having to look at me. I felt her to be arrogant and extremely ill-disposed towards the "creatress" who had filched two hundred performances of *The Capture* from her. And I privately insulted her without opening my lips; I stared at her superciliously, soundlessly calling: "Dwarf, tobacco-jar, half-size siphon, white negress, cheap little miming tart." We were excessively prim and dignified with each other and gave a perfectly ridiculous display of conventional politenesses. I wanted to hit Brague, who went on stroking his stage moustache and looking as conceited as a cock over whom two hens were quarrelling.

"This time, it's our bell! Are you going in front, Rat dear? Shall I tell them to give you a seat?"

"Certainly not! I'm part of the 'swinish paying public' these days. I insist on producing my five francs!"

"Quite right, I keep forgetting she's made of money these days, this Rat! Hear that, kid? She wants to squash us with her five bob! All right, we'll let her have her way!"

I left them, laughing, and bitterly hurt. He had said "we" as if on purpose. To banish me in so many words from the kingdom that was once mine. Once the first warmth was over, he had been oblivious, complacent, egotistic. He had found not only a satisfactory understudy, but also, quite obviously, an easy-going, dissolute partner who gave him and demanded from him a trivial sexual pleasure. He had told me the story of Bordeaux and promised me the story of Brussels, but *my* "stories", of Nice and elsewhere, were not worth his enquiring about. Henceforth nothing would ever make me regain my lost prestige in the eyes of Brague. If I were to tell him: "I'm marrying a millionaire", or "I'm becoming a nun", he would reply: "That's your business; but just listen while I tell you about my affair with the leader of the claque at the Kursaal, in Lyons, you'll split your sides."

"Not through there, Madame! That door's only to be used by people working in the theatre. The staircase on the right, if you please."

I turned away meekly, with the submissiveness of an ordinary spectator, which is what I am now. Ah, they don't have to tell me to my face that I'm no longer anything in the theatre. A year ago I'd have answered that Genevan stage-manager back in rich Parisian language in which every word is an outrage to respectability. But I've quickly lost the particular insolence that is the hallmark of "the profession". A quite inoffensive insolence, really; a childish flouting of convention that is satisfied by such things as dining at a smart restaurant in a coat and skirt, reading the paper while eating and using a shy, over-familiar tone with the waiters. I no longer had the courage to assert myself. I obeyed the stage-manager's direction; I went down the staircase on the right which I knew as well as he did and eventually reached my five-franc stall. There I found myself wedged between two stout male neighbours who smelt of beer and tobacco. I could hear their heavy breathing and, do as I would, I could not help brushing against their knees and their arms. These prudish Genevans would have told me, had I asked them, what they thought of the "immorality of the stage".

When I came away, after *The Capture*, my heart was swollen with misery and jealousy. Anonymous among the crowd, I let myself be swept along towards the exit and out into the square that was glistening with rain, chewing the bitter cud of one of the last things my sister-in-law Margot had said to me: "You will lead a dignified life, and a dignified life for woman is one that leads her, unnoticed by almost everyone, to her grave."

Unnoticed! Poor Margot, she might well be gratified. Unnoticed. Was I ever more so than here, more so than tonight? Forgotten, dispossessed! There was no more place for me beside Brague and La Carmencita than between the two lovers back there in Nice.

If I were in Nice at this moment, I should have the bright lights of suppers at the *Bonne Hôtesse*, music that banishes thought, bubble-spangled wine, May's chatter and Masseau's lunacy. I should also have, to give value to every gesture, every glance, every word of mine, a man's desire, desire that would enrich me with everything I did not grant.

The best thing to do is to set off once more. What is the point of seeing Brague again here? Tonight's experience has been enough for me. My pride, both as a friend and as an actress, rebels too much, in the presence of Mademoiselle la Carmencita, at not being the leading lady in Brague's affections and the attraction on the posters: I do not want to become petty, spiteful, unjust. The brand-new railway time-table bought in Nice offers me its precious collaboration and my open window frames a patch of pure, rain-washed sky, above the black lake which mirrors drawn-out reflections of lights on the bridges and quays.

Set off again? . . . It is strange that, free and alone as I am, I give the impression of someone who is escaping, or being chased away. It seems as if there never is enough room for me in any place where there are people who embarrass me. Nice has become uninhabitable on account of May and Jean; Geneva cramps me because La Carmencita is playing here with Brague. I am ripe for a season in Paris and even a season of economy. A Golden Rat can live richly on two thousand francs a month, all the same she must not squander too much of it on railway fares.

I have almost run through my quarterly allowance and the only remedy for that is Paris. Paris, and not some corner of Normandy or Brittany, already green under the spring rain; Paris, because I have neither the energy nor the inclination to choose another refuge and, most of all because . . . because . . . I will have the courage to formulate a truth I have already known for a year . . . because I do not know how to travel.

No. I really do *not* know how to travel. Years of touring may have taught me how to pack a trunk, how to read a time-table, how to get up between midnight and six in the morning without shilly-shallying or moaning, but all that was only the experience of any commercial traveller. Even the craving for fresh landscapes and new cities only signifies in my case the freedom of the tramp or the restlessness of the homeless who have no ties and who keep endlessly assuring themselves: "*There*, I shall be better off than here; *there* I shall find what I lack!" I no longer have the right to doubt it.

Yet how ardently I longed for complete freedom in the days when I walked round and round in a circle at the end of a string! How I sang its praises, with the lyricism of those who, living alone, re-write their own lives in long monologues, in "effusions", admirable in their way, but a trifle artificial.

I could safely lament, for I had foreseen everything, except that the string would break.

The intoxication was, none the less, genuine, but it did not last long; it was disturbed almost at once by a strange kind of nostalgia for the treadmill which expressed itself in sudden starts, in an obsessive need to ask: "What time is it?" I still find it difficult not to yield to this torture that afflicts the amputated, which drives me to lunch earlier and more hurriedly on Sundays, to put my little Swiss watch beside my plate, well in sight, when I am having dinner.

I went through some hateful weeks when every place seemed to me tiresome and pointless because I no longer had to find out, as soon as I arrived, which street the beloved music-hall was in and the times of rehearsals and performances. Frankly, it was during that time, and not during my stage career, that I nearly became exactly like Miss Herculea, the woman who was shot from a cannon, who used to say in a gloomy voice: "All these holes are the same. There's always a *house* where you're playing, a bad hotel where you sleep and a German brasserie where you blow yourself out with sauerkraut."

I struggled with myself, I scolded myself severely: "What, am I going to come to that too, to having no existence outside the theatre, am I going to come to that?" and that arrogant "I" meant "I, who am sensitive to the changing landscape, to the striped shawl passing by, to the crumbling, yet still solid red ruin; I, with my cultivated mind, my delicate perceptions."

Serenity returned; it always does. I had recourse to no one, except, mentally, to Maxime Dufferein-Chautel because I had to appeal to the man I regret more than anyone in the world and to Brague, Brague my friend, my scathing comforter, my thorny support. But the latter was gadding all over the place and fighting to make a living and the former had taken a wife, and it served me right.

Serenity always returns, on condition I buy it at a price. Each time I am the one who pays, or who gives in. A little walk round the town, then, the moment the intolerable staleness and uneasiness sets in, departure. It has become a habit, a hygienic measure I adopt

without rhyme or reason. Jean and May quarrel, Masseau compli-
cates the situation: I depart. Brague invites me to stay in Geneva,
but Mademoiselle la Carmencita would derive only a mitigated
pleasure from my staying and I myself am irritated by the presence
of Mademoiselle la Carmencita: I am going to depart. It is very convenient, especially for the others, who never have to displace themselves.

Yes, I argue very sensibly about all these people and about myself,
for it is not common sense that I lack. What I continue to lack is
light-heartedness; I take everything seriously, as old maids do. The
attentions of a Gentleman-on-his-own embarrass me, I make a tragedy out of Brague's indifference, and, on my oath, if one slightly sensual gesture to vent his spleen against May did not make me believe
for a moment that Jean was about to offer me his life!

Three white swans are resting against the quay, not asleep, because
I can make out the movement of their folding and unfolding necks
and their treading the water disturbs the surface with frequent ripples. When do they sleep? This landscape of black water, garlanded
with street-lamps, is pleasant to me because of all it contains of the
already-seen, of the almost familiar. When I leave it, I shall go off to
seek some other known setting, where the spire of a church, the silhouette of a mountain—not even as much as that; a noisy street, the
welcoming face of a hotel proprietor who will call me by my name
—will give me, for an hour, the illusion, not of arriving, but of *coming home.*

FIVE

THE hotel omnibus did not leave for half-an-hour. Faithful to old rites of departure, I locked my two trunks and packed my bag so as to give myself the pleasure of having breakfast in peace, digging into the pot of honey and the lump of butter with methodical greediness. The lake was the colour of a sick pearl, even paler than the sky in which one could feel the sun quite close, ready to burst through the clouds. A nice morning for going away!

"Come in!"

It was my bill and a letter, a letter with the flap hardly stuck down, that was not from Brague.

"I am downstairs in the hall. I want to speak to you. Can I come up?

Jean."

"Just a moment! Waiter! Waiter! Can't you wait for the answer? It's amazing, such shocking service! Tell this gentleman . . . No, I'll come down. On second thoughts, no. I'll give you a note to take. Stay outside in the corridor a minute. I'll call you."

There was nothing to lose my head about, yet I felt as if both my ears had been opened and a draught was blowing right through my brain. I grabbed my gloves, I put them back on the table, I flung the wet towels trailing about on the carpet into the bathroom, then I stared at myself in the glass, unable to put two simple ideas together. During this moment of idiotic confusion, I became aware of someone standing in the frame of the open doorway, someone who was not Jean, but Masseau.

"Masseau! What on earth are you doing here?"

He had no overcoat on and was wearing his felt hat that was too small for him and grey kid gloves, ceremonial gloves without stitching and with overcast seams like a woman's gloves. Doffing his hat, he waited bareheaded, looking respectful and utterly fantastic.

"Whatever's going on now? For goodness sake come in. Is Jean downstairs?"

"No, Madame!"

"Oh! Well then?"

He came in, put down his hat and ungloved his delicate small yellow hands which he proceeded to rub together.

"He is not downstairs. For, had he been downstairs, he would already have been upstairs. And, if he were upstairs, I could not have replied to you, without jeopardising the truth: 'Yes, Madame, he is downstairs.' Now, one of two things . . ."

I cried out, exasperated: "No! No! Stop it. I haven't got time for fooling! Why are you here?"

"Why? Because I love you!"

"Idiot! Was it you again—writing that note? Does it amuse you, that sort of . . . mystification? (I'd like you to observe I'm using a polite word!) At least, one can't accuse you of varying your methods. They're very low, my poor friend!"

The poor friend, extremely calm, was eating the remains of my pot of honey and muttering, with a disgusted expression: "Three teaspoonfuls every two hours. Heavens, how nasty this medicine is!"

Then, having carefully wiped his moustache with my napkin, he deigned to reply: "My dear friend, one of two th . . ."

"Masseau! I shall smash a vase in a minute!"

"Either . . . I have committed a forgery in private correspondence, or I have not committed one. That is what we shall learn from the enquiry. But first it is incumbent upon us to know if: One, I have the right—Oh, boiling sap, oh hidden spring!—the—oh, lubricious awakening of an exacerbated male!—the right, I say, to be in love with you. Two, the right devolving on any thinking being of the masculine sex, Catholic and vaccinated, to bear the Christian name of Jean."

"What on earth do you mean?"

"My name is Jean," repeated Masseau in a fluttering voice.

He had marked, in the air, the commas and dashes of his speech and seemed enchanted with himself. I sat down opposite him, feeling all at once very tired.

"Oh Lord, how exhausting life is with all you lot! How much truth is there in this story, and why are you here?"

"My name is Jean," repeated Masseau.

And, throwing back his head, narrowing his gaze between his lids, thrusting his chin out insolently, he achieved, for a couple of seconds —in spite of his goatee and his withered yellow skin—such a prodigious resemblance that I leapt up, roused by an inexplicable resentment.

"That is too stupid for words! Do you imagine I'm going to miss my train for the pleasure of admiring your portrait gallery? My dear Masseau, stop being horrid and tell me how you knew I was in Geneva? Lord, how stupid of me! I got the porter at the Impérial to get my ticket! So tell me, instead, *why* you came?"

I was using kindness and patience now, as one does with mad people. There must have been some cogent reason for that man to leave his white mats, his pipe and his lamp. But he was subtler than I was and I could not "pump" him so easily. He was not taken in by my cordiality and, besides, he had seen me just now, through the open door.

"Be off, dear lady, be off! The anecdote is not really worth your missing your train. And yet Jean wanted . . ."

"What?"

"No, no, it's too late, be off!"

This sharp-nosed fox, this sham madman was pouncing on me, letting me go, then pouncing on me again, all in virtue of a name, the name of a man with whom, for the past four days, I ought to have been less obsessed.

"And look . . . here's the porter come to fetch your luggage."

"Tsst! Leave it there, will you? I shall take the . . . the two o'clock train."

"But, Madame, there isn't a two o'clock train," objected the bare-armed, red-faced lout.

"That's none of your business. I'll have a special put on!"

When the door was shut again, I slipped Masseau a humble, conniving smile; a discreditable smile that awaited the explanation. With one finger at the corner of his mouth, he gave a revolting smirk.

"I will tell all!" he cried. "But I want you to come and lunch with me at Ouchy."

"At Ouchy? Why at Ouchy rather than . . . all right, at Ouchy, I'm quite willing. But we've plenty of time; it's only nine o'clock. Between now and then . . ."

"Between now and then I want you to play bezique with me!"

"Bezique? Oh, cut it out!"

"I want to! I want to!" yapped Masseau, draped in my Indian bedspread. "Or the child I bear in my bosom will be born with a three-thousand-five-hundred on its nose."

He broke off his dramatic pacing to and fro and murmured, transfixed with admiration before the long glass of the wardrobe, "Oh! Eleanora Duse!"

Until it was time to catch the boat, I played six-pack bezique with the most cowardly complaisance and without extracting the faintest gleam of information from Masseau.

"Where are we lunching in Ouchy, Masseau?"

"At the Hôtel du Château, with Jean."

"With Jean?"

"My name is Jean," he said suavely. "Forty in knaves, without prejudice to a twenty in hearts I wouldn't discard for a medal blessed by the Pope."

I had stayed on and he was taking advantage of it. I stayed on as if Masseau were the devil in a morning-coat and as if, between our two fans of cards, lay a stake that we never mentioned. I stayed on, most of all, because Masseau, with a madman's cunning, was helping to reawaken my dormant curiosity, my taste for intrigue and adventure, the desire to be desired: there is room for all these in my life and for things still worse and still better. I was not unaware of this; but the main thing was for them to turn up at the right moment, like this providential buffoon.

Nevertheless I played faultlessly and I even won, with my combinations of marriages and sequences; the superficial complications of this game of a hundred and ninety-two cards suited my present state of mind. "A game for old caretakers," Brague called it. A game, anyway, for women with nothing to do; with the bezique pack in the middle, a bag of chocolates to one's right, a glass of liqueur to one's left, time passes.

"Masseau! What about May?"

Obviously, I might have put this question before the boat left the quay. Anyway, Masseau was making his farewells to the land and was not listening to me. He was busy exchanging handkerchief-waves with a Swiss family—grandmother, mother and four daughters—who replied conscientiously to his signals. The boat was crowded—it was Sunday—with proud young men of the male-voice choir and girls of all ages, carrying umbrellas and hold-alls embroidered in cross-stitch.

There was an abundance of "big girls", female children who had grown too fast and who were dressed with an immodesty you do not see in France: short dresses revealed women's legs, bare and downy above ankle-socks; prematurely-developed breasts swelled out childish brassières. They were embarrassing and ingenuous, at once more innocent and more shameless than French girls.

"How charming!" said Masseau. "Here at last we have a nation that seems to understand and encourage love in its two most convincing forms: rape and sadistic murder! Wait a moment, I want to offer that sturdy young person in the very inadequate skirt a collection of postcards."

"Masseau, don't be disgusting! Masseau, I'm asking you: what about May?"

His only reply was a glance, a spontaneous glance that revealed the true Masseau, subtle and contemptuous. For the first time, I was conscious of feeling ashamed in his presence, as if in the presence of a man. Five minutes later, he was sitting between a girl of fifteen and her mother and chatting with them. With his hands crossed on the knob of his umbrella, he was imitating the sanctimonious expression, the furtive gaze and confidential mien of a bad priest and seemed to be no longer aware of my existence.

Drowsiness overcame me, the exquisite drowsiness of the open air; the drowsiness you feel on board ship, in a hammock or in an open car. The painted sides of the steamer, the sky and the far side of the lake were all the same muted greyish-white and the still air had the sweet, enervating smell of water with no salt in it.

Where was I going? I should know soon enough. At least I was being taken somewhere and for a few brief moments I recovered a peculiar sense of peace, the inert security of being simply a piece of luggage. I could feel the approach of an unknown will to which my own was already magnetised, like a sensitive needle. And since there was no question—at this moment—of fighting against it, I was aware only of its distant compulsion, its hypnotic charm.

How far would I have pursued that vague dream as I dozed with my eyes half-open, pleasantly conscious of the undulating line of misty green banks but not distracted by it? It was a shock to my optic nerves that awakened me; the sudden impingement on my sight of a massive obstacle, tall, square and capped with red tiles: the tower of the ancient castle of Ouchy.

"Say what you like, the Riviera is a gigantic sell! We've just had lunch out-of-doors, in Ouchy, at the end of February. How many times can one risk doing that before March or April in . . . well, anywhere in the entire Midi?"

I had not said "Nice", I had made a tiny little detour to avoid the word, like an ant going round a cinder, because I was thinking of that lunch at the Impérial, the one at which May was missing and I was aware that one of my companions was thinking of it too. Two men all to myself as back there, and, now that we had reached the coffee and brandy stage, the same odours, all the more evident when the faint breeze dropped, of the aftermath of a feast. How soon a good lunch begins to smell nauseating!

A ray of pale sunlight made the sparkles of the diamond I wear on my little finger dance on the table-cloth in bright, tiny rainbows.

"Pretty hands," observed Jean, with a smile.

I looked at him reproachfully, shocked to realise how closely his memories were following mine.

"Oh Jean, not really!"

I hoped he understood that far from being a coquettish protest, this was an attempt to head him off from recalling and re-acting a recent scene.

Conversation languished, now that we were no longer eating. Sitting at a table, stimulating themselves a little with food and drink, is not that the only pleasure people who have nothing to say to each other can share? Masseau was reading a Geneva newspaper and apparently taking no notice of us, as if his mission were accomplished. The delicately grey sky, the horizon of dull silver mountains that bounded the lake made a setting the colour of thawing snow against which our three faces took on the yellow tinge of fever. I powdered my face and reddened my lips with the inefficient aid of a pocket mirror, too small to be of much use.

"The left cheek," advised Jean. "It has as much right to it as the other. Wipe your eyebrows. There!"

Secretly humiliated, I guessed that this morning he did not find me pretty, that he was comparing me with the Renée of Nice, and I nervously responded by "pulling together" my tired features. Any woman instinctively performs this defiant feat of facial gymnastics—which consists in faintly smiling to refine the shape of the lips, raising the eyebrows, expanding the nostrils and tightening the muscles under the slightly slackening chin—even for the uninterested eye of a passing stranger. I had inopportunely forgotten it because I was tormented by the desire to go to sleep and the need to understand the situation. Had I dared, I would have asked these two men, one of whom had just constituted himself the accomplice, almost the servant, of the other: "I implore you, tell me what is happening, or going to happen between us. Here we are in this bare garden, all three of us come from a very long distance, as if for a diplomatic conference or a conspiracy. A conspiracy against May? Then how is it I feel more involved and more menaced than the woman who is absent?"

But those were the things one could not say. Had Masseau been questioned, he would have disguised himself as Machiavelli and as to Jean, I know no one who inspires less confidence or with whom it would be more impossible to be frank and spontaneous. Moreover, at this moment, he was feeling resentful towards me. He had come by himself and, for four days, had been longing for the two of us to be alone together. For four days I had been constantly growing, in his mind, more beautiful, more mysterious, more seductive; for four days he had been incessantly cultivating his last image of me: a Renée Néré in a low-necked black dress who had pink cheeks and sparkling eyes. He had arrived to find a woman in travelling-clothes, a woman of thirty-six of whom people say "she definitely doesn't look her age", but mention the probable date of her birth.

His bright grey eyes scrutinised me impatiently as if they were searching for my vanished glory. In those eyes even love would not kindle the generous glow I remembered in Max's—Max who had cherished me all the more when I was ravaged by our rough games; my powder all rubbed off, my nose shiny, my cheeks marked with kisses and the traces of his teeth.

To greet our arrival, Jean had put on the charming, ingratiating smile of a man who hopes both to charm and to be forgiven and had promptly burst into a flood of gay chatter and explanations: May was returning to Paris but Jean had branched off at Lausanne to buy a boat, "look, here's a snapshot—pretty little craft, isn't she?" I had not found much to say, apart from one blundering remark: "So you're not angry with each other any more, you and May?"

"Angry? Why, I'd be a perfect brute if I were! Angry with May? Poor kid, she's had enough of being dragged hither and thither, she's gone back to her little perch in Paris."

He brought all this out with unwonted frankness, with a kind of paternal solicitude for May, as if she were a convalescent. He kept deliberately bringing her name into every sentence, as if to make sure

I understood the implication: "May is still there, we are doing nothing clandestine, let us innocently enjoy ourselves and above all, above all don't be afraid, don't withdraw into your shell!" He soon dropped his manufactured exuberance. The great thing, now, was to reassure me! The attention he was focusing on me had not diminished but, as time went on, it had changed its character. Now it was tinged with a sternness to which it had no right; that is to say, not one that I ought to acknowledge.

I riposted as best I could. My gaze searched out and rested on every imperfection that marred this man's handsome face: the cheekbones that were too high and too broad for the delicate chin and gave him a slightly Mongolian look; the bull-like protuberance above the nose. Today, on the edge of the almost black hair, I could easily make out the blue of a narrow shaved margin, the trace of a discreet pruning back that daily heightened an ennobled brow! The rest I merely glanced at casually, avoiding the mouth, thick, but with sensitive corners, and the eyes, brighter than mine because moister. On account of the small, but round ears and the short lower teeth that looked as if they had been filed, I diagnosed: "Degeneracy!"—all the while envying this "degenerate" his beautiful pale nostrils, unspoilt by redness or blackheads, whose wings were welded to the face by a deep, well-chiselled groove. When he is silent, he has—I am exaggerating but I am not self-deceived—he has an air of distinction but he becomes commonplace when he talks and smiles. At that moment, I positively longed for him to make that mischievously gay grimace, to throw back his head and laugh in the way certain men pick up from living with loose women.

Brusquely, he snapped the catch of his cigarette-case as if he meant to put an end to our mutual critical examination. I stood up to go. Jean rose too; my gesture had reawakened his dormant instinct of the chase.

"Where are you off to?"

"Why . . . I'm going back."

"Back where?"

"First to Geneva, then to Paris."

"Good idea. But . . . little motor drive first?"

"No thanks. The road by the lake is too boring for words."

"Little expedition in a sailing boat?"

"What boat? The one you're buying?"

"N . . . no. How about one of those charming little local craft

making up that picture-postcard scene down there by the landing-
stage?"

I hesitated, then accepted, but not because I particularly wanted
to go for a sail. Ever since my arrival in Ouchy, my day had been
spoilt by a sense of frustration, of having made a false start and put
myself in a false position. Perhaps, if I made haste, there was still
time to dissipate this uncomfortable feeling by some means or other.
I no longer knew what I had come here for, but I knew very well
that I had not had it; perhaps it needed only a moment, a word, a
brief rest on the smooth water for me to go away calm and appeased.

The shore was receding but the sail still flapped feebly against the
mast, slow to fill and heel over. Masseau, who had tried to make a
sylph-like leap into the boat and fallen into two feet of water, had
been left behind on the quay. He stood there, dripping like a wet
umbrella and shouting nautical commands.

"Shorten sail! Mind the boom! Haul in the stern sheets! Let go
the starboard anchor!"

We did not even laugh and our fresh-water sailor, who was handling the boat with the help of a small, bare-footed boy, stared at the
"madman" with an inscrutable, impassive politeness, like a good
Swiss, accustomed to put up with the ways of tourists.

"Masseau will catch cold," I said, merely for the sake of saying
something.

"Oh, it doesn't matter," replied Jean, absent-mindedly. His tone
was apologetic, as if I had stepped on his foot.

"What do you mean, it doesn't matter? After all, that man isn't
your servant!"

"That's why. If he were my servant, I'd be annoyed if he caught
cold."

"What a sweet, kind nature you have!"

"Kind enough to lend a coat to a woman who hasn't enough on.
Take this one, I can't bear to see you looking frozen."

It was true, I could feel myself turning pale, for the wind had
brought the boat to life and it yielded to it with a screech of its taut
canvas and a pleasant creaking of wood as it suddenly heeled over. I
was cold and I buttoned myself into Jean's mackintosh coat; it smelt
faintly of rubber, tobacco and a perfume that was not May's.

"I hope to goodness you're not feeling lake-sick?"

I laughed, my chin embedded in a turned-up collar that scratched like straw-matting.

"Good heavens, no! Only, you know, I had a very short night and ever since this morning I've had no chance to rest, so . . ."

"True, poor thing . . ."

He said no more, suddenly at a loss for words when it was a question of showing sympathy. I remembered a day when May was ill and he was looking after her. His face was indignant and he handled the cushions and the cups of hot drinks roughly, with a kind of enraged clumsiness. I never thought of that day till now and did not realise I had remembered it. The picture had just come up, clear and complete, in my mind, because Jean had said, "True, poor thing . . ."

"But you, Jean—aren't *you* going to freeze now?"

"I'm quite all right, thanks."

If I had exclaimed, in the typical manner of May: "Dear friend, don't you think the cold will play hell with your fatal beauty, braving the elements like that without your overcoat?" Jean would have replied in the same vein, and not with that curt, irritated "thanks". What had literally "cast a chill" over us was that sudden show of normal solicitude, simply expressed. Instead of that very natural gesture of masculine protectiveness bringing us closer, it made me want to call him "Sir".

The rudimentary accommodation of the boat—a small hard bench and soaked boards under our feet—increased our moral discomfort and reminded me of the days before I took to my wandering life. It brought back memories of moving house, of the misery of installing oneself in unfamiliar rooms, among furniture that has suddenly become unrecognisable. However hard I tried, I could not destroy that impression of some new and difficult *beginning*.

The water glided along either side of the boat in two slender, curling scrolls of very pale, very pure green, it felt almost warm to my cold hand.

"Why do all women trail their hands in the water when they are in a boat?" asked Jean.

I shrugged my shoulders.

"I don't know. I think all women make the same gestures at certain moments—confronted with a mirror, or a stretch of clear water —or passing by a flower or a very velvety fruit or material. They yield to their two invariable temptations. To adorn themselves—in other words, offering themselves. And to touch, which is the same as taking."

"All women—that makes a lot of women. . . ."

"Not as many as you think."

"But more than you say, muse of false humility."

"Of false . . ."

"Yes, I mean it. I don't find it attractive, this way you have of treating women with contemptuous pity, as poor little creatures, not very complicated and not very interesting. And to make it convincing you add: 'I know something about them, since I'm like all the others. . . .' So, logically, the simple-minded listener concludes that you're not like any of them."

"But, Jean . . ."

"And when you generalise, as you've just been doing, it's neither from modesty nor conviction. It's just out of calculating laziness, to produce the maximum effect with the minimum of effort."

"But, Jean . . ."

"And when you answer me, if you do answer me, you'll restrict yourself to a few clever, facile words, but admirably supported by a look that means a hundred times more than what you say. For your trick—excuse the word—your particular personal trick is reticence, all the business of the lowered eyes, the secretive smile, the hand quickly withdrawn—in fact you convey everything in dumb-show, my dear, pure dumb-show! Lord, I'm hot! I knew I shouldn't need that overcoat. And now you can crush me with superior silence, but I shan't take back one word of what I've said."

"But, Jean, on the contrary! I'm listening, I'm amazed . . . I'm even impressed! It's not stupid at all, what you've just been saying!"

"And you can't conceal your amazement: 'Miraculous! He talks, he thinks! Joy, he's bullying me a little!' "

It was a singular spot for a conversation of this kind, our first, perhaps our only one. For he had just gone further in "generalising" than I authorised, by overestimating my pleasure in being bullied. The wind had freshened and now our boat was swallowing the crests of the waves and a little sea slushed in the bottom, wetting the edge of my skirt. But Jean, excited, held up his cheeks to the fine spume and licked the tasteless water off his lips as it splashed us. The tower of Ouchy looked so tiny, back there on the land. I wanted to go back because I was feeling slightly ill; my back was tired and my head heavy, unlike this robust young man, swaggering in his unbuttoned jacket. But I dared not say so.

Illness is clement to very beautiful animals and very young human beings, the only creatures it does not disfigure. May used to admit, shamelessly: "My children, I'm tied up in knots with the gripes" or "I warn all present I want to vomit" and, in her state of physical collapse, she preserved a cynical grace that was not in the least repugnant; I can see the beautiful anguished eyes, ringed with black, and her green cheeks one rather too festive night.

I repeated feebly: "Miraculous! he speaks, he thinks. . . . Let's say, instead of 'miraculous', it's a surprise, and leave it at that."

Then I became mischievous again and I imitated Jean, the Jean of yesterday.

"'Snothing more than a wretched pub, 's Hôtel Paradenia!" "Forty horse-power's no use to me, I want a car with some speed." "Wine-waiter, have you any more of that Mouton-Rothschild you had last year?" "May, old girl, you're making a bloomer. That woman isn't thingummy's mistress, she's what's-his-name's late one, the one he used to call his old body—I recognise her necklace and the folds under her chin."

Jean's sensitive nostrils quivered slightly but his grey eyes, faintly green like the lake, began to smile.

"Well, why not? When I'm travelling, I try to speak the language of the country. Just as other people talk pidgin-English, I spend three quarters of the year talking pidgin-tart, pidgin-Jew, pidgin-playboy. But, all the same, I have a native language. And there are countries where I find it without having to look for it—yes, my dear, we'll go back, you had enough, eh?—charming countries where no one seems to know who I am, which put up their barriers at my approach, but which, at a word, I recognise as my own. Countries where I make my way, slowly—slowly you understand? as if I were going along a familiar path I'd allowed to become overgrown with briars."

SIX

WHEN I was a child, I was very seldom taken to the theatre or to the circus. But on those nights the approach of evening found me in such a state of nerves that my hands were cold and I could not eat any dinner. The shock of the theatre lights, the first gust of music affected me so acutely that at first I could not look at anything; I was too busy keeping back the passionate tears I longed to shed and which I sensed would have been a delicious indulgence.

Just as my childhood has left me with unusual control over my tears, so I have also retained, with an intensity scarcely diminished by time, the ability to be moved by certain moments, and not only by those which irresistibly combine such things as the sound of a perfect orchestra, moonlight reflected on shining box-leaves and laurels and the smells of the earth when a summer storm is brooding. There are moments of idle weakness when brief, very old visual memories of contrasts of light and shadow are enough to melt some of the aridity of a heart that has deprived itself of loving. Thus the warm rosy glow of a lighted window in the side of a dark house, that oblong glow projected outside on to a sanded path or filtered through black foliage, has a special significance for me. It symbolises love, sheltered love, home, precious and lawful privacy.

When I leave the cold night outside and enter a bright, warm, welcoming room, it is not only my senses that are dazzled. I feel a compulsive inner excitement, a brief flutter of happy expectation, as if I were going to meet a lover. It does not last long, for I am never expecting anyone; anyway, it has never lasted as long as it did to-night. The moment all three of us sat down at the table on the glaringly-lit veranda, such a wave of sheer joy went over me that I had to smile and clench my teeth to stop myself trembling. I thought I was utterly exhausted but I had no desire to rest. Moreover, it seemed to me that the state I was in depended entirely on myself and that the man sitting opposite me could have been removed and replaced by another without making the slightest difference. It seemed so, yet at the same time, I *knew* this was not true. I knew that my pallor, my tiredness, my slight aberrations of taste and touch—the iced champagne seemed to me tepid and the fork I was handling froze my fingers—had an obvious cause and were not accidental. They were the results or—to be frank—the victories of a silent, effective will which would weary perhaps, but which meanwhile was breaking me down.

I could not feel humiliated by this, since I was faced with such a strong adversary. The white shirt-front and dinner jacket set him off to advantage, with his smooth chin, his supple hair and those eyes, lighter than his skin, which make him look younger and give him an air of freshness and bloom. It was he who was dressed up tonight, for I had to keep on my travelling-suit, my wilted linen jabot and my toque with two little pointed wings. Masseau, drab and chilly, wrapped in unspoken thoughts, served as a second foil to him. I had to accept the fact that, though I was a woman dining with two men, I was not the high-light of the trio. It would have been so simple to go back to Geneva before dinner! But I had not wanted to.

Pleased that I had stayed, conscious of what it signified, Jean allowed himself to make coquettish gestures, a trifle suggestive of a tart displaying her charms. He smoked, with his elbow on the table and his little finger, which is slim and much shorter than his ring-finger, extended. He ran a finger between his collar and his Adam's apple, to draw attention to his neck which has stayed remarkably fresh, and, when he laughed, he deliberately prolonged his laugh in a canine grimace, with his lip curled up to show off his teeth.

Nevertheless, these little tricks, picked up from women, did not shock me. I came from a milieu where masculine and feminine beauty ranked equal, where you used the same appreciative words for the marvellous legs and narrow hips of a handsome gymnast as for the shapeliness of a female acrobat or dancer. Moreover, however little I had frequented "society" in my past life, I had had no difficulty in catching the men of that world using the same methods of attracting as the women and doing so every bit as obviously. So I let Jean parade in front of me like a circus horse, arching his chest, flashing his eyes and his teeth, and I refrained from checking him with a sarcastic word or a critical look. He was giving a performance for my benefit which I found anything but displeasing. And it was common honesty on his part that, neither at Nice nor this afternoon in the boat, had he mentioned the word "love" to me.

Honesty! Let us say a proof of good taste, or at least of tact. "I love you," Max had declared, in the very first hour. And, in his mouth, that great absolute word had seemed quite simple. He might have uttered it while eating, while blowing his nose, without provoking laughter or amazement. But Jean! I had only to imagine him murmuring the avowal to react at once with the incredulity of the offended surprise with which one greets a "bloomer". I had sometimes seen him behave like an ill-bred man, but never like a clumsy one.

The meal was soon over; we were the only diners in the almost empty hotel. The habit of being together, apart from the customary hours of eating and drinking, made us ask simultaneously: "What shall we do now?" And it was I who went on, without waiting, "Oh, Jean, there's only one thing for me to do, take the next train back to Geneva!"

"Go back? Again?" (His grey eyes hardened.) "This morning Masseau found you all set to go back to Paris. After lunch, you wanted to go back to Geneva; in the boat, you wanted to go back to the hotel. And now, this evening, you're starting it up all over again! Anyway, we'd better find out. Masseau, you haven't got a railway time-table on you?"

"I always have," said Masseau. "Lausanne . . . Lausanne. . . . Ah! here we are. Lausanne, 19.23, that's too late. Lausanne, 21.7, which gets you to Geneva about midnight. Or else there's the still better train that leaves at 22 hours exactly and arrives at Geneva three-quarters-of-an-hour later."

"Three-quarters-of-an-hour later! ! !"

Suspicious, I leaned over and observed that Masseau was "improvising" at sight from a little Ouest-État time-table.

"Masseau! Is that what you call a Swiss time-table?"

"It's quite good enough for you," said Masseau, unmoved. "For, one of two things. . . . Ow! Either you are going back to Geneva or you are not going back. Therefore, you are not going back. This hotel's as good as the one in Geneva and . . . What? You haven't got even the most rudimentary luggage? Somewhere in a corner of my suitcase I have some delicate pink soap, stolen from a bathing establishment, which floats on the water."

"And I," said Jean eagerly, "have Indian silk nightshirts—white stripes on purple or green—and straw sandals."

"And I," said Masseau, going one better, "have a precious waist-coat knitted in maroon wool and a flannel belt unrivalled for keeping the lumbar regions warm. All this is yours, comma, if you will deign to accept it, full stop. You need add nothing to it but the contents of your 'little' handbag, yes, none other than that one, which could accommodate an entire roast lamb in its maw. And when one is such an experienced traveller as you are . . ."

I knew better than he that my handbag contained "all the necessaries". I am no longer twenty-five, to set out on a journey without my powder-puff! The debate did not last long; I gave in quickly, so as not to make my consent seem in any way important, and I asked Jean eagerly: "So what shall we do now, then? What shall we do?"

I caught sight of myself in the glass, fagged out, pale, with hectic, painted red lips. I was afraid Jean might feel sorry for me and advise me to go straight to bed. No, no, I could not bring myself to finish this day like that, I *would* not!

"Oh Jean, up there, in Lausanne, there's a music-hall where I played two years ago, a ghastly beer-soaked, smoky hole, where you can see films and pathetically bad performing animals and twentieth-rate singing-turns and . . ."

"Closed," interrupted Masseau. "Gone bankrupt."

"Did you get your information from the Ouest-État time-table?" I asked acidly.

"No. The Ouest-État time-table is a well-composed anthology, the fruit of a first-class mind, but, in some respects, incomplete. I had to have recourse to the hotel porter."

He addressed himself again to scribbling goodness knows what in a little black notebook, his right shoulder hunched up in the classic pose of a quill-driver deformed by long habit. One could see nothing but his thin nose, pinched like a sick man's, and the top of his bald head, sparsely striped by long plastered-down hairs like flattened grass. Old devil that he was! Satan disguised as a provincial notary, his cleft foot in a square-toed shoe, and trafficking in haunted castles. It seemed to me that his claw, clutching the fountain-pen like a crab, wished me now good, now a little ill.

"Well, Jean, what shall we do, since . . ."

"Ssh!" interrupted Masseau.

"What is it now?"

Masseau raised a finger, unveiled his small eyes and blinked in the direction of the garden.

"Rain."

I listened to the sudden shower that was beating on the veranda and my resentment turned against Masseau.

"You did it on purpose!"

Jean's laugh made me think I had said something funny, but I added sulkily, as if personally offended, "Since that's that, I'm going to bed. Masseau, go and ask for a room for me, that's the least you can do!" He disappeared and I realised, too late, that I had spoken to him more as if to a servant than to an obliging friend.

"I really might have done it myself. . . ."

"Don't worry," said Jean. "It amuses him."

They had just switched off half the lights on the veranda, an obvious hint that drove us into the hall, a covered-in courtyard of the old castle where ferns and stork's bill clung to the jointures of the stone walls. Against their massiveness the English furniture looked frail and flimsy.

I sat down at a little desk, and propped myself up on my elbows in a careless, provisional attitude. Jean half-seated himself on the arm of a chair. Obviously we were going to leave the hall in a moment, yet I did not even look as if I knew it was cold and deserted and that the miserly light was rebuking us for being still up at this hour. I stayed where I was, and Jean did not stir. And behind both our faces was the same fixed will: this interminable day, which for me had been harassing, spoilt by reticences and banalities, this empty, humiliating day—since my part in it was that of a woman who had come a long way to meet a man—had to be brought to a close by some word or some gesture that would ratify it or erase it. I had reached a point where I would have been content with very little. A false confidence would have sufficed me, one of those stories in which the anecdote is hardly more than a pretext for such remarks as "I don't know if you think as I do . . ." or "I've always been like that . . ." or "I only need to look at you to realise . . ."

But nothing came; neither word nor gesture. Nothing but nervous yawns and idiotic remarks about English taste in furniture.

I felt ashamed for him and of him, this man sitting side-saddle on the edge of an armchair, swinging one foot and staring at his patent leather shoe and the silken mesh of his sock.

I was ashamed of myself obviously *waiting* and I could feel the exasperating moment coming when this flagrant waiting would assume the force of a mute invitation, almost of deliberate provocation. I hated myself, and I hated Jean. Yet there I remained, stuck; laughing and listening to myself talking. I gave a glance at Jean sitting there, a glance at the door through which Masseau should be returning any moment, a glance at the clock. Another five minutes, and I would go —yet another five minutes, but those would definitely be the last.

"That's just like me. I remember my husband once gave me some Dutch furniture. Like everyone else, I had 'the first Dutch furniture ever seen in Paris'; you get sick of it at once, that furniture without any style."

"When I furnish seriously, *I* shall allow that sort of fancy stuff in a smoking-room or a dressing-room."

"Or a kitchen."

"Yes, it could go in a kitchen too."

He had stood up; I felt it rather than saw it, for I was turning over the pages of a magazine. He was behind me; my whole back was watching him.

"A kitchen, now, one can do charming things with that. What always ruins a kitchen is the cook."

He had had his hand in his pockets; I had just heard him withdraw them.

"All the same, Jean, I remember, when I was staying in a very simple country house in England, admiring the delicious uniforms the servants wore—blue linen for the kitchen staff and pink linen . . ."

With his two free hands, Jean had seized me firmly by the elbows so that the nape of my neck understood at once what was wanted of it and bent forward—a movement to escape, if you like, but very convenient for choosing the place to kiss. A good kiss, warm, not too devouring; warm, long and tranquil; a kiss that took time to satisfy itself and that gave me, after the first shiver right down my spine, a slightly lethargic contentment. A good, static kiss, well given and well taken, which did not disturb the balanced poise of our two bodies, and to which I submitted, with eyes and mouth closed, with an inward sigh of relaxation: "Ah, how good I feel!"

". . . And pink linen for the housemaids."

"Charming," replied Jean, in a voice hardly lower. "A bit like a pink fondant, perhaps. Ah, there comes our Masseau in person! Well, Masseau, have you got her a room?"

Masseau rubbed his hands and stared at us between the eyes as if he hoped for some remarkable revelation. There was nothing to discover. We were very calm, just as calm as before and I no longer looked bad-tempered. Jean had his arms outstretched, but he might have been yawning.

It might have been sleepiness too that made me so hurriedly say goodnight to my two companions and give them an absent smile as I proffered a warm, limp hand.

What I have done is, I believe, what is known as putting one's head in the lion's mouth. All right. There I am, there I stay. It is quite comfortable there and I feel, at the moment, as calm as if I had already been devoured. Jean? . . . Jean is on the floor below, in his room. Or else, since it is no longer raining, he is taking a walk by the lake. He is wherever he chooses to be. It is as if he were less in my thoughts tonight than he was this morning or these past few days.

With a sigh of exhaustion, I have just locked myself into my room, which is at the top of the tower and all windows. Gothic scrolls painted on the walls and the ceiling would provide me with information about the history of the ancient castle of Ouchy, but I am more interested in the dressing-room and the steaming water lashing into the bath.

The day that has just ended has drained all my energies and I resent these fifteen hours of moral tension, anxiety and defensive coyness. Defensive? I might just as well not have been! My inveterate romanticism had been all prepared to be lyrical or scathing about Love. As if this were a question of love! Let me take a deep breath and consider—while my head is still just clear enough not to let avidity muddle it—the thing I know least about: the brief adventure. There are other names for it, but I reject them because they are vile; the thing itself is none too beautiful as it is! I can only congratulate myself in those feeble, slightly brutal phrases people use to a child who has burnt itself playing with matches or come a cropper while running: "Well, are you satisfied now? Have you got what you wanted? Goodness knows you asked for it! Still, all's well that ends well!"

Someone was walking about, down below. It was Jean, or Masseau, or some other man. The thought that Jean might come up and knock at my door did not make me so much as raise my head. It was not insensibility, no, no, far from it! But what strange resignation! A kiss, and everything becomes simple and enjoyable and superficial—and also a trifle coarse. A kiss, and the soaring spirit comes down to earth like a cloud of summer midges beaten down by the first drops of a storm. For nothing could have been more explicit than that silent kiss. Not a tender word, not a whispered entreaty, not even the

murmur of my name, nothing but that kiss given treacherously from
behind and received with smug insincerity. I had barely interrupted a
banal remark for it; I had neither hindered it or returned it. And
how equally careful Jean had been to *forget* it so promptly afterwards! Our honest bodies have clung together with a mutual thrill of
delight they will remember the next time they touch, while our souls
will withdraw again behind the barrier of the same dishonest but ex-
pedient silence. Jean's signifies: "There's nothing to worry about;
simply a question of pleasure, pleasure and still more pleasure. As to
the rest, let's be careful to keep it out of it." And mine replies: "So
there *is* a 'rest'? The idea hadn't even occurred to me. But don't
worry, you're not the man who's likely to remind me of it."

Yet why should delicacy not play almost as great a part in our attitude as cynicism? I grant that Jean may want to safeguard my touchy
independence as well as his own liberty; I may well concede him that,
provided he understands what I am offering and what I am with-
holding: "You are reassuring me, but let me reassure you. Set your
mind at rest. I do not intend to lean on you any more heavily, or any
longer, in the future than I did just now in your arms. My weight is
no more than the weight of a plant, momentarily broken down, and
needing support only enough to revive and stand upright again." He
will understand; if necessary I shall have to tell him in so many
words, if there is no other way. We are not, I sincerely hope, going
to indulge in long bouts of "lovers' talk" or the mawkish confidences
of schoolgirls. It is our silence, the silence of higher animals, that
raises our hasty affair a little above the commonplace. Let us remain
silent. We should not, we cannot talk of the past; the past is betrayed little May, and other little Mays before her; it is my regretted,
yet dreaded, Max—solid, without a flaw or a crack in him anywhere
like a splendid, insuperable wall! We must not talk of the future; to
talk of the future is to talk of love. Oh! let us go on being silent!

A great soothing calm pervades my whole body. It is as if I had
suddenly done with thinking. I feel as if I had just arranged the
minutest details of a project, all the rites of a ceremony that must be
performed soon, and inevitably. I shall probably go right off to sleep
but I do not want to. What is the point of blind, total sleep? If I do
not close my rigid eyelids, tenuous pictures flit across the dark blue
screen of the windows. These coloured projections are the comfort of
my disturbed nights, the joy and entertainment of my calm ones.
Landscapes, known or invented, animated by very few figures, illuminated by such varied lights shed by such fabulous stars that their

splendour or their mysterious gloom make me proud of them, as if I were painting them; that is all, that is enough.

I am about to fall fast asleep; real sleep and real dreams, ordained, realistic, impervious dreams—*the other life*—solicit me urgently. I resist, because I know I am powerless to choose the scenery of that subterranean kingdom and the sad figures that people it, chosen from among the peaceful dead, friends long vanished and forgotten children who played with me. My recent friends and the casual acquaintances of my present life do not descend into those depths. I resist so as to remain with my frail apparitions of the upper world, the ones I summon up on the blue screen of the windows. Jean!

It is a faint summons, but it is answered. Here he is, standing on a white terrace above a formal hotel garden. Here he is, looking exactly like himself, but I have lost the key to his face and his gestures, which have become to me unintelligible. In his anonymous perfection, he is the Unknown Stranger. He follows me and disappears as soon as I turn round, but I am aware of his wish to be seen. I am walking along a path through a park, a path he has just trodden before; elder-flowers and pink spikes of tamarisk dangle, broken, at the level of my face, as if chewed by some tall straying animal.

I come to a circular clearing, flooded with pale sand. Where can he hide himself here? There is no cover for him except these little low bushes, fragrant and black in the sunlight. But he hides himself in my shadow, like those devoted dogs who cling to their master's heels. He revolves with my shadow, insistently, almost abjectly, following my every movement to keep his shadow lying on mine.

I must keep walking! I am not fleeing but the inexorable unfolding of the dream drives me on. Unknown stranger, do you hear me? I am not fleeing. You would reckon my flight as a victory to you. I go further and further until I am in a bedroom which is mine, as all hotel bedrooms are mine, and into which you do not enter. Against the background of blue-grey sea that fills the space of the open window, I can see the bluer smoke of your cigarettes rising up like incense. If I were to lean out of the window, you would vanish again, leaving the air disturbingly redolent of smoke and of perfume. You have a sprig of heliotrope in your buttonhole. I cannot see it but I recognise its scent.

I must keep on walking! The dream, even if unconscious of time, is painfully aware of its own frailty and hurries on to a logical end which is at the mercy of a creaking board, the scrape of a rat's claw or a nervous jerk of the dreamer's body. I must walk on, so that I can feel you are tracking me, not like a swift, alert poacher, but with the sullen air of a half-wakened beast pursuing its prey out of lazy hunger. Ah! you are not giving yourself any trouble over me. Yet, all the same, you use one stratagem—beauty.

You are beautiful and I do not know who you are. You were the one thing lacking in this torrid landscape and you had to appear. You complete the scenery of my dream, a necessary adjunct of it like the poplar standing up like a stiff plume on the hill, like the purple rock, like the green wave that suddenly bursts into white flame as it hurls itself on it. Do you demand more? It is enough, since you embody neither sorrow nor love, and moreover your face, your look, your irritating passivity reveal your true nature.

I do not know who you are and yet I insult you and I talk to you as if we were intimates. Now your shadow, unknown stranger, is growing larger beside mine on the path. You are going to overtake me; I can hear your long, lazy tread that makes a soft sound like the padding of heavy velvet paws. Overtake me, go ahead of me so that my eyes can wander down your shaven nape, all blue with black hairs, to your bare hands clenched and menacing. Let us go on walking, follow me, precede me, but do not speak. Why are you not dumb, beautiful ghost? Encompass me, surround me on all sides, let us hasten on together to the end of the dream, but do not speak to me.

Take advantage of this labyrinthine park, blazing with white sunshine and scarlet flowers, take advantage of this dull, inexorable music that comes from I know not where and drifts heavily on the breeze. Be content to remain, for a brief space neither you nor I can measure, a figure in a landscape.

I give you a tryst on this terrace beyond which there is nothing but the sea and the end of the dream. Come to that tryst slowly and in such silence that I may misjudge the distance between us, that you may come on me so suddenly and unawares that there is no room for me to stretch out my arm and thrust you away. Come, beautiful rock in my tranquil path; come that I may climb over you, since I do not want to avoid you.

SEVEN

"Yes, we're coming into Paris," said Jean.

He wiped the pane with a corner of the blind and tried to make out what was going on outside. The darkness showed him nothing but his own reflection and I could see his two faces, one light, one dark, forehead to forehead like two rams about to butt each other.

He stayed like that, glad perhaps to rest his weary gaze by fixing it on nothing but darkness. We had had enough of travelling sitting opposite each other.

With May, it had not been so tiring. I remembered a Jean fast asleep in the corner of a compartment, his head leaning sideways and his mouth half-open. I had pulled my veil down to my chin and retired from circulation while May, her right eye hidden by the peak of a leather cap, smoked twenty cigarettes, crumpled up newspapers and watched us with envy, wide-awake as a little owl. But today . . . To be honest, we had had some delightful interludes. It had been fun, for example, pretending to be a couple in the restaurant car, searching the list together for a wine that would console us for the Breton leg-of-mutton and saying to Jean under my breath with hypocritical reproach: "For goodness sake, don't look at me with that amiable expression! People will think we've just picked each other up in the corridor!"

We were alone in the compartment; I hardly counted the presence of the lady in pince-nez and of her little dog who refused to lie down, went to sleep standing up, toppled forward on its nose and woke itself and started all over again, just like Fossette, my deceased Fossette. I said to Jean: "If only you had known Fossette . . ." and I proceeded to quote some examples of canine intelligence. He received any brief anecdotes of my past with a polite, patient, faintly disgusted expression. All right, I'd be silent! Better still, I'd be angrily silent, passionately silent! On my side, I noticed that Jean put on a special expression when he spoke of his family or of himself.

He said: "My father . . . My uncle La Hourmette . . ." in a consciously flippant way, he said: "It was the year my poor good mother died," in a tone of kindly contempt and added, jestingly: "To a certain extent, we all make our mothers die of grief!"

I felt like retorting "*I* didn't", just to see his astonished expression: raised eyebrows and thrust-out chin. Do music-hall actresses *have* families? Good Lord, whatever can they be like? On the other hand, every allusion to May was greeted without the faintest embarrassment, even with enthusiasm. "We'll all three have lunch together this week, naturally."

I found *naturally* going rather too far and I replied with one of those "complicated" looks, into which Jean accuses me of putting too much. He applauded it, not without irony: "Excellent! Perhaps not absolutely an 'off-stage' look, but very good, all the same."

In a twelve-hour journey one can learn a good deal, even with very little talking. This contempt Jean did not hesitate to display for my former profession indicated that he thought about it enough to want to forget it and that he cared sufficiently to be preoccupied with something more than the desire of the coming night.

Twice he had abruptly got up as if he were going to stop the train and get out; then he had sat down again, very sedately.

"I apologise. Travelling in a train makes me bad-tempered. In a car, I'm delightful; but a train, this internment which . . ."

"Which goes on for ever . . ."

"Yes, exactly, which goes on for ever! We'd be better anywhere than here. And, to begin with, your patience would exasperate a saint."

"I'm accustomed to trains, you know."

"Yes, I know, I know! Don't start the saga of your touring days again or I'll do something desperate!"

I laughed, because I was thinking of Max and because I already enjoy deceiving Jean about the causes of my mirth. I am certainly not acquiring a taste for virtue in his company.

Yet we were quite comfortable in this compartment that smelt of peeled oranges, dust and fresh newsprint. Only we had had enough of it. Our mutual attraction allowed us neither long silent rests nor long conversations nor prolonged disregard of it. Our sail had exhausted my patience, our meals together seemed to me interminable and he could not endure another second of this twelve hours'

tête-à-tête. If he had dared, he would have exclaimed: "Let's play at something else."

Fickle passer-by, Unknown Stranger of my dream, I knew the game that would please you, and I was thinking of it too.

"It's easier," Jean had said. That is a word that covers much. Obviously it was easier for me to leave my baggage ticket with his manservant so that he could take my trunks to the Hôtel Meurice. To get into Jean's car and drive off at once over the greasy road surface was easier than waiting for a taxi. It is always easier to let oneself go than to restrain oneself.

Besides, nowadays, my trunks are merely my trunks and I entrust them to anyone. I no longer trail round that precious, shabby old object that contained our stage costumes, that treasure which gave Brague and myself such agonised qualms every time we arrived in a new town. "Look here, this infernal Railway Company has let the trunk go astray *again!*" Its tarred canvas displayed prominent wooden ribs, like a half-starved cab-horse; its corners, which we had had brass-bound at our common expense, defied the malevolence of theatrical wardrobe-men whose idea of "bringing down" a trunk is to give it one good shove at the top of the stairs as if they were chucking out some mug of a stage-door Johnny. Its sides, plastered with a patchwork of labels, attracted the eye; open, it exhaled an odour of naphthaline, wool that had been dyed and re-dyed, and slightly mildewed leather.

"We'll go to my place first, shall we?" Jean said. "For one thing, it's almost on your way, and, besides, we can see if May has telephoned or written. If you're thirsty, you can have a drink and you can pinch some of my fruit. It'll probably be better than what you'll get at the hotel."

As I said nothing, he added carelessly: "I'm not inviting you to tour the premises tonight. My little place is so much more attractive in broad daylight!"

He seemed extremely gay; he was humming. He kept leaning forward, then sitting up straight again, displaying at every moment a delight in coming home again which I could only watch, without sharing. In the old days, when we returned from a tour, Brague would begin to fidget excitedly as we approached Paris: "Dear old hole, bless it!" Even Fossette, if I had taken her with me, would sniff the first suburbs, sneezing and shaking an imaginary mane. But I?

You could hardly expect my heart to soften at the first sight of the Hôtel Meurice, like a homecoming Breton's catching the first glimpse of his village steeple! With a start, I felt a familiar, comradely slap on my knee, then a gloved hand imprisoned mine as it had in Nice.

"What on earth's come over you?"

"I don't know, I'm happy. I'm very fond of my neighbourhood. I like coming back to it with you."

"I know your neighbourhood. I lived in it a . . . a long time ago."

"Really!"

The intonation amused me. It was disapproving and showed no desire for further information. The car stopped and I jumped out, without being invited to, from sheer need to stretch my limbs and breathe; it was an involuntary movement that committed me all the more to continuing this journey together. It was a dark, damp, mild night. I recognised, from very long ago, that nocturnal smell of the Boulevard Berthier, where the passage of flocks often leaves the warm, musty odour of stables and sheepfolds.

Jean lives in one of the last little houses on the boulevard. I must have visited this one, in the old days, when I was a young married woman. Yes, I am sure I have. The narrow stairs, the dining-room on the left, the drawing-room on the right. But now there is a light paper on the walls and a waxed wooden staircase that smells of furniture-polish.

"Funny, it doesn't look like a man's house!"

"Yet I've made it into a bachelor's house. When I offered to furnish it for May she told me I had a damn cheek offering her this tart's poky hole. The little house has never recovered from it!"

"Oh! A fire!"

A lovely blaze of logs lit up the room Jean had just opened. My exclamation was so excited and greedy that Jean gave me an inquiring look, his eyebrows raised and his chin thrust out in that way that gives his expression of surprise an air of disapproval.

"Of course, you don't understand. . . . No, don't switch on the light, you can see the fire better. You don't realise that . . . we're nearly in March, aren't we? Well, I haven't seen a wood fire for a whole year."

"Are you joking?"

"No. Where do you expect I'd have seen a wood fire? In the bedroom of 'good' hotels they don't even have fireplaces any more. So . . ."

I fell silent out of laziness, out of well-being, as I stretched out my hand to the fire. It was such a glorious, generous fire, the fire of a bachelor whose man-servant does not worry about expense. It made a magnificent, varied noise on the hearth; from time to time a charred twig jumped out and burnt black on the marble, like a joss-stick, sending up its thin skein of smoke that smelt of creosote and sandal-wood.

I sat down cross-legged in front of it and Jean went out of the room. Was this a drawing-room? Yes, or a smoking-room. In the dancing firelight, I could make out gleaming wood surfaces, the curved legs of some charming old pieces of furniture, the dim greens of a tapestry hung on the wall, the belly of a blue vase.

But nothing meant so much to my weariness, to my trembling audacity—the audacity of a woman about to fall and watching her-self fall—nothing meant so much as that fire against which I was tak-ing refuge.

"Don't you want a cushion? I'm doing the waiting, Victor hasn't come back from the station."

Jean put a tray loaded with grapes and oranges down beside me.

"Winter fruits; a meagre supper, eh? There's some not very excit-ing dessert wine in this decanter and some fresh water in the jug."

"Oh! you shouldn't have bothered! Anyway, I'm going in a min-ute. . . ." I glanced up at him with a look that must have been despairing but he seemed not to notice and sat down cross-legged like myself, after having carefully pulled his trousers up at the knees. The dancing red light turned his face into that of a terra-cotta statue with silver eyes. He sucked grapes and threw the empty skins into the fire with a childish gravity, while I drank the juice of a split or-ange. Then he poured himself out a large glass of water, wiped his fingers and said "Ah!" in a way that implied: "Well, we've got to make up our minds to do *something!*"

And I suddenly realised that he too might be frightened and unde-cided, that his reserve, ever since the kiss he had given me, might be due more to hesitation than diplomacy. At the exact moment when I was losing even the outward appearance of calmness, a providential malice restored my self-control.

I reiterated: "Ah!" in the exact tone he had used, and I added: "That was the transitional phrase I was searching for! It leads on quite naturally to the next one—viz: "Eh! eh!" In all languages, that means: "Goodness, it's already past midnight!"

The fire was crumbling into embers; in the thickening shadow I could see the silver eyes gleaming with a slightly negroid ferocity and I began to reckon less on my host's shyness and apprehension. To fortify myself and also to insult Jean mentally, I conjured up the memory of Max, so amenable, in spite of his strength, and so honourable, even in the attack, that I was never frightened of him. Promptly, I shook the memory off with an ungrateful jerk. 'Ah, no, leave me in peace; I've quite enough to cope with with this one.'

This one had lain down flat on his stomach and was propping himself on his elbows, his head close to my knees. He turned his eyes towards the door and muttered, as if he had not heard me: "It's Victor with the luggage."

"So?"

"So don't move. What does it matter to you if Victor has come back with the luggage? Nobody comes in here unless I ring. Don't go, unless you really want to."

This direct challenge to my sincerity left me dumb and stupid. I really wanted to tell the truth but it seemed to be breaking up into separate strands inside me like a haycock swept away by a stream. Which one should I choose? Admit to him that his lightest word would keep me here? and that, at the same time, I felt cold and gentle, my senses asleep, very different from how I felt last night? It was all true, and all impossible to put into words.

Perhaps he guessed this, as he stroked my ankle through my silk stocking. But it was hardly a caress, it was like the mechanical movement of tracing a pattern on a material or a wall-paper with the tip of one's finger.

"Tell me," he reiterated, "tell me if you want to go?" He had crept a little closer still; I could feel his chin on my crossed knees. I looked him straight in the eyes and answered sadly, "No."

There was only one expiring flame left in a corner of the fireplace. It would sink down on to the glowing mass of pink and black embers and seem as if it were quenched for good, then once again it would escape and shoot up, flickering. Now concealing it, now modelling it clearly, it was the perfect light in which to study this man's face, so close to mine yet almost the face of a stranger. My voice had been so sad when I made my admission that it had prevented him from leaping on me; he had hesitated, then decided to adopt an affectionate, courteous tone to say eagerly: "Then you'll stay?"

With a feeble gesture, I indicated my surroundings, this unknown room in this unknown house; I drew attention to the travelling suit and hat I had been wearing all these hours and I tried to make a joke of it all.

"Honestly, Jean, you must realise that with the best will to immorality in the world . . ."

Then I abruptly broke off and reserved my strength to fight him off, for he had begun to overwhelm me; he was climbing round me, paralysing both my arms. He made himself purposely heavy, he made himself as clinging as a tenacious weed. I could not get up or even uncross my legs; I struggled conscientiously, half-pushed over backwards, supporting myself on one arm and muttering under my breath: "This is idiotic . . . this is really too idiotic!" until my simple, female sentimentality suddenly burst into that resentful, indignant cry: "You don't even love me!"

Still holding me tight in both arms, Jean raised himself up and looked down at me with a severe expression.

"Well, and what about you?"

Then he bent forward and kissed me delicately on the mouth. It was so sweet after those two minutes of struggling that I allowed myself the respite of it and let my head drop back on the carpet. How sweet it was, that naked mouth on mine, those full lips that resisted the kiss and had to be crushed a little to make them part. I wanted to stay prone like that, with my heart pounding in my throat, while the rosy fire warmed my cheek and its glow was reflected above me in two silver-grey eyes. How sweet it was, the moment of losing myself enough to think: "I am freed from the trouble of thinking. Kiss me, mouth for whom I am only a mouth." But that mouth was the mouth of an enemy whom the kiss was making ruthless, who knew I was conquered and would give me no quarter.

Arrogant, completely assured of his triumph, he displayed a barbarous contempt of methods. Hair, skirt, fine linen were all rumpled and crushed together as if he had not time to undress me. It was I who muttered, in shame: "Wait!" It was I who undid buckle and ribbon and removed pins that might hurt; it was I, lying on my back on the carpet, who made my slightly bruised body a cushion for Jean. Yet when he lay resting his head in the hollow of my shoulders with his hair tumbled over his forehead, his eyes closed and his mouth half-open, it was I who was the happier.

"Are you all right?"
"I am all right."

I seemed to have fallen from a great height into the middle of that bed where I lay prone, motionless and crushed. A fresh breeze, a ray of the setting sun came in through the open window and, every time a lorry or a motor-car passed, I saw the reflection of the water in a glass dancing on the ceiling. I felt a little giddy because my head was lying lower than my chest but I remained, out of laziness and by design, in this attitude which concealed my face and revealed all the rest.

All I could see through my tangled hair was the ceiling and the dancing reflection. Long ago, when I was a child, I used to stare at the sky like that, between criss-crossed barley stalks above my head.

A bare arm slid against my hip and I murmured feebly: "Stay still, do, you're not cramping me."

The arm raised itself to support the back of my neck and I accepted it. I nestled against this body which lay close to mine, making use of it as if it were a cushion or a piece of carpet. Then I lay still and laughed very softly.

"What's making you laugh?" asked Jean in a careless voice.

"I'm laughing because I can hear your movements. You've just stretched your arm out to the table the fruit is on and you couldn't reach it. Now you've let your arm fall back on the bed, regretfully. Tell me, isn't that so?"

"You're quite right. But come a little closer to me. You've slid right into the middle of the bed, I can't see you any more."

I moaned like a wounded person: "Oh no, no no! I implore you. I shall break to bits if I budge now; go on being patient."

He was silent and I went on waiting blissfully for my strength to return.

How long was it since we had rolled interlocked on the carpet in front of the dying fire? A day? A year? Only one day and that seemed so long ago. I came back today, I had lunch with Jean and after lunch I followed him into his bedroom. He did not close the window; he did not draw the curtains. How well I co-operated with him! So well that our embrace was like a harmonious wrestling-bout, planned in advance.

This is something I have never known before, this intelligent pleasure of the flesh that instantly recognises its master and responds to him by quickening for him and becoming pliant, docile, ardently reckless. It is so delightful, so easy, so totally unlike love.

At the mere impact of our bare knees, at the interlocking of our arms in a purposeful grip, I felt I was entering on hours of delight without danger. I was proud that I had given him as much as he had given me. Everything had been so perfect; I did not want our repose to be any less completely satisfactory than our pleasure. That was why I nestled comfortably against Jean and at the same time verified that his long leg lay quietly confident beside mine, neither tensing politely nor drawing away.

We had not spoken much but we had said necessary, pleasant, truthful things to each other. He had told me: "What lovely arms you have and how I like to feel you solid and heavy in mine when I lift you up!"

And I had declared to him in my turn: "How perfectly you suit me! You have a skin that's smooth and warm and dry, like mine."

And he had remained serious when I told him he was beautiful and I thought him the more modest for not protesting, since his face and his body . . .

I was imperceptibly worried as I tried to recompose exactly the features of his face that had just eluded me like a capricious word. Let me see . . . I could draw the nose from memory, and the dimple in the chin. The mouth—oh! the mouth! I knew the colour of the eyes, and . . . No, the face would not coalesce into a whole. Did I have to make the appalling admission I had forgotten it?

With a jerk I sat up in the bed and bent anxiously over Jean as if I really had been frightened I would no longer recognise him. Thank goodness! There he was as I *knew* him. No doubt his face had been too close to my eyes all today, mouth against mouth, his hard, cool nose against mine; his features had been blurred.

"Why are you laughing again?"

"I'm not laughing, I'm yawning. I feel good. Your room smells of carnations. How brown you are on that white sheet!"

He stretched out his limbs and let himself be stared at. The curve of his eyelids makes him look as if he were smiling when he closes his eyes. Very lightly, I touched everything that attracted and intrigued me in that exposed face; the small shaved area that makes the hairline recede, the feminine lips, the neck that was so young, so flawlessly smooth. So young! It was the first time I had thought of his age, of him as a person.

"Is that a scar—there—on your temple?"

"Yes, I think so."

"And there, is that a birthmark in the middle of your chest? A beauty-spot, if you prefer. No, let me see. Your veins are green in the bend of your arm and at your wrists—green, green! Goodness, I *am* enjoying myself! How about you?"

"Renée . . ."

"What?"

I looked at him with slight astonishment when he used my Christian name. Previously, I had not noticed.

"Do you want to get up, Renée?"

"No, what for?"

I fished out my handkerchief-puff from under a pillow and powdered my nose and cheeks without feeling inclined for other repairs.

"What for? I don't want a bath or to comb my hair or to go out. All I want to do is keep the good warmth and the smell of you, to sleep in them and to wake up when we've had enough. How about you, Jean?"

"Me too."

He rolled against me like a round, heavy tree, seeking a comfortable place with his shoulder and the back of his neck. He closed his eyes, then opened them again when he thought I was not looking, and it seemed to me that those beautiful grey eyes were demanding something of me, reproaching me for something.

"Are you sleepy? Lie there, then."

When did I last feel a man's head lying so heavily and trustfully on my shoulder? With my nostrils and lips I inhaled the slightly burnt smell of the harsh black hair.

"Laughing again?"

"But I'm not laughing! Why do you want me to laugh all the time?"

"On the contrary, I don't want you to," he sighed. "*I* don't feel like laughing."

"You're unhappy? You're tired? You're dissatisfied with me?"

He indicated "No" by rubbing his head against my breast. Soon night would hide him from me, but sleep would give him to me more completely. He would forget my cheerfulness, my companionable ease after love-making. Perhaps he wanted me to be happy, but more respectful of his prowess, more broken, more vanquished. I was not vanquished, I was contented.

"You'll come tomorrow, Renée?"

"Why, of course I'll come."

"And the other days?"

"I don't know, how do you expect me to know?"

"Don't you want to, then?"

With all my recovered strength, I clasped the strong body that lay relaxed in my arms.

"I swear I do."

He muttered, as if he were already dreaming. "You see . . . I love you."

I shook him gently: "What's that you're telling me?"

"Why yes . . . you realise . . . love . . ."

I closed the beautiful, indiscreet mouth by pressing my cheek against it.

"Shh! Not that word! Goodbye. Don't talk any more. Let's go to sleep."

EIGHT

If Hamond were still alive, he would listen to my confidences, then he would shake his head and say: "This isn't an honourable liaison!"

I could see his long face with its big, bold nose, I could hear his voice; in short I missed them badly enough to be offended by the opinion he would have had and I defended myself against it as if he were present.

"Not an honourable liaison! And, pray, what *is* an honourable liaison?"

My old friend would have inevitably replied, with that reserved sincerity that stood up to all my rebuffs: "It's, quite simply, a liaison which, whether people know about it or not, you can feel does you honour."

His answer, which I had invented, offended me as he had offended me by suddenly letting himself die. An angry, intolerant grief had made me hot with resentment during the first weeks after his death: "To do such a thing to me, to *me*, to *me!*"

I still miss him. It is a selfish grief that afflicts me when I need not advice but intelligent, disinterested conversation to distract me from my exhausting interior monologue. When I am in that state I do as I am doing now: I resurrect my dead friend and imagine that he is talking. However, this bears no relation to a "psychic phenomenon"; it is simply a question of making the voice of Hammond speak for the conscience of Renée Néré.

There are days when, having left Jean's arms, I go away and walk along the fortifications which are beginning to show signs of green, days when I secretly exclaim: "Is this all?" Yes, this is all. "It is quite enough!" replies the languid body. How sensible it is, this contented, heavy-footed body!

A dishonourable liaison. Why cast an unnecessary slur on the ill-assorted but well-matched couple that we are? Why not throw myself into this as whole-heartedly as Jean, who is so charmingly rash as to want to live under the same roof—strangers as we are with nothing in common but physical delight? I am touched that he will not much longer tolerate the overnight luggage concealed in a "small" handbag: a nightdress and two silk slippers; nor my comings and goings between the Boulevard Berthier and the Hôtel Meurice. I am touched when I suddenly see him leave his lunch and rush upstairs to the first floor, three steps at a time. When he talks of "our future life", I shall never interrupt him to tell him: "These aren't plans for the future you're making; they're furnishing estimates." I shall not tell him that, in deciding to do what seems to him open and honourable, he risks compromising the frail—but perhaps durable—bond between us. Frankly, I like the discomfort of these sporadic meetings. I must not let him know this. I must commit myself to the same extent as Jean which, after all, is not saying much: he is only giving me a definite place in his home. I still do not know if he has finally broken with May.

All the evidence points to it and I am convinced he is no longer her lover but he has not *invited* me to know it. What is he waiting for? The installation of the new bed and the carpet the colour of silvery mouse-fur? Furnishing estimates!

Ever since our embrace in the glow of the dying fire, I seem to have been holding in my hands, in my arms, everything that Max neither could nor would give me in those days: physical love for physical love, a splendid adversary well suited to me, a passion into which one entered, as into a secret room, already throbbing with anticipated pleasure. The preparations for our meetings would have occupied part of my days which would henceforth be idle and I can imagine how swiftly the time would pass, divided between expectations, possession and greedy memory. It is a great deal. It is enough. I have heard young women declare trenchantly: "In love, my motto is *all or nothing*." Well, well, a charming nothing, admirably presented, is anyway something.

Jean wants more, and I acquiesce, not to be outdone in generosity. The remarkable thing about our relationship is that all day we outdo each other in cautious reserve about the most trivial subjects.

"Would you like to go to the theatre?"

"Yes, I'd quite like to."

"But perhaps you don't really want to?"

"What about you?"

"I want to do whatever *you* want . . ." etc., etc.

Before we were lovers, we were not so formally polite to each

other. Yet, on the other hand, what a warm urge to come close together, what sincere throwing off of reserve, if he presses his mouth
to mine, if his hand caresses me tentatively! Then an inimitable
confidence, if not the other. "Is that all?" Why yes, that is all. And
who would not be content with it?

"What are you going to do? Aren't you coming with me to
Levallois to see the garage man? The car's had a nasty bash, you
know."

I made my habitual grimace and the glass in front of me warned
me: "Take care! That's an expression you'll have to avoid in the very
near future."

"No . . . the garage man doesn't tempt me."

"Where are you off to, then?"

"Don't know. Taking a little walk . . . maybe as far as the
Meurice. The laundress should have brought back some of my
blouses."

"Why don't you stay here and make yourself at home?"

I straightened the bent shaft of a hatpin and stared at Jean in
blank perplexity. Why, in fact, didn't I stay where I was? There were
books in the smoking-room-cum-drawing-room downstairs, a chaise-
longue, the almost insipid cigarettes I prefer, and Victor, the man-
servant, would surround me with discreet attentions which signified:
"Mind you, I'm not wild about *you*, but I couldn't stick *her* at any
price". For even the silence of this Parisian servant has a common accent.

"No . . . You see, I'll get a headache if I stay shut up indoors."

"You mustn't do that, you mustn't do that!"

"I'll just go a couple of steps, then I'll come back. Anyway . . ."

I was lying. I was going to the Hôtel Meurice.

I would check my linen and spray it with scent to disguise the
odour of chloride and chilled iron, I would open the papers they
bring me every morning and glance through them rapidly, sitting in
an armchair, with my feet on the table: I would dawdle about my
room, polishing my nails and listening to the familiar music of
crockery and glass being got ready for dinner that rose from the
courtyard and the distant violins playing in the glass-roofed hall.
Then it would be time and I would return here with a freshly
"done" face, in which for some hours nothing would be lacking; on
the contrary, I should have put on a little too much of everything. In

fact I should do nothing bad and nothing good, but I should go to the Hôtel Meurice. It was my right, my habit, my dull and hygienic interlude. I should return there tonight, for I am not sleeping in the Boulevard Berthier—not yet. . . .

All we have experienced together is daytime sleep that descends suddenly and as suddenly departs. I am apprehensive about a whole night; it is not Jean who has anything to fear from the surprises of waking up, the revelations of the broad daylight of morning. We often sleep in the afternoon, through the sunlight or the spring rain, while down in the basement kitchen Victor raises his rat's head to the level of the pavement the moment anyone rings and guards us against the possible return of May.

May . . . a name that, ten days ago, we mentioned every other minute and that, little by little, we are eliminating from our vocabulary; a name around which a rather suspicious uncertainty is gathering. I have not written to May; throughout our haphazard intimacy we have never corresponded with each other. But I believe that, if I had been able to say to Jean: "Keep May, don't defraud her of anything but the secret hours you devote to me", this dishonest solution would have given me a very honest satisfaction. What would those "all-or-nothing" ladies, those intransigent suffragettes in the cause of love, think of me? But I am not speaking of all Love, I am only claiming my share of the . . . of . . . in fact to be allowed to keep what I have and which, for me, is so new and light-hearted, which pacifies my mind and gives a fresh, warm glow to my skin. I know all about the great transports and the great agonies; like everyone else I went through all those when I was a young, inexperienced woman. At the moment, I felt I wanted to please everybody, even May.

"Hi! . . . Renée, Renée!"

She had so suddenly appeared there in front of me, at the very second I was mentally pronouncing her name, that my first thought was to blame myself. 'Serves you right, that's what comes of summoning her.'

She caught me up as I was walking along by the Tuileries. She had jumped out of an orange motor-car, a curious little vehicle with a bare, rounded behind, like one of those sick hens that has lost its back feathers. I did not flee, but while May was running after me with constricted little steps, I imagined myself lying down, well-guarded, in Jean's smoking-room. I sighed and resigned myself to the shock.

"So I've found you, you quitter!"

Quitter? She sounded effusively pleased to see me, not angry, did that mean she knew . . . everything—everything except about me?

"Come in here, I've got some very serious things to tell you."

She dragged me into the melancholy garden, naked of grass and greenery, and, to fill up the silence, I made such remarks as were strictly necessary.

"Well, honestly . . . You always drop from the sky like a thunderbolt. Where have you sprung from?"

It was as much as I could manage. May's scent, her arm tucked in mine, the sudden physical contact with *Jean's mistress* disturbed me in a most painful, unexpected way. Most intolerable of all was feeling that rounded arm clutching my own, knowing it was the arm of Jean's mistress.

"Very serious things, I tell you. You look marvellous. I'm pale, aren't I?"

She was as pink as an azalea, but it was a pinkness that doubtless concealed an authentic pallor. I thought she was looking very pretty. She seemed to me prettier than ever: a regimental ribbon encircled her straw cap, her neck was bare under her jacket that was at once skimpy and loose, a strand of hair gleamed like a streak of gold braid on her temple. Never, no never had her twenty-five years so deliciously glamourised the faults of an idiotic fashion. I could think of nothing else. I had to make a mental effort to recall myself to reality and tell myself: 'You have taken this young woman's lover. She might be brandishing a weapon in her hand, instead of a rolled umbrella!' I felt no terror, except one of subtle repugnance whenever May pressed my arm closer as she talked or laid her ungloved hand on my hand.

"You know what happened?"

"Happened when?"

"After you departed from Nice?"

"No. . . ."

"Jean left me."

"Yes. . . ."

"You knew that? Was it Masseau who told you? After I returned here—I'll spare you the details, shall I? Jean came to see me twice, as charming as could be."

"Ah!"

"But that's not paying him any compliments because every time he becomes very charming, it's a bad sign. I wasn't taken in, I got the letter five days ago."

"What letter?"

"*The* letter. The letter to say it's all finished."

"Ah! And didn't you do anything?"

A bitter wind was sweeping the terrace and blowing stinging dust in our faces. May clutched the brim of her hat and my eyes were streaming. But it did not occur to us to go anywhere else.

"What d'you mean, I did nothing? Ah, you're talking of . . . of revolvers, laudanum, navaja, all that bag of tricks! Just imagine! With a boy like Jean!"

"What's so special about him?"

May turned her back on the yellow Seine and leant on the balustrade. Clinging to her hat, with her skirt plastered against her knees and her stomach she looked like a passenger on a yacht heeling over in the wind.

"If you like, he hasn't anything special about him, yet, in one sense he has everything. He's a man, that's all. The more you see of men, the more you tell yourself they're all alike in everyday life . . . then when something happens, some quarrel, some misunderstanding, you stand there gaping at them as if you'd never known more than one. Don't you think there's some truth in that?"

"I'm sure there is."

"I had that feeling with Jean even more than with the others. I even had it all the time with him."

"One would never have guessed it."

May gave a sidelong smile, her golden lock blown into her eye; she had taken my sarcastic remark for a compliment.

"I had it all the same. He's a fellow you're all at sea with. Rotten with pride, to begin with."

"Is he?"

"Goodness me, yes. When he's made a mistake, just try rubbing his nose in it and making him own up to it, you just try, you'll be astonished! His Lordship knows everything, His Lordship's so bloody cocksure! Because His Lordship's ruined himself a little bit in motors, a little bit on the stock exchange, and in politics too—for hardly long enough to mention it he had a government job in Ille-et-Vilaine— a little bit here, a little bit there—he's more infallible than the Pope."

"Just fancy that!"

"And secretive, my dear! When you think he hasn't got a bean, he's got money. When you see him flinging cash about in handfuls, it means he's on the rocks. Always the same thing—pride! Like his way of saying nothing sometimes when I was telling him off good and proper. That way of smoking without saying a word, holding his cigarette in his teeth and sticking his chin out."

I could not imagine anywhere where I would feel worse than I did where I was. The wind, May's words, the shame of listening to them, all these combined to produce a physical misery that was a blend of migraine, sea-sickness and cramp in the stomach. Alas! I could not doubt that this woman was suffering. She was suffering as much as she could, to the full of her small capacity.

". . . And to smile like that, you know, as if he were gazing right through the wall at something you couldn't see. 'Joan of Arc and her visions', as I used to say to him. . . ."

But what right had I to assess the quality of her suffering? And what was I doing here, listening to humiliating confidences? The most trivial of my questions and exclamations that invited or prolonged an answer of May's were as bad as listening at doors or prying open a letter.

The only honourable words, the brave exclamation: "Don't say any more, Jean is mine now," refused to cross my lips. . . .

"Let's walk a little, this spot is impossible. Mind you, all these things I'm telling you about Jean aren't crimes. He's ever such a character, too. When a woman has said of her lover that he's conceited and 'superior' and rather underhand and none too generous, that doesn't make him a scoundrel. But there's something worse about Jean."

"Whatever's that?"

The wall of the Orangery sheltered us. Quick, during this respite of the wind, let me bend down to catch the last vile whisper, the best one, the one the little deserted mistress was keeping for a *bonne bouche*. How cold I was!

"The worst thing about him is the way he f——s off."

"Yes?"

"He f——s off like no one else and you never get him back. I can talk about it now because the first effect's worn off, thank God. But what Jean did to me is no more and no less than he did to Marthe Byse, famous star as she is, no more and no less than he did to Madame . . . oh hell, my memory for names. . . . A widow, that pretty blonde? . . . well, it doesn't matter. He f——s off, that's the frightful thing. When you chuck each other, it's after a scene, isn't it? . . . Or coming unstuck, little by little? Well, my dear, *he* f——s off in the middle of a sentence, closing the door behind him, or else he goes out to buy cigarettes and you never see him again except in the form of a farewell letter, very well written, simply marvellous. . . . I don't know if you're like me but that affects me much more than the gentleman who stages a big scene: 'Since we must part . . .' Jean's way is the worst way of f——g off because, mark you, he doesn't do it like the gentleman who snatches your purse and disappears in smoke, oh no, not at all! You write to him, you ask him to come and see you and someone turns up who's called Jean, and is wearing a suit and tie you know very well. You recognise the stick, the cuff-links, even the sound of the voice. But the gentleman—he's f——d off so completely that you stare at him, you open your eyes as big as saucers and you ask yourself: 'Well, honestly, *did* I sleep with this man or didn't I?' Listen, I'm not spiteful, but I'd like to see the face of the woman who's pushed me out when Jean f——s off again! . . . Now it's raining. We only needed that. Come along, I'll run you home in my car, a yellow car . . . that's appropriate or I'm a Dutchman. But a character like me isn't superstitious. The car and the person who's waiting in it is a try, a feeble try. . . ."

"I can't, I've some shopping to do, under the arcades."

"Let's run then! I offer you half my umbrella."

"No, run on ahead! I've got nothing on that rain will spoil. Run! Yes, yes, I'll telephone you. . . ."

She ran with short quick steps, her skirt hitched up round her knees like a little pair of knickers. She went off, lightened by all the load she had left with me. Ah, it was then that I wanted to speak, to own up, to come out with everything I had been choking back a few minutes earlier.

"May!"

Luckily, she did not hear. A taxi came by; I managed to gasp out the address in the Boulevard Berthier: "And drive fast!" Suppose, in my absence, Jean had "f——d off"?

NINE

"Jean! . . . Ah! you're there!"

"Why of course I'm here! What's the matter?"

"Nothing. Just imagine, I let myself get caught in the rain, so I came back here instead of going and dressing myself. Too stupid of me."

"It's never stupid of you to come back here."

"But I wanted to make myself beautiful. And here I am again just as you left me."

"I should hope so! You look very much like a certain traveller who sat there on the floor one night. I like you."

"As much as she?"

"Better."

Slowly, I pulled myself together. By talking, by saying pleasant nothings, I concealed the anxiety that had sprung up when I left May and that had grown, on the way back here, into an irrational panic: "Jean has gone . . . I can feel that he's gone, I'm convinced of it."

May's words had followed me all the way with the malevolent force of a *spell:* "He f——s off and you never get him back!" The narrow house, blinded with shutters, looked to me deserted, and I called out "Jean!" in the voice one uses in nightmares.

There he was, very much present, very much alive, between the fire he was stoking up for me and the lamp topped with a shade like the luminous roof of a little pagoda. The twisted feet of the armchairs reflected the flame and the silk curtains were a mellow, sumptuous red.

"What's the matter with you? Odd for a woman who was supposed to be taking a couple of steps, to arrive in a taxi, looking as if you'd returned from heaven knows where."

"I think I've caught cold. Oh! it's nice here, in your home."

"There are hazel-hens for dinner and a Viennese tart—a big, heavy tart."

"Really? What luck! And what did he say, your garage-man?"

"He said, seeing the crack that splits the door from top to bottom: 'The door's cracked'."

"You can't hide anything from him."

He wandered about the room, pushed forward an armchair, pulled the curtains and "tidied up" with the good grace of a bachelor host. As he passed me, he stroked my knee and caught hold of my ears, like two handles, so as to kiss me better. His hands, his body, his smooth cheek—they were all warm and firm, all infinitely, preciously alive. I contemplated him admiringly: so close, so free, perhaps all mine, perhaps already lost to me.

"And . . . how many days will he take over it?"

"Will who take over what?"

"Why, the garage-man."

To Jean's surprise, I let a long time elapse between his question and my obvious answer. A very long time indeed, during which I stalked round him, taking a bitter pride in seeing him so intact, so little touched by life, so well-equipped to hurt, as I might have said yesterday. Today, I said to hurt *me*.

"Help me, Renée! Look how unhappy those roses look laced up in their tight string corsets."

"It's not worth the bother. Roses from Nice, they only last two hours in a room where there's a fire."

"Two more hours of beauty in front of you—don't you think that's worth having?"

I flushed in the shadow and gave him a vindictive look, but he had spoken in all innocence.

"There! Is that all right?"

"Very nice indeed. But I had to ask you! I'm always surprised. Come and sit on my knee . . . surprised to see how few feminine ways you have."

"Go on, tell me I ill-treat you!"

"You don't arrange flowers in vases, you don't pull the table cloth straight when it's crooked, you don't pat the sofa cushions. You sit down, you cross your legs."

"Don't exaggerate!"

"Well, anyway you behave like a lady paying a call and that annoys me."

"Me too."

"Aren't you my lover then? Don't you want to belong to me as I belong to you? There are days when you humiliate me with your hurry to get undressed before and get dressed again after. Days when one really wouldn't think that you love me, but that you're using me."

I listened complacently, without the least resentment. Sitting on his knee, I gazed at him from close to, breathing in the smell of his hair that tongs daily scorch a little; at last I had him! "I have him," I thought. "Let that be no more than the affirmation of my senses— not a thought, not a hope which the future is already withering. . . . Oh, let it express only the pleasure of this hour and not commit me further than here and now!"

He sulked, with more grace than conviction, but he was not very pleased. He would lose his temper, if I egged him on.

I caressed him with growing melancholy, for I was beginning to realise that his changes of mood had very little effect on me. Jean in a temper, or Jean disdainful and sarcastic, or Jean crafty and a little cautious as he always is when he turns very gentle, what did it matter, provided it was Jean? The marvel of his *presence*, the unutterable security of all one's senses.

"Understand me!" he said impatiently. "You only seem interested in what I take from you, not in what I am!"

"And you?"

He lowered his brows like an animal and his whole forehead seemed to come down. I guessed from the relaxing of the knee I was sitting on that he wanted to throw me on the floor.

"Me? You know perfectly well that I . . ."

"Say it!"

"I've said it to you already! I said it first!"

"That could have been a reflex. There are moments when the expression 'I love you' is no more than an involuntary nervous twitch."

We laughed, half-angry with each other. I had no scruple in contradicting him, even in bad faith. I was hungry tonight for everything he could give me; lies, obstinate perplexity, offensive gesture or too tender look. Had I not had this identical conversation long ago with Maxime? It was a distant echo that died away if I listened, a memory so faint that it cast no shadow on my present.

Nothing in my past dares impinge any more on my present. Why? Why should this utterly fresh Jean, often still as hard and closed as a tardy oak-bud, enjoy this outrageous immunity? Outrageous, because it does something worse than merely protect him; it rears up in front of him, not a faithful likeness of Max, but a distorted, almost comic picture of him. I see a Max who looks stiff and awkward, with his features drawn geometrically inside a rectangle, like the faces in Sadi Carnot's old caricatures.

Though Jean is neither handsomer nor better than Max, I never compare the two men to Jean's disadvantage. The only excuse I can offer for this is the mysterious, obtuse, feminine objection: "It's not the same thing."

He was there, close against me. I held him in proud silence, as he leant heavily and confidently against one of my breasts, crushing it with his weight. We had learnt already that whenever our minds or our consciences awoke and defied each other the only thing to do was to clasp each other tight and be silent. Embracing gives us the illusion of being united and silence makes us believe we are at peace.

"I'd like to know the evil you think of me," he sighed.

"Guilty conscience!"

"No, but I'm listening to you thinking. Your breathing's uneven, it stops when you come to a cross-roads of ideas. And when you turned your face over on the cushion, your eyelashes gave a quick flutter that scratched the silk."

"Not bad, not bad!"

"It isn't, is it? I'm so intelligent! Is something worrying you?"

"Yes: you. Do you want to know what I'm thinking? I was thinking I shall never have the courage to go back to the hotel tonight."

Almost imperceptibly he tightened his arms round me. He did not even look up but I could see a smile of delight slide down from his eyelids to his mouth. He relaxed and grew heavier, as if he were already on the point of falling asleep. I did not regret having spoken. A little sooner, a little later, the ordeal of the long night and of waking up together awaited me. And tonight I felt so cowardly at the thought of being alone in a darkness that would echo till dawn with May's voice: "He f——s off, and you never see him again."

Dinner passed quickly: we chattered with unwonted coherence and sparkle. It was as if, by using the excuse of such things as an antique sideboard and a monogram on some silver to document me about his family, Jean wanted to give me a bigger share in his home, to *invite* me more urgently into it. The way he said "My father" in a tone of impatient respect, like a schoolboy kept short of pocket-money, made him seem amazingly younger.

"How old are you, Jean?"

"Ssh! I've stopped admitting it for the past two years!"

He was joking, but I promptly imagined that he was concealing his age out of delicacy, to stop me from making comparisons . . . so I did not dare insist; I remained silent, feeling a little shaky.

"My blessed father, I can't get out of spending three days with him next week. Including the two journeys that means I'll be away five days. If I missed my mother's anniversary, the Autocrat would have a seizure. Will you find that odd, five days without me?"

"I don't know, I can't very well imagine myself, at this moment. . . ."

"What will you do with yourself all that time? Who will you go and see? Your family—your friends?"

It was the first time he had shown any direct sign of interest in me, or at least of a curiosity that was not purely sensual. Taken aback, I stared at this young imperious face that was questioning me; a family . . . friends . . .

"You know, I haven't any relatives left since my sister-in-law Margot died."

"And friends? Haven't you any friends?"

I mastered a shaming sense of being a wanderer with no one belonging to her and defied him.

"Indeed I have! I've got Brague. And I also used to have a little dancer but she's travelling abroad at the moment. An unmarried mother called Bastienne."

He was about to say something insulting, then changed his mind.

"Well . . . don't let's think about that five days ahead. Anyway, I'm not sure I won't take you with me."

"If I'd like to come?"

We laughed, and our eyes caressed each other, not very frankly. *He* is born to please without effort, to seduce, and to make his escape. *I* . . . I am like the grey mare my father had; a good cut with the lash did not frighten her but the shadow of the whip on the road, beside her ears, made her crazy with terror.

He brought his chair closer to mine and shared my dessert.

"Do you split oranges in two? *I* peel them and sugar them."

"Sugar on an orange, how revolting! I'll make you fruit salads in the summer, you'll see I'm an expert."

"I absolutely forbid you to do any such thing! Fruit salads have always made me think of . . . of dessert rejected by an intolerant stomach!"

Every time we disagreed, we were seized with immoderate gaiety. And suddenly I was stupid enough to say: "One thinks those little things don't matter a bit. All the same I used to get furious in the old days at the mere sight of my husband dipping his bread in his soup."

But Jean was not in the least interested in my husband. He had heard the clock strike half-past nine and he gave a stretch and yawned with an excellent imitation of common bad manners, showing the whole fresh interior of a well-furnished mouth. A splendid red jaw that could bite up anything. He caught my eye and the expression in his own changed, to an urgent, unsmiling gaze that said: "Come . . ."

He was asleep. He does not sleep as he does in the daytime. He can sense, through his slumber, the long night ahead and the chill that precedes the late dawn of March; he sleeps in stern immobility, covered right up to his shoulders. He breathes very slowly. I could see him dimly by the light of the street lamp outside, for the window was wide open. I breathed in, as if I were in the country, the smell of wet grass and mist; a cold air that seemed pure and that made our amorous bedroom chaste.

He had left me a wide place beside him in which I dared not stir. I felt tired, forgotten until he woke up, but patient and peaceful. He no longer knew I was there. Once, I touched him very lightly; he drew his arm away with a childish, irritable gesture.

Nothing had changed. Only my inability to sleep gave a touch of solemnity to our first night whose delights equalled those of our afternoons; nevertheless it was a "first night". Before that night lay the past sealed off for me, but what did I know of our future?

Did I even foresee a future, as I kept my submissive vigil, careful not to disturb Jean's rest? I do not know, but I kept vigil because it was the *first night*. I kept vigil as any woman, raw or experienced, might do who is apprehensively beginning life or beginning it afresh at the side of a sleeping man.

"Goodbye for a little while! You've got your handkerchief, your key?"

"I was sure you'd forget it! Victor, bring down the key Monsieur left on the dressing-table."

"I'll be back early, you know."

"I hope so."

Jean studied himself once again in the looking-glass in the hall and once again smoothed his hair with the gesture of an actor settling his wig.

"Leave your head alone! It's ugly enough as it is. This fashion of plastered-down hair!"

He did not believe a word of it and his face expressed an earnest complacency, an unsmiling satisfaction that prevented his vanity from being odious. The piece of mirror that reflected me beside him seemed to be of a darker glass, greenish and warped.

He came back late this afternoon, exclaiming: "I'm dining with the Autocrat!" and tearing off his jacket and tie the moment he got upstairs. The dress I was putting out ready to wear for dinner with him remained on its hanger, holding out its two short sleeves as if it were saying: "There's nothing we can do about it. . . ." For the pleasure of following Jean and assisting at his toilet, I had stopped attending to my own, and now I saw myself in a loose dressing gown, with my hair in becoming disorder. But my figure, beside the streamlined tails, the starched shirt-front, the pale, clean-shaven face, looked sluttish and untidy; there was a heaviness about it, an indefinable air of voluptuous maturity.

"Do hurry and get off, Jean!"

"Yes, but I want you to be sorry for me."

"Because?"

"Because I'm dining with the Autocrat!"

He held out his sulky mouth one last time, before jumping, on one bound, down the steps that led to the street. I laughed and shrugged my shoulders, and, in spite of myself, I thought that he did not affect this boyish manner with May. With May, he spoke sharply and raised his hand to her, and it was May who acted like a little girl; only May was twenty-five.

The motor drove off. I remained for a moment in the doorway, leaning out and smiling as if he could see me. Above the mound of the fortifications, the sky was still a little pink and against it the black trees thrust up their swollen buds, just on the verge of opening. Neighbours, peaceful inhabitants of this ill-famed Boulevard, were calling their dogs and strolling about bareheaded, like villagers, before leaving the place to problematical "apaches". It was a very mild evening, without a breath of wind. I could not have chosen one that better suited my desire to be alone.

For some hours, Jean will be away. And, though I kept saying over and over again: "Be off with you, you'll be late!" he did not sense how much I wanted to get rid of him. He did not realise how well chance had served my purpose tonight, for I have a purpose. The way I hurried over dinner was sufficient proof of it and so, now that I have shut myself up in my room again, is this face I see in the glass, the face of someone unscrupulously plotting a crime? Yet I do not want to write secretly to anyone nor, in spite of that hateful look in my eyes, do I want to kill or to steal; I want to be alone; if he were to come in unexpectedly at this moment, or if he were hidden behind the curtains, I should scream. I should scream like any other woman, surprised by her lover when she is day-dreaming alone in her bedroom; scream with terror and rage and blaze up with the chaste wrath of an outraged priestess. Suppose he were to come in and find me something worse than naked—find me altered beyond recognition?

I have been living here only a month. And never did mistress move in with less commotion; three trunks of clothes and underwear, some papers in a box and a beauty-case. It was all done so quickly, so simply, that a sceptical lover would have suspected the expertness of long habit. But Jean, mistrustful as he is, is not a sceptical lover. The day I arrived, I shyly set down my two essential pieces of furniture on the pretty desk in the bedroom: a fountain pen and a very ancient little Chinese knick-knack, a polished jade fruit, so worn that it seems to be melting away but exquisitely smooth to the touch.

And straight away I had begun my initiation into an existence quite unknown to me; the only one that, under a surface of unconventionality and illusory freedom, involves outdated customs and an almost oriental dependence: the existence of the *kept woman*.

When the kept woman, like myself, has no family and no intimate friends, and is brave enough or heedless enough to entrust herself entirely to the man whom chance has selected for her, she may find her new life a mixture of pleasures and mortifications. She may have the impression of being simultaneously a convalescent in a nursing home, a novice in a dissolute convent—or a harem—and a "trusty housekeeper" burdened with a thousand domestic cares. Idleness gives me a taste for arranging things; Jean's daily absences now that "the Autocrat's" state of health involves his spending some hours every day with his family oblige me to make each of his returns a little festival; flowers on the table, some delicious fruit just in season, or the sudden appearance of a euonymus hedge in the little neglected garden. . . .

After all, the good fairy who looks after nomads keeps me from being impatient and bad-tempered by whispering in my ear: "This will last as long as you want it to, and no longer." No longer . . . so I reassure myself and bask in the present with the belated improvidence of a passionate woman to whom love was miserly in the bloom of her youth. I have grown a little fatter, I savour my food with pleasure; like Jean, I sleep long hours. In the daytime, my preoccupations are more or less the same as Victor's, the man-servant's: "Is Monsieur going out with Madame? Or without Madame? Has Monsieur come home? Is Monsieur dressing tonight?"

The first days, during Jean's absences, I made my way back to my usual eating places; the little Italian restaurant where the ravioli sizzles with butter and piping hot cheese, and the brasserie whose hot sausages and velvety beer Brague so highly commends. But I could no longer enjoy them in quite the same way, with the frank pleasure of a greedy old bachelor. "One doesn't go to such places all by oneself!" Jean would exclaim. "One doesn't deliberately give the impression, when one is a woman like you and one has a lover like me, of being reduced to sauerkraut and beer dives! Gracious, you've got a house at your disposal and a cook who's not too inefficient and yet off you go traipsing all over Paris", etc., etc., etc.

On the first rainy evening, sitting all alone in front of my ravioli, I rebuked myself with the docility of a happy, malleable animal: "Gracious, I've a house at my disposal, a cook who's not too inefficient", etc., etc. . . . and I admitted Jean was justified on every count.

If I dine at a restaurant, it is with Jean. If I go to the theatre, it is with Jean. In the old days, when I was legally married, I was allowed to have outside acquaintances, but the code of "living in sin" is far more stringent. To accompany me, I have a lover, Jean, or a bodyguard, Masseau. The same code regulates my comings and goings so exactly and to such a strict minimum that it amuses me; I am secretly flattered that such rigour should dictate the actions and behaviour of an ingénue of thirty-six, and when I risked observing one day: "But when you were May's lover, I don't think you . . ." I promptly received the stiff answer: "May didn't live with me. And besides, May was May and you're you."

"This will last as long as you like and no longer. . . ." I accept my new condition with interested curiosity. I am contracting the habit of hasty acquiescence and of childish fibbing. I content myself with what satisfies other women in my position, the free time Jean procures me by going out.

Realise this, you who say you love me: the most loving mistress turns away from her lover during certain hours which she mysteriously arranges should come and which she cherishes in anticipation. The most beautiful woman, if you perpetually spy on her, will not survive undamaged. The most faithful one needs to hide herself, if only to be able to think freely.

"Freely! To be free! . . ." I am speaking out loud to try and make that beautiful faded word come alive again and shimmer with the green of wild woodlands, echo with the beat of wild wings. In vain!

You pretend to love me; this means that all day long I must bear the burden of your anxiety, your watch-dog vigilance, your suspicion. Tonight I am not off the chain, but it has slipped from your hand and trails behind me so that I do not feel the pull of it.

You pretend to love me, you do love me. Every minute your love creates a woman better and more beautiful than myself whom you force me to resemble. I put on, along with your favourite colours, the tone of voice and the smile you like best. You have only to be present for me to give a miraculous imitation of all the characteristics and charms of my model—all that I dread is certain hours like this one when I suddenly want to scream at you: "Get out! My princess's dress and my radiant face are going to drop off simultaneously, get out!" This is the moment when the cloven hoof is going to appear under the hem of the skirt, the twisted tip of a horn under the silken hair. I am possessed by the demons of a silent, inner Sabbath. I must curse and reject the gentle shape in which you have imprisoned me.

It is growing late; I must have been alone for a very long while. How many times have I paced to and fro in front of this mirror? Each time I pass, it shows me my guilty face with its false, sidelong, anxious smile. One shoulder droops slackly, the other is hunched up to the ear as if to ward off an unexpected blow.

Just now I squatted down in front of my reflection in the attitude Jean dislikes: with my arms crossed on my knees and my breast crushed against them, I rocked myself like a sick bear.

I remember having frantically scratched my head like a real flea-riddled gipsy. I must also have fixed my gaze on the glittering belly of a little copper vase that glows in the shadow like a red-hot poker, for I can still feel its luminous point hurting me between my eyebrows. And during that time I must have been utterly blank and forgotten to think.

A little shock roused me, a disagreeable little mental shock: "What is Jean doing?" With marvellous promptness, a mental picture followed the question. It was not Jean in the arms of May, or bending over an unknown woman; it was Jean all by himself, walking along gaily, his nose in the air, exactly as he might be walking about the streets at this moment. He too is alone. Why hadn't the thought occurred to me before? And why should "Ah! so he is alone!" seem an amazing, alarming discovery? Why shouldn't he be alone? I have wanted it often enough lately haven't I? Whatever imbecility has replaced for this whole past month my fear of seeing him "f—— off?" I make use of him, of his house, of his table, of his car. I retreat, at his expense, into lairs of solitude from which I defy him and where I sometimes almost forget him. In fact I behave towards him with that selfish stupidity which women agree to call masculine. "There are two kinds of love," says Masseau: "Unsatisfied love which makes you intolerable to everyone and satisfied love which makes you idiotic."

So Jean is alone too. Intoxicatingly alone, like a student staying out all night, or deliberately and sullenly alone, resigned to finding the same woman at home as yesterday?

Let me be just—and to be just is already proof of great humility in a woman—whether our adventure continues little or long, all I can reasonably count on is Jean's resignation, for that is all I deserve. For a month I have been giving myself to him each time he wanted me, each time we wanted each other. The rest of the time, what does he know of me? Am I Venus or the Queen of Sheba that I need only lie on a bed to satisfy this beautiful young man to whom I owe more than he owes me? The rest of the time, I study him, without sounding his depths and I judge him as if he were still May's lover, not mine. That counts and weighs too, the rest of the time, and it adds up to a great many hours.

When he has been reticent, I have judged him as empty. And, when he has questioned me about myself, I have fobbed him off with a would-be superior irony, so whose fault is it, if, instead of being here with me at this moment, Jean is walking the streets or sit-

ting on a lighted terrace, and breathing in the soft night air with a
face that does not belong to me?

He does not know that I am kind and loving, that I have the mak-
ings of a stalwart friend. I attribute to him the defects which make a
certain type of man successful: duplicity, unscrupulousness, laziness;
but it is I alone who impose them on him like some flashy adorn-
ment that would suit his slightly brutal face.

I think my profound mistake is that, up to now, I have never tried
to dissociate Jean from the idea of sexual pleasure. When the appetite is gorged, the thought of sex arouses coldness and indifference.
Famished, it wants nothing but what appeases it.

Jean . . . oh, obtuse brute that I am! There is a Jean who is not
Renée's lover, a Jean who is neither mysterious nor sexually exciting.
And that Jean—so young still, with his caustic laugh—has matured
and developed from the boy he was in the past and whom I never
knew. Jean's thoughts, Jean's soul—did I really believe these had any
place in our brief exchanges of words or in the frenzied silence of our
nights?

I have insulted this lover, out there alone in the soft spring night,
restoring his own identity; I have insulted him by giving him my
body and supposing that this was enough. He has returned the insult. I only hope he will not come home at this moment; I would be
quite capable of crowning my folly by being absurdly effusive. Far
better he should go on wandering, alone and pure, as remote from
me as if he had never met me.

When he returns, I shall be in his bed and perhaps I shall be
asleep. I am aware of worse dangers now than sharing my sleep with
him. My slumbering shell belongs to him and does not succeed in
forgetting him. Without leaving the deep realms into which I plunge
in my dreams, I grip his hand tighter or make room for his head on
my shoulder. Nestled against him, I sleep easily and naturally. Alas,
he is not here yet and already he is taking possession of me. That
swift, hastily averted glance is the one he finds attractive.

Standing upright, with her feet together and her bosom held high,
with a growing radiance mounting from her lips to her forehead, the
woman you wanted, the woman whom perhaps you love, resurrects.
You may return.

TEN

"What's the time, Masseau?"

"Quarter to."

"Quick, gather up the cards. Leave that ashtray, I'll empty it myself. And pass me that glass of anisette, there, on the table. I'd no idea the days were drawing out so much. He'll say again that the place reeks of stale tobacco smoke."

"That window's been wide open all the time."

"That makes no difference, he's got a nose like a hound. You've let a card drop on the floor."

"'He that is down need fear no fall'," quoted Masseau sententiously. "I'll pick it up. It's a nine of spades. 'Troubles'."

"Get along with you, you old sleepwalker! What's that I hear? Is it he?"

"Why no, it's a taxi. For one thing, he wouldn't be coming from that direction."

"Why? He goes to the office every day now because the Autocrat isn't getting any better."

"To please him?"

"Yes . . . no . . . to replace him."

Masseau gave a little snort. I said: "After all he's his father's son, he's the one who'll succeed him. You seem to think it funny that he should go to the office."

"Not in the least, my dear, not in the least. Better than just anyone, as good as the next, no worse than Tom, Dick or Harry."

"Shut up!"

"I can form a very clear notion of banking."

"Can you? Oh, *really*, Masseau . . ."

"And to prove it . . ."

He turned up the points of his detachable collar in the old-fashioned way, pushed up his tie and tried, by puffing out his cheeks, to make one believe he had dewlaps.

"Laffitte!" he exclaimed.

"Did Laffitte look like that?"

"I don't know. I hope so. Give me three francs and twenty centimes which you lost at the game of bezique. Thank you. May God repay you a hundredfold."

"That will make precisely sixteen louis. That knock, is that he?"

"No, it's the ice-man."

"You'll stay to dinner?"

Masseau cast an avid glance at the folded card-table.

"I'll play you for my dinner. If I win, I'll stay. And if I lose, you'll keep me to console me."

Frustrated of his game, he followed me into the dining-room where I absent-mindedly make little adjustments to the laid table, pinching the stalk of a flower, spacing out the glasses. The solitary tree in the garden, a chestnut, pressed its leaves against the bare window-pane; the electric light bleached them to the pale green of a young pod.

"Look, Masseau, it's a pink chestnut. You can see the colour of the buds—already!"

He agreed, nodding his melancholy bald head. The scalp showed yellow under the parsimonious strands of long hair, patiently divided up to cover it evenly. I hastily averted my eyes which were used to lingering caressingly on Jean and looked instead at the open door.

"It isn't he," said Masseau, with sardonic acuteness.

"He . . ." Masseau had not spoken Jean's name. And I too say "He" like a woman obsessed with her man. But I am ashamed that we should say it in hushed voices, with a slightly degrading complicity, like Victor the manservant, leaning over the food-lift and whispering down to the invisible cook: "*He* says the sweet was a failure. *He*'s noticed the fruit dish has been stuck together."

An intolerable ringing broke out in the hall.

"Oh, that infernal telephone! I'd smash the beastly thing if I had my way. Hallo, is that you, Jean?"

I knew already what that far-off little voice was going to tell me—Jean's voice, clear but with a twang in it, as if he were joking.

"Hallo! Yes, it's me. Listen, don't wait dinner for me, they're keeping me here at Papa's. He's not too good tonight."

"Ah?"

"Yes. Can you hear me? Hallo! Whatever's the matter with this line? Hallo . . . You know, I'll be back immediately after dinner. Are you alone?"

"No. Masseau's here."

"Oh well, if Masseau's there . . ."

"What did you say?"

"Nothing. Goodbye for the moment!"

"All right. Goodbye for the moment."

Savagely, I hung up the detestable instrument whose function is to receive and to bring bad news. Heard on it, the voice seems to become pregnant with meaning, and to betray unspoken thoughts. "Oh well, if Masseau's there . . ." What did that mean? That Jean would take his time and come home at two in the morning? I am beginning to know his "Goodbye for the moment!"

I turned out the light in the hall—an old, economical habit I have never entirely broken. Besides, the face of a disappointed woman who is mastering her irritation is not a very pretty sight. . . .

"Let's sit down and have our dinner, Masseau. Jean's dining with his family."

To make the table look symmetrical, Victor had put Masseau in Jean's usual place. An unspeakable depression, nigh to tears, overcame me at the sight of his face opposite me. Instead of the firm, low-browed face with its well-cut mouth and discontented nose, I had to look at the sharp, twitching features of an ageing, almost bald man, riddled with nervous tics. . . . I wanted, oh, how I wanted at that moment!—just to be May or any other little "character" who could relieve her feelings by childish tears, by smashing plates, by screaming alternately: "I want Jean, now this minute!" and "I'll never see him again, he makes me sick!" But exhibitions of that kind have to be left to the Mays of twenty-five summers who can laugh after their tears, display a little pink nose and lovely wet eyelashes and look as artlessly fresh as a wild-flower. For Renée Néré, tears are a disaster.

"What are you looking for under the table, Masseau?"

"An animal, to give it something to eat."

"You know perfectly well there isn't one here."

"I do know it, and that surprises me."

"Oh, nonsense! Imagine starting all over again to train a puppy or a little cat, getting fond of it, dragging it about from hotel to hotel. . . ."

Masseau blinked faster. "What do you mean, from hotel to hotel?"

"Yes, I know there's no question of hotels at this very moment. But one never knows, we aren't chained to each other for life, Jean and I. We haven't sworn eternal fidelity, thank heaven!"

I felt I was being rude and clumsy, using that false voice, putting on that unconvincingly cynical expression. My off-handedness might have deceived an idiot but not Masseau who, embarrassed by all that I did not admit, gave up trying to make me laugh. I do not confide in him but he has become a habit with me. I remember that it was he who brought me to Jean and, in my familiarity with him, I display a little of the shameless unreserve one might feel in talking to a eunuch or an unscrupulous nurse.

It seems endless—a dinner at which nobody eats. Yet Victor kept going to and fro with an affection of silent alacrity that got on my nerves. His discreet rat-like face and his airy footsteps were at such pains to convey to us that we must pay no attention to his presence that we saw and heard nothing but him.

"Coffee in the drawing-room, don't you think, Masseau?"

A moment or two later, I collapsed in my favourite soft armchair.

"Ouf! Alone at last! When I say *at last*, that makes three dinners without Jean I've regaled myself with this week. What can one do? That man makes a positive cult of his family!"

"His father is ill," said Masseau gently.

"Oh, I know he is. But even if you told me his father had golden hair and wore divided skirts, I shouldn't make a tragedy out of it."

"In that case, I shan't tell you any such thing," said Masseau, still very gentle.

"Do you think I'm asking you to, my good man?"

"I do think so, and I shall confine myself to answering you this: One of two things, either I am the repository of Jean's secrets and I ought not to betray them or I am ignorant of them, in which case, in spite of all my desire to strike death into your soul, I can only keep silent and, at this point, enrich my great *Treatise* with a few notes."

"What great Treatise?"

"Hush! . . . and affirm my superiority at bezique by winning some money off you."

"But you won't go as far as helping me or taking my side! If I asked you to do something for me and tell Jean . . ."

"Nothing doing!" interrupted Masseau with such vehemence that some of the strands of hair came unstuck from his scalp. "Nothing doing!" He added, almost in a whisper: "You realise, my dear, that opium is expensive."

I understood. I understood only too well. Poor Masseau! I was quite aware that Jean gave him money to buy the drug, exactly as he might have given him good cigars, with the serene unscrupulousness of a friendly poisoner.

"Obviously . . . my dear old Masseau, I'm not the person who'd be officious enough to tell you: 'Give up smoking and get cured'."

"Any more than I would advise you: 'Leave Jean if you're not satisfied with . . . the state of his father's health. Or make him happy once and for all.' But that last suggestion is beyond the powers of an intelligent woman!"

"I know. What you mean is it needs those of a maid-servant who's been promoted to her master's bed. So we'll make Jean marry his cook."

"Like me," said Masseau, without moving a muscle. "But there is no urgent hurry and we have time to think only of you. What you have to deal with is a boy, who is fundamentally rather simple. Arrogant from birth and brought up to be despotic, because he always saw Mama tremble before Papa. A little humiliated by having dabbled in everything and not stuck to anything; a little young to be good and still deluded enough to rebel at the idea that woman can occupy the most important place in a man's life and heart. To sum up, Gentlemen and valued colleagues, we have occasion to offer our warmest congratulations to our town-council. Let us now affirm, with one voice: 'This is a great day for the Republic!' "

"What on *earth*?"

"It's the peroration of one of my speeches at Saigon in 1893. As you see, it's as good as new."

I listened, smoking a cigarette. I nodded approval and thanked him with a connoisseur's screwed-up glance.

"It's very good, you know. The 'instructions herewith' are first-class. You haven't added the 'Directions for use' which, in any case, was unnecessary."

"Why?"

"Don't know . . . Have an idea . . . Jean is charming . . . So am I . . . We shall remain charming . . . on condition we don't exaggerate anything. . . ."

I had lit another cigarette, an indispensable property when one is giving a classical performance of carelessness, slightly cynical detachment and civilised immorality.

I said, between puffs: "Charming, I assure you. That's exactly why I want to preserve a memory of our . . . adventure . . . that will be worthy of it. No chain, not even a chain of flowers—it's so ugly, a withered garland! Something I'll call 'an infallible instinct' warns me that Jean and I have everything to gain by going back to being just good friends. We rushed into bed together . . . excuse the expression . . . too quickly, almost without knowing each other and . . . you'll understand me when I say there's a certain unpredictable temper, certain oddities of character, certain . . . in fact certain things that I can't accept."

I stopped short and blushed to the roots of my hair: that last phrase was May's private property. How often she had used it in the days when, having been soundly thrashed in private, she redressed herself in public, glowing pink with freshly-scrubbed pride.

As if to make the analogy all the more cruel and before I had had time to hear the car drive up, there were steps on the sanded path and Jean opened the front door. The next moment, he was in the room.

"It's you!"

My loud, startled exclamation embarrassed all three of us and made Jean grow red.

"Yes, it's me. It's me once again. Goodness, to hear you scream like that when I come home, anyone would think it wasn't me you were expecting!"

He was wrong, but I took advantage of his mistake.

"You realise I wasn't expecting you so soon. You look tired. How's your father?"

"Better. Well enough to have become intolerable again. And to think I'll be like that at his age! What did you two have to eat to-night?"

He sat down and stretched. He talked. I knew he would not pro-nounce the words that would unite or sever two destinies. But there he was, as he said, "once again". I could feel Masseau's eye on me but even that sarcastic little eye could not prevent me from follow-ing—in the most doglike sense of the word—all Jean's movements. All I did was to raise my head a trifle and turn my gaze and my body towards the man who was talking. But I knew that every movement of mine was as significant as the tilting of a flower towards the sun or the yielding of a ribbon of seaweed to the curve of the wave.

There he was, the man whom just now I had wanted to leave—but did I want to leave him? The contrast between my lying words a lit-tle while ago and the burning truth of this moment was so violent that I shivered. There he was, fidgeting or sitting still in his usual way, and everything seemed simple between us and around us. Yet I knew that he was more hidden from me than a god in his cloud.

From now on, he was interposed between me and all the rest of a clear universe in which he alone was opaque. There was no piercing his mystery which existed only for me and for which I was almost wholly responsible, since he was my lover. Love is that painful, ever-renewed shock of coming hard up against a wall which one cannot break. We might have remained two friends, walking parallel with each other on either side of that crystal barrier, without realising that it divided us. But love was going to impel us towards each other and I trembled lest I, the more fragile one, should be the first to shatter myself against it.

Sleep eludes me and you lie asleep beside me. You go on sleeping under the lamp I have just turned on—Psyche's torch does not awaken you. Are you dreaming? No. I cannot see on your cheek or your brow that quiver like the reflection of running water, that ripple from the well-spring of your being that betrays the swift passage of a dream in your deepest consciousness. You do not dream when I am there. It is as if you do not want to. How well you defend yourself! This is the time when I wander all round you as under the walls of a locked palace. Where can I reach you? What breach can I open in your smooth, unlined forehead? Speak, avid mouth, and tell me in your sleep what you will never say in the brightness of day! Tell me what they hide, those sly smiles of yours, like the smile of an animal caught thieving and still licking its chops. I have so often seen you with eyes that are suddenly empty; eyes paler and blanker than a vast stretch of sea without ships.

Leaning over you, I catch back a fluttering piece of lace against my breast for fear it might brush your cheek, and I scarcely breathe. But can you not hear the buzzing of my angry thought as it beats vainly against the deaf shell of your ears, against your insensible nostrils and mouth?

The time is past when I used to admire your capacity for sleep and smile whenever I glanced at you! Beside you, I could read and think undisturbed; pleasantly aware of you like a treasure lying strewn on the bed. I could forget you and then recollect you again; you were neither more precious nor more galling to me than my other possessions.

Something has happened between us which has poisoned all that. Is it love, or only the long shadow love casts before it? Already I can no longer see you as luminous and empty.

I measured all the danger, that day when I began to despise what you gave me; a gay, facile pleasure that left me ungrateful and frivolous, a slightly ferocious pleasure like hunger and thirst and as innocent as they. One day, I began to think of all that you did give me; I entered into the chill shadow that travels ahead of love.

And here I am, humiliated, spying on your sleep. Oh, my treasure, strewn there on my bed, can it be that I disdain you because I am beginning to love you? Oh, Beauty, can it be that I prefer the soul perhaps unworthy of you, that inhabits you? Are there words now, Beauty, that dull the lustre of your name—such words as jealousy, betrayal, fidelity?

Once again, I have consumed the night in contemplating you, you who were my pride, my succulent and unloved prey. I can see the time close at hand when the growing shadow of love will have covered me, the time when I shall be still more humble, when I shall think such deplorable things as: "Does he love me? Is he deceiving me? Heaven grant that I know all his thoughts!"

I am not wholly deluded, not yet. I still have enough strength to leave you—if I want to. You wake up slowly—I know so well how your eyelids reluctantly open, showing a thin, wavering line like the streak of light on the horizon that heralds the dawn. . . . And you would find yourself alone, you would pick up this ribbon that ties my nightdress. . . . Never again would you hear that quiet, very quiet song, always the same, that I sing for myself alone and to which you listen behind the closed door.

No. I shall stay. A kind of obtuse heroism keeps me here, on the verge of my ruin. I shall stay. Sleep while I lie awake, calmly imagining the best fate that could befall you! A merciful death that would petrify the image of my new love forever in your pose of impenetrable sleep.

ELEVEN

"No, I don't agree with you."

That was all I had said. He was politely silent and I stared at the sea, dotted with islands. We had not quarrelled, there was nothing to quarrel—or even to argue—about. That was all I had said, yet it was enough to make us both feel we had parted forever.

At our feet lay a narrow sandy beach, still wet between boulders that had been bored through over and over again by the waves and whose base was blue with tightly packed little mussels. Beyond it, the ebbing tide was uncovering bare, peaked rocks. As far as the eye could reach there was not a single detail to mar or ruffle this Breton landscape; not a storm cloud in the sky, not a ribbon of wrack or a fringe of flotsam on the edge of the sea, not a house on the coast except this one, Jean's. It is a low, grey house, with a sparse wood behind it and, in front, a blaze of red geraniums and a scanty field that slopes down to the sea and blossoms with wild roses, stiff, fragrant pinks and gorse-bushes through which the wind whistles.

It is a perfect place, right at the edge of the land from which it seems to be trying to escape and take refuge in the sea which is gradually wearing it away. High tide encroaches on it till there is nothing left but a narrow strip of sand, rocks and grass, then, as it ebbs, it concedes it an insecure territory of beaches and reefs that never have time to dry. It leaves behind tiny, populous lakes whose bitter water is incessantly agitated by the claws of crabs and lobsters and the swishing tails of sea-perch and shrimps.

We came here last week. We arrived at the hour of twilight, a twilight whose rosy glow seemed to be shed equally by the setting sun, its reflection in the sea and an early-risen moon riding high and pale in the sky. We were not proof against the intoxication of the sea air which, those first nights, disturbed our sleep, quickened our blood and prolonged our hours of lovemaking under the febrile blue light of the full moon.

Everything was new to me, or unrecognisable; the salt on Jean's lips and mine, the noonday smell of the west wind which had passed over half-opened shellfish and that of the land wind, sweet with the scent of warm hay; the seaweed, the clams with their quilled valves, the sand-eels like mother-of-pearl whips, the furious crabs; the water that rose up and clasped, first one's ankles, then one's knees, in two heavy, icy bracelets. Last of all there was Jean himself, gentle and half-naked, like a faun. Every day he went down to the sea and I watched him admiringly as his step sent rippling shadows over his back and that magnificent muscular V that one sees in beautiful statues.

But already he was wearying of the holiday routine, of the sand clinging like a warm shroud to the drenched skin, of the silent siesta, almost blank of thoughts, under the softly-flapping canvas awning. Already we were being invincibly drawn back to our awareness of each other and the words I had just uttered seemed to be those he was expecting.

"No, I don't agree with you."

I do not know whether my tone made it sound more portentous or whether it was Jean's expression when he heard me say it that transformed it into a sentence of doom.

We fell silent and he lowered his eyes, for a curious kind of dignity forbade him to look, like myself, at the ebbing sea and the huddle of red rocks. That path of light, opened up between two clouds and running right to the horizon, was the path down which I was escaping. To have followed my gaze would have been, for Jean, almost tantamount to giving in and acquiescing. He would not give in so soon.

I had just offended him gravely, since I did not agree with him.

"Jean, are you angry? You think that I'm wrong?"

He protested, without raising his eyes: "Not in the least! I bow to your decision."

Yes? Or was he being crushing?

Goodbye, goodbye, I do not agree with you. Once again we were separated; far, far away from each other. By stretching out my hand, I could have touched his hair on which the salt water was slowly drying. A moment ago, our dark, drenched heads had emerged from the sea together and now we were so far apart. Goodbye, goodbye! Was it for the last time?

For I could feel that he despaired of me. One word, and our life in common had become intolerable to him; he would give up the journey he had planned and the tempting night that lay ahead. It was not that he hated me, no: he was shaking me off.

I did not speak. I used the exasperating weapon of the weak and the calculating: patience. I behaved as if I had forgotten Jean's existence. But he was not entirely deceived. During our first quarrels, my excellent imitation of the unself-consciousness of an animal which knows it is all by itself used to delude him completely. But he soon learnt that I merely wanted to offend him and he took offence. Now, perversely, I take care to talk and to keep silent just enough—enough to ruin everything. Instead of consciously trying to bring about our complete union, I want this to come about through a catastrophe, through some providential disaster and I keep incessantly piling up the clouds over our heads. My poor lover, how can I make you a sign across this barrier my false pride is building up between us, and what chance remains that you would recognise the sign?

You excuse everything in me which in any way resembles you. You overlook my lying, my bad temper and a certain frivolity that breaks out in bursts of wild gaiety for, in any extremity, whether of pain or pleasure, I depend on you. But today, you are utterly baffled, "I don't agree with you".

I said those words. I think I uttered them with a theatrical slowness, with a kind of deliberate security to show that they were something more than an evasion, that they implied a retreat, a return back to what Jean sometimes calls *my people*.

"*My people*" is an expression he uses to designate all the unknown side of my life. He says "my people" as if he were talking of a hostile tribe whom he instinctively hates. It is about "my people" he is thinking with deep mistrust at those moments when his eyes ask me so clearly: "Where do you come from? Who are you?" when he seems to be searching in my shadow for the indecipherable, paler shadow of so many vanished forms, the shadow of so many strangers who have made me in their image. They, too, "*do not agree with him*". Is it solely because of them that, in moments like this one, Jean gives me up in despair?

Passion—the only thing that brings us together—lay dormant, withdrawn into some dark refuge—and there we were confronted with each other, two people who were neither friends nor relatives. Anything—invective, wounding words, even separation—would be better than our dismal game which can go on forever, in spite of Jean's quickly-exhausted patience: if he is the dog, I am the cat at the top of the tree.

Jean, my ill-loved one. . . . Once again, our thoughts were running in opposite directions. I was going back bitterly to the time when I called my brief adventure love with a Passer-by. But he must have been going back to the days of my first perfection and reliving them, adorning them with a posthumous poetry. He must have been dreaming of the first weeks of our love when he suddenly began to believe in me, in my permanence, in my total submission, and repeating the words he found to flatter my pettiness. My opaque silence was elevated into "pensive wisdom" and the laziness that he irritably sees today as the inertia of a worn-out gipsy impressed him as regal.

So we sat there, patient, in front of the island-dotted sea. Once again, we were vaguely expecting that some chance would bring us together again as just now it had separated us. Or else the impure tide of desire which had been secretly mounting would sweep us both away till it stranded us once again on a barren shore. What point have you reached? Have you finished heaping abuse on me? Go on, magnify all my defects! When you have made me an enormous, blackened monster, loaded with more evils than a cloud swollen with hail, you will have gone a long way.

I myself have reached the symbolic halt in the journey which brought us here; I am back at that beautiful day on the mountain. Right on the top, standing on the red ruin, you drank in the blue air that whistled between the stalks of lavender. With genuine enthusiasm, invigorated by a little reading, you raved aloud over the open expanse, the towns, the villages, the shape and the clearly defined limits of a province girded with mountains and hills. You traced it through its history and you searched its soil to find the footsteps of its conquerors.

I was there, close beside you, and the grip of your strong hand on my arm stressed your words. I was there, rebellious and out of tune with you, far more interested in the magical appearance and disappearance of a lizard, in a tuft of marjoram swaying under a hornet buried in it, in the cry of an invisible shepherd. I was observing the mountain with the narrow range and the eye for small, sometimes subtle details, of a woman and a short-sighted woman at that.

When you realised this, all your excitement dropped dead and, as you stared at me dubiously, I felt at once far away, yet dangling in your clutches—small enough for you to carry me off yet heavy enough to impede your flight.

Were you thinking, as I was, of that day on the mountain? Were you counting, beginning from that day, the hours when we crazily supposed we had wrenched ourselves apart?

I did not know. But your silence despaired of me. Under your outraged stillness you were conscious of a regret that made you feel like a waning god, the furious regret of not having created me.

Today, I escaped from him by a path through furze-bushes that clawed at my dress. I reached an echoing shelter in the rocks, inhabited by a whirling wind. Down below, among the long narrow reefs, the ashen sea was boiling and writhing with the violence of a dammed-up stream.

From the height of my breached tower, I could spy on the house, draped with dark, glossy ivy. Jean was down there. He was reading, with his forehead rammed between his fists like a schoolboy. He would not come; up here I had leisure to calm myself. I was chewing a wisp of bitter little grass that made my saliva taste of box-leaves and turpentine. The wind dried the spray on my arms and cheeks and my fingers were rough and green from twisting the spikes of broom that had brushed against my hands all along the path. On me and in me I bore the smell and the savour, the bitterness and salt of my jealousy.

I was—if jealous was the right word—jealous, festering from something Jean had said, a terrible thing he had said hesitantly, as if he were spelling it out: "I'm afraid we don't need each other enough. . . ."

At that rather cowardly "we" that did not dare to be "I", I ran out of the house. When I returned there, he would give me all the usual things: the reassuring word, the convincing caress, the sworn promise. He would find it easy to exculpate himself because he feels blameless and because he still believes—poor simple man!—that fidelity should be sufficient to engender trust. He will not know, he must not know, *in what way* I am jealous. For him, jealousy means physical unfaithfulness, picking up a crumpled letter—it means the hope of winning back a disputed possession. To be jealous is to see all the time behind a woman, the shadow of a man. I envy him.

But I, *I* . . . if he does not need me enough, what have I been doing all this time and what future have I with him? He is more necessary to me than air and water, I prefer him to the brittle possessions a woman calls her dignity, her self-esteem. Only his single, solitary figure rose up before me on the ravaged field of my memories, rose up between me and the short waves of the absinthe-coloured sea. I could forget his last love and the face he kissed before mine; I could thrust all that away with careless impatience. He was all that I gazed at, all that I reviled. I was jealous of him alone.

I do not know how or when this thing first came over me. I remember one day turning round and finding him standing behind me, and, all at once, it was like seeing him for the first time. The sight of him startled me into a peculiar rage, a mixture of a sudden premonition of losing him and the humiliation of being more his than he was mine.

I suddenly saw him, with his typical stance, stooping forward a little like a man about to break into a run; with his voluptuous way of breathing in the scent of a flower. It was then that, muttering angrily to myself, I began to realise—too late—how much he meant to me.

Too late! Already, had he known it, he could have tyrannised over me in scandalous immunity. Had he known it, he could have made imperious demands on me and found my generosity inexhaustible. He could have expanded and ripened in me as in some beautiful province that nourishes every fruit. Had he known it, I could have been, according to his whim of the moment, the warm silent mouth or the sisterly arm or the friendly voice of a wise adviser. Everything —I could have been everything, flawlessly and effortlessly, and you have no inkling of it.

At this point my jealousy surged up again, inflamed by an imaginary notion of poetic justice, and burst into a bitter lament: "What I have been to you, *you who do not need me enough?*—you are destined to be for another woman." Does she exist? That is irrelevant. But I foresee that I am preparing a lover for another, a love whose splendour I alone know; a love in the image of my own love for you which I hide from you.

"I perish at the thought that one day you will equal me, you whom I might fill to overflowing. You will equal me, only to overwhelm another woman with love, or to live with her as I live with you. When I create you as you will be then, you dazzle me. It is as if I took off all my secret jewels so as to assess their worth better: when I see them glittering on you, I weep to see how precious they are.

"I left you just now because I had not the strength to hurt you. I have come, by a thorny path, to this dungeon of rocks where the wind lashes me like my sorrow. There is nothing left in me, above me, below me but churned-up sea, crumbling stone, gusty clouds.

This tempest of sea and wind, this debris of shattered rocks might have been created by my own inner confusion to honour and glorify you, you who have just appeared in the doorway of the house. You look so small in the distance, a slim, tiny, clear-cut shape—tiny and terrible."

TWELVE

THE darkness is ebbing. A faint wind stirs the trees, bringing a green smell of trampled grass. Behind the plane-trees, the mound of the fortifications is emerging from the dusk and the sky is taking on the colour of a field of blue flax, the subdued, slightly grey, slightly melancholy tint of a summer dawn over Paris.

A lean tom-cat, on the nearest bench, is savouring the peace of this cool hour and taking no notice of me. I make so little noise that he does not know I am watching. Now and then he raises his head and gazes at the sky with a blank, poetic gravity, untroubled by wariness or fear. Both of us are waiting for the dawn.

It will be hot. It will be a long day, like yesterday. Paris is already humming regularly and mysteriously with a murmur like the sea at low tide on the margin of a flat beach. For me, it will be a very long day. I know in advance all its phases; already, as a deserted woman, I have my fixed routine and now and then I take a curious interest in my plight like an incurable invalid who distracts himself with his illness. I know that in a few minutes, in an hour at most, I shall have got through what is perhaps the worst period of my day, the one that follows my brief sleep.

Before I wake up, before the lucid moment of remembering, there is a confused whirl in my mind in which shreds of dreams mingle with a hazy reality; my whole being defends itself and refuses to *know* Jean is gone. This very struggle and the pitiful unconscious movement I make to huddle myself together and hide in the hollow of the bed only bring back more clearly the memory of everything. Then I give up struggling; I meekly get up from my bed and go over to the window, pink with an August dawn or blue with heavy, beneficent rain.

Then I take to pacing up and down the room, from one wall to another. I bow my head for this is truly the awful hour. I use what little strength I have left to stop myself from beating my head rhythmically against the cool wall of the bathroom, to stop myself from moaning "Oh!" every time I take a new breath. I am patient. I move noiselessly about this bedroom that does not belong to me, I avoid looking at Jean's portrait which the triumphant dawn is bringing to life again on the mantelpiece. I give a wide berth to the table on account of the cigarette-case Jean has left behind there, a leather case whose smell I suddenly caught the other day as I passed. I had not time to master myself and the next moment I was nothing but a lost animal, whimpering over its master's scent it had picked up again.

And then I go over to the window and lean my elbows on the sill in an attitude which is already habitual and I begin to suffer as a matter of routine, to suffer in the same way as yesterday and all the days before. I do not want to weep: I look at the avenue, the scorched grass, the dawn colours brightening in the sky: I am interested in a passing flock of sheep kept together by mute, panting dogs. Sometimes I smile as I watch the games of the prowling cats; why not? Everything I see is registered against the solid background of my grief but my reactions to it remain the same.

The "pain of absence". . . . By dint of compulsively repeating, over and over again, those three words, always the same, always at this same window, I have come to distort their meaning in the strangest way. Because I always lean sideways on the bar that is too low and obstinately persist in bruising my left side on it, I identify the "pain of absence" with a physical pain, here, in my side below the heart, in that place I crush against the wooden bar, tenderly, as if I cherished the hurt.

The pain of absence. . . . It is such a simple form of suffering. How far removed I feel from the base tumults of jealousy and its homicidal madness! Everything is so simple in my mind, as simple as my grief; he was with me, he has gone. I have no other desire, no other hope, except for his return. If only he would come back, loving or not. If only he would come back. . . . If only he would come back.

A thrush whistles softly. The voices of a thousand dusty sparrows accompany his song with a sustained twitter that can barely be called musical, a cool noise like wet gravel being swept. The sky and the pavement reflect the same fleeting whiteness before the sun rises; it is that virginal moment the gardeners in my native province, who took care to pick the fruit firm and cold, used to call strawberry hour.

Strawberry hour. . . . There are certain old expressions like this which touch off some mysterious spark in us and kindle our imagination. Quick, let me carry this one while it still rings in my mind with all its delightful associations back to my crumpled bed. Perhaps, for a little while, its magic will fend off the, alas inevitable, return of a ghost. Due to the strain of standing so rigid here by the window, I am shivering as if with cold. Suppose I am going to fall ill? But, madmen do not fall ill, nor do those who are being inwardly devoured by a single obsession.

Slowly I go back to bed and defiantly get between the sheets of this bed in which there still lingers a vague scent that is not my own. Now I have to force myself not to give in to anguish, not to upset the sad equilibrium of my day by a storm of tears. In any case, the sun is rising. The first metro train will soon be passing, then there will be the milkman's knock at the basement window, then at last the step of the first postman. He will bring me nothing, nothing from Jean. But, after him, there will be other postmen whose footsteps I shall listen to as they approach and recede, footsteps that punctuate my day with rising and ebbing tides of hope.

So in turn will come all the other hours to be worn away; bathtime, luncheon-time, the siesta behind the closed shutters, the dragging, spun-out walk, dinner with Masseau and then the night. Once again the night, the arid night of a Paris summer; what would I not give for a film of damp mist, for a ground fog smelling of dew and earth? Once again night, solitude, insomnia, the inevitable awakening.

Sometimes I tell myself: 'There is no reason why all your days and nights should not go on like this to the end of your life if he does not come back.' But the suggestion smacks too much of ordinary commonsense to frighten me: all I look forward to is the wildly improbable . . . his return.

He has been gone a month. He left me with a kiss: his family was expecting him in the country; his father, ill or not, had summoned him there. I said to him: "Mind you write and let me know how you are!" in the gaily incredulous voice one uses to a forgetful young brother who is going away for a week. He replied: "As if I wouldn't!" But, as I watched him crossing the broad pavement, his whole back was lying. I called him back: "Jean! No, I'm wrong; I thought we'd forgotten to put your mackintosh in the car."

He turned round quickly and I had time to read the expression on that handsome, obstinate face and in those eyes, almost green in the shade of the plane trees. They showed treachery, impatience and a kind of affectionate cowardice, the cowardice of those from whom the sight of the hurt they inflict draws tears.

If I myself had been sincere at that moment, I would have held out my arms, I would have burst out with those extravagant words that come quite naturally to lovers: "If you go away, I may die. Truly, truly I may just cease to exist without you, because I love you. You couldn't do anything more appalling to me than what you're doing by just walking away from me. Forgive me for having taken so long to realise it."

He went off, calling out one last time, "Au revoir!" He was lying. I went back into his house and I began to wait for "the letter" as May said, "the letter that means it's all over".

Nothing has come, not even that, against which I might have defended myself, pleaded—if necessary, threatened. Nothing, except two ambiguous telegrams, whose content in itself was trivial, and which were sent only to find out whether I was still there, whether I was still obstinately encumbering the house that was not my own. When the second arrived: *"Be kind enough ask Victor send riding clothes and boots. Much love."*, I "translated" it and meekly put on my hat to go over to Batignolles and look out the few pieces of furniture I had kept. They were piled up in the sinister gloom of a two-roomed "flatlet" that I use as a furniture store. I stared at them, I wiped the dust off the cracked glass of a pastel with my finger, and I shook my head, saying almost aloud: "No; I can't", and I returned to Jean's house.

The next day I went to the Hôtel Meurice and asked for one of those blue or cream or peppermint green rooms which had been old haunts of mine for three years. And while one of the staff was vaunting the recent improvements in the hotel, and calling me "Madame Renée" as he talked, I listened with horror to the violins in the lounge moaning out a hackneyed waltz. From now on that languorous waltz would be entwined with too searing a memory.

That moment was one of my worst and weakest. I was conscious of an icy terror—the fear of the unseen snake you have nearly trodden on and which escapes from under your foot, the fear of the hole with crumbling edges, the reminder at every step, every moment, of what I had lost. "No, I can't." And I returned to Jean's house.

Here, nothing distracts me from Jean. As to the waltz, I sing it myself.

"What's the matter with you?"

"With me? Nothing."

One of us would sometimes ask the question, sometimes make the reply; we had almost reached a point where our conversation consisted entirely of these few words.

We could no longer communicate except through uneasiness, for nothing is exchanged in the sexual act. Speech gradually withdrew from us as the sound of shouting and singing, all the warm, irrelevant noise of living creatures must die out on a frozen planet. Our love which had begun in silence and the sexual act was ending in the sexual act and silence. One day, I dared to ask Jean: "What are you thinking of?" and then promptly began to laugh and talk without waiting for his answer; I was as much terrified of a lie as of an admission. I could feel him fluttering at my side, beating his wings and on the point of escaping from me like a bird already airborne. Yet every night brought him back to me and not once did I find the courage to repulse his desire. He made love to me only in total darkness and in sombre silence and I imitated his mute activity. At the height of the struggle he wrested an angry pleasure from me, and abandoned me afterwards, sickened. Then the ditch between us, hollowed a little deeper by the weight of our two bodies, separated us for the rest of the day.

I reached the point of looking with envious admiration at the sealed letters the post brought him, thinking that there were people in the world who corresponded with him, who exchanged ideas and plans with him, who talked to him about the future. People who, although they had met and known and loved Jean, continued to live and think and act normally. I even envied May, who had got off so lightly. Retracing our short, abrupt path, I would deny that a strong healthy love could be born, after a few weeks of false comradeship, from a kiss on the nape of the neck. Yet at the same time, the memory of that heavy kiss would bow me down more than ever. But since this is love, Jean, why does it not make us happier?

It is too late to ask myself that question now. I did not dare ask him "why" and perhaps he realised it. I did not dare. He was merely the man to whom I displayed myself naked.

He has gone. Does May know? Has he seen her again? She was only a poor little innocent prophetess, yet, now that fate has put me in her place, I think of her harshly. I accuse her and her kind, her and her predecessors, of having exploited Jean without knowing I existed, of having moulded him for some unknown woman, in no way like me, whom he is pursuing through all of us. Is he seeing May again? My pulse does not beat faster, no offensive picture rises up before me: the idea of betrayal plays so little part in my torment. This is neither nobility nor disdain, but simply the result of an odd sense of security. I do not feel any woman between Jean and myself. He has gone off exasperated, unable to bear our secretive, overcharged silence any longer but there is no one but myself in his mind. This does not rouse any glimmer of hope in me, it only spares me a slightly keener pain by relieving me from the wretched anxiety of *comparing*, of seeking and finding, in some young, well-made passerby, reasons for despising what beauty remains to me. Although it is beginning to fade, my physical charm does console me, though I do not deceive myself about what is going and what is still left. If grief consumes one, as they say, by now I should be an old woman. Yet, in spite of insomnia, in spite of the tears I cannot always restrain, in spite of an obsession more wearing than tears or insomnia, I keep myself up to the mark, ready, from the moment I get up to the moment I go to bed, for any surprise appearance. Even Masseau himself has never seen me look slatternly.

Nowadays, I cherish this curious friend. I suspect that Jean writes to him or at least that he writes to Jean. If he is no longer the messenger, almost the go-between, he once was, I hope that he is still the spy and that he reports my words, the look on my face, my elegant decline, to Jean. I resurrect every night for Masseau. Out of dignity, I take care not to display my misery to him, but I act, almost unconsciously, in a way to stress this dignity of a deserted woman, too proud to show her feelings. I play bezique gaily—a little too gaily. I am hearty—a little too hearty—at dinner. I act "naturally" as they say in the theatre, with the "naturalness" of a juvenile lead who affirms, biting his lip and clutching his breast, that he is "perfectly all right".

Play-acting—but if I did not act, if I let myself go, Masseau would find me waiting in the doorway, pale and trembling, crying: "You've seen him? He's talked to you? He's mentioned me? He's coming back? Tell me! Tell me! Bring him back to me, bring him back to me! Let him know, through you, that everything will be easy, everything will be a joy, if he comes back. Tell me that if he comes back, I shall feel him coming, that if he were only out there at the end of the street, I should know it as infallibly as a parched leaf knows it is going to rain! Tell him that, but, above all, tell him to come back because I am getting weak and all hollow inside and I am afraid of dying without him."

"Hallo, dear old Masseau."

"Pray accept, Madam, the assurance of my most cordial esteem. P. Masseau."

"Literally?"

"Literally. Why, if one writes as one speaks, not speak as one writes? I once—but this is a tale of my brilliant youth—put myself under a cloud with Madame Auberon—for having thought I was talking to her when I was writing to her, so my note ended: 'Well, so long! See you next week!' Is that what's making you laugh?"

"No; it's your hat."

Masseau was reflected full-length, from his straw hat to his shoes, in the hall mirror which always seems a little tarnished on account of the meagre light that filters through the fanlight and the greenish canvas that covers the walls. I saw myself standing beside him, as I had stood beside Jean when he was going off to dine with his father and I waited for the sharp twinge of memory—a contraction of my sides as if I were plunging into a cold bath—to subside before continuing my laugh.

"What's wrong with my hat?"

I had no idea. It was a straw boater. In the hand, it looked like any other boater. Neither did Masseau's tie differ intrinsically from any other tie nor his jacket from any other jacket. But on him the unobtrusive cloth, the inoffensive rice-straw and the conventional tie took on a malevolent life of their own. At a sign from Masseau, would they not come running—the hat bowling alone on its brim, the jacket limping on its empty sleeves, and the tie wriggling like a hissing snake?

"General Boulanger!" Masseau curtly informed me, as he stood planted before the mirror. "Bad business."

Turning to me and touching the lymphatic swelling above his beard, he consented to explain, "When I look like General Boulanger, it means my liver is out of order."

"The heat, no doubt?"

"Yes, the heat of the summer, the summer of 1889 which was terrible in Saigon."

He rubbed his hands and I preceded him into the smoking-room.

"It's nice in here, isn't it?"

I was lying. Everything in it was sinister, behind the half-closed shutters. A place without a master, a deserted woman.

"Very nice," agreed Masseau, sitting down.

He has a manner of his own of sitting on one buttock, like someone who has come to ask a favour.

"The days are drawing in already," he said in his old lady's voice.

And, for some reason, just those words threw me into a frenzy of despair which I succeeded in hiding.

"Why yes, my dear Masseau. One must expect that now. Anything new?"

He blew his nose before replying and I sat rigid and crazily tense, saying to myself: "If only he will take a long time blowing his nose! If only he will leave me for just another moment the possibility, the hope that *there is something new!* If he was very malicious, he might leave me in doubt and not tell me till the end of his visit that *there is something new.*

But he was not very malicious. He answered at once: "No, nothing. And you? No news?"

"No news." And I added weakly: "Why?"

Masseau raised his writer's hunched shoulder higher in token of impotence and I grew bolder.

"After all, whatever you say, he really might . . . Just common politeness. And even common rudeness, yes. I'd infinitely prefer that—the gentleman who writes: 'Look here, I've had enough of this!' After all, Masseau, I'm not a woman who . . . I mean, you understand."

"No," said Masseau.

The fact was I was searching for words like a foreigner. I did not want to give any trace of lyrical expression to my grief.

"I mean, he had nothing to reproach me with."

"Yes, he had," said Masseau.

"That's perfectly ridiculous! Besides, even if he'd been dealing with a . . . a woman like May . . ."

"He is," said Masseau, "dealing with a woman like May."

I opened my mouth to protest, but Masseau's attitude reduced me to silence. He had seated himself like a fakir and his little yellow hand was raised in command or in blessing. From where I was sitting, I could smell his breath, the breath of a man who hardly ever eats.

"I am about to speak! I am about to say imperishable things! I am overwhelmed with a burning desire to tell you a fable. Once upon a time there was a man in the valley of Bois-Colombes who was returning to his home. As he approached, he heard an appalling din of screaming and drumming going on inside his house. He blasphemed and stopped up his ears as he crossed the threshold. There, a filthy stench offended his nostrils; he blasphemed and stopped up his nostrils, then he called to his wife: 'Wobad,' he said, still keeping his nostrils stopped up, 'Tell me where this filthy sdench ad this did cobes frob?' The wife smiled and said: 'The stench is this unctuous cheese, all runny under its rind and the din is your son who is playing at being a soldier with his trumpet and drum.' Then the man glorified Allah and exclaimed: 'In truth, my son was born to be a warrior, to beat the drum and to sound powerful blasts on the trumpet! And, as to the cheese, pearly drops of ambrosia cannot equal its rich sweat whose very odour makes the mouth water!' Then he sat down at the table, cut the cheese and embraced his son."

"And then?"

"That's the end. It's a fable."

"Obscure, Masseau."

"If it were not obscure, it would not be a fable. Obscure, comma, dash, but the meaning is accessible, even to a feminine brain. Jean is the turbulent son, Jean is the odorous cheese."

"You're trying to make out that I ought to find everything he does charming, just because *he* does it? That's silly."

The oriental story-teller, now embellished by a little copper paperclip that pinched the bridge of his nose, shook his head.

"It's not so silly as all that. I am trying, with the aid of a drum and a Pont l'Évêque in prime condition to make you realise what love is."

"I was waiting for you to say that!"

"You're waiting for me to say something else. And you might have waited a long time but for my weakness of being interested in Jean. Do you love him, woman-like-May?"

"I . . . Yes, Masseau."

"And he loves you, forgive me, he loved you? Now, now, keep

calm. My child, remember that a doctor is like a confessor. And a confessor is like a doctor. In any case I am neither a doctor nor a confessor. Ha! Ha! Let us continue. Have you written to him?"

"Of course. Very little. Only once at length, last month."

"And what did it contain, your esteemed of the ult.?"

My nerves were on edge. Two troublesome little tears pricked my eyelids. I let myself be probed with the tense docility of a dog whose wound is being dressed.

"I can't remember now, Masseau. That I was unhappy. That I was astonished at his behaviour. That he ought not to have treated me like that. That . . . that one has dignity as a woman."

"Henough! Henough!" yapped Masseau. "I was sure of it!"

He uncrossed his lean legs, re-tied the lace of his shoe and said coldly: "You can stew in your own juice. I'll leave you do so at leisure."

After three steps towards the door, he came back.

"*Your* unhappiness, *your* misery, *your* loneliness! Your dignity! To begin with, dignity is a masculine defect! You, you always you. All that demanding and moaning and sulking and brooding of yours is no more than a disguise for your eternal deficiency—the inability to possess! Pooh! and even Fi! Demanding, and always a little bit at a time!"

I could not repress a smile.

"A little bit? But I want everything! It's not *my* fault if . . ."

My familiar demon cut me short by slicing the air with the flat of his hand.

"*Your* fault! *You* again! I said a *little bit* because all you wanted of Jean was his love. No, that isn't 'quite a tall order'! You spend your time putting Jean *opposite* you. That's the attitude of coition, no more. But it's another thing to inhabit him, to take him inside you! To take him inside you, to carry him inside you to the point where his radiance, his warmth, his manifestations of gaiety, anger, suffering, sensuality no longer appear to you as *someone else's*, but as the result of sublimest, most arrogant error, as the projections of your own innermost feelings! Does that bovine expression on your countenance indicate comprehension?"

"Yes . . . wait, Masseau, I'll put it another way: I'm in the dark but it doesn't frighten me, if I'm the one who's carrying the lantern? Is that it?"

"That's a faint, rough approximation."

"But . . . what about him, Masseau?"

"What do you mean, him?"

"I mean, will he do the same for me? Ought he to carry me inside him, as you say, to such a point that, for example, if he found me in the arms of another man, he'd exclaim: 'Ah, how passionately that emanation of myself . . . loves!' "

"That's none of your business. Such things don't concern you at all. As if feminine love had any connection with ours!"

"Ours . . ." He rocked to and fro on one foot, like a plucked heron. Yet this creature who looked so little like a man was speaking of love with emphatic authority.

"Woman, if the love you devote to your lover engages him in any way whatever towards you, it is no longer genuine love."

"What you're demanding of me in that case, Masseau, is mother-love."

"No," said Masseau. "The maternal instinct does not progress. It is born instantaneously—complete, fully armed and bleeding. Whereas love has the gift of tending towards its own perfection."

"Is that a piece of advice?"

"It is only an opinion. But it is based on observation."

"Frankly, you can't often have met her, this ideal female."

"Often, no. Only once. Therefore I married her. She was my housekeeper."

"So let us sing: 'He hath exalted the humble!'."

"I leave that sort of facile cynicism to you, my dear. You ought to go down on your knees and pray the good God that I wasn't mistaken when I judged you and Jean to be 'humble' enough to make a united couple. You, thank heaven, are not a genius and maybe Jean will never have his picture in the papers. You dream of obeying, on condition that you're allowed to go off all by yourself, with a great air of independence, to buy haberdashery at the Louvre. He likes to command, provided he is protected. In fact, you were—and how I regret having to employ that past tense!—you were both of you ordinary enough to engender a marvellous love."

A marvellous love! All those words he had spoken to me were the words of a man. It was all very intelligent, too intelligent for me. Instead of following his thought along the lines he suggested, I stopped short at the practical aspect of his discourse. I spoilt it by searching for a *recipe*, by trying to detect in it my lover's covert wishes. I reduced Masseau once more to his inferior status of messenger and in the admirable feminine self-sacrifice he proposed to me I saw only a means of luring Jean back.

THIRTEEN

THE sun is going down into the island-dotted sea. No aftercrop has grown in the meagre field that ends up as a beach and the trees in the copse blaze red in this rainless autumn. All the fresh colours of the landscape, red, grass-green, flaming pink, blue and mauve seem to be gathered together in the sea and in the clear sky it reflects.

A healthy tiredness has kept me sitting here on the terrace since lunch. The off-land breeze brings me the smell of meadows and burning weeds. It will not be long before Jean comes back. He will be carrying some sea-bird, hanging by its limp claws and swaying its slender dead neck. In spite of his scratched leggings and his faded old jacket, there will be something slightly unconvincing about this handsome hunter's appearance, as if he were only playing at being a sportsman. I shall receive his smile of greeting; I shall also receive his swift glance that will search out anything amiss in me and my surroundings; for example, this little coffee-stain on my white dress and the colchicums I gathered this morning lying fading on a bench.

The fact that we have been living together again for the past two months is a miracle which I humbly accept, as one must accept any prodigy, without seeking for an explanation. When I was a child, I was given a tree-frog which, instead of being green, was blue, and when I asked "But *why* is it blue?" the reply was: "Nobody knows. It's a prodigy."

He did not want to come back to me and I felt myself gradually dwindling away. I was already regretting my own death. I told myself: "What a pity! It would be better if some other human creature perished. There is still so much vigour in me; this body here, the brain behind this forehead—it is all good and sound, it could all be happy and useful."

But one day my sadness entered into a phase of compulsive activity, a blind, unreasoning determination: to see Jean again, to do everything possible to see him again, to have recourse to any conceivable means, to reject all calculations except those needed to work out an immediate, practical plan. The one I adopted was ingenuously simple: a pretended departure, then patient vigilance and, at the right moment, return.

A telephone call nearly ruined everything because once, knowing he had returned home, I yielded to the longing to hear his voice. In the booth at the hotel, I heard him exclaiming: "Hallo? . . . Well? . . . Who is that on the line?" and I stood silent, holding my breath as if the slightest movement would be fatal. He sensed it was I, for his voice changed register and I heard, in a lower tone: "Hallo, I say . . . Hallo . . ." Then he said hesitantly: "Is. that . . ." and checked himself. And I heard nothing more but the sound of the receiver being hung up.

I had the connivance of Masseau and also, though not gratis, that of Victor the manservant. And I waited for Jean in his home one night, on the very day a letter from me, posted by Brague, assured him that I had gone to Le Havre where I was returning to my former profession.

I waited for him, with all the lights out, in our bedroom that was dimly illuminated by the gas lamp in the Boulevard Berthier. I listened to the passing hours striking, immune to weariness and fear, even to the fear that my romantic ambush might make me look ridiculous. No doubt, had I written to Jean: "I must speak to you", I should have seen him the next day but that was not the Jean I wanted.

I waited, conscious of a calm I had never known, as if I had reached the end of my life. I waited, sitting in the darkness. The scent of a rose tucked in my belt mounted insistently to my nostrils in the still air. I listened to the wheels of every car and to the sound of every footstep. And each time I said tranquilly: "It isn't he." Towards midnight I heard a slow footstep approaching, the footstep of a man who was not in any hurry, and my exquisite calm changed into a kind of madness. What should I do? Run away? Scream? Rush downstairs and open the ,door? Hide myself at the top of the house? I was on the point of doing any of them. And yet, when the same slow steps climbed the stairs, I was still sitting in the same place. I thought, as in a dream, that he might be frightened when he entered the room and, before he opened the door, I called out quite audibly: "Jean!"

He had certainly heard but he did not answer. He came in, closed the door behind him, turned on the light and we found ourselves standing face to face, shading our eyes with our hands.

"So here you are!" he said, after a moment.

"Here I am. I called out to you so that you wouldn't be too surprised to find me."

"Then this is an ambush?"

He broke into quiet laughter and I began to despair because he looked so affable, so carelessly at ease, as if he were paying a call. He seemed to me taller and handsomer and not so young as my memory pictured him. I was thinking, as far as I remember, on three different planes: first, he is there, before my eyes. Then: before the night is over, I shall know my fate. Finally: he already has two lines ruled on his forehead, he is not a child, he is not a cruel adolescent, he is a man, he is a being of my own kind and my own age, there must be means of communicating, of *treating* with him on a human basis.

I smiled too, and I said: "Why of course! With my old instinct for theatrical situations, what else would you expect?"

Something descended from his forehead and down over his whole face, a brutal shadow that was the forerunner of anger but he pulled himself together and invited me to sit down. And, as he thrust out his hand to me, I took that hand and shook it gaily.

"Good evening, Jean."

"Good evening . . ."

On his face I could read deep perplexity and, at the same time, relief to find me gay—no tears, no dramatic cries, no threats. I was concentrating so hard on what I *ought* to do that it seemed to me I hardly loved him any more. I had entirely ceased to suffer. He sat down and ran his hand over his forehead.

"You look tired, Jean."

"Yes, just fancy, I'm working now. My father will never be able to go back to the office. I haven't acquired the habit of work—or the taste for it—yet. It's rather like being kept in to do an impot at school. I don't know why I'm telling you all this; it doesn't interest you in the least."

Behind the deliberately detached tone there was already reproach. At last reproach, at last the prelude to a lover's scene. I took my cue promptly.

"But it does interest me, Jean; it interests me very much, like everything else that concerns you."

I had spoken my line with too much conscious care; he saw the path I was trying to lure him into and dropped the subject. After this tactless blunder of mine, there was a quarter-of-an-hour of commonplaces and forced politenesses. The late hour, the unwonted light thrown through the wide-open window on to a scorched tree in the avenue, above all our unspoken thoughts gave this imbecile dialogue between a gentleman in evening dress and a lady in a tailor-made suit a hue of tragedy. I did not weary—"Dignity is a masculine defect", and it was Jean who gave the first signs of fatigue. He yawned nervously and, far from offending me, that yawn conjured up a Jean I had disdained to know—a serious Jean, at work, his plump, greedy man's neck bent over a page full of figures. His greedy man's neck . . . A savage sensuality suddenly burst up my innermost depths, sending the blood rushing up to my throat, making me cough, throbbing in my ears like a drum. It was the blind, primitive, instinct of the animal crying frenziedly for its master. I know that, at that moment, I sprang to my feet, that the violence of my movement overturned my chair and that I said furiously: "So then?"

He had risen too; and, having seen my face, he was watching my hands.

"You're wrong," I said curtly. "Don't be frightened. I only meant to say: 'So then it's finished? It's finished, us two?' "

He looked at me sombrely, resenting most of all that I was forcing him to reply.

"What do you mean, finished? What do you mean, finished? Haven't you had enough of this existence? Did you find it funny, our life? You want to start all over again?"

At last our positions had been logically reversed; he was the one who talked, the one who complained and accused, all I had to do now was to listen, while inwardly answering with my whole heart: "Start all over again, oh yes! Start again, no matter how, provided it's with you." All I did was to slip in an occasional "But, Jean . . ." to make him go on, to make him sweep it aside like a river surging over some obstacle too feeble to dam it.

He was pacing up and down the bedroom.

"Start that existence all over again. I certainly beg your pardon if I have hurt you in any way," he said, with a venomous expression. "But I think we're quits."

"You feel bitter against me, Jean?"

He stopped still, as if to defy me.

"Yes, I feel bitter against you. I can't deny it. I can't even say whether I'm right or wrong, but I feel bitter against you."

"My darling . . ."

Low as I murmured it, he heard. But he grasped too that I was staggering with gratitude under this resentment that made me his again. The meek, cringing gratitude of a bullied wife, May's beaming face after he had knocked her about! In his turn, he undeceived me and said craftily: "No. You are free. But if it satisfies what you called in your letter your 'dignity as a woman', let me tell you you are the worst memory of my love life."

I had sat down again, and leaning my head against the familiar silk of the armchair, I kept muttering, with closed eyes: "Yes . . . talk . . . talk . . ."

" 'Talk'! It's high time! After months of superior silence, now you say to me: 'Talk'! You boast of *listening to me think*: what need have you of my talking to you?"

"Oh, Jean! Listening to you think. . . . I might have said that in fun but . . ."

"Don't lie!" he shouted. "You're lying! You did listen to me thinking, or rather you attributed thoughts to me that conformed to the false idea you built up for yourself not of me, but of *man, man,* your enemy, your *bête noire.*"

"Yes . . . go on talking."

"The best I gave you—in the physical sense—only served you as a pretext to insult me the more. You conferred on me the merits of a boor and the deficiencies of an imbecile! Ah! did you think you were the only one of the two of us who heard the other thinking?"

He moved away to pour himself out a glass of water and I heard the neck of the water-jug rattling against the rim of the glass. I did not stir, I did not open my eyes for fear of stopping him. But, mercifully, he had not finished.

"And even if your Delphic priestess's vanity had not been constantly in the wrong, even if I had been the shifty swine you married once and for all long ago, listening to me think is a perpetual offence against my mental peace, against my security as an intelligent being, against the sacred imperviousness to which I have a right and which you ought not to violate!"

I did not open my eyes. I gently nodded my head, inwardly saying approvingly: "That's good. That's very good. And, besides, he had said: 'You ought not to' and not 'You ought not to have'."

He fell silent and I looked at him admiringly again, as he paced to and fro, palpitating with a resentment of which I was beginning to feel proud. 'To take him inside you, to carry him inside you to the point where his radiance no longer appears to you as *someone else's.*'

"But, Jean, why didn't you defend yourself? Why didn't you explain yourself, reveal yourself?"

He rounded on me as if he were going to hit me.

"Defend myself! Explain myself? Judge's words, d'you hear? Judge's words after a judge's silence! To begin with, why me and not you?"

I rejoiced in that childish expression, like a thwarted schoolboy's. In any case I was rejoicing at being where I was, in the full spate of a lover's quarrel and that this one looked like lasting a long time.

"Fair enough," I said loyally.

He had seated himself on a little sofa and made no attempt to hide all the weariness on his face. Not once, since I had been there, had he had a lustful impulse; there had been not one of those vindictive kisses that had been our only language. As if he were thinking the same thing, he let fall these despondent words: "It's so meaningless, just going to bed together."

And I was not offended that, in my presence, he had reverted to an innocent being who wanted nothing from a woman except perhaps feminine warmth, the still, living shelter of two cradling arms. But that I dared not offer and it seemed to me only too certain that I would never dare to again.

"Is it true that you're going away again?" he asked in the same tired voice. "That you're returning to the stage, to your former profession?"

I shook my head.

"No, Jean, it isn't true. It's just one more lie. I haven't got a profession any more."

And, in my mind, I continued with sad sincerity: "I no longer have one, and there no longer exists any profession for me. There is only one aim in my life and it is there in front of me—this man who does not desire me and whom I love. To capture him, to tremble for fear of his escaping, to see him escape, to stalk him again patiently and recapture him—henceforth that is my only profession, my only mission in life. Then everything I loved before him will be restored to me; light, music, the whispering of trees, the shy, ardent appeal of tame animals, the proud silence of suffering men—all these will be restored to me, but *through* him and provided only I possess him. He seemed so near to me, so closely coupled to me that I thought I did possess him. I foolishly wanted to surmount him, taking him for an obstacle when, in fact, he was the limit of my universe. I think many women, at the outset, make the same mistake as I did, before they resume their right place which is *on this side* of a man."

"Then what do you propose to do?"

I tried to put all my reply in a look, but his eyes refused mine as definitely as if he were saying: "No, no, it's too soon." His expression, at that moment, was excessively severe as if he wanted to discourage me for good and all. I nearly smiled; he did not know I had all the rest of my life in which to wait.

"What am I going to do? That's going to depend a little on you, Jean, and when I say *a little* . . . I'm going to begin by leaving you to get some sleep, because it's late and you're working."

I had picked up the very ancient, half worn-away jade fruit and I was fondling it as I looked round for another trace of my passage through this bedroom. I caressed its cold, smooth surface, then I slipped it into my handbag.

"Aren't you going to say anything to me, Jean?"

His eyes followed my hands, aware of their symbolic gesture of taking back, of departing.

"Goodbye, my silent one."

Standing there, I felt my confidence and my stubborn resolution on the verge of collapse, like my body. I secured my hat more firmly to leave, saying to myself: 'He's going to let me go. But I haven't gone yet. I'll cling to any straw. I haven't gone yet.'

He had stood up too and towered above me. I raised my eyes and I was seized with an odd feeling of extreme respect for myself, for the woman I was a few weeks ago, the Renée of last season, the woman who had had this man.

"My silent one, you never speak and you write even less. You've left me in such silence."

He lowered his brow and he averted that suddenly evasive glance that made him less beautiful.

"What did you want me to do? Answer your letter, write more scenes, exchange abominable words one doesn't forget? At a moment when neither of us could tolerate each other a moment longer, put more poison between us?"

"It's true that . . ." I conceded slavishly. But I was thinking: "I know very well that he isn't perfect. If fate gives him back to me, I shall often see that thieving animal's smile of his again, that recoil from a painful truth, from having to make an effort. I know very well that, before giving a little of himself, he is capable of demanding everything of me while gracefully apologising for not demanding more. But since, just as he is, I find in vulgar parlance 'as good as I'll get' and since I have neither the wish nor the right to belong to a hero, my imperfect self wants this imperfect Jean and none other."

"Then, au revoir, Jean?"

I held out my hand, and, as he bent down to kiss it, I saw the charming cleft in his upper lip quiver under his nostrils. I hesitated only a second: I must get him back, no matter by what means. I must gain time! I must throw him down, along with myself, not this time to drain and exhaust each other but to try and make a clear jet spring up out of the mud of our sad, sombre sensuality—the pure jet of love of which we might one day be worthy.

And, as a beginning, I ran a swift, caressing finger over his delicate ear. He started and turned away, with the gesture of a tempted woman.

"My darling . . ."

He shook his head, and warned me in a dull voice: "Take care! Once more, it's only desire."

His gaze took possession again of what he found attractive in me; my shoulders, my bosom, my hands which were clasped so as not to caress him too hastily.

"I tell you—do you hear?—that it's only desire!"

I nodded to signify, "Yes, I know."

The hand of my master fell heavily on me.

"Is that enough for you? Is that enough for you? Is that all you want of me? Is that all you bring me?"

Too exhausted to lie, I threw myself into his arms and I closed my eyes so that he should not see that it was my soul I was giving him.

The sun is going down and drawing out the conical shadow of the reefs over the sea. An hour has passed and I am still here under the canvas awning, against the sun-gilded wall. Over there, very far away, on the top of a jagged cliff is a tiny figure which moves capriciously; now coming closer, now stopping, now going away again. It is he. He too can see my white dress. He will come without hurrying himself, since I am waiting for him. Only when I see him down there, dark and clear-cut on the pale yellow beach, shall I get up and go down to meet him. I shall not hurry either, since he will be coming towards me. He will put his arm round my shoulder and say it has been a splendid day, he will tell me about the birds he went after, about the ferret that escaped. We shall exchange few words, because all our words enrich us with a little more of each other.

He will go off again tomorrow, anxious to enjoy every hour he can of this countryside he loves during his brief holiday. Here, he walks strenuously and displays the energy of a contented peasant. I follow his example, but in his wake and at a slower, gentler pace than my old one. It seems to me, as I watch him launch out enthusiastically into life, that he has changed places with me; that he is the eager vagabond and that I am the one who gazes after him, anchored for ever.

ABOUT COLETTE

Sɪᴅᴏɴɪᴇ Gᴀʙʀɪᴇʟʟᴇ Cᴏʟᴇᴛᴛᴇ was born in Saint-Sauveur-en-Puisaye, a small village in the Burgundy region of France, in 1873. Her mother, Sidonie (nicknamed "Sido" by her husband Jules-Joseph Colette, a pensioned army officer), surrounded her family with flowers, animals, and a love of life which profoundly influenced her daughter. In 1893 Colette moved to Paris to marry thirty-eight-year-old Henri Gauthier-Villars ("Willy"), well-known publisher and writer. He urged her to write, the result being the successful Claudine novels. To support herself after their divorce in 1906, Colette became a music-hall mime and actress. She married Henri de Jouvenel, ambitious, handsome, young editor-in-chief of *Le Matin*, in 1910. Her only child, a daughter named Colette but called "Bel-Gazou," was born in 1913 when Colette was thirty-nine. This second marriage ended in divorce in 1925. Between 1925 and 1935, when she married for the third time (to Maurice Goudeket, many years her junior), Colette traveled, acted, wrote, and lectured widely. In her later years, Colette was confined to her bed with crippling arthritis but she wrote prolifically —and gained new fame. When she died in Paris in 1954 at the age of eighty-one, she had written more than forty works of fiction, criticism, reminiscence, and journalism. Colette was the first woman elected to membership in the Goncourt Academy, and the second woman in history to be made a grand officer of the Legion of Honor.